STEPHEN JONES lives in London, England. He is the winner of three World Fantasy Awards, four Horror Writers Association Bram Stoker Awards and three International Horror Guild Awards as well as being a twenty-one time recipient of the British Fantasy Award and a Hugo Award nominee. A former television producer/director and genre movie publicist and consultant (the first three *Hellraiser* movies, *Nightbreed*, *Split Second* etc.), he has written and edited more than 120 books, including *Coraline: A Visual Companion*, *The Essential Monster Movie Guide*, *Horror: 100 Best Books* and *Horror: Another 100 Best Books* (both with Kim Newman) and the *Dark Terrors*, *Dark Voices* and *The Mammoth Book of Best New Horror* series. A Guest of Honour at the 2002 World Fantasy Convention in Minneapolis, Minnesota, and the 2004 World Horror Convention in Phoenix, Arizona, he has been a guest lecturer at UCLA in California and London's Kingston University and St. Mary's University College. You can visit his website at www.stephenjoneseditor.com

Recent Mammoth titles

The Mammoth Book of SF Wars
The Mammoth Book of One-Liners
The Mammoth Book of Ghost Romance
The Mammoth Book of Best New SF 25
The Mammoth Book of Jokes 2
The Mammoth Book of Horror 23
The Mammoth Book of Slasher Movies
The Mammoth Book of Street Art
The Mammoth Book of Ghost Stories by Women
The Mammoth Book of Best New Erotica 11
The Mammoth Book of Irish Humour
The Mammoth Book of Unexplained Phenomena
The Mammoth Book of Futuristic Romance
The Mammoth Book of Best British Crime 10
The Mammoth Book of Combat
The Mammoth Book of Quick & Dirty Erotica
The Mammoth Book of Dark Magic
The Mammoth Book of New Sudoku
The Mammoth Book of Zombies!
The Mammoth Book of Time Travel SF
The Mammoth Book of Angels & Demons
The Mammoth Book of the Rolling Stones
The Mammoth Book of Prison Breaks
The Mammoth Book of Westerns
The Mammoth Quiz Book
The Mammoth Book of Erotic Photography Vol. 4
The Mammoth Book of ER Romance
The Mammoth Book of More Dirty, Sick, X-Rated and Politically Incorrect Jokes
The Mammoth Book of Best New SF 26
The Mammoth Book of Hollywood Scandals

THE MAMMOTH BOOK OF BEST NEW HORROR

VOLUME 24

Edited and with an introduction by

STEPHEN JONES

RUNNING PRESS
PHILADELPHIA · LONDON

Constable & Robinson Ltd.
55–56 Russell Square
London WC1B 4HP
www.constablerobinson.com

First published in the UK by Robinson,
an imprint of Constable & Robinson Ltd., 2013

A copy of the British Library Cataloguing in Publication Data is available from the British Library

UK ISBN: 978-1-47210-027-6 (paperback)
UK ISBN: 978-1-47210-028-3 (ebook)

1 3 5 7 9 10 8 6 4 2

First published in the United States in 2013 by Running Press Book Publishers,
A Member of the Perseus Books Group

US ISBN: 978-0-7624-4943-9
US Library of Congress Control Number: 2012944639

9 8 7 6 5 4 3 2 1
Digit on the right indicates the number of this printing

Running Press Book Publishers
2300 Chestnut Street
Philadelphia, PA 19103-4371

Visit us on the web!
www.runningpress.com

Printed and bound in the UK

CONTENTS

ix
Acknowledgements

1
Introduction: Horror in 2012

91
Witch Work
NEIL GAIMAN

94
The Discord of Being
ALISON LITTLEWOOD

113
Necrosis
DALE BAILEY

121
The Hunt: Before, and the Aftermath
JOE R. LANSDALE

138
The Cotswold Olimpicks
SIMON KURT UNSWORTH

154
Where the Summer Dwells
LYNDA E. RUCKER

167
The Callers
RAMSEY CAMPBELL

182
The Curtain
THANA NIVEAU

196
The Fall of the King of Babylon
MARK VALENTINE

207
Nightside Eye
TERRY DOWLING

227
The Old and the New
HELEN MARSHALL

241
Waiting at the Crossroads Motel
STEVE RASNIC TEM

251
His Only Audience
GLEN HIRSHBERG

274
Marionettes
CLAIRE MASSEY

283
Between Four Yews
REGGIE OLIVER

311
Slick Black Bones and Soft Black Stars
GEMMA FILES

330
The Other One
EVANGELINE WALTON

351
Slow Burn
JOEL LANE

360
Celebrity Frankenstein
STEPHEN VOLK

378
Blue Crayon, Yellow Crayon
ROBERT SHEARMAN

397
October Dreams
MICHAEL KELLY

400
The Eyes of Water
ALISON LITTLEWOOD

422
Necrology: 2012
STEPHEN JONES & KIM NEWMAN

482
Useful Addresses

ACKNOWLEDGEMENTS

I WOULD LIKE to thank David Barraclough, Kim Newman, Vincent Chong, Mandy Slater, Amanda Foubister, Rodger Turner and Wayne MacLaurin (*sfsite.com*), Peter Crowther and Nicky Crowther, Ray Russell and Rosalie Parker, Gordon Van Gelder, Andy Cox, Ellen Datlow, Charles Black, Debra L. Hammond, Douglas A. Anderson, Merrilee Heifetz and Sarah Nagel of Writers House, Nicholas Royle, Johnny Mains, Andrew I. Porter and, especially, Duncan Proudfoot, Max Burnell and Dorothy Lumley for all their help and support. Special thanks are also due to *Locus*, *Ansible*, *Entertainment Weekly* and all the other sources that were used for reference in the Introduction and the Necrology.

No. 701, May/June 2012. Reprinted by permission of the author.

THE HUNT: BEFORE, AND THE AFTERMATH copyright © Joe R. Lansdale 2012. Originally published in *Trapped in the Saturday Matinee*. Reprinted by permission of the author.

THE COTSWOLD OLIMPICKS copyright © Simon Kurt Unsworth 2012. Originally published in *Terror Tales of the Costswolds*. Reprinted by permission of the author.

WHERE THE SUMMER DWELLS copyright © Lynda E. Rucker 2012. Originally published in *The Magazine of Fantasy & Science Fiction* No. 703, September/October 2012. Reprinted by permission of the author.

THE CALLERS copyright © Ramsey Campbell 2012. Originally published in *Four for Fear*. Reprinted by permission of the author.

THE CURTAIN copyright © Thana Niveau 2012. Originally published in *From Hell to Eternity*. Reprinted by permission of the author.

THE FALL OF THE KING OF BABYLON copyright © Mark Valentine 2012. Originally published in *Terror Tales of East Anglia*. Reprinted by permission of the author.

NIGHTSIDE EYE copyright © Terry Dowling 2012. Originally published in *Cemetery Dance Magazine* Issue #66, 2012. Reprinted by permission of the author.

THE OLD AND THE NEW copyright © Helen Marshall 2012. Originally published in *Hair Side, Flesh Side*. Reprinted by permission of the author.

WAITING AT THE CROSSROADS MOTEL copyright © Steve Rasnic Tem 2012. Originally published in *Black Wings II: New Tales of Lovecraftian Horror*. Reprinted by permission of the author.

HIS ONLY AUDIENCE copyright © Glen Hirshberg 2012. Originally published in *The Raven of October*. Reprinted by permission of the author.

MARIONETTES copyright © Claire Massey 2012. Originally published in *Marionettes*. Reprinted by permission of the author.

BETWEEN FOUR YEWS copyright © Reggie Oliver 2012. Originally published in *The Ghosts & Scholars Book of Shadows*. Reprinted by permission of the author.

SLICK BLACK BONES AND SOFT BLACK STARS copyright © Gemma Files 2012. Originally published in *A Season in Carcosa*. Reprinted by permission of the author.

THE OTHER ONE copyright © Debra L. Hammond 2012 as literary heir to Evangeline Walton. Originally published in *Above Ker-Is and Other Stories*. Reprinted by permission.

SLOW BURN copyright © Joel Lane 2012. Originally published in *Where Furnaces Burn*. Reprinted by permission of the author.

CELEBRITY FRANKENSTEIN copyright © Stephen Volk 2012. Originally published in *Exotic Gothic 4: Postscripts 28/29*. Reprinted by permission of the author.

BLUE CRAYON, YELLOW CRAYON copyright © Robert Shearman 2012. Originally published in *Remember Why You Fear Me: The Best Dark Fiction of Robert Shearman*. Reprinted by permission of the author.

OCTOBER DREAMS copyright © Michael Kelly 2012. Originally published in *Supernatural Tales* 22, Winter 2012. Reprinted by permission of the author.

THE EYES OF WATER copyright © Alison Littlewood 2012, 2013. Originally published in slightly different form in *The Eyes of Water*. Reprinted by permission of the author.

NECROLOGY: 2012 copyright © Stephen Jones and Kim Newman 2013.

USEFUL ADDRESSES copyright © Stephen Jones 2013.

This one is for "the boys" –
Kim, Paul, Barry, Baz and Chris
– for the lunches, beers, DVDs
and camaraderie over the years.

INTRODUCTION

Horror in 2012

FOLLOWING THE ABRUPT departure at the end of January of its sole remaining editorial staff member, Dorchester Publishing finally closed its doors after seventy-five years. Amazon Publishing acquired the rights to more than 1,000 titles from the bankrupt publisher, as authors who chose to go with the new company received the full back royalties they were owed.

Those who did not want to sign with Amazon had the rights to their titles reverted back to them, although Dorchester apparently found it difficult to track down some of the (long-dead) authors on its list.

Amazon also purchased the Avalon Books imprint, founded in 1950, including its backlist of around 3,000 titles.

At the end of May, Houghton Mifflin Harcourt Publishing Co., whose authors include Mark Twain and J. R. R. Tolkien, sought bankruptcy protection with estimated debts of more than $3 billion.

That same month Terry Pratchett told a newspaper that text messaging and Twitter were damaging children's ability to write sentences correctly. He suggested that parents should consider restricting access to mobile phones and social networking sites to encourage their offspring to go back to talking to each other face-to-face.

Despite a reported last-minute decision by Rupert Murdoch's News Corporation make a bid, in late October it was announced that Pearson's Penguin imprint would be merged with Bertelsmann's Random House to create Penguin Random House. The deal was not expected to be finalised until the second half of 2013, and the new company would control a 25% market share of book sales in the English language and generate estimated annual revenues of around £2.5 billion.

Meanwhile, Poland's Catholic Archbishop Andrzej Dziega branded Hallowe'en "irresponsible and anti-Christian fun". Despite the growing popularity in his home country for carving pumpkins and dressing up on October 31st, he complained that the celebration introduced young people to "a world of darkness, including devils, vampires and demons".

As that was kind of the point, in 2012 a record $8 billion was spent by Americans – notably an increasing numbers of adults – at Hallowe'en, making it the second biggest consumer spend for decorations after Christmas.

James Herbert brought back his psychic investigator David Ash from *Haunted* and *The Ghosts of Sleath* to investigate a series of hauntings at Scotland's Comraich Castle in *Ash*. In the UK, publisher Macmillan issued a free chapbook sampler of the novel.

About an all-American family hiding a terrible secret involving their twin children, Stephen King praised *Breed* by Chase Novak (aka best-seller Scott Spencer) as "a total blast".

R. L. Stine's first adult novel, *Red Rain*, was about a woman who took a pair of orphaned twins into her home with gruesome results, and a young captive fought back against his sadistic abductor in Joyce Carol Oates's harrowing *Daddy Love*.

Strange happenings surrounded an archaeological dig at an Egyptian pharaoh's tomb in Lincoln Child's thriller *The Third Gate*, while Vlad the Impaler ended up in modern-day

Mexico City in Carlos Fuentes's literary novel *Vlad*, originally published in Spanish in 2010.

A former journalist may have murdered his wife in Gillian Flynn's best-seller *Gone Girl*, which relied on the trick of an unreliable narrator.

Odd Apocalypse was the fifth in the series by Dean Koontz, while the author's *Odd Interlude* was originally serialised in three parts in e-book format.

The Wrath of Angels was the eleventh in John Connolly's Charlie Parker series.

Tim Powers's historical chiller *Hide Me Among the Graves* was a sequel-of-sorts to his 1989 novel *The Stress of Her Regard*, as Pre-Raphaelite siblings Christina Rossetti and Dante Gabriel were haunted by the vampiric ghost of their uncle, John Polidori, and the undead incarnation of Dante's late wife.

Photographer Cass Neary found herself involved in ancient Icelandic myths and the hunt for a serial killer in Elizabeth Hand's *Available Dark*, a sequel to the author's *Generation Loss*, while the schizophrenic narrator of Caitlín R. Kiernan's *The Drowning Girl: A Memoir* was haunted by a ghostly woman she found wandering naked near a river.

A sixteen-year-old boy searched for his missing father amongst a vaudeville show that hid a terrible secret in Robert Jackson Bennett's *The Troupe*.

A film-maker was commissioned to make a documentary about a notorious cult in Adam Nevill's *Last Days*, and police detective Cass Jones finally discovered the true origins behind the shadowy cabal of The Network in *The Chosen Seed*, the third volume in Sarah Pinborough's ambitious The Dog-Faced Gods trilogy of crime/supernatural thrillers.

A paranoid schizophrenic started to believe his monsters were real in *The Hollow City* by Dan Wells, while a hungry devil stalked the halls of a medical institution in Victor LaValle's *The Devil in Silver*.

A new manager and his daughter found themselves dealing with the ghostly inhabitants of the *Deadfall Hotel* in Steve Rasnic Tem's often touching novel.

Chaz Brenchley's *House of Bella* was the third in the Keys to D'Esperance series and, under his pseudonym Ben Macallan, *Pandaemonium* was the urban fantasy follow-up to *Desdaemona*.

Simon R. Green's *Live and Let Drood* was the sixth volume in the Secret Histories series about the Drood family and their ongoing battle against the forces of darkness.

Dave Zeltserman's *Monster: A Novel of Frankenstein* was a revisionist version of Mary Shelley's novel, as narrated by the scientist's creation, while a group of teens teamed up to track down a monster killing high school girls in Brian McGreevey's *Hemlock Grove*.

An old Hollywood movie monster came to life and started killing in Heather Graham's *The Unholy*, featuring FBI paranormal forensics investigator Sean Cameron. Meanwhile, paranormal investigator Katya Sokolov investigated a series of undersea deaths around a legendary shipwreck in the same author's *The Unspoken*.

Guy Adams's *Sherlock Holmes: The Army of Dr. Moreau* pitted the great detective against the beast-men from H. G. Wells's novel.

The formula that created Jack the Ripper was rediscovered in *Ripper*, the latest thriller in David L. Roper's Event Group series, and a super-secret military force protected the USA against supernatural threats in *Seal Team 666* by Weston Ochse.

Survivors of the sinking of the *Titanic* found greater horrors awaiting them on the rescue ship in Matt Forbeck's *Carpathia*, and Harper Blaine investigated the reappearance of a mysterious lost ship in Kat Richardson's *Seawitch*, the seventh title in the Greywalker series.

People were vanishing from a mist-shrouded northern town in Simon Bestwick's *The Faceless*, while Gary McMahon concluded his Concrete Grove Trilogy, about the eponymous haunted housing estate, with *Silent Voices* and *Beyond Here Lies Nothing*.

A series of bizarre suicides and an outbreak of gruesome murders by children were linked in Liz Jensen's horror/SF novel *The Uninvited*, and a tattoo artist found himself involved in the hunt for a serial killer in Aric Davis's *A Good and Useful Hurt*.

A "Collector" of souls for Hell had to prove that a woman accused of torturing and killing her family was innocent in Chris F. Holm's *Dead Harvest*.

A San Francisco detective hunted a serial killer beneath the city in Scott Sigler's *Nocturnal*, and a witch-turned-Boston cop used her magical heritage to investigate a series of ritual killings in *The Thirteenth Sacrifice* by Debbie Viguié.

In Kate Griffin's *Stray Souls*, the first novel in the Magicals Anonymous series, an apprentice shaman and her crew of magical misfits had to find London's soul and save the city from supernatural creatures. Orbit published a chapbook excerpt from the book back-to-back with an extract from Francis Knight's *Fade to Black*.

A backwoods woman was believed to be a witch in *The Cove* by Ron Rash, and a young woman discovered that she was a "Necromancer" in Michelle Sagara's *Silence*, the first volume in the Queen of the Dead series.

Witchy historian Diana and her 1,500-year-old vampire husband Matthew travelled back in time to 16th-century England to search for an enchanted manuscript in *Shadow of Night*, Deborah Harkness's sequel to her best-seller, *A Discovery of Witches*.

A woman discovered that her house contained a dark history linked to a famous singer in *The Ghost of Lily Painter* by Caitlin Davies, and an American teenager discovered that his English public school was haunted by *The White Devil* in Justin Evans's ghostly novel.

Daniel Polansky's *Tomorrow the Killing* was the second in the author's Low Town series, Wayne Simmons's *Doll Parts* was a sequel to *Drop Dead Gorgeous*, and *Juggernaut* by Adam Baker was a prequel to the author's *Outpost*.

Jason Hawes, Grant Wilson and Tim Waggoner collaborated on the novel *Ghost Town*, and Wayne Simmons had two new horror novels published, *Parts* and *Fever*.

The Apocalypse Index was the fourth volume in Charles Stross's humorous Laundry series about British spies battling Lovecraftian horrors, and Seth Grahame-Smith re-imagined the birth of Jesus as a fantasy adventure with Egyptian zombies and black magic sorcerers in *Unholy Night*.

Orange Prize-winning historical novelist Helen Dunmore's *The Greatcoat*, a ghost story set in early 1950s Yorkshire, was the first new book from Random House/ Arrow's Hammer imprint. It was followed by Jeanette Winterson novella *The Daylight Gate*, based on Lancashire's seventeenth-century Pendle Hill witch trials, and Tim Lebbon's novel *Coldbrook*.

Kronos by Guy Adams was the second novelisation based on the 1974 Hammer movie *Captain Kronos Vampire Hunter*, featuring an introduction by creator Brian Clemens, and an updated version of the 1971 film *Hands of the Ripper* from the same author came with a foreword by Hammer expert Jonathan Rigby. Mark Morris pulled the same stunt with his contemporary version of the 1972 film *Vampire Circus*, while Shaun Hutson novelised Hammer's obscure 1958 SF movie *X the Unknown*.

Alan Goldsher's *My Favourite Fangs: The Story of the Von Trapp Family Vampires* was a humorous mash-up of bloodsuckers with *The Sound of Music*.

A vampire William Shakespeare was stranded on a mystical isle in Lori Handeland's *Zombie Island*, the follow-up to *Shakespeare Undead*, and a vampire Jane Austen found her wedding plans disrupted by murder and the supernatural in *Jane Vows Vengeance*, the final volume in the trilogy by Michael Thomas Ford.

Gena Showalter's *Alice in Zombieland* was a YA mash-up and the first in The White Rabbit Chronicles.

* * *

Deadlocked was the penultimate Sookie Stackhouse novel by Charlaine Harris, while US Marshall Anita Blake was on the trail of a fifteen-year-old girl abducted by vampires in *Kiss the Dead*, the twenty-first book in the series by Laurell K. Hamilton. *Beauty*, a deleted scene from Hamilton's novel, was available as a bonus "eSpecial" and was added to the paperback edition.

Twin sisters planned to escape the blood camps set up to feed hordes of vampires in *The Farm* by Emily McKay, and surviving humans battled virus-created vampires in a post-apocalyptic world in *The Twelve*, Justin Cronin's sequel to his 2010 best-seller *The Passage*.

John Redlaw travelled to America to investigate a series of attacks on vampire immigrants in *Redlaw: Red Eye*, the second in the series by James Lovegrove.

In *Incarnation*, the second book in the historical vampire history series by the pseudonymous Emma Cornwall, Lucy Weston set out to discover why Bram Stoker lied about her in *Dracula*.

Daughter of Light was the second book in the Kindred vampire series, following *Daughter of Darkness*. It was credited to the long-dead V. C. Andrews®.

Red White and Blood by Christopher Farnsworth was the third in The President's Vampire series, and former cop Laura Caxton concluded her war with ancient vampire Justinia Malvern in *32 Fangs*, the fifth and final book in David Wellington's series that began with *13 Bullets* in 2006.

Jeanne C. Stein's *Haunted* was the eighth in the series about vampire Anna Strong, while *Undead and Unstable* was the eleventh volume in Mary-Janice Davidson's humorous Betsy the Vampire Queen series and the third in a trilogy.

Set during the French Revolution, *Commedia della Morte* was the twenty-fourth volume in Chelsea Quinn Yarbro's series about vampire Count Saint-Germain.

Titan Books continued its reprint series of Kim Newman's *Anno Dracula* alternate history series with *The Bloody Red*

Baron and *Dracula Cha Cha Cha*. Both attractive trade paperbacks contained exclusive bonus material, including new novellas in both.

Need was an erotic gay vampire novel by Todd Gregory.

Anne Rice turned to the werewolf genre with markedly less success than she enjoyed with vampires thirty-six years earlier. Based on a forty-page TV treatment, *The Wolf Gift* involved the transformation of a young newspaper reporter into a lycanthrope.

The Craving was Jason Starr's humorous follow-up to *The Pack*, featuring former family-man turned werewolf Simon Burns, while Gregory Lamberson's *The Frenzy War* was the second book in the Frenzy Wolves Cycle following *The Frenzy Way*.

The Germans used "corpse gas" to create an army of zombies during the First World War in Joseph Nassise's *By the Blood of Heroes*, the first in the Great Undead War alternate history series.

Kevin J. Anderson's humorous *Death Warmed Over* was the first in a series about zombie PI Dan "Shamble" Chambeaux, and *Plague Town* was the first volume in Dana Fredsti's Ashley Parker series.

Deck Z: The Titanic by Chris Pauls and Matt Solomon featured zombies on the famous sinking liner, a struggling actor woke up as a zombie in *Husk* by Corey Redekop, and a young man was being groomed to lead the human survivors in the post-apocalyptic zombie novel *This Dark Earth* by John Hornor Jacobs.

Created by Stephen Jones, *Zombie Apocalypse! Fightback* was the second volume in the "mosaic novel" series, with contributions by Peter Atkins, Anne Billson, Jo Fletcher, Christopher Fowler, Brian Hodge, Reggie Oliver, Sarah Pinborough, Robert Shearman, Michael Marshall Smith, Lisa Tuttle and others, including an original comic strip by Neil Gaiman and Les Edwards that was adapted into a short animated film available online.

Variations on the zombie apocalypse continued in *Devil's Wake* by Steven Barnes and Tananarive Due, while Madeleine Roux's latest heroine was stuck in Seattle following the zombie apocalypse in *Sadie Walker is Stranded*, a companion volume to the author's *Allison Hewitt is Trapped*.

K. Bennett's *The Year of Eating Dangerously* was the second legal thriller featuring Mallory Caine, Zombie at Law. It was followed by *I Ate the Sheriff*, which also featured a werewolf fighting a difficult child custody battle.

Even White Trash Zombies Get the Blues was the second in Diana Rowland's series about zombie Angel Crawford.

Day by Day Armageddon: Shattered Hourglass was the third book in J. L. Bourne's zombie series, *Survivors* was the third volume in Z. A. Recht's The Morningstar Strain series, and *Siege* was the third in Rhiannon Frater's originally self-published As the World Dies trilogy.

Autumn: Aftermath was the fifth and final volume in David Moody's zombie series, as an army of corpses attacked the human survivors taking refuge in a fortified castle, and *Blackout* was the final volume in the near-future Newsflesh trilogy by Mira Grant (Seanan McGuire), set decades after the zombie apocalypse changed the world.

I Saw Zombies Eating Santa Claus was a humorous novella by S. G. Browne set in the same world as *Breathers*.

A gay actor came back as a cannibal zombie in Corey Redekop's literary comedy *Husk*, while *Eat Your Heart Out* was a lesbian zombie novella by Dayna Ingram.

A man searched for a possible cure to a zombie plague in a US split into two hemispheres of the living and the dead in *The Return Man*, a first novel by V. M. Zito that was originally serialised on the Internet.

Susan Dennard's first book, *Something Strange and Deadly*, was a YA steampunk zombie novel set in the 1800s, while *Cannibal Reign* was a post-apocalypse horror novel by debuting author Thomas Kolonair.

Stephen McGeagh's debut urban horror novel *Habit* from Salt Publishing came with a glowing cover blurb from Ramsey Campbell.

A young woman found herself caught up in an escalating war between the angels and the Fallen in Lou Morgan's debut novel *Blood and Feathers*, the first in a series.

Alison Littlewood's first novel, *A Cold Season*, followed the classic Faustian bargain format, a couple tracked supernatural creatures in Lee Collins's *The Dead of Winter*, and A. G. Howard's debut *Splintered* was a dark Gothic retelling of *Alice in Wonderland*.

A young girl feared that she would succumb to the supernatural homicidal madness that affected random female teens in her hometown in Mary Atwell's YA debut novel *Wild Girls*.

A vampire fan was ready to become the real thing in Helen Keeble's humorous YA debut, *Fang Girl*, a werewolf enforcer fell in love with a wild woman who had lost her powers to shift in Rhiannon Held's debut *Silver*, and a boy believed he was transforming into a worm-like creature in Mary G. Thompson's debut YA novel *Wuftoom*.

Curious Warnings: The Great Ghost Stories of M. R. James was a 150th Anniversary Edition edited by Stephen Jones and illustrated by Les Edwards. The handsome leather-bound hardcover from Jo Fletcher Books included all James's supernatural stories, along with the children's novel *The Five Jars*, a number of articles by the author, the most definitive versions to date of various story fragments, and an extensive illustrated afterword by the editor.

M. R. James's *Collected Ghost Stories* from Oxford University Press contained thirty-three stories (three more than in the original 1931 edition) along with an introduction and story notes by editor Darryl Jones.

Constable & Robinson published a numbered and slipcased facsimile edition of Bram Stoker's *Dracula* to commemorate the hundred-year anniversary of the author's death. The book contained a new introduction by author Colm Tóibín (which was more concerned with Stoker's life than the novel's place in horror history), and as an added bonus there was a colour reproduction of the original 1897 hand-written contract between Stoker and his publisher.

Yet another new edition of *Dracula* from Harper Design was illustrated by Becky Cloonan.

With historical introductions by Stephen Jones, *The Lost Novels of Bram Stoker* was an omnibus of the author's not-very-lost novels *The Jewel of Seven Stars*, *The Lady of the Shroud* and *The Lair of the White Worm*.

The Great God Pan/Xelucha was an omnibus of the two short novels by Arthur Machen and M. P. Sheil, respectively, from Creation Oneiros. Illustrated by Austin Osman Spare, the book came with three different introductions plus a foreword by H. P. Lovecraft.

From the same imprint, *Skullcrusher: Selected Weird Fiction Volume One* collected eleven stories by Robert E. Howard along with an introduction by editor James Havoc, a foreword by D. M. Mitchell and a memoriam by Lovecraft.

Barnes & Noble reissued Stephen King's *Three Novels: Carrie, Salem's Lot, The Shining* in an attractive leather-bound, silver-edged edition.

In a poll to celebrate World Book Day on March 1st, Roald Dahl was chosen as Ireland's favourite children's author of all time.

A Monster Calls, written by Patrick Ness from an idea by the late Siobhan Dowd, won the CILIP Carnegie Medal for "the most outstanding book for children" in the UK in June, while Jim Kay's illustrations for the book received the CILIP Kate Greenaway Medal for illustration. It marked the first time since the Greenaway award was founded in 1956 that both prizes went to the same title.

The following month, best-selling YA author G. P. Taylor called for a ratings system for children's books, as he believed that they had gone "too far" towards disturbing horror. The Anglican vicar and author of the Vampyre Labyrinth trilogy admitted that he felt the same about his own work and would rather go back to writing books like *Shadowmancer*.

Scholastic reissued a number of *Goosebumps* books by R. L. Stine to celebrate the series' twentieth anniversary.

Stuck on a remote island for the summer, a man was haunted by a foreboding black mansion in *The Turning* by Francine Prose.

Following a near-death experience, a teen believed that she had brought something dark back with her in Graham McNamee's *Beyond*, while a girl apparently received messages from her dead twin brother in *The Vanishing Game* by Kate Kae Myers.

Everybody could now see ghosts in Daniel Waters's *Break My Heart 1,000 Times*.

A girl was repeatedly brought back from the dead as part of a secret drug experiment in Cat Patrick's *Revived*, and a boy discovered that magic really worked in Jeff Strand's humorous *A Bad Day for Voodoo*.

Cara and her friends had to fight an elemental threat that wanted to cleanse the planet of all life in *The Shimmers in the Night*, the second volume in Lydia Millet's The Dissenters trilogy.

Dark Eden: Eve of Destruction was the second book in the series by Patrick Carman, and Jeyn Roberts's post-apocalyptic novel *Rage Within* was a sequel to *Dark Inside*.

Such Wicked Intent by Kenneth Oppel was the second in The Apprenticeship of Victor Frankenstein series, a prequel to Mary Shelley's novel. *As Dead As It Gets* was the third in Katie Alender's Bad Girls Don't Die series.

Another Jekyll, Another Hyde was the third in the series by Daniel and Dina Nayeri about pupils at an upscale New York school, while James Reese's *The Strange Case of Doctor Jekyll & Mademoiselle Odile* was a prequel to Robert Louis Stevenson's novel, about the orphaned daughter of a witch.

Masque of the Red Death was a post-apocalyptic

"re-imagining" of Edgar Allan Poe's story by Bethany Griffin.

The Saga of Larten Crepsey: Brothers to the Death was the fourth title in the prequel series to the Cirque du Freak books by best-selling author Darren Shan (Darren O'Shaughnessy). Shan was also the author of the illustrated novellas *Zom-B* and *Zom-B Underground*, the first two volumes in a new series.

The Spook's Blood (aka *The Last Apprentice: Lure of the Dead*) was the tenth volume in The Wardstone Chronicles by Joseph Delaney, illustrated by Patrick Arrasmith. It was followed by *Spook's: Slither's Tale*, which included an interview with the author.

For younger children, *Tales from Lovecraft Middle School #1: Professor Gargoyle* was written by Charles Gilman and illustrated by Eugene Smith.

Sara was a gay-themed YA horror novel by Greg Herren, from Bold Strokes Books.

An adopted girl travelled to London to discover the fate of her sister in *The Vampire of Highgate* by Asa Bailey.

The Slayer Chronicles: Second Chance was the second volume in a parallel series to Heather Brewer's The Chronicles of Vladimir Tod, told from the viewpoint of vampire slayer Joss Macmillan.

Richelle Mead's *The Golden Lily* was the second in the Bloodlines series, a spin-off from the author's Vampire Academy series, and K. J. Wignall's *Alchemy* was the second book in the Mercian trilogy.

Department 19: The Rising was the second book in the vampire series by Will Hill, while *Suck It Up and Die* was Brian Meehl's sequel to *Suck It Up*.

Nick Lake's *Blood Ninja III: Betrayal of the Living* was the final book in the trilogy about sixteenth-century Japanese vampire ninjas.

Balthazar was the fifth volume in the Evernight vampire school series by Claudia Gray (Amy Vincent), and Mari Mancusi's *Soul Bound* and *Blood Forever* were the seventh and eighth books, respectively, in the Blood Coven Vampire series.

Hidden was the tenth title in P. C. Cast and Kristin Cast's House of Night YA vampire series, while *Black Dawn* and *Bitter Blood* by Rachel Caine (Roxanne Longstreet Conrad) were the twelfth and thirteenth volumes, respectively, in The Morganville Vampires series.

A girl investigated the death of her best friend, who was killed by a white werewolf, in *Hemlock*, the first volume in a trilogy by Kathleen Peacock, and *Taken by Storm* was the third book in Jennifer Lynn Barnes's Raised by Wolves series.

A suicidal teenager and five others took refuge from zombies in a local high school in Courtney Summers's *This is Not a Test*, and a group of school kids on a field trip in the mountains came across zombies in *Gravediggers: Mountain of Bones*, the first in a series by Christopher Krovatin. Sean Beaudoin's *The Infects* was also about a group of teens battling zombies.

Ilsa J. Bick's *Shadows* was the sequel to the author's post-apocalyptic *Ashes*, while *Flesh & Bone* was the third in Jonathan Maberry's post-apocalyptic YA zombie series that began with *Rot & Ruin*.

The Sacrifice was the fourth book in Charlie Higson's The Enemy zombie series.

Ellen Datlow and Terri Windling edited *After: Nineteen Stories of Apocalypse and Dystopia* for Disney's YA Hyperion imprint. Among the authors included were Carol Emshwiller, Caitlín R. Kiernan, Garth Nix and Jane Yolen.

Translated by Marlaine Delargy, *Let the Old Dreams Die and Other Stories* was the first English-language edition of a 2006 collection by John Ajvide Lindqvist. It included eleven stories (including a sequel-of-sorts to *Let the Right One In* and a novella follow-up to *Handling the Dead*), along with the author's foreword to the original Swedish edition and a new afterword.

Night & Demons collected twenty-eight horror stories by David Drake along with extensive story notes.

21st Century Dead: A Zombie Anthology edited and introduced by Christopher Golden contained nineteen original stories about the walking dead from Mark Morris, Orson Scott Card, Amber Benson, Simon R. Green, Brian Keene, Rio Youers and others.

Edited by Sam Weller and Mort Castle, *Shadow Show: All-New Stories in Celebration of Ray Bradbury* contained twenty-six stories by Margaret Atwood, Neil Gaiman, Harlan Ellison, Joe Hill and others, along with a foreword by Bradbury himself.

V-Wars was a shared-world anthology in which a plague had turned humans into vampires. Edited by Jonathan Maberry, contributors included Nancy Holder, James A. Moore and Scott Nicholson. Dacre Stoker supplied the introduction.

Edited by Marie O'Regan, *The Mammoth Book of Ghost Stories by Women* contained carefully chosen reprints by Mary Elizabeth Braddon, Caitlín R. Kiernan, Mary E. Wilkins-Freeman, Alison Littlewood, Mary Cholmondeley, Cynthia Asquith, Amelia B. Edwards, Elizabeth Gaskell and Edith Wharton, along with sixteen new stories by Sarah Pinborough, Kelley Armstrong, Elizabeth Massie, Lisa Tuttle, Nancy Holder, Marion Arnott, Nancy Kilpatrick and Muriel Gray, amongst others.

O'Regan also teamed up with her husband, Paul Kane, to co-edit *The Mammoth Book of Body Horror*, which featured twenty-five "stories of transformation, mutation and contagion" along with an introduction by *Re-Animator* director Stuart Gordon. Once again, the best thing about the book was the terrific reprints by Mary Shelley, Edgar Allan Poe, H. P. Lovecraft, John W. Campbell, George Langelaan, Richard Matheson, Stephen King, Clive Barker, Robert Bloch, Ramsey Campbell, Brian Lumley, Nancy A. Collins, Richard Christian Matheson, Michael Marshall Smith, Neil Gaiman, James Herbert and Christopher Fowler. Grouped at the end of the book were also eight original tales by Graham Masterton, Gemma Files, Simon Clark, Conrad Williams and others.

Magic: An Anthology of the Esoteric and Arcane edited by Jonathan Oliver featured fifteen stories by Audrey

Niffenegger, Will Hill, Steve Rasnic Tem and Melanie Tem, Thana Niveau, Alison Littlewood, Christopher Fowler, Storm Constantine, Gemma Files, Robert Shearman and others, and boasted a terrific cover illustration by Nicolas Delort, which was re-used nicely throughout the text.

Edited by John Skipp, *Psychos: Serial Killers, Depraved Madmen, and the Criminally Insane* contained thirty-eight stories (eighteen original) by Ray Bradbury, Neil Gaiman, Kathe Koja and others, along with two non-fiction articles.

Blood Lite III: Aftertaste edited by Kevin J. Anderson contained thirty humorous horror stories presented by the Horror Writers Association.

Westward Weird edited by the late Martin H. Greenberg and Kerrie Hughes contained thirteen weird Western stories, while *The Big Book of Ghost Stories* was a big reprint anthology compiled by Otto Penzler, featuring seventy-nine tales by Ramsey Campbell, M. R. James, August Derleth and others.

Edited by Ellen Datlow, *Best Horror of the Year Volume Four* from Night Shade Books contained eighteen stories along with a summation of the year by the editor.

The Mammoth Book of Best New Horror Volume 23 edited by Stephen Jones featured twenty-six stories (two by Ramsey Campbell), along with an overview of 2011 and a Necrology by the editor and Kim Newman.

The Year's Best Dark Fantasy & Horror 2012 edited by Paula Guran included thirty-three stories.

There were no crossover tales between the Datlow and Jones volumes, although Alison Littlewood did appear in both with different stories. Guran and Datlow also had no stories in common, although both did feature work by Stephen King, Margo Lanagan and Glen Hirshberg. Guran and Jones shared the same story by Joan Aiken and included different tales by Joe R. Lansdale.

In January, Apple released the iBooks Author app, which allowed desperate would-be authors to automatically format their novels, including adding photographs and film footage! As if that wasn't bad enough, "books" created with the app could only be sold through Apple's own iBookstore or iTunes sites.

That same month, Barnes & Noble, Books-A-Million and Canada's Chapters Indigo announced that they would not stock Amazon Publishing titles (including those from the SF imprint 47North) because of the company's restrictive e-book policies.

J. K. Rowling's long-awaited Pottermore website was launched on March 27th, selling the first *Harry Potter* e-books. The site took £1 million in its first three days and trebled that total during the first month.

In April, the US Department of Justice filed an antitrust lawsuit against Apple and publishers Hachette, HarperCollins, Macmillan, Penguin and Simon & Schuster, alleging they colluded in fixing the price of e-books by adopting a similar type of business model. Hachette, HarperCollins and Simon & Schuster agreed to settle, and were forced to cancel any contracts with retailers using restrictive practices (such as Amazon) and forbidden to use the agency model contract for two years. The other three publishers decided to fight the charges in court, although Penguin subsequently agreed to settle so as not to affect its proposed merger with Random House.

The following month, Britain's biggest book-selling chain, Waterstones, surprised the industry by announcing that it was linking up with Internet retailer Amazon to sell Kindle e-readers through its 294 high street stores.

In August, Amazon UK announced that, for the first time ever, its digital book sales had outstripped traditional print sales in Britain. Just two years after the downloadable format was first launched in the UK, 114 Kindle editions were being sold for every 100 hardcover and paperback printings.

A US study found that the number of Americans who owned an e-reader or tablet computer was up from 18% in 2011 to 33% a year later. However, although 89% of regular readers (aged 16+) read at least one print book in the preceding twelve months, only 30% read at least one e-book. Despite that, print sales in the US declined by 9% in 2012.

Best-selling American author Terry Goodkind controversially took his revenge on a fan who had openly pirated his latest fantasy novel by posting the offender's photo and details on Facebook after attempts to privately contact the individual had been ignored. The pirated web pages were quickly removed.

The French-owned Byook app for iPhones and iPads was launched with a version of Sir Arthur Conan Doyle's 1892 Sherlock Holmes mystery "The Adventure of the Speckled Band" that was visually and aurally "enhanced" with blood and screams.

Available as an e-book from BBR, Simon Clark's debut collection was reissued as *Blood and Grit 21* to celebrate its original publication twenty-one years earlier. The new edition included an original Skinner Lane story, a new introduction by Andrew Darlington and an illustrated afterword by the author.

In October, editor John Joseph Adams and Creeping Hemlock Press launched *Nightmare Magazine*, a new monthly online and e-book periodical featuring original and previously published fiction. A companion title to *Lightspeed: Science Fiction & Fantasy*, stories from both electronic magazines were featured in a chapbook sampler containing work by Jonathan Maberry, Laird Barron, Sarah Langan and others.

Alan Baxter's novella *The Darkest Shade of Grey* appeared as a web serial on the electronic journal *The Red Penny Papers*.

With traditional print books in America facing growing competition from e-books, it was reported that 45% of all print books published in the US in 2011 were self-published (a total of almost 150,000 titles).

Improved technology and falling costs meant that 2012 saw an explosion in print-on-demand (PoD) books in the horror genre. Although this allowed many older titles to come back into print, it also resulted in anybody being able to publish their own "book" (often under spurious imprint names) – whether or not they had any actual talent.

Perhaps the most high-profile of the PoD imprints was executive editor Don D'Auria's Samhain Publishing, which issued numerous titles throughout the year, including Brian Moreland's *Dead of Winter*, *House of Sighs* and *The Fallen Boys* by Aaron Dries, *Hedge End* by Peter Mark May, *Evil Eternal* and *Swamp Monster Massacre* by Hunter Shea, *The Nightcrawler* by Mick Ridgewell, *Sacrifice* by Russell James, *Malevolent* by David Searls, *Daughter of Evil* by Nile J. Limbaugh, *Amongst the Dead* by David Bernstein, *A View from the Lake* by Greg F. Gifune, *A Dark Autumn* by Kristopher Bufty, *Jin Village* by Vincent Stoia, *Video Night* by Adam Cesare, *NightWhere* by John Everson, *Donor* by Elena Hearty, *Sorrows* and *House of Skin* by Jonathan Janz and *Bloodthirst in Babylon* by David Searls.

Nightmare City and the third Department 18 book, *The Eighth Witch*, both by Maynard Sims (who seem to have now become a single entity), were both available from the same imprint.

David A. Sutton's Shadow Publishing issued a new edition of the veteran author/editor's 1975 anthology *The Satyr's Head: Tales of Terror*, which featured ten stories by Ramsey Campbell, Brian Lumley, David Campton, Eddy C. Bertin and others, along with a new introduction.

To launch his Writers from the Shadows series, Sutton also selected and introduced *The Female of the Species and Other Terror Tales*, the first volume of stories by Richard Davis (1935–2005). This welcome collection of twelve tales additionally included a 1969 interview with the author, the complete text of a 1971 speech about horror fiction, and a bibliography of Davis's books and stories.

Shadow Publishing also issued the latest collection from Johnny Mains, *Frightfully Cosy and Mild Stories for Nervous Types*, which contained twelve stories (five reprints), an introduction by Stephen Volk and a foreword and story notes by the author.

Karōshi Books was a new imprint from Mains and others dedicated to bringing out work by new and unpublished authors. Its debut publication was *Glory and Splendour*, which contained eight weird stories by Alex Miles and a foreword by Michel Parry.

For Noose & Gibbet/Airgedlámh Publications, Johnny Mains edited and introduced *Party Pieces: The Horror Fiction of Mary Danby*, which included thirty-one stories (one original) for adults and children, along with an interview with the famed British anthologist of the 1970s and 1980s.

As usual published in trade paperback by editor Charles Black under his Mortbury Press imprint, *The Ninth Black Book of Horror* contained sixteen original stories in the style of *The Pan Book of Horror Stories* by John Llewellyn Probert, Simon Bestwick, Gary Fry, Anna Taborska, Paul Finch, Thana Niveau, Marion Pitman, David A. Riley and others.

Donald Sidney-Fryer's *The Atlantis Fragments: The Existing Chronicle: A Vision of the Final Days* from Hippocampus Press was more accurately titled *The Atlantis Fragments: The Novel* on the cover. From the same author and PoD imprint, *The Golden State Phantasticks: The California Romantics and Related Subjects* included essays on Clark Ashton Smith, George Sterling, Ambrose Bierce, F. Marion Crawford, Robert E. Howard and Nora May French.

Hippocampus also issued two collections by Richard A. Lupoff, which were also available in hardcover from Mythos Books: *Dreams* contained fifteen stories (one original) with an introduction by Cody Goodfellow, while *Visions* featured thirteen stories (five original) with an introduction by Peter S. Beagle. Both books contained not-always-accurate story notes by the author.

Portraits of Ruin collected thirty-nine stories (nine reprints) by Joseph S. Pulver, Sr. with an introduction by

Matt Cardin, while *At Fear's Altar* was a collection of thirteen stories (six reprints) by Canadian author Richard Gavin.

W. H. Pugmire's *Uncommon Places: A Collection of Exquisites* included twenty-two stories (eleven original), and *Intimations of Unreality: Weird Fiction and Poetry* contained all Alan Gullette's Cthulhu Mythos stories, together with two original novellas, an extensive sampling of the author's poetry, an introduction by Robert M. Price and interior art by Denis Tiani.

Also from Hippocampus, *Forever Azathoth: Parodies and Pastiches* was a revised edition of Peter Cannon's Lovecraftian-lite tales with an extra story added, while *The Nemesis of Night*, was the fifth novel in the Lovecraftian Shaman Cycle by the late Adam Niswander.

For Miskatonic River Press, Joseph S. Pulver, Sr. edited and introduced *A Season in Carcosa*, an anthology of twenty-one stories inspired by Robert W. Chambers's *The King in Yellow* that featured Joel Lane, Simon Strantzas, Don Webb, Gary McMahon, Richard Gavin, Gemma Files, Richard A. Lupoff, Michael Kelly, John Langan, Allyson Bird and others, including the editor.

From the same publisher, *The Strange Dark One: Tales of Nyarlathotep* collected eight Lovecraftian stories by W. H. Pugmire, including the title novelette.

Two of the year's best anthologies – PoD or not – were *Terror Tales of East Anglia* and *Terror Tales of the Cotswolds*, both edited by Paul Finch for Gray Friar Press. A follow-up to the editor's previous *Terror Tales of the Lake District*, the two volumes contained thirteen and fourteen stories, respectively, interspersed with "real" supernatural tales from their particular areas. The impressive line-up of writers for both books included Roger Johnson, Simon Bestwick, Steve Duffy, Mark Valentine, Johnny Mains, Alison Littlewood, Reggie Oliver, Gary McMahon, Simon Clark, Thana Niveau, Steve Lockley, Joel Lane, Ramsey Campbell, Simon Kurt Unsworth, John Llewellyn Probert and the editor and publisher.

From the same imprint, *Enemies at the Door* collected twelve short stories and novellas (three original) by the busy Paul Finch, but in far too small type.

The Gray Friar imprint also launched its New Blood series with Stephen Bacon's *Peel Back the Sky*, containing twenty-one stories (six original) along with an introduction by Nicholas Royle and story notes by the author. The second title in the series, *From Hell to Eternity*, was the impressive debut collection by Thana Niveau. It contained sixteen stories (half original), along with story notes by the author and a glowing introduction from Ramsey Campbell.

Produced as a charity anthology to raise funds for the Baltimore Poe House and Museum, which had its funding cut by the city, *The Spirit of Poe* from Literary Landmark Publishing contained forty-seven stories and poems, two by Poe himself, along with a foreword by Barbara Cantalupo, editor of *The Edgar Allan Poe Review*.

Chiral Mad: Anthology of Psychological Horror was yet another charitable anthology, this time with profits going to Down syndrome charities. Edited by Michael Bailey for Written Backwards, it featured twenty-eight stories (five reprints) by, amongst others, Gord Rollo, Andrew Hook, Gary McMahon, Monica J. O'Rourke, Gary A. Braunbeck, Gene O'Neill, Jeff Strand and Jack Ketchum.

Edited by Jan Edwards and Jenny Barber, *The Alchemy Press Book of Ancient Wonders* contained fourteen stories (two reprints) about magical monuments by Adrian Tchaikovsky, Peter Crowther, Adrian Cole, William Meikle and others, along with an introduction from Kari Sperring. For the same imprint, Mike Chinn edited *The Alchemy Press Book of Pulp Heroes*, which featured seventeen stories (two reprints) about heroes and heroines from, amongst others, Mike Resnick, Adrian Cole, Joel Lane, Peter Crowther and Peter Atkins.

Available from Nodens Books, *Above Ker-Is and Other Stories* was a welcome collection of ten tales by Evangeline Walton (1907–96), edited with an introduction and fascinating story notes by Douglas A. Anderson. Four of the stories were previously unpublished.

What Monsters Do was a slim PoD collection of seven stories (one reprint) by former *Hellraiser* actor and comics writer Nicholas Vince, available from Bibliofear.

Michael V. Gleich's *Jawbone* from Damnation Books was based on Native American folklore, about a Mohave demon who fell from the stars.

Night Terrors II: An Anthology of Horror from Blood Bound Books was edited by Theresa Dillon and Marc Ciccarone and featured twenty-eight original stories by David Bischoff, Jason V. Brock and others. K. Trap Jones's *The Sinner* from the same imprint involved a farmer isolated in a cave and his encounters with the Seven Deadly Sins and their attendant demons.

"Produced, directed and edited" by Eric Miller for Big Time Books, the unwieldy-titled *Hell Comes to Hollywood: An Anthology of Short Horror Fiction Set in Tinseltown Written by Hollywood Genre Professionals* featured twenty stories by authors you'd probably never heard of, with a brief foreword by SPFX make-up artist Roy Knyrim.

For the on-demand Science Fiction Trails imprint, David B. Riley edited and introduced *Low Noon: Tales of Horror & Dark Fantasy from the Weird Weird West* and *Gunslingers & Ghost Stories*. Containing twelve and eleven stories, respectively, the two anthologies featured fiction by Don D'Ammassa, C. J. Killmer, cover artist Laura Givens and others, including the editor himself.

Edited by Julie Ann Dawson for Bards and Sages Publishing, *Return of the Dead Men (and Women) Walking* contained fifteen stories about the various undead, while editor Lorraine Horrell's *Sowing the Seeds of Horror* from Static Movement contained twenty-one tales about bad things growing.

Valentines for the Dead from Shadowfall Publications featured thirteen stories by writer and poet Corrine De Winter and came with no less than three introductions, by

Thomas F. Monteleone, James Sclavunos and the author herself.

Billie Sue Mosiman's novella *Mourning Mansion* from DM Publishing involved an investigation into a number of missing boys and was loosely based on a series of true crimes that occurred along the Gulf Coast in the mid-1980s.

From Books of the Dead Press, *Best New Werewolf Tales Vol. 1* edited by Carolina Smart featured twenty previously unpublished stories and a comic strip by, amongst others, Michael Laimo, William Meikle, David Niall Wilson, Nina Kiriki Hoffman and Anna Taborska.

At the Gates of Madness collected eighteen stories by Canadian Shaun Meeks, while *These Old Tales: The Complete Collection* from Distressed Press contained short stories, flash fiction and poetry by Kenneth W. Cain. Both authors also supplied an "Afterward" [*sic*] to their books.

Two men's fates were bound by an ancient entity that thrived on suffering in Ennis Drake's novella *28 Teeth of Rage*, while ghosts still haunted the location of a vanished town in S. P. Miskowski's *Delphine Dodd*, both from Omnium Gatherum.

From the same California imprint, *Hunter's Moon: Visceral Tales of Terror* collected nineteen stories (twelve reprints) by R. Scott McCoy. Kate Jonez and S. S. Michael edited *Detritus*, featuring fifteen original stories about collecting by Kealan Patrick Burke and others and, with L. S. Murphy, Jonez also edited *Fortune: Lost and Found*, containing twelve stories (three reprints) about money and wealth.

Second Thoughts: Tales of Horror and Suspense from Spinetinglers Publishing collected seventeen stories by British writer Richard Moule.

Available from Curiosity Quills Press, *The Green-Eyed Monster* by Mike Robinson was about a literary rivalry that resulted in death and something worse, while a fallen angel used his network of advertising agencies to do Satan's work in Dina Rae's novel *Halo of the Damned* from Eternal Press.

Edited by Paul Genesse, *The Crimson Pact Vol. 3* and *Vol. 4* were the latest two volumes in the anthology series available from Alliteration Ink, who also published *Dangers Untold* edited by Jennifer Brozek and "presented" by The Horror Society.

Dark Tales of Lost Civilizations, edited and introduced by Eric J. Guignard for Florida's Dark Moon Books imprint, featured twenty-five new stories about lost lands and ancient cities.

William Patrick Maynard's *The Destiny of Fu Manchu* from Black Coat Press was based on the character created by Sax Rohmer.

From Ramble House/Dancing Tuatara Press, *The Unholy Goddess and Other Stories* was the third volume in the Collected Weird Tales of "shudder pulp" author Wyatt Blassingame. *The Devil's Nightclub* from the same publisher contained eight stories by fellow pulp author Nat Schachner, *House of the Restless Dead & Other Stories* featured nine previously uncollected pulp stories by Hugh B. Cave, and *Hands Out of Hell* collected eight weird menace pulp stories by John H. Know.

The Strange Thirteen was a reprint of Richard Gamon's 1925 collection of thirteen stories set in India, and D. H. Olsen contributed an introduction to H. B. Gregory's 1940 novel *Dark Sanctuary*, which also included an interview with the author. All the books included introductions by imprint editor John Pelan.

Midnight and Moonshine from Australia's Ticonderoga Publications collected thirteen stories (one reprint) by Lisa L. Harnett and Angela Slatter, with an introduction by Kim Wilkins. A 100-copy hardcover edition was signed by all the contributors and cover artist Kathleen Jennings.

From the same publisher, *Bread and Circuses* collected fifteen tales (four previously unpublished) by Felicity Dowker, with an introduction by Trent Jamieson.

Liz Grzyb teamed up with Amanda Pillar to edit and introduce *Damnation and Dames*, which contained sixteen tales of a paranormal *noir* by Jay Caselberg, Robert Hood and the Hannett and Slatter team, while Pillar was also the solo editor of *Blood Stones*, an anthology of seventeen stories about unusual creatures with an introduction by Seanan McGuire.

Also for Ticonderoga, *The Year's Best Australian Fantasy & Horror 2011* edited by Grzyb and Talie Helene contained thirty-two stories by Lucy Sussex (twice), Terry Dowling, Angela Slatter, Stephen Deadman, Lisa L. Harnett and Margaret Mahy, amongst others, along with a look at the year in review by the editors, a recommended reading list, and a list of Australian and New Zealand fantasy and horror awards.

No longer co-editor of *Dark Discoveries*, Jason V. Brock launched his own on-demand paperback magazine with S. T. Joshi as Managing Editor. The colourful and busy premiere edition of *[Nameless]: A Biannual Journal of the Macabre, Esoteric and Intellectual . . .* featured six stories by Gene O'Neill and others, various articles (including tributes to Ray Bradbury), interviews with artists Demetrios Vakras and Lee-Anne Raymond, and various reviews.

A stage comedian discovered that there was more to his uncle's childhood tales of magic than he could have realised in Ramsey Campbell's latest novel from PS Publishing, *The Kind Folk*.

A previously unpublished version of Basil Copper's 1976 Gothic mystery *The Curse of the Fleers* came with the author's original working notes, an introduction by Stephen Jones and cover art by Stephen E. Fabian.

When a woman attempted to transport her murdered friend's ashes to the destination of her dreams, she soon found herself in danger from various factions, including an all-too-real legendary killer, in Joe R. Lansdale's *Edge of Dark Water*.

As usual, PS also issued a number of short story collections, including *Trapped in the Saturday Matinee* by Joe R. Lansdale, *Born with Teeth* by Conrad Williams, *Leave Your Sleep* by R. B. Russell, *Where Furnaces Burn* by Joel Lane, *The Pottawatomie Giant and Other Stories* by Andy Duncan, *Angels and You Dogs: Stories* by Kathleen Ann

Goonan, and *Nothing As It Seems* by Tim Lebbon. All included new and reprinted material, and were available in signed and numbered editions of between 100 and 200 copies each.

Commissioned by editor Peter Crowther for the Humber Mouth Literature Festival 2012, *Four for Fear* contained a quartet of spooky stories by Ramsey Campbell, Christopher Fowler, Alison Littlewood and Nicholas Royle. The slim hardcover was limited to 200 copies and signed by all the contributors.

Once again edited with an introduction by S. T. Joshi, *Black Wings II: New Tales of Lovecraftian Horror* contained eighteen original stories, often loosely inspired Lovecraft's work, by Tom Fletcher, Caitlín R. Kiernan, John Langan, Don Webb, Nicholas Royle, Steve Rasnic Tem, Chet Williamson and others.

Edited by Marie O'Regan and Paul Kane, *A Carnivàle of Horror* brought together sixteen stories (four original) about circuses by Ray Bradbury, Joe Hill, Muriel Gray and others.

Flying Fish by Randall Silvis was a novella from PS about an island woman who may have been more than 200 years old.

Volume 28/29 of *PostScripts* was also, somewhat confusingly, *Exotic Gothic 4* edited as usual by Danel Olson. Along with a footnotes-filled Preface by the editor, the hardcover anthology featured twenty-five stories (one reprint) from Margo Lanagan, Reggie Oliver, Simon Kurt Unsworth, Robert Hood, Steve Rasnic Tem, Terry Dowling, Paul Finch, Anna Taborska, Scott Thomas and Stephen Volk, amongst others.

Produced as a collaboration between PS Publishing and Cemetery Dance Publications, Stephen Jones's anthology *A Book of Horrors* was available as both a limited edition, signed by the editor and artist Les Edwards, and a deluxe edition signed by all the contributors (including Stephen King and John Ajvide Lindqvist) for £595/$999.

From PS Publishing's Stanza Press imprint came *The Foliate Head*, a collection of thirty-six poems by Marly Youmans with illustrations by Clive Hicks-Jenkins, along with a reprint of Brian Lumley's 1982 poetry collection *Ghoul Warning and Other Omens*, illustrated by Dave Carson and with a 1999 afterword by Dave Sutton.

PS also launched a new mass-market paperback imprint, Drugstore Indian Press, with new editions of Ramsey Campbell's *The Darkest Part of the Woods*, *The Overnight*, *Secret Story* and *Told by the Dead*.

From Cemetery Dance Publications, Brian James Freeman and Bev Vincent's revised and updated *The Illustrated Stephen King Trivia Book: Revised & Updated Second Edition* was illustrated by Glen Chadbourne and included more than 100 additional questions.

The search for a missing child led to a man claiming to be a mythological monster in Lee Thomas's *Torn*, which was available in a 750-copy signed edition.

A couple took a trip up the Amazon in 1906 in the novella *Amazonas* by the late Alan Peter Ryan. It was available from CD in a signed edition of 1,000 copies. Peter Straub's 1990 novella *The Buffalo Hunter* was reissued by CD as a regular hardcover value priced at $19.99 and in a signed, limited edition.

The Woman contained the 2010 horror novel by Jack Ketchum along with a new sequel novella. It was also available in a traycased, signed and lettered edition of fifty-two copies ($175).

The 20th Anniversary edition of Bentley Little's *The Mailman* was available in a 1,000-copy signed edition and a traycased lettered edition ($400), while *The Circle* from the same author was a short novel in which the residents of William Tell Circle started doing unimaginable things to each other.

Edited by Joe R. Lansdale, *The Horror Hall of Fame: The Stoker Winners* from Cemetery Dance Publications collected thirteen award-winning stories by Robert Bloch, Harlan Ellison and others. Illustrated by Glenn Chadbourne, it was also available in a signed, limited edition.

Professional problem-solver Matthew Corbett ended up aiding his arch-enemy Professor Fell in discovering the identity of a traitor on a Caribbean island in *The Providence Rider* by Robert McCammon, from Subterranean Press. McCammon's 1980 novel *Bethany's Sin* was reprinted in a signed edition of 750 copies and a twenty-six copy lettered edition ($250).

Ad Eternum was a novella in Elizabeth Bear's New Amsterdam series, set in an alternate 1960s America that included vampires, werewolves and detective sorcerers.

The Woman Who Married a Cloud: The Collected Short Stories of Jonathan Carroll contained thirty-eight tales, the earliest dating from 1982, while Bentley Little's *Indignities of the Flesh* collected ten stories (one original) with story notes by the author.

Mira Grant's *When Will You Rise: Stories to End the World* contained a novella in the author's Newsflesh series with an unrelated story, both previously published as e-books.

Confessions of a Five-Chambered Heart: 25 Tales of Weird Romance collected stories that originally appeared on Caitlín R. Kiernan's subscription website *Sirenia Digest* between 2007 and 2009, along with a new introduction by the author and an afterword by Sonya Taaffe.

Also from Subterranean, *No Sharks in the Med and Other Stories: The Best Macabre Stories of Brian Lumley* contained twelve reprint tales and a new introduction by the author in a limited edition of 1,500 copies and a traycased, leatherbound edition of twenty-six ($250) signed by Lumley and artist Bob Eggleton.

The Janus Tree and Other Stories collected eleven stories by Glen Hirshberg in a 750-copy signed and limited edition, and Thomas Ligotti's 1994 collection *Noctuary* was reissued as a signed, leatherbound edition limited to 250 copies.

Available in a 500-copy signed edition and twenty-six lettered copies, *Shadows West* was a collection of three unproduced "weird Western" screenplays by Lansdale and his brother John R. Lansdale, while Subterranean's deluxe anniversary edition of Lansdale's 1981 novel *Act of Love* added a new novelette, an interview with the author, and illustrations by Glenn Chadbourne. A 200-copy signed, leatherbound edition was also available for $100.

Set between *Wizard and Glass* and *Wolves of the Calla*, *The Dark Tower: The Wind Through the Keyhole* was the eighth volume in Stephen King's long-running epic fantasy series from Donald M. Grant books. It was published in a 5,000-copy slipcased edition signed by artist Jae Lee ($75.00) and an 800-copy deluxe cased edition signed by both author and artist ($350).

Two young mothers infected with vampirism found themselves on the run from the mysterious Whistler and his companion in Glen Hirshberg's *Motherless Child* from Earthling Publications.

An oversized deluxe 25th Anniversary Edition of Clive Barker's *Weaveworld* was also available from Earthling in a very limited print run, illustrated with thirty new illustrations by Richard Kirk.

After a publishing hiatus following the tragic death of its co-founder, the Fedogan & Bremer imprint was back with a new anthology, *Worlds of Cthulhu*, edited with an introduction by Robert M. Price. Containing eleven original prequels and sequels to H. P. Lovecraft's work by Richard A. Lupoff, Darrell Schweitzer, Will Murray, Adrian Cole and Gary Myers, amongst others, the hardcover boasted dust-jacket art by Gahan Wilson and interior illustrations by Tim Kirk.

Best known for its series of chapbooks, Spectral Press also started publishing hardcover titles, beginning with *The Respectable Face of Tyranny*, the first in the Spectral Visions series containing two novellas and an afterword by Gary Fry.

The Nine Deaths of Dr. Valentine from the same imprint was a fun tribute by John Llewellyn Probert to Vincent Price and his *Dr. Phibes* films, while *The 13 Ghosts of Christmas* edited by Simon Marshall-Jones contained thirteen stories (one reprint) by Jan Edwards, William Meikle, Thana Niveau, Paul Finch, Gary McMahon and others, along with an introduction by Johnny Mains and a preview of Stephen

Volk's Peter Cushing-inspired novella *Whitstable*. All Spectral Press books were limited to 100 numbered copies.

William Meikle's novella *Professor Challenger: The Island of Terror* was available from Dark Regions Press in a signed, leatherbound and slipcased edition of just thirteen copies for $99.00.

Dark Regions also launched its Black Labyrinth imprint in June with *The Walls of the Castle* by Tom Piccirilli, the first of ten psychological horror novels and novellas illustrated by Argentinean artist Santiago Caruso. The Black Labyrinth titles were available in a variety of signed and numbered editions, including an oversized and traycased "ultra-deluxe edition" limited to just thirteen copies.

Published in a numbered edition of just 150 hardcover copies under the Enigmatic Press imprint, *A Haunting of Ghosts: A Collection of Ghost Stories* collected six original tales written over a two-month period in 2012 by (L. H.) Maynard (and M. P. N.) Sims with photographs by Emily Rose Sims.

Amongst a raft of titles put out by Centipede Press were *Where the Summer Ends* and *Walk on the Wild Side*, two volumes of thirty-five stories comprising *The Best Horror Stories of Karl Edward Wagner* edited by Stephen Jones.

A city became the hunting ground for humanoid creatures with claws and completely white eyes in Paul Kane's short apocalyptic novel, *Lunar*, from Bad Moon Books. Ramsey Campbell contributed the introduction.

After an anthrax attack wiped out half the population of Atlanta, the spirits of the dead started to possess the living in Will McIntosh's novel *Hitchers* from Night Shade Books.

In an alternate Naples where magic worked through holy music, a secret society planned to raise the Devil himself in *The Black Opera: A Novel of Opera, Volcanoes and the Mind of God* by Mary Gentle.

Inspired by the works of Arthur Machen, *The Croning* was the first full-length novel from Laird Barron and was about the strange things that exist on the periphery of our existence.

In Mark Teppo's *Earth Thirst*, the first volume in the Arcadian Conflict series, vampires fought back against humans who were destroying the planet, and a man returned to face his childhood nightmares on Catalina Island in *Terminal Island* by Walter Greatshell.

Edited by Ross E. Lockhart for Night Shade, *The Book of Cthulhu II* was a follow-up to the acclaimed anthology based on the concepts of H. P. Lovecraft and included twenty-four stories (four original) by Neil Gaiman, Kim Newman, Caitlín R. Kiernan and others.

Other Worlds Than These: Stories of Parallel Worlds edited with an introduction by John Joseph Adams was a hefty anthology of thirty mostly recent reprints along with a foreword by Lev Grossman and a further reading list compiled by Ross E. Lockhart.

Available in a printing of 300 copies, *Black Horse and Other Strange Stories* from Tartarus Press was the debut collection of American author Jason A. Wyckoff. Unfortunately, the sixteen original stories read more like pastiches of other, better works.

One of the best debut collections of the year was poet Helen Marshall's first prose book, *Hair Side, Flesh Side*, from Canadian imprint ChiZine Publications. Containing sixteen original stories based around different parts of the human anatomy, the book came with a glowing introduction by Robert Shearman and illustrations by Chris Roberts.

From the same publisher, *Remember Why You Fear Me: The Best Dark Fiction of Robert Shearman* included twenty-one superior stories (seven original), along with an introduction by Stephen Jones, while Ian Rogers's debut collection *Every House is Haunted* contained twenty-two stories (seven original) and an introduction by Paul Tremblay.

The first book in the How to End Human Suffering series, *Ninja Versus Pirate Featuring Zombies* was a humorous novel by James Marshall, a psychic threat from the Cold War resurfaced in David Nickle's *Rasputin's Bastards*, and

A Tree of Bones was the third in Gemma Files's weird Western Hexslinger series.

All ChiZine titles were also available in signed, limited hardcover editions through pre-order.

From Prime Books, *Witches: Wicked, Wild & Wonderful* edited by Paula Guran featured twenty-three stories (two original) by Neil Gaiman, Kelly Link, Ursula K. Le Guin, Tanith Lee, Jane Yolan, Madeleine L'Engle and others. *Obsession: Tales of Irresistible Desire* from the same editor featured nineteen stories by authors including Elizabeth Hand, Joe R. Lansdale, Fritz Leiber, Storm Constantine, Pat Cadigan and Lawrence Block.

Along with three other anthologies for Prime, the busy Guran also edited *Extreme Zombies*, which included twenty-five tales of the walking dead by Nancy A. Collins, Edward Lee, Brian Keene, George R. R. Martin, Joe R. Lansdale and others, and *Ghosts: Recent Hauntings*, a compilation of thirty stories (one original) by, amongst others, Peter Straub, Tim Powers, Caitlín R. Kiernan and Karen Joy Fowler.

Future Lovecraft edited by Silvia Moreno-Garcia and Paula R. Stiles featured twenty-eight SF stories (three reprints) and ten poems (one reprint) inspired by HPL's work, from authors including Don Webb and Nick Mamatas.

Edited by Russian-born author Ekaterina Sedia, *Circus: Fantasy Under the Big Top* included twenty stories by Peter Straub, Howard Waldrop, Holly Black and others, while *Bloody Fabulous: Stories of Fantasy and Fashion*, from the same editor, featured fourteen tales (seven original) of sartorial suspense from authors including Kelly Link and Holly Black.

Also from Prime, *At the Edge of Waking* was the second collection from Canadian author Holly Phillips, containing eleven stories (one original) with an introduction by Peter S. Beagle, while Elizabeth Bear's collection *Shoggoths in Bloom* included twenty stories from the past six years (one previously unpublished) and an introduction by Scott Lynch.

From Small Beer Press, *Errantry: Strange Stories* collected ten reprint tales published over the same period by Elizabeth Hand.

David Britton's latest Lord Horror novel, *La Squab: The Black Rose of Auschwitz*, came in a stunningly designed (by John Coulthart) hardcover from Savoy, profusely illustrated by Kris Guidio and with a CD reading by veteran British actress Fenella Fielding.

The publisher also issued a companion disc, *The Savoy Sessions*, on which the husky-voiced Fielding gave her own unique interpretations of sixteen songs.

Yet another tribute to *The Pan Book of Horror Stories* series, *The Screaming Book of Horror* was a hardcover edited with an introduction by Johnny Mains for Screaming Dreams. It contained twenty-one stories by John Llewellyn Probert, Alison Littlewood, Bernard Taylor, Anna Taborska, Paul Finch, Rhys Hughes, Alison More, Reginald (Reggie) Oliver, David A. Riley, Steve Rasnic Tem, Christopher Fowler, Charlie Higson and others, including posthumous contributions from John Brunner and John Burke, and a story by the editor.

A Certain Slant of Light from Robert Morgan's Sarob Press was a collection of eight ghost stories (three original) by Peter Bell, along with an afterword by the author. The limited, numbered hardcover was illustrated by Paul Lowe.

For the same publisher, Rosemary Pardoe edited and introduced *The Ghosts & Scholars Book of Shadows*, which featured twelve sequels and prequels to M. R. James's stories, originally submitted as competition entries, by Rick Kennett, John Llewellyn Probert, Reggie Oliver, Mark Valentine, David A. Sutton, Peter Bell and others, including Christopher Harman's winner, "Quis est Iste?".

Edited and introduced by Anne C. Perry and Jared Shurin, *A Town Called Pandemonium* featured ten stories set in or around the eponymous Texas town by Will Hill, Joseph D'Lacey, Jonathan Oliver and others. Illustrated by Adam Hill, the shared-world anthology was available from Jurassic

London as a trade paperback and a 100-copy numbered hardcover edition.

Terry Martin's *Probably Maybe Perhaps: A Collection of Near and Future Short Stories* contained nineteen tales by the editor-in-chief of The House of Murky Depths.

Sam Stone's *Zombies at Tiffany's*, from Telos Publishing, was set in New York City in 1862.

From Megazanthus Press, *The First Book of Classical Horror Stories* edited by D. F. Lewis contained twenty-one stories inspired by classical music from Andrew Hook, Stephen Bacon, John Howard, Mark Valentine and Rhys Hughes, amongst others.

Darker Minds: An Anthology of Dark Fiction was the second volume in the anthology series from the collective Dark Minds Press, featuring new stories by Stephen Bacon, Simon Bestwick, Gary Fry, Gary McMahon and others. Ben Baldwin contributed an impressive cover image.

Ottawa's Ex Hubris Imprints published *Postscripts to Darkness 2* edited by Sean Moreland and Aalya Ahmad. This thin anthology contained sixteen stories, an interview with American author Lee Thomas and an afterword by the editors.

Vampyric Variations from Canada's Edge Science Fiction and Fantasy Publishing collected ten vampire stories (one original novella) by Nancy Kilpatrick, along with an introduction by Tanith Lee. Kilpatrick also edited and supplied an introduction to *Danse Macabre: Close Encounters with the Reaper* for the same publisher, containing twenty-six stories by Lisa Morton, Lucy Taylor, William Meikle, Tom Piccirili, Brian Hodge, Tanith Lee and Brian Lumley, amongst others.

Mark Leslie edited and introduced *Tesseracts Sixteen: Parnassus Unbound*, which contained twenty-eight stories and poems (five reprints) from authors such as Robert J. Sawyer, Sean Costello, Michael Kelly and Steve Vernon.

Edited by Tehani Wessely for Australia's FableCroft Publishing, *Epilogue* contained twelve stories about the end of the world.

Night Shadows: Queer Horror was a gay- and lesbian-themed anthology from Bold Strokes Books edited by Greg Herren and J. M. Redmann and featuring fourteen original stories.

William Holden's *Words to Die By* and Felice Picano's *Twelve O'Clock Tales* appeared under the Liberty imprint of the same lesbian/gay/bi/trans/queer publisher.

Originally written in 1976 as an outline for a movie, and lost twice in the intervening decades, Ray Bradbury's *The Nefertiti-Tut Express* finally saw print as a handsome oversized chapbook from Terence McVicker's The RAS Press with numerous line drawings by Gary Gianni.

Simon Marshall-Jones's Spectral Press issued Simon Kurt Unsworth's chapbook *Rough Magic*, Alison Littlewood's *The Eyes of Water*, David Tallerman's *The Way of the Leaves* and Mark West's *What Gets Left Behind*. Each booklet was limited to just 100 signed and numbered copies.

Nicholas Royle's Nightjar Press issued two chapbooks by Claire Massey, *Marionettes* and *Into the Penny Arcade*, along with David Rose's *Puck* and Alison Moore's *Small Animals*. Each booklet was published in a signed edition limited to 200 copies.

Nodens Books launched its Nodens Chapbooks series with *Sable Revery: Poems, Sketches and Letters* by Robert Nelson (1912-35), a contributor of verse to *Weird Tales* and a correspondent of H. P. Lovecraft and Clark Ashton Smith. It was followed by *The Ghost in the Tower: Sketches of Lost Jacobia*, a historical booklet about south-western Michigan by Earl H. Reed (1863–1931). Both print-on-demand chapbooks were introduced by Douglas A. Anderson and available in trade paperback and hardcover formats.

Algy Black and Artie Mack were back in Earthling Publications's *The Raven of October*, the latest chapbook by Peter Atkins, Glen Hirshberg and Thomas St. John Bartlett to tie in to performances of The Rolling Darkness Review at Los Angeles' Theatre/Theater during October and November.

From Rosemary Pardoe's Haunted Library, *Ex Libris: Lufford* contained a number of Jamesian pieces by Daniel McGachey, inspired by "Casting the Runes".

Edited by Gary William Crawford, *Insufficient Answers: Essays on Robert Aickman* from Gothic Press collected three essays about the life and works of the late author.

The six bi-monthly issues of Gordon Van Gelder's digest *The Magazine of Fantasy & Science Fiction* featured the usual stellar line-up of authors, including Ron Goulart, Albert E. Cowdrey, Lewis Shiner, Michael Blumlein, Peter S. Beagle, Tim Sullivan, Steven Utley, Geoffrey Landis, Fred Chappell, Dale Bailey, Kate Wilhelm, Rachel Pollack, Andy Duncan, Richard A. Lupoff, Peter Dickinson, Lynda E. Rucker, Alan Dean Foster and Lewis Shiner.

There were also book and film review columns by Charles de Lint, Elizabeth Hand, Kathi Maio, Chris Moriarty, Lucius Shepard, James Sallis and Michelle West, while Don Webb, Frances Grimble, Jack Womack, Bud Webster, Chris DeVito and David Langford all contributed more obscure titles to the always-fascinating "Curiosities" page.

The first issue of *Weird Tales* from the new editorial team, sporting a double-covered "Elder Gods" theme, restored the title's classic logo and featured a new Cthulhu Mythos novella by Brian Lumley, along with stories and poetry by Michael Shea, Michael Reaves, Darrell Schweitzer, Parke Godwin and Jessica Amanda Salmonson, amongst others. The flip-side contained a special tribute section featuring various works by Ray Bradbury, along with a personal reminiscence by editor Marvin Kaye.

However, the magazine ran into controversy when plans to run an excerpt from Victoria Foyt's controversial YA novel *Save the Pearls Part One: Revealing Eden* – set in a world where black people have become the dominant race – had to be pulled following an online furore that led to the resignation of senior contributing editor Anne VanderMeer "due to major differences with the existing editors".

Andy Cox's *Black Static* managed just five issues during the year, but this was because it changed to a more compact format in July and synchronised its publishing schedule with companion title *Interzone*.

Along with the usual opinion columns by Stephen Volk, Christopher Fowler and Mike O'Driscoll, the UK's best horror magazine also featured fiction by Stephen Bacon, Simon Bestwick, Joel Lane, Nina Allan and others, plus interviews with Alison Littlewood, Christopher Fowler and Nicholas Royle.

The two issues of Michael Kelly's visually much-improved paperback magazine *Shadows & Tall Trees* featured original fiction by Nina Allan, Don Tumasonis, Andrew Hook, Gary McMahon, Stephen Bacon, Reggie Oliver, Alison Moore, Robert Shearman and others, along with a key book review per issue.

Also looking better were the two issues of David Longhorn's *Supernatural Tales*, which featured stories by Steve Rasnic Tem, Iain Rowan, Steve Duffy, Michael Chislett, Michael Kelly and others. Unfortunately, due to financial pressures, the editor announced that the title would change to print-on-demand in 2013.

The two issues of James R. Beach's glossy *Dark Discoveries* included fiction by Thomas Ligotti, Kurt Newton, Lisa Morton and Clark Ashton Smith, along with some very lurid limericks by Ramsey Campbell. As well as a number of interesting articles and various reviews, there were also interviews with W. Paul Ganley, Joe R. Lansdale, Lisa Morton and Ellen Datlow. The magazine found a new publisher with issue #21.

After an almost twenty-year hiatus, John Gilbert revived his *Fear* magazine with a "Special Collector's Edition" in October, and followed it up with another thin issue the following month. Featuring interviews with James Herbert, Stephen Jones, Tom Fletcher and Nicholas Vince, along with articles by Mark Morris and Stephen Volk and a selection of book reviews, the magazine also sponsored a ghostly short story competition.

The September issue of *Fortean Times* celebrated the 150th anniversary of the birth of M. R. James with an article by Robert Lloyd Parry and commentary from Ramsey Campbell, Stephen Jones, Kim Newman, John Connolly, Stephen Volk, Gary McMahon and Adam Nevill.

The six issues Tim Lucas's *Video WatcHDog: The Perfectionist's Guide to Fantastic Video* included tributes to actress Lina Romay and director Robert Fuest; a look at Tim Burton's *Alice in Wonderland* and an adult version of the story; a retrospective of *Dark Shadows*; an overlong interview with actress Daliah Laví; a look at the *Universal Classic Monsters Essential Collection* on Blu-ray, and an interesting history of *Exorcist II: The Heretic*, along with all the usual reviews and the "Ramsey's Rambles" column by Ramsey Campbell.

Canada's *Rue Morgue* put out its usual eleven glossy issues, including a bumper fifteenth-anniversary Hallowe'en edition celebrating 100 years of Universal Studios. Other features included articles on Hammer's *The Woman in Black*, the new version of Clive Barker's *Nightbreed* and the anniversaries of *Poltergeist* and *Prince of Darkness*.

Among those interviewed were writers Anne Rice, Sarah Pinborough, George Clayton Johnson and John Skipp, along with actors and directors Carla Laemmle, Julie Adams, Sidney J. Furie, William Lustig, Tommy Lee Wallace, Tim Burton and the cast of the original *Dark Shadows* TV show, and the late Jean Rollin, David Friedman and Ray Bradbury.

Bob Eggleton illustrated a fantasy smack-down between Godzilla and Gamera on the cover of the *kaiju*-themed issue of *Famous Monsters of Filmland* #262. The artist also contributed an article on the 1958 movie *Varan the Unbelievable* to the same edition.

The March 16th issue of *Entertainment Weekly* included an exclusive excerpt from Justin Cronin's vampire novel *The Twelve*, a sequel to *The Passage*.

The forty-fourth anniversary issue of *Locus* was a special "Science Fiction and Fantasy Art" edition that included interviews with (Gerald) Brom and John Picacio, along with commentary from an impressive roster of other artists, while the July issue was a "Young Adult Fiction" special featuring interviews with Holly Black, Tamora Pierce and Rae Carson. Other writers interviewed in the magazine during the year included Claude Lalumière, Joe Haldeman, Paul Di Filippo, Sarah Pinborough, William F. Nolan, Jack Vance and Tim Pratt.

The British Fantasy Society managed to get only two issues of its *BFS Journal* out in 2012, but they were both hefty trade paperback editions packed with columns and articles by Lee Harris, Ramsey Campbell, Mark Morris, Simon Bestwick, Michael Marshall Smith, Amanda Rutter, Stephen Volk, Gillian Redfearn, Paul Kane and others, along with interviews with Sarah Pinborough, Nina Allan, Rhys Hughes, Mike Barrett, David A. Sutton and artist Chris Roberts.

There was also fiction and poetry from, amongst others, Jonathan Oliver, Marie O'Regan, Allen Ashley, Garry Kilworth, Christopher Golden, Gary Fry and Peter Crowther, plus the usual BFS news and views.

The *FantasyCon 2012* souvenir book was a hardcover edited by Paul Kane and Marie O'Regan, while Christopher and Barbara Roden edited the *World Fantasy Convention 2012* softcover souvenir book, which reflected the event's theme of "Northern Gothic and Urban Fantasy". Both featured fiction by and articles about the various Guests of Honour. There was also apparently a hardcover edition the WFC Souvenir Book, but that was only available to a select few.

The two issues of Rosemary Pardoe's *The Ghost & Scholars M. R. James Newsletter* included Christopher Harman's winning entry in a short story competition, an article about the influence of dreams in James's fiction, and the usual Jamesian news and reviews.

After taking over the subscription list for the now-defunct *Realms of Fantasy*, Hildy Silverman's *Space and Time* entered the magazine's forty-sixth year of continuous publication with fiction by Scott Edelman and others, along with an interview with Kevin J. Anderson.

John Meaney was interviewed in Ireland's *Albedo One*, which also featured fiction by Todd McCaffrey and others.

Thirty years after he ceased publication, Jon M. Harvey revived his Spectre Press as an imprint for charity. The first new publication was *The Weird and the Wonderful Portfolio 1: From the Collection of Jon Harvey*. It contained an explanatory booklet and eleven prints by Stephen E. Fabian, Brian Frost, Dallas Goffin, Alan Hunter, David Lloyd, Martin McKenna, Jim Pitts (the only one in colour), SMS, John Stewart and two by the publisher. The portfolio, which was also available as a CD-Rom, was followed by *Alan Hunter 1929–2012*, a slim chapbook featuring a haphazard selection of artwork by the late British illustrator.

Morpheus Tales finally improved its print design as it put out four issues featuring fiction by, amongst others, Stuart Hughes and Matt Leyshon.

Edited by June M. Pulliam and Tony Fonseca, and issued twice a year by Hippocampus Press as a slim on-demand paperback, *Dead Reckonings* was a surprisingly entertaining compilation of book reviews from diverse hands, along with regular columns by Ramsey Campbell and S. T. Joshi.

Edited by Daniel Corrick and Mark Samuels for Hieroglyphic Press, *Sacrum Regnum 1* was a literary paperback magazine containing fiction, poems, essays and reviews by Samuels, Mark Valentine and others.

Published in full colour, it was a shame that Justin Marriott's attractive and informative *The Paperback Inferno* had to go to subscription-only due to increased Royal Mail charges. Issue 22 was a bumper special edition dedicated the Tandem and Award book imprints and included articles on authors R. Chetwynd-Hayes and Charles Birkin, Occult books of the 1970s, *Planet of the Apes* tie-ins, and the UK edition of *Galaxy* magazine. It also included an impressive gallery of Robert Bloch covers, along with a lively letters column.

* * *

S. T. Joshi's wide-ranging study *Unutterable Horror: A History of Supernatural Fiction* was split over two hardcover editions (and nearly 800 pages) by PS Publishing in *Volume 1: From Gilgamesh to the End of the Nineteenth Century* and *Volume 2: The Twentieth and Twenty-First Centuries*.

Joshi also edited a revised and updated edition of H. P. Lovecraft's *The Annotated Supernatural Horror in Literature* for Hippocampus Press, and with David E. Schultz he co-edited and introduced *Letters to James F. Morton*, a collection of Lovecraft's letters to one of his numerous correspondents, along with an appendix, index and various articles about Morton.

Jenifer Paquette's *Respecting The Stand: A Critical Analysis of Stephen King's Apocalypse Novel* was published by McFarland, as was *The Subversive Harry Potter: Adolescent Rebellion and Containment in the J. K. Rowling Novels* by Vandana Saxena.

Edited by Tracy L. Bealer, Rachel Luria and Wayne Yuen, *Neil Gaiman and Philosophy* for Carus Publishing/Open Court collected fourteen essays, while the equally esoteric *Feminism in the Worlds of Neil Gaiman: Essays on the Comics, Poetry and Prose*, edited by Tara Prescott and Aaron Drucker for McFarland, contained sixteen essays.

Christopher M. O'Brien's *The Forrest J Ackerman Oeuvre* from McFarland was subtitled *A Comprehensive Catalog of the Fiction, Nonfiction, Poetry, Screenplays, Film Appearances, Speeches and Other Works, with a Concise Biography*. A checklist of more than 3,000 items that was likely to only appeal to the most hardcore Forry fan, it came with a foreword by Dennis Billows and included a selection of black and white photos.

Terry Earl Kemp's *The Anthem Series: A Guide to the Science Fiction, Fantasy, Horror and Weird Specialty Publishers of the Golden Age* from The Last Stand was a bibliographic listing of the publications of more than forty small press imprints, including Arkham House, Shasta,

Fantasy Press and others, along with numerous colour cover reproductions.

A Natural History of Ghosts: 500 Years of Hunting for Proof was a terrific examination of the British fascination with ghost-hunting by film critic and former horror writer Roger Clarke.

In May, a pastel version of Edvard Munch's painting *The Scream* was sold to an anonymous buyer at Sotherby's in New York for a record-breaking $119.9 million (£74 million), making it the most expensive piece of artwork ever sold at auction. Three other versions of the picture are known to exist.

Edited with a Preface by Joseph Wrzos for Centipede Press, *Hannes Bok: A Life in Illustration* was a massive tome that collected hundreds of examples of the pulp artist's work, including all of his early illustrations for *Weird Tales*, much of it in full colour. There was also a reprinted memoir by Ray Bradbury, along with tributes from other artists and additional biographical and critical material.

From IDW Publishing/Desperado, *Jeffrey Jones: A Life in Art* contained text by the late artist and Cliff Biggers.

Written and illustrated by Brom, *Krampus: The Yule Lord* involved a failed songwriter and the eponymous demon, who was plotting to destroy Santa Claus on Christmas Eve.

Mike Mignola and Christopher Golden's novella *Father Gaetano's Puppet Catechism* was also illustrated by Mignola.

From Underwood Books, *Spectrum 19: The Best in Contemporary Fantastic Art* edited by Cathy Fenner and Arnie Fenner included reproductions of more than 500 pieces of art from over 300 artists, along with a profile of Grand Master Award-winner James Gurney.

PS Art Books continued its successful series of full-colour pre-code comic book reprints with *ACG Collected Works: Out of the Night Volume One* with a foreword by Roy

Thomas and *ACG Collected Works: Skeleton Hand* with a foreword by Peter Normanton, while Christopher Fowler contributed the foreword to *Harvey Horrors Collected Works: Black Cat Mystery Volume One*.

Kim Newman and James Lovegrove supplied the forewords to the fourth volumes of, respectively, *Chamber of Chills* and *Witches Tales*, the latest titles in PS ArtBooks' "Harvey Horrors" series of comic-strip reprints.

Roy Thomas Presents was a new series that began with *The Heap Volume One*, a reprint collection of the 1940s monster comic strip with a personal and historical introduction by Thomas.

From the same imprint, *The Casebook of Bryant and May: The Soho Devil!* was a hardcover graphic novel written by Christopher Fowler and illustrated by Keith Page.

Compiled by comic book historian Tim Pilcher, *The Little Book of Vintage Horror* from ILEX featured full-colour covers, pages and strips from *Adventures Into the Unknown*, *Forbidden Worlds*, *This Magazine is Haunted* and other pre-code titles, along with a free fridge magnet. Companion volumes covered *Sci-Fi*, *Crime*, *Combat*, *Romance* and *Sauciness*.

For fans of pre-code horror, Yoe Comics/IDW launched *Haunted Horror*, which reprinted a number of stories in a regular comic book format.

Through interviews with more than 150 insiders, Sean Howe looked at the stories behind the history in *Marvel Comics: The Untold Story*.

A gillman monster was influenced by the torn pages from Shakespeare he found inside a bottle in Jonathan Case's *Dear Creature* from Tor Books.

Judge Dredd: Cry of the Werewolf from Rebellion collected four strips dating from 1983–2010.

Road Rage from IDW was a four-issue adaptation of the novella by Stephen King and Joe Hill, inspired by Richard Matheson's *Duel*.

Steve Niles wrote the sequel to Mary Shelley's novel and the great Bernie Wrightson illustrated it in IDW's

Frankenstein Alive, Alive! while the same imprint also re-launched *Godzilla* and *Mars Attacks* titles.

Howard Lovecraft and the Undersea Kingdom from Arcana Studio was a child-friendly sequel to co-writer Bruce Brown's *Howard Lovecraft and the Frozen Kingdom*. It involved the youthful protagonist and his tentacled pet Spot travelling to the planet of Yuggoth.

Veteran illustrator Ernie Colon adapted four stories from the 1940s radio show for NBM's *Inner Sanctum*, while Richard Corben illustrated Edgar Allan Poe's *The Conqueror Worm* for Dark Horse.

The same publisher also revived Warren's *Eerie* title from the 1970s with a mixture of new and reprint material.

Dynamic Entertainment's *Vampirella vs. Dracula* was actually a sequel to a 1997 story by Alan Moore while, in another major cross-over, Vampirella teamed up with Barnabas Collins to battle Jack the Ripper and Elizabeth Bathory in the *Dark Shadows/Vampirella* series.

Killings in a small Minnesota town were committed by a werewolf in Avatar Press's *Ferals*, and Bluewater Comics' *Dorian Gray* was an updated version of Oscar Wilde's original.

The Infernal Man-Thing from Marvel was a three-part series based on an unpublished script by the late Steve Gerber.

Comics writer Dan Slott received death threats after killing off Peter Parker at the arms of Doctor Octopus in the 700th and final issue of Marvel's *The Amazing Spider-Man* in December. However, it was announced that the narrative would continue in a new title, *Superior Spider-Man*.

In an ironic twist of fate, the original cheque for $130 with which Detective Comics (later DC) bought all rights to Superman from creators Jerry Siegel and Joe Shuster sold at auction in April for $160,000.

Battleship by Peter David, *Snow White and the Huntsman* by Lily Blake and *Resident Evil: Retribution* by John Shirley were all original movie tie-ins.

Gareth Roberts's *Doctor Who: Shada: The Lost Adventure by Douglas Adams* was based on the unproduced TV scripts by Adams. Other tie-ins to the show included *Doctor Who: Magic of the Angels* by Jacqueline Rayner, *Doctor Who: Dark Horizons* by J. T. Colgan and *Doctor Who: The Wheel of Ice* by Stephen Baxter.

BBC Books also reissued a number of *Doctor Who* novelisations from the 1970s that featured additional material, including new introductions by Michael Moorcock, Alastair Reynolds, Mark Gatiss, Steven Moffat, Tom MacRae and Gary Russell.

The Walking Dead: The Road to Woodbury by Robert Kirkman and Jay Bonansinga was the second in the series set in the world of the comics and TV series, while Nancy Holder's *Teen Wolf: On Fire* was based on the MTV show.

The Vampire Diaries: Stefan's Diaries 5: The Asylum and *6: The Compelled* were the latest uncredited tie-ins to L. J. Smith's YA books and the TV series created by Kevin Williamson and Julie Plec.

Meanwhile, *The Vampire Diaries: The Hunters, Vol. 2: Moonsong* and *Vol. 3: Destiny Rising* were the second and third volumes, respectively, in the uncredited spin-off series The Hunters, also based on Smith's original books.

The Secret Circle: The Divide and *The Secret Circle: The Hunt*, both by Aubrey Clarke, were based on another YA book series created by Smith and were tie-ins to the already-cancelled TV show.

S. D. Perry's *Resident Evil: Caliban*, *Resident Evil: City of the Dead* and *Resident Evil: The Umbrella Conspiracy* were all set in the world of the video game franchise, while Nate Kenyon's *Diablo III: The Order* was based on a computer game.

Arkham Horror: The Lies of Solace by John French was the second book in the Lord of Nightmares gaming trilogy, and Graham McNeill's *Arkham Horror: Bones of the Yopasi* was the second in the Dark Waters trilogy.

Lisi Harrison's *Monster High 4: Back and Deader Than*

Ever was the fourth book in a series based on a range of Mattel dolls.

The usual slew of new film titles from McFarland & Company included *Werewolves and Other Shapeshifters in Popular Culture: A Thematic Analysis of Recent Depictions* by Kimberly McMahon-Coleman and Roslyn Weaver, *The Zombie Movie Encyclopedia Volume Two: 2000–2010* by Peter Dendle, *Going to Pieces: The Rise and Fall of the Slasher Film* by Adam Rockoff, *Hammer Films: An Exhaustive Filmography* by Tom Johnson and Deborah Del Vecchio, *Caroline Munro, First Lady of Fantasy* by Robert Michael "Bob" Cotter with a foreword by the actress herself, *Gutter Auteur: The Films of Andy Milligan* by Rob Craig, *American Silent Horror, Science Fiction and Fantasy Feature Films 1913–1929* by John T. Soister, Henry Nicoletta, Steve Joyce, Harry H. Long and Bill Chase, *Character Actors in Horror and Science Fiction Films 1930–1960* by Laurence Raw, *Australian Horror Films 1973–2010* by Peter Shelley and *Regional Horror Films 1959–1990: A State-by-State Guide with Interviews* by Brian Albright.

From the same imprint, *Now a Terrifying Motion Picture: Twenty-Five Classic Works of Horror Adapted from Book to Film* by James F. Broderick was an idiosyncratic selection of filmed fiction that included chapters on *The Amityville Horror*, *The Birds*, *Dr. Jekyll and Mr. Hyde*, *The Exorcist*, *The Fly*, *Frankenstein*, *Ghost Story*, *Jaws*, *The Masque of the Red Death* and *The Night Stalker*.

Published by BearManor Media, *Invasion of the Body Snatchers: The Making of a Classic* by Mark Thomas McGee was a look behind-the-scenes at the 1956 movie.

Unfortunately, the imprint also thought they could just rip-off old movie tie-ins if they couldn't trace the copyright holders. As a result, they issued what were basically pirated editions of *Bride of Frankenstein*, *Brides of Dracula*, *Dr. Terror's House of Horrors*, *The Raven* and *The Revenge of Frankenstein*, featuring new material "edited" by Philip J. Riley.

More positively, Riley and BearManor also put out a series of books under the Filmonster imprint based on unproduced Universal movie scripts, including versions of *Cagliostro* starring Boris Karloff, *Frankenstein* and *Dracula's Daughter* starring Bela Lugosi, and *The Wolf Man vs Dracula* with Lugosi and Lon Chaney, Jr.

The Mammoth Book of Slasher Movies: An A–Z Guide to Over Sixty Years of Blood and Guts by Peter Normanton was a guide to around 250 films from more than twenty countries. The trade paperback also included a full list of the "video nasties" that the UK government tried to ban.

David Konow's *Reel Terror* was a look at 100 years of horror movies, while Blair Davis charted the rise of the genre second feature in *The Battle for the Bs: 1950s Hollywood and the Rebirth of Low-Budget Cinema.*

Edited by Richard Christian Matheson for Gauntlet Press, *Stephen King's Battleground* was a commemorative volume of the Emmy Award-winning TV adaptation scripted by Matheson himself for the premiere episode of TNT's *Nightmares & Dreamscapes.*

In *Un-Dead TV: The Ultimate Guide to Vampire Television*, Brad Middleton listed vampires in small-screen series, movies, episodes and documentaries. Vampire expert J. Gordon Melton contributed a foreword.

Edited by Wayne Yuen for Carus Publishing/Open Court, *The Walking Dead and Philosophy* contained twenty essays about the philosophical concepts to be found in the comics and TV series.

Mark Cotta Vaz wrote *Breaking Dawn Part 1: The Official Illustrated Movie Companion.*

After protecting their fast-growing but ludicrously named vampire daughter Renesmee (Mackenzie Foy) from the villainous Volturi, a trick ending failed to save the boring protagonists of Bill Condon's *The Twilight Saga: Breaking Dawn – Part 2* from all living happily ever after. The fifth and final film in the fatuous franchise had a depressing $141 million debut and went on to gross $751 million world-wide after just four weeks, making it the most successful *Twilight* entry of all time.

For an audience too young to remember its numerous SF precedents, Gary Ross's version of Suzanne Collins's best-selling YA novel *The Hunger Games* featured Jennifer Lawrence as a teenager forced to compete in televised fight-to-the-death tournaments in a dystopian future. Older members of the cast included Woody Harrelson, Elizabeth Banks, Stanley Tucci, Lenny Kravitz and Donald Sutherland.

The film became the third-biggest opener at the time when it took $152.5 million (£100 million) at the US box-office over its first weekend in March, making it the highest-grossing opening of any "non-sequel". Outside America, where the books are less well known, the movie did not perform quite so spectacularly, but in the US it managed to out-gross all the *Twilight* and *Harry Potter* movies.

Finally bringing together Iron Man (Robert Downey, Jr), Thor (Chris Hemsworth), Captain America (Chris Evans), the Hulk (Mark Ruffalo) and a bunch of other heroes nobody cares about, Joss Whedon's 3-D *The Avengers* (bizarrely retitled *Marvel Avengers Assemble!* in the UK to stop it being confused with the 1960s TV series) opened to an incredible $207.4 million (£123.7 million) at the US box-office in May, breaking all previous opening-weekend records. The film also became the first movie to reach $150 million in only two days, $200 million in three days and $450 million in seventeen days. It went on to become only the third film (along with James Cameron's *Avatar* and *Titanic*) to pass the $600 million mark in domestic release.

Meanwhile, Marc Webb's *The Amazing Spider-Man* was a likeable 3-D reboot of the recent franchise (last seen in 2007) that was aimed at the chick-flick market and recast British actor Andrew Garfield as the angst-ridden web-slinger. At least a subdued Rhys Ifans was on hand as mutant reptilian villain The Lizard.

Five years after he last played the role, Nicholas Cage was back as Marvel's motorcycle-riding avenger battling Ciarán Hinds's suave Satan in 3-D in *Ghost Rider: Spirit of Vengeance* which, if anything, was more bonkers than the original.

Christian Bale's sombre Batman battled Tom Hardy's masked terrorist Bane and teamed up with Anne Hathaway's slinky cat burglar Selina Kyle/Catwoman in *The Dark Knight Rises*, the $250 million concluding chapter in Christopher Nolan's revisionist trilogy.

Tragically, a masked gunman went on a rampage at a midnight screening of the film in a suburb of Denver, Colorado, and used legally purchased semi-automatic weapons to kill twelve people and injure fifty-eight more. As a consequence, the film's remaining premieres around the world were cancelled, advertising was pulled, and the studio decided not to announce box-office figures during that opening weekend.

It subsequently emerged that *The Dark Knight Rises* took $160.9 million at the domestic box-office over its inaugural weekend. Although this was the best debut ever for a non-3-D movie and the third-best weekend at the time, it still fell below industry expectations. The film went on to take $300 million domestically in just twelve days, with only *The Avengers* and *The Dark Knight* getting there faster.

In Peter Jackson's *The Hobbit: An Unexpected Journey*, the highly-anticipated prequel to *Lord of the Rings*, the wizard Gandalf (Ian McKellen, recreating his role) enlisted Bilbo Baggins (Martin Freeman) and his band of fellow hobbits in a quest to reclaim the lost Dwarf Kingdom of Erebor from the dragon Smaug. The first in a trilogy, it also featured Andy Serkis's Gollum and blink-and-you'll-miss-'em cameos by Ian Holm, Elijah Wood, Hugo Weaving, Cate Blanchett and Christopher Lee.

Meanwhile, J. R. R. Tolkien's estate and publisher HarperCollins sued Warner Bros, New Line and the Saul Zaentz Company for $80 million (£50 million) for causing "irreparable harm" to the author's legacy and reputation by registering various trademarks "to which they are not entitled", including a *Lord of the Rings* online slot machine. The case dates back to the granting of merchandising rights in 1969 (with amendments in 1975 and 1981).

Having excised "*of Mars*" from the advertising for reportedly commercial considerations (it's still on the end titles), Disney's overlong $250 million version of Edgar Rice Burroughs's *John Carter* starred former fashion model Taylor Kitsch as the titular Confederate Civil War hero accidentally transported to the red planet. After costing $250 million to make and around a further $100 million in distribution fees and marketing, the movie opened in the US to a disastrous $30.2 million weekend gross and went on to take around $184 million world-wide, making it the most expensive movie flop in history.

Kitsch was also one of the stars of Peter Berg's $209 million alien invasion movie *Battleship* (along with Liam Neeson and singer Rihanna), which was based on the board game from Hasbro, who were also responsible for the *Transformers* franchise. It had the worst US opening ever for a picture costing at least $200 million.

A crew of scientists (including Charlize Theron, Noomi Rapace and Michael Fassbender's sardonic cyborg) found themselves stranded on a distant planet that held the answer to mankind's origin in Ridley Scott's epic 3-D prequel-of-sorts *Prometheus*, which was set in the same universe as the director's classic *Alien*.

A futuristic assassin (Joseph Gordon-Levitt) was hired to kill his older self (Bruce Willis) in Rian Johnson's twisty time-travel thriller *Looper*.

Fifteen years after the first film and a decade since the forgettable sequel, Will Smith's Agent J travelled back in time to 1969 to save a young Agent K (Josh Brolin, expertly channelling Tommy Lee Jones) from an alien assassination plot in Barry Sonnenfeld's reportedly troubled 3-D *Men in Black 3*.

Colin Farrell, Kate Beckinsale and Jessica Biel were the stars of *Total Recall*, Len Wiseman's schlocky $125 million remake of the 1990 Arnold Schwarzenegger film, also based on the novel by Philip K. Dick.

Meanwhile, Karl Urban was the future cop who dispensed extremely rough justice in Mega City One in the 3-D *Dredd* which, like the 1995 film starring Sylvester Stallone, was based on the British comic strip *Judge Dredd*.

The addition of 3-D and a CGI Yoda added little to the re-release of the 1999 misfire *Star Wars Episode One – The Phantom Menace*, as George Lucus looked to wring every last cent out of the franchise.

He need not have worried – in October, Lucas agreed to sell his production company, Lucasfilm Ltd., to Disney for $4.05 billion (£2.5 billion) in cash and stock, thus paving the way for the Mouse House to immediately announce three more *Star Wars* sequels with Lucas serving as "creative consultant". The new *Episode VII* is due to be released in 2015.

Sam Worthington returned as Perseus, who travelled to the Underworld to rescue his father Zeus (Liam Neeson), in the unexpected 3-D sequel *Wrath of the Titans*.

Directed by Drew Goddard, who co-wrote the script with producer Joss Whedon, *The Cabin in the Woods* defied audience expectations as five college kids explored the titular fright-house. The film, which featured future *Thor* star Chris Hemsworth, was originally shot in 2009 but delayed after the bankruptcy of original studio MGM.

Hemsworth also led a band of attractive young Americans defending their country against an invasion by North Korea in *Red Dawn*, an updated remake of the 1984 film.

As nobody seemed to remember the 1989 TV movie scripted by Nigel Kneale, Hammer remade Susan Hill's 1983 novel *The Woman in Black* starring a post-*Potter* Daniel Radcliffe as a widowed lawyer stuck in a haunted house in Yorkshire.

Unbelievably, according to the British Board of Film Classification, it became the most complained-about film of the year in the UK, as more than 120 idiots protested that it was "scary and sinister" and not what they were expecting from a 12A-rated film starring Radcliffe. Apparently they failed to notice from the publicity that it was a horror movie.

Co-written by Seth Grahame-Smith and based on his own best-selling 2010 mash-up novel, the future sixteenth US President (Benjamin Walker) battled Rufus Sewell's secret Southern cabal of bloodsuckers in Timur Bekmambetov's 3-D *Abraham Lincoln: Vampire Hunter*, produced by Tim Burton.

Also lazily scripted by Grahame-Smith, Burton's own *Dark Shadows* was a stylish re-imagining of the 1960s TV soap opera, with Johnny Depp as 200-year-old vampire Barnabas Collins, out of his depth in the modern world of 1972. The formidable supporting cast included Michelle Pfeiffer, Helena Bonham Carter, Eva Green and even Alice Cooper.

John Cusack's alcoholic Edgar Allan Poe teamed up with a local detective (Luke Evans) to track down a serial killer who used the author's stories as inspiration in James McTeigue's curiously muted *The Raven*.

Anthony Hopkins portrayed the director of *Psycho* in *Hitchcock*, which also featured Scarlett Johansson as Janet Leigh and Helen Mirren as the director's long-suffering wife Alma.

Inspired by the video game franchise, Michael J. Bassett's *Silent Hill: Revelation* in 3-D was a belated Hallowe'en sequel that nobody wanted featuring Malcolm McDowell, Carrie-Anne Moss and a returning Sean Bean.

Milla Jovovich was back kicking monster and mutant zombie arse across a series of virtual realities in her husband Paul W. S. Anderson's 3-D *Resident Evil: Retribution*. Previous cast members Michelle Rodriguez, Oded Fehr and Colin Salmon also returned in the fifth movie in the video-game-inspired franchise, which opened at #1 in the US.

Kate Beckinsale also returned in the skin-tight leather catsuit for the 3-D *Underworld: Awakening*, the fourth entry in the puzzling vampires vs Lycans series, co-scripted by her husband Len Wiseman. It also debuted at #1 in the US.

Twenty years after the release of the original, Jean-Claude Van Damme and Dolph Lundgren were back as resurrected warriors in *Universal Soldier: Day of Reckoning*.

Two years after Alexandre Aja's sly remake, *Piranha 3DD* was bigger if not better with a cast that included a returning Christopher Lloyd, along with David Hasselhoff, Gary Busey and veteran Clu Gulager, the father of director John Gulager.

Ashley Green and Tom Felton were haunted by a blurry entity in *The Apparition*, while Jeffrey Dean Morgan and Kyra Sedgwick's daughter (Natasha Callis) was inhabited by an evil dybbuk demon in *The Possession* (which was also apparently "based on a true story"). It was #1 at the US box-office over the Labor Day weekend.

Elizabeth Olsen starred in *Silent House*, an American remake of Gustavo Hernández's real-time Spanish thriller, and Clive Owen starred in *The Intruders*, a haunted house story set in both Spain and the UK.

Returning home to her late mother's haunted house, a biker girl (Caity Lotz) had to face her childhood traumas in Nicholas McCarthy's low budget debut *The Pact*, which also featured Casper Van Dien.

After moving into a house where a number of gruesome murders were committed, Ethan Hawke's true-crime writer found his family endangered by a murderous spirit in Scott Derrickson's *Sinister*, while Kelly McGillis turned up as psychic actress staying at a 100-year-old Connecticut inn haunted by a dead bride in Ti West's *The Innkeepers*.

Set in Yorkshire during the 1970s, *When the Lights Went Out* was "based on the true story of the most terrifying poltergeist haunting in British history". In a desperate attempt to drum up some publicity, the film's producer called in the exorcists when two screenings were interrupted by power cuts, which were put down to the effects of "demonic possession".

Also based in Yorkshire, *Imbred* was about an encounter between a group of young offenders and the locals that led to bloody violence.

A psychopathic marksman was killing people on the top floor of a soon-to-be-demolished high-rise in *Tower Block*, starring Sheridan Smith.

Maryland beach-goers were infected by horrific parasitic isopods in Barry Levinson's eco-warning *The Bay*, while Rutger Hauer, Doug Bradley and Shane Richie were among the unlikely cast gathered for Neil Jones's low budget vampire film *The Reverend*.

Jessica Biel uncovered the legend of *The Tall Man* while searching for her missing child, and a killer targeted his victims via Internet chats in *Smiley*.

A psycho killer *may* have kidnapped Amanda Seyfried's sister in *Gone*, and new kid in town Jennifer Lawrence discovered odd things going on at the home of a boy and his sister in *House at the End of the Street*.

Richard Bates, Jr.'s body horror comedy *Excision* featured Traci Lords, John Waters, the busy Malcolm McDowell, Marlee Matlin, Ray Wise and the offspring of many well-known actors in a tale of a psycho student (Anna-Lynn McCord).

A pair of hitmen discovered more than they expected in the remote house of their intended victim in Sean Hogan's talky *The Devil's Business*, while debuting director Alastair Siddon's ghost movie *In the Dark Half* was made for even less money.

A couple teamed up to battle zombies in Keith Wright's comedy *Harold's Going Stiff*.

Paranormal Activity 4 was actually a "found footage" follow-up to the first sequel (the previous entry being a prequel), as a Nevada family came to regret taking in their neighbour's kid.

Paranormal Activity creator Oren Peli produced and co-scripted *Chernobyl Diaries*, in which a group of "shock tourists" were chased around the former Russian nuclear facility by murderous mutants, while Noel Clarke scripted and starred in *Storage 24*, a low budget British thriller in which a group of friends ran around a storage unit being pursued by an alien monster.

Acquired by Paramount for just £1 million, the R-rated faux-documentary *The Devil Inside* opened in the US at #1 with a record-breaking $33.7 million – the third-biggest January opening ever, despite poor reviews.

From Eduardo Sanchez, co-director of *The Blair Witch Project*, *Lovely Molly* was another "found footage" farrago about a woman literally haunted by her past.

V/H/S was a "found footage" horror anthology of six stories by six directors, including Sanchez, David Bruckner and Ti West, while more "found footage" revealed that a British explorer (Richard Dillane) and his stowaway son discovered prehistoric creatures in the Congo in *The Dinosaur Project*.

British stand-up comedian Ross Noble played a reanimated killer clown in Conor McMahon's Irish slasher flick *Stitches*, and Jon Wright's comedy *Grabbers*, in which getting drunk was the only defence from a tentacular alien monster, also hailed from the Emerald Isle.

Cillian Murphy and Sigourney Weaver's sceptical scientists investigated Robert De Niro's blind psychic in Spanish writer and director Rodrigo Cortés's paranormal thriller, *Red Lights*.

"Presented" by Luc Besson, futuristic French thriller *Lockout* was basically *Escape from New York* in outer space as charisma-challenged Guy Pearce had to rescue the president's daughter from an orbiting prison.

A French adaptation of the 1796 Gothic novel by Matthew Gregory Lewis, *The Monk* starred Vincent Cassel as the titular seventeenth-century Spanish friar tempted by the Devil (Sergi López).

Bickering survivors of a nuclear attack took refuge in the basement of a New York apartment building in the German-made *The Divide*.

Halle Berry's South African boat owner lost some stupid tourists to the sharks in *Dark Tide*, while Moscow was overrun by alien invaders in *The Darkest Hour* in 3-D.

Bhoot Returns was a Bollywood sequel involving ghosts and an exorcism.

Salman Rushdie's script of his novel *Midnight's Children* downplayed the book's magical realism, while the Wachowskis' and Tom Tykwer's epic version of David Mitchell's literary SF novel *Cloud Atlas* juggled six storylines simultaneously with the help of a cast that included Tom Hanks, Hugh Grant, Halle Berry, Jim Broadbent and Hugo Weaving in multiple roles.

Frank Langella's former cat burglar enlisted his mechanical housekeeper as a partner-in-crime in the sentimental *Robot & Frank*.

Ben Stiller, Vince Vaughn and Jonah Hill were members of an oddball neighbourhood watch patrol who discovered that an alien invasion was happening in their suburban neighbourhood in the misjudged comedy *The Watch*.

A lonely novelist (Paul Dano) struggling with writer's block willed into existence of the girl of his dreams (scriptwriter Zoe Kazan, the granddaughter of legendary director Elia) in *Ruby Sparks*, which also featured Antonio Banderas, Annette Bening, Steve Coogan and Elliott Gould.

Willem Dafoe's character just got on with things while the ozone level evaporated in Abel Ferrara's *4:44 Last Day on Earth*, and Steve Carell and Kiera Knightley went on an apocalyptic road trip together as a massive asteroid plummeted towards the planet in the oddball romcom *Seeking a Friend for the End of the World*.

Julia Roberts's pantomime evil queen plotted the death of her step-daughter (a bland Lily Collins) in Tarsem Singh's *Mirror Mirror*, while Charlize Theron's immortal wicked queen was far more alluring than Kristen Stewart's pouty heroine in Rupert Sanders's all-flash-but-no-substance *Snow White & the Huntsman*, which also featured Chris Hemsworth as the hunky huntsman and the cream of British character actors as *eight* dwarves.

Loosely based on the Jules Verne novel, the 3-D *Journey 2: The Mysterious Island* was an enjoyable family-friendly follow-up to the 2008 *Journey to the Center of the Earth* and featured Dwayne "The Rock" Johnson and Michael Caine.

Three teens emerged with telekinetic powers after an alien encounter in the low-budget *Chronicle*, which was presented in video diary format. The film beat *The Woman in Black* to #1 in its opening week at the US box-office.

Based on his 1984 live-action short film, Tim Burton's *Frankenweenie* was a 3-D stop-motion fable about a ten-year-old horror film fan named Victor who brought his beloved dead dog Sparky back to life. Catherine O'Hara, Martin Short, Winona Ryder and Martin Landau helped provide the voices.

Adam Sandler's Count Dracula was over-protective of his 118-year-old daughter (voiced by Selena Gomez) in Genndy Tartakovsky's 3-D animated comedy *Hotel Transylvania*. It achieved the best September opening weekend of all time in the US, debuting at #1. Tartakovsky's hand-animated short *Goodnight Mr. Foot*, about Bigfoot checking into the same hotel, was shown as support in some cinemas.

The ability of an eleven-year-old outcast (voiced by Kodi Smit-McPhee) to talk to ghosts came in handy when his cursed Massachusetts town was overrun by zombies in the delightfully spooky 3-D stop-motion children's film *ParaNorman*, from the same studio that created *Coraline*.

The 3-D animated *Dr. Seuss' The Lorax* had the third-best March opening ever, grossing $70.2 million in its first week and keeping *John Carter* off the top spot in its second. The colourful cartoon ended up taking almost three times what the Burroughs adaptation did at the US box-office.

Other children's animated films included *A Monster in Paris* and, in 3-D, *The Pirates! In an Adventure with Scientists!*, *Rise of the Guardians* and *Wreck-It Ralph*.

Rodney Ascher's fascinating feature documentary *Room 237* looked at the conspiracy theories surrounding Stanley Kubrick's *The Shining*, including supposed references to the Holocaust, the genocide of Native Americans and Kubrick's admission that he helped fake the *Apollo 11* moon landing!

As part of its extensive Alfred Hitchcock retrospective, the BFI reissued a restored version of the director's superb

1927 silent thriller *The Lodger: A Story of the London Fog*, which starred matinee idol Ivor Novello as a suspected Jack the Ripper killer. Nitin Sawhney provided a new music score.

Meanwhile, for the first time ever, Hitchcock's overrated *Vertigo* (a ghost story without a ghost) replaced *Citizen Kane* at the top of *Sight & Sound*'s poll of the best films ever made, as voted every ten years by a jury of international film critics (who should be ashamed of themselves).

The 84th Academy Awards were announced on February 26th at the temporarily renamed Hollywood and Highland Center in Los Angeles. Although it did not pick up any of the major awards, Martin Scorsese's delightful children's fantasy film *Hugo* was the big winner of the night, collecting technical Oscars for Best Cinematography, Best Art Direction, Best Sound Editing, Best Sound Mixing and Best Visual Effects.

The Girl with the Dragon Tattoo won for Best Film Editing, and the Best Animated Film Oscar went to *Rango*. "Man or Muppet" from *The Muppets* won Best Song, while *The Fantastic Flying Books of Mr Morris Lessmore* collected the Best Animated Short Oscar.

At $499.99 the *Harry Potter Wizard's Collection* not only contained all the films in DVD, Blu-ray and Ultra Violet versions, but also five hours of new extras, including a conversation between J. K. Rowling and screenwriter Steve Kloves. The packaging also featured various "artifacts", and even the box itself was a magic trick.

Almost as entertaining, *Indiana Jones: The Complete Adventures* included new high-definition transfers of all four films and a new making-of documentary about the 1981 original.

The Blu-ray of Marvel's *The Avengers* included Louis D'Esposito's spin-off short film *Item 47*, in which a young couple discovered a discarded alien gun from the climax of that film and went on a crime spree. A pair of S.H.I.E.L.D. agents were dispatched to stop them.

Released for the first time on Blu-ray, the limited edition *Universal Classic Monsters: The Essential Collection* featured eight discs, twelve hours of extras and a forty-eight-page book, *The Original House of Horror: Universal and a Monster Legacy*.

A pair of evangelical American Christians (Brittania Nicol and Henry Garrett) discovered that pagan beliefs survived in a remote Scottish border village in *The Wicker Tree*, Robin Hardy's ambitious companion piece to his cult classic *The Wicker Man* (1973). The direct-to-DVD release included a blink-and-you'll-miss-him cameo by Christopher Lee, who starred in the earlier film.

Udo Kier's Nazi launched an invasion from the dark side of the Moon in the deliriously bonkers *Iron Sky*, while *Outpost II: Black Sun* was a sequel to the 2008 *Outpost* that once again featured Nazi zombies.

Seiji Chiba's *AvN: Alien vs Ninja* was not the only clever direct-to-DVD title of the year. Alejandro Brugués's *Juan of the Dead* was about the titular Cuban zombie-killer, while Jonathan Glendening's *Strippers vs. Werewolves* did exactly what it said on the box and featured an eclectic cast that included Robert Englund, Steven Berkoff, Sarah Douglas, Lysette Anthony and Martin Kemp.

Meanwhile, Michelle Ryan, Honor Blackman, Tony Selby, Georgina Hale, Dudley Sutton and Richard Briers were among the British thespians dealing with an outbreak of the living dead in London's East End in Matthias Hoene's *Cockneys vs. Zombies*.

Toby Jones's sound engineer found life imitating art as he worked on a 1970s Italian horror movie in *Berberian Sound Studio*, and former "Pinhead" Doug Bradley starred in the unnecessary sequel *Wrong Turn 5: Bloodlines*.

Somehow Lance Henriksen and Art Hindle found themselves involved in *Monster Brawl*, Jesse T. Cook's wrestling monsters movie that also featured wrestling legends Jimmy Hart and Kevin Nash.

A night in Dartmoor's haunted Wistman's Woods didn't work out well for a trio of hikers in *A Night in the*

Woods, a poor man's British version of *The Blair Witch Project*.

When it came to 1980s remakes, Elijah Wood starred in Franck Khalfoun's *Maniac*, which was shot entirely from the killer's point of view. Rebecca De Mornay starred in *Mother's Day*, a remake of the psychological thriller from the director of three *Saw* sequels, while Malcolm McDowell was the star of *Silent Night*, a remake of the Santa Claus slasher *Silent Night Deadly Night*.

Even Stephen King was impressed with the low budget independent film *Entrance*, about the peculiar life of a female barista (Suziey Block).

Cashing-in on star Noomi Rapace's appearance in *Prometheus*, the direct-to-DVD *Babycall* (aka *The Monitor*) was a Scandinavian chiller about an apparently haunted baby-monitor.

Paco Plaza's *[Rec]3 Génesis* was the second sequel in the Spanish zombie franchise, while *Kill Zombie!* (aka *Zombibi*) was a comedy/horror hailing from the Netherlands.

Executive produced by Roland Emmerich, *Hell* (aka *Das Ende der Nacht*) was a German post-apocalyptic thriller set in 2016, when the world had been turned into a scorched wasteland by global warming.

Resident Evil: Damnation was an original CGI movie released on Blu ray and DVD

In August, the British Film Institute launched its new M. R. James series *Ghost Stories: Classic Adaptations from the BBC* with a disc containing both the 1968 and 2010 versions of *Whistle and I'll Come to You*, and a double-bill of *The Stalls of Barchester* and *A Warning to the Curious*.

From 1971 and recalling the work of Nigel Kneale, *The Dæmons* was one of the best *Doctor Who* stories ever. The five-part series was digitally remastered for a two-disc DVD that also included a making-of documentary and another looking at the career of producer Barry Letts.

Although the BBC wiped most of the original tapes of another Jon Pertwee *Doctor Who*, the welcome DVD release of 1970s *The Ambassadors of Death* was pieced together from various sources.

Released on DVD to tie-in with Tim Burton's misunderstood remake, the three-disc set *Dark Shadows – The Original TV Series (The Barnabas Collins Episodes)* contained just eighteen episodes from the 1960s daytime soap opera that featured Jonathan Frid's 175-year-old vampire.

Peter Bogdanovich, Joe Dante, Bruce Dern, Robert De Niro, Peter Fonda, Jack Nicholson, Martin Scorsese, William Shatner and Quentin Tarantino were among those who paid tribute to the career of influential producer/director Roger Corman in Alex Stapleton's documentary, *Corman's World: Exploits of a Hollywood Rebel*.

Lara Pulver was without doubt the sexiest Irene Adler ever in "A Scandal in Belgravia", the first of three new contemporary *Sherlock* films from the BBC starring Benedict Cumberbatch and Martin Freeman as Holmes and Watson. Unfortunately it was followed by Mark Gattis's misguided riff on "The Hound of the Baskervilles", but the series picked up again for the final showdown between Holmes and his nemesis Jim Moriarty (Andrew Scott) in "The Reichenbach Fall". The latter featured a brief appearance by Douglas Wilmer – a BBC Holmes in the mid-1960s – as an elderly member of the Diogenes Club.

There was an argument to be made that the Syfy channel was the new Monogram/PRC as it churned out a string of low budget TV movies in all genres, some of which bore an uncanny resemblance to bigger and better-known works.

A magnetised Mercury threatened to crash into the Earth in *Collision Course*, a Miami mountain could wipe out all life in *Miami Magna* (aka *Swamp Volcano*) and a mystical snow globe created *Snowmegeddon*. The planet was knocked off its rotation by exploding white matter in *Earth's Final Hours* starring Bruce Davison, and more superstorms threatened the Earth in *Mega Cyclone* (aka *Space Twister*).

Giant spiders attacked New Orleans in *Arachnoquake* featuring Edward Furlong, and Dominique Swain and Jake Busey's scientific researchers were kidnapped in Antarctica by *Nazis at the Center of the Earth*, who were creating a cyborg Adolph Hitler.

American Battleship (aka *American Warships*), starring Mario Van Peebles and Carl Weathers, could not possibly be confused with a more expensive summer movie, as the crew of the last battleship confronted an alien invasion of Earth.

Even by the (low) standards of Syfy movies, *2-Headed Shark Attack* starring Carmen Electra and *Jersey Shore Shark Attack* featuring Jack Scalia were rubbish.

However, these Syfy movies offered once-famous movie and TV actors an opportunity to still add to their credits as poor Michael Madsen found himself stuck in the Roger Corman-produced hybrid *Piranhaconda*, and Rae Dawn Chong looked on as *Pegasus vs. Chimera*.

Paul Ziller's *The Philadelphia Experiment* was actually a sequel to the 1984 time-travel movie of the same name, featuring Nicholas Lea, the ubiquitous Malcolm McDowell and the star of the original, Michael Paré, in a different role.

Hansel discovered his grown-up sister (Shannen Doherty) was working for the evil witch in *Witchslayer Gretl*, *Grimm's Snow White* featured Jane March as the wicked Queen, and Ben Cross turned up in *Black Forest*.

Aliens attacked the Earth with electromagnetic tornadoes in *Alien Tornado* (aka *Tornado Warning*) starring Jeff Fahey and Kari Wührer.

A demonic dead school principal wanted revenge in *Haunted High* (aka *Ghostquake*) starring Danny Trejo and Charisma Carpenter, and Morgan Fairchild was the house-mother from Hell (literally), harvesting the souls of sorority pledges in *American Horror House*.

Poachers Yancy Butler and Robert Englund discovered a lake was full of man-eating crocodiles in *Lake Placid: The Final Chapter*, while TV sitcom veterans Danny Bonaduce and Barry Williams were joined by Bruce Davison, Sherilyn

Fenn, Howard Hesseman and Alice Cooper playing himself in *Bigfoot*.

Emma Samms's chief of police had to stop the *Boogeyman*, and the Syfy channel celebrated St. Patrick's Day with *Leprechaun's Revenge* starring Billy Zane and William Devane.

Of course the Roger Corman-produced *Attack of the 50ft Cheerleader* was shown in 3-D on EPIX. At least the cast included Sean Young, Treat Williams and Mary Woronov, with cameos by John Landis, Ted Raimi and Corman himself.

In *The Girl*, Toby Jones's lecherous Alfred Hitchcock was obsessed with Tippi Hedren (Sienna Miller), his leading lady in *The Birds*, in a distasteful HBO movie made with the co-operation of the actress herself.

Olivia Holt's teenager discovered that she was descended from a family of monster hunters in Disney's *Girl vs. Monster*.

Delayed from its intended Hallowe'en debut, the BBC's three-part *The Secret of Crickley Hall*, written and directed by Joe Ahearne and based on the novel by James Herbert, made heavy-going of its story about the eponymous haunted house. Suranne Jones, Tom Ellis, Douglas Henshall and David Warner starred.

Matthew Rhys starred as the opium-addicted choirmaster John Jasper in the BBC's two-part adaptation of Charles Dickens's final, unfinished novel *The Mystery of Edwin Drood*.

"Presented by" Ridley Scott and Tony Scott, Lauren Ambrose, Geena Davis, James Woods, Ellen Burstyn and Richard Dreyfuss starred in A&E's two-part remake of *Coma*. It was based on the novel by Michael Crichton, which had previously been filmed in 1978.

Matt Smith's third season as *Doctor Who* began promisingly with Steven Moffat's psychotic zombie Daleks, but the BBC show soon returned to its annoyingly juvenile roots with a spaceship full of dinosaurs, a cyborg gunslinger and an invasion of Earth by alien cubes. Before the seventh new series went on hiatus after only five episodes, the Doctor travelled back in time to New York City, where he confronted the Weeping Angels and companions Amy and Rory (Karen Gillan and Arthur Darvill) finally and thankfully bowed out. Guest stars included Rupert Graves, Mark Williams, David Bradley, Jemma Redgrave, Steven Berkoff and Alex Kingston as River Song.

Meanwhile in May, children's show *Blue Peter* aired an exclusive *Doctor Who* mini-episode featuring Matt Smith and Karen Gillan, reputedly scripted by three young viewers who took part in a competition earlier in the year. *Children in Need* in November included a sneak preview of the Doctor's new companion Clara, played by Jenna-Louise Coleman, who had already turned up as a sassy disembodied intelligence in that first new episode of the year, "Asylum of the Daleks".

Another version of Coleman's character was introduced in the *Doctor Who* Christmas Day special, "The Snowmen", set in Victorian London. Guided by the "Great Intelligence" (voiced by Ian McKellen), Richard E. Grant's sinister Dr Simeon tried to take over the world with an army of pointy-toothed snowman.

After a brief appearance by Russell Tovey's George and an intriguing flash-forward to a dystopian future ruled by vampires, the ghostly Annie (Lenora Crichlow) was joined in the fourth season of the BBC's increasingly darker *Being Human* by new housemates – werewolf Tom (Michael Socha), bloodsucker Hal (Damien Molony), new ghost Alex (Kate Bracken) and a mysterious baby – as the vampiric Old Ones (led by Mark Gattis's campy Mr Snow) finally showed up to take control of humanity. Among the guest stars was Mark Williams, while Craig Roberts returned as Adam, the forty-year-old vampire trapped in the body of a teenager.

At the end of its resumed second season, AMC's *The Walking Dead* killed off its two most interesting characters before Hershal's farm was overrun by zombies and Sheriff Rick Grimes's (Andrew Lincoln) depleted band were scattered. As Season 3 began, the bickering survivors took refuge in an abandoned prison, while David Morrissey joined the cast as the obsessed governor, who held his zombie-free town of Woodbury in a lethal grip with the help of a familiar face.

Unexpectedly, a second six-part season of the supernatural soap opera *Bedlam* turned up on Sky Living in June. Most of the original leads were gone as Lacey Turner played a weepy paramedic who had inherited the power to see ghosts in the haunted luxury apartment block converted from an old insane asylum. At least the show created its own bogeyman.

And then there were nuns . . . Despite featuring a number of returning actors from the first series, FX's *American Horror Story Asylum* (no colon) was a totally unrelated tale about a madcap Church-run asylum set (mostly) in the mid-1960s. Into a heady mix of sex and the supernatural, the producers threw a lesbian journalist, alien abduction, bloody-faced serial killers, a mad doctor and his mutant experiments, demonic possession, a homicidal Santa and spanking nuns. Actors such as Zachary Quinto, Joseph Fiennes, James Cromwell, Jessica Lange, Ian McShane and Chloë Sevigny must have wondered what they had done wrong to end up in this mess.

Following the killing of series regular Bobby Singer (Jim Beaver) by Leviathan leader Dick Roman (James Patrick Stuart) on The CW's much-improved *Supernatural*, Dean Winchester (Jensen Ackles) travelled back to 1944 to team up with proto-hunter Eliot Ness (Nicholas Lea) while Bobby's angry spirit returned Topper-like to help the boys out when they needed him. After a cliff-hanger ending, Season 8 revealed in flashback what happened to Dean after he spent a year in Purgatory and what caused his brother Sam (Jared Padalecki) to give up monster-hunting.

For Season 5 of HBO's *True Blood*, Christopher Meloni joined the cast as the 400-year-old head of the Vampire Authority, an undead faction that wanted to live in harmony with humans. However, he met his true death at the hands of a resurrected Russell Edgington (Denis O'Hare), who wanted just the opposite. Meanwhile, Rutina Wesley's increasingly annoying Tara found herself transformed into an unwilling vampire to save her life, and Sookie (Anna Paquin) and Jason (Ryan Kwanten) discovered a secret about their parents' death in a fairy burlesque club. Creator Alan Ball announced that he was stepping down as show-runner if *True Blood* was picked up for a sixth season.

Bi-sexual succubus Bo's (Anna Silk) attempts to prevent a civil war amongst the Fae led to the deaths of two major characters in Season 2 of Syfy's *Lost Girl*.

Terry O'Quinn and Vanessa Williams were the devilishly attractive couple out to steal the souls of a young couple (Rachel Taylor and Dave Annable) hired to manage their cursed Manhattan apartment building in ABC's *666 Park Avenue*.

Despite a slowly emerging conspiracy plot, NBC's *Grimm* was never more than a mythological creature-of-week series. The first season ended with Detective Nick Burckhardt (David Gluntoli) discovering that the mother he thought dead (Mary Elizabeth Mastrantonio) was alive and kicking monsters. The second series shook things up a bit, as Nick's annoying girlfriend (Bitsie Tulloch) awakened from a magical coma with no memory of who he was, and a mysterious cabal sent some nasty critters to kill the monster-hunter.

After Artie (Saul Rubinek) used a stolen artefact to turn back time and restore *Warehouse 13*, the investigators encountered people who thought they saw H. P. Lovecraft's tentacled monsters, and series regular Leena (Genelle Williams) was apparently killed by someone she trusted at the end of the third season of the Syfy show.

With its final thirteen-part season, Syfy's *Eureka* (aka *A Town Called Eureka*) upped its game considerably in the opening two episodes, with the crew of the *Astraeus* trapped inside a dark virtual reality created by renegade scientist Beverley Barlowe (Debrah Farentino), which lead to the shocking death of one of the show's most likeable characters.

However, that character was subsequently resurrected in a new body and the series quickly returned to its usual lightweight format as a couple of townsfolk were revealed to be saboteurs, and Sheriff Carter (Colin Ferguson) finally married Allison (Salli Richardson-Whitfield).

After five seasons the series ended on a perfect note, with a number of characters returning for the bittersweet finale.

Unfortunately, the fourth season of Syfy's *Sanctuary* was the most disappointing yet, with its tedious overarching plot about abnormal terrorists from Hollow Earth. After an opening episode in which Dr Helen Magnus (Amanda Tapping) travelled back in time to stop Adam Worth changing history, the show reached its nadir with a cringe-worthy musical episode.

Despite being executive produced by J. J. Abrams (*Lost*), *Alcatraz* was cancelled by the Fox network after just one season. A young San Francisco detective (Sarah Jones) teamed up with a geeky historian (Jorge Garcia) and a taciturn government agent (Sam Neill) to investigate why 302 prisoners and staff who mysteriously disappeared from the island prison in 1963 were returning to modern San Francisco unchanged. Unfortunately, we never found out in the cliff-hanger final episode.

In its third season, Syfy's *Haven* continued to build upon its complicated mythology as Audrey (Emily Rose) discovered more about her own mysterious history, the origin of the Troubles and the truth behind the Colorado Kid. In the perplexing season finale, she finally entered the mysterious barn as the predicted meteor shower struck the town.

The seventh season of Showtime's *Dexter* opened with the show's highest-rated premiere to date as the serial killer's sister, Lt Debra Morgan (Jennifer Carpenter), tried to come to terms with her brother's true nature, and Yvonne Strahovski turned up as the former girlfriend of a dead killer who had her own secrets to hide.

Although not quite up to the standard of BBC's *Sherlock*, CBS's *Elementary* was still an enjoyable updating of the consulting detective, as an addictive Holmes (Jonny Lee

Miller), fresh out of rehab, teamed up with his sobriety monitor, Dr Joan Watson (Lucy Liu), to solve not-too-baffling crimes in New York City.

Perhaps the biggest problem with Season 2 of HBO's *Game of Thrones* was that there was *too much* plot – and plotting – as everybody and their brother (often literally) attempted to seize control of King's Landing before the horrific threat behind the Wall was revealed in a stunning final sequence.

ABC's *Once Upon a Time* continued to have some problems blending its real-life and fairy tale narratives, but Lana Parrilla was a terrific Evil Queen/Mayor Regina and Robert Carlyle had fun as the scheming Rumpelstiltskin/Mr Gold. In a clever twist, Meghan Ory's Red Riding Hood turned out to be the Big Bad Wolf herself, while genre veteran Brad Dourif guest-starred as a dark sorcerer.

In the show's second season, despite the queen's curse being lifted on Storybrooke, the fairy-tale characters recovered their memories but were still trapped. Meanwhile, Sheriff Emma Swan (Jennifer Morrison) and her mother Mary Margaret/Snow White (Ginnifer Goodwin) were transported to the other reality, where they encountered a number of characters familiar to fans of Disney films, including Captain Hook (Colin O'Donoghue), along with a certain Dr Frankenstein/Dr Whale (David Anders). Barbara Hershey also joined the cast as Regina's even more evil mother Cora.

The CW's drippy *Beauty and the Beast* wasn't a patch on the 1980s show as Kristin Kreuk's brittle NYPD detective became involved with Jay Ryan's military experiment while also trying to solve the murder of her mother.

Pouty heroine Elena (Nina Dobrev) died and came back as a vampire at the end of the third season of The CW's increasingly convoluted *The Vampire Diaries*, while the fourth season kicked off with Connor (Arielle Kebbel) trying to uncover the secrets of Mystic Falls.

The teen witches of *The Secret Circle* were almost convinced to tap into their dark magic by the manipulative

John Blackwell (Joe Lando) before The CW thankfully cancelled the charmless show after just one season.

ITV's equally dull *Switch* featured Lacey Turner, Hannah Tointon, Nina Toussaint-White and Phoebe Fox as four friends living in the London borough of Camden who used magic to try to sort out their love lives. Caroline Quentin turned up as a batty older witch in the six-part series.

After being saved from cancellation by a last-minute co-financing deal, *Primeval* returned to ITV with a fun fourth season. After a year trapped in the Cretaceous period, Abby Maitland (Hannah Spearritt) and Connor Temple (Andrew-Lee Potts) returned through an "anomaly" to their own time, only to discover a rebuilt ARC (Anomaly Research Centre) with a new dinosaur-hunting team in place. Alexander Siddig joined the cast as a mysterious billionaire.

One door closed, as Steven Spielberg's *Terra Nova* was justifiably cancelled after one season by Fox, and another briefly opened, as Spielberg went on also to executive produce ABC's faux-documentary series *The River*, in which a shaky camera crew followed the trail of a missing wildlife-TV host (Bruce Greenwood) into the Amazon jungle. The creepy show was co-created by *Paranormal Activity* director Oren Peli but was still also cancelled after a single season.

Meanwhile, we were treated to a two-hour season premiere for the second season of TNT's ten-part *Falling Skies*, which Spielberg also executive produced. After escaping from an invader's ship, Noah Wyle's dour history professor found himself not trusted by his fellow rebel fighters and not trusting himself. After a slow start, the show picked up as a number of supporting characters were killed off before the 2nd Mass arrived at an underground headquarters in Charleston (governed by Terry O'Quinn and Matt Frewer, which should have been a warning) and teamed up with a revolutionary force amongst the skitters to assassinate a powerful alien Overlord.

Thrown back in time from a dystopian future to the twenty-first century while pursuing a group of urban terrorists in Syfy's *Continuum*, future cop Kiera Cameron (Rachel

Nichols) discovered that to save the future she had to control the past.

Despite combining the creative talents of J. J. Abrams, Jon Favreau and Eric Kripke, along with an interesting opening premise in which all the power of Earth suddenly stopped working, NBC's *Revolution* quickly ran out of juice and turned into just another post-apocalyptic drama with horses and crossbows set fifteen years after the planet went dark.

The second season of MTV's twelve-part *Teen Wolf* grew up quickly to become the year's darkest YA genre show. Scott (Tyler Posey), Stiles (Dylan O'Brien) and Alison (Crystal Reed) found themselves battling a merciless team of Hunters and a deadly new werewolf clan, while at the same time trying to identify a "Kanima" – a legendary reptilian shape-changer. By the season finale, old foes had joined forces to confront a common enemy, and plenty of interesting new characters had been introduced.

Aimee Smith starred in the BBC's seventeen-part YA series *Wolfblood* as the member of a lupine race with heightened senses and abilities that have lived amongst humans for centuries.

In Season 4 of BBC Wales' *Young Dracula*, Vlad (Gerran Howell) attempted to broker a truce between the Vampire High Council and the Slayers' Guild as he struggled to overcome his blood-thirst and track down a murderous shape-shifter.

Nickelodeon's *House of Anubis* returned for a second season of forty-five fifteen-minute mysteries set in a strange English boarding school.

There was more than a touch of *Game of Thrones* to the two-part opening of the fifth and final season of BBC's *Merlin*. Set three years after end of the previous series, King Arthur (Bradley James) and his faithful knights rode north to rescue their comrades from the clutches of Morgana (Katie McGrath) and Mordred (Alexanda Vlahos).

After a series of final adventures, that included Gwen (Angel Coulby) being "possessed" by the vengeful sorceress, the two-part Christmas finale brought the show to its inevitable conclusion, with an added contemporary twist. Liam Cunningham and Julian Glover turned up in both fantasy shows, and during the thirteen-part series there were memorable appearances by Lindsay Duncan, James Fox, John Shrapnel and Anthony Head as a resurrected Uther Pendragon.

Sky's *Sinbad* may have been a too violent for small children and too dull for adults, but the spectacular-looking twelve-part Arabian Nights series boasted a likeable performance by newcomer Elliot Knight as the young thief cursed to sail the seven seas with a multinational crew by his grandmother (Janet Suzman). Naveen Andrews was the vengeful Prince Akbar, Orla Brady played the scheming kohl-eyed sorceress Taryn, while Timothy Spall turned up as a sly personification of Death. In the season finale, the companions travelled to the Land of the Dead, with unexpected consequences.

Co-created by Russell T. Davies and Phil Ford for the BBC, *Wizards vs. Aliens* featured boy wizard Tom Clarke (Scott Haran) and his science-geek school friend Benny (Percelle Ascott) battling the Nekross, a race of alien invaders.

Based on the DC Comics character Green Arrow, The CW's *Arrow* was a gritty and stylish reboot of the character (played by Stephen Amell), out to wreak revenge on Starling City's criminals after being shipwrecked on a remote island for five years. John Barrowman portrayed a ruthless crime boss, while Jessica De Gouw showed up as the homicidal Huntress.

After revealing the existence of his super-powered *Alphas* at the end of Season 1, Dr Lee Rosen (David Strathairn) was tasked with bringing the team back together in the unanticipated thirteen-part second season of the Syfy series.

E4's fourth season of *Misfits* saw the community service superheroes gaining two new gang members as, over eight episodes, they encountered zombies, a giant White Rabbit and the Four Horsemen of the Apocalypse.

ITV's six-part *Eternal Law* was about two angelic lawyers (Samuel West and Ukwell Roach) supplying celestial legal aid to the people in the city of York.

For anybody who didn't remember TV's *Early Edition* or the 2009 movie *Knowing*, Kiefer Sutherland's autistic son (David Mazouz) helped strangers sort out their lives through his ability to see patterns in numbers in Fox's thirteen-part touchy-feely *Touch*.

The show surprisingly went to a second season as the father–son duo helped a mother (Maria Bello) track down her presumed-dead daughter and we learned more about the mysterious Aster Corporation.

Meanwhile, following a fatal car crash, detective Michael Britten (Jason Isaacs) travelled between two alternate realities in the high-concept *Awake*. In one, his wife was alive, and in the other his son survived the accident, while he also had different therapists and different police partners in each world. NBC cancelled the show after just thirteen episodes.

Iraq war veteran Walter Sherman (Geoff Stults) suffered a brain injury and mysteriously acquired the ability to find missing things in Fox's *The Finder*, which also lasted just one season.

The fifth and final season of NBC's *Chuck* came to an end in January with guest appearances from Carrie-Anne Moss, Bo Derek and Linda Hamilton.

CBS's *A Gifted Man*, in which a successful surgeon (Patrick Wilson) received advice from his dead ex-wife (Jennifer Ehle), had nowhere to go and was cancelled after a single season as well.

Leonard Nimoy voiced a Mr Spock action figure in an episode of CBS's *The Big Bang Theory*, and the actor also returned as the scheming William Bell for the fourth season finale of Fox's twenty-two-episode *Fringe*, as he tried to bring the two worlds together in a catastrophic event to create his own personal reality.

As *Fringe* entered its fifth series, the show jumped forward in time to the dystopian world of 2036 run by the time-travelling Observers for a final fifteen-episode run.

Based on the books by Douglas Adams, the gently amusing *Dirk Gently* returned for a second season of three one-hour episodes starring Stephen Mangan as the holistic detective and Darren Boyd as his despairing side-kick before the BBC announced that the show was being cancelled because of the government freeze on the licence-fee. Guest stars included Helen Baxendale and Bill Paterson.

Doug Naylor's comedy sci-fi show *Red Dwarf* was surprisingly resurrected by Dave after a three-year hiatus for a six-episode tenth season reuniting the original cast.

Horror directors Adam Green and Joe Lynch starred alongside Dee Snider in Green's macabre sitcom *Holliston* on the cable-based FEARnet, while the infantile *Todd & the Book of Pure Evil* returned to the same channel for a second series in March.

Hunderby was a decidedly odd eight-part macabre comedy series from Sky starring and created by Julia Davis, while just like in *Coneheads*, ABC's sitcom *The Neighbours* was about a family of aliens moving into suburbia.

The third season of ITV's *Whitechapel* saw Rupert Perry Jones and Phil Davis's East End detectives uncover a lost Lon Chaney, Sr. film that reputedly drove its audiences mad while investigating murderers committed by a mythical bogey-man.

In what really should have been a Hallowe'en show, the penultimate episode of the third season of ABC's *Castle* had the eponymous author (Nathan Fillion) and Detective Kate Beckett (Stana Katic) investigating a murder that was apparently committed by a zombie.

The fifth season of *Murdoch Mysteries* featured episodes in which the smug turn-of-the century Canadian detective (Yannick Bisson) investigated the apparent curse of an ancient Egyptian tomb and a man who claimed to have invented a time machine.

Harold Perrineau voiced the "daywalker" vampire hunter in the animated *Blade* on G4, and Brent Spiner guest starred on a robot-themed episode of Fox's *The Simpsons*.

Although the 1999 series *Eurotika!* covered the subject matter in more depth, the BBC's feature-length documentary *Horror Europa* was a bright and breezy stroll (literally) through nearly eighty-five years of European horror cinema thanks to the urbane charm of writer and presenter Mark Gattis, who interviewed cult directors Guillermo del Toro, Dario Argento, Jorge Grau, Harry Kümel and Narciso Ibáñez Serrador, amongst others.

Hidden away late on Hallowe'en night, Channel 4's hour-long documentary *Frankenstein: A Modern Myth* looked at the enduring influence of Mary Shelley's novel, with emphasis on Danny Boyle's recent stage play at the National Theatre and the various movie versions. Benedict Cumberbatch, Jonny Lee Miller and John Waters were among those interviewed.

An entertaining Christopher Lee was the first subject of Sky's hour-long series about *British Legends of Stage and Screen*. Other episodes of the show were devoted to the careers of Diana Rigg and Michael York.

Final Curtain, a recently re-discovered pilot made in 1957 for a proposed anthology TV series by the legendary Edward D. Wood, Jr., was shown at Utah's Slamdance Film Festival in January. This was reputedly the script that Bela Lugosi was reading just before he died.

In October, BBC Radio attempted a half-hearted cross-station celebration of Gothic horror. On Radio 4 that included *Classic Serial: The Gothic Imagination: Dracula*, which was the convoluted title of Rebecca Lenkiewic's new two-part adaptation of Bram Stoker's novel starring Nicky Henson as the Count and John Dougall as Dr Van Helsing. It was somewhat unimaginatively followed by Lucy Catherine's two-part dramatisation of *Classic Serial: The Gothic Imagination: Frankenstein* featuring Jamie Parker as the titular scientist and Shaun Dooley as the Monster he created.

Saturday Play: The Gothic Imagination: Bloody Poetry was Howard Brenton's ninety-minute dramatisation of the evening on the shores of Lake Geneva when Mary

Wollstonecraft Godwin (Clare Corbett) first came up with the idea for *Frankenstein*.

Over on BBC Radio 4 Extra the celebration continued with *The Gothic Imagination*, which featured three half-hour plays: "Looted" by Lucy Catherine, "The House on the Hill" by Nancy Harris and "The Winter House" starring Annette Crosbie.

Also broadcast on Radio 4 as part of The Gothic Imagination, the half-hour *Scream Queens* featured Reece Shearsmith interviewing Barbara Shelley, Madeline Smith, Jane Merrow and other actresses about the changing role of women in horror films.

Earlier in the year on the same radio station, a new strain of bird flu wiped out half the human population in John Dryden's three-part *Pandemic*. The cast included Alison Steadman and Louise Jameson.

Sebastian Baczkiewicz's dark fantasy series *Pilgrim* returned for four new episodes with Paul Hilton as the 950-year-old William Palmer, cursed to live between the human and faerie worlds.

Alastair Jessiman's Glasgow psychic detective Thomas Soutar (Robert Laing) returned to investigate a woman's obsession with her late father in *Afternoon Drama: The Sensitive: Queen of the Dead*.

Matthew Beard starred in John Wyndham's post-apocalyptic novel *The Chrysalids*, which was dramatised by Jane Rogers over two hour-long episodes at the end of July.

Radio 4 also adapted Wilkie Collins's 1878 Venice-set novel *The Haunted Hotel* into an hour-long drama, while *Wilkie Collins* was a five-part abridgement of Peter Ackroyd's recent biography of the Victorian author of *The Woman in White*, read by actor Michael Pennington.

As part of the station's "More Than Words Festival", *The Hound of the Baskervilles* was a comedic version of the story performed by the Peepolykus Theatre Company and featuring Javier Marzan as Holmes and John Nicholson as Watson.

Hattie Naylor's *The Forgotten* was a twist on the "Sleeping Beauty" story, set during the aftermath of an unnamed war, while Frances Byrnes's *Saturday Drama: Red Shoes White Snow* was a two-part story also based on traditional fairy tales.

15-Minute Drama: Modesty Blaise: A Taste for Death was a five-part adaptation of Peter O'Donnell's novel with Daphne Alexander as the female super-spy, Carl Prekopp as her assistant Willie, and Alun Armstrong as Sir Gerald Tarrant, head of a British secret service agency.

Narrated by Charles Dance and broadcast over Christmas, *A Little Twist of Dahl* featured five daily dollops of Dahl with "Taste", "The Way Up to Heaven", "The Hitchhiker", "Edward the Conqueror" and "The Neck". Mark Heap, Kenneth Cranham, Celia Imrie and Jamie Glover were amongst the featured players.

Presenter John Waite celebrated the centenary of Edgar Rice Burroughs's character in the half-hour Radio 4 documentary *Tarzan: Lord of the Jungle*.

Crime writers Frances Fyfield and Simon Brett investigated *The Mystery of The Mystery of Edwin Drood* with Charles Dickens expert Jenny Hartley and, in *Was Dracula Irish?*, novelist Patrick McCabe looked at the links between Dublin-born Bram Stoker's creation and the Emerald Isle.

Billy Boyd narrated the story of the first musical stage production in 1967 of J. R. R. Tolkien's novel in *The Hobbit, the Musical*.

Angela Carter's 1984 novel *Nights at the Circus* was named the best of all past winners of the James Tait Black Prize, Britain's oldest literary award, as a one-off honour to mark 250 years of English literature study at the University of Edinburgh.

Claire Skinner was the voice of the author in the five-part *Book of the Week: A Card from Angela Carter*, in which theatre critic Susannah Clapp read from her portrait of her late friend. To mark the twentieth anniversary of her death, Clapp, Carmen Callil, Marina Warner and Christopher Frayling discussed the writer's passion for audio adaptations of her work in *Writing in Three Dimensions: Angela Carter's Love Affair with Radio*.

Marina Warner also marked the bi-centenary of the first edition of the Grimm brothers' *Children's and Household Tales* with the ten-part *Grimm Thoughts* on Radio 4.

In *Happy Day: The Children of the Stones*, writer and comedian Stewart Lee looked back at the spooky 1977 children's TV series *The Children of the Stones*, with contributions from series creator Jeremy Burnham, surviving cast members and fans.

Academic Hugh Haughton drew upon a 1919 essay by Sigmund Freud to explore the concept of *The Uncanny*, with help from novelist A. S. Byatt, writer and actor Mark Gattis, psychotherapist and essayist Adam Phillips, architect and critic Anthony Vidler, and composer Tarik O'Regan.

For an episode of Radio 4's *Off the Page* in July, writer and critic Kim Newman, clinical psychologist Linda Blair (no, not *that* one . . .) and writer Ian Marchant discussed the fascination of "The Dark Side" with host Dominic Arkwright.

BBC Radio 4 Extra's short series *The Female Ghost* featured half-hour dramatisations of "The Cold Embrace" by Mary Elizabeth Braddon, "Man-Size in Marble" by E. Nesbit and "Afterward" by Edith Wharton. The station also broadcast a half-hour dramatisation of Braddon's titular 1860 story towards the end of the year.

Ghost Stories of E. Nesbit featured readings of "The Shadow", "John Charrington's Wedding", "The Violet Car", "Man-Size in Marble" and "The Ebony Frame", while Toby Jones, Richard E. Grant, Kenneth Cranham, Anthony Head and Julian Wadham read "Seaton's Aunt", "All Hallows", "Crewe", "A Recluse" and "The Almond Tree", respectively, for *Ghost Stories of Walter de la Mare*.

In June, *The Late Alfred Hitchcock Presents* . . . featured fifteen-minute adaptations of A. M. Burrage's "The Waxwork", Saki's "Srendl Vashtar", Margaret St. Clair's "The Perfectionist", Arthur Williams's "Being a Murderer Myself" and Jerome K. Jerome's "The Dancing Partner".

The half-hour anthology series *Weird Tales* featured

Melissa Murray's "Out of the Depths" and "Connected", Chris Harrald's "The Loop", Ed Hime's "Bleeder", Lynn Fergusson's "The Fly" and "Split the Atom", Richard Vincent's "The House of Pale Avenue", Christopher William Hill's "Original Features" and "The Burial of Tom Nobody", Amanda Whittington's "Louisa's" and Lizzie Nunnery's "Night Terrors".

Over Hallowe'en on Radio 4 Extra, *A Short History of Vampires* included readings of Bram Stoker's "Dracula's Guest", Kristine Kathryn Rusch's "Hero Dust", Tanith Lee's "Israbel" and Tanya Huff's "Quid Pro Quo".

Sylvester McCoy's Time Lord joined up with a Nazi scientist sidekick (Elizabeth Klein) from an alternate future in Jonathan Clements's four-part serial *Doctor Who – Survival of the Fittest*, and the duo battled shark-like alien invaders in Steve Lyons's four-part *Doctor Who – The Architects of History*.

Paul McGann's "forgotten" Doctor was the star of the two-part audio serials *Doctor Who – Orbis*, *Doctor Who – The Beasts of Orlok*, *Doctor Who – The Scapegoat* and *Doctor Who – The Cannibalists*. The strong supporting cast included Sheridan Smith, Phil Davis, Phil Jupitas, Miriam Margolyes and Samantha Bond.

Meanwhile, former Doctor Tom Baker read David Fisher's seven-part *Doctor Who and the Creature from the Pit*, and the late Elisabeth Sladen narrated *The Sarah Jane Adventures: The Thirteenth Stone*, an hour-long adventure about her character's alien son Luke being menaced by the spirit of an evil king trapped inside a standing stone.

Nicholas Courtney starred in a new four-part series of *The Scarifyers*, and the late actor also turned up in a re-run of the 1980s John Wyndham adaptation "Survival" on *Fear on 4*, introduced by Edward de Souza.

Blake's 7: The Early Years: Eye of the Machine, *Point of No Return*, *Blood and Earth*, *Flag and Flame*, *The Dust Run*, *The Trial*, *When Villa Met Gan* and *Liberator* were all half-hour dramas based on the cult 1970s TV series. Benedict Cumberbatch, Stephen Lord, Carrie Dobro, Jan

Chappell, Colin Salmon and Geoffrey Palmer were all featured.

A psychiatrist received a frantic telephone call from a patient who claimed to have been buried alive in Carey Harrison's half-hour drama *A Call from the Dead*.

In July, Radio 4 Extra's *Book at Beachtime* featured a five-part reading by Hattie Morahan of Sadie Jones's supernatural novel *The Uninvited Guests*, set in Edwardian England.

Never the Bride was a three-part dramatisation of Paul Magrs's Gothic novel, while Garry Kilworth's seasonal story *A Ghost for Christmas* was broadcast on Radio 4 Extra over the holiday season in two episodes.

BBC Radio 3 commemorated the 100th anniversary of the Irish author's death with the five-part *The Essay: Bram Stoker*, in which a handful of essayists – Dr Catherine Wynne, novelist Colm Tóibin, Christopher Frayling, Professor Roger Luckhurst and Dr Janath Killeen – looked at different aspects of Stoker's life and work.

In the half-hour *Five Meet to Make Up Myths*, Gyles Brandreth explored the connections between Victorian authors J. M. Barrie, Arthur Conan Doyle, Robert Louis Stevenson, Bram Stoker and Oscar Wilde, who all knew each other.

The soundscape for Lizzie Mickery's Hallowe'en ghost drama *The Wire: Adventures of the Soul* on Radio 3 featured recordings of original electronic voice phenomenon (EVP).

Also broadcast on the same station during Hallowe'en week, *Drama on 3: The Midnight Cry of the Deathbird* by poet Amanda Dalton re-imagined F. W. Murnau's silent *Nosferatu* for radio in poetry, prose, song, monologue and dialogue, with Malcolm Raeburn as the vampire Count Orlok.

Pseudopod, the free-to-download horror fiction podcast, continued to offer weekly readings of new or classic horror fiction by such contemporary authors as Michael Marshall Smith, Mark Valentine, Jay Lake, David J. Schow, Mort Castle, Brian Hodge and Lynda E. Rucker, along with offerings from older names such as M. R. James, Guy De Maupassant, E. F. Benson and J. Sheridan Le Fanu.

The audio CD *Timepieces: Stories by the Stop-Watch Gang* featured fiction by narrator Richard Baldwin, Tony Pi, Brad Carson, Stephen Kotowych, Costi Gurgu, Ian Donald Keeling, Mike Rimar and Suzanne Church.

Over April and May, writer/director Dan Bianchi's RadioTheatre! presented five stories by H. P. Lovecraft in repertory at New York's The Kraine Theater. "The Curse of Yig", "The Shadow Over Innsmouth", "The Lurking Fear", "The Hound" and "The Rats in the Walls" were each performed with award-winning aural design and an orchestral score.

After repeatedly missing its opening dates, receiving a savaging by the critics, and having a fifth performer – actress T. V. Carpio, who replaced Natalie Mendoza as the evil "Arachne" – suffering an on-stage injury, Julie Taymor was finally removed from her position in March as director of the $60 million Broadway musical *Spider-Man: Turn Off the Dark*. A new team was brought in to help re-stage the show.

A stripped-down version of William Peter Blatty's *The Exorcist* opened at Los Angeles' Geffen Playhouse starring Emily Yetter as the demon-possessed Regan MacNeil. Brooke Shields played her movie-star mother, while Richard Chamberlain was veteran exorcist Father Merrin.

After running for just five performances on Broadway in 1988, a new version of the musical adaptation of Stephen King's *Carrie* premiered off-Broadway on March 1st. Starring Marin Mazzie and Molly Ranson, with music and lyrics by Michael Gore and Dean Pitchford, the $1.5 million revival closed after just eighty performances – two weeks earlier than scheduled – as a result of poor ticket sales and mostly negative reviews.

Written by King, with songs by John Mellencamp, the two-act musical *Ghost Brothers of Darkland County* premiered in April at Atlanta's Alliance Theatre to generally lukewarm reviews.

Another revival was Jonathan Kent's 1930s-set version of Stephen Sondheim's *Sweeney Todd* at London's Adelphi Theatre. Michael Ball stepped out of his comfort zone in the role as the titular murderer, and he was ably supported by Imelda Staunton as a creepy Mrs Lovett.

Also re-set in the 1930s was Simon McBurney's production of *The Master and Margarita*, staged at London's Barbican Theatre. Based on the cult novel by Mikhail Bulgakov, Paul Rhys played the novelist trapped in an insane asylum, Sinéad Matthews was his devoted lover, and Angus Wright turned up as Koroviev, the Devil's associate.

Also updated was a revival of Thomas Middleton's *The Revenger's Tragedy* at London's Hoxton Hall. First performed in 1606, the gruesome Jacobean morality tale starred Jaime Winstone and was re-set in 1915.

London's wet summer didn't dampen the enthusiasm for Rupert Goold and Michael Fentiman's spectacular production of C. S. Lewis's *The Lion, The Witch and The Wardrobe*, presented in a waterproof tent in Kensington Gardens from May to September.

Kristin Atherton portrayed the teenage author of *Frankenstein* in the Shared Experience company's production of *Mary Shelley*, which played at London's Tricycle theatre over the summer.

At the beginning of October, Chicago's WildClaw Theatre presented Charley Sherman's world premiere adaptation of Clive Barker's *The Life of Death* at the DCA Storefront Theater, directed by Carolyn Klein.

The Barbican's Hallowe'en presentation was the Polish company T. R. Warszawa's *Nosferatu*, a new stage version of Bram Stoker's *Dracula*, with Wolfgang Michael as the worn-out vampire.

Sarah Douglas starred in Cigarette Burns's portmanteau production of *The Hallowe'en Sessions*, which related the stories of five patients who were apparently held in an insane asylum. Inspired by the old Amicus anthology movies, and scripted by Kim Newman, Stephen Volk, Maura McHugh, Anne Billson, Paul McAuley and director Sean Hogan, it ran for six nights over Hallowe'en at London's Leicester Square Theatre as part of AlleyKat's inaugural 13th Horror Festival, which included theatre, comedy, music, lectures and storytelling.

Meanwhile, Theatre of the Damned took over the unrefurbished upstairs room of Whitechapel's crumbling Wilton's Music Hall over Hallowe'en for *The Horror! The Horror!* Theatre-goers were taken back to 1904 for a sneak-preview of a mysterious music hall company's new season of variety acts – not least, Mr Merrick's Miraculous Performing Puppies and their unfortunate fate.

Alexandra Spencer-Jones's highly physical version of Anthony Burgess's *A Clockwork Orange* made the transition from the previous year's Edinburgh Fringe to London's Soho Theatre at the end of the year, while choreographer Matthew Bourne's acclaimed reinterpretation of *Sleeping Beauty: A Gothic Romance* at London's Sadler's Wells added vampires and faries to Tchaikovsky's ballet.

Veteran British rock 'n' roll singer Tommy Steele starred in a seasonal revival of Leslie Bricusse's 1992 stage musical *Scrooge* at the London Palladium for a limited ten-week season.

Warner Bros. Studio Tour London opened *The Making of Harry Potter* at the end of March near Watford, twenty miles north-west of London. Tickets, which ranged from £21.50 for a child aged five and above to £29.00 for adults sixteen and above, had to be purchased in advance.

The Opening Ceremony of the London 2012 Olympics at the end of July was marked by director Danny Boyle's somewhat skewered and overblown £27 million celebration of Britain. Author J. K. Rowling popped up to introduce a sequence combining the National Health Service with children's literature, although it sometimes seemed more to do with movies than books as the latter included a giant puppet Lord Voldemort, Captain Hook from *Peter Pan*, Cruella Deville from *One Hundred and One Dalmations*, the Queen of Hearts from *Alice in Wonderland*, the Child Catcher from *Chitty Chitty Bang Bang* and a squadron of flying

Mary Poppinses. Most people seemed to prefer a filmed insert in which Daniel Craig's James Bond briefly interacted with the real 86-year-old Queen Elizabeth II.

At the equally chaotic Closing Ceremonies two weeks later, a scary-looking Annie Lennox and some impressively undead dancers performed a song from the movie *Bram Stoker's Dracula* (1992). Meanwhile, for no apparent reason, after Caliban's speech from William Shakespeare's *The Tempest* was read by Kenneth Branagh (in character as Isambard Kingdom Brunel) during the opening event, Timothy Spall's Winston Churchill popped out of a mock-up of Big Ben to do the same thing during the finale.

In March, the video games retailer Game Group went into administration. The company had 610 shops in the UK and a further 663 overseas, employing 10,000 people. It was thought that the company was hurt by the shift to digital downloading and competition from specialist online sellers and supermarkets.

Capcom swamped the market with a number of new *Resident Evil* games in 2012. *Resident Evil: Operation Raccoon City* had the same setting but not the same gameplay as *Resident Evil 2*, while a new pathogen called the C-Virus created zombies that could use automatic weapons in *Resident Evil 6*, which abandoned the series' survival roots and could randomly pair the player with others online.

Resident Evil: No Hope Left was released later in the year, along with HD updates of two earlier entries in the series, *The Umbrella Chronicles* and *The Darkside Chronicles*.

A viral zombie infection had decimated London in the survival game *ZombiU* from Ubisoft, and there were more zombies to shoot in *Call of Duty: Black Ops II*.

Tellrale Games' *The Walking Dead* was a five-game series based on the comic book rather than the dull TV show, while *Deadlight* was a survival zombie game that didn't live up to its graphics.

Konami's *Silent Hill: Downpour* was not up to previous entries in the series, and a woman escorting a mysterious young girl on a train discovered everyone around her turning into zombies in *Amy*.

Based on the comic book, *The Darkness II* once again followed the exploits of Mafia hitman Jackie Estacado and his monstrous tentacles, while you had the ability to become a nine-foot tall vampire lord that could teleport via a swarm of bats in the multi-player game *The Elder Scrolls V: Skyrim – Dawnguard*.

Vampires, zombies, and every other mythological creature existed in *The Secret World*, set in a contemporary world of magic and munitions, and there was more monster-hunting to be played in *Torchlight II*.

The great detective was framed for crimes he didn't commit in *The Testament of Sherlock Holmes*.

In July, the free online interactive game *RuneScape* became the first in the world to total 200 million players – almost the combined populations of the UK, France and Germany.

The Amazing Spider-Man video game for multiple platforms was set directly after the new film reboot and featured an innovative "web rush" option that allowed the player to jump around the screen at incredible speed.

It was certainly a lot better than *Battleship* – a game based on a movie which itself was based on a game – and the disappointing *The Dark Knight Rises* for iOS, which came with in-app purchases.

Based on the 1980s movie trilogy, the boxed set of *Back to the Future: The Game* featured the voice of Christopher Lloyd as a motion-capture Doc Brown and a cameo by original star Michael J. Fox.

Hotel Transylvania was another film tie-in game, which could be played in 3-D.

Lego's Monster Fighter sets included versions of Dracula, the Frankenstein Monster and a werewolf, while the Mummy Minimates Box Set was based on the classic 1932 movie.

Moebius Models' Bela Lugosi Dracula Model Kit was based on the 1927 stage play with a base modelled on actual props from the production, and for $35.00 you could buy a replica of Lugosi's Dracula ring, once owned by Forrest J Ackerman.

Round 2 Model's *Dark Shadows* statues of Barnabas Collins, the Werewolf and Vampire Van were exact replicas of the 1969 model kits down to the retro box art.

The thirty-six ounce Cthulhu Tiki Mug was created via a Kickstarter campaign.

On February 23rd, Britain's Royal Mail issued a new set of ten stamps honouring "Britons of Distinction". Amongst those who were considered to have made a major contribution to society was M. R. James, "scholar and author of ghost stories".

The March set of "Comics Characters" stamps included first-class stamps depicting Dan Dare from *Eagle* and Judge Dredd from *2000 A.D.*

Ireland marked the centenary of the death of Bram Stoker on April 19th with a set of two stamps commemorating the creator of *Dracula*.

Over Hallowe'en, the Royal Armouries museum in Leeds put on show a "Vampire-Slaying Kit", thought to have been commissioned in the 1890s by an unknown owner. It included wooden stakes, a mallet, holy water and a pistol, and was estimated to be worth £7,500.

In November, a recently discovered presentation copy of the first edition of *Frankenstein; or, The Modern Prometheus* (1818), signed by author Mary Shelley to Lord Byron, was sold in London for an undisclosed sum to a UK collector, with the proviso that the book would be made available for future viewings by the public. The Chelsea auction house selling the copy had invited bids "in excess of £350,000".

That same month, at a sale of pop culture memorabilia at Christie's in London, one of Indiana Jones's kangaroo-hide bullwhips sold for £20,000. A Holy Grail prop made for *Indiana Jones and the Last Crusade* went for £11,875, while a diary kept by Sean Connery's Henry Jones fetched £18,750.

T. E. D. Klien was the recipient of the Grand Master Award announced at the 2012 World Horror Convention held in Salt Lake City, Utah, over March 29th–April 1st. Guests of Honor included author Sherrilyn Kenyon, artist Mike Mignola and editor Scott Allie, along with a raft of "special guests". P. N. Elrod was Toastmistress.

The event was held in conjunction with The Horror Writers Association 2011 Bram Stoker Awards weekend, which additionally had Joe R. and Karen Lansdale, Robert McCammon, Dacre Stoker and Jeff Strand as guests.

The award for poetry went to *How to Recognize a Demon Has Become Your Friend* by Linda Addison, while Rocky Wood's *Stephen King: A Literary Companion* won for Superior Achievement in Non-Fiction. *The Corn Maiden and Other Nightmares* by Joyce Carol Oates picked up the Collection award and the Anthology award was collected by editor John Skipp for *Demons: Encounters with the Devil and His Minions, Fallen Angels and the Possessed*.

Stephen King's "Herman Wouk is Still Alive" won for Superior Achievement in Short Fiction and "The Ballad of Ballard and Sandrine" by Peter Straub won in the Long Fiction category. The Young Adult Novel award was a tie between *The Screaming Season* by Nancy Holder and *Dust & Decay* by Jonathan Maberry, the First Novel went to Allyson Bird's *Isis Unbound*, and Joe McKinney's *Flesh Eaters* won the Stoker Award for Superior Achievement in a Novel.

Rick Hautala and Joe R. Lansdale were given Life Achievement Awards, and Derrick Hussey of Hippocampus Press and Roy Robbins of Bad Moon Books each won Specialty Press Awards. The HWA's Silver Hammer Award for outstanding service to the organisation went to Guy Anthony DeMarco, while Karen Lansdale received The President's Richard Laymon Service Award.

As if all that wasn't enough, for one time only the HWA, in conjunction with the Bram Stoker Family Estate and the Rosenbach Museum & Library, presented a Vampire Novel of the Century Award to Richard Matheson for *I Am Legend*.

FantasyCon 2012 was held in Brighton, England, over September 27th–30th. Guests of Honour were authors Joe R. Lansdale, Muriel Gray and Brent Weeks. Veteran anthology editor Mary Danby, writer and actor Mark Gatiss and film director Robin Hardy were Special Guests, while Tim Lebbon was Master of Ceremonies.

A whole slew of winners of British Fantasy Awards were announced at the banquet on the Sunday afternoon. The Karl Edward Wagner Special Award went to Peter and Nicky Crowther for PS Publishing, and the Sydney J. Bounds Best Newcomer Award went to Kameron Allen.

Woody Allen's *Midnight in Paris* won for Screenplay, Joe Hill and Gabriel Rodriguez won Comic/Graphic Novel for *Locke & Key*, Magazine/Periodical went to *Black Static*, and Chômu Press received The PS Publishing Independent Press Award.

Daniele Serra won The Artist Award, The Non-Fiction Award went to Grant Morrison's *Supergods: Our World in the Age of the Superhero*, Robert Shearman's *Everyone's Just So So Special* won for Collection, and the Anthology award went to *The Weird* edited by Ann and Jeff VanderMeer. Angela Slatter's "The Coffin Maker's Daughter" won for Short Fiction, and Novella went to *Gorel and the Pot Bellied God* by Lavie Tidhar.

With the Novel award for the first time split into two categories, the August Derleth Award for horror went to *The Ritual* by Adam Nevill, while the winner of the newly created Robert Holdstock Award for fantasy was presented to *Among Others* by Jo Walton.

Despite claiming to be held in Toronto, Canada, the 38th World Fantasy Convention actually took place in the suburb of Richmond Hill from November 1st–4th. Guests of Honour were Elizabeth Hand, John Clute and Richard A. Kirk, with

Gary K. Wolfe as Toastmaster. Special Guests included Charles de Lint, Tanya Huff, Patricia Briggs, Mercedes Lackey and Larry Dixon.

At the World Fantasy Awards Banquet on the Sunday afternoon, the Special Award – Non-Professional went to Raymond Russell and Rosalie Parker for Tartarus Press, and Eric Lane of Dedalus Books received the Special Award – Professional for publishing in translation.

John Coulthart won the Artist award, Collection went to Tim Powers's *The Bible Repairman and Other Stories* and the VanderMeers once again picked up the Anthology award for *The Weird*. Ken Liu's "The Paper Menagerie" won for Short Fiction, the Novella award went to "A Small Price to Pay for Birdsong", and Lavie Tidhar's *Osama* was deemed the best Novel.

Lifetime Achievement Awards had earlier been announced for Alan Garner and George R. R. Martin.

As I mentioned above, in recent years there has been a huge increase in PoD (print-on-demand) and digital publishing, particularly in our genre. However, greater choice does not always lead to better quality.

As never before, the publishing industry is in a state of upheaval. While publishers' profits are beign squeezed by falling sales and closing bookstores and libraries, advances in new technology such as the insidious Apple iBooks Author app and Amazon's digital text platform are creating a generation of self-published authors who think they can write.

In most cases, they can't.

At a time when writers such as Anthony Horowitz have questioned the role of the publisher in modern publishing and the UK's latest children's laureate, Malorie Blackman, has spoken out against those who criticise the quality of Stephenie Meyer's Twilight series, we need publishers like never before.

We need the experienced agents, editors, proof readers, designers, advertising and marketing departments, and booksellers. In short, we need all the things that sort the wheat from the chaff. This is not being elitist – it is simply the best method of filtering out the good stuff from the bad.

The rise of self-publishing and e-books might mean that it is now easier for the neophyte author to potentially reach a much wider audience, but at the end of the day it is no substitute for creativity, technique and knowledge. And all that only comes from working with professional publishers.

It was once said that everybody has a book in them. But really, you know, they don't.

The Editor
July, 2013

NEIL GAIMAN

Witch Work

NEIL GAIMAN has co-scripted (with Roger Avary) Robert Zemeckis's, motion-capture fantasy film *Beowulf*, while both Matthew Vaughn's *Stardust* and Henry Selick's *Coraline* were based on his novels. Next up, his Newbery Medal-winning children's novel *The Graveyard Book* is being adapted for the movies, with Gaiman on board as one of the producers.

The busy author also has out a book of poems, *Blueberry Girl*, illustrated by Charles Vess; *Crazy Hair*, a new picture book with regular collaborator Dave McKean, and the graphic novel compilation *Batman: Whatever Happened to the Caped Crusader?* (with art by Andy Kubert). *The Tales of Odd* is a follow-up to the 2008 children's book *Odd and the Frost Giants*, while *The Absolute Death* and *The Complete Death* from DC/Vertigo feature the character from the Gaiman's *Sandman* comic. He is also working on a non-fiction volume about China, following his visit to that country in 2007.

About the poem that opens this volume, Gaiman says: "I wanted to write something that seemed to be about the person it was about, while it was actually about the person telling it. I wanted something that felt like a nursery rhyme and which echoed. In my head, this is probably a Dunsany story I never actually wrote . . ."

The witch was as old as the mulberry tree
She lived in the house of a hundred clocks
She sold storms and sorrows and calmed the sea
And she kept her life in a box.

The tree was the oldest that I'd ever seen
Its trunk flowed like liquid. It dripped with age.
But every September its fruit stained the green
As scarlet as harlots, as red as my rage.

The clocks whispered time which they caught in their
gears
They crept and they chattered, they chimed and they
chewed.
She fed them on minutes. The old ones ate years.
She feared and she loved them, her wild clocky
brood.

She sold me a storm when my anger was strong
And my hate filled the world with volcanoes and
laughter
I watched as the lightnings and wind sang their
song
And my madness was swallowed by what happened
after.

She sold me three sorrows all wrapped in a cloth.
The first one I gave to my enemy's child.
The second my woman made into a broth.
The third waits unused, for we reconciled.

She sold calm seas to the mariners' wives
Bound the winds with silk cords so the storms could
be tied there,
The women at home lived much happier lives
Till their husbands returned, and their patience be
tried there.

The witch hid her life in a box made of dirt,
As big as a fist and as dark as a heart
There was nothing but time there and silence and
  hurt
While the witch watched the waves with her pain and
  her art.

(But he never came back. He never came back . . .)
The witch was as old as the mulberry tree
She lived in the house of a hundred clocks
She sold storms and sorrows and calmed the sea
And she kept her life in a box.

ALISON LITTLEWOOD

The Discord of Being

ALISON LITTLEWOOD was raised in Penistone, South Yorkshire, and went on to attend the University of Northumbria at Newcastle (now Northumbria University). Originally she planned to study graphic design, but "missed the words too much" and switched to a joint English and History degree. She followed a career in marketing before developing her love of writing fiction.

She is the author of *A Cold Season*, published by Jo Fletcher Books, an imprint of Quercus. The devilish novel was selected for the UK's Richard and Judy Book Club, where it was described as "perfect reading for a dark winter's night". Her second book, *Path of Needles*, published in May 2013, combines a crime story with a look at the more horrific side of fairy tales.

"'The Discord of Being' is really my version of a love song to Morocco," reveals the author. "I spent a short holiday there a couple of years ago, and it completely got under my skin. I loved the colour and the life and the sense of adventure it engenders. It's also stunningly beautiful, with completely contrasting landscapes wherever we went.

"There's always a sense of discordance, though, when you're in a strange place and don't entirely understand its ways. All of those things found their way into 'Discord', along with a flavour of the local folklore. The thing that remained with me longest, though, was an odd sense of being homesick for somewhere that was never home – it's probably unsurprising that the phrase found its way into the characters' dialogue."

EMMA HADN'T BEEN to Morocco, the place her mother was buried and her father still lived, since she was little more than a child. All the same, as she stepped off the aeroplane it seemed familiar, despite the strangeness of the low, decorated terminal, the palm trees waving flag-like branches in the breeze. It was the sky, she decided. A grey covering of clouds rolled away into the distance; it was an English sky. Even so, her skin prickled with sweat as she walked towards immigration with the other passengers – holidaymakers, their children, and people going home.

In the terminal, where families waited, one man stood among the others, holding a sign that bore her name. Her father had sent a colleague to meet her, a tall, neatly dressed man named Ibrahim. She shook hands with the stranger, remembering her father's words on the telephone: *You don't need to come*. She felt he had been offering an escape route for them both.

The call had come late one night, the ring tone sounding just like any other. That was what seemed strange afterward, that the sound had carried no warning: that she hadn't known.

Disturbed, her father had said, and all Emma could think of was being pressed close to her mother's body, safe, warm. *Her grave has been disturbed. I just – I thought you should know*. And then that eternal mantra: *You don't need to come*.

The thought of it angered her. How could he have done this? For it was her father she blamed, at once and entirely. He had brought her mother here, leaving Emma to stay with an aunt, just for a little while. And then her mother died and he decided to stay, just like that, not seeing Emma save for when she came for her mother's funeral. How could he let her mother die like that? How could he let her die *here*? And how could he live among people who would do this to her grave?

Emma opened her mouth to say something to Ibrahim, then closed it again. It was as if he read her thoughts. He turned to her with sympathy in his eyes. "The Moroccan people would not do this."

She scowled. "Then who?"

It was his turn to subside. He shook his head, led her to the car.

It wasn't long before they reached the foothills of the Atlas Mountains. Emma watched the colours flash by. She had imagined somewhere sepia and bleak, without growth and life; instead there was this red land, with grasses and straw and brilliant yellow flowers, everything dotted with dark green argan trees.

The engine protested as the road grew steeper, heading up towards the grey sky.

"It will rain," Ibrahim said, trying to lighten the mood. "I think you brought it from England," and she smiled back at him as he was proved right; droplets speckled the windscreen. The wipers scraped and Emma wound down the window to see a river rattling down a narrow gully, palm trees darkening in the rain.

They wound upwards until they reached a narrow track. To one side great boulders were piled atop one another, their ochre streaked with red and grey and orange. To the other side was a sheer drop. Emma glimpsed the road they had travelled far below, a village nestled into the hillside beyond, the mosque's minaret towering over everything else.

In front of them, an inlet was cut into the rocks. Buildings slotted into it, filling every inch, their wooden doorways painted bright colours. One opened and a man stepped out. He wore a point-hooded *djellaba* and had yellow *babouches* on his feet. He had a grey beard and was turning something in his hand; a piece of stone. With a tremor, Emma realised it was her father.

When she turned to Ibrahim, he gave a sympathetic smile.

Her father did not hold out his arms or say anything at all. Instead he raised his watery eyes, nodded, and led the way inside.

The room was dark, its concrete floor strewn with threadbare rugs. There was a simple wooden table, shelves holding rocks and grit and tools: hammers, chisels, brushes. A mobile phone lay among them, dust-covered like the rest. The room smelled of damp stone and something sweeter; honey, perhaps. Emma felt a twinge of anger. As far as she'd known, her father had left England for a good job, a prestigious job, working with the fossil mining concerns that dotted the mountains. But this – was this why he had left? Her desk at work was just one grey cubicle among many, but the walls were smooth, the floor clean. She had a computer and a telephone, air conditioning.

Then she saw a small bottle balanced on the lintel over the door, its contents dark red, muddy looking. She snatched it down and sniffed, thinking of alcohol, but the scent was of meat.

Her father looked apologetic. "It's for the *djinn*," he said. "It keeps them out." He shrugged.

Emma snorted, banging it back onto the ledge. "Is this it?" She could barely keep the fury out of her voice. She waved a hand around the room, encompassing everything.

Her father lifted his arms, let them fall. He still clutched something in his hand and he held it out. An ammonite, tight whorls inscribed in stone. "A new species," he said. "New to science, anyway. I saved it for you."

She reached out and his fingers closed over it. "I meant I could name it for you."

Emma shook her head. He had named her. *Her*. And then he had left her for this shack with its dirt and its rocks.

Her father nodded, as though it was what he had expected. "It is good to see you, Em."

"Emma." She barked out the word, though he was right; Em was what people called her. It was what her mother had called her. Her stomach twisted.

"Emma." He nodded.

"Are you going to tell me what happened?"

"I will," he said. "But first you can get settled. We'll have tea together. I'll show you around."

Emma glanced at the room. She had seen everything already.

"No," he said. "Not in here. Out there."

The mountains swirled around them, fading into the distance. Rain still pattered down but the sun shone through it, the light soft and delicate, turning the slopes to pastel. Wild flowers sparked in brilliant pinks and yellows. And everywhere, leaning against the building, lying on the ground, were ammonites and trilobites, some of them several feet across.

Her father was talking about how the mountains had formed. Emma imagined him burrowing into the miles of fossils under his feet, chipping at the vastness until he had found each one, his home long forgotten. Out here, she could almost forget it too. The air was clean and smelled of rain, the mountains sweet, beguiling. And something he said struck her: *it was all under the sea*, and she felt a wave of vertigo, imagined fathoms of salt water above her head, stretching into the sky. She had a sense of the earth beneath her shifting and shattering, thrusting upwards over the millennia, movements on a scale impossible to imagine.

"And you study all this." She looked at the shapes on the ground, the spirals and lobes. She reminded herself that they were familiar from museums and nature programmes, known, catalogued. And yet he had been here for years. He worked for a company who dug up these creatures that had turned to stone and bought and sold them.

"I study all this."

"So you understand it all."

He smiled. "No. No, I'll never understand it all."

She scowled. "What happened to my mother?"

He was silent.

"What happened?"

"She was at peace. She still is, Em."

She did not correct him. She only waited.

Her father's throat clicked as he spoke. "They dug up the ground."

"Who did?"

"We don't know."

"How far?"

He didn't answer, though Emma knew he'd understood what she meant. How far *down*, is what she'd wanted to ask. He said nothing, raised his hands again and let them fall. Emma remembered the fossil in his hand, the delicate life written in stone, a species never before seen or numbered. That dizziness took her again. Amazing there could be anything new left to discover. A different kind of life, long turned to rock, held for a moment in the palm of his hand.

"I want to see it," she said. "I want to see everything."

The journey passed in bursts of rain and sunshine, blue patches of sky meeting and joining as they left the mountains. Emma's father sat up front with Ibrahim. He hadn't wanted to come, but Emma had insisted. She had felt like a geologist herself, fighting his reluctance, as though prising a fossil from its hole in the ground.

Now the men exchanged occasional words in Darija, the Moroccan Arabic, low and quick as though they didn't want to disturb her. Before they departed they'd packed the boot full of bags of fossils, so that Emma's things wouldn't fit; they were beside her on the seat.

Emma looked out at the horizon and saw the higher peaks of the Altas, capped with snow. She remembered that somewhere out there lay the dunes of the Sahara, home of Tuareg and Bedouin, and felt again a wave of disorientation.

Marrakesh, when they reached it, was something else again: a line of terracotta coloured rock walls. "The Red City," said Ibrahim, and she imagined it being carved from the earth, the buildings rising like something organic.

The grave was in a cemetery on the outskirts of the city, sectioned into Moslem, Jewish and Christian. The cemetery was narrow, spread around a hillside that had probably been no use for anything else. There were buildings opposite, shops with narrow alleys leading away.

Emma was suddenly reluctant, but her father held out his hand. "It's all right," he said. "I told you." She followed, glancing back to see that Ibrahim had stayed behind.

Emma had been fifteen when her mother was buried, an event that was oddly and comprehensively missing from her memory, as if she'd tried to blank it out, or never really taken it in. A heart attack, they'd said; a Western death in a country far from home. Now Emma stood in the cemetery, though the recognition was strong and total, a knife in her gut. The headstones were lit by sharp, hard sunlight. She saw the one that was her mother's, but it wasn't right: it looked intact, a little crooked perhaps, but there was nothing to show that anything had happened. She stared at the words: *Beloved wife and mother*.

"But it's fine," she said, her voice faltering. She felt she had been robbed, as if everything should be torn and uprooted and twisted.

"It has been put right," her father said. And then, hesitant: "I'm sorry."

"I wanted to see. I wanted to know everything."

Her father sighed. "No one really knows, Emma. It happened at night. The stone was overturned, the grave—"

"Dug into."

"Yes."

"So did they find her? Did they reach the body? Did it happen to other graves, or just hers?" Emma waited, but the answer didn't come. She scowled. It was as if he didn't want to know, didn't *need* to know. As if something was broken and had been fixed and he had already moved on.

"It won't do any good. Look, it's all right now. No one seemed to know what happened. Sometimes – it's difficult to find things out." He sighed. "You didn't need to come. I told you."

I told you. As though that was the answer to everything.

"Did you upset someone?"

"What?" He looked surprised.

"In your job. Or whatever. Have you done something? Made someone want to hurt you – hurt my mother?"

"Of course not." He shook his head. Then, slowly: "Not like that. Sometimes I think, with the digging – we have gone too far." His voice went distant. "The *djinn* . . ."

She snorted, rolled her eyes. "For God's sake."

He paused. "So I suppose you will go now. We can take you to the airport. We have business – we will stay awhile, now we are here, Ibrahim and I. Whenever you like—"

Emma remembered the bags in the boot of the car. Of course, he had brought his work with him. Even her mother's desecration was a reason to study his precious fossils, dead things dug from the ground. She shivered as she turned from the grave. She couldn't get that out of her head: dead things, dug from the ground. She didn't know how he could bear to look at them.

Marrakesh was life and sound and noise. Emma stood at a crossroads full of cars all trying to turn at once, beeping their horns, missing each other by millimetres. Perhaps because her father seemed so willing for her to leave, she had decided to stay until she was ready. She turned her back, passed under an arched gate set into the city walls, and entered the old town or *medina*. There were no cars here, but although the sounds changed, the bustle was the same. The streets were narrow and full of people: tourists, locals in colourful *djellabas*, women with *shaylah* scarves over their hair or veiled faces. Donkey carts plodded along, unfazed by the motorcycles that gunned through it all, edging everything else out of the way.

Emma had left her father and Ibrahim at the hotel, though they had offered to show her around. She hadn't wanted to be shown around. She had wanted to walk and to think. Now she found thinking impossible. Everything was new, different. She passed a shop with brightly coloured sacks of spices on the ground, casting rich scents into the air; another with hundreds of shoes hanging outside, forming a solid curtain.

She took a narrower turning into the *souk*, a roofed passageway so crowded with goods it felt like a tunnel. Stalls were hung with leather belts and *babouches* and wallets and bags in every colour. Everything smelled of leather. Men sat outside their shops, stitching or waiting to trade. Emma jumped out of the way of a motorcycle, the rider clutching a live chicken by its feet. Then leather gave way to lamps, every conceivable shape and size, each stall shining like a genie's grotto. Emma let the colours and sounds play over her, the constant flow of Darija and Berber and French from the crowds, the blare of a radio, the tapping of stall-holders working on their wares and the bark of haggling. She felt stirred, overwhelmed, the sounds thrumming. *All of life is here*, she thought. It was naked in its intensity. People wanting to trade, needing to trade, to fleece a tourist so their children could eat.

Emma kept wading through it all, drowning in it, seeing everything and thinking of nothing: not her father, not what had happened to her mother's grave. And then someone turned in the crowd ahead, looking back so that Emma saw their face, and everything stopped.

Someone knocked into her, muttered some apology or imprecation, but Emma couldn't move. She stared at the figure and it looked back at her with her mother's eyes. It *was* her mother. After a long moment she turned and melded with the crowd.

Emma started to push her way through, trying to keep the figure in sight. Everywhere were faces, some indignant, some curious. And then the alleyway ended and Emma stumbled into an open space. It was thronged with people. She took a step forward, looking about. What had her mother been wearing? She couldn't remember. Her breath came hard and fast. She couldn't see her anywhere, didn't know which way to go.

Emma stepped forward into the square, into the strains of discordant music. She knew where she was from the pictures she'd seen: Djemaa el Fna, the most famous square in Morocco, perhaps in the world. And everywhere were people. Traders sitting on stools or carpets, stalls with fair-ground games, storytellers' tents, people crossing from one place to another, friends meeting, kissing on the cheeks, men holding out water snakes or Barbary apes to tempt tourists to part with their *dirhams*. And everywhere, groups of musicians; flowerings of notes competed with throbbing drums and soothing pipes. She scanned it all, seeing nothing she could recognise. The woman who had looked like her mother had gone.

Emma caught one of the city's petit taxis back to the hotel, knowing she'd never find the way on her own. She hammered on her father's door. It opened and she saw his lined face, his faded eyes. And Ibrahim, always there, a fossil and a magnifying glass held in his hands.

"I saw her," said Emma. In spite of herself she felt tears spring into her eyes.

Her father squinted, as if he hadn't yet adjusted to looking out at the world. "Who?"

"I saw *her*." Emma was suddenly furious. "I saw my mother." Then her body sagged and she leaned against the door. Her father took her arm, led her to the only chair. A foot away was his bed, tousled and scattered with fossils. "This is ridiculous," Emma snapped, and her father shrugged, helplessly.

Ibrahim stepped forward. "A little tea, perhaps," he said. "You thought you saw something. The heat, maybe. Morocco can be a strange place to those who do not know her."

Emma gave him a look, wiped at her eyes. "I saw my mother," she insisted.

"Someone who looked like her. There are many English in Marrakesh."

"I *know* that."

"She is in your heart, of course. In your thoughts." Ibrahim's voice was gentle, the kindness in it cutting through her, and Emma bit back a sob.

"A drink, perhaps," Ibrahim said again, this time to her father. Emma knew he was Moslem, wouldn't touch alcohol, and had a sudden image of what she must look like: a stupid foreigner, overwhelmed by the noise and the heat. She closed her eyes and felt her father pushing a glass into her hands. It was wine, poured into a cheap hotel tumbler.

"I'm sorry, Em." Her father said. His voice seemed different when he said it. His eyes were rheumy, the wrinkles gleaming with moisture. "I never was a good father to you."

Emma looked away, drew deeply on the wine. Her hand shook. She couldn't remember a time when he had said such things, and now she didn't want to think about him at all; only of her mother. She remembered the face in the *souk*. She would have given anything to speak to her, longed for the woman whose funeral she had attended; not this father who stood in front of her.

A crowd gathered around a tent, laughing and jeering. Emma stood on tiptoes, though she didn't stand a chance of seeing anything. Ibrahim, a head taller, looked over and laughed. "It is an old Moroccan joke," he said, "about a man and his wife. The wife is also played by a man, of course."

The crowd convulsed with laughter. And the image that sprang into Emma's head was of Punch and Judy, sitting on some frigid English beach while a puppet's neck grew longer and longer. She grimaced.

"It is an old tradition," Ibrahim said, and she nodded.

She followed him as he pointed out men rigging tents for the evening barbecues, ladies offering henna tattoos. He didn't pause, assuming she wouldn't be interested, and Emma peered down at the photographs of flowered hands and feet. She was half tempted to stay, but daunted by the women's harsh invitations.

Ibrahim had offered to show her around, and he was taking his role as tour guide seriously. "Djemaa el Fna," he said, "the centre of Marrakesh; at least, of its spirit. Hundreds of years old. Once, they sold slaves here, stolen from their homes and bound for Europe. Or the other way around."

Emma blinked. Ibrahim smiled at her. "Europeans were stolen too," he said. "Some were brought here by the corsairs. Not so many as Africans, of course."

Emma frowned, trying to understand the import of his words, but he went on. "*Djemaa* means congregational mosque," he said. "*Fna* is courtyard, or death. No one agrees what it means. It could be mosque with a courtyard. Or it could be assembly of death, place of death. You see? Morocco has many meanings." He waved a hand, taking in the snake charmers, the street dentists with human teeth laid out on rugs, Moroccan teenagers buying dried apricots and figs.

"But which?" asked Emma. "What does it mean? They must know."

Ibrahim smiled. "It is for you to choose."

"No, it's not. It's—" but Emma's voice faded. She had seen someone across the field of paving slabs, someone who was standing quite still amidst the movement.

"Emma?"

"It's her." Emma started walking, was jerked back when Ibrahim caught her arm.

"You mustn't," he said, urgently. "It isn't her. Do not."

She wriggled free and started across the square, hampered by the press of people, the haphazard placing of tents and rugs. She didn't call out; she knew her mother would never hear. Then she saw that the figure had stopped. Her mother was pale, her skin white against the dark, straight hair. Her eyes were hollow, their expression impossible to make out.

Emma began to run. She had to know, to understand what her mother was trying to tell her. The woman was in a narrower part of the square now, heading for the road that marked its edge, moving easily between throngs of tourists. Emma wove in and out as people stopped in her path to check that their bags or their children were safe. She heard the road, its honking and screeching.

There: a flash of dark hair. Then it was gone. Emma let out a cry, felt Ibrahim's hand close once more on her arm. She struggled and he let go, spreading his hands in the air.

"Please." Ibrahim looked hurt, anxious. He glanced around to see who might be watching.

Emma clenched her hands on nothing, pressed them against her face.

"I am sorry. But you mustn't. It is not a good thing. You should not follow. You must not look for her, Emma."

"It was my *mother*." She choked on the words, and as she did, she knew what she needed to do. Before Ibrahim could react, she turned and ran once more for the road. A taxi was parked at the kerb, discharging passengers. Emma grabbed the open door, jumped inside. When the driver looked at her with startled eyes, she gave the name of the cemetery where her mother was buried.

Emma couldn't find the caretaker anywhere. Eventually she asked in a local shop and the shopkeeper led the way down narrow streets to a small tumbledown house. He banged on the door until another man came, but it was the shopkeeper who asked what she needed and Emma realised he had stayed to interpret. He looked at her kindly, and tears welled in her eyes. Suddenly there was a chair, a glass of hot, sweet mint tea. They brought flatbreads, a dish of honey. Their generosity made everything worse.

"I have to know what happened to my mother," she said. "I have to know if the grave was empty."

They exchanged looks, speaking to each other in rapid Arabic. Eventually the shopkeeper explained. "No," he said, "your mother's grave was not empty. But it was – opened, yes?"

Emma stared down at her glass of tea, feeling hot vapour on her cheeks. "But if she *was* there – what happened?"

There was more conferring. This time the shopkeeper's voice was gentle. "He says there may have been animals. A hyena, maybe. But they did what they could for her."

"Animals?" Emma looked up. The man's eyes were fixed

on hers and they were dark, almost black. She saw the message in them, and suddenly felt sick.

"He is very sorry." The man indicated the caretaker. "He would watch all the time, but he has a family. He says they took care of it."

Emma nodded. She knew they'd filled in the grave, fixed it, as her father had said. *No need for you to come.* She hesitated. "But how do you know it was my mother? And where is she now?"

This time, the translation came quickly: "But of course it was your mother. And she is back in the ground. We buried her again."

Emma shook her head, staring at the floor. Hyenas, this close to the city? It didn't make sense. And she thought of what she had seen in the shopkeeper's eyes, when he had said it: he was protecting her. His expression had been gentle, as if the truth he was hiding was somehow worse than his lies.

When Emma got back to the hotel, her father was waiting. He ushered her into his room. This time, Ibrahim wasn't there. "Emma, what you did. It was reckless." He put a hand on her arm and she pulled away. "I know you think you saw your mother."

She turned on him, her eyes fierce. "I *did* see her. I went to the cemetery. I know what happened."

"I am sorry." Her father didn't say if he was sorry for what happened, or sorry that she had found out.

"You left her for the animals. *Animals*."

Now her father looked angry. "I did *not*," he said. "I loved her. I buried her. Do you understand that?"

She was silent.

"Your mother lived, and now she is dead. It was not your mother you saw. Your mother is safe, wherever she is."

"I *saw* her."

"No. It was not your mother."

"Her ghost, then. Her spirit."

"*No*. You come here, seeing nothing." He looked away at last. "I told you of the *djinn*, Emma. I have – dug too much and too far. I fear I have angered them. And now one of them has come to punish me."

Emma stared, astonished.

"They are everywhere, Emma. And one of them – an evil *djinn* – has tasted your mother's body and now it has taken her form."

She shook her head. "You're—"

"Crazy, yes. But I know what I know. This thing has your mother's face, but it is not her. It is a grave robber, a *ghul*, Emma. And if you follow it—" he looked away. "It will take you too."

Emma lay awake, listening to the anodyne sounds of a hotel in the early morning: the clanking of the maid's cart, banging doors, the distant buzz of the lift. She pressed her hands against her face, remembering her mother as she had last seen her; dark-smudged eyes set into white skin, an expression she couldn't read. If she had been closer, perhaps she would have known what her mother had been trying to say. She would have been able to tell if her father's words were true.

She screwed her hands into fists. If she had seen her dead mother in England, would she then only have been a spirit – a ghost? Could she have spoken to her – had her father robbed her even of that, by bringing her to a place where the *djinn* walked?

Emma shook her head, rose, and headed for the lobby. When she reached it she heard a familiar voice. She turned to see Ibrahim, dressed smartly, a heavy-looking sample case at his feet. "Emma," he said, only that, but his tone said everything.

She shook her head. "I'm going back to the square. Just once more. And then I'm going home." She paused. "I have to understand."

He looked at her, his gaze steady, until she had to look away. He spoke only once before picking up his case and turning to leave. "I do not think it is a place you understand," he said. "I think it is a place that you feel."

She thought of those words as she left the hotel and headed for the square. She hadn't been talking about the place, at all: it was her mother that had been in her mind. All the same, as she entered Djemaa el Fna, she knew that he was right. The bustle was there, but it was different. She saw now that the square wasn't the paving or the mosque or the buildings that marked its edge; it wasn't even its history. It was the people who filled it, selling and buying and entertaining, telling their stories, filling the air with charcoal-smoke and music, so that every moment it changed, becoming somewhere new. She couldn't understand this place, would never understand, because it was never the same. And if she couldn't understand this place, something man had made and torn up and remade, how would she ever understand what she had seen?

The discord of music filled her mind, confusing everything. The square was a whirl of people going about their lives, their daily dance. *All of life is here*, she thought, and remembered her mother's face looking back at her: *No. All of life and death*.

Emma started to walk. Despite her earlier resolve, she was no longer sure she wanted to see her mother. All that was left was hollowness, and a strange kind of yearning. Yet as she passed through the square, she realised her mother was there: she was walking ahead of her through the throng, clearing a path for Emma to follow. This time she looked back and smiled, and it was the old smile, clean and good. This time no one got in Emma's way; the crowds drew back as the spirit passed, as though they saw or sensed what it was.

Emma's heart beat faster, the music around her transforming into light and air, rising and falling in perfect rhythm. This was where she was meant to be. She *knew* this place, belonged in this moment. She scarcely noticed as her mother entered a narrow alleyway, a shadow falling across her features. She pulled a layer of fabric from her dress, drawing a veil across her face; then she stepped back into a recess, her back to the stone, and beckoned her daughter in.

* * *

There were images behind Emma's eyes, a multitude of them: the chaos of goods in the *souk*, curious faces, men staring or calling out in Darija, intricate tiles on a floor or wall, donkey carts, delicately whorled stones. There were sounds, too: the deep call of the muezzin, the higher wail of the pipers. Their music no longer made sense to her. She moaned, putting her hand to her forehead, trying to wipe away the things she saw or didn't see. There was pain there, but she realised it was not a headache. She touched a hand to her neck, lower down, the hollow place above her shoulder blade. She felt something dry under her fingers. When she looked at her fingertips, she found them powdered with blood.

She opened her eyes and saw the plain, blank ceiling of her hotel room. By the harsh light slashing the rectangle, she knew it must be about mid-day. Then a sound began to register. Someone was hammering on the door.

When she opened it her father was standing there. Emma opened her mouth to greet him then closed it again. What was the use? There was no name she could call him. "Father" was too formal, like something out of a book; "Dad" was too familiar. Instead she stared as he guided her back inside and felt her forehead. Emma caught a glimpse of herself in the mirror, her skin pale, her eyes nothing but dark smudges.

Her father had her lie down, brought her water to drink, rubbed life into her hands. He kept talking, though Emma didn't listen to the words. Eventually, she spoke.

"Why did you stay here?" she asked.

This time, his words were halting. "Because I had to," he said. "Because it would have killed me not to."

Emma let his words drift over her.

"Sometimes a place takes hold of you. And you know you have to stay, because anywhere else – the homesickness—" he paused. "You are homesick for somewhere that was never your home."

For a while, there was silence. The knife of sunlight drew across the ceiling. Emma pushed herself up; found her father resting his head on his arms. He stirred and looked back at her. She put out a hand and touched the whorls of skin around his eyes, thinking of the ridged curls of an ammonite.

"What did you call it?" she asked.

He looked puzzled; then he understood. "Emmaceras," he said, and smiled. "You know, Emma, ammonites are named for the Egyptian god Ammon. The god of procreation. Of life."

She nodded. She pushed herself up and examined her neck in the mirror. The wound was shallow and surrounded by scratches, but it was clean. Her father must have washed it.

"Do you think it's happy now?" she asked.

He merely sighed, raising and lowering his hands. He didn't try to explain, just looked at her face, his gaze steady. And then he said: "You should stay here."

Emma started. Touched a hand to her neck. She had expected him to say she should go home, get as far away from Morocco – and the square – as she could. And yet, now the words were out, she felt she understood. *All of life is here*, she thought. *And all of death*. She knew this, had been touched by it. And yet the heart of it, the sound, the chaos – it was inside her, too.

Life and death. Death and life. Vivid and loud and bright and dangerous. Not something to be ignored, to be analysed or regulated or wrapped in plastic, layers and layers of it, so that when either of them surfaced, it was frightening.

The thought made her dizzy, made her want to laugh. She looked at her father's face, feeling the ties that ran between them despite the years and the distance. She caught his hand in hers, felt the thinness, the bones beneath the papery skin.

When she closed her eyes, though, what she saw was a doorway; a large, beautiful doorway in the shape of a keyhole, dusty and grimed. On the other side of it was her desk at work: clean, bare, organised. And she knew that she could step through, take her seat, resume her life. And then what? Would she turn again, look back the other way, to see – what? Already there was an odd pang in her stomach, a deep sort of longing she couldn't understand but that she could feel.

She opened her eyes and she didn't know for whom or what she felt it.

Her father was watching her. He smiled. "It's very simple," he said, and when she looked back into his eyes, she knew that it was true.

DALE BAILEY

Necrosis

DALE BAILEY lives in North Carolina with his family, and has published three novels: *The Fallen*, *House of Bones* and *Sleeping Policemen* (with Jack Slay, Jr.). His short fiction, collected in *The Resurrection Man's Legacy and Other Stories*, has won the International Horror Guild Award and has been twice nominated for the Nebula Award.

He has recently published stories in *Asimov's Science Fiction*, *The Magazine of Fantasy & Science Fiction*, *Queen Victoria's Book of Spells* and *Oz Re-Imagined: New Tales From the Emerald City*, and has work forthcoming at Tor.com.

About the tale that follows, he recalls: "This story was spurred by a close encounter with an essay about flesh-eating bacteria – truly a horrifying malady – in Atul Gawande's *Complications: A Surgeon's Notes On An Imperfect Science*.

"In writing it, I posed a dual challenge to myself: I wanted to compose an old-fashioned club story, and I wanted to try out an unusual point of view, first-person collective. I can only hope that I succeeded on both counts."

IN RETROSPECT NONE of us could say with any precision when it began. Condon had never been part of our set. Grandfathered into the club by one of those old robber barons whose fortunes had declined, he was essentially nondescript – capable of maintaining a decent conversation, pleasant enough to be around, but not the kind of man with whom one formed deep and lasting relationships.

When we met him, we were friendly. When we didn't – which was the norm, Condon not being ubiquitous in our circles – we didn't think of him at all. So it was hard to say, as we thought the thing through among ourselves, when precisely it had begun – a task complicated by the fact that none of us had known anything *had* begun, until it was over.

Westfall claimed it had started in the late fall. He'd run into Condon Christmas shopping – we usually trade small gifts among ourselves – and had detected a faint unpleasant smell around the man. But the rest of us disagreed: the scent could have been nothing but some poorly chosen cologne, and besides, in the thronged department store in late November, the smell, which even Westfall admitted was subtle and brief, might have belonged to someone else altogether, brushing past in the crowded aisle where they stood conversing.

Symes put the date a little later. He'd run into Condon on the street outside a bakery, and had concluded that Condon looked splotchy and pale, rather wrung out. He'd thought nothing of it at the time. But in retrospect—

Nothing, the rest of us agreed.

Who doesn't look splotchy and wrung out when the city bustles with the holiday season, and a mere passing hello – which Symes confessed was the extent of their intercourse that mid-December afternoon – hardly provided the opportunity for the concentrated study needed to identify something as subtle as what Condon must have already been experiencing in its early stages.

No, the true start of it must have been just prior to Christmas when we met at the club to exchange the small gifts that spoke of our esteem for one another, and our pleasure at being privileged to enjoy one another's company. We were in our late twenties then – old enough to have reached some accommodation with life, young enough to still partake of the many pleasures it afforded. And though there were women in most of our lives, they hovered at the periphery; not yet had that marital drift begun which gradually unravels a rare circle of friendship like ours. In any case, Condon had stopped in for a drink, and seeing us at the bar, he joined us. We welcomed him kindly enough, and he stood among us as presents were unwrapped, nodding in appreciation of the perfect understanding each gift represented: a platinum cigar cutter for Lewis, a bottle of Delemain Extra for Gibson, an exquisite array of silk ties and pocket squares for Banks, the dandy among us.

After the last gift, Condon excused himself to the restroom. "I say," Gibson said, "did you smell the man's breath?" No one else had been standing as close to Condon as Gibson, so there was some good-natured dissension among us. "He'd been drinking," someone – it must have been Morrison – said, and several of our group nodded: it had been the alcohol, nothing more. Besides who wanted to smell the man's breath – or indeed anyone's breath? But Gibson demurred: "It's positively rancid," he said, and so, as we shook hands with Condon before departing, several of us leaned in for a private word – best wishes for the season and all that, a moment of eye contact (Condon's were a pale, pale grey, as nondescript as the rest of the man) and a squeeze of the shoulder.

Condon looked round once more at the gifts and smiled a closed-mouthed smile. "Well, I'll see you again, I'm certain. Until then" – another tight little smile – "I wish you the best." Then he turned, and Harris – the doorman, a tall cadaverously thin Negro who had preceded our tenure at the club – saw him out.

Another round ensued and those who had stepped close to Condon took up Gibson's cause. So the man's breath was sour, someone said, and Lewis, a doctor, noted that halitosis was hardly a novelty among men. What of it? "But it was rancid," Gibson said again. "Like something spoiled, or rotten." Really, it was, several others – those who had leaned close to shake his hand – attested. Intolerable actually. Lewis frowned: it's rarely a matter of serious concern, he said. And then Symes lightened the mood. "Too bad for the woman in his life," he said, and some question arose about whether anyone had ever seen Condon with a woman, provoking another round of drinks and debate (the consensus was that no one had). And so – after a joke that Condon had lately haunted us – the subject was dropped and we departed the club, gifts in hand, with a merry round of good wishes.

Condon didn't come up again, either in our lives or in our minds, for several weeks. The new year was underway and winter besieged the city: snow clogged the sidewalks and merchants scattered salt to melt the ice before their storefronts. Several of us booked passage for warmer climes: Italy, the French Riviera, Spain. Those hardy enough to stay and brave the elements hugged the buildings as we walked to avoid the parabolas of slush flung up by passing automobiles, unleashing spectacular arrays of colour.

Westfall had been mulling their beauty, he later told us, when he encountered Condon mid-street. Hellos were exchanged, a quick grip of gloved hands; and then they strode off to their separate sidewalks before the onslaught of traffic consumed them. Westfall didn't notice the faint powdering of grey dust on his glove until later in the afternoon, and even then he had no cause to associate it with Condon – not until that evening at the club, when he seemed to recall that Condon's shoulders had been lightly dusted with the same material, and that once again there had been a faint unpleasant odour about the man. But Morrison, the attorney among us, said that *ex post facto* evidence was hardly evidence at all, and that the grey dust on the glove was suspect itself, since it might have come from anywhere – especially since Condon had himself been gloved. Perhaps it sifted down his shirtsleeve, someone suggested, but Morrison merely lifted an eyebrow, and thus the conversation drew to a close.

Several more sightings followed, the tales duly returned to us at the club. Banks encountered him at a restaurant, pausing at the table where Condon dined alone. Despite the unpleasant odour that seemed to cling to the man, a brief conversation ensued: the usual social niceties, how are you doing, I hope that work goes well, we'll have to get together some time – though both of them must have known that such promises were hollow, that men not of the same order in life do not mix. Banks introduced his date. Smiles and greetings were exchanged. They shook hands as they departed, and Banks felt the grip of rubber in his palm: the man was wearing latex gloves, such as a surgeon might wear. And now that he thought of it, Condon's face had looked splotchy and reddened, as by wind; under that, like a palimpsest, a greyish pallor reigned.

On the whole, he told us that night at the club, it was a most unsettling encounter. Nor would it be the last. Perhaps three months later, Hynes came to the club with a strange story. He had run into Condon at the bookseller we occasionally frequented, an antiquarian known for his personal service and his eclectic collection. Hynes had dropped by to pick up a travel volume; he'd lately begun planning a sojourn abroad, several months in southern Italy and Greece. As he passed, he happened to catch sight of Condon perusing the shelves. Striding over, he was surprised to see that, despite the warmth of the spring day, Condon was clad in a hat and a light overcoat; and shaking hands he found, as Banks had reported, that the other man wore latex gloves. Despite these precautions, a faint hint of decay hung about him. "You're not ill, are you?" Hynes asked, looking into Condon's face, which appeared grey, almost spongy in texture. Condon had responded in the negative, Hynes reported, but his voice – his voice was ravaged, a deep gravelly whisper, as though it was all he could do to speak. Unnerved, Hynes made a hasty departure, his travel book forgotten, and as he narrated the tale later at the club, he looked unnerved still.

And so the mystery of Condon deepened. He became for the first time a subject of conjecture that fascinated us all. Lewis speculated about a diagnosis, but in the end could produce nothing concrete, to his palpable discomfort. The rest of us began to debate where the thing had begun – in the department store or outside the bakery or that night not long before Christmas, when he had interrupted us as we exchanged our small gifts. Or perhaps it had begun earlier still, when none of us had been around to perceive it. In the end – though Westfall and Symes held out – we agreed that the first time it became perceptible was that night in the club, though it might have been going on for weeks and months before that, as the condition incubated, when few of us had seen Condon and none of us had noticed anything awry.

It might have rested there but for the final encounter, when Morrison ran into Condon at a coffee shop. He waited in line behind a man dressed unseasonably in overcoat and hat, a man he took for one who lived on the street, both because of his attire and his smell, a heavy, oppressive odour that Morrison – wrongly as we would discover – associated with the stench of a long-unwashed body. He backed away a step, and when the man turned, his order in hand, Morrison saw that his face had been wrapped tightly in a white scarf, prickled here and there by bright red pinpoints that could have only been blood. Nothing could have surprised him more, Morrison later reported, than such an apparition speaking his name. Yet speak his name the creature did, and when Morrison gasped, "Who are you?", it was Condon's name that was returned. "You – you don't look well," Morrison said, and in a hollow rasp of a voice, Condon said, "I am as well as can be expected." That was the end of the conversation. Morrison, to his shame, he admitted, wished the man improved health, turned on his heel and departed.

And now we sat in the club – where we had not seen Condon for months, since that night just before Christmas – pondering these mysteries. Someone suggested that we should let the matter go altogether; someone else that we should seek Condon out, assure ourselves that he was indeed well, and if he was not, to offer what aid there might be in our power to provide. This view won out in the end – though in truth it was curiosity that drove us. Harris was prevailed upon for Condon's address, and we departed upon the minute.

Condon's neighbourhood was in the first stage of the city's eternal cycle of decay, collapse, and gentrification. Apartment windows were barred, others broken, dooryards in disarray. Abandoned buildings thronged the street, their façades cracked and sagging. Grey-faced Negroes congregated on stoops. Condon's family had fallen further than we had thought – as had Condon himself. His building, four stories of eroding brick, stood next to an overgrown lot behind a chain-link fence. The concrete steps were crumbling. Though the men clustered there drew away from us in deference, a sense of shared apprehension possessed us. The lobby was shabby. Condon's name appeared over a long-corroded buzzer. The door to the stairs hung open. We climbed them in silence. When we knocked on his apartment door, it swung open at our touch.

Condon was in the bedroom, supine upon the bed beneath a single sheet. The stench of rot was overpowering. It was all several of us could do to master the impulse to throw up. Condon's hair had come out in patches; his face was grey and eaten away by decay. His nose had collapsed altogether, leaving only a pair of identical slits. Through the flesh of his jaw, one could see teeth that hung loose in his jaw. "My God," Lewis said, stripping away the sheet, and we saw then that his body had begun to deliquesce. Through vents in his abdominal cavity, we saw the pulse of organs – and these too had gone grey – that only Lewis could identify. "My God," he said again. "What has happened to you?"

For a long time, Condon did not reply. An oppressive silence clogged the room. Just as several us concluded that he was beyond speech, he opened his mouth. Skin gave way along the jaw, as soil might subside into a rift opened by an earthquake. His voice, when it came, was a ravaged whisper, barely perceptible.

"I have awaited your coming," he rasped.

And it is to that moment that we date our membership in a new and more hideous fraternity.

JOE R. LANSDALE

The Hunt: Before, and the Aftermath

JOE R. LANSDALE is the author of more than thirty novels, numerous short stories, articles and comic and film scripts. He has won numerous awards, among them The Edgar, nine Bram Stoker Awards, The Lifetime Achievement in Horror, Grandmaster of Horror, and many others. He is a member of The Texas Literary Hall of Fame and is Writer in Residence at Stephen F. Austin State University. His novella, "Bubba Ho-Tep", was made into the popular cult film of the same name directed by Don Coscarelli and starring Bruce Campbell.

As the author admits: "Oddly, though I'm worn out with zombie stories, I've written a few, and each time I've tried to approach it from a different angle.

"I decided to stop thinking so much about the zombies and think about a world where people are not only learning to live with their presence, but in fact the focus of the story is on the living people. I don't care much for the idea of zombies becoming human again, but I wanted to see if the humans could stay human. Thing is, humans can be good or bad, or they can have the most common of problems, no matter what kind of world they live in.

"This was my attempt to write a story that might have been written by someone writing during a time of zombie infestation, but a time when the world had put itself back together and zombies were a truism of everyday life, same as disease."

WE RODE THE famous Fast Train out west, all the way from New York City.

Went out there with men and women packed in all the cars along with all our baggage and the guns, and they were good guns, too. All of us had good guns. That was a perquisite. We had paid for the hunt and our guides made sure we had the best of everything, and that included the guns. They wanted us to have good weapons, not only because we were about to hunt and were paying heavily for the privilege, but because they thought if we had excellent weapons and ammunition, it less likely that something might blow up in someone's face, killing them. There were insurance policies, of course. But there's always trouble and always challenges from the insurance, especially on these types of hunting expeditions. Part of the reason the hunting was so expensive was because the insurance the hunting company paid was very high.

I brought along my wife, Livia, and we left the kids with their grandparents – my parents. It was a good trip out, and there were excursions along the way, and we even did a bit of bird hunting in Arkansas. Stopped there for a couple of days and stayed in some cabins up in the mountains where the woods were thick.

It was September, and there were some brisk mornings, some warm mid-days, and then at night there was the cool again. But it was never miserable. We spent the nights in the cabins, but before bedtime we all sat around a campfire that was prepared by our guides, and there was entertainment. Singers and even some skits that weren't really all that good but seemed a lot better under the circumstances.

As I said, it was a good trip in that everything went smooth, but it wasn't good when it came to Livia and I, and considering all that had gone before, I didn't expect it to be, but it was good that the trip itself wasn't bad to make matters worse. At least we had that going for us, the smoothness of the trip.

During the day while we were in Arkansas we hunted. Mostly we were done by noon, and when we came in the guides would have the birds cleaned right away and put in the refrigeration car, and that night they would be our meal, that and some good beans and fresh baked cornbread.

Frankly, though I like shooting birds, I don't much care for the meat. But I ate it well enough, and by the end of the day, tromping around with the hunting dogs that had been provided by the Arkansas cabin owner where we stayed, I most likely could have eaten anything and thought that it was good. I think I would have thought that cornbread was good anytime; I'm a big fan of cornbread.

The first night in the Arkansas accommodations, Livia and I went to our cabin and decided to take showers, since we smelled of smoke from the campfire. Livia wanted to go first. She began to undress. I watched her. Even though she was nearing the age of forty, she had a youthful body, and I enjoyed watching her take off her clothes and pause before a mirror in the bedroom to shake out her hair, which had been tied back in a ponytail.

When she walked to the bathroom, I enjoyed the view, and was sorry that even though we were sharing a bed, we wouldn't be sharing one another. I wished then that I had things to do over, but I didn't, and it was my hope in time that we could reconcile things, and not just so we could have sex, but so we could have peace and things would be like they used to be; that was the purpose of the hunt; time together and reconciliation.

Anyway, she showered, and came into the room, and pulled a huge red night shirt over her head, and without putting on panties got into bed. A year ago, that would have been a kind of silent invitation, but tonight I knew it was just a tease, something to make me feel bad about what I had done, and about what I wasn't going to get tonight because of it. It had been that way every night since she found out about the infidelity. That was eight months ago, but things hadn't changed much in that time, except we could talk a little more civilly most of the time.

I showered, and while in the shower I masturbated, thinking it would be a lot better to do that than to lie in the bed and think about what was under her night shirt all night. There was also in me a bit of defiance. I was truly sorry for what I had done, and I had tried in every possible way to make it up.

I didn't think just because I was sorry that should be the end of the matter, as that kind of betrayal is serious and nothing anyone can get over easily. I know I would have had problems, but damn it, I was trying, and I didn't seem to get points for trying. I felt she was enjoying punishing me a little too much.

By the time I had satisfied myself and washed the results down the drain, I was feeling less bold, and understood exactly why she felt the way she did. I took a long time drying off and brushing my teeth, and by the time I got in bed, Livia was sound asleep.

We stopped in Palo Duro Canyon in northern Texas, and that night there was a play about statehood. It was performed in a beautiful part of the mountains, and there were lots of lights, and there were horses and cowboys and they rode the horses along the rim to the sound of tiny, but inspiring music, that seemed to be as loud as the canyon was normally silent.

It was a good show, and it even included the changes that had occurred, and there were people dressed up like the dead people, shuffling along, and there were a few comic bits associated with it, and then it was over.

As we were bussed back to where the tracks were, and where our hotel was, Livia said, "You know, that was hokey, but I really enjoyed it."

"So did," I said, though that wasn't entirely true. I had begun to see that Livia was looking at other men in a way she hadn't before. I don't know if it was because she was thinking about cheating to even up the score, or if what I had done had just opened her mind to someone other than me. Anyway, I had watched her and I thought I had seen something in her eye when she was watching some of the male actors in the plays. They were all young, and most likely gay, I told myself, but still, Livia was watching. I felt certain of it. Nonetheless, I liked that she had spoken to me in that way, as it seemed natural, and for a few seconds it seemed as if she had forgotten all about being mad at me.

But, back at the room we went straight to bed, and I lay there and looked at the ceiling for a long time. Eventually I heard Livia breathing evenly as she slept, and I turned and looked at her.

There was enough moonlight through a part in the curtains to fall on her face and make her look angelic. I thought she was the kind of woman that could easily attract a much younger man, and I was the kind of man that if I managed to keep my business and money, could most likely attract a younger woman, but only if they didn't know I was in debt. She had options, and I didn't have any real ones. Just ones I might be able to lie about.

I think that's what it had been about, the infidelity, a feeling that I was getting past it all and needed some assurance of my manhood. It hadn't been a classic sort of infidelity, and I told myself that because of the uniqueness of it, it didn't count. But if it had been the other way, Livia instead of me that had done it, I know I would have been insane with jealousy.

It didn't work the other way, though. I might have been better off had I had an affair, and not just an encounter – and an encounter I paid steeply for, both financially and emotionally.

I hoped when we got to the hunt, everything would be better. That I could make it better and she would accept that. I lay there and tried to think of all the clever things I could do to make her happy, but all of them were fantasy and I knew none of them would work.

* * *

We had a private car on the train with food and alcohol and most anything that we seriously needed. There would be the hunting car later, but on the way out and back, when we weren't stopped along the way at some site or entertainment that was planned, we had the room and a fold-down berth, and it was all nice and clean and private.

The humming of the train over the tracks had become soothing, and maybe that was why Livia was able to talk about it. She came at me with it out of nowhere, and it was the first time she hadn't yelled at me when she brought it up.

"Was it because I didn't satisfy you?"

I was sitting at the fold-down table with a drink of well-watered whisky. I said, "Of course not."

"Then why?"

"I've told you, Livia."

"Tell me again."

"I've told you again and again."

"Make me believe it."

I sat for a moment, gathering my energy for it. "I suppose it has to do with getting older. I don't feel all that attractive anymore. I'm a little heavy, going bald. I wanted to feel that I could be with another woman."

"But that woman . . . That doesn't work, Frank. She didn't want you back. She was paid for. And she was . . ."

"I know," I said. "But it was the fantasy that she was someone who cared for me and that it was a secret rendezvous. It was the idea of it more than the actuality of it. It was stupid, but I did it and I'm sorry, and I am so sad it ever happened."

"Childish."

"Yes," I said. "Very much so. I know that now. But I just felt it might give me a boost, so to speak."

"I don't give you a boost?"

"You do."

"I know I'm older—"

"You look fantastic," I said. "It wasn't that. It was me."

"And that's supposed to make me feel better?"

"I don't think that – no. It won't make you feel better.

But it's an answer, not an excuse, and it's the only one I have. There is no good answer. I was foolish. It's just that . . . I love you, Livia. But I just wasn't satisfied."

"It wasn't like I didn't make love to you."

"No," I said. "You did. But . . . it wasn't all that passionate."

"We're not eighteen anymore."

"I guess that's what I wanted, something more passionate. Something that would make me feel eighteen again."

"The only thing that could make you feel eighteen again is being eighteen," she said.

"I know. I just wanted something besides the usual, you know. I don't mean that offensively, but I wanted to feel something akin to the old passion."

Livia turned her head away from me when she spoke. "Why didn't you ask? We could have experimented."

"I hinted."

"Hinted?" she said. "Isn't it men who always say that women don't say what they want? That they beat around the bush? Don't you always say, 'how am I supposed to know what you want if you don't ask'?"

"I suppose it is."

"No supposing to it."

We sat silently for a long time. I didn't even pick up my drink.

"Do you think you can ever feel good about me again?" I said. "That you can ever trust me and feel that things are right again? Can we ever be okay?"

"I don't know," Livia said.

She went to the cabinet and pulled the latch and took out a glass and a bottle of some kind of green liquor. She poured herself a drink and put everything back, and went to sit on the fold-down bed.

"You'll try?" I said.

"I try every day," she said. "You don't know how hard I try."

"This trip . . . was it a mistake?"

"I don't know. I'll see how it makes me feel when it's all over."

I nodded and drank the rest of my drink. I couldn't think of anything else to say or do, except get another drink, and I didn't even do that. I just sat there, and in time Livia took a magazine from her suitcase and lay on the bed and read.

I finally got up and got another drink and sat down at the table with it. I sipped it and thought about how I had ruined everything that had ever meant anything to me for a piece of overpriced heavily lubricated ass.

I began to hang all my hopes on the hunt, and that the enthusiasm of it would excite her as it did when we used to deer hunt together. That had been years ago, and this was different, but I think, except for those times when we had been young and in bed together, it was the time when I felt the most bonded to her.

I suppose it was the thrill of the hunt, and mostly the thrill of the kill. I never deluded myself into thinking hunting was a sport. Killing was what it was all about, and to kill something was to satisfy something deep in the soul, something primal. And it was a strange thing to see in that primitive nature in a woman, and to observe her face when she stood over the body of a dead deer; her eyes bright, the deer's eyes dull, and on Livia's face an expression akin to the one she had when she had an orgasm and lay in my arms, happy, satisfied, having experienced something that was beyond intellect and rationalisation.

It was a cool, crisp morning when we reached Montana. The air felt rich with oxygen and the sky was so blue it was hard to believe it was real. There wasn't a cloud in the sky. By mid-day it would be relatively warm, if still jacket weather, but we would be in the hunting car, perched at the windows with our rifles, so it would be comfortable enough, stuffed as the car would be with other hunters, adrenaline and passion and the desire to kill.

Though, perhaps, kill was the wrong word here, and that's what made the whole thing somehow acceptable. You can't kill what's already dead, but you can enjoy the shooting, and maybe it wasn't as good as a live deer brought down and made dead, but to shoot the living dead, a human, and not have any remorse because it was all sanctioned, there was something about that, something about the fantasy of killing a human being instead of just bringing down a walking thing that was the shell for someone who had once lived.

The train parked on the tracks and some of the guides went to the storage car where the dead people were kept. They would let them out and drive them to the centre of the plain, and they would throw sides of beef in the dirt to keep them in that area, bloody beef that the dead could smell and want.

When they went for the beef, when the guides said it was time, we could point our guns out the window and take them as fast as we could shoot. Sometimes, the guides said, the dead would come to the window, and that you had to be careful, because you could get so caught up in the shooting, you could forget that they wanted you as much as you wanted them. If your arm was out the window, well, you could get bit, and the waiver we had signed said that if that was the case, we went out there with them. We wouldn't necessarily be dead, but we soon would be, so there was a chance to shoot someone who was actually alive; someone already doomed. It was considered practical and even humane, and it was covered by insurance money that your family would receive.

Livia and I settled into our shooting positions. We had benches by a long window, and the window was still closed. We were given our rifles. They were already loaded, and we were told to keep them pointing up, which, of course, we knew without being told. Everyone here had gone through the program on how to handle the weapons and how to deal with the dead, and Livia and I were already hunters and we could shoot.

I had paid dearly for this event, and I hoped it would make a difference. When it was all over, I would be deep in debt, but I would have saved my marriage if it worked. Money was easier to regain than the loss of a good marriage.

The guides came through and told us the basic rules again, gave us reminders, the same stuff I told you about not getting so caught up in the kill that we forgot to watch for the dead slipping through, getting hold of us through the windows. They said everything was very safe, but that it had happened, and they would be outside, on the fringes, with weapons to take down any of the dead that seemed to be getting through the line of fire and presenting a problem.

My hands were sweating. Not from fear of the dead, or even anticipation of the shoot itself, but thinking how it would be between Livia and me when it was over.

"What's she wearing?" Livia asked.

I was startled out of my thoughts.

"What?

"I said, what is she wearing?"

"I bought an orange jump suit for her."

"How does she look?"

"Dark hair, tall . . . well built."

"That could be me."

"I suppose that had something to do with it," I said. "Her reminding me of you."

"A dead woman?"

I knew then my tact had backfired, and I could have kicked myself.

"Just the appearance," I said. "But it's been awhile. And even with refrigeration, she's gone down hill. She still looks close to being alive. Not as much as before."

"You mean when you fucked her?"

We were seated pretty close to other hunters, and I glanced to see if any of them had heard her, heard anything we might have said.

They all seemed preoccupied with their weapons and their thoughts and their eagerness, and I realised that Livia wasn't as loud as I thought she was.

"I don't know how to describe her so that you will know right off," I said. "I'll try and point her out."

"You do that," Livia said. "I want to be the one."

"I know."

"I thought maybe I'd want you to shoot her, just to show me it didn't matter, but then I thought that wouldn't do. I want to shoot her."

"Of course it doesn't matter," I said. "It wasn't like she was alive."

"I want to shoot her," she said.

"It could be anyone that shoots her," I said. "There's no guarantees it'll be you that gets her."

"It better be me," Livia said. "You paid to fuck her, now you've paid for me to shoot her. It better be me."

"You don't just want to shoot her," I said. "You want to finish her. A shot through the head to destroy the brain."

"Think I don't know that? Everyone knows that. And I can shoot. You know I can shoot."

I couldn't say anything right. Everything I said was like stepping in shit and being forced to smell my shoe.

"Yes," I said. "Of course you can shoot."

The guides were moving back along the aisle of the rail car.

"All right," one of them said. "We are going to open the cars, and when the dead come out – and listen to me. Do not shoot! Not at first. The beef is in place. You see the yellow chalk line we've laid in the grass? You can not, and will not, shoot until the dead are beyond that, on the beef. If some do not go past the line, the outside guides will work them that way with the push poles, and if they can't get them to go, they may have to put a few down themselves. After the dead are over the line, you can fire at will. And if they start to come back over the line, you can still fire. But you have to wait until they are first over the line. Does everyone understand?"

We all called out that we understood.

"Any questions?" asked the guide.

There were none.

"Then," the guide said, "ladies and gentlemen, the windows will be lowered. Do not put your rifles out the windows until the dead are all past the yellow line, and when they are, then its open season."

The automatic windows rolled down. The windows gave plenty of room for propping the rifles and for laying your elbows on the sill.

We heard the train cars opening on either side of us, and we could hear the dead, moaning. Then we saw them coming out of the cars. The guides had big heavy poles and they pushed the dead with them to make sure they went toward the yellow line. But they didn't need much pushing. The bloody meat smelled even better than we did to them, and the dead went for it right away.

Livia said, "Point her out. I want to shoot her a few times in the body before I take the head."

"Someone might beat you to it," I said.

"Just point her out."

In that moment I thought about the night I had had with the woman who had no name and was for a while part of the dead brothel down on 41st Street. She was only part of it while she was fresh, and then they had to let her go to the sale market for the hunts, and I was lucky to buy her. I almost didn't win the bid, and I had to keep raising it, and pretty soon I had my bid way up there and it was really far more than I could afford. But I bought her for the hunt. But even then, she was just mine to place in the hunt, not mine or Livia's to shoot. That was up to circumstance.

It was said many a husband or wife had bought their dead spouses to shoot at because of past grievances, and it even occurred to me Livia might turn the rifle on me. It wasn't a serious thought, but it passed through my head nonetheless.

I thought about the dead woman now, of how she had been fastened to the bed and her mouth was covered over with a leather strap; how she had writhed beneath me; not because she enjoyed or felt anything, but because she was trying to break loose and she wanted to bite me. I could hear her grunting with savage hunger under the mask, and it was exciting to know what I was doing. I had paid for her with a charge card, and though the card didn't say brothel on it, Livia was able to figure it all out. It took her awhile, but she got it doped out and then she confronted me, and I didn't even try to lie. I think on some level I had wanted her to find out, had wanted her to know.

But the young woman beneath me that night at the brothel was still firm and she wasn't falling apart. She hadn't been dead long, and what had killed her was heart failure, some inherited condition that took her out young. When she died the dead disease took her over, and her mother sold her to the brothel then; had them come out and capture her and take her there.

A few years back such a thing would have been thought horrible, but now it happened all the time. It was part of the government plan to dehumanise them after they were dead, to make people think of them as nothing more than empty shells that walked and were a threat and were sometimes entertainment. It was an indoctrination that was starting to take hold.

Yet, when I saw the dead out there, wandering over the line, in all manner of conditions, some fresh, some with their skin falling off, some little more than skeletons with just enough viscera and flesh to hold them together, I felt sick. My parents had died but a few years before the flu came that caused so many to become what these poor people were, and I thought if they had lived just another year, they might have been victims, they might be out there. Someone's parents, brothers, sisters, husbands, you name it, were out there. It was only luck that had caused us and so many others to take flu shots that year, and the flu shots saved us, even though there had never been a flu like this one. Just that simple thing, a flu shot, had saved many from dying and coming back. Those who hadn't taken the shot, and got the flu, they got worse, died, and came back.

All of this was running through my head, and then I saw the woman. She had on the orange jump suit I had bought for her, and she was staggering toward the meat on the other side of the line.

"There she is," I said. "The orange jump suit."

"There are a lot of orange jump suits," Livia said.

"Not like this one," I said. "It's bright orange. She's off to the side there. She has long black hair. Very long, like yours. Like all the others, her back is to us."

"I see her," Livia said.

She lifted her rifle and fired right away. It was a miss. But she fired again and she hit the woman in the back. The shot knocked the woman down. She got up rather quickly, and started walking again, toward the beef.

"I want to see her face," Livia said.

"That might not happen," I said.

Livia fired again, hit the woman in the right knee. It was a shot that not only knocked her down, but as she fell, her face turned toward us. It was still a good face, somewhat drawn, but still the face of someone pretty who had once been very pretty in life. And then she caught another shot from Livia's rifle, this one in the face, just over the upper lip. The woman spun a little, and I think the blow from the heavy load made her neck turn in such a way that it snapped her spine.

When she was on the ground, she began to crawl toward the smell of the meat again. Her head was turned oddly on her neck, and the side of her face dragged the ground as she went.

"I want you to shoot her once," Livia said. "Then I'll make the kill. You shoot her in the body."

Now there were explosions everywhere as the dead targets took hits, and even Livia's target, the woman I had fucked, was being shot at. Bullets were smashing into the earth all around her and one took off part of her right foot.

"You shoot her," Livia said. "You shoot her now."

I fired and missed.

"You better hit her," Livia said.

I fired again, hit the woman in the body. She kept crawling.

Livia just sat there, watching her crawl.

"You want to finish her, better hurry before someone else gets her," I said.

Livia looked at me. Her eyes were cold. "You better hope no one else does," she said.

She lifted her rifle and fired. The woman's head exploded.

After that, we began to fire at will, and I think I blew the heads off four, though someone else's shot might have taken one of them. I couldn't be sure. Livia hit at least seven in the head and dropped them. She hit several more in the body, and dropped them. Eventually, someone firing at the same targets got the head.

When it was all done, the guides gathered up the bodies with hooks and carried them to a large and long pile of lumber that had already been laid out and had weathered some. They put the dead on the pile and poured gasoline over all of it and set it on fire.

When the fire was going, the rifles were gathered and stored and the windows went up, and we broke for clean-up and then dinner, just as the train was starting to move.

Back in our little room we could really smell the gun oil and the stink from the firing. We decided to shower and dress for dinner. There was to be a big formal dinner in the dining car tonight, a celebration of the completion of the hunt. On the way back the train wouldn't stop, but would run full speed night and day until we arrived back east.

Before I got in the shower, I looked at Livia, and she was obviously different, relieved, as if a poison had been drained from her. I went to the bathroom and undressed. It was tight in there and the shower was close. I turned on the water and began to soap up and shampoo my hair.

I heard the curtain slide back, and there was Livia, naked. She didn't smile at me. She didn't say a word. She got in and pulled back the curtain and took hold of me and got me ready and then before I knew it was happening, I was inside of her, pushing her up against the shower wall, going at her for all I was worth.

She was amazing, animal-like even. It was over quickly for both of us. We leaned together, panting. Then Livia was out of the shower, and was gone, and I was left dazed and amazed, satisfied and confused.

When I came out of the bathroom, drying myself with a towel, the lights were on, but Livia had already gone to bed. She was lying in our little bunk beneath the sheets with her back to me, her face turned to the wall. The blanket was folded back to her feet.

I was about to put on my pyjamas, when she said without turning toward me, "Don't bother with your pyjamas. Put out the light and come to bed."

I did. And we did.

It was a great, long night of love, and even as I mounted her, and enjoyed her, and she squirmed beneath me and moaned, I couldn't help but somehow be reminded of that night with the woman we shot. Like that night, what Livia and I did was not so much making love as it was a pounding of each other's genitals. It was a savage pelvis fight that left bruises and redness and utter exhaustion.

Later, lying beside Livia, holding her, listening to her breathe, I wondered how long it would be before things went back to the way they used to be. Not just how we could be together without the thing I had done not hanging before us in the air, but the sex, as well; how long before it became mild again, as common as a subway ride, and as boring.

I thought of that and I thought of the strange time I had had with the dead woman in a room on 41st Street, and I told myself that such a thing couldn't happen again, but I knew, too, that while Livia and I had been at it this night, when I closed my eyes, it was not Livia I saw. It was the dead woman I imagined beneath me.

What in hell were the desires of man?

No profound revelation presented itself in answer to my question.

I closed my eyes and thought about many things, but mostly I thought about that dead woman, and how she had been, and how it had been to shoot her today, and how it had made Livia and me fill up with the lava of passion. I tried to think of Livia, and our life, and how much I loved her, but in my mind all I could see was that dead girl being screwed by me or shot by us, and the Fast Train fled eastward.

SIMON KURT UNSWORTH

The Cotswold Olimpicks

SIMON KURT UNSWORTH was born in Manchester in 1972 and has not yet given up the hope of finding that the world was awash with mysterious signs and portents that night.

His work has been published in a number of anthologies, including Ash-Tree Press's *At Ease with the Dead, Shades of Darkness* and *Exotic Gothic 3*, Dark Horse's *Lovecraft Unbound*, PS Publishing' *PostScripts* and Gray Friar Press's *Where the Heart Is*. This is his fifth appearance in the *Mammoth Book of Best New Horror* series, and he has also appeared in *The Very Best of Best New Horror*.

His first collection of short stories, *Lost Places*, was released by Ash-Tree in 2010 and was (along with Angela Slatter's *Sourdough*) *Black Static* magazine's reviewer Pete Tennant's collection of the year. His latest collection, *Quiet Houses*, was long-listed for the Edge Hill Short Story Collection prize, and he has two further collections due: *Strange Gateways* from PS Publishing and an as-yet-unnamed volume that will launch the Spectral Press "Spectral Signature Editions".

As he admits: "When I was asked to contribute to *Terror Tales of the Cotswolds* (in which 'The Cotswold Olimpicks' first appeared), I agreed without having thought through the fact that I'd never actually been to any of the places that constitute the Cotswolds.

"I started to research the area, coming eventually across a reference to 'The Cotswold Olimpicks'; the name stuck in my head, and when I read an article about the games and the man who set them up, the story appeared in my mind pretty much fully formed. It seemed to fit perfectly with my new-found love of folk music, with my sense of old notes stretching tendril fingers back into the past, with my realisation that folk tunes are darker than I'd ever understood – full of sex and rebellion and anger.

"I liked the idea of the Cotswold Olimpicks, of the unofficial histories of places and the curious traditions that pepper the UK like secret blisters, and I wanted to write something that not only celebrated these folk traditions but that also poked and played with their origins. It is, I suppose, my version of *The Wicker Man*, only without Summerisle, Britt Ekland's dancing, Christopher's Lee's suavely evil urbanity and kilt, Sergeant Howie's dour and unforgiving Christianity and unattractive pyjamas, or crowds in a pub bursting into bawdy song.

"It's a story about the past and the now and the dancing we do when we get caught between the two; it's also a story about tradition and alcohol, and I'm rather proud of it.

"Robert Dover's poem at the end of the story is, incidentally, genuine."

FILLINGHAM FIRST SAW the women by the *dwile flonkers*. He had spent the day walking around Dover's Hill, the shallow amphitheatre where the Cotswold Olimpick Games took place and had taken, he thought, some good photographs so far. The place was heaving and he had captured some of that, he hoped; the shifting bustle as people flocked from event to event and laughed and shouted and ate and drank. The sound of cymbals and mandolins and violins and guitars filled the air about the crowd, leaping around the brightly costumed figures and the smells of roasting meat and open fires.

There were five of them and they were watching as a circle of men held hands and danced counter-clockwise around another group of men. The men in the centre of the circle had a bucket and were dipping cloths in it and hurling them at the dancers; every time one of the cloths hit its target, the crowd laughed good-naturedly. When the cloth missed, arcing into the people beyond, a cheer went up and a man dressed in a costume of rags and wearing a hat that was too big for him would shout, "Ha! Jobanowl declares a penalty!" and the cloth thrower was given a large glass of ale to drink. The women were smiling as they watched, clustered tightly together, dressed similarly in white shift dresses and with their hair long and loose. Fillingham wondered if they were some kind of act and took their photograph, thinking that if he could catch another one of them later, in performance, it might make a nice pair, *Artists at rest and work* or something.

The women were definitely a group, seemed to be in tune with each other somehow, their heads bobbing to the rhythms of the music slipping through the air around them, their bodies turning in the same direction as though responding to invisible currents like birds wheeling through the sky. When one of the sodden cloths, the *dwiles*, came towards them, they danced aside as though choreographed. The crowd cheered again as Fillingham lowered his camera, a knot of people jostling between him and the women as they tried to avoid the dripping missile, and when they moved aside the women were gone.

Fillingham let the press of the crowd drift him along the field, taking more photographs, this time of men dressed in smock shirts and clogs kicking at each other's shins, and then of another team of men destroying an old piano as people around them cheered and chanted a countdown. As dusk crept across the valley, his images took on a sepia tone, bleached of colour's vibrancy, becoming timeless. This was what he was after, he thought; a set of pictures that captured some of the sense of history of this event, of people stepping back for a day to celebrate nothing but tradition and enjoyment itself. This was a folk event, owned by everyone here.

On the cusp of the gloaming giving itself to darkness, someone appeared as Robert Dover, the founder of the games some time in the early seventeenth century. He was riding a huge chestnut horse, was dressed in a tunic with a heraldic crest on his breast. A yellow feather bristled jauntily from the brim of his wide hat, bobbing as he rode around. His face was a white mask hanging down from under the hat, gleaming like bone, and he was waving a wand above his head that glittered and spat sparks. It was a sign that the bonfire was to be lit and the crowd began to move back towards the huge pile of wood at the far side of the fields, following the horseman as he capered and called exhortations for people to *hurry*, to *dance on*. Fillingham took more photographs, catching a good one of Dover rearing his horse in the centre of a mass of people, like some ancient leather-bound general, all buckles and gleam and leadership.

Moving with the crowd, Fillingham found himself walking behind the women in white and spent a few moments appreciating the sway of their buttocks under the thin dresses before realising they were barefoot; mud was spattered up the pale skin of their bare calves in dark, irregular tattoos. The hems of their dresses were damp and dirty as well, he saw, the material swinging in sinuous patterns as the women moved. It was surprisingly erotic, this shift of skin and muscle under skin and cotton and dirt that crept up to where Fillingham's eyes could not follow, and he suddenly felt guilty, as though he was peeping. Feeling himself blush and glad of the darkness to cover his embarrassment, he raised his eyes to deliberately look away.

The fire caught quickly, leaping orange into the sky and throwing its heat across the crowd, creating a fug of temperature and sweat. Dover cantered around the blaze, crying "To ale! To ale!" as people cheered and shouted, his motionless face reflecting the fire's colours. Fillingham took more pictures, wishing, not for the first time, that his camera could somehow catch sound and smell as well, that it could trap the intensity of the heat and the noise and the scents of mud and flame and grass, and preserve them.

From huge bags on the ground near the fire, stewards in reflective tabards began to take long white candles and hand them out. The first few they lit and then let people ignite each other's, a chain of flames that stretched out in a long, snaking line as the crowds began to walk slowly back towards Chipping Campden. Fillingham declined a candle and let the line carry him, snapping all the while.

The procession ended up in the small town's market square, where more revels were starting up. Most of the shops were still open, filling with tourists buying souvenirs, and stalls along the sides of the square did a brisk trade in food and drink. Down the streets off the square, small canvas tents with open fronts nestled between the shops, offering people the opportunity to play chess and draughts, or games of chance like three card marney or craps. The square soon became busy, clusters of people spilling out into the surrounding streets, drinking and talking and shouting, filling the tents and shops, moving, and Fillingham photographed as many of them as he could.

He had been in the square for around an hour when he saw one of the women again; she was moving through the crowds holding a beaten pewter flask and stacks of small plastic cups. Fillingham followed her, intrigued; this wasn't what he'd expected. The women had looked like a singing group, as though they were about to launch into madrigals or choral songs at any moment, but now they were separated and were doing . . . what? The woman he was following, tall and dark, was doing little other than giving drinks away, pouring small amounts of liquid into the cups and handing them out. Fillingham took photographs of her, watching as she distributed the cups, dipping her head and saying something each time someone drank. Fillingham moved closer, hoping to get a clearer image and hear what the woman was saying, but he kept losing her in the press of bodies. Her white dress glimmered in amongst the shifting masses like a faltering beacon, and he followed.

The woman moved surprisingly quickly, without apparent effort, slipping along the alleyways around the square, darting through knots of people and giving out her drinks, nodding and speaking. Fillingham wondered where the other women were; doing the same thing throughout the crowds, he supposed, giving out their drinks and adding to the atmosphere. The day's games were over; now the celebrations started in earnest. He took more photographs as he followed the woman, of stall-holders serving, of a group of Morris Men drinking beer from tankards, their bells jangling as their arms moved. Fillingham saw that the tankards were attached to their belts by lengths of string or leather cord; some of the Morris Men had more than one, spares hanging to their side as they supped. Children ran between the legs of adults, chasing and chased and laughing.

"Would you like a drink, sir?" The voice was friendly, the accent difficult to place, not local but redolent of somewhere hot and dry and surrounded by embracing blues seas. It was the woman, holding out one of her cups to Fillingham. He took it and sniffed at the liquid it held; it was sweet and rich and pungent. The woman was looking at him expectantly, but he held the cup back out to her. "No, thank you," he said. "I'm not drinking at the moment." *Not drinking alcohol*, he almost added, but didn't. Instead, he indicated his press badge in its plastic sheath dangling against his chest and gave her a rueful smile, saying, "I'm working. Perhaps later."

"The celebrations go on for many hours," said the woman. Above her, in the sky, a firework exploded, showering multi-coloured flames across the stars. "You can pay fealty at any time." Another firework tore open the sky, streams of colour painting the woman's shift blue and green, throwing their shadows downwards. For a moment, the woman's shadow self moved against the shadow Fillingham, pressing to him, and then another explosion above them sent them dancing apart, wavering, their edges rimed with yellows and reds, and then the woman was moving again.

She stopped at the people next to Fillingham, offering them drinks which they took. As they drank, she dipped her head again and spoke, and this time he was close enough to hear what she said. It was doggerel, some old rhyme he presumed, intoned as though it were a prayer. *Atmosphere*, he thought, snapping a last picture of her before her head rose from its penitent's pose. On the screen in his camera's rear, she looked small and pale, the swelling of her breasts only just visible under the cotton of her dress, her hair draping down in front of her face, her neck exposed and delicate. She lifted her head, giving Fillingham a last look that he couldn't quite fathom, and then she was gone.

By the time Fillingham decided to go back to his hotel, the atmosphere was definitely changing; most children and their parents had emptied from the crowd, leaving only the adults who were drinking seriously. The amount of dancing had increased and the town-square was full of moving figures and noise. Three or four different groups of musicians were playing, with more in the pubs, and the sound of violins and guitars and differing beats and voices was creating a discordance that Fillingham didn't enjoy.

The fireworks display had lasted for a few more minutes after the woman had left him behind, and had culminated in a huge explosion of reds and greens and blues and Dover using a megaphone to cry "To ale!" again, the wand above his head spitting like some giant sparkler as he waved it around, creating endless looping patterns in the air above him. Fillingham had taken more photographs, trying one last time to catch the feelings and the sounds and the smells of Chipping Campden, with its twisting streets and cobbles and stalls and *olde worlde* charm that managed, somehow, to seem vibrant and real and not clichéd or faked. After, he had put his camera in his bag and gone back to his room.

He was staying in a chain hotel, and not an expensive one either. He used the cheap chains unless he was on a commissioned assignment and could charge the room to someone else, and had grown used to their uniformity. Each room was the same; identical cheap veneer with its wood-grain pattern to make up for the fact that the surfaces were all plastic, identical small TVs bolted to the wall with a limited number of channels available, identical beds and bedding. Everything the same, from city to city, even down to the pictures screwed to the corridor walls and the carpet with its not-too-subtle pattern of brown and skeined red. He had become almost fond of it, in the knowing what to expect and surpriselessness of it all. At this end of the market, there were no individual flourishes in the room, no soap or shampoos in the bathroom, only two sachets of coffee, two cartons of milk, two tea bags by the small white kettle that each room came equipped with.

Like most of the hotels Fillingham stayed in, part of the reason it was cheap was that it was out of the town centre. Chipping Campden was small enough to be charming at its heart, but even it had a business district and some minor industry, and the hotel was in this area, a ten-minute walk from the cobbled lanes and town-square. The view from his window was of a car-park for an office block and, beyond this, the corrugated roof of a garage. The garage was also part of a chain, Fillingham noticed, his mood oddly low; after a day amongst so many people, so many colours and tradition and vibrancy, looking out on identikit companies from an identikit hotel was depressing. It wasn't how he usually felt, and it was unsettling in a way he couldn't quite identify. Dropping the blind down, he went and lay on his bed. The mattress was unpleasantly soft and moved under him, his book and camera, lens cap on, bouncing gently beside him. He turned on the television, turned it off again after hopping through the channels and finding nothing but blandness. Finally, he sat up, sighing.

Distantly, the sound of revels reached him and Fillingham wondered about going back and joining them and then decided against it. By the time he had left, most of the people there had been drunk and pairing off, and he'd end up feeling left behind, stood to one side and watching but unable to join in. He'd end up miserable, wishing he'd brought his camera and seeing things in terms of their composition, their visual attractiveness as flat images; the lens stood between him and these things, even when it wasn't actually there. He sighed again and put his shoes on.

Although it was late, the shop along the road was still open and happy to serve him; Fillingham bought a bottle of white wine, taking one from the refrigerator so that it was cold. He didn't drink alone often, but tonight he would, and try not to think of the women in their shift dresses covering muddy legs and taut thighs and high breasts. There was no one to betray if he did so, no wife or girlfriend; he simply knew that thinking about them would make him feel worse.

Walking back to the hotel, Fillingham smelled the scents of the day's games and the ongoing party, burning wood and paper and powder, meat, malty beer, spices and wine. The skyline ahead of him glowed orange, the dark shapes of buildings painted in shadow between him and the bonfire at Dover's Hill. Here and there, tiny yellow flickers bobbed through the gloom as people moved distantly with their candles. It would make a good picture, he thought, fireflies of light set against the solidity of the angular buildings, skittering and indistinct, a perfect metaphor for the way folk traditions survived in the modern world. He wished he'd brought his camera, and then sighed again at his own inability to detach himself from his lens.

Fillingham's room was on the third floor of the hotel, the uppermost, on the opposite side from the entrance. He was too tired to take the stairs so used the lift, emerging into a corridor decorated with featureless watercolours. He went past doors with DO NOT DISTURB signs hanging over their handles, past the muffled dissonance of televisions and conversations, before coming around the corner to the stretch that contained his room.

One of the women was at the far end of the corridor.

It wasn't the one Fillingham had spoken to earlier in the evening; this one was taller, blonde instead of dark, fuller-figured, but she too was carrying a beaten flask and had a bag hanging at her side. As Fillingham watched, she took a small plastic cup from the bag and poured a measure of liquid into it from the flask; the drink looked thick and viscid.

"A libation," she said, holding the cup out. Her voice was deep and mellow, filled with sly amusement. He glanced down at his bottle of wine, sheened with condensation, the neck cold in his fist, and said, "Thank you, but no. I don't like to mix my drinks." He sounded prissy, even to himself, but couldn't help it; it was late and he was tired and miserable, and whatever opportunities he had hoped the night might present felt old and lost to the past. This woman was a tendril of the event occurring down the road without him, reaching out, and her presence in the hotel was jarring, throwing his lowering mood into even sharper relief.

"You refuse?" she asked.

"Yes," said Fillingham, and went to his room door. As he unlocked it, he was conscious of the woman simply watching him; just before he opened it, she said, "It is a small thing, a simple toast. Join me?"

"No," said Fillingham again. Even from the other end of the corridor, he could smell the drink, pungent and spicy, and the mud that was smeared across the woman's legs. The odour was cloying, unpleasant, made saliva squirt into his mouth as though he was about to vomit. He swallowed, glancing at the woman to find her still staring at him and holding the cup out. Her nipples were prominent through the material of her dress and he had a sudden strong impression that she was naked under the thin cloth. She stepped forwards, still holding the cup out towards him. Fillingham swallowed his own spit, warm and swollen, and then opened his door, stepping into the room without looking at the woman again.

Its banality was reassuring. Fillingham poured some of his wine into one of the cheap white porcelain mugs and took a large swallow, unsure of what had just happened. Why was he so bothered? Ordinarily, the sight of an attractive woman, and she had been attractive, no doubt about it, would have pleased him. Even if nothing had come of it, he could have flirted, hopefully made her smile. Instead, she had disturbed him in a way that was unclear even to himself. She was out of context, yes, away from the games and celebrations, but that couldn't have been it. Her smell was strong, not pleasing but, again, it couldn't have been just that. He took another mouthful of wine and realised.

Darkness. The woman had been in darkness.

The hotel, like all the others in the chain, had corridors whose lights did not remain on all the time; instead, they were triggered by movement, yet the woman had been standing in a pool of shadow. She had come into the corridor, moved along it as she spoke to Fillingham, and the lights had remained off. He drank more wine, was surprised to find he'd emptied the mug, and then started as someone knocked hard on his room door.

Hot saliva leapt into Fillingham's mouth and he swallowed again, tasting something like electricity and an afterimage of wine, and thought, *Why am I afraid? It's a woman, and a near-naked one at that! What harm can she do me?* He went to the door as the knocking sounded again, picking up his camera off the bed as he went.

The woman was standing away from his door, perhaps twenty feet along the corridor, still in darkness. Her dress glimmered in the shadows, a white smear toped by her pale face. Her lips were red, almost as dark as the shadows crowding her shoulders, and she was smiling.

"What do you want?" asked Fillingham.

"You to celebrate with us," she replied, holding out the cup again. The liquid inside slithered up and then down again, and even in the poor light Fillingham saw the residue it left on the clear plastic sides, glistening and clinging like oil. "Devotions must be paid."

"What?" said Fillingham. "Look, I appreciate you've got this weird acting gig at the games and you're only doing your job but, please, it's late and I'm tired and I don't want to drink whatever that is."

"A last enquiry: you refuse?"

"Yes! I refuse! Now, just leave me alone." To emphasise what he was saying, Fillingham lifted his camera and took a photograph, the light of the flash filling the corridor with a leaching whiteness that painted the woman into a colourless mass for a moment. As the dancing ghostlights cleared from his eyes, the woman nodded and then lifted the cup to her lips and drank the liquid it contained. Keeping the cup at her lips, she thrust her tongue out into it and Fillingham saw it writhe within, licking at the remaining drips of drink. It should have been erotic, he thought; he was sure it was *meant* as erotic, but somehow it wasn't, it was crude and unpleasant. Her tongue was dark and looked slimy, glittering inside the clear plastic walls of the cup. Finally, she dropped the cup to the floor, lowered her head and muttered something that sounded Latin or Greek. Before she could look up at him again, Fillingham shut his door.

Still unsettled, Fillingham sat at the counter that ran across the room under the window, shifting the mess of magazines and coins that he had dropped there and putting the camera in its place. He poured himself another mug of wine and sat, intending to look through the pictures he had taken that day. He always found it calming, seeing his images scrolling before him, seeing the life in them reduced to tiny rectangles of colour and composition like butterflies pinned to card. He hoped that he had managed to capture the sense and energy of the Olimpick Games and the celebrations afterwards, and anticipated that he could sell some of the pictures and use others for his portfolio.

The last picture he had taken, of the woman in the corridor, was the first one he looked at, and he saw immediately that it was . . . wrong. It was difficult to see it clearly on the small screen, but the air around the central figure of the woman was filled with shapes. No, with a *single* shape that had lots of pieces, he thought, something that writhed behind the woman with too many limbs to count. He wished he had brought his laptop with him in order to look at the image on its larger screen, but he hadn't wanted to carry the extra weight for an overnight trip, so he was left with the camera's display. Squinting, he tried to make out details; was that skin? Fur? Teeth? Hands, or clawed feet? There were things curling around the woman's legs from behind her, as though the dirt on her skin had gained mass and was lifting itself towards the camera. What was going on here?

The woman herself seemed normal except for her eyes, which were entirely black and much wider than he remembered them being; it made little sense, because if she was reacting to the flash, her pupils should have contracted not expanded. Quickly, he scrolled back to the earlier pictures, to the ones of the other woman distributing drinks and then to the ones of the five females standing together by the dancing men; the same distortions were evident in all the photographs, things fluttering and shifting in the air behind them. They were clearest in the picture he had taken of the woman bending her head after giving the group of people her drinks; it was still impossible to see what it was, but it gave an impression of limbs, too many limbs, claws that curved back on themselves, eyes that gleamed like dark bone, a pelt, or skin that was rough and ridged, or possibly feathers.

Fillingham pushed his chair back and went to rise, and that was when the hands fell on his shoulders.

They pushed him down into his chair, clenching around his shoulders painfully. Fillingham tried to twist and managed to shift a few inches, craning his neck around. His room door was open and the five women were standing in his room; the blonde one was holding him and the brunette he had photographed earlier was by the door. The others were motionless by the bed. "What—" he started but the women, speaking as one, interrupted him.

"You must pay obeisance to partake in Dover's Bacchanalia," they said, a single voice from coming from all their mouths. "You refuse to partake in the tribute yet drink wine. This cannot be." One of the women, shorter and red-haired, reached out without appearing to move and lifted his wine from the table. She lifted it to her nose and sniffed and then upturned it, pouring the remaining liquid across his bed, dropping the bottle into the puddle when it was empty.

"Who are you?" Fillingham said, gritting his teeth against the pain of the grip; the woman's hands were extraordinarily strong and felt unlike a human hold, as though her skin were a mere covering for something else, something muscular and old and venomous.

"We are Dover's Children," they said, still in unison. Outside the room, something heavy crashed and the floor vibrated. "He is our father, the father of games themselves." There was another crash and a long, low noise like a howl scrambled and put back together with its innards showing.

"I don't understand," Fillingham said, still trying to twist free of the woman's hold. There was yet another crash from somewhere out of the room but closer, and this time everything shook, the wine bottle rolling to the edge of the bed and falling to the floor with a dull thud.

"The games were a gift to Dover from that which comes, given to him in dreams so that he might, in turn, gift it on," the women said. "A gift, and all that people need do on this one night is to take the drink in honour of the gift-giver, to drink and then to worship in inebriation and heat and the movement of flesh. You refused the drink three times."

There was another crash from the corridor, still closer. Another, and the door shuddered, dust vibrating from its top and hanging in the air. The lights flickered. Another crash and the lights went out completely. In the sudden darkness, one of the women moved and the blind was torn from the window, falling to the desk in a noisy tangle. Leaping orange reflections filled the room. *How is no one hearing this?* Thought Fillingham, pulling uselessly against a grip that was getting tighter, was digging into him and tearing.

"It only comes for you," said the women, as though hearing his thoughts. "All others have given honour, or do not join the revels. All around, those who drank the tribute and heard the prayer are communing with each other through song and flesh and note, or they sleep undisturbed because they take no wine or beer." The room was suddenly filled with noises, with grunts and shouts and moans and tunes, with the images of dancing and clothed flesh and naked flesh, of people losing themselves to pleasure, and then the sounds and images began falling away, layer after layer stripped to nothing as though lenses were falling between Fillingham and them, distancing him, swaddling him away from the rest of the world.

"Give me the drink now," he managed to say.

"Offence is already taken," the women said, and the one holding him let go of his shoulders and stepped back. Fillingham snatched up his camera as he started to rise but something lashed into him, a hand tipped with claws or bone, and he pitched sideways into the wall, falling to his knees as he bounced away from it.

"He comes," intoned the women. There were more crashes from the corridor, closer and closer, faster and faster, and then the doorway was filled with a huge figure.

It was Robert Dover, only it wasn't. It was massive, having to stoop as it entered the room, and the women took up a low moan, swaying. Its head brushed the ceiling as it straightened, the huge moon of its mask face glowing palely. Its eyes were completely black and in them Fillingham saw something roiling and twisting about itself, something that glittered and rasped and sweated. It stepped fully into the small space, and green and red and blue fire boiled across the ceiling above it, gathering in streamers and falling to the floor in long, sinuous fronds. Fillingham screamed and tried to rise but again one of the women struck him, sending him sprawling. He managed to raise his fist, still holding the camera, and fired off a single picture. The glare of the flash leaped across the room and for a brief moment the fire was gone, the women reduced to pale shades, Dover to a ragged and spindly thing that capered in the light, and then the fires were back and Dover's shape was gathering, thickening, the mask dancing with the colours of the flames and it was coming towards Fillingham with its arms open wide in a lover's embrace.

I cannot tell what planet ruled, when I
First undertook this mirth, this jollity,
Nor can I give account to you at all,
How this conceit into my brain did fall.
Or how I durst assemble, call together
Such multitudes of people as come hither.

– Robert Dover, 1616

LYNDA E. RUCKER

Where the Summer Dwells

LYNDA E. RUCKER is an American writer currently living in Dublin, Ireland. Her fiction has appeared in such places as *The Magazine of Fantasy & Science Fiction, The Mammoth Book of Best New Horror, The Year's Best Dark Fantasy and Horror, Shadows and Tall Trees, Nightmare Magazine* and *PostScripts.* She is a regular columnist for *Black Static*, and her first collection, *The Moon Will Look Strange*, was recently released from Karōshi Books, an imprint of Noose & Gibbet publishing.

"This story was, I suppose, born the summer that I was fifteen years old," recalls the author, "which my best friend Scott and I spent driving all over the dirt back roads of Elbert County, Georgia, where I grew up, exploring old cemeteries and fallen-down houses.

"A couple of decades later, I started writing 'Where the Summer Dwells' when I was living in Portland, Oregon, and feeling homesick for the South. Although I ended up putting it away for awhile, and not returning to it until I actually moved back to Georgia, where I was finally able to finish it.

"A title eluded me for nearly as long as the story itself, because I couldn't get the one already claimed by the late, great, fellow Southerner Karl Edward Wagner out of my head – 'Where the Summer Ends' – which told a much darker tale of what lurks beneath the kudzu.

"Once I figured out that the summer in the story wasn't so much at an end as it was simply elsewhere, I finally had my title – and a nod to one of my favorite horror writers."

LITTLE WAS LEFT now of the abandoned railway save for the rails themselves, two steel bars emerging from brambles and weedy clumps of grass. Seth, walking backward, followed them, clutching his digital camera ("1440 by 1080 pixels," he'd told Charlotte breathlessly, like she was supposed to know what that meant, and be impressed), calling for Larkin to lie down between them so he could film her. The first hint of unease brushed Charlotte then, stroked her hair, caressed her cheek, and was gone almost as quickly – for no unease could exist here on this cloudless day, with skinny overeager Seth springing about, his hair flopping in his eyes, Lee perched on the hood of the car, head thrown back so his face was turned up toward the sun, and Larkin in her white eyelet sundress, stretched between the rails, arms above her head, miming bound wrists and revealing dark unshaven underarms, unexpectedly erotic.

Seth said, "Charlotte, give her your necklace thing to wear."

She knew what he was after: against Larkin's pale skin, the three copper disks would glint golden in the sun, but Charlotte, already wandering, pretended not to hear. The heavy grass, grown high enough to graze her fingertips dangling at her sides, scratched her bare legs. Seth said again, "Charlotte, Charlotte," but she didn't stop, snatching her hands back from the tops of the grasses and slipping her fingers round the disks.

She disliked seeing Larkin there where before it had been her and Cade and Victoria, lost in that summer a dozen years ago now, happy times, when they'd finally been old enough to drive and they'd get lost on these back roads, looking for fallen-down houses and forgotten cemeteries, pulling off on abandoned sawmill lanes, listening to music like Elliot Smith and Andrew Bird – which had gotten them labelled fags at school. (*And how can you and I be fags? We're* girls, Vic had said, like the insult was supposed to make some logical sense.) In a collapsing one-room schoolhouse their fingers skated above the rotting keys of an abandoned piano. Cade found a pile of handheld fans in one corner, the kind funeral homes gave out with their addresses printed on one side and a crowd of pink-cheeked cherubs on the other. How did such things get left behind and forgotten? they asked one another. In what must have been the cloakroom, someone had started a fire at one point, for the wall was scorched beneath the rows of little wooden pegs. The forest had crept right up to the window; Charlotte had tried to imagine what scene the schoolchildren had looked out on one hundred years ago, but the past seemed remote, inaccessible, even in a place that was trapped there.

So long ago, and all of them grown up and gone away. She'd long known better than to come back here.

It had started like this: the day was born sticky and hot, and she and Lee and Seth and Larkin had stumbled into it – and into Seth's battered '79 Impala – early, just past dawn, out of the motel rooms they'd taken in exhaustion after driving straight through several nights. The shabby motel was just east of Muscle Shoals and bade them by way of copy board to SUPPORT OUR TROOPS and added that YOU'LL NEVER BE LONELY IF YOU "FRIEND" JESUS. Larkin, at the wheel, snorted, "Fanatics," but Seth said he got some good shots of it as they nosed out of the parking lot and back onto the highway. As noontime came and went and they crossed the state line from Alabama into Georgia, the day had not improved. Charlotte thought stifling summer days in the South often felt old and stale, as though someone had forgotten to freshen things up, to air the place out. You'd be outside and wish you could ask someone to open a window.

Once they hit Bydell County, opening the windows had left them choking on clouds of red clay dust. Back in Oregon

Seth had probably bought the Chevy for its white-trash hipster-chic aesthetic, and its lack of air-conditioning seemed negligible; here, as Lee pointed out, they faced a choice of asphyxiation by dust or dying of the heat like bugs trapped under glass. They had bounced along back roads, alternately coughing and sweltering, while the speakers crackled with the raw pickings of Mississippi bluesmen. Those guys – R.L. Burnside and T-Model Ford and Junior Kimbrough and all the rest on the Fat Possum label those were the real sounds of the South, Seth said, at least before Fat Possum sold out and started signing all those indie bands instead. Never mind that the Delta was hundreds of miles to the west of them; the whole region might as well have been a figment of Seth's imagination, for all the resemblances his notions of the place bore to reality.

Charlotte had dutifully taken them to the places she recalled: the schoolhouse – now unsafe for entry, its roof caved in – and the Civil War-era cemetery with its toppling monuments and graves of former slaves granted the dubious honour of burial with the master, and the abandoned barn surrounded by junked farm equipment: rusted tractors and broken tillers. Seth shot it all with a bland enthusiasm, and then they'd crossed these tracks, and it was her own fault they were here. "Wait," she'd said. "Stop," she'd said. And so they did.

Back *then*, August had that winding-down feeling about it. The air remained sultry as ever; insects whirred in the brush and the sun rose relentlessly, day after day, as though it might never rain again. But they felt the end, Vic and Cade and Charlotte, felt the dark dull hallways of school-again looming near, the clanging lockers and the shrieking bells, textbooks on trigonometry, composition folders, laps around the gym, and smelly lunchrooms. The indignity of it all. *But not yet.* Some days still separated freedom from captivity. "We will make the most of it," Vic had announced, throwing herself back into the clover that grew wild and ragged along the train tracks. Cade was rolling another joint, flapping one hand at a persistent hovering bee, but Charlotte had a headache and didn't want to smoke anymore. "We should do something," Vic went on, "some kind of ceremony to mark this summer. To mark us all."

She made up the words. She was good at making things up. Charlotte could no longer remember what exactly Vic had said, but could still see her as she'd looked that day: red hair twisted on top of her head, wearing shorts and a black Neutral Milk Hotel T-shirt, and somehow regal despite it all.

Now Charlotte kicked at decaying ties, at scattered spikes. She had not been home in such a long time, and something almost like regret broke over her. Lee touched her on the back and made her jump.

"All right?"

She shrugged. He nodded. He always knew. They were closer than siblings. They plucked one another's thoughts out of thin air. He knew her better than anyone, better than any lover – and lovers always left her, claiming she held some part of herself remote from anyone's reach. She and Lee had met freshman year of their first day of college, when the housing department mistakenly assigned them to share a room in the co-ed dorm. Housing had reacted with considerably more horror than either of them and quickly found them gender-appropriate roommates, but they grew closer than siblings. Now Lee, exaggerating the Southern accent he'd left behind when they moved to the West Coast together, cried, "Oh mah gahd! It's a train track!" and they were both cracking up without really knowing why, because it was one of *those* jokes, its origins lost in time, probably rooted in mockery of someone they'd disliked but impenetrable to outsiders and now to them as well. While they were still laughing he said, "I'm sorry. You didn't have to come."

"No, don't be." She could imagine how events had unfolded before she entered the picture: the three of them, Lee and Seth and Larkin, getting high in Lee's living room and talking about Seth's idea for a documentary – something about the South (Seth had never been there) and a road trip, something he could enter into a film festival, maybe South by Southwest, when Lee, stoned and rash and half in love with Seth, blurted out Charlotte's name, said she'd be into it, she was between jobs now anyway and kinda depressed (he'd said something like that, she was sure of it). Lee had grown up in a faceless Atlanta suburb but Charlotte hailed from a hick town. *She* could take them into Southern Gothic country, all right.

The Southern Gothic that Seth imagined didn't really exist any longer, if it ever had, but he'd never know that. Nonetheless the three of them came pounding on the door of her Sellwood studio that same night. Five days and a world ago: it had been one of those idyllic Portland summer evenings, just warm enough for an outside table at the brewpub round the corner (to which the four of them had repaired, because Charlotte's studio was hot and stuffy and both alcohol and space were in short supply there). Safe in the lush green of a Pacific Northwest August, downing her third Ruby Red Ale, she could not remember the burnt-up humidity of Georgia in summer. Furthermore, she and Lee had both made the tactical error of assuming that Larkin, the only one of them with a real job – she worked at the advertising agency that made all the Nike commercials – would not be joining them. Larkin was okay but she had a way of assuming a blameless, bright, and superficial *let's-be-kind-to-the-help* sort of air whenever she talked. "It's *so* good to run into you," she would say, smiling brightly while somehow still managing to signal that the exact opposite was true.

At some point in the evening, maps had been produced, highlighters sketched ambitious routes along interstate highways. "It's freaky down there," Larkin warned, "*Deliverance* country," but nobody paid her any attention. By nine the next morning, when the phone jangled Charlotte awake, she was hungover and regretting the promises she'd made, but they were on their way over and backing out felt impossible.

Now Seth called back to them. "Let's follow the tracks! This is good stuff!"

"Excellent," Lee said. "Now he'll be hoping to encounter some backwoods eccentric he can get on camera."

"Some latter-day Hazel Motes."

"Nah, that's a little *too* eccentric. Maybe another Howard Finster. Religious fanatics are a lot more palatable when they're folk artists."

"And we grow 'em on trees here, those loveable eccentrics."

They watched the two for a moment. The sight of Larkin picking her way along the tracks in inappropriately flimsy red flip-flops made Charlotte feel meanly glad for just a moment. She said, "You know, it's a lost cause, darlin'. I don't care who else he might be sleeping with, he's utterly devoted to her."

"I know. I'm an idiot."

Charlotte shrugged again. "The things we do for love, right?"

That made him laugh. "You've never been in love in your life, how would you know? You're the one who does the heart breaking!"

"Shut up," she said, lightly, steadily. She'd never told him about Cade and Vic, which meant she'd never told anyone. "Let's go." Seth and Larkin went over a rise and vanished on the other side. They followed. A field stretched to the left of them, its grasses yellowing and dying in the summer drought; to the right, the ground dipped and fell away into already dead forest blanketed by kudzu.

When the kudzu covers something it leaves the shape behind and takes the thing itself down into the underworld, said Vic's voice in her head. Cade said, *My spooky girl*. Vic drew macabre sketches of things rising from the forest floor, of rooms empty but for unsettling shadows in wrong places, of faces that floated at windows and figures made out of bits of tin can and leaves and bones. She posted her work to her webpage, where it had lingered ghostlike for years until the free webhosting company shut down altogether. Charlotte used to visit there often, imagining that *this time* she'd find a message embedded somewhere in the pixels.

They'd thought to sleep out here under the stars that night. After half-an-hour of slapping mosquitoes they'd tried to squeeze into Cade's pup tent, without success. Since nobody could sleep, Cade pointed out constellations and told them fantastic stories about gas giants and collapsing black holes. When they ran out of stars to name, Vic took over the storytelling.

"Once upon a time," she said, "I came walking here when I was a little girl. I found these same tracks and I started to follow them. They took me deeper and deeper into a forest. I was growing tired and then I looked down and I saw that the metal rails had turned to bone. The bone was smooth and polished like someone took loving care of it. I wondered who would do a thing like that."

Cade said, "You didn't have to wonder long, though." He brushed damp strands of hair from her forehead.

"Not fair," Vic said, "you've heard part of the story before." Charlotte hated it when one of them reminded her it had been two of them before it became three of them, even though they meant nothing by it. Vic went on. "Three scruffy black dogs, uncollared, wild and hungry-looking, came slinking through the trees and waited a few yards away from me. Their flanks were thin and their ribs stuck out like this." Vic held her hands in a way that mimicked protruding ribs. "And then the biggest dog spoke to me. It wasn't a talking animal like in a children's story. It was the most awful thing I've ever heard in my life. It had blackened teeth and a blackened tongue and its voice sounded like something savage and wild and malformed."

Charlotte couldn't wait. "What did it say?"

"It said, *Little girl, my brothers and I are going to eat you up. We're going to eat your feet first so you can't run away, and then we're going to eat your hands so you can't hurt us. We'll eat your stomach and your eyes, your elbows and your knees. We'll eat up every bit of you, slowly, and then we'll be filled up with pieces of you and you'll be part of us, Vic.*

"But what he and his brothers didn't notice was that while he was doing all that talking, I was filing my teeth into sharp needles. I filed my fingernails into claws and I took off my shoes and did the same for my toenails – he was a really long-winded dog – and when everything I could make sharp was as sharp as could be, I made my move. I leapt on the talking one first and tore out its throat. Then I killed the others with my sharp new claws.

"By then I was all covered in blood and other awful things, and I wanted to bathe. I kept walking and I came to the railway trestle, and the river running beneath it. I took off all my clothes and I dived in, but while I was swimming I felt someone watching me from the shore. At first I thought it was just a water-spirit but then I knew for sure it was something else. So I came to the surface of the water and I saw a woman standing there. She was the most beautiful woman I've ever seen, or ever will see. I knew then that she was the one who cared for the tracks, who kept the bones polished and free of kudzu. She said, 'You have killed my three best companions.'

"I told her it wasn't my fault. It was kill or be killed, after all. She nodded and said that she understood but she had to take something from me anyway. She said that, and then she turned and started to walk away. I called after her; I asked her what she was taking. She said I'd find out one day."

"And did you?" Charlotte again, leaning forward, eager.

Vic said, "I'm still waiting."

Before they fell asleep at last Vic had suggested that they lay pennies on the tracks for trains to flatten, and even though they knew that nobody had used those tracks in decades, maybe a century, they did it anyway. They all heard the whistle in their dreams, and they woke to the sight of three smooth, flat disks balanced along the rails. Vic had scooped them up, laughing, and scraped little designs on them then and there, using her grandmother's diamond engagement ring that she always wore on her right ring finger. In later years Charlotte wondered if Vic had done it herself, replaced the pennies with already-flattened ones she'd brought with her. But they agreed they had all heard the train passing, had felt the night air shiver, and anyway, it wasn't the kind of thing Vic would do. She liked stories, not hoaxes.

Seth and Larkin must have gotten farther ahead of them than either Lee or Charlotte had realised. They passed over the rise and saw no sign of them. Charlotte jumped when a flock of birds burst from a nearby copse of trees and climbed into the sky, shrieking. The only cloud they'd seen all day passed before the sun; it lessened the heat's intensity but left her feeling breathless and hemmed in. They walked on. Ahead of them the railway vanished into a pine forest.

Lee put a hand up to his mouth and called, "Seth! Larkin!"

They waited. Only insects sang in reply.

In the forest, the needles felt soft and slick underfoot. They had to leave the tracks in places where the undergrowth grew too thickly. Aluminium drink cans bleached shiny and anonymous by the sun and rain littered the railbed and gave way to other bits of garbage, twisted metal, rotting lumber. They really should turn back now. Charlotte felt it uncurling in her gut, the sense of crossing borders into stranger places.

"I was in love," Charlotte said to Lee. "Once."

"You lie. What happened?"

"People leave," she said. "You know." It was almost true.

They had parted that morning in high spirits, filled with plans for the week ahead. But Cade's parents had lain in wait for him, as parents do. They sent him away – some kind of military boarding school, maybe, or worse, one of those boot camps like you saw on TV for troubled kids.

Vic's voice took on a bleak quality Charlotte had never heard in it as she reported what little she knew. And then Vic was gone as abruptly: IMs and emails went unanswered, the phone rang and rang for days, until at last Vic's mother answered it. She was doing fine, she told Charlotte in a tight voice, and she could talk to her friends when she was better. Vic messaged her once after that, hastily: *i did something stupid. tried to cut open my wrists*. While Charlotte was typing a reply Vic added, *gotta run, they're back, they never leave me alone*. Of course, Vic's mother had been lying; Vic had never returned to school that year, and Charlotte, so clearly *not our kind of people* in a way that made Vic's mother wrinkle her country-club nose, had not been told what became of her. And that had been the end of that.

Or so it seemed. The following summer, two weeks into a waitressing job down at Hilton Head, she'd gotten a phone call.

"It's an emergency," groused her manager Mac. He towered over her, all six-foot-five of him, in the narrow passage between the kitchen and the dining room where the staff phone was located. "Or it damn well better be."

"Char, it's Vic."

"*Is* it an emergency?" Mac demanded, hands on hips. "You know you can't take personal phone calls here!"

"Jesus," Vic said. "Char, listen, you have to come here tonight. Me and Cade are in town."

"Five minutes!" Mac mouthed, holding up a splayed hand, wiggling his five fingers in case she hadn't gotten the message.

"We're going out to the train tracks. I know how to get through. I figured it out."

Something metal clattered to the floor in the kitchen. Wes, the sous chef, shouted, "Fuck!" The kitchen door jostled her in the back. "Your table sixteen is up, Char!"

"Figured what out?"

"How to cross borders. How to get to the other side. On purpose this time, not by accident." Vic was impatient.

"Meet us at moonrise. Sometime after midnight. We'll wait for you."

An abrupt click was followed by silence. Mac leaned against the wall, one finger on the phone's cradle. "Table sixteen wants their shrimp," he smirked.

Charlotte untied her apron and flung it at him. "Better take it to them." In the parking lot her heart raced. She called both Vic's and Cade's home numbers from her cell phone, but the lines on the other end merely rang and rang, as she expected. Bydell was five hours away and she had no idea when the moon would rise. At first luck was with her as she raced through the night, her headlights swallowing the centre-line and not a cop in sight. Outside of Augusta, disaster: the clean-up from a multi-car accident blocked every lane and she sat at the back of a long line of cars. Crawling forward, she could see highway patrolmen carefully waving motorists to detour one by one onto the interstate's shoulder, but by the time her turn came and she was moving at a steady speed again, the moon showed its face. "Waning gibbous," she whispered, knowing the words because Cade had taught her the moon phases like incantatory phrases. *Waxing gibbous. Full. Waning gibbous. Half-moon. Waning crescent. Dark.* She kept driving. She didn't know what else to do. Once she reached her destination, she sat by the tracks until sun-up. The first rays of light picked out something glinting on the tracks: their pendants. They had left her a message, but she didn't know what to do with it.

"The trestle's just ahead," she told Lee, but they spotted it before she finished speaking, its wooden planks spanning the gully below. Only a trickle of water suggested that it had once been a Broad River tributary. "God, this drought. It's like the whole state is gonna catch on fire." They walked to the edge of the trestle. Slats in the middle had rotted into the parched channel.

They both spun round at the sound of crashing undergrowth, and Seth's voice reached them. "Hey, guys! We got some great stuff!" He and Larkin made their way back over to the tracks. "That trestle," Seth said. "It's amazing. Like, almost haunting. Look."

He showed them a long shot of the trestle, standing some way upstream – or what would have been upstream, had there been any water. Next, a shot of broken boards, looking down into the ravine below. "I walked out to the middle," he said, "as far as I could go."

Larkin faked a shiver. "You made it look creepy."

Seth shrugged. "Hey, I think we're done here. I'm hungry. Are you hungry?" He turned to Charlotte. "You must know, like, some pretty cool place around here we could eat, right? Barbecue or something? Or like soul food?" He didn't wait for an answer but turned with Larkin and started back along the tracks.

"Right," Charlotte said, watching them go. "They're done, so we are too, I guess."

"I guess," Lee said.

She walked to the edge of the bank and closed her eyes. She could hear the soft whistle of the train approaching. She took hold of the pennies. In her hand they felt warm, almost alive. Maybe the train would slow, maybe Cade and Vic would lift her up into their arms. She could smell that summer coming nearer. It would be as though no time had passed. Why had she waited so long?

Lee touched her on her back. She knew it was Lee; she could smell his cologne.

"What really happened?" he said. "You were in love and then what happened?"

Charlotte opened her eyes. She said, "I think they went away with the fairies, you know? I just couldn't go with them."

The drone of the cicadas and the tree frogs rose to a crescendo, and fell again. She and Lee stood there, the sun dappling through the trees and onto their skin. Their arms glowed golden in its light. Behind them, the trestle groaned and creaked in a wind that did not reach them, and grew silent like the missing and the lost.

RAMSEY CAMPBELL

The Callers

RAMSEY CAMPBELL was born in Liverpool, and still lives on Merseyside with his wife Jenny. His first book, a collection of stories entitled *The Inhabitant of the Lake and Less Welcome Tenants*, was published by August Derleth's legendary Arkham House imprint in 1964, since when his novels have included *The Doll Who Ate His Mother*, *The Face That Must Die*, *The Nameless*, *Incarnate*, *The Hungry Moon*, *Ancient Images*, *The Count of Eleven*, *The Long Lost*, *Pact of the Fathers*, *The Darkest Part of the Woods*, *The Grin of the Dark*, *Thieving Fear*, *Creatures of the Pool*, *The Seven Days of Cain*, *Ghosts Know*, *The Kind Folk* and the movie tie-in *Solomon Kane*. His short fiction has been widely collected and he has edited a number of anthologies.

More recent publications include two novellas from PS Publishing, *The Last Revelation of Gla'aki* and *The Pretence*, and a new collection from Dark Regions Press in America entitled *Holes for Faces*.

Now well in to his fifth decade as one of the world's most respected authors of horror fiction, Campbell has won multiple World Fantasy Awards, British Fantasy Awards and Bram Stoker Awards, and is a recipient of the World Horror Convention Grand Master Award, the Horror Writers Association Lifetime Achievement Award, the Howie Award of the H. P. Lovecraft Film Festival for Lifetime

Achievement, and the International Horror Guild's Living Legend Award.

About the following story, the author admits: "I'm afraid it betrays how I spend my morning break. By the time *The Jeremy Kyle Show* comes on TV I've usually been working for several hours and have a bit of breakfast then. His show is or used to be sponsored by foxybingo.com, and one of their ads started me thinking about bingo calls.

"That sort of passing thought can be all I need to come up with a story, and here it is. *The Jeremy Kyle Show* also led to the opening scene and indeed my initial thoughts for *The Kind Folk*. Nothing is wasted . . ."

MARK'S GRANDMOTHER SEEMS barely to have left the house when his grandfather says "Can you entertain yourself for a bit? I could do with going to the pub while I've got the chance."

Mark wonders how much they think they've entertained him, but he only says "Will grandma be all right coming home on her own?"

"Never fret, son. They can look after theirselves." The old man's hairy caterpillar eyebrows squirm as he frowns at Mark and blinks his bleary eyes clear. "No call for you to fetch her. It's women's stuff, the bingo." He gives the boy's shoulder an unsteady squeeze and mutters "You're a good sort to have around."

Mark feels awkward and a little guilty that he's glad he doesn't have to meet his grandmother. "Maybe I'll go to a film."

"You'd better have a key, then." His grandfather rummages among the contents of a drawer of the shaky sideboard – documents in ragged envelopes, rubber bands so desiccated they snap when he takes hold of them, a balding reel of cotton, a crumpled folder stuffed with photographs – and hauls out a key on a frayed noose of string. "Keep hold of that for next time you come," he says.

Does he mean Mark will be visiting by himself in future? Was last night's argument so serious? His mother objected when his grandfather offered him a glass of wine at dinner, and then her mother accused her of not letting Mark grow up. Before long the women were shouting at each other about how Mark's grandmother had brought up her daughter, and the men only aggravated the conflict by trying to calm it down. It continued after Mark went to bed, and this morning his father informed him that he and Mark's mother were going home several days early. "You can stay if you like," she told Mark.

Was she testing his loyalty or hoping he would make up for her behaviour? While her face kept her thoughts to itself his father handed him the ticket for the train home like a business card, one man to another. Mark's mother spent some time in listing ways he shouldn't let anyone down, but these didn't include going to the cinema. Wearing his coat was among the requirements, and so he takes it from the stand in the hall. "Step out, lad," his grandfather says as Mark lingers on the pavement directly outside the front door. "You don't want an old crock slowing you down."

At the corner of the street Mark glances back. The old man is limping after him, resting a hand on the roof of each car parked with two wheels on the pavement. Another narrow similarly terraced street leads into the centre of the small Lancashire town, where lamps on scalloped iron poles are stuttering alight beneath a congested late April sky. Many of the shops are shuttered, and some are boarded up. Just a few couples stroll past deserted pristine kitchens and uninhabited items of attire. Most of the local amusements have grown too childish for Mark, though he might still enjoy bowling or a game of indoor golf if he weren't by himself, and others are years out of bounds – the pubs, the clubs waiting for the night crowds while doormen loiter outside like wrestlers dressed for someone's funeral. Surely the cinema won't be so particular about its customers. More than one of Mark's schoolmates has shown him the scene from *Facecream* where the girl gets cream squirted all over her face.

As he hurries past the clubs he thinks a doorman is shouting behind him, but the large voice is down a side street full of shops that are nailed shut. At first he fancies that it's chanting inside one of them, and then he sees an old theatre at the far end. While he can't distinguish the words, the rhythm makes it clear he's hearing a bingo caller. Mark could imagine that all the blank-faced doormen are determined to ignore the voice.

The Frugoplex is beyond the clubs, across a car park for at least ten times as many vehicles as it presently contains. The lobby is scattered with popcorn, handfuls of which have been trodden into the purple carpet. A puce rope on metal stilts leads the queue for tickets back and forth and twice again on the way to the counter. When Mark starts to duck under the rope closest to the end of the queue, a man behind the counter scowls at him, and so he follows the rope all the way around, only just heading off two couples of about his own age who stoop under. He's hoping to avoid the disgruntled man, but the queue brings Mark to him. "*Facecream*, please," Mark says and holds out a ten-pound note.

"Don't try it on with me, laddie," the man says and turns his glare on the teenagers who have trailed Mark to the counter. "And your friends needn't either."

"He's not our friend," one of the boys protests.

"I reckon not when he's got you barred."

Mark's face has grown hot, but he can't just walk away or ask to see a film he's allowed to watch. "I don't know about them, but I'm fifteen."

"And I'm your sweet old granny. That's it now for the lot of you. Don't bother coming to my cinema." The manager tells his staff at the counter "Have a good look at this lot so you'll know them."

Mark stumbles almost blindly out of the multiplex. He's starting across the car park when somebody mutters behind him "He wants his head kicked in."

They're only words, but they express his feelings. "That's what he deserves," Mark agrees and turns to his new friends.

It's immediately clear that they weren't thinking of the manager. "You got us barred," says the girl who didn't speak.

"I didn't mean to. You oughtn't to have stood so close."

"Doesn't matter what you meant," she says, and the other girl adds "We'll be standing a lot closer. Standing on your head."

Mark can't take refuge in the cinema, but running would look shameful and invite pursuit as well. Instead he tramps at speed across the car park. His shadow lurches ahead, growing paler as it stretches, and before long it has company, jerking forward to catch up on either side of him. He still stops short of bolting but strides faster. He's hoping passers-by will notice his predicament, but either they aren't interested or they're determined not to be. At last he reaches the nightclubs, and is opening his mouth to appeal to the nearest doorman when the fellow says "Keep walking, lad."

"They're after me."

The doorman barely glances beyond Mark, and his face stays blank. "Walk on."

It could be advice, though it sounds like a dismissal. It leaves Mark feeling that he has been identified as an outsider, and he thinks the doormen's impassive faces are warning him not to loiter. He would make for the police station if he knew where it is. He mustn't go to his grandparents' house in case they become scapegoats as well, and there's just one sanctuary he can think of. He dodges into the side street towards the bingo hall.

The street looks decades older than the main road and as though it has been forgotten for at least that long. Three streetlamps illuminate the cracked roadway bordered by grids that are clogged with old leaves. The glow is too dim to penetrate the gaps between the boards that have boxed up the shopfronts, because the lanterns are draped with grey cobwebs laden with drained insects. The only sign of life apart from a rush of footsteps behind Mark is the amplified voice, still delivering its blurred chant. It might almost be calling out to him, and he breaks into a run.

So do his pursuers, and he's afraid that the bingo hall may be locked against intruders. Beyond the grubby glass of three pairs of doors the foyer is deserted; nobody is in the ticket booth or behind the refreshment counter. His pursuers hesitate as he sprints to the nearest pair of doors, but when neither door budges, the gang closes in on him. He nearly trips on the uneven marble steps as he stumbles along them. He throws all his weight, such as it is, against the next set of doors, which give so readily that he almost sprawls on the threadbare carpet of the foyer.

The caller seems to raise his voice to greet him. "Sixty-three," he's announcing, "just like me." The pursuers glare at Mark from the foot of the shallow steps. "You can't stay in there," one girl advises him, and the other shouts "Better not try."

All the gang look determined to wait for him. If they don't tire of it by the time the bingo players go home, surely they won't dare to let themselves be identified, and so Mark shuts the doors and crosses the foyer. The entrance to the auditorium is flanked by old theatrical posters, more than one of which depicts a plump comedian with a sly schoolboyish face. Mark could imagine they're sharing a joke about him as he pushes open the doors to the auditorium.

The theatre seats have been cleared out, but the stage remains. It faces a couple of dozen tables, most of which are surrounded by women with score cards in front of them and stumpy pencils in their hands. The stage is occupied by a massive lectern bearing a large transparent globe full of numbered balls. Mark might fancy that he knows why the posters looked secretly amused, because the man in them is behind the lectern. He looks decades older, and the weight of his face has tugged it piebald as well as out of shape, but his grin hasn't entirely lost its mischief, however worn it seems. Presumably his oversized suit and baggy shirt are meant to appear comical rather than to suggest a youngster wearing cast-off clothes. He examines a ball before returning it to the globe, which he spins on its pivot. "Three and three," he says as his eyes gleam blearily at Mark. "What do you see?" he adds, and all the women eye the newcomer.

At first Mark can't see his grandmother. He's distracted by a lanky angular woman who extends her speckled arms across the table nearest to him. "Lost your mammy, son?" she cries. "There's plenty here to tend to you."

For an uneasy moment he thinks she has reached for her breast to indicate how motherly she is, but she's adjusting her dress, her eagerness to welcome him having exposed a mound of wrinkled flesh. Before he can think of an answer his grandmother calls "What are you doing here, Mark?"

She's at a table close to the stage. He doesn't want to make her nervous for him if there's no need, and he's ashamed of having run away. The uncarpeted floorboards amplify every step he takes, so that he feels as if he's trying to sound bigger than he is. All the women and the bingo caller watch his progress, and he wonders if everybody hears him mutter "I went to the cinema but they wouldn't let me see the film."

As his grandmother makes to speak one of her three companions leans forward, flattening her forearms on the table to twice their width. "However old are you, son?"

"Mark's thirteen," says his grandmother.

Another of her friends nods vigorously, which she has been doing ever since Mark caught sight of her. "Thirteen," she announces, and many of the women coo or hoot with enthusiasm.

"Looks old enough to me," says the third of his grandmother's tablemates, who is sporting more of a moustache than Mark has achieved. "Enough of a man."

"Well, we've shown you off now," Mark's grandmother tells him. "I'll see you back at home."

This provokes groans throughout the auditorium. The woman who asked his age raises her hands, and her forearms sag towards the elbows. "Don't keep him to yourself, Lottie."

The nodding woman darts to grab a chair for him. "You make this the lucky table, Mark."

He's disconcerted to observe how frail his grandmother is by comparison with her friends, though they're at least as old as she is. The bingo caller gives him a crooked grin and shouts "Glad to have another feller here. Safety in numbers, lad."

Presumably this is a joke of some kind, since quite a few women giggle. Mark's grandmother doesn't, but says "Can he have a card?"

This prompts another kind of laughter, and the nodding woman even manages to shake her head. "It's the women's game, lad," the caller says. "Are you ladies ready to play?"

"More than ever," the moustached woman shouts, which seems somehow to antagonise Mark's grandmother. "Sit down if you're going to," she says. "Stop drawing attention to yourself."

He could retort that she has just done that to him. He's unable to hide his blazing face as he crouches on the spindly chair while the bingo caller elevates the next ball from the dispenser. "Eighty-seven," he reads out. "Close to heaven."

The phrase earns mirth and other noises of appreciation as the women duck in unison to their cards. They chortle or grunt if they find the number, grimacing if they fail. Nobody at Mark's table has located it when the man at the lectern calls "Number forty, old and naughty."

"That's us and no mistake," the moustached woman screeches before whooping at the number on her card.

"Number six, up to tricks."

"That's us as well," her friend cries, but all her nodding doesn't earn her the number.

"Forty-nine, you'll be fine."

The third woman crosses out the number, and flesh cascades down her arm as she lifts the pencil. "He's that with bells on," she says, favouring Mark with a wink.

He has to respond, though the smile feels as if his swollen lips are tugging at his hot stiff face. "Three and twenty," the man at the lectern intones. "There'll be plenty."

Mark's grandmother hunches over the table. He could think she's trying to evade the phrase or the coos of delight it elicits from the rest of the players, but she's marking the number on her card. She seems anxious to win, staying bent close to the card as the bingo caller consults the next ball. "Six and thirty," he says, and a roguish grin twists the left side of his mouth. "Let's get dirty."

He pokes at the grin with a finger as if he wants to push the words back in, although they've raised appreciative squeals throughout the auditorium. The fleshy woman falls to her card so eagerly that every visible part of her wobbles. "That'll do me," she cries.

Presumably she means his suggestion, since she hasn't completed her card. Mark sees his grandmother glance nervously at it and then stare at her own as though striving to conjure up a number. "Four and four," the caller says and almost at once "There's the door."

The moustached woman rubs her upper lip so hard that Mark fancies he hears the hairs crackle. "Never mind that," she tells the caller.

He blinks at her and stares around the hall. Mark feels more out of place than ever, as though he's listening to jokes too old for him – beyond his comprehension, at any rate. The caller's drooping face grows defiant as he identifies the next ball. "Ninety-five," he says. "Leave alive."

This brings no laughter, just a murmur that falls short of words. At least Mark's grandmother has found the number on her card. She needs three more to win, and he's surprised by how much he hopes she will. He puts the wish into his eyes as he gazes up at the stage. "Number fifty," the caller says in a tone that seems almost as mechanical as the dispenser. "He'll be nifty."

"Aye," several women respond, and the quivering woman gives Mark another wink.

"Eighty-one, nearly done."

"That's me," the nodding woman agrees, bowing to her card as if the motion of her head has overtaken the rest of her.

Perhaps she means her age, since the irregular cross she makes doesn't finish off the card. "Twenty-nine," the caller says, keeping his eyes on the ball he's raised between the fingertips of both hands. "See the sign."

If the players do so, they keep quiet about it, not even greeting the number or bemoaning their luck. The caller displays the next ball like a magician and puts a finger to the edge of a grin that's meant to appear mysterious. "Sixty-three," he says. "Time to flee."

The murmur this provokes is unamused, and he concentrates on the ball that rolls out of the dispenser. "Twenty-four," he says. "Can't do more."

His gaze is drifting towards Mark when the fleshy woman emits a shriek that jabs deep into the boy's ears. "We're done," she cries. "It's mine."

The caller shuts the globe and extends a hand. "Give us a look."

As she mounts the steps to the stage a series of tremors passes through her body, starting at her veinous legs. Having checked her numbers against those that came up, the caller says "We've a winner."

She snatches the card and plods back to the table, where Mark sees how the crosses resemble sketches of gravestones, at least until she turns the card the right way up. She lowers herself onto her creaking chair and says "I claim the special."

The caller doesn't look at her or anywhere near her. "It's not time yet," he tells whoever needs to hear.

While he leans on the lectern to say so he puts Mark in mind of a priest in a pulpit, though the comparison seems wrong in some way Mark doesn't understand. He's distracted by his grandmother, who lays down her pencil next to the card scattered with the kind of crosses all the women have been drawing. "I'll do without my luck tonight," she says and grasps his arm to help her stand up. "Time someone was at home."

"Don't be like that," the fleshy woman says. "You can't just go running off."

"I won't be running anywhere." As Mark wonders whether that's defiance or the painful truth his grandmother says "I'll see you all another night."

"See us now and see yourself." The speaker nods so violently that her words grow jagged. "You're still one of us."

"I'm not arguing," Mark's grandmother says and grips his arm harder. "Come along now, Mark."

He doesn't know how many women murmur as she turns towards the exit. While he can't make out their words, they sound unhappy if not worse, and all of them are closer than the exit. Nobody moves as long as he can see them, and he finds he would rather not look back. His grandmother has almost led him out, clutching his arm so tightly that it throbs, when the lanky woman who first greeted him plants a hand on her breast again. Though she could be expressing emotion, Mark has the unwelcome fancy that she's about to bare the wizened breast to him. His grandmother hurries him past, and the doors to the foyer are lumbering shut behind them when a woman says "We aren't done."

Mark hopes she's addressing the man on the stage – urging him to start the next game – but he hasn't heard the caller by the time he and his grandmother emerge onto the steps. The street is deserted, and he suspects that the couples who followed him from the cinema are long gone. Outside the clubs the doormen keep their faces blank at the sight of him and his escort, who is leaning on him as much as leading him. She's quiet until they reach the shops, where she mutters "I wish you hadn't gone there tonight, Mark. We're meant to be responsible for you."

He feels guiltier than he understands. She says nothing more while they make their increasingly slow way home. She's about to ring the doorbell with her free hand when Mark produces the key. "Isn't he in?" she protests.

"He went to the pub."

"Men," she says so fiercely that Mark feels sentenced too. She slams the door by tottering against it and says "I think you should be in your bed."

He could object that it isn't his bedtime – that he doesn't know what offence he's committed – but perhaps he isn't being punished, in which case he isn't sure he wants to learn her reason for sending him to his room. He trudges up the narrow boxed-in stairs to the decidedly compact bathroom, where every item seems too close to him, not least the speckled mirror that frames his uneasy face. The toothpaste tastes harsher than usual, and he does his best to stay inaudible while spitting it into the sink. As he dodges into the smaller of the two front bedrooms he sees his grandmother sitting at the bottom of the stairs. He retreats under the quilt of the single bed against the wall beneath the meagre window and listens for his grandfather.

He doesn't know how long he has kept his eyes shut by the time he hears the front door open below him. His grandmother starts to talk at once, and he strains to catch her words. "Did you send Mark to fetch me tonight?"

"I told him to stay clear," Mark's grandfather says not quite as low. "What did he see?"

"It isn't what he saw, it's what they did."

"Are you still up to that old stuff? Makes you all feel powerful, does it?"

"I'll tell you one thing, Len – you don't any more." Just as righteously she says "I don't remember you crying about it too much when it was your turn."

"Well, it's not now."

"It shouldn't be our house at all." This sounds accusing, especially when she adds "If there's any talking to be done you can do it."

Apparently that's all. Mark hears his grandparents labour up the stairs and take turns to make various noises in the bathroom that remind him how old they are. He finds himself wondering almost at random whether they'll take him to the celebrations tomorrow on the town green; they have on other May Days. The prospect feels like a reward if not a compensation for some task. The door of the other front bedroom shuts, and he hears a series of creaks that mean his grandparents have taken to their bed.

For a while the night is almost quiet enough to let him drift into sleep, except that he feels as if the entire house is alert. He's close to dozing when he hears a distant commotion. At first he thinks a doorman outside a club is shouting at someone, perhaps a bunch of drunks, since several people respond. There's something odd about the voice and the responses too. Mark lifts his head from the lumpy pillow and strives to identify what he's hearing, and then he realises his efforts are unnecessary. The voice and its companions are approaching through the town.

Mark does his best to think he's misinterpreting what he hears. The voices sound uncomfortably close by the time he can't mistake them. "Seventy-four," the leader calls, and the ragged chorus answers "Knock on his door." Mark is additionally disconcerted by recognising that the caller isn't the man who was on the stage. However large and resonant it is, it's a woman's voice.

"Number ten," it calls, and the chant responds "Find the men." The chorus is nearly in unison now, and the performance puts Mark in mind of a priest and a congregation – some kind of ritual, at any rate. He kicks the quilt away and kneels on the yielding mattress to scrag the curtain and peer through the window. Even when he presses his cheek against the cold glass, all of the street that he can see is deserted. His breath swells up on the pane and shrinks as the first voice cries "Sweet thirteen" and the rest chant "While he's green."

They sound surer of themselves with every utterance, and they aren't all that troubles Mark. Although he knows that the houses opposite are occupied, every window is dark and not a single curtain stirs. Is everyone afraid to look? Why are his grandparents silent? For a few of Mark's breaths the nocturnal voices are too, but he can hear a muffled shuffling – the noise of a determined march. Then the caller announces "Pair of fives," and as her followers chant "We're the wives" the procession appears at the end of the road.

It's led by the fleshy woman. As she advances up the middle of the street she's followed by her moustached friend and the nodding one, and then their fellow players limp or trot or hobble in pairs around the corner. The orange glow of the streetlamp lends them a rusty tinge like an unnatural tan. Mark doesn't need to count them to be certain that the parade includes everybody from the bingo hall except the man who was onstage and Mark's grandmother. As his grip on the windowsill bruises his fingers the fleshy woman declares "Ninety-eight."

She has a handful of bingo cards and is reading out the numbers. "We're his fate," the procession declares with enthusiasm, and Mark sees eyes glitter, not only with the streetlight. The moustached woman wipes her upper lip with a finger and thumb while her partner in the procession nods so eagerly that she looks in danger of succumbing to a fit. "Eighty-nine," their leader intones as if she's reading from a missal, and the parade almost as long as the street chants "He'll be mine."

They're close enough for Mark to see the fleshy woman join in the response. He sees her quivering from head to foot with every step she takes towards him, and then his attention is caught by the lanky woman in the middle of the procession. She's by no means alone in fumbling at a breast as though she's impatient to give it the air. That's among the reasons why Mark lets go of the curtain and the windowsill to huddle under the quilt. Once upon a time he might have believed this would hide him, but it doesn't even shut out the voices below the window. "Twenty-four," the caller shouts and joins in the chant of "Here's the door."

This is entirely too accurate for Mark's liking. It's the number of the house. As he hugs his knees with his clasped arms and grinds his spine against the wall he hears a muffled rumble close to him. Someone has opened the window of the next bedroom. Mark holds his breath until his grandfather shouts "Not here. Like Lottie says, you've been here once."

"That was a long time ago, Len." Mark can't tell whether this is reminiscent or dismissive, but the tone doesn't quite leave the fleshy woman's voice as she says "It's either you or him."

After a pause the window rumbles shut, and Mark finds it hard to breathe. He hears footsteps padding down the stairs – whose, he doesn't know – and the front door judders open. This is followed by an outburst of shuffling, first in the street and almost at once to some extent inside the house. As it begins to mount the stairs Mark hears the caller's voice, though it's little more than a whisper. "Number one," she prompts, and a murmuring chorus responds "Let's be mum." Is it proposing a role to play or enjoining secrecy? Mark can't judge, even when the procession sets about chanting in a whisper "Mum, mum, mum . . ." The repetition seems to fill the house, which feels too small for it, especially once the front door closes behind the last of the procession. The chorus can't blot out the shuffling, which sounds like the restlessness of an impatient queue. All Mark can do is squeeze his eyes so tight that the darkness throbs in time with his pulse, and he manages not to look until he hears a door creep open.

THANA NIVEAU

The Curtain

THANA NIVEAU lives in the Victorian seaside town of Clevedon, Somerset, where she shares her life with fellow writer John Llewellyn Probert, in a Gothic library filled with arcane books and curiosities.

This is her third appearance in *The Mammoth Book of Best New Horror* series. She is the author of the collection *From Hell to Eternity*, where "The Curtain" originally appeared. Other stories have been published or are forthcoming in *Exotic Gothic 5*, *The Burning Circus*, *Sorcery and Sanctity: A Homage to Arthur Machen*, *Steampunk Cthulhu*, *Sword & Mythos*, *The 13 Ghosts of Christmas*, *Magic: An Anthology of the Esoteric and Arcane*, *Terror Tales of the Cotswolds*, *The Black Book of Horror* (volumes 7, 8, 9 and 10), *Death Rattles* and *Delicate Toxins*.

"I started this story after my first experience of scuba diving," explains the author, "but I wasn't able to finish it until years later, when I'd been diving many more times. Shipwrecks are some of my favourite sites to dive. They have an unearthly beauty and I'm never able to shake the feeling that ghosts are watching me, touching me as I glide through the wreckage. There's a sense of Lovecraftian awe without the cosmic terror.

"The *Thistlegorm*, resting in her watery grave at the bottom of the Red Sea, is one of the eeriest places I've ever been. Time stands still there, and you're literally surrounded by history. You also hear strange things while diving. Fish nibbling on reefs, bubbles and your own breathing all conspire to make the experience even more otherworldly than it already is. Sometimes you even hear voices. I was sure I heard whispering on the *Thistlegorm*.

"As I was drifting through the holds of the ship, I imagined peering into one of the rooms and seeing rows of bodies just like the ones Martin sees. It wasn't a frightening thought at all (which in itself is probably frightening), but it was so vivid it almost seemed like a vision. I had the sense that I had passed between worlds, that while I was there, I was a ghost myself."

"MEET ME BY the pinnacle," Martin said as he spat into his mask and rubbed the lenses. "And save me some beer."

Carlos tossed his empty bottle into the floor of the boat and yawned. "Better whistle. I might be asleep."

"Then you'd better wake up. I'm not swimming all the way back."

Martin fitted his mask and looked out across the bay between Laberinto Island and the mainland. The water was unusually still and the early hour lent a sickly quality to the light. Or perhaps it was just the aftermath of the storm.

"Looks weird, doesn't it?" Carlos said, as though reading his brother's thoughts.

"Yeah. But maybe it always looks like that. I can't remember the last time I watched the sun come up."

Martin tested his regulator and tightened the straps on his fins. "Okay," he said. "Fingers crossed for some not-too-buried treasure. Want anything while I'm down there?"

"Bring me a mermaid," Carlos murmured sleepily. "Preferably a blonde."

Martin grinned. "See ya." With that he rolled backwards into the water with a splash. The sea closed over his head and he became weightless as he slipped beneath the waves.

Martin pinched his nose through the mask and blew to equalise the pressure in his ears. A high *squeee* sound filled his skull as his ears popped and then he was alone with his breathing. Each deep sibilant inhalation was followed by a soft stream of bubbles as he released the breath. The bubbles rose like thousands of tiny balloons racing into the sky. Above him the boat was a vague oblong shadow belonging to a different world. Down here he was part of the silence.

Greenish cloudy water engulfed him as he descended. For two days the hurricane had sat just off the coast, churning the sea and damaging the reef. Then, like an angry god, it had swept across Laberinto Island, knocking aside anything in its path as it headed inland.

Although the island had been evacuated, the hardier residents had stayed put, refusing to be driven out by what was only the second storm of the season. Laberinto was their home and livelihood and they weren't about to abandon either one to the elements or the looters who would follow. Let the tourists seek shelter on the mainland; the locals would take their chances, as they had year after year.

Martin had been in the water the day before the storm hit, fascinated by the curious behaviour of the fish that seemed to know something was coming. They darted erratically, oblivious to his presence. Wide-eyed gulping groupers drifted as if in a daze, ignoring the frantic smaller fish flitting all around them. Easy prey, ignored. A line of crabs saluted him from behind the waving fingers of an anemone, then disappeared so quickly Martin wondered if he'd even seen them at all.

Today only murky clouds of debris and pulverised coral drifted around the disfigured reef. The underwater world felt as deserted as the island.

Martin and Carlos had weathered the storm behind the boarded-up windows of their parents' house as they thrilled to the most dramatic hours of the hurricane's passage. They'd stayed up all night, drinking and blaring music on Martin's laptop until the battery died. Then there was only the screaming wind and the occasional thump as something was blown against the house.

It was just like when they were kids, deliberately stranding themselves in their treehouse during rainstorms. The treehouse would become a pirate ship lost at sea as the wind and rain lashed the flimsy wooden structure. There always came a point where genuine fear replaced the excitement, where they worried that their ship might truly sink. But the tree's fort had always held and so did the house, a veteran of many such storms.

The treasure hunt had been Martin's idea. Storms like this one nearly always took a few boats with them, but he had to get in the water before the salvage crews arrived. Here was a chance to explore while Laberinto was still a ghost town.

Martin kicked his fins and dived deeper, following the curve of the reef wall and equalising the pressure in his ears as he went. He had always felt at home in the ocean. From the moment he'd taken his first breath underwater he'd felt as though he belonged. On land he was graceless and ordinary; down here he could fly.

He swam through an icy patch and then the water was warm again. The strata of ocean currents seemed to have new and strange edges this morning. It was like passing through undiscovered rooms in a familiar but invisible mansion.

A cluster of menacing shapes loomed in his peripheral vision and he started with alarm. But they were only arms of coral and clumps of kelp, floating dead in the soupy water. There was bound to be a lot of that. As violent as the storm had been on land, it must have been positively demonic down here.

He soon came to the Three Sisters, an underwater cavern with three entrances. Each jagged passage led down into the labyrinth that gave the island its name. Thousands of years ago the entrances had been above ground, but flooding had submerged the entire cave system. It had never been fully penetrated. The natives believed it was a portal to the underworld.

The colony of Gorgonian sea fans that flanked the three openings had been destroyed. Fierce currents and clumsy divers often broke fingers off them but the hurricane had completely uprooted the elegant corals. They lay like fallen trees on the seabed.

Peering into the cave, Martin could see evidence of collapse. The first two entrances were obstructed by debris but the third was only partially blocked. He moved cautiously just inside and switched on his underwater torch. The light revealed stalagmites that now leaned crookedly or that had been crushed by falling rubble. Knots of seaweed clung to the outcroppings of rock, trailing like reptilian hair into the darkness within. It might be a sunken mine blasted into ruins. With a sad shake of his head Martin turned away from the cave and swam into the blue.

He checked the dive computer on his wrist. The Vyper's display showed that he'd nearly hit forty metres. Going deeper would limit the time he could spend on the bottom, but there was an extra scuba tank in the boat in case he needed to make a return trip.

It was a shame Carlos didn't dive. The world beneath the waves offered so much beauty and adventure and Martin wished he had someone to share it with. It was a privilege to be down here, gifted with sights and experiences most people would never know. Moving in three dimensions was an experience shared only by divers and astronauts in zero gravity. It was spectacular. But Carlos had never been able to see the magic in it; for him the ocean was simply a hostile environment. A cold unforgiving place fraught with danger.

"If we were meant to be down there we'd have gills," he often said, sounding like their father. "No way am I putting my life in the hands of some machine to feed me air."

Sarita had felt exactly the same. During their short-lived summer romance she had gone into the water with Martin only once, wading like a terrified child into a sheltered lagoon with him. She knelt down in the shallow water, hesitantly submerging her head, but she just couldn't bring herself to breathe in through the regulator. Martin waited patiently, squeezing her hand for reassurance and gesturing up at the surface mere inches above them. Finally, she drew in a breath. Behind the mask her eyes widened with a kind of primal fear, as though she'd inhaled poison gas. Her instant exhalation was so violent the bubbles broke the seal on her mask and water leaked in. She panicked and shot up out of the water, tearing away the mask and regulator and gasping for air like someone nearly drowned.

Martin had never been able to understand the terror of the silent depths. Surely submersion was as natural for humans as for any aquatic species. Did we not spend nine months floating in warm water before the trauma of entering the gravity-bound world? Wasn't there a theory that we'd evolved from the sea ourselves? Breathing enriched air through a hose made it possible to go back.

The visibility improved as he descended, but the murky water above him blocked the sunlight as effectively as a canopy of trees. He scanned the shadowy landscape with his torch as he dropped another few metres. In the dim glow he saw a flash of silver and as he swam closer a glittering curtain of fish parted to admit him. It was the first sign of life he had seen. They reformed and hovered, flickering, over a bulky object resting on the bottom about fifteen feet away.

He glided through thin strips of icewater that made him flinch as he neared the dark shape. Something gleamed brightly beside it. The slimy caress of a tentacle brushed his calf and he whirled to discover he'd tangled his fin in a length of seaweed. He kicked free of it and turned back to the shape. The fish danced just ahead of him.

A wooden crate had smashed into a large brain coral on its way down, gouging chunks out of it. Bottles of dark wine lay scattered amongst the splintered boards. Martin floated above, playing the torch beam over the debris. Reflected metal glinted from between the bottles on the sandy floor. Excited, he dropped down for a closer look.

He lifted a bottle out of the way and frowned at his discovery. A spoon. Beneath the other bottles lay forks and knives. His treasure was nothing but a jumble of spilled cutlery.

Dispirited, he held up one of the wine bottles and peered closely at the label. All he could tell was that it was from Chile and it wasn't especially old. He didn't know much about wine but he guessed that lying on the seabed wouldn't have done it any good. He hadn't exactly expected to find a Spanish galleon with a chest full of jewels but he'd hoped for something a little more interesting than some worthless plonk and flatware.

Something flashed past him with such surprising speed that he dropped the bottle. It fell silently, raising a cloud of sodden dust as it hit the bottom. Martin swept the beam around him in a circle, but couldn't find anything in the gloom.

He checked the Vyper, relieved to see he still had plenty of time for a leisurely exploration. The computer would calculate the amount of time he could stay at any given depth without needing a decompression stop and it would warn him when he needed to surface.

A soft munching reached his ears, but he couldn't tell which direction it was coming from. It was never entirely silent in the deep. The sea had its own voices. As he swam towards more debris his beam illuminated a school of blue pinstriped surgeonfish, nibbling on bits of wreckage, investigating every nook and cranny. They swam languidly aside as he passed among them, as though he were one of them.

Another shoal of silver fish hung suspended before him. Unless the same one had followed him. The small fish dispersed and rejoined like liquid metal, reforming into a curtain. Mesmerising. He swam towards them, expecting them either to scatter in fright or flow around him as the surgeonfish had done. But these fish didn't move.

Martin floated in the water, staring as they held their position. He waved his hands at them as though shooing away flies. Their tails flickered, but the fish remained in place. Unnerved, he tried to swim around them but the shoal moved to block his path. He'd never known fish to behave so strangely, storm or no storm. He had the distinct feeling that he was not wanted here. But that was ridiculous. Their illusion of choreography was merely the work of a hive mind; there was no conscious decision, no sentience.

After watching them steadily for a few moments he charged straight at them, arms out in front of him, Superman-style. Their slick bodies brushed against his bare arms as he penetrated the blockade and once he was through they scattered in all directions.

A boat had come to rest here, all right. Smashed bits of the hull littered the seabed, its jagged points like bayonets at the ready. His torch unveiled a mangled instrument panel, a circuit board, part of a propeller.

Dark shapes slid past the wreck, just out of range of the light. Probably just some of the larger fish that lived in the bay – barracuda, jacks or tuna. None of them were aggressive. But what if they didn't want him here either?

Martin picked his way around the splintered boards, finding only more cutlery and banal household rubble. His beam danced over a collection of ruined, soggy books. The shadows leapt, wavering.

The boat had come to rest on its port side. Hovering above the wreck, Martin used a finger to steady himself against the edge of a doorway as he peered closely into the main cabin. He checked his gauges and saw that he had plenty of air. The Vyper gave him ten minutes. If he went over that he'd be forced to stay under even longer for a decompression stop near the surface. With no time to waste, he propelled himself inside.

Something jumped in his torch beam and he watched in amazement as a butterfly glided past, its powdery wings all but disintegrated. Behind it bobbed a bloated caterpillar, like a woolly worm adrift in outer space. After a moment's disorientation he saw that a framed insect collection had broken open and the occupants roamed free, their pins protruding like tiny weapons.

He swept his beam through the rest of the cabin, illuminating a few curious fish but nothing of interest or value.

Beyond the main cabin was a bedchamber with two berths. The bedding had come loose and the sheets floated like aquatic ghosts in the dancing light. The head of an eel protruded from a hole in the floor, its sharp-toothed mouth opening and closing, its eyes cold and empty.

Martin poked around the berths, unearthing only crabs and fish. There was a surprising amount of sea life here for such a recent wreck. He had no idea how long a sunken boat took to form a natural reef but he wouldn't have guessed so many creatures would move in overnight.

He turned to go and found himself snared by tendrils of seaweed. It coiled around his leg and took some pulling to remove. It seemed to have established itself in the cabin, looping in through the portholes and covering the walls like ivy. His torch revealed the extent of the coverage. Astonishing. The entire cabin was a jungle of vines. He brushed aside another creeper before it could get tangled in his hoses.

He swam out through the smashed hull, circling round to the main part of the wreck. And stopped short. A body was lying there.

It was a woman, lying on her back, arms outstretched like a sleepwalker. The gentle current rocked the body, giving it the illusion of life as the arms drifted back and forth with an eerie grace.

Martin had never seen a dead person before and the sight both frightened and fascinated him. He approached her slowly. Wisps of dark hair floated around her face and her long skirt billowed softly, as though stirred by a breeze. She might have been asleep but for her staring eyes. There was something inexpressibly sad about this person lying here, reaching up like a child wanting to be carried to bed.

Martin checked the Vyper. Five minutes. He should go up now and signal for Carlos, then contact the authorities and tell them about the body.

He was beginning his gradual ascent when he noticed another shape a few feet from the woman. He aimed the torch beam at it. It was another body. A man. He was positioned in exactly the same way as his companion – lying on his back, arms floating upward. Beside him lay a little boy. Beyond the child, there were more bodies.

Martin grew cold as the light showed him body after body. The people lay scattered along the ocean floor like sleepers in a huge dormitory, arms reaching up and swaying gently, eyes like those of the eel, gazing blankly. His breathing had become fast and shallow and when he realised it, he forced himself to calm down. He couldn't afford to waste air like that.

As he slowed his breathing he tried to count the bodies. There were at least twelve that he could see, with more skeletal shapes just beyond the range of his torch beam. The sight chilled him. All those grasping arms, like some strange coral garden.

He looked back at the first body. Was he imagining it or had the woman's head turned slightly towards him? His breathing suddenly seemed oppressively loud. There was something very wrong here, something important he felt he should have noticed.

An image came to him of Jonestown, its maze of boardwalks strewn with corpses. There was a kind of hellish peace about these underwater sleepers, as though they'd gone to their fate without a struggle. With a sinking feeling he realised what was wrong. They hadn't floated.

He aimed his torch at the nearest bodies and his stomach twisted. They were trapped. Coils of seaweed encircled the legs and torsos like ropes, holding them all in place, binding them to the wreckage. And there was something else. Although their clothes were in tatters, the bodies themselves were untouched.

Martin shuddered, suddenly feeling watched. He could actually hear the shoal of strange silver fish behind him, their tails flickering softly in the water. Slowly he turned, sweeping the light around him in an arc. The fish were there. Staring at him.

A chilly trickle seeped into his mask and he readjusted it, expelling the water with a sharp snort that sent a torrent of bubbles to the surface. The boat was up there somewhere, invisible beyond the turbid water.

He kicked upwards rapidly, ignoring the warning beeps from the Vyper that he was ascending too fast. He didn't care. He had to get out of there. His heart was pounding wildly and again he had to slow his breathing. He was nowhere near the agreed meeting point and if Carlos had fallen asleep Martin would have to swim to the boat. He could get there faster just below the surface than on it, but only if he didn't waste his air.

He could see no sunlight through the murk. Tangles of seaweed drifted in every direction, winding around his arms and legs as though trying to restrain him. He thought of the bodies down below and fished out his knife, slashing at the vines as he kicked his way upwards.

A dark shape was swimming down to meet him and he froze. It couldn't be Carlos but perhaps his brother had been intercepted by another boat. Well, if it was a salvage crew they could have this wreck; Martin wanted no part of it.

The shape became more distinct as it neared, approaching faster than a man could swim. Surely a fish wouldn't dive straight down like that. As the object sank past him he saw with surprise that it was a scuba tank. He only had time to register what that meant before another shape began spiralling down towards him, this one trailing a dark cloud of ink. It was a man's leg.

Martin screamed, losing his regulator and flailing wildly for a moment before regaining it. He watched helplessly as pieces of the boat began to appear through the darkness above him. The sea seemed stained with blood. A deafening howl filled his head as another shape, this one much bigger, much darker, began to descend. Not with the wild trajectory of a sinking object but with terrible, purposeful aim. Martin fled in the only direction left to him – down.

Again the Vyper bleeped urgent warnings at him but he'd have to take his chances with the bends now; he had no choice. Perhaps he could skirt the wreck and try to surface further away, as slowly as possible to allow the gases to leave his body safely. If he ran out of air and had to go up quickly he'd just have to hope someone was manning the decompression chamber on the mainland. If he could even get there.

The wreck and her sleeping crew slowly emerged as Martin reached the bottom again. He stared helplessly into the blue. The openness froze him. He would be completely exposed out there. Perhaps he was safer here for now, hiding from whatever had destroyed his brother's boat. He hardly dared imagine what could have done it. He crouched behind a jutting piece of the hull and waited, trembling.

An arm with a familiar tattoo thumped silently to rest in the silt beside him. Martin's eyes blurred with tears.

His torch hung loosely on a lanyard around his wrist, its beam casting aimlessly about in the gloom. He thumbed it off, worried it would give away his position. The darkness wasn't total but even so it was constricting. The entire weight of the ocean pressed in around him, making him aware of just how small and insignificant he was in this alien world. Martin calmed himself as much as he could, slowing his breathing to conserve air, but the bubbles he expelled meant he couldn't make himself invisible. He was the outsider here. Small dark shapes continued to rain softly down from above and he closed his eyes for a while so he wouldn't have to see them.

There came a distant throbbing noise, a soft pulse of sound. At first he thought it was a boat's engine but there was an unmistakable animal quality to it. It was the sound of something living. A voice. And with the voice came the certainty that whatever was hunting him had not just purpose but intelligence. It would find him and kill him. Or worse – keep him. As it had the others.

There was one place he might be safe – the Three Sisters. If he could reach the cave he could hide inside where his bubbles couldn't give away his position to anything in the open water. Martin readied himself to make for the reef. He switched the torch on again. The fish were back.

They hovered, perfectly still, a screen between him and the reef wall. Watching him. As though they knew what he'd been planning. Their flat black eyes glinted with unnatural awareness, cold and calculating.

He lunged forward and pushed against their bulk but it was no use. Like quicksilver the fish surrounded him, creating a wall he couldn't penetrate. Their scaly bodies scraped against his hands, scoring his palms with tiny cuts. He turned and tried to swim around them but they were too fast. They closed around him like a net, forcing him deeper, back to the wreck, past the area he'd already explored. He stared in horror at what lay beyond. The seabed was strewn with bodies as far as he could see.

The awful howl came again. Martin could feel its vibrations through the water in every direction. His body ached with the sound as the darkness pressed against him, crushing him. Disoriented, he swung his torch around but there was only emptiness. He lost his bearings, gasping for breath and unable to tell which way was up. He hung in the black abyss, powerless and frightened. From somewhere far away he heard the Vyper, but there was no need to look; he knew he was past the point of no return.

Slowly the pain subsided and the angles of the boat came into focus. He sank to the sandy bottom and knelt there like a penitent. He thought of the cave again, now impossibly distant. He was never meant to be here, never meant to see what he'd seen. The fish had tried to stop him seeing but now it was too late; they wouldn't let him leave.

He peered into the distance and saw he wasn't alone. The dead were sitting up, their heads turned towards him, their vacant eyes watching him. The torch guttered like a flame and went out.

Although he could no longer see clearly, Martin felt he was seeing more clearly than ever. The cave. He understood now, with a terrible clarity. A portal had been opened by the storm and something had emerged. Something that had been trapped there for a very long time.

He was going to die. Just like all the other islanders who had stayed behind. He accepted the realisation with calmness and something approaching euphoria. The water felt alive with movement and gradually the sense of an even deeper black began to swell in the distance. Martin felt himself straining to reach it, to become part of it. Oblivion.

He wondered if he could breathe without the scuba gear. So he released the catches of his buoyancy vest and eased the tank off his back. He peeled off his mask. He spat out the regulator and hesitated for only a moment before taking his first breath. The water entered his lungs easily and painlessly, warm and silky.

A glow flickered like candlelight beside him. The silver shoal. His guardians, his guides. The curtain parted as he swam through to take his place with the others. Then it closed behind him in the liquid dark.

MARK VALENTINE

The Fall of the King of Babylon

MARK VALENTINE has written biographies of the fantasy writers Arthur Machen (Seren, 1990) and Sarban (Tartarus Press, 2011) and several volumes of supernatural short stories. His most recent books are *Selected Stories* (Swan River Press, 2012) and *Herald of the Hidden* (Tartarus Press, 2013), a collection of episodes in the career of Ralph Tyler, Northamptonshire occult detective. He is also the editor of *Wormwood*, a journal of fantasy, supernatural and decadent literature, short-listed for a World Fantasy Award in 2012.

As the author explains, "'The Fall of the King of Babylon' was inspired by a part of the Isle of Ely, cut off from the city by changes to the Great Ouse river in medieval times. This area became known as Babylon, a lawless and lonely place, embellished a bit in the story.

"It could have been entitled 'Eel Meet Again', but thankfully the temptation was resisted."

THE THICK DARK water sucked greedily at the oars each time they dipped into the river's jaws, as if it was reluctant to let them go. He could tell by the way the boatman pushed hard against them that the current was offering him no help at all. It was as well that they did not have far to go. It was only a few minutes since they had left the banks of the city, and already the tall warehouses on the other side glowered above them. The towers of Babylon, he thought. Dark-bricked, dimly lit on the bank side, with barred windows, and with foundations and lower chambers sunk deep in the ooze of the river, they were more like outgrowths than buildings.

The night was moonless and clouded, and the wind was riding in from the black marshes to the south. There had been heavy rain for days, and the river was broad and high, bloated. Its deep bed mud had been stirred up, and had darkened and soiled the waters. He sniffed at the rich, loamy miasma that had been released. The moisture in the air, squatting just above the water, seemed to stick to his face like a grease, in silvery streaks.

They thudded against the old quay: it consisted of slabs streaked with green spittle like a sick man's tongue. There were a few great rusted iron rings: much bigger vessels than this had once tied up at the side. The boatman grunted and held the barque almost steady in the water, though still the river seemed to grip at it, as if it wanted to pull it under.

His passenger looked up at the dank wall: there was a narrow set of rungs, dripping with green weed and oily moisture. He swung himself out onto one of these, and caught hold of the cold rail. The boat began to move away at once. But its passenger was quicker. With a swift twist of his limbs, he kicked out, and caught the boatman a heavy blow on the head. He followed it with another.

There was a baffled cry, and a gurgling of the waters as the boat thrashed about, out of control. Then there was a heavy crash and a great jet of the green water thrust upwards, flicking over him. He watched carefully, licking at the rank liquid on his face: little sparks of light glinted in his dark eyes. Nothing came to the surface. The boat began to drift away, empty.

Good, he thought: I won't be needing you again anyway. Already he could feel his skin longing, and the river and its mud summoning him. Just a few more tide-hours, just a few.

He heaved: briefly, he was not sure he could haul himself up further without his soles or his fingers slipping, but he clung on and gasped to the top and onto the dank slabs, filling his breath with their ripe stench. Then he scrambled to his feet. He had business in Babylon.

That was what they called it, this mudbank of a place, an island of sorts, a backwater within the Isle of Ely itself, cut off from the city when they diverted the river centuries ago.

It was a huddle of slimy buildings: the warehouses, twenty or so hovels, a few boatyards, the shed where they made osier baskets, and one pub. Some of its people were the ancestors of those who had always lived here, the original "exiles". The freemen beyond the water, that's what the city people had called them. Some of those families were still stubbornly clinging to the place. But most of the inhabitants had come later, drawn by its isolation, the way it was left alone, a law to itself, by the "mainland", as they sardonically called the city. And so Babylon had been built outwards onto the spit of mud, and upwards, with ramshackle attachments to the older structures: and there were also tunnels and archways between buildings, so that even here, necessary things could be carried on clandestinely.

And Babylon had a king, or that's what they called him. The boss. He liked the title. Elias Smith, his real name, it was said; but it didn't do to use it. He wasn't worried about a crown or a throne, but he did want the power, and the deference. Nothing moved on this mudbank without him knowing about it. Nobody lived there without paying his taxes, and those were set at whatever rate he pleased.

In the city there was a bishop and a soaring cathedral, with its great lantern tower, the glory of the Fens. But here in Babylon, there was no church, no chapel: just the eel warehouse, a ruined ziggurat of red bricks. And at its very top, in his own vaulted chamber, there resided the king. You had to be conducted there: no set of stairs led straight to it.

There were different iron flights for each floor, and linking corridors, and empty halls, which you were hustled through in a blur. You went back, if you went back, a different way. But rumour said that from a concealed door in the king's reception room, there was a chute, a steep chute that went down, down, straight into the Great Ouse. And at such force that nothing sent down ever surfaced again.

In the warehouse, above smouldering pits of slow-burning alder-wood, skinned silver eels were being smoked in long rows of round gallows like dark chandeliers. The columns of flesh swayed and twisted in the draughts, as if they were still alive. There was an acrid smell from the embers and also, still, the deep dank odour of river mud, not yet burnt out of the bodies of the eels. The two together were almost overpowering. In the cellars, frequently flooded, and always dripping with damp and mould, were the slabs where the catch was first reamed of its gleaming skin. A streaked tin tub of eel heads stood in one corner; the black eyes still glinted in the dim light.

The King of Babylon owed a vast wealth to this gruesome river harvest. But he was restless this night. There was something wrong in his realm, he knew that, and although he could not say exactly what, there were signs. There hadn't been a catch in days. The women in the weaving-sheds were murmuring amongst themselves; they shut up too quickly when they saw him. The river was too solid; he did not like the look of it. And from over in the city, there was too much talk of a foreigner seen, staring across at Babylon, asking questions. He had a strangeness in his tongue, the king's spies said, and probably came from beyond the seas.

The king's heavy form paced about his high room, and he glared down from this eyrie to the darkened alleys and empty yards below, through the small panes of smeared grey glass. Like the bricks of his building, his face and hands were a blackened red. Abruptly, he turned away, and tugged at a bell-rope. A cracked clangour sounded. Boot-steps stumped in the stairwells and along the corridors. A young woman, with cropped hair, and dressed in rough black clothes, presented herself. She had a white scar on her left cheek. It gleamed silver in a face already a dirty pale, the colour of congealed candle-wax.

He stared at her. She lowered her dark eyes, and fidgeted.

"Who's in Babylon tonight?"

"Forty-two souls, sir. Eighteen down below, doin' the skinnin', smokin' and saltin'. Balin, patrolling the building, with Den and Pulver. Twelve in The Anchor: that's nine o'the fishing men, the potman, the barmaid, old Agar talking to 'imself. Then there's Mother Shearn in her cottage . . ."

"What's she doing?"

"Playing at cards, sir."

"Playing? Or reading them?"

"Couldn't tell, sir. Looked like playing though. She didn't have that funny look in her eyes."

But you do, the king thought, that's why you won't look in mine. Hiding something. He gestured to her to go on.

"Four o'the women in the basket shed. And then there's them two men you put on the wharves, looking out. That you didn't tell me, nor nobody about. But I spotted 'em. And then me, and you, see, sir, makes forty-two."

He grunted. "Been everywhere?"

"Everywhere."

"Would you like to be skinned, Nix?"

Still she would not look at him.

"I have been everywhere," she repeated, slowly.

"Skinned, salted, smoked alive on one of the eel-gallows?"

"Everywhere," she murmured.

Mother Shearn did not tarry long in the brick hovel she called her home, where dirty lace tried to escape through cracks in the smeared windows. After she saw Nix's pale face glimmer in the grey panes, then vanish, she blew out the candle. She continued to count out the cards in their rows and columns, knowing them by touch in the gloom. She had been in Babylon longer than anyone remembered, and was rumoured to be the only one on the isle that the king, Elias, was afraid of: wisely, perhaps, she had never put this to any great test. Her face was silted and brown like the river's leavings.

She hunched over the cards for some time, then hastily gathered them up and stuffed them in a little pouch of frayed red satin, which hung from the thick leather belt at her waist. She wrapped a bundle of tawny shawls around her shoulders. Outside, she sniffed the dank night air. Her thick greasy nostrils seemed to suck in and sift the stench. Then she made a gurgling noise at the back of her throat, and shuffled towards The Anchor. Its door unleashed a babble, then swung closed behind her.

Old Agar was reciting to himself from the Bible again: he seldom did anything else. At least, it sounded like the Bible. There was a lot of muttering about the things to come. He barely registered her arrival.

A group of men in the corner looked up from their beer as she moved towards them. She thrust her face into their hoarse-throated circle.

"Eels is risin'," she said, quietly.

They fell silent for a few moments then started to mutter.

"Can't be."

"Naw, not tonight, Mother."

"Have another look at they cards o'yours."

"Get her a gin."

"Eels is risin'," she repeated.

Reluctantly they began to get to their feet, clumsily lace up the boots they'd eased loose, and climb into heavy, soil-streaked coats, gather up kit bags. From a corner, they took up nets, clubs and the shining gleaves, long, speared forks, like primitive weapons. Grumbling and spitting, they headed for the door.

She watched them go, and then signalled with a quick jerk of her head for a double genever. She felt the spirit graze her throat. Yes, they were rising, all right, swimming up from the silt and the mud, following some instinct old and blind. She knew that; she always did. Whatever the instinct was, she could catch its dim echoes, like a coiling of green miasma in her mind. But this time there was something else she could not fathom. There was a cold gap. She could not tell when the rising would end, when they would return to the slime, to the river's depths. She shivered, drew her shawls closer about her, and signalled for another spirit.

The men trudged, then waded, down to the shallows where the boats were kept. They lurched and jostled against each other. They could already tell the hag was right: the smell in the air was heavy enough to get through the beer in their heads. They bundled the eel-tools in a pile on the mudbank and hauled the boats toward them on their sodden ropes. The brown slime stuck to their hands. The coracles seemed heavy in the swollen waters, were reluctant to come. They heaved harder, their boots sinking into the clinging clay. At last, with a jolt and a surge, the dank wooden shells began to move towards them.

Ben Crawke got his in first, but the sudden impetus took him by surprise and when the boat bumped against his shins, his fuddled brain wasn't quick enough to react, and he toppled forward into the bottom of the boat. Cackles of laughter greeted his mishap, and were redoubled when Crawke screeched. The boat thrashed about in the water and in the dim light they could see his limbs flailing about comically. Why didn't he steady himself? He used to be able to hold his drink better than that. Still, it was worth watching.

After they'd let him mess about for a few moments, still bellowing fit to burst the moon, one of the men stooped down quickly and caught up the trailing boat-rope, and another helped to try to steady the juddering. It took both of them to tug the boat back once again to the bank. And then Crawke's head emerged.

The youngest fisher, Thom, had been sent against his will to an elementary school in the city for a year or two, before he slipped away back to Babylon, where they didn't come looking for him again. One day he had been shown a book of myths which he quite liked because it had a lot of pictures of strange things in it, things that even Babylon did not possess. And one of these was of a woman with a head all covered in snakes.

Crawke looked like that now. Except they weren't snakes. They were eels. And they weren't just in his hair, like that woman's. They were on his face too. No, not just on his face; in it. Some of the men stumbled forward, as if they could help, seizing their clubs and the long barbed spears.

Then the river current, which had been slow and sluggish, seemed to give a great surge, to rise up in a sudden swell, and the ropes dropped slack as the rest of the boats rushed to the bank.

And then they saw the writhing within them, a great mass of the dark coiling creatures. It would have been the greatest haul ever made, something to boast about in The Anchor for years to come. Except that it was all wrong: for the first, and last, time in their lives, they had no need to go out for the catch. It had come to them.

The river surged again, lunging at them. The strong waters sucked at their limbs. They tried to ground their boots in the mud, to grab hold of the mooring posts, even to clutch at the sharp, yellow-green reeds. Still, they were summoned into the depths. And when they finally gave way, they found out why the current was so fierce. It wasn't just the water that had sucked them under.

Nix crouched in a dark corner. She had five dark corners on the isle, where neither Balin nor Mother Shearn nor Elias Smith could know where she was. To get to this one, she had quietly moved aside a huddle of osier baskets, then a stretch of oilcloth, revealing an iron lid. This she forced up with a little knife she'd filched once from one of the fishermen; it had grey string round the handle for better grip. The blade dislodged the seal of grit and mud around the lid, and she heaved it up. Below was a narrow rung, and at the bottom of this a platform above a black channel of water. It ran under the warehouse and came out under one of the unused cellars. Even Elias did not know about this. When she was alone she did not call him the king, even though she belonged to him. She rubbed the scar on her white face.

They told her she had been born in Babylon, and so she belonged to him. There wasn't anybody else claiming her, that was for sure. But she did not call him the king because she knew, somewhere inside her, that there was another ruler of this isle, and always had been, and he would come again.

Maybe somebody had told her a story about it once, maybe she had overheard a few things and put them together, maybe she had always known it. But she was more certain of it even than the breath of the boss, Elias, when he took hold of her and pulled her close and stared at her.

That breath was the thing she feared the most, because she could tell from it what would happen next. His breath, heavy, rotten, rank, seemed to enter her like poison. And then his venom worked in her veins, all the way through her. But when she later lay quivering, trying to secrete the poison, trying to get rid of it, she also called, far in the depths of her mind, called and sang – to the unknown king, to the one that she knew would one day hear her.

Her body in its black clothes tautened, so tight, so intense she thought it might suddenly change, in a flicker, into something else. Footsteps. Coming steadily towards her. Heavy, too, sending echoes into the tunnel. His? Elias? She felt something surge in her, a burst of hot defiance. Her fingers tightened on the corded handle.

He could feel the waters rising. Already they would be filling up the underground channels, surging into the vaulted chambers, clawing at the walls. The deep, dark stench of the water called to him; already he had offered it two bodies he'd found prowling about after him. They'd been distracted by some babbling young fisher-boy, who clung on to them, shouting about a face he'd seen, a face that was writhing. The boy would have more to talk about now.

But there was a greater urging in him too, more overpowering than the river. He knew she was here: the sense coursed in his limbs like a shot of silver. He waited. Then his eyes seemed to form the image of an iron disk, and draw his body towards the shadow of the warehouse with insistent force.

She heard the grating noise, saw the lid rise up. A face of white shone in the gloom, and then a form slid easily down and dropped beside her. She felt her body become even more tense. And then stared at his black eyes, stared hard, and saw her own reflected back. She was seized and thrust into the dark waters. They closed about her head. For a few moments she was blinded and numb. Then she kicked out, thrust herself forward, and at once felt her body become part of the current. Around her, forms moved in the water.

When they emerged into the cellar, her breath was soiled at once by the burning smell from the smoking gallows above them in the building, which seemed to permeate every streaked brick. She felt a plunge of fear, and she wanted to cry out. But then a hard rage seethed through her and her eyes gleamed in hatred.

Her companion touched her, and beckoned. Their dark, dripping forms moved lithely to a stair and quickly ascended. Flight followed flight, in a crooked route through corridors that glistened as they left behind them a trail of the black slime.

And there was his door. Behind it, the man who liked to be called the King of Babylon. Now the hatred was so fierce in her that she knew it would change her forever: her body could not contain that dark fire. She heard the bell shout for her from its bronze throat; she heard that name bawled, "Nix! Nix!"; she heard the threats that followed. Her fingers felt the silver scar upon her face.

Her companion thrust her to the stone floor, and crouched beside her. Then, together, as if they were one being, they lunged, and burst through the door. There was a sharp, keening sound, and a barbed glieve thrust through the air toward them. They twisted with a wild instinct, and it clanged uselessly aside. It was raised again for another strike, but stopped: it was held before them, holding them at bay. But still within them, they felt that instinct surging strong.

Then the king saw the intruders' faces change. They seemed to pulse rapidly, to quicken and writhe before him. And the flesh began to turn colour. It had been white, like the skinned strips dangling from the gallows below. Now it was darkening, becoming brown, like the river water, rank green, like its weed, and finally black, black like its depths of mud. And the shape of their faces was changing too: becoming sleek, sharp, pointed; until at last he knew exactly what he faced, and stared into the utter glinting dark of the eyes.

Elias Smith, alias the King of Babylon, bellowed, and backed quickly into an ante-chamber. He spun an iron wheel in the corner of the outer wall. With a grating noise, a door swung heavily open. There was a large arched tunnel, like an open mouth, with a brick throat, sloping steeply down. He leapt into its maw, skimming its streaked surface, feeling the foetid air rising to fill his breath as he descended at reckless speed.

Behind, he could sense the things slithering even faster after him.

TERRY DOWLING

Nightside Eye

TERRY DOWLING is one of Australia's most respected and internationally acclaimed writers of science fiction, dark fantasy and horror, and author of the multi-award-winning "Tom Rynosseros" saga. He has been called "Australia's finest writer of horror" by *Locus* magazine, the country's "premier writer of dark fantasy" by *All Hallows*, and its "most acclaimed writer of the dark fantastic" by *Cemetery Dance* magazine. *The Year's Best Fantasy and Horror* series featured more horror stories by the author during its twenty-one-year run than by anyone else.

Dowling's award-winning horror collections include *Basic Black: Tales of Appropriate Fear*, *An Intimate Knowledge of the Night* and *Blackwater Days*, while his most recent titles are *Amberjack: Tales of Fear & Wonder* (Subterranean Press, 2010) and his debut novel, *Clowns at Midnight* (PS Publishing, 2010), which the *Guardian* called "an exceptional work that bears comparison to John Fowles's *The Magus*." He has also written three computer adventures (*Schizm: Mysterious Journey*, *Schizm II: Chameleon* and *Sentinel: Descendants in Time*), and co-edited both *The Essential Ellison* and *The Jack Vance Treasury*, amongst many other titles.

"As so often happens, 'Nightside Eye' is the result of a number of separate ideas coming together at just the right time," explains Dowling.

"A tactic I often use to prompt the creative unconscious is to keep a list evocative titles and check on them occasionally to see if any speak to me and reveal how they might be resolved. It can be a good way of blind-siding yourself and coming up with all manner of unexpected treasures. One such title was 'The Delfray Mantel', a deliciously old-world title if ever there was one.

"Even as I was pondering how such an architectural feature might be explored in narrative terms (things like where you might find such a mantelpiece, what you might put on it or find missing from it), and as the idea of poltergeist events became ever more compelling, I learned how old-time mariners quite likely preserved a useful day- and night-sightedness when going below-deck from the bright light of day by wearing eye-patches and swapping them from one eye to the next as needed. The elements connected, became intriguing, then irresistible.

"Meanwhile, the marvellous Hydro Majestic Hotel at Medlow Bath in the Blue Mountains outside of Sydney had stood vacant for many years awaiting renovation. It was the perfect place to locate such a haunted mantelpiece. I visited the old Hydro and photographed key features, hoping, hoping, hoping that the resulting story would see print before the long-overdue renovations began. I thank the unseen occupants of the Delfray Room for letting this be exactly how it happened."

THE FACT THAT the guest lounge, ballroom, whatever it had originally been, was devoid of furniture only intensified the feeling of something waiting to happen.

Jared had read the latest tender updates for the old Hydro Majestic Hotel, knew that they all listed the Delfray Room as a minor function room.

"So that's it?" he said, indicating the mantelpiece above the handsome fireplace in the eastern wall.

"That's it," Susan answered, clearly intrigued, possibly even disconcerted at knowing someone who actually wore an eye-patch like the traditional black one over Jared's left eye. Jared was thirty-six, lean enough, his features regular enough, to make him attractive to many women at first glance. The patch lent him an unexpectedly rakish air, friends and colleagues said. Susan Royce was in her late twenties, with ginger hair in a pixie crop, and was clearly taken with him – in spite of the patch, because of it, who could say? Now she led the way across the parquetry floor to the black iron fireplace, looking for a moment as if she were actually going to touch the unadorned marble ledge. "Put anything on it, it ends up on the floor."

Jared did reach out and touch the cold smooth marble. "But not immediately, I understand. It takes time."

"Not immediately, no." Susan seemed interested, well-intentioned. She was a different heritage representative to the one assigned to Martin Rathcar fifteen months before. Without Rathcar's media brouhaha, the scale of that whole publicity circus to draw attention, she may have had only a token briefing on what this evening's proceedings were all about. "But an hour, two hours later. It always happens. Used to take days, weeks, months, but it's much more frequent now, a matter of hours, sometimes minutes. Even heavy weights end up being shifted. They say it's something electro-magnetic, a freak of nature."

"You've seen it?" Jared asked. Though he'd been hoping he'd get Cilla Paul, the same heritage rep Rathcar had dealt with, things seemed to be shaping up well regardless.

"Only on CCTV. I'm still pretty new."

The Delfray Room seemed larger from this angle than it actually was. Being painted a stylish off-white probably helped create that effect. At the far end, the western end near the double doors, four long sash windows were curtained with light brown drapes, gathered back with the same tasselled silken cords as on the other westward-facing windows in the hallways of the old Hydro Majestic. Like those hallway windows, these too looked out over the vastness of the Megalong Valley, gave the spectacular views that had made the place so famous in its heyday. Now the Hydro was in its third year of being closed, officially awaiting restoration to all its former glory as a world-class spa resort if only the appropriate government, licensing and restoration bodies could agree. Having read the various tender documents, Jared knew how dauntingly expensive it was going to be. The old Victorian and Edwardian buildings made a gentle chevron along the ridge-line, set fifty metres in from the main highway that led across the Blue Mountains from Sydney out to Lithgow, Bathurst and beyond. It was the sort of white elephant that was so costly to maintain yet too dramatically part of the local landscape and local history to be ignored.

The late-autumn sun had already set beyond the last of the ranges. The famous view was gone from the long windows now, their old panes turned to so many mirror reflections by the light from the Deco wall sconces and the chandelier overhead. The black iron fireplace, clean but inevitably dusty, was the room's most distinctive feature, the mantel a modest afterthought by comparison, even more simple and functional than the CCTV footage had shown it to be.

"The previous owners must have become fed up with the whole thing," Jared said.

Susan nodded. "None of the various management groups ever said much about it but, you know, who wanted the publicity? It could happen at any time. It was always there. And, like I say, it's been getting more frequent."

"Hard to live with."

"They only used the Delfray Room as an overflow room for special occasions, last-minute wedding bookings, that sort of thing. They just made sure they put nothing on the mantel. Records show that the occurrences – you call them 'events', don't you? – started soon after the hotel was first opened in 1891 as the Belgravia Hotel, though very infrequently then. When it became the Hydro, only a few people knew about them. Management had to consider their more refined and sensitive clientele, so hushed things up pretty quickly. There was originally a large mirror mounted over it, quite ornate, so no one really questioned the lack of other adornment."

"Except the occasional guest who suddenly found his drink on the floor."

Susan laughed. "Exactly. The ultimate party trick. I imagine it's a bit like trying to sell or lease out a murder house. Something you just don't mention, just work around as best you can. Mr Ryan – Jared – if you'll excuse me asking. I understand that you're not blind in that eye. You're just masking it for what's being done tonight. Is what Cilla said true? This whole thing is about *seeing* what's doing it?"

"That's right."

"You don't mean it's someone? A person? A ghost?"

Jared shrugged. "We can't know. Martin Rathcar proceeded from the certainty that *something* was doing it – whether resident poltergeist or freak of nature. He found serious funding to develop a method for seeing anomalies like this a different way."

"But the patch. I understand that—"

"Dr Rathcar called it the Nightside Eye as a media draw-card in 2008, back when the funding proposals went in. Made it sound sexy, mysterious. He got the idea from one of those myth-buster programmes on TV."

"Really. How so?"

"It seems veteran seamen aboard sailing ships in the seventeenth, eighteenth and nineteenth centuries often wore a patch over one eye when they went below-deck. They swapped the patch from one eye to the other so they were nightsighted and could see immediately. It let them find things quickly, stopped them bumping their heads. Very practical."

Susan looked sceptical. "That really happened?"

"It's highly likely. Dr Rathcar expanded on the idea, kept one eye completely isolated from all the customary vision tasks for nine months, took injections of several quite powerful, very specific neurological regulators to intensify the 'nightside' function in that particular optic nerve."

"Biased it?"

"Many claimed so, though the regulators weren't known to be hallucinogens. More like the drugs used in eye surgery, optical trauma events, sight retrieval situations.

Increased receptivity and adaptivity. Intensification of the optic process."

"I remember now. Rathcar's the guy from Sydney University who wouldn't say what he saw. He took his own memories with another drug. I remember that interview on *60 Minutes*."

"That's the guy. Martin Rathcar."

"You're doing what he did?"

"As best I can." Jared touched the smooth marble ledge again. There were no *frissons*, no untoward sensations, nor had he expected any. He took his hand away. "When he injected the Trioparin, took his memories, he breached quite a few legal agreements. He ended up being locked out of his own facilities, forfeited his database and research material. But some preliminary theory was already published. There was even a popular article in *New Scientist* to generate interest. The rest of the procedure was relatively easy to duplicate. The main thing was getting access to the same location he used a year ago. You can see why I'm so grateful to you and your office."

Susan smiled. "Cilla briefed me as well as she could before she left for London. Her mum is unwell, all last minute. She said I just have to be here and watch. Make sure rules are followed."

"You're doing more than you realise. You and the security guards rostered on tonight become impartial observers as well."

"Hey, I like that. Independent witnesses!"

"I'm glad you think so. I wonder if you'd be okay with us using your names in our observation log? It could really help."

"Sure. It's exciting. I'll ask Geoff and Amin later."

"My camera and sound people will be here soon, Sophie and Craig, my volunteer assistants and official witnesses. It's six o'clock now. Once we're set up, we'll begin at 7:00 p.m., the same time Dr Rathcar did fifteen months ago. We'll do the whole thing twice if we can, put several objects here on the mantel – a plastic bottle, a child's wooden block, a toy train – and simply record what happens. Second time through, if we *are* lucky tonight and the phenomenon occurs, the moment they're moved, disturbed in any way at all, I shift the patch from one eye to the other and see what I get. It shouldn't take long."

"You do that *once* it happens?"

"As soon as it happens. As close to. The first time is a control to establish parameters: event frequency and duration, lighting levels, things like that. But the second time round I stand over here by the fireplace and shift the patch, just as Rathcar did."

"But the camcorders will only catch your reactions. Not *what* you see."

"Right. But whatever we get may match reactions in the CCTV footage from the Rathcar attempt. Rathcar's own footage hasn't been made available yet, but may be released once we do this. Rathcar called out a single word – 'Kathy!' – his assistant's name. We don't know why now, and of course he can't tell us."

"Or won't."

"Or won't. But there may be some key detail or other that emerges. Later spectrographic analysis may show even more, who knows?"

"It's all very uncertain," Susan said, looking at him intently, or possibly at the eye-patch that was to play such a key role in what was about to happen.

"True. But it's all we can expect in a situation like this, and hopefully what we do tonight will actually duplicate Rathcar's results, whatever those ultimately were. All we know is that there was an event and that Dr Rathcar shifted his patch, reacted strongly to something, called out Kathy Nicholls's name, just her first name, then shifted the patch back. It's what he did afterwards that caused the fuss. Gave himself the injection."

"So you're doing this to help Dr Rathcar?"

"In a sense. Not out of some noble motive or anything; I've never even met the man. But I have to allow that he saw *something*. A respected research scientist took his own memories of what seems to be the key moment in a serious experiment. Grandstanding aside, something probably significant happened to make him do that."

"The resident poltergeist," Susan said.

"I'll settle for that, whatever it is."

"You hope to see it?"

"That's the idea. Hopefully see something."

"So why do it at night? It happens in daylight too. Surely that'd be easier?"

Jared had to smile. "Rathcar did it at night, so we do likewise. I think it was Channel 9's idea, having the night-shoot. Spookier. More dramatic."

"I can understand that. The smallest things are scarier at night."

"Exactly."

"But whatever you see may just be sensory overload. All those drugs you mentioned."

"I know. Large-scale perceptual trauma. But those optical regulators aren't known for that, have been deliberately tailored to avoid it in fact. Ah – here are my long-suffering volunteers!"

Sophie Mace and Craig Delmonte had appeared at the doorway to the Delfray Room, laden with camcorders, audio equipment and a portable lighting stand, assisted by Geoff and Amin, the security guards rostered on for the evening.

Jared and Susan walked back to the double doors, where Jared completed the introductions then helped the security men carry in chairs and a table so Craig and Sophie could set up their video monitors just inside the entrance. Susan left them to it, going outside to discuss the evening's schedule with the guards.

"Give us twenty minutes to get the settings," Craig said. "Won't take long."

"Listen, Craig—"

"Jared. Let's do this like we discussed. You're pumped, I can tell. It's only natural. Go for a walk and calm down! Sophie and I can handle this."

"Right."

They had talked about it, about remaining composed, focused, letting others help. This footage would be seen, closely scrutinised. Objectivity and detachment were everything.

Jared stepped out into the corridor, walked the short distance to the corner and turned left into the long axial hallway for the whole wing. It was dimly lit, and so quiet, stretching off into shadow at its farthest reaches. Jared started along it, moving soundlessly on the old carpet, with locked doors to his left and long darkened windows to the right. He knew that beyond the steady mirror reflections in those panes the land fell away over sheer crags, buttresses, blurrings of eucalypts, a great gulf of darkness, all invisible now. In daylight it was the sort of panoramic view that caught your breath, weakened you in the knees, made any attempts to capture it in photographs impossible. Photographs never caught the scale, the dimension, the vast uncaring emptiness.

Now that he was finally doing it, everything seemed intensely unreal, and he had to counter that feeling. He took several deep breaths, made himself consider where he was. The old spa complex was all around him, stretching away like a bleached wishbone here by the highway at Medlow Bath, an antique ivory clasp opened and laid out along the ridge, arms pushed back against the incredible drop. The phrase "abandoned in place" had never been more appropriate.

This fabulous old hotel was meant to be restored, maintained, fêted, if only as something as second-rate yet cherished as the Carrington Hotel in nearby Katoomba. But *used*, for heaven's sake. Though no one was saying so officially, there was already the distinct feeling that it might all prove too hard, that these empty rooms, forgotten lounges, deserted balconies and silent staircases would stay like this indefinitely, the only thing moving in the halls by day the motes of dust glittering in the westering sunlight, by night the shadows made by the moon as it fell down the sky. Now and then security guards would come and go, trying the locks, checking the fire-doors, running the aircon in various rooms to counter mildew and mould, helping to replace the fire-extinguishers as they reached their use-by dates, escorting the planning people who seemed to come less and less frequently now.

Jared turned to face his own reflection in one of the long casements, stood distracted by the familiar shape with the eye-patch. For a moment it made him forget the great darkness beyond the glass, but then he forced himself to think of it, savour it: the fact that two things could be true at the same time, his image *and* the other. It calmed him, anchored him somehow.

When he finally did check his watch, he saw it was 6:51, time to get back. He re-traced his course, returned with the same silent tread to the Delfray Room, welcoming the soft murmur of voices as Sophie and Craig made final adjustments, calmly explaining what they were doing for Susan's benefit. The security guards were off making last-minute checks of the exits.

Everyone knew to leave Jared be now, and he distanced himself, found focus by reviewing how well it had gone so far. The Rathcar duplication was nearly complete: his taking the exact regulator doses across nine long months, the grooming of the monocular separation followed to the letter. The logistical requirements had been met too: securing the Hydro for the evening, keeping the costs well down. The guards were rostered on anyway. Only Susan had to be paid a fee for the two or three hours it should take, and she had turned out to be so interested that if he'd bothered to arrange to meet beforehand she might well have done it for free.

At 6:56, Jared called for Stand-by. Susan took out her mobile and contacted the security men. "Geoff, get Amin. We're about to start."

The guards appeared in the doorway moments later, took their places on the spare chairs, interested and attentive.

"All right," Jared said. "So everyone is clear on the sequencing, we roll cameras at 7:00 sharp, do the control run to make sure our visitor is with us. We set up our things on the mantel, let our guest have a free go at them. Once it happens, *if* it happens, we then take the thirty-eight minute break and do it all again, this time with me standing over by the mantel and swapping the patch as soon as I can after the event occurs."

"Is the thirty-eight minutes necessary?" Susan asked.

"Again, it's what Rathcar did. It wasn't planned. He just had more things to co-ordinate. But we're duplicating his sequencing as closely as possible."

"Understood."

"Okay, Sophie, Craig. It's 6:59. Begin recording. I'll go put the things on the mantelpiece."

Jared did so, once again crossing the empty dance-floor to the fireplace. First he stood the plastic bottle on its end, then set down the wooden block a short distance along from it, finally placed the red toy locomotive. Though tempted to stay by the mantel even for this first run, pulling his patch aside at the first sign of any disturbance, he made himself return to the monitors by the doors.

The vigil proper began at 7:02.

It was exciting at first, full of a new and understandable tension, an intensification of everything. The objects sat there – so ordinary, so comical in that ordinariness, both unreal yet super-real, but growing more and more unsettling, even disturbing somehow in their stillness.

As long minutes passed, the waiting soon became unbearable, of course. In most modern cultures, human senses were rarely accustomed to being strained this way. What once might have been essential for hunting and for vigilance in the face of danger and strife now brought only a worrying hypersensitivity. Jared watched the monitors, then the mantel across the room, monitors and mantel, glance up, glance down, the cycle repeating over and over. He found himself afraid to blink, straining to catch the slightest movement, the smallest disturbance, keenly aware of the gulf beyond the windows, of the chill autumn darkness all about them, thought of the empty rooms and hallways, the locked bars and dining rooms, the kitchens, closets, the empty pipes, the utterly still interiors of the hotel outbuildings scattered along the ridge. He imagined movement a dozen, two dozen times, but there was nothing, certainly no confirmation from Craig and Sophie at their monitors, watching the test objects in both long-shot and close-up. Geoff and Amin sat quietly behind him, Susan to his right, close by the monitor screens, no doubt staring too.

Jared had not forbidden talking, but that's what had resulted. There was barely a sound.

Ten minutes became twenty, thirty, and the silence grew to be a layered thing. Sounds not noticed at first gained a striking new intensity: the hum of the recording equipment, the smallest cough, the rhythmic cycle of their breathing, the occasional tick of temperatures shifting, of masonry cooling, old pipes settling, whatever traces came in from the great emptiness beyond the windows.

It was so sudden when it happened – as alarming, dramatic and violent as everyone had said it would be. One moment the objects sat unmoving, exactly as placed. The next they were gone, clattering on the parquetry floor as if an unseen arm had swept them aside.

"First event, 7:46," Craig said for the audio log, then: "Stand by. Stand by. Counting to the thirty-eight-minute repeat at 7:47 – now!"

Everyone relaxed then, began talking all at once. It was happening. They were in the thirty-eight-minute time-out.

To Jared's surprise, one of the security guards, Amin, was suddenly at his elbow, handing him a folded note. "When I started my rounds earlier, Jared, a guy parked out by the highway asked me to give you this the moment something happened."

"What's that?" Jared said, even as he took the note, opened and read it.

Mr Ryan

I am waiting in front of the hotel in a white Camry.

Please give me fifteen minutes of your time. It is very important that you do so.

Martin Rathcar

Jared passed the note to Craig, said: "Keep to the countdown. I'll be back in time." Then he left the Delfray Room, hurried out to the front exit, out through the *porte-cochère* to where, sure enough, a solitary white Camry was parked by the highway. As Jared approached the vehicle, the passenger window lowered, revealed a man behind the wheel leaning over, smiling.

"Jared Ryan? I'm Martin Rathcar. Thanks for coming out. Please get in for a moment."

Jared climbed into the passenger seat and they shook hands. "Dr Rathcar, I have to say this is truly a surprise! Really quite marvellous! But why are you here?"

Martin Rathcar looked older than his fifty-two years. He sat with his hands on the steering wheel, his narrow face partly shadowed, partly lit by the highway lamps. His eyes glittered. "I know you don't have long. My one-time assistant, Kathy Nicholls, let me know that you'd duplicated the monocular separation and were doing this tonight."

"Using your Nightside Eye."

Rathcar gave a wry smile. "To call it that. I enjoyed the theatricality, I suppose."

"I've read all the interviews, all the *available* transcripts."

"That's all there are."

"I accept that. But I thought – since you asked to see me – that there was something you remembered and were prepared to share."

"Jared, I remember nothing of what I saw, just that it was enough to make me obliterate the memory of whatever it was. It's strange to find myself asking you to abandon the whole thing now when I have no memory of what it is I'm warning you away from. Feels a bit silly really, especially when it puts me in the position of wanting more than anything to know exactly what I *did* see. But I have to allow that there were vitally important reasons. Please reconsider going ahead with this."

The request surprised Jared. "What about your own reply to Sandra Cartwright on *60 Minutes* in July 2009? 'This is science. Learning about the world.'"

"I won't insult your intelligence by giving the line that was put to me in the same interview, that there are things we are simply not meant to know. I still hold with what I said. If we can know it, it's science and there to be known. It's only right that I should wonder now about what I saw that night that led me to take the final step. Theatricality is one thing, melodrama quite another, and I really do hate sounding this way after years of advocating rigorous investigation myself. But it had to have been important. I pretty well committed professional suicide with what I did."

"Surely not. It was always going to be a case of their having to take your word for whatever you saw. You just pissed off a lot of people. Deprived them of an answer to something they would have called inconclusive anyway."

"Which, nevertheless, many say was because I saw nothing. That this was my intention all along."

"Dr Rathcar – Martin – your reputation, your previous work in perception, suggests otherwise." Jared hesitated. "It really did take your memory of it?" He had never been truly convinced, he realised.

"That's the thing, isn't it? I should have insisted on a second subject doing it with me from the beginning, or at least waited until whatever I saw could be verified in a subsequent procedure. But Trioparin is effective only on recent memory. I was told it affected only an hour, ninety minutes tops. It's like a mind-shock that way, very different to Diprovan and other amnesiacs. Whatever I saw made me decide that I could *not* by any means wait for subsequent verification."

"It bothered you that much."

"I have to allow that it did. I desperately needed to forget. Anyway, the drug worked better than expected. My short-term memory of the twenty-six hours preceding the injection was lost. Twenty-six hours, can you believe it? Far longer than anyone expected. Part of me wants to know what it was I saw, now more than ever given your intentions tonight, I can't deny it. But I have to accept that I gave myself that injection knowing what it was I did."

"But to have arranged for that contingency in the first place, you must have seriously suspected – sensed – that something could go wrong. Trioparin is a last-resort trauma amnesiac. Prohibitively expensive."

Rathcar nodded. "At the time I simply allowed that there could be intense trans-perceptual trauma. It seemed entirely likely. You deprive one eye of its normal tasks for months on end, suppress at least three key neurotransmitters in doing so, then suddenly restore sight to that – let's use the pop term – Nightside Eye. Well, you know the outcome, though now I wish I'd never *mentioned* arranging such a precaution. The media seized on it, had a field day."

Though he hadn't automatically expected it, Jared found himself liking this man. "You didn't just accept that whatever you saw might be dismissed as hallucination, hyper-perception. It suggests you *believed* what you saw."

"It does, doesn't it? I'm glad you think so."

"You wanted it *all* gone regardless, though you knew in advance that it would be intolerable for you afterwards. The *not* knowing."

Rathcar gave a forbearing smile. "That's what made me drive up here tonight and ask to see you. Weird position to find myself in, like I say, but I have to allow that it really is as serious, as important, as my subsequent behaviour suggests. I was never much given to pranks or over-reaction, believe me."

"But what could it be? What must you have seen – even as an hallucination – that could possibly make you want to forget it forever?"

Rathcar sat with his hands on the wheel for a time, staring at nothing. Then, noticing Jared glance at his watch, he continued. "You understand my dilemma. I have to allow that it was either an hallucination for me, something purely subjective, or a reality for us all. They're the alternatives, the least I can claim. But, Jared, you stand to face the problem I faced: failing in your duty as a scientist. I clearly didn't want even the *possibility* of it being real in the objective sense. You see the extremes here, why I can't help but be fascinated with what you're about to do. I knew it might happen in time, but now, tonight, I keep reproaching myself for not seeking corroboration *before* taking my memories of what I saw."

Jared smiled grimly at the implications. "It really must have been something."

"Well, no matter. At least you're doing it at the same place I did. And I understand you've duplicated my procedures for fostering the Eye precisely."

"That was the whole point, duplicating what you did."

"Again, I'd be lying if I didn't say that I'm fascinated to know what will happen. Maybe I was wrong to do what I did. But that's the other reason I wanted to see you. Would you consider using a lethophoric like Trioparin to take your memories?"

"Frankly, Martin, I'm more the budget operation. You had institutional funding. I can't afford luxuries like that."

Rathcar smiled again. It was a good smile. They truly did like each other. He took one hand from the wheel, patted the pocket of his jacket. "I have some here in case. The last of my supply, pocketed that night, thank goodness. Everything else was confiscated. I'll wait out here in the car."

"Come inside."

"No, I must *not* be in there. You must appear unbiased. But just remember that it's here. I'm here."

"If I do come out to you, you won't ask what I've seen?"

"I'll want to more than anything in the world. But, no. I promise I won't. I must believe in myself to that extent. You say you're not doing this for me, and I believe you. In a sense, I'm not just doing this for you either. It's because I have to trust myself – trust that I acted for the right reasons. I do not need to know what you see. But if you come out and ask for the Trioparin, I will at least know that you've seen something as unbearable and that I was right in doing what I did that night. Right now that means everything."

Jared made it back to the Delfray Room with seven minutes to spare. Both Sophie and Craig wanted to ask about what had happened, but Jared raised a hand.

"He just wanted to wish me luck and try to talk me out of going through with it."

"Really?" Sophie said. "No insights?"

"Unfortunately not a thing," Jared told her. "But we can talk about this later. It's nearly time."

At 8:24, Jared crossed to the fireplace again, retrieved the bottle, the wooden block and the toy locomotive from the floor where they had fallen, and began setting them back on the mantel, making sure that the placing of the train coincided with Craig's 3-2-1 countdown to 8:25 exactly. Jared then moved to the right of the fireplace, watching the three objects, wondering how long it would be – *if* at all.

It was a different sort of vigil now, of course, marked by a wholly new kind of tension, such a definite – *pressure* was the only word. Jared's breathing was so loud in his ears. He could feel his heart thumping, his pulse racing, was aware again of the silence out in the room, of how far away the others were across the dull sheen of the parquetry. A quick glance showed Sophie and Craig at their monitors, faces ghost-lit just a touch, showed Susan looking up from the screens to him, the screens then him. Geoff and Amin sat behind them, darker shapes in the open doorway, eyes fixed and glinting.

The pressure became everything. It could happen at any moment, any instant. He felt he could almost guess when. It was like the waiting tension in a game of Snap or that kids' game where closed fists were placed knuckle to knuckle against one another, and the kid who was it got to hit the other's hand before it could be snatched away.

Jared's thoughts raced. What was it? *Who* was it? Was it really something as simple as electro-magnetic fluxes, atmospheric and geomorphic glitches, nothing supernatural at all? Or was there motivation behind it? Purpose? That was the real question here. What was out there drawing ever nearer, was even now preparing to sweep the objects aside, so dramatically, so brutally. Where did it come from? How far did it have to travel to do this simple, mindless thing? Is that what the delay meant, or was this poltergeist always here, holding back out of a sense of mischief? But *why* did it have to be done – this furious sweeping aside? That remained the issue. The real priority wasn't just shifting the patch to see what there was *after* the event, but shifting it in time to catch who or what was doing it *just as it was about to happen*!

It would be departing from Rathcar's procedure, certainly, but this was about finding answers, seeing the process as process. *Complete* process, with more than just an ending, an outcome. With a beginning, a definite lead-up and possibly – could it be? – with intent.

The pressure *was* building, definitely growing stronger, Jared was sure of it. Something was about to happen, was beginning even now out there in the room, there to be seen if he dared risk it, dared throw it all away on a conviction, this *felt* certainty, totally unprovable.

Jared felt his hand clench, felt himself preparing to take that risk, commit that violation.

This was what it needed to be! Knowing what it was *before* it happened, *as* it happened, not afterwards. Seeing the cause, not the effect.

The pressure was too much.

His hand was at the patch, shifting it from one eye to the other, uncovering the different kind of seeing.

Jared reeled at what he saw, had to reach out and steady himself with one hand on the mantel edge.

There was no sign of Susan or the others, none of the equipment, not even the spotlight. The room was crowded, too crowded, with row upon row of dead-white forms, pallid near-human shapes pressing shoulder to shoulder with not a space between them, dozens, hundreds of sexless, minimalist things like mannequins, but with mouths hanging open and dull red eyes fixed mindlessly ahead, looking beyond him, fixed on nothing.

He was frantically registering the enormity of what he was seeing when there was a commotion in the throng, a sudden rippling forward as someone, something came pushing through, finally thrusting aside the figures in the foremost row to stand slavering, heaving. It was another of the pallid shapes, but this one had eyes that were wildly animated, blazing red, and a mouth stretched wide in a grotesque toothless grin.

No sooner was it there than it raised one long white arm and swept everything from the mantel. The familiar clatter echoed in the room, in no way muffled by the crowding forms.

Jared stared in utter dread. It wasn't just the dead-white face, the grinning, gaping mouth, the imbecilic, red-eyed glare. It was the idiot glee in those eyes, the look of absolute manic delight at having done this single, simple, stupid thing yet again. It was like a puppy waiting for the next throw of a ball, a witless automaton for whom only this had meaning.

And worse still was the sense that the rest of the crowding, slack-faced throng had their special things too, tasks waiting to be triggered and just as mindlessly resolved, whatever they were, however long they had to wait, however long it took.

"Susan!" he shouted, not to Sophie or Craig, but to the young woman who was nearest in his thoughts, had been the focus of so much recent attention.

And there she was, visible now, moving from the back of the shapes, moving forward *through* all the still figures, but not alone. One of the pallid, gaping forms moved with her, followed close behind, in attendance, her eager companion.

We all have them, Jared realised. Following, always following, always there, biding their time.

Are they what waits for us? All that is left of us? What simply wears us down, brings us to death, what?

There was no way of knowing. But *this* was what Rathcar had seen. What Martin Rathcar had understood.

Jared couldn't help himself. He reached up, snatched the patch back over the Nightside Eye so the room, the hotel, the world became normal again.

Seemed to.

"What was it?" Susan asked, still moving towards him across the empty, never-empty room. "What did you see?"

"Nothing," Jared managed, giving the beautiful lie. "There was nothing. It was too much of a shock. Just too much disorientation for the brain. It didn't work."

And he gazed out at the welcome emptiness, the normal world, knowing it could never be that again, knowing that Rathcar was right and realising what had to be done.

If Rathcar had waited, kept his word, was still out by the highway.

Jared ran to the double doors, rushed out to the main entrance. Susan hurried behind. Sophie and Craig abandoned their monitors and ran after him. Geoff and Amin exchanged glances and followed.

Behind them the abandoned equipment hummed quietly. The things from the mantel lay scattered where they had fallen. The windows reflected only the empty room, showed not a trace of the darkness beyond the old, old panes.

HELEN MARSHALL

The Old and the New

HELEN MARSHALL is an award-winning author, poet, and medieval book historian. Her writing has been published in a range of anthologies and magazines including Tor.com, *Lady Churchill's Rosebud Wristlet*, *The Year's Best Canadian Speculative Fiction and Poetry* and *The Year's Best Dark Fantasy and Horror*.

In 2012, ChiZine Publications released her debut short story collection, *Hair Side, Flesh Side*, an exploration of history, memory and the cost of creating art, which has recently been short-listed for an Aurora Award. Her second collection, *Gifts for the One Who Comes After*, will be published in 2014.

As the author recalls: "When I was seven, my parents took me to see the crypt beneath the church of Santa Maria della Concezione dei Cappuccini in Rome – a place where the bodies of nearly four thousand monks had been nailed to the walls to form intricate and macabre murals.

"This is, one might argue, not the best tourist-stop for a kid, but my mother is a forensic pathologist and so perhaps it seemed more run-of-the-mill at the time. What can I say? I adored it.

"Twenty years later, I found myself in Paris trying laughably to mime the word 'catacombs' to my French-speaking concierge while my boyfriend of the time looked on with some bemusement. (He thought I wanted, in order, an escalator, a night club, or a pirate ship.)

"At the current count, there are over six million dead bodies exhumed and arranged in the subterranean catacombs beneath Paris. This struck me as a strangely wonderful place for a date. Thus, this story was born."

THE CATACOMBS WERE dark, and Becca felt a chill settling over her entire body the moment she emerged from the narrow, spiralling staircase. She could hear a rheumatic gurgling in the distance. Or perhaps it was close by. It was very hard to get a sense of the space, and Becca wanted to reach out and take John's hand but the staircase had been too narrow, so she had had to go it alone, John in front, enthusing about the quality of the light, the patterns of the shadows on the stones.

John loved the play of the light on the stones here.

"Look at this," he said. "We don't have anything this old back home." He patted the walls affectionately. "Nah, everything's brand new – so shiny it could be made of plastic. But this –" *pat pat* "– this is the real thing, this is *old*. This reeks of history."

Becca looked around a little bit sceptically – not too sceptically, she *wanted* to be here, really she did, or rather, she wanted to be with John and John wanted to be here, and so, by association, she wanted to be here as well. She made an encouraging noise, kind of like an ooh-aah all run together. The stones really were old . . . very old. They had that sort of rough-hewn look to them, as if they were carved by peasants. They probably were, she thought. Not a sandblaster or an electric drill or anything like that, just hammers and chisels, or maybe even fingernails – who knew what the peasants might have been given to work with?

"But that's the problem with North America, isn't it?" John asked. "Nothing old, nothing that sticks around that long. Nothing but teepees before the Europeans showed up, and they don't last for more than a couple of years at best. Maybe you get a lighthouse here, a church there, but that's nothing. This is it. Right here." John had a happy look in his eyes, and so Becca smiled with him, and she oohed and aahed at the walls and the creeping dampness, and the smell of rot and dead things that had lived and died years and years before her country had even become a proper country.

But then they hit the bones, and the rocks were nothing – the rocks were meaningless, because here were over six million dead Frenchmen (and women, probably, but Becca couldn't remember if women were buried properly back then – maybe it was just the men, but the women *had* to be buried, didn't they?).

And the bones were . . . something. They were lined up, row upon row upon row of them, all these smiling bone faces with black eyeholes like another set of little caves for her and John to explore. But that's what the brochure had said, some unreadable stuff in French and then in big letters, STOP! THIS IS THE EMPIRE OF DEATH!

There were so *many* of them – that's what amazed Becca the most, how many there were. Six million. Six million people had been buried here in the catacombs. Becca couldn't even fathom that number. If she squinted her eyes she could almost pretend that they were rocks, that they hadn't been people at all, they were just rocks that might look a little bit person-shaped.

Becca didn't like the way they smiled at her. It was creepy, all that smiling in a place where over a six million dead people had been put on display.

When John slipped his hand into hers, Becca almost yelped, and she was thankful that the hand gripping hers had flesh and was warm and even a little sweaty. She was glad for it, that warm hand. So glad she gave it a little squeeze. Then Becca looked at John, she smiled but a shiver ran over her spine when John smiled back because right behind him were row on row of eyeless, skinless heads smiling right along with him.

* * *

Paris was beautiful in a way Becca hadn't expected it to be. Montmartre. The Eiffel Tower. All those lights winking at her from across the dark cityscape. She hadn't thought much of Paris, really, until John had said he wanted to go, had always wanted to go, and that he wanted *her* to go with him. Then Paris seemed magical, everything about it seemed magical – the city of light, *la Ville-Lumière*, he had called it.

Becca thought quite a lot of John, had always thought of him. She used to watch him while she was at the photocopier back when she first started working for the firm, fetching coffee and the like. Becca suspected that John hadn't thought very much of her initially. John was one of those easygoing handsome sorts who tended to work at firms, effortlessly charming in conversation, with little streaks of silver running at his temples. John never spoke to her, but that was all right because John was married, and so Becca watched him while she did the photocopying. She didn't talk to him. Others did. There were always people stopping by his office for a chat or a coffee. His wife, sometimes, with bags of take-out food from Pusateri's or some other expensive place. They'd eat together in the office. She'd sit on the desk, and she'd kick her legs, long legs, perfectly slim beneath some sort of frippy little summer dress, and John would look at her and smile. She was a pretty woman. Prettier than Becca, with small slim hands and blonde hair Becca would have killed for.

Not Becca though, she never talked to John. She was just an intern, so she didn't exist; his eyes just skipped over her. When they rode together in the elevator there was nothing but silence between them; he wouldn't even look up, not once. He only had eyes for *her*, his beautiful, blonde wife.

One day, it was news round the office that John wasn't married any more. No one quite knew what happened – if she'd left him or what or why or for whom. But the ring was gone, and so was the charming smile, and the little streaks of silver became a bit more than that, like someone had smudged them, like he had aged ten years overnight. Becca felt sad as she watched him after that; people didn't stop by his office anymore, they didn't bring him coffee. Well, they did at first, all curious to know what had happened, but John would simply get a look on his face – a sad look – and then he would smile a sad smile, and they would feel bad that they had asked, bad that they were disturbing him. Pretty soon, they stopped visiting altogether.

Becca felt sad for him too, sad for the way he shuffled around the papers on his desk now as if he didn't quite know what to do with his hands, as if he had forgotten why they were there, ringless. Once, when he was out on his morning smoke break, she snuck into his office and she left a coffee for him – two sugars, the way he liked it. She waited by the photocopier. She copied things. She decided that she had copied those wrong, that there was a smudge on the page, and her boss wouldn't like a smudge on the page. So she copied those things again. But then that load didn't look quite right either, so she decided there must have been something on the copying panel. Becca made quite a show of cleaning the copier, and she copied the pages a *third* time because that was what her boss would have wanted. John didn't come back to the office though. And the third set of copies didn't have a smudge. Not even a hint of a smudge, nothing smudgy or blotted or wrong with them at all. So Becca fiddled for a moment, hoping for something, for *anything* to be wrong with them, but there wasn't so she retrieved her papers, and left.

"How about a photo?" John said, smiling, but he wasn't really looking at her; his eyes were rapt with the camera.

"I don't think so." She said it with a smile so he wouldn't think she didn't want a picture taken with him, just that she didn't want a picture with . . . *them*. All of them.

"Just one. It'll be nice. Just one? I don't want to forget this. I don't want to forget our first trip to Paris. We want to remember this, don't we? We'll never see anything like this again, and just think, we can be a part of it for a little while. We can show the folks back home that we were really, *really* here."

Becca didn't want a picture, but John wanted it, and she wanted John to be happy.

"All right," she said. She squeezed his hand and let him manoeuvre her to the nearest shelf of bones.

"Not that group," John said after he had held up the camera. "The light's no good there. Try this one – well, maybe this one. Much better ones here. Whoever did that lot wasn't good," and he laughed. "Probably didn't get a promotion for that lot of bones. Must have been the dull one out of the bunch."

Finally, it was right and John was happy and he held the camera up and said, "Smile!" so she smiled and he smiled – and when he turned the camera around to show the tiny digital display, a thousand dead Frenchman smiled and winked alongside them.

John didn't come back from his break. Becca watched his office from her tiny desk – it wasn't a proper desk, just a table set up for her. From where she was seated, she could see the steam rising from the coffee, and then, after a little while, there was no steam.

He didn't come back after lunch either, and when Becca went to do the afternoon copying, the coffee was still sitting there, untouched. It had to be quite cold. It had been several hours. But she didn't want to give John cold coffee, did she? What if he thought she did it on purpose? What if he got back in the afternoon from an important meeting with his divorce lawyer and he found a cup of cold coffee? *She* used to drop off coffee, he would think to himself, my wife, Laura, whatever her name was, *she* used to drop off coffee and now I won't ever have a hot coffee in my life, only cold coffees for me from now on. As if a broken heart wasn't enough.

That would be a little bit cruel, a little bit sad. And Becca wanted him to be happy. John deserved to be happy. He was a good man, a kind man, the kind of man you ought never to leave. And so she left the copying to go, and she went back into the office.

She just meant to grab the coffee. Just the coffee and that was it. But then she couldn't help it, she saw on his desk a photo – a photo of a woman smiling. Laura. Or whatever her name was. His wife. The picture didn't look old. It looked quite recent, and she was smiling at the photographer, really smiling, not the kind of fake smiles that most people did for cameras. It was a real smile, and there was so much love in it, more love than Becca had ever put into a smile before. Most of her smiles were littler things than that, she didn't show her teeth ever, she thought they were big and horsey. But Laura had nice teeth. Nice little even rows of super-clean, white teeth.

Becca found herself hating that picture. Why would he even have the picture up still, when Laura, or whatever her name was, had left him – had just up and vanished? She picked up the picture, and she slipped it out of the frame. There it was, on the back. *Laura*. That was her name after all. Laura. No date, no other words, just Laura. Laura was a bitch, Becca thought, how could she have left him? She was a slut. Becca didn't like the word, would never say it out loud, but somehow it seemed right. Becca picked up a magic marker, and she wrote across the back of the photo SLUT in wobbly writing. Then she put it back into the frame, but you could see the word across it, SLUT, all across that smiling, perfect face. And then in the corner, Laura. Just a name, nothing more.

Becca picked up the coffee cup. It was cold. She sipped it, and the coffee was sweet, too sweet for her, but it was just how John liked it. She drank the entire cup.

She couldn't leave the picture there. How would John like it if he were to come back to his office and find the word SLUT across his picture? The ink was starting to bleed through, black smudges growing darker and darker across Laura's face. Becca slipped the picture frame into her purse, and she went out to the copy machine.

It was quite close to closing now, and Becca was looking forward to getting out – light and sunshine, bottles of wine, a quaint European hotel room . . .

The tourists had trickled off but John's enthusiasm hadn't. Not even a little. Row on row of the faceless heads and he snapped away, merrily *click-click-clicking*. "It's strange," John said, as he rounded a pillar composed entirely of femurs. "No names. Six million people but not a single one has a name. There should be a list of them somewhere – do you think there is, in the hall of records? I once did a shot of The Wall in Washington, you know, the big one. All those people running their fingers alone as if it was Braille. But it was just names.

"There was this kid there –" *snap snap*, he was snapping away quite urgently now "– and I thought his grandfather must have died, and he's crying as if it just happened, as if it were a tombstone. But it wasn't. It wasn't anything like that. It was just a list of names, and he's crying and so I put my hand on his shoulder and I ask him why he's crying. You know what he says? He says his girlfriend just broke up with him." John shook his head in disbelief, but he stopped snapping very suddenly, and he clenched Becca's hand hard.

"I think I'd like to go now," Becca said. She could smell the hint of fresh air. She almost ran toward it. In fact, she did jolt forward but John was still holding her hand and she was yanked back a pace.

"What's the rush?" he asked. And his eyes said, "Please say this is great." But he wasn't smiling. There was something wrong with his smile.

She tried that ooh-aah trick again, just let her mouth make a series of encouraging sounds that weren't quite words. He seemed to brighten up. What she was really thinking was that it was just bones. Rooms and rooms of them, skulls mounted on piles of tibias, giant circular ossuaries. Sometimes they would be artistically arranged – a line of skulls outlining a block of thighbones, all the knobby ends pointed outwards. In one place, a giant stone cross was set in the middle. As if we didn't get the point. Stop! This is the Empire of the Dead! It was all a bit melodramatic, wasn't it? A thousand skulls would have been enough, but six million? Six million was overdoing it a bit. Six million was too many.

They stopped being people at that point; they were just bits of debris, bits of things that had died.

"We can't go yet," John said softly, and there was something in his voice, that something edging toward desperation. He tugged on her hand and it might have been playful, but maybe, just maybe, it wasn't. "What about that chapel, that was pretty good, wasn't it? And the light – the light didn't do it justice. I want to try again. I think I could make it work if I gave it another go."

Becca felt something inside her crawling. She didn't want to go. It was awful, the chapel was awful, and she just wanted to get out. But John tugged again on her hand, drawing her back, and he smiled that smile of his – the one that was mostly happy, but maybe just a little bit sad.

Becca was returning with coffee for her boss when she had her first, *real* conversation with John. They were both waiting for the elevator, standing awkwardly next to each other in the lobby of the building. His eyes flicked up and then away. She almost thought he didn't recognise her, but then they flicked back. A hint of a smile. Did he know her? She couldn't be sure. She tried smiling back, but he had already looked away. She bit her lip, waited, tried smiling again but now he was looking at his shoes, and then the floor display, and then he was pressing the button again impatiently.

"Coffee?" she asked. It was her boss's coffee – black, the way she liked it. He wouldn't like it though; that wasn't how he took his coffee.

At first, he didn't respond. Nothing. Eyes on the floor. Then, as if the words had taken a long time to penetrate, he turned to her and blinked once. "Yes, thanks," he said, and then that hint of a smile became an actual smile, a real one. Not as real as the one in the picture, not as full or as genuine or as happy as that one, but maybe it had a little of that in it. She handed him the coffee. She had no coffee to bring her boss now, but that was all right, she was doing good for the firm, keeping up morale. She dug into her pockets.

"Two sugars, right?" She produced them, and he smiled a little more, so she ripped the tops of the packages, both at the same time, and she dumped the sugar in. "Sorry," she said, "no spoons on me."

He took the coffee. The elevator door opened, and they both stepped inside. "You're Becca, aren't you?" he asked. "Beth's new intern."

Becca nodded. He sipped the coffee, smiled again, sipped again. Silence.

It was the sugar, Becca thought, a good thing I brought the sugar. He wouldn't like it black, and then we wouldn't be talking now. And she smiled back, and she surreptitiously patted the pocket of her jacket, crammed full of sugar packages.

But now John wasn't talking and the elevator was moving inexorably toward the top floor. Becca counted out the floors as they passed them – fourteen, fifteen, sixteen. John sipped. Becca fidgeted. She tried to look at him out of the corner of her eye, squinted so he couldn't see her doing it. Seventeen, eighteen. She was looking at his hand, his left hand, ringless, like there had never been a ring. Twenty.

"Where did she go?" She didn't mean to say it. John looked surprised at first, his mouth went through a little series of silent ohs, before it bunched up into a look of intense pain.

"I don't know," he said. His eyes dropped. "I really don't. They ask me sometimes, ask about the ring. I don't know. One day she was there, and then suddenly, she wasn't anymore. Pieces of her started to go missing. First it was an eye. Her hand. The whole left side of her body. No one noticed except me, but I could see her slipping away, a little bit at a time. And then she was gone. And then the ring was gone. And then . . . her things. The clothes in her drawer . . . her picture on my desk . . ." he turned and he looked at her, but he wasn't really looking at her, he was looking past her, not seeing her. "I think I might be going mad."

Becca didn't say anything, he looked so sad right then, so terribly, terribly sad. She put her hand on his, touched him very, very lightly, so lightly she didn't know if he could feel it.

"You're not going mad," she said. "Shhhhh, it's all right. Don't worry, don't worry." Inside, though, she was thinking, she's gone, she's really gone, you never had a wife, John. You never knew her, you never loved her.

He looked up, very tentatively, met her eyes for the first time, smiled. The door opened with a cheery *bing* and he startled guiltily. Half-jumped out of the elevator. But then he paused, turned and put a hand across the door. "This coffee wasn't for me, was it? I haven't gotten you into trouble?"

"It's *your* coffee now," she said. "Just for you." And saying it she felt happy, just happy, and solid. Like he could see her at last. Like she was real to him.

"Right," he said, "thanks." But as the doors closed again, she saw that look in his eyes, something speculative, something wondering a little bit – who was the girl in the elevator? – but a happy kind of wondering, a curious sort of wondering, a maybe-maybe sort full of hope and excitement. She saw it there, in the eyes, in the smile. And then elevator began to drop away underneath her with a feeling that might have been a little like love.

And now she felt anger, just the barest hint of anger that he should be sad, here, in Paris, the city of lovers, *la Ville-Lumière*. He was the one who had wanted all these fucking bones, these fucking dead Frenchman, what right did he have to be unhappy? He should be smiling, he should be smiling, and she should be smiling, like in the picture. But he wasn't. There was something missing from his face, some part of him that wasn't quite there, wasn't quite with her. He should have been smiling.

John was snapping away furiously now, and Becca wanted to go; she didn't want to be in this dank dark place any more, she wanted to be where there was light, where there were bottles of wine.

"There's supposed to be something here," he said, and he was staring at a place in the wall where an ancient skeleton had been composed on a little shelf. "A name. There's supposed to be a name here." Becca looked at John, looked at that handsome face, but the eyes were wrong, they were wide and staring. She wanted to be kissing John, but he was interested in all those bones, all those stupid, fucking bones. They *weren't* people anymore, they couldn't be. They couldn't talk, they couldn't fuck, they certainly couldn't *love* you anymore. Dead people couldn't love you. That was the point, why didn't he understand that? Dead people were gone, they were vanished forever.

John was muttering something now, and his breathing was hoarse. "I can't find any names, there must be names here, mustn't there? Who were all these people? Where did they come from? Where?"

"John," she said, "we're going now."

And he took a picture. And another picture. And another picture. So many goddamn pictures. And then he wasn't taking picture anymore, he was putting away the camera, and Becca thought, thank god, at last, he's done with it. He doesn't need pictures anymore, he can just have me. But he was picking up the skull, he was staring at it.

"It's Laura," he whispered, and his face made a thousand silent, painful ohs. "I think it's Laura." He paused, and he was rubbing his ring finger then, and Becca stared at it, the band of light, untanned skin where that ring used to sit. In the washed-out light, he seemed to be a stranger, she didn't recognise him anymore, there were dark smudges across his face, the eyeholes deep and sunken. And full of something. Wonder. Love.

"She's here – she always said . . . Paris . . . she wanted to go to Paris. *La Ville-Lumière*. She wanted to make love in Montmartre. She wanted to stand at the top of the Eiffel Tower and see all those lights, all those little lights winking at her. She wanted to . . ."

And he was looking at Becca now, and he was holding the skull in his hand, and suddenly Becca could see it too, it was Laura, it had the same loving smile, and it was looking at him, and the word SLUT was written across it in large wobbly writing. And she was angry. You don't exist, she thought, you never existed. You weren't real. He never loved you.

"I remember. I remember her, she was there, and then she . . . Why are we here?" he asked, and he was staring, and his eyes were wide and dark as caverns. "Why are we in this *fucking* place? Why did you—?"

Becca found that she didn't want him to be there anymore, he wasn't *nice*, he wasn't kind, he wasn't the kind of man you ought never to leave. Because he was leaving her. She knew it, she could see it, she could feel the little pieces of herself disappearing. He was leaving her, and all for his wife, for his *dead* wife. She wasn't a person, she wasn't anything. There were six million dead people buried here, six million, and how many more? How many more everywhere? Throughout all of time? The dead are nothing, she wanted to scream at him, they aren't anything at all, just a little whiff of air, a thing that was there and then gone. She was nothing. She was a stone. She was a memory. She was band of white flesh wrapped around his finger.

"She's dead, John, she's just fucking dead!" And Becca felt it happening, felt that look in his eyes, felt the darkness of those caverns swallowing her up.

And he kissed the skull, he leaned over and he planted his lips on it, the warm flesh ones against cold, hard, gleaming bone. He didn't shiver. She thought he should be shivering, that he should be cold, that it would be awful to kiss a dead person but it wasn't. There was a look on his face. Happy. A smile that was a real smile, and the skull was smiling too. Nice little even rows of super-clean, white teeth.

Why are you doing this, John? she wanted to scream. Why are you doing this? Why can't you just love me, why am I not enough, why am I not real to you? All those skulls, all those skulls around her were laughing now, they were saying, "You mocked us but you are one of us. You are one of us, you are dead, you are among the dead and now we shall have you." The teeth. All those dark eye holes and smiles full of teeth.

And then John was looking at her again, really looking. Becca felt herself falling into pieces under John's terrible stare. And maybe it was a bit like love, that feeling of dropping away.

STEVE RASNIC TEM

Waiting at the Crossroads Motel

STEVE RASNIC TEM followed his 2012 collection *Ugly Behavior* and the novel *Deadfall Hotel* with no less than three new collections in 2013: *Onion Songs* (Chômu Press), *Celestial Inventories* (ChiZine Publications) and *Twember* (NewCon Press). 2014 will see the appearance of his latest novel, *Blood Kin* (Solaris), and his stand-alone PS Publishing novella, *In the Lovecraft Museum*.

"This story started with a character," he reveals. "It's always struck me that someone who believed in the realities posited by H. P. Lovecraft – possibly the most paranoid scenarios imaginable – might be similar to some fathers I've known: steeped in conspiracy paranoia and willing to drag their families wherever their fantasies took them."

WALKER NEVER THOUGHT of himself as any kind of genius, but he knew that at least his body was never wrong. If his body told him not to eat something, he didn't. If his body told him not to go into a place, he stayed outside. If his body wanted to be somewhere, Walker let his body take him there. He figured he got his body from his father, whom he never knew, but he knew his father had been someone remarkable, because his body knew remarkable things.

"Blood will tell," his mother used to say, in pretty much every situation when an important decision had to be made. He eventually understood this referred to the knowledge he had inherited from his father, held in his blood, and which informed his body which seemed to know so much. Walker's blood never said anything too loudly – it whispered its secrets so softly he couldn't always hear. But he could feel it pull in this or that direction, and that had been the compass that had brought them here.

The motel was small, all one story, just a row of doors and square windows along the inner side of an L-shaped building, with a dusty parking lot and no pool. Walker heard there used to be a pool, but they'd had a hard time keeping the water sanitary, so they'd filled it in with sand. A few cacti and thorny bushes now grew in that faded bit of rectangular space, but none too well.

The maid – a withered looking woman well into her seventies – tried confiding in Walker from day one. "There's something wrong with this dirt, and the water ain't never been quite right. You buy bottled water for your family while you're here – especially them kids." But Walker made them all drink right out of the rusty taps, because that was the drink his own blood was thirsting for.

If anything Walker felt more at home at the Crossroads than he had anywhere in years. He'd drink the water and he'd breathe the dry desert air, taking it deep into his lungs until he found that trace of distant but unmistakable corruption he always knew to be there. He'd walk around outside barefoot at night, feeling the chill in the ground that went deeper than anyone else could know. He'd walk around outside barefoot during the middle of the day letting the grit burn into his soles until his eyes stung with unfamiliar tears.

Angie had started out asking nearly every day how long they'd be staying at the Crossroads, until he'd had enough and given her a little slap. He didn't really want to (he also didn't want *not* to), but it seemed necessary, and Walker always did what his body told him was necessary.

That was the thing about Walker – he could take people, or he could leave them. And he felt no different about Angie. His body told him when it was time to have sex with her, and his body told him to hide her pills so he could father some kids by her, but Walker himself never much cared either way.

"The four of us, we'll just stay here in the Crossroads until I hear about a new job. I have my applications in, and I've been hearing good things back." She never even asked how he could have possibly heard good things, waiting there in the middle of nowhere. He never called anyone. But she'd never asked him any questions about it. Angie was as dumb as a cow.

Somehow he'd convinced her that the Crossroads Motel was the perfect place for them to be right now. From the Crossroads they could travel into New Mexico, Arizona, Utah, or turn around and head back towards Denver. They could even go back home to Wyoming if they had a particularly desperate need to visit that state ever again. In order to do any of those things, though, they'd have to get a new car – theirs had barely made it to the Crossroads before falling apart. "But we have a world of choices." That's what he told her. Of course he'd lied. She was an ignorant cow but the dumbest thing she ever did was fall in love with him.

Their fourth day there he'd made an interesting discovery. He'd always whittled, not because he liked it particularly, he just always did. He'd grabbed a piece of soft wood and gone out to that rectangular patch where the cacti grew and the swimming pool used to be – he called that area the "invisible swimming pool" sometimes, or just "the pool" – and sat down cross-legged in the sand, the sun bearing down on him like a hot piece of heavy iron pressing on his head, and started to carve. He was half-way through the piece – a banana-shaped head with depthless hollows for eyes and a ragged wound of mouth – when suddenly the hand holding the knife ran it off the wood and into the fatty part of his hand – slow and deliberate and unmindful of the consequences.

He permitted the blood to drip, then to pour heavily into the sand before stopping it with a torn-off piece of shirt-tail. Then it thickened, blackened, spread into four flows in different directions. Then each of those flows hardened and contracted, rose from the sand into four legs attempting to carry the now rounded body of it away. It had begun to grow a head with shining eyes when the entire mass collapsed into a still shapelessness.

Not strong enough, he thought. *But that will change.*

Walker spent most of the next few days sitting in an old lawn chair he'd set up behind the motel. The cushion was faded and riddled with holes – rusty stuffing poked through like the organs of a drowned and bloated corpse. The whole thing smelled like sea and rot – odd because it was so dry here, miles from anything larger than a car wash puddle – but it was an aroma he'd always found comforting. It was like the most ancient smell of the world, what the lizards must have smelled when they first crawled out of the ocean.

He had the chair set up so he could gaze out across the desert that spread out behind the motel, away from the highway that fed out through the south-west corner of Colorado and into the rest of the West. That desert was as flat and featureless and as seamlessly light or as seamlessly dark as the ocean, depending on the time of day and the position of the sun and the moon. So much depended on those relative positions, and the things that waited beyond, much more than most human beings were destined to know.

Out on the distant edges of that desert, out at the farthest borders the sharpest human eye could see, lay shadowed dunes and hard rock exposures, ancient cinder cones and mesas, flat top islands in the sky. He had never been to such a place, but it had been a location fixed in his dreams for most of his life.

Every day Walker sat there in the chair, the eaves of the motel roof providing some minimal protection from glare, a notepad in his lap, a blue cooler full of beer at his feet, and watched those barely distinguishable distant features, waiting for something to change or appear, or even just for some slight alteration in his own understanding. "I'm working out our future plans and finances," was what he told Angie, and of course she'd believed him. If she'd only taken a peek at that notepad she would have seen the doodles depicting people and animals being consumed by creatures whose only purpose was to consume, or the long letters to beings unknown using words few human tongues could say. But no doubt she would not have understood what she was seeing, in any case. If he had a sense of humour he might say, "It's a letter from my father." But since he had never seen the utility of humour he did not.

Angie had never asked him why they had to travel so far just to wait for the results of some job applications, especially when there were no jobs at Crossroads or anywhere within a hundred miles of that place. He hadn't even bothered to concoct a story because he'd been so sure she wouldn't ask. This woman was making him lazy.

Once or twice he'd told her directly how stupid she was. She'd looked as if she might break apart. Part of him wanted to feel sorry for what he'd said. Part of him wanted to know what the feeling was like, to feel like your face was going to break. But he didn't have the capacity in him. He supposed some people were born victims. And some people were born like him. *Predator* was a good word for people like him, he supposed. There were a great many predators on this planet.

Their two kids had been climbing the walls. Not literally, of course, but that's the way Angie had expressed it. The only place they had to play was the motel parking lot. As far as he was concerned they should let them loose out there – the children could learn a few lessons about taking care of themselves. If they saw a car coming, let them learn to get out of the way. But Angie wouldn't allow it. He was their father, of course – they had his wise blood in their bodies. He could have insisted. But sometimes you let the mother have the final say where the care of the children is concerned.

Walker's own mother let him wander loose from the time he was six years old – that had been her way. It didn't mean she had no caring in her for him. Actually, he had no idea how she felt. She could have felt anything, or nothing. That was simply the way she was.

He'd never met his father, but he felt as if he knew him – certainly he could feel him. She'd lain with a hundred men or more, so it could have been anyone, or anything he supposed. But Walker felt he'd know his father if he saw him, however he manifested himself. It never bothered him. And if he did see this creature, his father, he wasn't even sure he'd say hello. But he might have questions. He might want a sample of his blood. He might want to see what happened if he poured his father's blood onto the grounds of the Crossroads.

The boy – they'd named him Jack – threw something at the girl. Gillian, or Ginger, depending on the day. Walker had never quite found a name he'd really liked for her, or even remembered from one day to the next. Walker didn't know what the boy tried to hit her with – he never saw anything. He didn't watch them very closely. And there was no sense in asking them – they were both little liars. That was okay with him – in his experience most human beings didn't respond well to the truth in the best of cases. These children were probably better off lying.

But Angie wouldn't stop. "They're going to grow up to be monsters! Both of them! Jack slaps her. Gillian kicks him. This crap goes on all day! Do you even care how they might turn out?"

"Of course I care," he'd lied. Because it would have been inconvenient if Angie had fully understood his basic attitude toward their children. He couldn't have her attempting to take the children and leave before things had completed. "I'll talk to them." The relief in her face almost made him smile.

The children looked up at him sullenly, defiantly. This was good, he thought. Most children were naturally afraid of him. "Jack, what did you throw at her?" he asked.

"It was a rock," Gillian or Ginger said. Walker slapped her hard across the face, her little head rocking like a string puppet's.

"I asked Jack," he explained.

She didn't cry, just stared at him, a bubble of blood hanging from one nostril.

"It was a rock," Jack said quietly. Walker examined his son's face. Something dark and distant appeared to be swimming in his light green eyes. Angie's eyes were also that colour, but Walker had never seen anything swimming there.

"Would it have made you feel badly if you had really hurt her?"

Jack stared up at him dully. Then the boy turned to his sister and they looked at each other. Then they both looked back up at Walker.

"I don't know," Jack replied.

"If you continue to behave this way where other people can see you, eventually you may be detained and imprisoned. It's your decision, but that is something to think about. Right now, you are upsetting your mother. You do not want to do that. You upset her and she becomes troublesome for me. You do not want that, do you understand?" Both children nodded. "Very well, go play quietly for awhile. Stay out of my field of vision."

After they left Walker saw that a couple of drops of his daughter's blood were resting on top of the sand. He kicked at them and they scurried away.

When they'd first checked in the Crossroads had been practically empty, just a single elderly couple with a camper who'd checked out the very next day. But since then a series of single guests and families had wandered in, almost unnoticeable at first since they mostly came in during the night, but the last couple of days there had been a steady stream, so by week's end the motel was full. Still, more people came into the parking lot, or stopped in the empty land around the building, some on foot with backpacks who set up small tents or lean-tos, others in cars they could sleep in. Despite their numbers these new visitors were relatively quiet, remaining in their rooms or whatever shelter they'd managed, or gathering casually to talk quietly amongst themselves. Many had no particular focus to their activities, but some could not keep their eyes off that horizon far beyond the motel, with its vague suggestion of dunes and mesas shimmering liquidly in the heat.

"Why are they all here?" Angie eventually came around to asking.

"They're part of some travelling church group. They'll be on their way after they rest, I'm told."

For the first time she looked doubtful about one of his improvised explanations, but she said nothing.

As more people gathered his son and daughter became steadily more subdued, until eventually they were little more than phantom versions of their former selves, walking slowly through the crowd, looking carefully at every one of them, but not speaking to them, even when some of the newcomers asked them questions.

This continued for a day or two, and although Walker could see a great deal of nervousness, a great many anxious gestures and aimless whispering, and although his sense of the bottled-up energy contained in this one location unexpectedly made his own nerves ragged, there was no explosion, and no outward signs of violence. Some of the people in the crowd actually appeared to be paralysed. One young, dark-bearded fellow had stood by the outside elbow of the motel for two days, Walker was sure, without moving at all. Parts of the man's cheeks had turned scarlet and begun to blister.

He noticed that the longer the people stayed here, interacting, soaking up one and another's presence, the more they appeared to resemble one another, and him, and his children, as if they had gathered here for some large family reunion. Walker wondered if he were to cut one of them whether their blood would also walk, and he was almost sure it would.

He took his morning barefoot walk – why his own feet hadn't burned he had no idea; he didn't really even care to know – by the invisible pool. An old woman crouched there like some sort of ape. At first he thought she was humming, but as he passed her he realised she was speaking low and rapidly, and completely incomprehensibly. She sounded vaguely Germanic, but he suspected her speech wasn't anything but her own spontaneous creation.

He gradually became aware of a rancid stink carried on the dry desert wind. Looking around he saw that those who had sought shelter outside the poor accommodations of the Crossroads were up and about, although moving slowly. When he went toward them, it quickly became obvious that they were the source of the smell.

A tall woman with long dark hair approached him. "You seem familiar," she said weakly, and raised her hand as if to touch his face. He stepped back quickly, and it wasn't because he now saw that a portion of the left cheek of her otherwise beautiful face appeared melted, but because he'd never liked the idea of strangers touching him. He knew this made little sense because he'd always been a lone figure among strangers. Angie, certainly, was a stranger as far as he was concerned, and his children Jack and (what was the girl's name?) little better.

Then an elderly man appeared beside her, and a young boy, all with bubbling, disease-ridden skin. Walker darted past them, and into a crowd of grasping, distorted hands, blisters bursting open on raw, burnt-looking skin. He squirmed his way out, but not without soiling himself with their secretions.

He felt embarrassed to be so squeamish. Was he any different than they? He'd seen the dark familiar shapes swimming in their eyes like the reflections of still-evolving life forms. Clearly, he was no longer alone in the world, because what he had seen in them was both familiar and vaguely familial. But it was an uncomfortable, even an appalling knowledge.

He was some kind of mongrel, a blending of two disparate species, and yet so were they. He doubted any of them had known their fathers. His own children were their blood kin, but at least they knew their father.

The two most familiar children came out of the crowd and gazed at him, their faces running with changes. He felt a kind of unknowable loss, for a kind of kinship that had never been completely his, for the simpler Sunday afternoon picnic world of humanity that would now be forever out of his reach.

Angie came outside for her children then, bellowing the dumb unmelodic scream of a despairing cow, and he struck her down with indifferent blows from both suddenly-so-leaden hands. She had been his last possible door into humanity, and he had slammed her irrevocably closed. Her children looked on as unconcerned as an incursion of sand over an abandoned threshold.

And now they've come out of those distant mesas and deserts, on their astounding black wings, on their thousand-legged spines, their mouths open and humming like the excited blood of ten thousand boiling insects, like the secret longings of the bestial herd, like his blood preparing to leave the confines of vein, like his blood crawling out of the midnight of collective pain, the liquid horizon unfolding.

And out of that shimmering line the fathers come to reclaim their children, the keepers of their dark blood. And Walker must collapse in surrender as these old fathers out of the despairing nights of human frailty, in endless rebellion from the laws of the physical universe, these fathers, these cruel fathers, consume.

GLEN HIRSHBERG

His Only Audience

A Normal and Nadine Adventure

GLEN HIRSHBERG'S story collections include *The Janus Tree and Other Stories*, *American Morons* and *The Two Sams*, and have earned him a Shirley Jackson Award and three International Horror Guild Awards.

His most recent novel, *Motherless Child*, originally published by Earthling in 2012, will be reprinted by Tom Doherty Associates/Macmillan in 2014 and followed by two sequels. He is also the author of two previous novels, *The Book of Bunk* and *The Snowman's Children*.

With Peter Atkins and Dennis Etchison, he co-founded the Rolling Darkness Revue, an annual touring show composed of live music, performance and ghost story readings that travels the west coast of the United States each autumn.

"'His Only Audience' appeared originally in *The Raven of October*, the 2012 Rolling Darkness Revue chapbook," explains Hirshberg. "It inaugurated a new, occasional series of occult detective-derived pieces featuring Normal (aka the Collector) and his long-time partner, Nadine.

"That gives me the excuse to write about pretty much everything I love thinking about when I'm not teaching, parenting or writing other stuff. In this case, that means sea stories, crazy collectors and subcultures, disappearing radio signals, music. And people, and their ghosts, of course . . ."

AROUND AND BENEATH them, the houseboat thumped and shuddered, and, as usual on their visits here, Nadine wished the Collector and his client would just turn off the shortwave and sit still for a while. Maybe, instead of hunching forever at the wooden table in this windowless hold, they could try the deck in the starlight, or the porthole down below, and let the world bring its wonders *to* them, for once. All those things down there in the bay, living or just floating. Knocking against hulls. Murmuring hello.

"Got one," Spook said, straightening in his chair as though called to attention. Out of the hiss and static, the spurts of Iranian classical music and snippets of BBC-wherever broadcasts, the dot–dash chirruping from ships so out of time that they still used Morse code as though anyone were out there to receive or translate it, a voice flared. Flickered out. Caught as Spook worked the console knob, locked in on the signal, and held.

Ice-voice. The voice ice would speak in, if ice spoke. Female, if ice had gender.

"*Seven. Three. Six. Eight. Five. No.*" Crackle. Empty frequency. And then again. "*Seven. Three. Six . . .*"

And by the third repetition, as always, Nadine felt herself leaning forward, too, forgetting the bay, uncrossing her legs, lowering her ear toward the receiver with its console knob and compass face, its wooden casing warped and blistered.

"A new one?" she said.

"I think so." Spook grabbed his notebook off the shelf behind him and scrolled quickly through his pages and pages and of charts. Lists, mostly, of all the numbers stations he'd ever located in decades of scouring the shortwave bands. Usually, he could tell just by the voice if he'd heard the signal before, though Nadine wasn't sure how, given that so many of them used identical, inflectionless tones. She wondered if there'd been a voice-over school for numbers stations right after World War II, when they were apparently in actual use, and not just left, forgotten, to bleat their coded messages into the air for absolutely no one. Had there been a Bletchley Park for blankness, where you learned to drain yourself entirely out of your own speech?

When he'd reached the end of his lists, Spook nodded. "Brand new." With his mechanical pencil, he noted down the number string.

"But not your dad's?" Nadine asked.

She'd said it so gently, and still the shadow swept over Spook's lined, sun-mottled, friendly face, the way it did every time anyone asked about his father.

"No," he said, and closed his notebook. Only then did he seem to notice his own posture, the ramrod attention the chanting ice-voice had drawn from him. He shook his head, and the second time he did it, the shadow fell away. "And there I was wondering why they call *me* Spook."

"You never were one, were you?" said the Collector, though his eyes and his attention remained fixed on the radio. Cataloguing, Nadine knew. Storing away information, though God knew into what sub-folder in which drawer in the bottomless pit of a file cabinet that passed for his head.

"Me?" Spook waved a callused hand across his forehead and through his white-grey hair. "I'm a carpenter. Houseboat handyman. That's all I've ever been or wanted to be."

"Son of Spook," Nadine said, even more lightly, and this time, Spook laughed.

"Son of Spook. Hey. Sorry. What are we drinking tonight?"

"Something Belgian," blurted the Collector, as though beating a televised *Jeopardy* contestant to an answer.

Nadine rolled her eyes. "Wow, Mr Smartie, you're on fire tonight. Now let's try, Something More Specific for $200?" But she grinned. These evenings, after all, were rare in their lives. Spook did, technically, qualify as a client. But unlike virtually everyone else who employed the Collector, he didn't want to beat anybody to a rediscovery or hoard away something esoteric. He simply wanted to hear, and maybe locate, numbers stations, and maybe one day pinpoint the one that had beamed out coded orders to his father the spy throughout the Cold War, and then brought him back. Home, but blank. Even more than he wanted that, though, Spook wanted company. And he served them Belgian beer, and sometimes warm Camembert. Which, in terms of her life with the Collector, almost qualified these evenings as social occasions. Couples Club.

"Rodenbach, I think," Spook said. "It's a Rodenbach night." And he smiled at Nadine, at the Collector, at his radio – which, okay, would have to do as Spook's contribution to the Couples part of the proceedings, but still – and got up.

"Can I hunt for a new one while you're gone?" said the Collector, gesturing at the radio.

"Sure. Like this." Spook put his hand on the knob at the base of the compass face, pushed it in, and started to twirl it. Spats of static filled the air. Boat-chirp. Guitar strum. BBC again, Arabic voice, static-spat—

"Wait," the Collector snapped. "Go back."

"Back where?"

But the Collector had seized the knob. When he'd finished futzing, he sat up, raised an eyebrow at Nadine, and she smiled in surprise.

"I love this song," she said.

"Me, too," he said. "So there."

"You love songs? There are songs you love? Or recognise as songs?" She was laughing, reaching for his hand when he burst out singing.

> *"She was gone when I first met her*
> *couldn't even find the floor."*

Nadine joined in, and to her amazement, Spook did, too.

> *"I helped her out, I brought her down*
> *but when I did she wasn't there anymore."*

Beer, she was thinking. *Group singalongs, to songs they had in common.* Maybe she and the Collector still lived on this planet, after all. They were positively harmonising as that exquisite verse arced towards its conclusion, their voices hitting the rise right on time at

"*Swept off down the . . .*"

Except that the voice on the radio *didn't* rise. It plunged, instead, off that so-familiar melody and down to a low, droning drawl, where it rooted furiously in a furrow of words Nadine had never heard before, gorgeous and wrong and strange. Something about "*mist in the bones*", about "*the heat under midnight*". Then – like a rabbit chased from a garden – it skipped from the song entirely, and the music grooved out on a skewed, broken acoustic guitar arpeggio. The Collector swivelled the volume almost all the way to silent.

"You knew that was going to happen," Nadine said, her voice somewhere between amazed and accusatory.

"I thought it might," said the Collector, fast, his fingers drumming the table. "Actually, I didn't really think so. I mean, frankly, I thought that particular search for that particular client was never going to . . . Spook, where's that signal coming from? Can we locate it?"

"You can if I'm involved," said Spook, beer and group singalong immediately discarded in favour of quest. Because he and the Collector were the same species, Nadine realised. And here she was sitting forward. Watching what Spook did. Calling up from her own formidable memory everything she already knew about Robert William Guthrie, and pulling the RAM-crammed netbook she never left home without from her nightpack. Because she was one of them, too, apparently. *Had she always been? Or had she changed when the Collector had – metaphorically – spirited her off? Like a selkie?*

From the long bookshelf above the galley sink, Spook had taken down some sort of cloth-bound reference volume.

He opened it and started flipping pages, asking, "What band? Can you read the number off the dial? I need the whole set of digits."

But when the Collector told him, he glanced up. "You sure?"

The Collector actually twitched in his impatience, like a bird dog with the scent in his nostrils, the leash all but strangling him.

"It's local," said Spook.

"How local?"

"Next door, practically. Right there." Spook gestured toward the front of the boat, the open water, as if pointing to a precise spot. "Hang on." He stood up, popped a latch on what Nadine had always taken for a breadbox – partly because it had the word BREADBOX engraved across the front – and drew down an impressively ridiculous piece of machinery. Another radio-type thing, two mini-dish antennae on top, some lights, the words COAST GUARD ISSUE stamped on the side. When he flicked a switch, the lights blinked.

"You *are* a spook."

Spook swivelled another dial, and the dish-antennae rotated. Rotated some more. The lights flashed. "Hello," he said, and looked up. "Not even fifteen miles out. Straight toward the Farallons."

"We need a boat," said the Collector, standing. "How do we get a boat?"

Spook glanced meaningfully around him. The Collector and Nadine caught the meaning at the same moment.

"This thing actually floats?" Nadine said.

"What would be the point of living on a houseboat if it didn't?" Spook was already halfway up the little stairway toward the deck, the Collector right behind him, leaving Nadine, for a single moment, alone in the hold. Rodenbach forgotten in the fridge. Robert William Guthrie song still echoing in her head, in her companions' voices.

"Having a house, maybe?" she murmured wistfully. To no one. "On a boat?"

Instead, she'd be spending the evening chugging out to sea, following the only known Pacific migration path of the giant Great Whites, but not to see them, either. No, she'd be chasing a signal, in the hopes of finding yet another arcane, lost thing for somebody else.

And that, she'd learned, years ago, turned out to be just how she liked it.

Grabbing her netbook off the table as the engines rumbled to life, she joined Spook and the Collector topside. The houseboat shrugged free of its moorings and slowly, cumbersomely – like a manatee, a domesticated one, something a Farallon Great White would swallow without even slowing – shuddered out of its berth and into the open water of the bay.

Earlier, on the way down from their cottage in the low Sierras to the harbour, both she and the Collector had remarked on the unusual absence of fog this night, the shadowy green of the grass valleys and then the ocean spreading unchecked all the way to the horizon and over it. But the moment the houseboat cleared the harbour's headland, with its automated light flashing clear and white into the dark, the first wisps of mist rose in their wake. By the time they were three miles out, the northern California coast had vanished behind them, and the rumble of the boat's engines had gone muffled, sunk into itself, as though swaddled in gauze. The mist wasn't particularly thick, and it wasn't cold, exactly. But the sensation it gave Nadine, wriggling along her skin and into her pores, proved no less unpleasant just because it was familiar. She'd last experienced it more than a decade ago, back in County Clare, on one of those winter nights when the fog streamed off Galway Bay and over the hillocks and all the way inland, causing this exact same painless ache. This dry damp. Even as a child, it had made her feel far from home. Long before she'd left.

Spook switched on an overhead flood, cut the speed, checked their course a lot. Once, he sent the Collector below to make sure the signal was still broadcasting. When the Collector assured him it was, he nodded.

"Be alongside him in twenty minutes. Maybe less. As long as we don't accidentally run him over."

Nadine held up the netbook. "Anything I can poke around for? Want to tell me what you heard?"

"Same thing you did," said the Collector, staring into the fog as though he were translating it.

"Right. But it meant something else to you."

"Not to me. To our client."

"Are you really going to make me do this one question at a time again?"

The Collector didn't look her way or anything. But he did smile. "Sorry. Habit. Plus, it's kind of fun hearing you get—"

"I thought we didn't do music people."

"It's not that we don't do them. It's that we're almost never what they need. I mean, either they're hunting rare pressings or stolen tapes or whatever, and those things usually aren't that hard to track, and then it's just a question of what someone's willing to pay. So, snore. Or else they're hunting something they've heard about, or been told stories about, and those almost always turn out to *be* stories. Apocryphal concerts, or mythical surprise shows no one actually saw but everyone somehow *knows* occurred. I really thought this was one of those. I mean, it's been years."

"At least eight, right?"

Now, the Collector did look at her. "How the hell did you know that?"

Nadine sighed. "Because I don't know about it. So, pre-me."

"Oh, yeah." His grin, she knew, was neither apology nor even acknowledgement. But there was love in it. Sometimes.

"Anyway," she prompted.

"You'd have liked this guy. Super-passionate Robert William Guthrie-freak."

"Aren't all Robert William Guthrie freaks super—"

"Yeah. But this guy . . . I mean, he built a tower on top of his house. An actual turret, so he could go up and lock a trap door and be alone with the music. He calls it the Tower of Song."

"*Do dum dum dum, de doo dum dum*," Nadine hummed, and when the Collector just stared at her, she drummed her hands against her legs. "Oh for God's sake, never mind, go on." Then she wrapped her arms to her chest as the tendrils of mist wriggled in deeper. Spook just peered straight ahead, looking credibly captain-like. That was comforting, anyway, though the waters over the side, under the grey-white mist, looked nowhere near green now, but black. Opaque. Probably, they were empty. Not full of monsters.

"The way this guy talks about Robert William Guthrie performing . . ."

"Most people hate Robert William Guthrie performing. Because he never just sings the songs the way people love hearing them. That's what I've always heard."

"Right. That's what this guy says. But he says people just don't understand. He says Guthrie's on this eternal quest. Because he knows there is a *right* way – and only one – for every single word, in every song, on any given night. The way those specific syllables, in that particular rhythm, to that individual tune, in *his* voice, are meant to sound *that day*. But he says catching all of that at the same time, in one performance, is like chasing a butterfly. Trying to get it to land on you. Some nights, it's there, for a single second, and then . . ."

The first bump against the bottom of the boat did little more than surprise them, knock Nadine sideways half a step, and cause her to clutch the netbook. And that was good, because the second bump rocked the ship fifteen degrees sideways, dropped the Collector to one knee, and caused Spook to hiss in surprise.

"The hell . . ." he said, straightening, standing on tiptoes to see over the bow. The Collector had straightened, turned toward Nadine, and his expression proved so completely clueless, so astonished – as though he'd only just remembered or maybe realised he was on a boat – that she relaxed. A bit.

"Was that a log?" she asked Spook. "Shark?"

He didn't answer right away, just held the wheel, watched the water. Every few seconds, it bumped against them, sometimes hard. Never too hard. Eventually, he shrugged. "It's just the water. Water's a little riled up. Just some chop."

Which didn't sound all that unusual to Nadine. She'd never seen any ocean without chop. And so while she noted that barely-there murmur of uncertainty in Spook's voice, she was able to make herself ignore it.

"Should be there in five," Spook said into the mist. "Maybe less."

The boat heaved again. Not too hard.

"So, our man," Nadine prodded the Collector. "Robert William Guthrie guy."

"Oh," said the Collector, blinked, and was off again. "Like I said, Nadine. You'd love hearing him talk. I'm not really a musico, as you know, but this guy made me get it. He made me understand. He talked about this one, legendary version – the version we just heard, I'm pretty sure – that Guthrie did of that song once, on some radio show, when he was very young, and then discarded for some reason. And it's never been heard since. By anyone. He says that when Guthrie gets it right, you can just *hear* the magic. And when you sit with this guy, our client, and you listen to him explain, you really can hear—"

"You can't, though," Nadine said, and the boat bumped, and Spook swore. The Collector wasn't surprised at her interruption. Or annoyed. He was waiting to hear. Because he was much more interested in what she might say than whether they might drown. Which was why they really were a team, as well as a couple. A little warmed, though no less damp or anxious, Nadine went on. "Not really. I know those guys. I've always known them. They're all over Ireland. They explain it to you. They point out the moment, they get all excited. They get so excited, you think maybe you really *do* hear something. But really, I think they just make you want to. Because *they* do, so badly. But the magic in music . . . it's not just in the singer. Not any singer. Not in any one way of singing, on one night, for everyone. It can't be. It's too simple. But maybe—"

"There," said Spook, and right as he said it, the boat – as though juddering down a launch into a glassy pond – levelled, and the bumping stopped. Moments ago, Nadine realised, without being told and on instinct, Spook had cut the motors. They floated now, so slowly, toward the little sailboat just taking shape in the mist. Seemingly forming out of it. "Will you look at that . . ."

It looked tiny, drifting there. Very nearly still. Its deck empty and silent, its mast tall, green sail slumping in the absence of wind, like some kid's toy sucked out to sea. As the mist closed around and behind them, blotting out the entire rest of the world, Nadine felt a shudder slide up her back, at least as much of awe as anxiety. As though she were on the Ark, and discovering the olive tree sticking up from the deluge. Abruptly, she turned around. Mist or no mist, she could see the water through which they'd come, swelling and flattening and slapping over itself as it churned.

She gestured toward the sailboat. "Isn't that awfully small to be out here?"

Spook, she saw, was watching the water, too. The glassiness beneath them, so still it seemed frozen over. The roil everywhere else.

"No," he said slowly. "But I see what you mean."

"It's like a hurricane," said Nadine. "Like we've reached the eye of one."

"A hurricane *in* the water?"

"Yeah. I don't know. Can that happen?"

"Sssh," the Collector snapped, and they shushed, and their houseboat drifted closer. And then they heard it. Somehow – because of the open air, the ocean, the mist, maybe – what reached Nadine's ears sounded remarkably like the signals that had streamed from Spook's shortwave. Same tinny compression. Same sense of travelling unimaginable thousands of miles on a rush of air. Even though this sound came from right in front of them.

Hands on the bow, head tilted forward to listen, Nadine felt the music lap against her. Flow inside. Felt her fingers tingle, then her spine. "Muddy Waters," she murmured. "Wow." And she listened. "Really early. God, so early. Listen – hear that? This has got to be like one of the first times with the amp, when everyone first heard that . . ." She looked up, at the Collector. "Unless this *is* the first time. But that recording's supposedly . . . okay, who *is* this guy?"

"Hallo, the ship," Spook called out, and Nadine froze, half-expecting rifle shots. Pirates boiling out of the hold. Jolly Roger flags, peg-legs.

Then she turned on Spook. "*'Hallo, the ship?'* People really say that?"

Spook's smile could be so shy, sometimes. A good fifty years younger than he was, somehow. "I'm pretty sure *somebody* says it."

But nobody answered. In surprising silence for such a long, lumbering craft, Spook's houseboat glided up to the little sailboat. With one more look toward Nadine – for approval, she realised, because like the Collector, he actually thought of *her* as captain, in his way – he took the coil of rope he'd already lifted from some deck-top receptacle, tossed it over the sailboat's rail, and in a few efficient passes of his hands, knotted the crafts together.

"How about, *'Permission to come aboard?'*" Nadine murmured to Spook.

"I don't know," said Spook. "A little *Star Trek*?"

"What's wrong with *Star Trek*?" said the Collector, and Nadine laughed, and Spook, too, and then Spook actually did it. Yelled it out.

And the music went silent. But just for a second. And only because a song had ended. Almost immediately, another one started. Some 1930s crooning thing. Violins warbling. Voice floating up from the warble and crackle to drift on the mist, hollow as mourning dove call, and all the lonelier out here, in the sea mist, amid what Nadine realised really might be albatross keening.

Almost until the end of that song, they waited. The music set all three of them swaying on that still water. If they stayed any longer, Nadine thought, the Collector might even ask her to dance.

Instead, he said, "I'm thinking permission granted."

"Normal . . ." Nadine warned, but the Collector ignored her.

"In fact, I'd say we were *invited*."

And with that, he stepped onto the deck of the sailboat, just as the crooning song melted into its own wavering. To be followed, instantly, by some spry banjo hurtling off at breakneck speed, with a whistling guy bobbing around on its wake like a water-skier.

"Maybe it's automated," Spook said.

"Maybe we should find out before your man there decides he can hornpipe," said Nadine, gesturing at the Collector, who'd already swung himself over some coiled ropes and was making for a small set of steps leading down into the sailboat's cabin. He was tapping his hands to the beat of the banjo. Or the thrum of the search.

Carefully, Nadine swung her own legs over the houseboat rail and onto the sailboat. Spook followed, and Nadine experienced a momentary but powerful misgiving. She almost asked him to go back. Just in case this *was* something pirate-y. Or stranger than it already seemed.

But in a different way than the Collector, Spook was in his element. Hunched, scuttling forward, his feet making almost no sound on the dry, nearly bare deck. Playing spook. Being his dad.

Neither scuttling nor hunching – but keeping her feet quiet, all the same – Nadine joined her companions, who stood together at the mouth of the stairwell. Whatever was down there, she saw right away, it was candlelit. The light warm and orange, but twitching, some. Wavering, like the voice of the crooner. Melting, constantly, into itself.

"Do we go down?" the Collector whispered, as if he weren't already on the first step.

The voice from below boomed in the near-silence, as though they'd hit a depth charge. "You've come *that* far. Seems ridiculous to stop now."

Right, great evening, thanks for having us, Nadine thought, but didn't even bother to open her mouth. The Collector had already skipped off down the stairs. Pulling her with him. Unless that was her own curiosity.

At a paint-spattered, grooved, and warped wooden table, behind a disappointingly Best Buy-looking set of broadcasting equipment and a cassette deck and a laptop and a lamp and one not-so-Best Buy reel-to-reel, sat a grey-haired black man in a white T-shirt. With a Jolly Roger on it. If he so much as glanced to see who'd boarded his boat, Nadine didn't spot it.

"We did call out," the Collector said, moving toward the table. "Didn't you hear us?"

The man shrugged. "Knew you weren't the Coast Guard. Probably weren't a shark. Didn't see much point in breaking the flow of my show." He had thin shoulders and even thinner arms, strung with veins that stretched, like strings down guitar necks, to surprisingly muscular wrists. And huge hands. Nadine stared at the hands as they flicked over the knobs of his board, cued up a track on the laptop, set it playing. Grimy, grinding mid-50s blues.

"They call me the Collector," said the Collector, and stuck out his hand, which struck Nadine as a bad idea.

But the man at the table just looked up. "Do they, now. Well. Always happy to meet a brother."

"And you?"

"Me? I'm the pirate radio DJ of your dreams. If you have proper dreams. And they have music in them."

All around the cabin, Nadine realised – all the way up the walls, built into the spaces where storage cabinets and utensil racks and life-vest hangars should have been – were narrow wooden shelves crammed to capacity with cassettes in clear cases. Their sides labelled with identical strips of red tape that caught the flickery light. Glowed, faintly. Black numbers stencilled into them. LA82235. BD112460.

Abruptly, Nadine glanced at Spook. Who'd seen them, all right. Was leaning closer. Looking for patterns he recognised. Yet again, that *sensation* wisped across and through her. As though she herself were mist, and the air was moving through her. Reshaping her.

Not pleasant.

Reaching behind him, Radio-man selected a case without seeming to look, popped out the cassette, and slid it into the deck. Spook – target acquired, sneaking about apparently finished for the evening – had taken up post against the doorframe through which they'd entered. He looked bored. Behind him, the flickering light seemed to catch and flit in the clear plastic cassette cases. The Collector had plunked himself on the table's edge, gaze flashing everywhere. Up the walls, over the broadcasting equipment, into the eyes of Radio-man.

Whose own eyes had levelled on the Collector's. Had not, as far as Nadine seen, left his face.

From the speakers mounted into the wall, thick, echoing Fender Rhodes chords sounded. The chords brooding, strange, not quite minor or major, the rhythm steady and slow and relentless as hammer-on-railroad-ties. And then that voice. Wavery as the candlelight, cartoon-deep, swooning. Dracula minus fangs and even hypnotic power. Lovelorn and hopeless, and so much sexier for it, at least if you were an Irish lass, attacked from all sides by pub versions of "The Fields of Athenry", out for a drive through the empty moonscape of the Burren with the boy from NUI Galway with the green flecks in his eyes.

"Holy shit, Blaine Fury," she murmured, then stopped. Leaned into the table, listening more closely. *Not a song she knew? There* were *no Blaine Fury songs she didn't know. And that whistling in the background. Not human whistling. Wind. Wind with snow. And no band at all?* Her mouth opened. To breathe, not to speak, and then she spoke, too. "Blaine Fury in Montreaux."

For the first time since the Collector had introduced himself, Radio-man's eyes left his face. Moved to Nadine's.

"Very, very good. *Not* home base for most of my listeners, I have to say . . ."

"1977," she said. "December? January?" Then her eyes leapt to the open cassette case. The red label. Which made total sense, now. BF122677. She did note, in some corner of her astonished brain, that the case was no longer glowing. But she didn't process that then. "My god, December 26th? What is that, the week after Mick stole his wife? The *day* after? Jesus, I heard about this session. Read about it. Him holed up in that castle with that guitar player he wouldn't even let in the studio, just playing and playing and playing. Songs he'd half-finished, other people's songs. But . . . I read he didn't even record it. Not one note."

"Yes," said Radio-man. "That's what you've read." And for the first time, he smiled. Strange smile. No glee in it. Not the kind you'd expect from a collecting man with a literal boat-full of treasures thousands of people might have wept . . . paid . . . bled to get their hands on. There was pride in the smile, all right. But not that sort.

Those specific syllables, she thought. *That particular tune, on any given day. Like chasing a butterfly . . .*

She stared around the rows and rows of plastic cases, their glow so faint. Like tea-lights. While something tickled, nagged, inside her. "So . . . what you collect . . . what you play . . . are *perfect* moments? There really is such a thing?"

Even before Radio-man spoke, the Collector started knocking his knuckles on the table. Not in rhythm with the music, but rapping them down, which drew Nadine's eyes to his face. His eyes narrowed, focused over her shoulder toward the stairwell or maybe nowhere at all. Lips compressed, head half-tilted in a shake.

Because she'd missed something.

Radio-man had pushed back from his broadcasting equipment, folded his veiny arms across his chest. Even sitting, he looked tall as a telephone pole. *And as dangerous to touch?*

"Don't know about that," he said. "No, what I collect are . . . hmm . . . *awakenings*. I think that's a word for it."

"*First* moments," said the Collector. And rapped his knuckles on the table hard enough that even Spook, gazing up the stairs at the mist and moonlight, glanced over.

And then Nadine had it. Knew what was bothering her. That tea-light glow and flicker, everywhere. But no tea lights. Or candles, either. Her eyes flicked back to the open Blaine Fury cassette case. Plain plastic. Not glowing. Which meant the glow . . . that low, lovely red light . . .

Radio-man's attention had snapped back to the Collector. And now, his voice swelled. Not so much in volume, but with a force that could have been joy. It approximated joy, Nadine thought, hand rising to her heart, which was doing its own rapping against her ribs. Also, she seemed to fighting back tears. "For them. For each of them. Yes. The moment they . . ." He gave a little grunt. It could have been throat-clearing, but came out as a giggle. ". . . *discover* . . . just what they have in them."

More tabletop-rapping. Hard. Pointless. Not like the Collector at all. With a sigh, he stopped, looked away from the stairs and back to Radio-man. "What you gave them," he said.

For Nadine, three things happened at the same time. Her mind went wild, thinking about hurricanes in the water, moments like butterflies, those gorgeous voices in that perfect mist, the glow in this room. Also, she started shivering, deep down in her shoulders, and couldn't get that to stop. And finally, she realised why the Collector was knocking. And why that wasn't working.

"Well, now," said Radio-man.

"Leaving only the question of what they offer in trade."

Unfolding his arms, Radio-man laid those huge palms on the table. Fanned out his fingers, like a poker player who'd been called. And then he really did smile.

"Wow," said the Collector. For the moment, he was genuinely amazed, head-over-heels for the thousandth time for the moment of discovery. Which always left him vulnerable.

"Normal," Nadine murmured, moving closer, trying to get his attention. Which was hopeless, just then.

"So, wait. Let me get this straight. There really *is* a crossroads? I mean, is that what they do? Meet you at the crossroads, go down on their knees?"

"We can do the Crossroads," Radio-man said. "I can come to your living room. Your rented castle in Montreux." He glanced at Nadine, halting her advance toward the table, and winked. "Hell, we can meet at 7/11 if that's most convenient."

Carefully, slowly, Nadine started edging forward again. Feet unsteady beneath her. Heart thudding. But as she did, her eyes leapt back to the tapes. The red glow radiating, faintly, from every single one of them. From *the tape itself*. From whatever it was this man had taken from all of these people and threaded onto the spools. She found herself studying the initials and dates, realised she knew or could guess them all. Because every person collected on these walls had gone on to become someone collected on walls. Every single one.

"And in return you get . . . their souls?" the Collector asked.

Radio-man snorted. "I don't exactly *get* anything. I accept what they offer. I remove what they no longer need. Or can't have."

Nadine had reached the Collector's side. Casually, so casually, she let her arms dangle down the back of his chair. Unlike the Collector's, her taps barely qualified as sound. She didn't need them to be sound. She just needed him to register that they were there. Understand what he'd been doing wrong. So he could finish whatever the hell he'd started, and then get them out of here, preferably with as little as possible *removed*.

"So, their souls. Like I said." The Collector was still focused entirely on his conversation. Paying no attention to Nadine whatsoever.

Radio-man rested his chin in those tremendous hands and pursed his lips. "I don't think they'd say that. I think they'd say their *souls* – whatever those are – are right there." He gestured at his speakers. The music streaming from them. "Wouldn't you?"

Partly to cover any noise she might make, but also because a sudden and profound disappointment had welled up, seemingly out of the floor of the cabin, and flooded her, Nadine said, "That can't be it."

For the second time, Radio-man lifted his eyes right to her. Nadine had to keep herself from shrinking back. The guy had barely moved. And yet the movement had surprised her, like the slither of a downed power-line. At least he was watching her, now. Not her hands. Not the Collector's face as he realised what she was doing. She finally felt that happen, in his spine. As shivers shook her again, and her eyes welled. *Beautiful Blaine Fury. So alone. The Heathcliff of her stupid, teenage dreams . . .*

"What can't, child?" The "child" not sarcastic, not even nasty. "And why can't it?"

"Music," she murmured. Made herself speak louder, because the Collector had lifted his own hands back to the table. Started tapping again. Still not in rhythm with the song on the radio. But in a rhythm of its own, now. *Dot-dot-dash. Dot-dot-dot-dash.* And even as she continued speaking, Nadine felt Spook look up. Comprehending, at last, that the Collector was communicating with him. Trying to tell him something. "Inspiration. Every great note anyone's ever played. That . . . it can't just come from you. I don't believe it."

Cocking his veiny arms behind his head, Radio-man barked out a laugh. "Good. Because I never said it. Who said anything about *all*? I'm just talking about these." And he gestured around him at the walls.

Dot-dash-dash. Dot-dot-dot . . .

"The ones who want it so badly, it's like a whistle in their blood. Like teeth in their hearts. Bites them every single time they breathe. The ones who want it like that, and don't quite have it. Or they have too much of . . . something else . . ." And there it was again. That smile. And this time, Nadine realised what it was, other than pride, that made the smile so unsettling. So *wrong*.

It was the kindness in it. Where no kindness should, or seemed, to be.

"Those are my charges," said Radio-man. "Children, almost." And then he glanced down, abruptly, at the Collector. At the same moment Nadine did. Because he'd realised, just as she had, that the knocking had stopped.

And because he was looking at the Collector, he didn't see – somehow missed – what Nadine glimpsed, out of the farthest corner of her eye. The lightning snatch of Spook's fingers. The single cassette disappearing into the pocket of his coat.

"Their souls, you mean," said the Collector. Fast. *To distract.*

Leaning across his mixing board, hands splayed, Radio-man half-rose. Like a panther coming out of his crouch, and Nadine grabbed at the Collector's arm to pull him away.

But the man didn't rise. Just stared. "That word again."

"You have a better one?"

"I think we should go, now," Nadine murmured, tugging at the Collector's sleeve. Nodding over her shoulder toward Spook. "Want to go get the boat ready?"

"Oh," said Spook. "Sure. See ya." And without so much as a nod, quick and sudden, he scampered up the steps onto the deck of the sailboat.

And Radio-man just let him go. Seemed to be thinking, still. "It's not that at all. No. It's really more . . ." Then he waved one huge hand over his equipment. "Like an extra antenna. Or, not extra. The one you're mostly born with. That allows us to . . . pick up signals, yes I like this." He was nodding, grinning. "To hear the people around us. Immerse in lives not our own. A valuable bit of ourselves, I admit, but if what you want, in your very core . . ." He stopped grinning, then. Pinned the Collector, half out of his seat, to his spot, and Nadine, halfway to the stairs, to hers. ". . . in your *soul* . . . If what you want is to pull down *other* voices . . . magic . . . out of the air . . . and then broadcast that out of yourself . . . well. That extra antenna can get in the way, don't you think? Pulling in all those ordinary, aggravating, everyday voices. Connecting you to each bland, dull, daily passing moment . . ."

Then, suddenly, the Collector was up. On the radio, those brooding Fender chords hammered away to nothingness, leaving just the faraway whistle in the Montreux winter wind. And Radio-man glanced down, sat back in his chair, hands flicking over the controls, cueing up another miraculous track. Nadine shot up the stairs. Felt the Collector right behind her. Waited for trailing footsteps. Heard none. Heard none.

"Hurry," she hissed, and was both relieved and amazed to see the Collector surging past her, for once.

"*You* hurry," said the Collector, leaping across the little gap onto the houseboat as Spook worked furiously at the knot he'd made, swung the ropes free. The Collector offered Nadine his hand, and she swatted it away as she jumped across and landed, skidding, beside him.

"You stole from that guy? You don't steal from anyone, ever, and you think *that guy's* an easy first mark?"

"I didn't steal. Spook did."

Nadine punched him in the arm as the houseboat shuddered back to life, the engines *loud* in the preternatural stillness, the motionless water that even their motor didn't seem to stir.

"*That's* what you were telling him to do? Are you crazy? Are you both crazy?"

"Did you get it?" the Collector barked, half-dancing in his excitement. "Spook, you have it?"

"Right here," he said. "Morse code. Genius."

"I thought so," said the Collector, flashed a momentary grin toward Nadine, and snatched the cassette case out of Spook's hands.

Nadine shook her head, shivered yet again. "What is Robert William Guthrie guy paying you, anyway?"

"It's not for him," said the Collector, fumbling with the cassette, clicking it open. "I wouldn't have done it for him."

Then the tape was in his hands. The glow faint, so faint. But there. The little throb occasional, and even fainter. Instinctively, the Collector had cupped his palm, and he held the cassette now as though it were a bird-chick. Only after a long moment of staring at that did Nadine look at the Collector's face and realise he was weeping.

"Normal, what the hell is—"

"He was one of the first who ever came to me, Nadine. One of the very first. And I laughed at him. I remember laughing. He said he was looking for . . . himself . . . that he'd lost a piece to a collector. That if I ever saw it, I would know. And could I please bring it back. God, I don't even know where he is, or if he's still alive. But if he is, and I can bring this—"

"Wouldn't, if I were you," boomed Radio-man's voice, and Nadine whirled, thinking he was right behind her, arms flying up to ward off the blow.

But Radio-man was standing on the deck of his own ship, in the dead water, fully ten feet away already. Giant hands folded behind him. Like wings.

Behind her, Nadine heard Spook gun the engine. But then the Collector said, "Stop."

"Stop?" Nadine snapped.

The Collector stepped to the rail of the houseboat. And Nadine noticed the mist. The way it seemed to slide down the air like raindrops down a windowpane. So that Radio-man and his ship began to blur. Waver.

"Why not?" asked the Collector. "Why shouldn't I return this to the man you took it from?"

"Well," said Radio-man. "Just what do you think will happen when you do? When you return all those ordinary, awful, beautiful, ravenous yearnings the rest of us feel so furiously when we're young . . . but without the lived-in years to temper them? That's a whole lot of hope and hunger you're holding, my friend. What you're *not* holding is the extra time, or wisdom, or experiences that would satisfy or lessen them. Help you learn to live with them, or let them go. The way the rest of us do. You sure you want to give that back?"

And there it was again. One last time, as the mist poured down on him. Filling the space he occupied. That smile. That terrible kindness radiating through it.

"Is that the kind of gift you give to a friend? Do you think, in the end, he'll say he preferred yours to mine?"

The Collector might have answered. Seemed to be starting to. But the first slap of open water banged into the hull then, knocked them sidelong, tilted them forward. And when he and Nadine had righted themselves against the rail and looked up again, there was only mist. Maybe the sailboat was still in it. But the music had gone.

Glancing toward the Collector, Nadine saw him slide the cassette into the case and close it. Then he dropped the case into his pocket. He didn't speak. At the wheel, Spook turned them toward shore. The water seemed to give way around them. Rocking them as they moved, but gently. Plain old sleepy night-time ocean. Seagulls above it. Monsters well down in it.

"What are you going to do?" Nadine murmured. Moved to touch his arm.

The Collector let her. Even squeezed back, once. Then he said, "I think I'm going to go down and listen to the radio."

And Nadine let him. And that's where she found him once they'd moored once more at Spook's berth. Sitting by the shortwave, still tuned to the band where Radio-man's station had been. Listening to the blankness. The spits of static on the empty air.

CLAIRE MASSEY

Marionettes

CLAIRE MASSEY lives in Lancashire, England, with her two young sons. Her short stories have been published in *Best British Short Stories* (Salt), *Murmurations: An Anthology of Uncanny Stories About Birds* (Two Ravens Press), *Still* (Negative Press), *The Screaming Book of Horror* (Screaming Dreams Press) and elsewhere.

"Marionettes" was first published as a limited-edition chapbook by Nightjar Press. Her other Nightjar story, "Into the Penny Arcade", was recently reprinted in Ellen Datlow's *The Best Horror of the Year Volume 5*.

"I have only visited Prague once," admits the author. "The marionette shop in the story was there, but I'm not sure I'd ever be able to find it again."

KARL WANTED TO keep looking for the American bar they'd had breakfast in seven years ago. It had been winter then. They'd stumbled into its warm fug from snow-coated cobbles. It was spring now and dusk.

"Can we just have a quick look in here first?" She lingered in front of the marionette shop's window.

He kept walking. "I'm starving."

"I don't know why we have to find that particular bar."

"Because I liked their omelettes. I don't feel like eating dumplings and cabbage. It's too warm."

The window of the shop was barely lit. A gathering of witches, flanked by shadows, peered out at her. It looked like a page from a storybook. "You wouldn't let me look in here last time."

"We never even saw this shop."

"We did." She moved towards the entrance and ducked slightly, ready to step beneath the jester marionettes strung from the doorframe. "Please."

Her heels clicked on the stone floor. The shop stretched back much further than she'd expected it to, a white walled cavern of dangling heads, legs and arms. It would be impossible to say the shop was empty because there were so many eyes watching her. There was no sign of a shopkeeper, though. No other customers. She glanced behind her and saw Karl's bulk silhouetted in the doorway.

The marionettes hung in tiers. She stuffed her hands into her coat pockets to prevent herself from touching them. Chiselled contours gave them impossibly soft-looking skin that rucked and wrinkled as though it stretched and sagged over bones. Each character's expression looked impermanent, as though it would shift the second you turned away.

"Look at this thing." Karl hovered over an antiquated till.

"Don't touch it." She heard herself use the same tone she would with the children.

There were more witches like the ones in the window, a row of wizened faces. She tried to avoid their canny gaze. There were simpering princes and princesses in medieval dress. Smiling devils thrust out bulbous tongues. But there were contemporary characters too. The attention to detail was amazing. One elderly man in a *cagoule* stooped under the weight of the rucksack on his back. A small boy in a perfectly miniaturised football shirt and shorts had grazed knees.

"Right, come on, you've had a look at the puppets now. We've been in Prague two hours and I've not had a beer. That's madness."

* * *

The next morning she left Karl in bed with his hangover. "We're on holiday, we can actually have a lie-in," he'd said. But when she opened the curtains onto a brilliant blue sky, she wanted to be down on the cobbled street below. She couldn't tell him the thought of wandering the city alone thrilled her. She said she wanted to shop.

It wasn't quite 9:00 a.m. and the Charles Bridge was already swarming with people. Jostled along in the crowd, she could barely see the sparkling surface of the Vltava, or the artists plying their work. Blackened statues punctuated the sky above the heads of American pensioners and Japanese students. There was a bottleneck in front of the statue whose bronze plaque it was lucky to rub if you wanted to return to the city. At the other end of the bridge rose the Old Town Bridge Tower. She remembered the view from the top of it in a biting cold wind. Karl with his coat unzipped wrapping her into it.

She entered the web of streets of Old Town. Streets too narrow for the number of tourists that surged though them. Sometimes she paused before a doorway or a sign and had the impression she'd stood there before, but with Karl, and talked about buying tickets for this recital, wondered where that alleyway led. The jumble of memories was confused by the fact that so many of the shops and passages looked the same, repeating themselves along with the cobbles.

When she came to the marionette shop she stopped. She hadn't realised she was so close to it. She'd already passed several other marionette shops that had cheap-looking Pinocchios in garish costume dangling outside. This was a proper marionette shop. The scene in the storybook window had changed. The gaggle of witches had gone and there were now just two marionettes behind the glass. A man and a woman. They had pale faces and dispirited eyes. They were both dressed in jeans. The man had a black coat on, the woman a green one. She touched her fingers to the glass as she realised it was a perfect, hand-stitched miniature of her own. The woman had brown eyes with dark shadows beneath them. Her eyes. And there was a line etched into her forehead between her brows. Karl always reminded her of that line when he saw her frown. The man had Karl's blue eyes, his mousey, receding hairline. The scar in his eyebrow from a teenage piercing. His marionette had hold of the string just above her marionette's hand.

"It was us."

"Don't be ridiculous."

"It was. They looked just like us."

"No one can carve a puppet that fast." He'd still been in bed when she got back to the hotel and was only just pulling on his jeans. "And anyway there was no one in that shop last night to see us."

"Your marionette had hold of one of my marionette's strings."

"Well that's definitely not us then; you do all the string pulling."

"Just let me show you."

They were planning to go to the castle so they could have lunch in the café with the vines painted on the ceiling, but a quick walk into Old Town wouldn't take long. They joined the stream of tourists on Charles Bridge. As they reached the Old Town Bridge Tower she saw Karl glance up at it but he didn't say anything. Her pace slowed as they wound through the alleyways. What if she'd been wrong? Or made too much of it? He'd love that. She paused outside shops selling wooden toys, saying they should get something for the children, although she knew they'd prefer something overpriced and plasticky from the airport.

"Are we nearly there yet?" He stuck out his bottom lip in perfect imitation of Meg, their youngest.

"It's just down this way. I remember that door." The arched wooden door was studded with ironwork. She didn't admit they'd already passed several very like it.

"Have you got the guidebook with you?" He looked like he'd had enough.

"I didn't pack it. I didn't think we'd need it. That shop wasn't in the book anyway."

They trawled the rambling maze of passages. When they emerged at one point into the Old Town Square, the sudden space and light above made her think of a glade in a forest. There was no escaping the crowds though. They passed the black house with the strange white sgraffito figures on the walls. A knot of people stood before the Astronomical Clock. There was an appreciative exhalation from them as the little Death dinged his bell. The parade of wooden characters began. Karl strode on, past the huts where they'd bought a Christmas bauble that had long since smashed, past the van selling mulled wine – it smelt cloying in the warm spring air.

A horse and carriage made lackadaisical progress round the square. An older couple sat in the back, a blanket on their knees, holding hands.

"It's not this way," she said. "We need to go back into the lanes, back towards the river."

"How can you tell which way the river is?"

She walked ahead and he trailed just behind. When she felt his presence missing, she turned. He'd stopped in front of a window full of tarnished silver jewellery set with garnets, or maybe red glass.

"I bought you a ring from here."

"You did. You didn't want me getting too many ideas, said it could be our engaged to be engaged ring."

"Where is it?"

"I had to stop wearing it when Charlie was born. I was scared I was going to catch him with it." She had no idea where she'd put it. Somewhere safe. "Come on, I give up, let's forget about the marionettes."

When they got to the castle complex and finally found the café with the vines on the ceiling it was closed for refurbishment. Karl didn't say anything, just stalked back in the direction they'd come from. As they passed though the courtyards she tried to take in the grandeur, the Gothic palaces, the ornate mass of St Vitus' Cathedral that towered over everything. "Don't you want to look at any of it before we go?"

"We've seen it all."

Outside the gates he stopped by the low stone wall, the red-roofed, blue-domed, grey-spired city spread out below them. The woods of Petřín Hill rose across from them, dark against the skyline. The Observation Tower pierced the canopy.

"We've stood here before," he said.

"Yes," she said. "We had an argument about a flag." She couldn't remember why. "Does the view look different to you?"

"We were different then."

The next morning she packed their things. She tucked empty bottles into the bin beneath some tissues, trying to disguise the fact Karl had drunk everything in the mini-bar. A tradition. She made the bed. They left their bags at reception saying they'd collect them later.

Karl had suggested they visit Petřín Hill. It was a drizzly day. As they walked through Malá Strana, along an unusually wide road, she didn't want to admit to herself that some of the pale pink and grey stone buildings looked drab. There was graffiti on the wall of a chemist's. Trams whirred past.

Too impatient to wait for the funicular railway, Karl led the way up a steep woodland path. Every so often, he'd pause beside a tree on the pretence he was taking in the view. She remembered him carving their initials. It wasn't into a tree, but a tree stump. She was sure she wouldn't have let him do it on a living tree.

Near the summit, they came to a stop on a grassy knoll. The air was damp and chilled. She wished she had a scarf. The castle was across from them. They were looking at the place where they had stood the day before. She almost wanted to wave to the memory of them, or at the memory of them stood there years before, to distract them from a pointless argument about a flag.

On the descent, they skirted the crenellated Hunger Wall. The whitish stone was stained with patches of lichen. Sodden mulch gave way beneath her feet.

"We should get a drink, something to eat before we have to get back for the transfer," Karl said. He must have given up on the trees.

She left him in a bar. Told him she still needed to pick up something for the children, something really from Prague, not just from the airport. Being pressed between the multitude of bodies and chatter on the streets of Old Town felt almost comforting after the stark quiet of the hill. She ambled round gift shops, fingered bright wooden animals, snow globes with miniature castles inside, tubes of colouring pencils. She eventually settled on a wooden duck and a crocodile. Each was wrapped in its own paper bag. She stuffed them into her handbag, which then wouldn't zip up, and stepped back out into the drizzle.

It seemed she could only find the shop when she wasn't looking for it. She headed down a narrow passage she thought would take her back to the bar and found herself in front of the familiar, dimly lit window. There was now only one marionette behind the glass, hers. She felt a strange release. A nervous weight settled between her chest and her stomach. The eyes of the marionette had more depth to them than paint on wood should allow. Tiny blood vessels crowded the whites at the inner corners. The indent of the frown line on the brow had softened. The arm strings were slack. The hands tucked into the coat pockets. She saw her own reflection overlaying the marionette that in turn mirrored her. She had her hands in her pockets. She stepped back. Where had Karl's marionette gone? Maybe he had got there before her, bought them both as a surprise. He was inside, and any minute now the shopkeeper's hand would reach her marionette from the window to wrap it and place it in the bag alongside his. She shrank back across the alley and shielded herself in the doorway opposite. It was a ridiculous fantasy, but she waited. Rain dripped from the eaves and pattered on the cobbles.

The flow of tourists slowed to a trickle. The shadowy glow in the window faded and she realised that on her previous visits the shop door had never been shut. There had always been marionettes strung up above the doorway. There weren't today. She crossed and tried the handle. It was locked.

The lanes had emptied. Everyone else was sheltering from the rain in warm bars and tea rooms. Faces watched her from the windows. She tried to retrace her steps but the tangle of passageways disorientated her. Her handbag was collecting rainwater. The paper bags inside it were disintegrating and the vividly painted wood of the toys poked through. She jammed them further down and managed to get the bag to zip up. She strode on and tried to sense which way the river lay. There was a door studded with ironwork that she definitely recognised, but she turned a corner and soon met its double. Bewildered, she stepped into another passage. It was as though the daily flood of visitors carved new alleys and inlets into the already labyrinthine folds of Old Town. Her heart beat faster as her heels struck the cobbles.

She found herself standing in front of the window again.

Her marionette remained in isolation on the bare sill, a crowd of shadows behind. Trying to smother her panic, she stared into her own eyes and willed the streets behind her to rearrange themselves, to let her go. Her breath touched the window and for a moment it hung on the other side of the glass.

Each raindrop found a new path down the pane. The string attached to her left hand had been pulled taut so that her palm was raised in a permanent wave. Faces peered in at her, bulbous and lined. A parade of witches and devils. No one waved back. The face she waited for didn't appear. The memory of his features dispersed into the flat grey picture of the world behind the glass. Behind her, the air stirred with silent breath and the beating of wooden hearts. She longed to turn around.

When she was lifted, the tug shivered through her scalp and hands and feet. She was swept across the stone floor to a recess near the back of the shop and strung up beside the elderly man with the rucksack. He was mute company. She could no longer see the window. In time she forgot it was there.

REGGIE OLIVER

Between Four Yews

REGGIE OLIVER has been a professional playwright, actor, and theatre director since 1975. Besides plays, his publications include the authorised biography of Stella Gibbons, *Out of the Woodshed*; two novels, *The Dracula Papers* and *Virtue in Danger*; and six collections of stories of supernatural terror, of which the fifth, *Mrs Midnight*, won the Children of the Night Award for Best Work of Supernatural Fiction in 2011 and was nominated for both a British Fantasy Award and a World Fantasy Award.

Tartarus Press has recently reissued his first and second collections, *The Dreams of Cardinal Vittorini* and *The Complete Symphonies of Adolf Hitler*, in new editions with new illustrations by the author, as well as his latest (and sixth) collection, *Flowers of the Sea*. His stories have appeared in more than fifty anthologies including, prior to this one, four in *The Mammoth Book of Best New Horror* series.

As the author explains: "This story was written for an anthology entitled *The Ghosts and Scholars Book of Shadows*. The brief was to write a 'prequel and/or a sequel' to a story by M. R. James. I chose to write both a prelude and sequel to James's 'A School Story', because it is one of the author's most enigmatic tales with plenty of gaps and loose ends to it that I felt needed filling.

"I wrote it also so that it could stand on its own and be understood even by a reader unfamiliar with the originating story. The title derives from the cryptic note that, in the original tale, the schoolmaster Sampson receives in class, saying (in Latin): 'Remember the well between four yews'."

"I AM SURE THEY have improved a great deal since my day," said Uncle Edward. "I sincerely hope so. In the fifties they were still remarkably similar to those described so vividly by Orwell and Waugh. At my public school we referred to them as our 'privates'."

His nephew Peter looked startled. Conversations with Uncle Edward often took unexpected turns as his view of the world was refreshingly indifferent to contemporary concerns and prejudices. It was one of the reasons why Peter liked to stay with him at his cottage near Aldeburgh. He used to refer to these sojourns, privately to himself, as "going on retreat".

His Uncle smiled. "No! Not those sort of privates. It may have been a term peculiar to Eton. M. R. James certainly used it at the turn of the century. We would say 'I did so and so at my private'. Short for private school. The usual term is of course 'prep' or 'preparatory school'. Curious how these locutions survive, though not perhaps surprising. Boys under the age of puberty are the most conservative of creatures. Where was I?"

"Your private, or prep school."

"Ah, yes. Well, they were very odd institutions in my day. I generalise, of course, but mine certainly was. Abbey Grove, it was called. They went in for these rather grand Gothic nomenclatures: it added cachet, I suppose. But there was nothing of the abbey about this one. It was more of an overgrown country house: 1820s, I should say. Attractive, slightly nondescript white stucco buildings; extensive rather fine grounds, as I remember. It was in the Thames Valley, not too distant from London. It's a housing estate now, of course. Every physical trace of it has been wiped out: it lives only in the memory of a dwindling few and when we who can still recollect it are gone it will have ceased to be altogether. Or possibly not."

"Your point being?"

They had reached the top of a ridge and were looking down over the gentle downward curve of a ploughed field towards a church on the rise opposite. There, in the graveyard among the yews, was a simple headstone commemorating Edward's wife Helena, who had died two years previously. Edward would walk there every day in all kinds of weather; and Peter was happy to go with him on his stays, especially on a day like this. It was mid-April, the sun was out, hawthorn was blossoming in all the hedges and the green on the trees was young.

"We are bound by chains of memory to the past. Some if not all of the memories are inaccurate, but they still make us what we are. When you lose these things, as my darling Helena did in the last years from dementia, you begin to die. To all intents and purposes you cease to be while still remaining technically alive. That is why I hardly ever throw anything away. It is not self-indulgence. It is a means of preserving what I am and what she was."

When they reached the churchyard, Edward went straight to the stone inscribed simply with his wife's name and dates and stayed there staring at it for several minutes, head bowed. Peter stood a few yards distant watching him. His uncle had brought no flowers to lay on the grave; there was not an ounce of sentimentality about his actions, but they were very deliberate. It seemed a passionless ritual, but was somehow all the more impressive for being so.

They had closed the churchyard gate behind them before Edward spoke again.

"I haven't much to leave you physically, Peter. A great deal of what I had in financial terms was used up in caring for Helena at the end, but there are memories and these are of value. I may lose them myself soon, as she did, so I want to pass them on. You may believe them or not: that is irrelevant. You may not like them: that too is unimportant. What matters is that they don't altogether die. *Non omnis moriar*, you know. Horace. Now that's one thing I do regret passing. The classical education. At least they gave us that at Abbey Grove."

When they got back to the cottage his uncle put the kettle on for tea. While he was busy in the kitchen Peter surveyed his surroundings. Uncle Edward had been too modest about his material wealth: there were still one or two items of value for him to leave. In his career as a diplomat Edward had made some judicious acquisitions in the countries where he had served. He had had an eye for such things. Some of the books too were worth a good deal. Edward had collected first editions to read rather than for their value, but he had kept them well, dust jackets and all. Peter took his eyes away from the shelves and tried to dismiss materialistic thoughts.

When Edward came in with the tea, he was also carrying an old-fashioned box file.

"We were talking about Abbey Grove, weren't we? So this may interest you."

Peter did not quite know why they had been talking about Abbey Grove, except that Uncle Edward had brought the matter up. It was true that Peter was a teacher, and so educational matters might be thought to be of interest to him, but he taught physics and chemistry at a Comprehensive and his view of fee-paying schools in general was dogmatic and dismissive. Naturally he kept these views to himself out of courtesy, but Edward, being no fool, must have been aware of them. Perhaps there was something on the old man's mind that needed to be unburdened.

While they were having tea Edward began to extract items from the box file. Here were some black and white snaps of Abbey Grove, taken by Edward with a Box Brownie. The angles were often askew, the focus less than exemplary, but Peter got the general idea. He took a mild interest in Uncle Edward's memories of his "private", as he insisted on calling it, but more in why Edward should be so preoccupied with them. It might have been a sign of approaching death.

Edward had said the school buildings were attractive, but Peter did not think so from the photographs provided. The architecture was regular, but plain and undistinguished and, Peter thought, faintly menacing. The grounds, fringed with trees, looked pleasant enough. On them distant figures of boys in grey shorts and white shirts could be seen playing impromptu games of French cricket. Edward handed him another snap, this time a close up of two boys, one of whom Peter recognised as his uncle, not so much from the features as from his characteristic manner of smiling and the way he screwed up his eyes when he did so.

"Photo of a young Edward," said his uncle.

"Who's that next to you?"

"Ah, that's my friend Macpherson. Claimed descent from the fraudulent creator of *Ossian*. One of those rather fey Scotsmen. He was my great chum at Abbey Grove. Don't quite know why. These youthful friendships are unfathomable, aren't they? Not that he was a bad chap by any means. Became a Presbyterian minister, I believe. Died not so long ago, as it happens, and left me something. But that will come later."

"Later than what?"

"That's what I'm going to tell you."

"Then perhaps you'd better."

Uncle Edward leaned back and nodded in acknowledgement that he had been found out. It was clear that he had been needing to tell someone and that Peter was the chosen vessel.

"I went to Abbey Grove in 1954 as a boarder. My parents' choice of it was not entirely arbitrary. It had been recommended to them vaguely by a friend of a friend, and it was near London, so visits to see me could be made without undue expense. It was not in any way an academically distinguished establishment, but I suppose it was fairly competent in performing its primary task, which was to get boys through the Common Entrance Examination and into public schools. It had the usual rapid turnover of teaching staff backed by a few long term old lags. The headmaster, a Mr Waterfield, had two sons who also taught at the school. The elder son, like his father, was a competent teacher and destined to succeed to the headmastership; the younger was less able. He taught Geography, in those days the dreariest of dreary subjects. He had a feeble, etiolated sort of body and a long narrow face. He was known throughout the school as 'Ratty', an epithet so appropriate in every way that it was almost officially recognised.

"Ratty had few designated powers and was not allowed to use the cane, the prerogative of Waterfield and his first-born alone. In spite of this Ratty managed to exercise a good deal of petty tyranny over the boys in his charge. One of the miseries he was allowed to inflict was something called 'punishment duty': boys who had displeased him in some way were made, under his supervision, to perform a menial task of service to the school.

"In the autumn term of my third year there Macpherson and I had been caught out by him in a minor infringement. It may have been only that we had been late for something or other. In any case we were put by Ratty on 'punishment duty', which was to sweep up the leaves on the hard tennis courts before evening prayers.

"It was a pretty futile exercise – there would be more fallen leaves there by the following day – but it pleased the mind of Ratty. He spent almost ten minutes contemplating our labours before sauntering off, sucking at the briar pipe which he fondly imagined gave him a manly air.

"As Macpherson and I continued with our task, which consisted of brushing the leaves into piles, putting them into a dustbin and then depositing its contents onto a nearby compost heap, dusk began to fall. The clear sky became a dull yellow colour and it turned very cold. The hard tennis courts were situated in a rather dingy part of the grounds which none of us really liked. Despite their displays of bravado young boys can be peculiarly susceptible to atmosphere. Uneasily we kept encouraging each other to 'get this stupid thing done as quick as possible'.

"I remember, we had almost scraped up the last pile of leaves when I happened to look up at Macpherson's face. He was standing facing me and appeared to be staring at something behind me and a little to my right. I remember thinking dispassionately that his features seemed unusually white and blank.

"'Crikey, who's that?' he said.

"I looked round and for a few seconds saw what he had been looking at. A face was peering at us through the wire mesh that bordered the tennis court, pressed so hard against the metal lattice work that parts of its pale, glistening flesh were bulging through the interstices.

"It was the face of a man of about thirty-five, I suppose, with a black beard, parts of which were also sticking through the fence, the ends dripping wet and greenish in hue as if they had been turned somehow into pond weed. But the thing that to us seemed most strange and alarming was the position of the head. It was only a few inches above the ground. It looked as though whoever it was had crawled towards the tennis court fence on his belly and was trying to get in under the wire. The eyes had no whites to them, but were as black and shiny as snooker balls.

"All this I took in in a few seconds. The next moment we had turned and were running towards the entrance to the court, mercifully at the end opposite to the dreadful face. After some frantic fumbling with the catch on the gate, we were through and racing up to the school buildings.

"When Ratty discovered that we had not completed our punishment duty he ordered us back to finish it off the following evening, but we both stubbornly refused. This act of defiance, for which we offered no explanation, baffled him. He little knew that what appeared to be courage was in fact sheer funk. After some consideration he decided to assign another task to us: that of clearing up a lumber room at the top of one of the school buildings next to the sick bay.

"This job suited Macpherson and me much better. We were both indoors sort of people and the idea of rummaging through ancient school detritus appealed to us. When Ratty turned up and found us almost enjoying ourselves he stayed for a very short while and walked off disconsolately.

"At first it was the novelty of the job that we liked. Most of the lumber was not very interesting. Apart from some decaying sports equipment, destined to be thrown away, there were piles of old examination papers to be put into boxes and ragged copies of *Kennedy's Latin Primer* and other textbooks to be sorted into neat piles. It was only when we managed to penetrate to the back parts of the storeroom that we began to discover items of real interest.

"There was a large number of mounted and framed school photographs from before the Second and even the First World Wars. We pored over these with fascination. You see, every Remembrance Sunday in chapel old Waterfield, the headmaster, would read out the names of those from the school who had died in the two World Wars. It was always a solemn occasion. Macpherson and I could, by consulting the legends on the mounts, put faces to those names and wonder at the fact that these innocent, confident young boys, their arms folded, cricket caps set jauntily on their heads would, in a very few years' time be dead, carried away in the maelstrom of war.

"In the farthest corner of the room, we found a set of framed sepia photographs dating from the very earliest days of the school in the 1870s. These, interestingly enough, were much less formally posed than later photographs, and included masters. Boys had no uniform and some wore top hats while the masters sported gowns and mortar boards.

"One of these pictures, dating from the year 1873, gave us a shock. A bearded man standing in the back row bore a striking resemblance to the face we had seen at the tennis court the previous evening. No names had been inscribed on the mount of the photograph, as with the later ones, but a few had been scrawled on the backing in pencil. From these inscriptions we could be fairly sure that the black bearded master was one G. W. Sampson. After a pause for reflection we continued with our tidying operation.

"There was one more thing. At the very back of the lumber room we discovered an old black japanned tin box about eighteen inches high and two foot square. On the top of it someone had pasted a label which bore a legend written in ink and firm if faded capitals: EFFECTS BELONGING TO G. W. SAMPSON ESQ. TO BE RESTORED TO HIM ON HIS REAPPEARANCE OR SENT TO NEXT OF KIN IN THE EVENT OF HIS DEATH BEING REPORTED, and then a date, JULY 15TH 1874.

"The box was locked but, conveniently enough, a key on a loop of string was tied to one of its handles. Macpherson was for opening the box; I was reluctant, but curiosity at length prevailed.

"There were a number of interesting items, some of them valuable, in particular a gold half-hunter watch made by Wormold of London. There were some jade cufflinks and a signet ring with a crest on it. A Greek New Testament bound in Morocco leather had been heavily annotated in pencil. Besides these there were a number of small curios, obviously of some antiquity. There were several cameos which I am pretty sure were Imperial Roman rather than later Italian copies; there was an ancient Babylonian cylinder seal in amber depicting a lion hunt in exquisite detail and an Athenian red figure calyx decorated with a scene of Heracles wrestling Cerberus, the three-headed guard dog of the Underworld. Though I saw all these treasures for only a matter of minutes over fifty years ago, they are still clearly etched in my memory. Last of all there was a black leather bound notebook on the cover of which the letters G.W.S had been stamped in gold. Being the honest boys that we were we replaced all the treasures reverently in the box, but the notebook Macpherson insisted on taking. I pleaded with him not to, but he said he would study the contents and then return it to the tin box at a later date.

"Over the next few days I was aware that Macpherson was in the process of reading the manuscript but I never saw him doing so. Whenever we met I would ask him to reveal to me something of what he had read, but he refused. I did not even know if, after reading the notebook, he had returned it to its rightful place, though I later found out that he could not have done so because Ratty had locked the lumber room after our tidying exercise.

"On a clear moonlit night, about a week after our adventures, something odd happened. We – Macpherson and I – slept in a dormitory at right angles to the main school building. Ratty slept in the main building on the first floor, so we could see his window from ours. At some time between one and two, I was woken up by Macpherson shaking me. He appeared to be in one of his fey moods: excited, frightened, exultant and troubled all at once.

"'Come over to the window and have a look at this,' he said. Dully, still half asleep, I obeyed. We looked out of the window and saw that on the drive below Ratty's window two figures were standing, monochromatic but clearly etched by the moonlight. One was a tall man in what might have been a schoolmaster's gown. His features were in shadow but you could tell that he had a beard. The other figure was smaller, slighter, thinner and appeared to be naked though it was impossible to determine the sex. Its skin seemed to glisten slightly as if it were wet. Then the bearded man turned his head to look full at us while he raised his right hand to point at Ratty's window. I glanced at Macpherson, who seemed to be transfixed by the vision. Slowly and almost imperceptibly he nodded towards the figure in the drive.

"'Mac, what on earth are you doing?' I asked.

"Macpherson stared at me, shook his head several times and said: 'Nothing. I didn't do a thing. I never thought they'd come.'

"'Who are "they"?'

"'I don't know. I don't know! Look, let's get back into bed and forget all about it.'

"I was happy to do so. Macpherson seemed to be in a state of shock.

"The following morning when I began to question him about the night before he gave me a blank look. I felt he was warning me not to broach the subject if I valued his friendship.

"Shortly after morning chapel we heard that Ratty would not, as usual, be taking us for Geography because he had become seriously ill during the night. Later in the day three of the boys told us they had seen an ambulance draw up in front of the main school house, and Ratty being put into the ambulance, not on a stretcher, but wrapped in a blanket and escorted by two tall men. The boys said that Ratty was struggling and the two men were having a job to get him into the vehicle.

"The following term Macpherson's parents took him away from Abbey Grove for reasons unspecified, but he and I did keep up a desultory correspondence. We never saw each other again as our paths diverged: I went to Eton and Oxford and thence into the Diplomatic, he from Fettes to St Andrew's and then the Ministry. The letters we exchanged were friendly and informative but not intimate and it was Macpherson who always seemed to initiate the renewal of contact. I had the feeling that there was something between us that he wished to recall and preserve, but what?

"The clue – if it is a clue – came when he died last year. Solicitors informed me that there was a sealed package which he had bequeathed to me. Inside the package there was no final letter from him. Simply this . . ."

From the box file Edward took an ancient black leather-bound note book on the cover of which the letters G.W.S had been stamped in gold. He handed it to his nephew.

"Read it tonight in bed, Peter," said Edward. "Even a stern rationalist like yourself might find it of interest."

Uncle and nephew spoke no more that day about Abbey Grove. They watched the news on television and then Edward, who was an excellent cook, made dinner and they shared a fine bottle of Pouilly Fumé. As they were going to bed Edward said to him: "Sleep well!" – something he never normally did – and there was a gleam of amusement in his eye.

Once he was in bed Peter dutifully opened the notebook. The handwriting in it was in that fine sloping style, characteristic of the mid- to late-nineteenth century. It took a little getting used to but was far from being illegible.

The first thirty or so pages consisted of random notes mainly about antiquities interspersed with occasional sketches in pen of coins, cameos and statuettes. There were jottings down of inscriptions in Greek and Arabic and one or two financial calculations. All this seemed only modestly interesting. Then Peter leafed through the book until he found what looked like a continuous narrative. He located the page where this began – it was headed MY TESTAMENT – and started to read in earnest.

MY TESTAMENT

I am Gerald William Sampson, though the last of these three is not my true name, but it is as true a name as any. I was born on the 24th of July 1838, the natural son of Martha O'Connor, kitchen maid and Sir Gerald Fitzgerald, baronet, of Cloyne House, County Cork, Ireland. My mother had been in service there but when she was found to be with child she was dismissed. Sir Gerald at that time was married but with no issue and he made some provision for the upkeep of my mother and myself. A couple of years later his wife gave him two sons in quick succession but he continued his payments to my mother, albeit on a reduced scale and took some interest in my education. When he found that I was academically proficient he paid for me to be tutored by a local priest. At the age of sixteen I was sent to Trinity College Dublin and from there, after two years, to St Mark's College, Oxford. At that time I called myself Fitzgerald.

It was at the beginning of my third year up at Oxford that the great tragedy befell me. Sir Gerald died suddenly in a hunting accident and I was summoned back to Ireland to attend the funeral. My mother was not present as she was, by that time, enduring the agonising illness that was to end her life some weeks later, and I was accorded no status at the obsequies. I was told to stay at an inn some miles distant from Cloyne.

On the day after the funeral I was summoned to Cloyne House where a most unpleasant interview took place in the library. Present were Sir Arthur Fitzgerald, the new baronet and Mr William Fitzgerald, his younger brother, together with the family lawyer Mr Broughton.

I was addressed by all three throughout as Mr O'Connor, my mother's maiden name with which I was barely familiar. This was galling enough, but there was worse. I was informed that no provision had been made for me in the late Sir Gerald's will, and that all allowances to me and my mother were to be stopped forthwith. I pleaded with them that my mother was seriously ill and that I should at least be allowed some funds to enable me to complete my degree, but they were adamant. I was too embarrassed to tell them that, in the careless way young people do, I had run up considerable debts with several local tradesmen in Oxford. To admit to my faults in front of these two popinjays was more than I could bear.

In my pride I knew that between them my half brothers had not a quarter of the intellectual abilities or strength of character that I possessed, and yet they were looking down on me. Worse still, they appeared to be enjoying my humiliation.

I remember how at the end of the interview I cried out: "But what am I to do?"

"You may go to the Devil, for all we care," said Mr William.

Sir Arthur, leaning carelessly against the library's great marble chimney-piece, laughed inordinately at this and though Mr Broughton looked decently ashamed by his clients' conduct he did not rebuke it. I turned on my heel without a word and left the house.

For a while I wandered the grounds of Cloyne, so distracted by shame and indignation that I barely knew what I was doing. After some hours, however, I remember finding myself towards dusk in a little clearing in the woods behind Cloyne where between four yew trees stood an old well. It was a gloomy place, but it suited my humour and there I found a measure of calm.

Out of that calm, however, there grew not sweetness and forgiveness but a great resolve. I would avenge myself upon my two siblings if it took me my whole life. The thought of it settled on my heart like a great cold weight but it seemed to give me strength.

By pawning the few valuables remaining to me I had enough resources to see that my mother was taken care of before I hurried back to Oxford. There I laid bare my situation before the college authorities in the hope that they might take pity on me and allow me to complete my degree, but they were unsympathetic. The Master of St Mark's was even pleased to be indignant with me for making myself out to be a gentleman when I was not. My reply, that I was at least a gentleman on my mother's side of the family, was not well received.

Only one person had a kind word for me and that was a fellow of St Mark's and my tutor in Ancient History, Dr Sampson. He told me that though he could not prevent my "going down", he could give me assistance in obtaining some means of gainful employment. He wrote for me a warm letter of introduction to Mr Julius Lagrange of Bond Street, London.

Mr Lagrange was a celebrated dealer in antiquities, his clients including connoisseurs, museums and learned institutions, even royalty. Being somewhat advanced in years and infirm, he needed a young and vigorous assistant to travel for him in Greece and the Levant in search of ancient treasures. A facility for languages and a good knowledge of the classical antique, both of which I possessed, were the essential requisites. I truly believe I was as much a godsend to Mr Lagrange as he was to me, and I began again to relish my prospects. In celebration of my new life (as well as to escape my creditors) I decided to change my name, and, to honour the kindness of my old tutor, I gave myself his: Sampson.

At some other time, if I live, I will write down all the adventures that I had in the next eight years as I travelled through Greece and the Near East. I found I had a natural ability for what I did, and made a considerable fortune for Mr Lagrange and a small one, if briefly, for myself. Through all that time, however, I did not once forget that my ultimate purpose was revenge upon the house of Fitzgerald of Cloyne.

Respectable, cultivated people and institutions will pay a great deal for antiquities and part of the price they pay, though they may not admit it, is for the privilege of ignorance. They must be spared the knowledge that these figurines were robbed from a tomb or that this ancient codex was cozened from a greedy abbot who had no right to dispose of it. When the very marbles of the Parthenon that rest in the sanctity of the British Museum enjoy a dubious provenance, you may be sure that their lesser brethren almost invariably have something to hide. It will come as no surprise, therefore, to learn that in the course of my travels I had intercourse with not a few very doubtful characters, and some outright villains. One of the strangest of these was a man I met in Smyrna who called himself Captain Kinnaird.

I believe it was Lagrange who first provided me with the introduction to this worthy. Undoubtedly he was of use to me in my business. For a price, naturally, Kinnaird was able to secure for me the services of every tomb robber, sneak thief and corrupt official in the neighbourhood. Everyone seemed to know "the Captain", as he was invariably called, and the captain knew everyone.

Occupying a large house in a disreputable quarter of Smyrna, he lived in a bewildering combination of opulence and squalor. He never seemed short of funds but he was always eager to acquire more, usually by the most irregular means. Through his establishment passed a motley selection of rogues, cutthroats, catamites and whores in whom he took a mild, almost paternal interest. To me, however, as a fellow Englishmen, he was especially welcoming and soon I got to know a little of his history.

One night at his house, after we had caroused into the early hours, I let him know something of my own life.

"We are brothers, then," said Kinnaird. "We are both scapegraces who have fallen foul of our families."

I was content to let that pass, though I considered myself a superior being in every way to Kinnaird, and presently my forbearance was rewarded when he told me his story. His full name was Talbot DeVere Kinnaird and he belonged to a minor branch of a noble family. After quitting Rugby he had obtained a commission in one of the smart regiments and had indeed reached the rank of captain but was cashiered for appropriating mess funds to pay off gambling debts. His family had guaranteed him a small remittance if he left the country and troubled their consciences no more. Wandering the earth in search of a place where his allowance would stretch furthest he found himself in Smyrna.

Looking round at the foetid luxury in which he was now ensconced I remarked that he seemed to have done pretty well for himself on such a small income. Kinnaird smiled.

"I have the means to augment my family pittance and I have created a world that suits me. But you, my dear Sampson, I can see, are still searching."

Rashly I admitted to him that I would never rest until I had avenged myself on the Fitzgerald brothers for the terrible wrongs they had done to my mother and to me.

"Believe me, old friend," said Kinnaird, puffing at a hookah pipe and squeezing the arm of one of the spangled *houris* who lolled on the divan beside him, "the old Spanish proverb is right. Living well is the best revenge."

"Then the best is not good enough for me."

"I am not unsympathetic. In fact I had to strive to reach the state I am in now."

I raised my eyebrows. The idea of Kinnaird striving to attain anything struck me as ludicrous.

"You mock me? I think you should not. Look over there." He gestured with the mouthpiece of his hookah to a corner of the room behind his left shoulder. "Tell me what you see."

I told him that I could see only a mass of shadows and something glinting within them.

"Wait. Look more closely. No! Don't get up and go over there. You'll disturb it. Tell me again what you see."

I concentrated my gaze on the corner of the room. Kinnaird was right. Something stirred there. They were not just shadows, but somehow, in an indistinct way, alive, and the more I stared at them the more I felt a kind of revulsion that is hard even now to explain or define.

"What is that?"

"You would not believe me if I told you."

"Kinnaird, I am drunk enough to believe anything."

"It is what in this part of the world is called a *djinn* or *vashnak*. The biblical term for it is 'familiar spirit'. You remember the Witch of Endor?"

"You are telling me that you have a familiar spirit? In God's name, why?"

"Why, to do my bidding, my dear Sampson. To keep me in cash and what you in your censorious way would call 'vicious enjoyments'. Mind you, I had the devil's own job, finding and securing it for my use. These things come at a price, you know, but that is why half the rogues and cut-throats of this stinking city come here to pay homage to me, and the other half are in mortal terror of what I might do to them."

My mind was too fuddled with drink to know what to make of this and the following day I left for Bodrum further down the coast in search of some Tanagra figurines – then just becoming fashionable with the cognoscenti – which I heard could be had for a reasonable sum. While on my journey South I had time to reflect on what I had been told and what I thought I had seen. At that time, as I have explained, I was possessed by an intense need to gratify my desire for revenge. As with our amorous urges, it is only when it has been sated that one can see how unreasonably this lust has dominated our lives, and what a monster it can make of us.

By the time I had got back to Smyrna my mind was made up. I went to Kinnaird and told him that I was determined to acquire a "familiar spirit" such as he had. Kinnaird smiled his queer little smile and said that he would see what he could do, but that I might have to wait up to a year before an opportunity arose. I said I was prepared to wait.

"There is a price you know," he said.

I said I was not short of funds and was prepared to pay the going rate for such things.

"Yes, that price too, but I meant another sort of price."

"You mean my immortal soul, or some such nonsense?"

"My dear Sampson, those are crude and superstitious terms that I would never deign to use in front of you. Nevertheless there is a universal and inviolable law which stipulates that for everything one gives one must receive and for everything received one must also give. In these cases the master can become the servant and the servant the master. Understand this and all may be well."

Thinking that I understood, I nodded. I left Smyrna in a few days' time, bound for Greece in search of Red Figure Attic ware.

In the two months that followed I almost forgot my conversation with Kinnaird and when I did remember it I wished it had never occurred. My enterprises prospered. Then one day I was on the quay at Patras overseeing the loading of some packing cases full of Ancient Greek vases for Lagrange when a boy came up to me and handed me a letter. It was from Kinnaird and God in Heaven knows how he had found me. The missive stated that if I wished to proceed with the enterprise we had discussed I was to take the next available packet and present myself to him in Smyrna as soon as possible.

I did not hesitate, though I have since often wondered why I did not, and the following evening saw me in the port of Corinth. The next morning I was sailing across the Ægean Sea, eastward bound for a tryst about whose nature and consequence I had not the least conception.

I feel I must give some account of what happened when I reached Smyrna. If I am to rid myself of this cursed thing, I will have to in some measure confess, if only to the pages of this book. But how I hate that word "confess"! It sounds so weak and simpering. Let me be as brief and to the point, then, as may be.

In a village called Bassarlik some ten miles from Smyrna in a mountainous region, there lived a wise man, or *Khof*, as they are called in those parts. From him Kinnaird had heard of a tragic incident in the village. A young girl of no more than fourteen, having been rejected by her suitor, had thrown herself down a well and killed herself. Now in Turkey, as in most societies I have come across, a suicide is considered to be a most unlucky thing for the neighbourhood in which it occurs. Equally, advantage may accrue if the restless spirit of the dead person can be disposed of. In short, the ghost of a suicide may be sold to the highest bidder as a familiar spirit: being no good for the next world, it may become a slave in this.

I will not describe the ceremonies by which the creature was invoked by the *Khof*, ably assisted by some of the village elders who were well paid for their trouble. Those interested in such anthropological curiosities may apply elsewhere. To me the details are too repellent to contemplate. It all took place at the well where the poor girl had drowned herself and in the early hours of the 24th of July 1865, which happened to be the day of my twenty-seventh birthday. I will only say that the sensations I felt when I saw a hideously emaciated arm, dead white and wet, rise above the well's parapet, were of the most profound horror and revulsion.

Slowly, by some mysterious process of levitation, the thing rose out of the well and then collapsed upon the earth beyond it. Immediately, as I had been instructed, I ran to it and placed round its neck a gold chain on which I had hung a token of my ownership of the spirit. It was a gold *solidus* of the Emperor Constantine Pogonatus, with the reverse rubbed smooth and my initials together with the date scratched upon it.

I then led my creature off to a grove about half-a-mile distant from the village of Bassarlik where was performed a second and private part of the ceremony. This I will not describe: it is too horrible to me, especially as while the ghastly act was being performed I realised that I was not alone. Halfway through the process I caught a glimpse of something in a dense thicket close to me. It was like a single luminous eye that glowed yellow in the dark, then faded to red, glowed, then faded again. It was Kinnaird's cigar.

With the aid of my familiar (as I shall now call her) my business as a trader in antiquities became prodigiously successful. By the year 1870 I was a rich man and was beginning to feel a pressing need to return home and fulfil my destiny.

My one anxiety concerned the familiar. Would it survive the journey to England and then Ireland? I consulted Kinnaird, albeit reluctantly, he being the only person who was in my confidence and might have some expertise in the matter. He told me that if I placed my familiar's desiccated remains – when inactive the thing returned to its corporeal entity as a corpse – in a box made of cedar and lined with lead, I could transport it overseas. Once landed, the familiar could be revived by the application of fresh standing water, preferably from a well, and the ritual practice which I will not describe.

In the year 1871 I arrived in Ireland and took a suite of rooms at an inn not far from Cloyne House. My skin was heavily tanned and I had grown a black beard so that I was confident that no one would recognise in G. W. Sampson esq., the insignificant young Mr Fitzgerald or O'Connor who had fled the scene so precipitately all those years ago. I pretended to be a young nabob who was looking to buy a property and settle down in the district.

Did I still feel the burning desire for revenge that had animated me all those years ago? Probably I did not, but the resolve had become a settled part of my existence and I could no more rid myself of it than I could have cut off my right hand. Everything I had done had been a prelude to this moment. So, one night I strapped the cedar box to the back of a hired nag and made my way to the old well between four yew trees at the back of Cloyne House.

Uttering the correct invocations I threw the contents of the box down the well and presently, by the light of my dark lantern, I saw the thing emerge, pale, wet, odiously thin. Once I had paid my part of the dreadful bargain I gave my familiar her instructions. It had been my whim to communicate with the creature always in Latin, so that we might keep our intercourse cloaked in the obscurity of a dead language.

One morning a few days later I was sitting in the parlour of my inn, enjoying a solitary breakfast, when the landlord entered and announced that a terrible tragedy had occurred. Mr William Fitzgerald, younger brother of Sir Arthur Fitzgerald, baronet and squire of Cloyne, had died on the hunting field. Accounts differed, but the general consensus was that Mr William's horse had taken fright at something and that in the ensuing wild career Mr William had been thrown from his mount and that his head had suffered a violent collision with a tree. Some accounts, admittedly not from the most reliable of sources, stated that someone or some thing had actually torn him from the saddle.

I consulted with the landlord, with whom I was now on excellent terms, and it was decided that, because I was beginning to become something of a notable figure in the district and was soon to be a permanent resident, it would be appropriate for me to pay a call on Sir Arthur to offer my condolences.

Sir Arthur, who had heard of me and my wealth, was prepared to receive me in the library. As I entered it the years seemed to fall away and I felt sure that he was going to recognise me, beard notwithstanding, but he did not. His manner was gracious if, understandably, distant. The years had not been kind to him. From being a heartily handsome young man, he had become florid and corpulent. The scarlet blooms of the habitual drinker showed on his cheeks. I had half a mind to pity him. He showed an interest in my doings and plans, which I suspected was not unconnected with the rumours of my fabulous wealth. I had noticed as I entered Cloyne House that the place was showing signs of neglect, and that there were a few naked patches on the walls where a valuable picture had once been.

As Sir Arthur and I were talking a woman in riding costume entered the room. She was introduced to me as Lady Felicia Fitzgerald, his wife: a tall lady with a slender figure and a face that was perhaps handsome rather than beautiful but which bore the unmistakable stamp of breeding and refinement. When she spoke her voice was low, melodious and somehow amused. I was captivated and wondered what she was doing with this clod.

Though our interview was brief, I believed a rapport had been established between Lady Felicia and myself. Soon after she had quitted the room I took my leave, having accepted an invitation to dine with them the following Saturday. When I made enquiries of my landlord about her he told me that Lady Felicia and Sir Arthur had been married barely a year, that she was the daughter of a local landowner, and that, as yet, she had not provided her husband with an heir.

At dinner on Saturday I think I managed to make a good impression. I regaled them with my traveller's tales of Greece and the Levant. Lady Felicia's eyes shone as she listened to me, for I fancy she was hungry for the kind of experience and cultivation which I could offer. Nevertheless I detected a certain reserve in her manner, as if she were not quite sure of my intentions. This only enhanced my admiration of her.

Sir Arthur fulfilled all my worst hopes. He listened to me at first with a dull sort of interest but then slowly, throughout the long evening, he managed to drink himself into a stupor. By the time the dessert was on the table he had fallen asleep in his chair at the head of the table.

Lady Felicia and I were now, in every meaningful sense, alone. Her skin glowed in the candlelight and I began to see her not simply as a fine specimen of womanhood but as a rare beauty. However, the possibility of a deeper acquaintance and intimacy was denied. With her husband's unconsciousness, Lady

Felicia had become more rather than less reserved in her manner. Perhaps she was afraid I might somehow take advantage of the situation, but nothing was further from my thoughts. Sensitive to this, however, I indicated that perhaps, under the circumstances, it would be best if I took my leave rather earlier than I might have done. Lady Felicia's face flushed with relief and gratitude and I knew I had made the right move.

Later that night I stood by the well between four yews and summoned my familiar. The instructions, as before, were simple.

A few days later the whole district was agog with the latest news: Sir Arthur was dead. Lady Felicia had been away, spending the night with relatives, and her husband had dined alone. When the servant had come in to collect the dishes at the end of the meal he found his master, as usual, asleep, or so at first he thought. But Sir Arthur's posture seemed unusually awkward and he was not emitting the stertorous snore which was the usual consequence of his potations. In short, Sir Arthur had died from some kind of seizure, perhaps brought on by a choking fit. Strange white marks had been observed around his throat, but, as nothing could be made of them by the men of science, they were dismissed as irrelevant. "Died of drink," was the general verdict.

I attended the funeral and paid a call on Lady Felicia as soon as a decent interval of time had elapsed. She received me very graciously, but still with that reserve I had found in her before. Once, I thought, she gave me a look that could almost be described as suspicious. I realised that I was in for a long siege, but the prospect did not discourage me.

It had been several weeks since I had had any communication with my familiar and for some reason this preyed on my mind. As far as I was concerned she had performed her task, unless perhaps she could aid me in my suit to Lady Felicia, and I had a vague notion of dismissing the creature, releasing her from her servitude to me, as Prospero did with Ariel. My mind, however, was not made up. It was too full of Lady Felicia to be occupied with much else.

One night – it was a full moon – I found I could not sleep. I was drawn to the window of my bedroom and there I saw, standing in the road in front of the inn, looking up at the window, the pallid, emaciated figure of my familiar. Slowly it raised an arm and beckoned.

By the time I was dressed and down in the street the thing was gone, but I knew where it would be. I walked – or perhaps ran – the five miles to the well at Cloyne in a daze, barely knowing what I did.

She stood by the well, the gold chain with its token of my possession glinting under the moon. I cannot say we spoke together. It is difficult to describe. Our communication was not so much in speech as in thoughts: certainly I cannot recollect the tone of my familiar's voice. I said I was grateful for her services but that our association must end. She replied that this could not be as we were bound to one another. I replied that if she could deliver to me Lady Felicia as my bride then she would have done me the last and greatest service. She said that I belonged to her and not Lady Felicia and – did I not know? – Lady Felicia was with child. She said that Lady Felicia must be destroyed like the others if I was to enter into my inheritance at Cloyne. I asked by what right she dictated to me what I should do with my life. With a thin skeletal hand my familiar held up the coin on its chain and said – or I think it said because I remember the exact words: "*Jure possessionis*" – "By right of ownership."

Enraged by this I grasped at the coin and tore the chain from her neck. Then I took hold of that bag of bones – how hideous and cold to the touch! – and made to hurl it down the well. The creature wrapped its limbs round me in a strangling grip and I felt my strength fade as it started to squeeze the breath from my body. I found myself being propelled towards the edge of the well with it. In a final desperate effort I steeled myself to bite through one of its arms. It was like cracking the shell of a lobster with one's teeth. An awful odour of decay filled my mouth but the arm fell away. A piercing high-pitched scream sang in my ears. Seizing the advantage, I began to tear the vile thing limb from limb and throw each individual part down the well.

Despite my fury I was thinking with icy clarity. Once the creature was dispatched I gathered branches of trees and rocks from all around – I even broke off boughs from some of the yews – and hurled them into the well. Eventually I managed to cover the mouth of the well so thoroughly with stones and pieces of wood I doubt if a mouse could have escaped from it. Having completed the task to my satisfaction I returned to the inn and slept soundly until midday the following morning.

The next day a letter arrived from Mr Lagrange, summoning me to London. Thinking that perhaps a break from Ireland might do me good I went willingly. My suit with Lady Felicia could be resumed at a later time, perhaps when she had been delivered of her child.

So it was with a light heart that I arrived in London, little knowing the disaster that awaited me. It turned out that some of the finest items which I had shipped, in all innocence, to Mr Lagrange had been looted from a Peer of the Realm by brigands while he was travelling through the Morea. The indignant milord was demanding full restitution and threatening worse. I was embroiled in several complicated lawsuits and, in short, lost my entire fortune. I was, of course, dismissed from Mr Lagrange's service and so once again found myself destitute. My only friend in the world, Dr Sampson, was able to supply me with an excellent academic reference so that, though my notoriety was still too great for me to apply to one of the more prominent educational establishments, I was able to secure a position as assistant master at Abbey Grove, a small private preparatory school not far from London.

Here, at long last, after many months of agony, I have begun to enjoy a measure of safety and serenity. It is for this reason that I now feel I can discharge myself of the burden that has been weighing upon me. Is it the burden of guilt? I cannot say. It is more like freeing oneself from the exhaustion of a long and arduous journey.

I can even amuse the boys with my traveller's tales, and I keep my familiar's token like a charm on my watch chain.

Later:

Something occurred in class yesterday that hints to me that I may not, after all, be away and free.

Parce mihi, Domine! Parce mihi, Christe, per tuam misericordiam! Parce mihi, Domine! [Spare me, o Lord! Spare me, o Christ, by your mercy! Spare me, o Lord!]

When Peter came down to breakfast the following morning his uncle was already up.

"You're looking a little pale this morning," said Edward. "Sleep all right?"

Peter threw the black notebook onto the kitchen table, saying as he did so: "I don't believe a word of it."

His uncle merely smiled and remarked: "I'm delighted to hear it. Tea or coffee?"

When Edward died suddenly the following year from a stroke Peter found that his uncle had been as good as his word and left him his entire estate. Though this was little more than the cottage near Aldeburgh and its contents, their total value was far from negligible. As Peter began to clear out the cottage he found a room full of papers and diaries concerning his uncle's life. These included the box file relating to Abbey Grove that contained photographs letters, old school reports and a black leather bound note book with G.W.S stamped in gold on the cover.

Peter made a bonfire in the garden of the cottage and incinerated all of Edward's papers. Much as he had liked his uncle, Peter did not share his views on the preservation of memory. He belonged to a different generation.

However, when he threw the Abbey Grove file onto the flames, he did, for a fleeting moment, have the odd sense that he was being watched. It was only for a moment, though. These things pass and normality, as we are pleased to call it, returns.

GEMMA FILES

Slick Black Bones and Soft Black Stars

GEMMA FILES was born in England and raised in Toronto, Canada. She has been a film critic, teacher and screenwriter. Her 1999 International Horror Guild short fiction winner (and Aurora Award finalist) "The Emperor's Old Bones" appears in her collection *The Worm in Every Heart*. Both it and her earlier collection, *Kissing Carrion*, feature two stories that were adapted into episodes of *The Hunger*, an anthology TV show produced by Ridley and Tony Scott's Scott Free Productions.

Recent short fiction appears in such anthologies as *Hauntings*, *The Grimscribe's Puppets*, *Magic*, *Mighty Unclean*, *Dark Faith Invocations*, *Clockwork Phoenix 4* and the previous edition of *The Mammoth Book of Best New Horror*.

Her first novel, *A Book of Tongues: Volume One of the Hexslinger Series* was a Bram Stoker first novel finalist and won a *DarkScribe Magazine* Black Quill Award for "Best Small Press Chill" in both the Editor's and Readers' Choice categories. *A Rope of Thorns* and *A Tree of Bones* complete the trilogy. She has also published two chapbooks of poetry, *Bent Under Night* and *Dust Radio*. The author is currently hard at work on a new novel.

"Writing someone else's Mythos, of any sort, is necessarily hard," observes Files. "You have to keep within the boundaries, coming up with something distinctive enough to be 'your own' while still staying true to the canonical spirit of the source material.

"And with this story I had a particularly difficult time of it, since Robert W. Chambers' *King in Yellow* stories, unlike those of his contemporary H. P. Lovecraft, create a mood of creeping horror mainly composed of lacunae, snatches of impenetrable dialogue and rhyme, names literally without faces – empty places, all waiting to be filled with images that can never truly hope to approximate the shadowy form behind the curtain conjured by Chambers' original words.

"So when I was set the challenge of writing something Chambers-esque for Joseph S. Pulver, Snr's *A Season in Carcosa*, I found myself moving away from simple pastiche towards a confluence of two real-life things I'd always wanted to write about, but never as yet found the right sort of glue to tie together: the grotesque yet weirdly fulfilling day-to-day grind of forensic archaeology and grave excavation, as outlined in Clea Koff's autobiographical memoir *The Bone Woman*, vs the odd latter-day history of Pitcairn Island, where the mutineers from *The Bounty* fetched up, as explored in Dea Birkett's *Serpent in Paradise*.

"I saw it as a bit of an experiment, both because I deliberately chose to tell the story in second-person present tense and because the notion of the Hali Islanders' extreme insularity, coupled with their physiological as well as philosophical 'slipperiness', seemed almost Kafka-like. The basic thesis: when you find yourself trapped by circumstance in a place so small it barely appears on maps, how can you ever be sure that *anything* any of the natives around you tell you is – or isn't – true?

"The story came out blessedly quickly after that, in a dreaming, trance-like rush, and I can only hope some of that feeling manages to communicate itself to the reader."

ALL GRAVES LOOK the same, generally: sunken or up-thrust, backdirt slightly looser than whatever lies around it, sometimes of a different colour, a different composition. Anything that shows something's been scooped out and reapportioned, piled back in atop what lies beneath.

You start with trowel and probe, cleaning the surface near what you suspect is the grave's edge, thrusting the probe in as far as it'll go, then sniffing it for decomp. If you strike something soft, that's a find. Satellite photos also help, as do picks, shovels; Ken Kichi sets up nearby to run the electronic mapping station, charting the site's contours, eventually providing a three-dimensional outline of every body and its position when found, while Judy Moss – your usual dig partner – shares process photography duties with Guillaume Jutras, head of this particular Physicians for Human Rights forensic anthropology team. Their shutters buzz constantly like strange new insects in the oven-door heat, *snap-flash, snap-flash, whirrrr.*

And you, meanwhile – you're crouched down in the stench feeling for bones, finding rotten cloth, salt-stiff flesh.

The grave is humid, seawater-infused. Sand clings to everything, knitting with bone itself. At the very top, exposed to air and scavengers alike – crabs, birds – the bodies are slimy, broken down for parts, semi-skeletonised. Down further, they're still fleshed, literally ripe for autopsy; those are the ones Jutras wants in the worst way. While down further still . . .

Each stratum is an era, a span of time between massacres. The numbers vary: twos and threes, five-person groups at most, as opposed to the first and second layers' twenty-three. Deeper than that is where your particular skills will come most into play, differentiating one body's bones from another's, telling male from female, adult from child. You try not to feel bad about wanting to get down there as fast as possible, to see just how far down it all goes.

This tower of murder, thrown down, inverted. To you, it's a mystery, a challenge; to the people whose fragments it's made from – their relatives, at any rate – it's an obscenity, a disgrace. But you can't think about that, because it'll only slow you down, make you sloppy. Sentiment breeds mistakes.

Crouching down, feeling with both hands, gently but firmly. And saying silently to yourself, with every breath: *keep working, keep quiet, keep sharp. Miss nothing.* Assuring them, at the same time: *lie still, we're coming, finally. At long last.*

We're coming to bring you home.

You reached the island of Carcosa seven days ago, at 6:35 p.m. by your watch, only to find what looked like two suns staring down, one centred, the other offset – an upturned pupil, cataract-white, with a faint bluish tinge. *It's an optical illusion,* Jutras told you, during your conference-Skype briefing; *Everyone sees them. There's other things, too.*

Like what?

Just . . . things. It's not important.

(The clear implication: *you won't be there long enough for them to matter.* An assumption you don't question, since it suits you fine; you'll remember it later, though. And laugh.)

So yes, it's strange, though not unbearably so – no more so than the incredible heat or the smell accompanying it, rancid and inescapable, though you haven't even come near the dig site as yet; the black beaches with their smooth-washed half-glass sand, the masses of shrimp-coloured flowers and spindly nests of stick-insects creeping up every semi-vertical surface. Actually, all the colours are different here, just ever-so-slightly "off": the green laid on green of its grasses, fronds and vines isn't *your* green, not exactly. More like your green's occluded memory.

There's a wet woodsmoke tang to the air, like they've just doused a forest-fire. Breathing it in gives you a languorous, possessive contact high – opium smoke mixed with bone-dust.

According to Jutras, the island – itself just the merest jutting peak of an underwater mountain-range ringed with black smokers, incredibly volatile – was once centre-set with a volcano that exploded, Thera-style, its caldera becoming what's now known as "Lake" Hali. The quote-marks are because the lake itself is filled and re-filled with seawater brought in through a broken end-section that forms the island as a whole into a wormy crescent. Carcosa City occupies the crescent's midsection, its highest peak, while the two peninsulas formed by the crescent's horns almost overlap. The longer of the two is called Hali-joj'uk, "Hali-door" or "-gate", in the island's highly negotiable yet arcanely individual tongue. Wouldn't think there could be quite so many sub-dialects supported on an island whose entire population has never historically topped four hundred, and yet.

It's like every family has their own way of saying things, Jutras told you. *And they all understand each other, but they know you won't. That's why we have the interpreter.*

They don't trust folks from Away, Judy chimed in. *That's how they put it: there's them, and then there's Away. Everywhere else.*

Yeah, it's a serious Innsmouthian situation round these parts, Ken agreed. *Some inbred motherfuckers we're dealin' with, that's a certified fact.*

Ken, Jutras warned him, but Ken simply snorted.

What, man? It's just true. These people been marrying their cousins for a thousand years, by definition; cousins if they're lucky, *and some years? I'm willing to take a bet the gene-pool maybe didn't stretch all that far. Like those Amish villages where the guys all have the same first name, and every dog's named "Hund".*

Not a lot of cultural contamination on Carcosa, in other words, which is good in some ways, not so much in others. To cite another history of similar colonial isolation, in 1856 – fifty-two years after being officially rediscovered by the British – Pitcairn Island, inhabited by the descendants of the H.M.S. *Bounty*'s mutineers, lost 100% of its population, gaining only sixteen of them back three years after. Since then, its numbers have fluctuated up and down – as high as two hundred and fifty in 1936, as low as forty-three in 1996. Yet numbers in Carcosa apparently remain steady, as though maintaining a strict death per birth replace-the-race policy . . . barring the occasional mass murder, that is.

Because that's what's brought you here, of course – like it always does, no matter where, no matter with who. Because this is your "business", the reckoning of mortality: to sex bones and extract DNA, to separate violent death covered up from more wholesome detritus, plague-pits or accidents or Acts of God alike, the dreadful human wreckage left behind whenever earth gapes wide, whenever the jungle sneezes up something that makes people cough themselves to death or sweat blood from every pore, whenever the sea rises up and bears away all in its path.

The whole island takes up approximately eighteen square miles, "lake" included. Nine of those take you from the airstrip to Hali-jo'juk, where the causeway to the dig awaits: Funeral Rock, yet one more island *inside* an island, a tiny chip barely a mile across split off from the main rim back into Hali itself, a shelf of bare black crag-slopes cradling a black sand beach which separates completely from the peninsula at high tide.

This is where it all happened; where no one will say how many of the island's otherwise rigidly documented population were herded over no one will say how long a period of time, never to return. From what Judy and Ken have uncovered thus far, they think it must've begun long before the island was charted, let alone visited, and continued intermittently long after, with only the sheer numbers of the last mass-murder finally revealing the true nature of this particular "memorial" tradition at last . . . along with the fact that those taken to Funeral Rock for "burial" were not, strictly speaking, usually *dead* before the rocks and sand were thrown in on top of them.

All they know is, there's no telling how deep it goes down, Jutras told you, before you even started packing. *Which is why I need my best girl, Alice – to turn this around, ASAP.*

What's the hurry? you asked. *Top layer's the only one they can press charges with, right? I mean, the rest certainly proves a pattern of behaviour, local prejudices, superstitions, maybe even religion-based motive . . . but in prosecutorial terms, just how useful is that?*

Jutras sighed. *Hard to say. It's a . . . weird situation, to say the least; slippery. Nobody knows who's responsible, or claims not to, so the authorities have just scooped up every able-bodied man within a certain radius; they don't have a jail, so they're holding them in the hospital's contagious ward.*

Because women *never kill* anybody, *right?* But since you both knew the answer to that one, you asked instead: *who* are *the authorities in this case, exactly, anyways?*

Um . . . Wikipedia says the Hyades Islands, "a sub-archipelago thirty miles off the coast of East Timor," so – Indonesia, I guess? It's all pretty up in the air. A pause. *Point is, they don't even have cops here, let alone a court, so whoever does get charged with anything is going to have to be taken off-island for trial, and nobody's happy with* that *idea; the local garrison commander needs hard facts to keep Carcosa from blowing up around him, literally. Thus, us.*

You've worked with Jutras seven times before, all over. United Nations International Criminal Tribunal digs to start with, co-ordinated through The Hague – Darfur, then Cote d'Ivoire. Then on to smaller matters in far more obscure places, balancing corporate internal policing with volunteer work for far-flung, resource-poor communities. Carcosa definitely falls under the latter rubric, and also promises something the other sites most often don't: Mystery. Even back when you were finishing your internship in the Ontario Forensic Pathology Service, the final verdict on any case was almost never in doubt from the moment you first viewed the body on, be it murder, misadventure or J-FROG (Just Plain Fuckin' Ran Out of Gas).

I've never heard of the Hyades, actually, you admitted, feeling stupid. *Carcosa either.*

Yeah, I'm with you there; had to look 'em up on the plane. But ours is not to reason, right?

And you might have disagreed with him, on that last part – should have, probably. But you were jet-lagged already, which never helps. One more dig didn't seem that big a deal.

Now here you are waist-deep in it, learning better.

Decomp clings to everything, in both senses of the word, just like the heat puts paid to modesty, prompting you and Judy to roll your coveralls to the waist over lunch, so you won't get corpse-rub in your food. Later, you'll pack today's "grave bra" into a plastic bag full of Woolite and choose tomorrow's from the rack it's been drying on in your hotel room closet. You buy seven new ones for every dig, colour co-ordinated by weekday, and leave them behind afterwards, so stink-saturated they're only fit for burning.

The famous interpreter Jutras hired, Ringo Astur, sits with you under the canopy, waving flies away. Round-headed, eternally cheerful, chain-smoking imported cigarettes; his skin is the same colour as Carcosa City's brick-work, a coral-tinged light brown, hair worn in short corn-rows. *How many today, Alice?* he asks you every noon and every night, eyes charm-crinkling, like it's some local version of *How* you *doin'?*

Three so far, Ringo. Why?

Oh, no reason. That's a lot, yes?

More and more, you want to tell him. More, and more, and *more* . . . Just what have these people been *doing* out here all this time, anyways?

Tell me about the other city, you say, instead. *The one from across Hali.*

Hm, he replies. *Well . . . that city's also named Carcosa, supposedly. It appears lake-centre, where the volcano used to be – not always, not every night, but sometimes. Where the first Carcosa City stood once, before it dropped inside.*

Then there's a whole other Carcosa City under this lake?

A shrug. *So they say. And it appears, sometimes . . . we'd be closer to it here than back over there, if it did. They come down to the quay when it does, the people who live in it, and beckon, try to get us to row across.*

People live there?

Well, they look like people, yes, supposedly. They say they wear masks, those who've seen them.

You look down at your hands then, still stained from the grave; the sand's black tinge never seems to wash entirely off. Remembering one skull, its back crushed in with an axe-like implement, so fragile that when you threaded two fingers through its eye-sockets and a thumb through the nose-hole, it came apart in your hand – shed itself by sections even as you fought to keep it intact, yellow-grey bone sliding to sketch an entire fresh new face with palm-pink eyes and an unstrung, mud-filled mouth.

Unsurprising how easy they come apart, considering what you discovered on those top-layer excavations: Carcosans are full of cartilage, like sharks or octopi, with the proportion of actual collagen-poor bone to extensive net of tissue creepily small; all of them come out flexible yet springy, like osteogenesis imperfecta without the fracturing. You can see the signs from where you sit, in Ringo's bluish sclerae, his triangular face, that certain blurred malleability of feature which comes from most of your cranial plates simply not fusing, a head full of fontanelles and no joint left un-double. Once, in Carcosa City, you saw a not-exactly-small ten-year-old squeeze through a cat-door and pop out the other side laughing, to bound away into the brush.

Not enough bones in some ways, too many in others. And you're the only person, thus far, who ever seems to have thought of putting the extra ones together . . .

(But that's a private project, at least for now. You haven't even shown Jutras.)

It happens on two-sun days, mostly, around suns'-set, Ringo continues. *That's what they say. You look across Hali and there it is, all lit up, with the masks, and the beckoning. And then when you look up you see black stars high above, watching you.*

Who's this "they" you keep talking about, man? Ken yells at him, from over by the cooler. *I mean, you're related to basically everybody here, right? All those other Asturs? Old John-Paul-George Astur from the post office, Miss Sexy London Astur from the kelp farm? That dude Kilimanjaro Means We Couldn't Climb It Astur, from the boat repair?*

Don't be an arse, Ken, Judy tells him. *Jesus! What's it to you, anyhow?*

Now it's Ringo's turn to look down.

They don't talk to me much anymore, he says, finally. *Because I went Away. So I can't really ask them about any of it.*

You never saw it yourself, then? you find yourself asking.

Well . . . I did, yes. Once or twice, I think. I was young, a long time back. It was before, and Away – well, Away makes things like that hard to remember.

Ever try to go over?

No, no. That would be – that's a bad idea.

You nod, take a swig of water. Then something he said earlier comes back, prompting another question, before you can think better of it:

Closer over here . . . is that why people really came to Funeral Rock, in the first place? So they'd have less of a way to row, if they wanted to make it to the other Carcosa?

Ringo looks at you hard for a long moment, not speaking. 'Til: *no,* he says, finally. *That's not why. They came to bury, or get buried. Like the King, in the story.*

. . . what story?

The King, Ringo tells you, once ruled in Other Carcosa City, before he was expelled and set adrift. He came from somewhere else entirely, far Away, further than anywhere – came walking through their gates on foot one two-sun day, at suns'-set, and when asked to remove his mask as a gesture of friendship, claimed he didn't wear one.

Couldn't they tell? you ask, reasonably enough. But Ringo just shakes his head.

He looked . . . different, supposedly. Pale, yellow, with horns, all over – no one could think that was really his face; that's what they say. And yet . . . That's why the volcano blew up, you know. So they say.

Because of the King?

Because he wouldn't leave. So the people in Other Carcosa City made it happen, to make sure he did.

Wouldn't that have destroyed them, *too?*

Ringo shrugs. Concluding, after a beat: *well, no, supposedly. They're – different.*

Later, back at camp, Judy maintains she's actually heard this same story a few times already, from other islanders. Which surprises the hell out of Ken, who – for all his bitching – probably hasn't tried talking to anybody without Ringo translating since he got here. Jutras easily confirms it, though, by pulling out an .mp3 he made on his phone of a woman (Miss Sexy London Astur?) telling the tale in Stage One Pidgin, the Malacca-Malay-inflected version of English Carcosans might've picked up from passing sailors, peppered with words you either can't hear or don't understand, your brain papering over the lacunae with whatever seems most contextually appropriate—

Many and many, one time there is to be being one [king] [magician] [warlord] [traitor], who is to be having all strength from the black pit of [stars] [salt] [silt], the bottom of every [hole] [mouth] [grave]. He is to be wearing no [mask] [face] [name]. He is to be being torn apart and ground down, thrown in seas, sunk deep, for fish to be eating. But then one time there are fish to be eating him, and islanders are to be eating the fish, with [pieces] [seeds] [bones] of him inside them. And then islanders are to be having children with [no bones] [no names] [no faces] . . .

You gulp, taste bile. *Jesus,* you say. *So . . . that's it, right? The motive.* That's *why?*

Classic Othering, with a fairytale spin, Jutras agrees. *I particularly like the whole Evil King deal that obviously keeps being trotted out every time these throwback genetic payloads pop up; you wait 'til it gets obvious, re-brand them as changelings spawned by the Enemy, then take 'em over to Funeral Rock and let "nature" take its course. "We 'had' to kill them, you see, because they weren't human, not really. Not like* us."

Look who's talkin', Ken mutters.

Judy frowns. *What I don't understand, though, is where this all came from, originally. The* idea *of this Evil King, of Other Carcosa City . . . all of it.*

"Away", I guess, Jutras replies. *Except . . . no, they were doing this long before anybody else ever came by here, so – some sort of primal phobia about the sea, maybe: all that water, everything underneath it, the earthquakes, all the instability. It has to be* somebody's *fault.* A pause. *That's the theory, anyways. Except it's hard to say, because, uh . . . nobody will say.*

You can't possibly believe—

Of course not, Alice, but they *believe it. Enough to kill twenty-three children, and God knows how many more . . .*

Now it's your turn to nod, to stare. And reply, eventually:

. . . I should show you something, probably.

Looking at what you've so neatly laid out on a canvas tarp in a shallow trench three feet from the grave's lip, elements-sheltered under a fresh new tent, Jutras says nothing, just stares down. You don't blame him, exactly; did it yourself, the first time you finally thought to stop and breathe. Now the words spill out in a similar rush, barely interrupted, monologue paced to an adrenaline rush tachycardia beat, so fast it barely seems to be *your* voice you're both hearing say these things, with complete declarative confidence – the same authoritarian, spell-casting rhythm which renders truth from lies, makes fiction into fact, simply by stating even the most ridiculous-sounding things out loud.

You study him closely as you speak, too, just in case: strain to read every minor shift, each muscle-twitch, each spasm. Almost as though you think that at some point his own eye-whites are going to turn blue, jaw and temples deforming, as the planes of his skull soften 'til they slide to form someone else's face entirely.

Remember how Ken kept saying these people weren't like us? Well, asshole that he is, turns out he's actually right. The adult human body has two hundred and six bones. These . . . have more. Best approximate total: just over three hundred and fifty, like a human infant, almost as though their bones never fused properly – and three times the normal amount of cartilage, so it doesn't much matter that they didn't. Like they were never meant *to; like they were* supposed *to reach adulthood able to squeeze themselves easily through spaces that'd break a normal adult human's neck.*

Also, the reason it's "just over" is because it seems each body's inevitably got two duplicates of one particular bone . . . except it's never the same one. This woman has two fibulae. This man has two second thoracic vertebrae. This child has two mandibles – must've made it hard to talk, especially since the second one is adult-sized. It's like God was smuggling a whole other person into Carcosa, hidden inside these people's bodies.

But – what can I say; I guess everybody caught on.

Oh, and now that we've reached the bottom – did that yesterday – you know how many corpses are in this grave, exactly? Three hundred and fifty.

Plus one.

It's that "plus one" Jutras' looking at right now, the nameless guest at this carrion feast, painstakingly pieced together in anatomical explode-a-view. On its own, it'd seem like some drunk pre-med student practical joke, a botched bastardisation Transformered together from three or more skeletons at once: spine articulated like a boa constrictor's, ribs everywhere, even in its limbs; skull like a Rubik's helmet, slabbed and fluted and interlocking, a puzzle-box with a million solutions but no answers. The fact that it proved surprisingly easy to assemble is the least of your worries, a strangeness so trivial it's barely worth sparing the energy to consider . . . not when there's just so much more about the whole exercise to avoid thinking about at all, in retrospect.

How long has that mould been growing on it? Jutras asks.

What mould?

He points, and you finally see it: grey as the bones themselves, furry. Hard to tell what you thought it was before, if you even registered its existence – moisture? Condensation?

I . . . don't know. Why?

. . . no reason.

But he's already backing away, step by step; peeling the flap without looking, shimmying himself free. You hear him take a long, shaky breath, almost like he's tensing against nausea, trying not to vomit. His walkie gives an almighty crackling howl.

There's something happening, he says, at last, after a hushed, one-sided conversation. *In the city. I have to go.*

And a minute later, it's just you and the bones again.

Jutras is out of contact for most of the next day, which means he isn't there for the undersea quake that rattles the island. Minor as tremors go, the epicentre's out by the black smoker ring that keeps Carcosa's shores so fertile, so teeming with fish and kelp-forests; closer to Carcosa City than Funeral Rock, thankfully, so the back-slop doesn't do much more than submerge the causeway far faster and for far longer than expected. You didn't even notice it yourself until you came out of the tent and found Ken and Judy on the horn with Jutras, yelling at him about being stuck on-site for the night until the causeway emerges again. Said prospect bothers you less than it should, but that could just be sheer exhaustion. Who knew watching mould grow could be so draining.

What *does* bother you – silencing Ken and Judy as well – is what Jutras finally tells you, when he gets a word in edgewise: the quake brought in a mini-tsunami that cracked the hospital apart, shearing off the wall of the contagious ward. In the confusion, most massacre suspects cut and ran, disappearing into a sympathetic web of back-rooms, basements, cliff-caves and other assorted hidey-holes. Surprisingly few injuries amongst the military guards, and all from natural causes rather than any sort of hostile action, but all of you can read between the lines; the garrison is confused and demoralised from the bottom up, perhaps even fixing to cut and run, and the islanders themselves . . . well, they aren't happy. To say the least.

They've heard what you're doing here, Ringo tells you, after Jutras signs off. *Putting the King back together – that's why this happened. They want to stop you.*

Ken snorts. *So these dudes in jail, what, called up a wave and surfed on out of there? C'mon, man. Army'll pick 'em up by tomorrow; this place ain't big enough to hide in, not for long.*

You don't know that. You don't know anything about *us.*

I know enough, man.

No. Ringo shakes his head, visibly struggling to keep polite. *It's . . . not safe for you here, not now, any of you. You should go.*

Go where? you ask, waving Ken silent, while Judy hugs herself. *Where should we go, Ringo?*

Without hesitation: Away, *of course. And take me with you, when you do.*

Though you're hardly a mycologist or sapro-phytologist by trade, anyone who works enough decomp learns to ID the key fungal players soon enough. The stuff that's growing over "the King"'s bones still doesn't match anything you recognise: too tough, spreading too fast, especially without an identifiable nutrient-source. You take a moment to look up the region on your tablet, looking for a local flora-and-fauna rundown, and pause at Wikipedia's disambiguation page for "Hyades". There are four entries: the islands, the band, the Greek mythological figures, and a star cluster in the constellation Taurus.

You look up in the dusk light, out across the lake. The "twin suns" sink towards the horizon in a blurry shimmer. A mirage, an illusion; the same thing that makes the suns look almost bluish-white, rather than red-gold. So Ringo says. You look back down to your tablet, and click on the entry for the star cluster. Thinking, as you do, about articles some of your geekier friends have sent to you, essays about such things as static wormholes, and equipotential space-time points; quantum tunnelling, black branes and folded space, negative energy densities.

The Hyades cluster is more than six hundred million years old, far older than most such stellar groups, a survivor of the aeons by orbiting far from galactic centre. At least twenty of its stars are A-type white giants, with seventeen or eighteen of them thought likely to be binary – double-star – systems. It appears in the *Iliad* on the shield that Hephaestus made for Achilles, and is named for the daughters of Atlas, who wept so hard over the death of their brother Hyas they eventually became the patron stars of rain.

Twilight deepens, and your tablet's glow increases in the growing dark. But your shadow grows sharp to one side, beyond what the tablet could illuminate, and you look up once more.

Above the centre of the lake, where the volcano exploded centuries ago, lights glow in a scattered matrix of green, blue, gold and red, clear and cold. The darkness between them seems to outline shapes – structures, blocks, towers. They're hard to look at, defying your eyes' focus almost painfully. Can't tell if the blur is distance, or atmosphere mirage, or the wake of motion too fast to follow. The blue-green, poisonous light of the setting suns behind it twists your stomach. You feel the whole thing *pulling*, physically, like a hook in the gut: some second force of gravity, pressing you towards the lake and the place you know isn't there, *can't* be there—

—not because it isn't real, but because it's somewhere else. Some utter, alien elsewhere, so far away its light is older than your species.

It's that pull, that nausea and that disbelief, which keeps you from hearing the tumult until it's too late. Distracted by Other Carcosa City's spectacular appearance, you simply haven't noticed the boats' approach, silent and sure – pontooned sea-canoes, anchoring themselves at Funeral Rock's base so their passengers can shinny up the handhold-pocked cliff and emerge through those cave-entrances you never even knew were there, almost under your feet.

A burst of bullets, muzzle-flare in the night, and Ringo's already up, hauling on your arm: *Alice, come, come on, Alice – now, now now, they're here! Leave everything!*

But – Ken, Judy, Jesus, Ringo! What about . . .

Too late, come on*! We have to* go—

Across Hali, behind Other Carcosa City's gleaming shoreline, you can just glimpse the "real" capitol going up in flames, a series of controlled explosions. Is one of those Jutras' field-office, the garrison, the sea-plane that brought you here? Over near the grave, meanwhile, Ken's scrabbling for his data, uploading frantically; one shot catches him in the shoulder, another in the upper back, sending him straight over the lip. You can hear him thrashing down below, desperately trying to cover himself in enough sand-muck to turn invisible. Ringo pulls you headlong while the attackers rush the camp, smashing and tearing, hurling equipment and evidence alike into the sea. Ripping up the tents, they riddle every prepped body-bag they uncover with yet more gunfire, as though they think something might be hiding in there.

Good thing I moved him, you find yourself thinking. *Good thing, good thing . . .*

Ringo drops to his knees, dragging you along with him; your knees jolt, painfully. *In here, Alice,* he says. *Come on! This one goes out the opposite side – we can swim, they'll never see us.*

Swim? *Where the hell* to?

Other Carcosa City, of course; no one will expect it. Can't you see them, beckoning?

But: that's just a bit too much crazy to stomach, even now. So here you pull back, wrenching yourself free, even as

Ringo worms his way slickly down into the earth, gone in seconds – you'd never make it anyways, is what you tell yourself. The gap's far too narrow, too twisting; you'd simply lodge fast, bruised and scraped and strained to breaking, to die crushed like a bug. You let him go instead, whispering *Goodbye*.

Why? Judy yells from behind you, uselessly, drawing another burst. *Why, why?*

Because some things are meant to stay buried, a voice replies, from deep inside.

Then: spotlights stab down out of the growing dusk, helicopter rotors roaring, as speakers filter what must be orders far past the point of comprehensibility. More gunfire strafes the camp, this time vertically; Judy's head explodes outright, GSW damage simultaneously shock-hammering away one half of your body in a series of consecutive hits to forearm, shoulder, hip, thigh. The downdraft wraps you in already-torn tent-fabric like a plastic bag shroud, momentum rolling you straight into the scrub where you stowed "the King"'s reassembled body, so you sprawl almost nose to whatever it uses for a nose with it.

No pain, simply shock, cold and huge enough to sharpen your observational skills to inhuman levels. The not-fungus has finished its work. The creature's skin is black everywhere but its pallid mask of a face, slick and soft, oily to the touch, almost warm; that's your blood it's soaking up, sponge-like, as if every pore is a feeding orifice, swelling with the sacrifice.

And its massive, horned head turns, yellow eyes cracking open. Locking upon yours.

I am here, it tells you; *look across the lake, where my city rises, and watch us beckon. You have done me great service, bringing me back into this world.*

Now: be not afraid, lie still, lie quiet. Your long wait is over.

Beyond the hovering 'copter, those two suns sink down, white-blue turning red, filling Hali's caldera with false lava. And when you slump over onto your back, looking up again by sheer default, you see stars: Soft black stars, almost indistinguishable, in a black, black sky.

The King lays one scaly hand on your brow, lightly. Almost affectionately.

I am coming, he promises, *to take you home.*

EVANGELINE WALTON

The Other One

EVANGELINE WALTON (1907–96) was the pseudonym used by Evangeline Wilna Ensley. Born to a Quaker family in Indianapolis, Indiana, she suffered from chronic respiratory illness as a child. Treated with silver nitrate tincture, her fair skin absorbed the pigment and turned blue-grey, which continued to darken as she aged.

She grew up reading the works of L. Frank Baum, Lord Dunsany, Algernon Blackwood and James Stephens, and most of her fiction was written between the 1920s and the early 1950s.

Inspired by the Welsh *Mabinogi*, her first novel, *The Virgin and the Swine* was published in 1936, but it was not until it was reissued as *The Island of the Mighty* in 1970, as part of the Ballantine Adult Fantasy Series, that the subsequent three books in the series – *The Children of Lyr*, *The Song of Rhiannon* and *Prince of Annwn* – saw print. All four novels were collected in an omnibus volume, *The Mabinogian Tetralogy*, in 2002.

Meanwhile, *Witch House* was published in 1945 as the initial title in the "Library of Arkham House Novels of Fantasy and Terror", and her other novels include *The Cross and the Sword* and *The Sword is Forged*.

During her lifetime, she was honoured with three Mythopoeic Fantasy Awards and two Locus Awards. She also received the World Fantasy Convention Award in 1985 and the World Fantasy Award for Life Achievement in 1989.

At the time of her death, Walton left behind a number of unpublished novels, poems and a verse play. The author's family has been working with Douglas A. Anderson in going through her papers, where they also discovered a handful of unpublished short stories. "The Other One" is one of these, along with her tale that appeared in the previous volume of *The Mammoth Book of Best New Horror*, and both are included in the posthumous collection *Above Ker-Is and Other Stories*.

In a letter to her agent dated August 7, 1950, the author seems to be referring to the story that follows: "If you think this story has any possibilities as a 'slick', but that it needs cutting or altering, I hope that you'll advise me . . . I think the central situation is appealing, but this type of subject matter is so foreign to me that I can't rely on my own judgement."

Centipede Press has produced an expanded edition of *Witch House* containing bonus material, while Tachyon Publications recently issued Walton's unpublished Gothic thriller *She Walks in Darkness* (written in the 1960s) with a cover by Thomas Canty.

I SHOULD HAVE LOCKED the door. You can't drag a solid body through a locked door. Fire would have finished the thing; without the body it couldn't have come back; not out of just ashes. But perhaps it is not there after all – the shape that comes whenever night comes. Maybe Anne was right, and the strain has been too much for me. Anne!

But it wasn't always all in my brain. Not last year, when I first met Anne MacNair. I'd sprained my wrist and couldn't finish a story that a magazine editor needed by a certain date. Somebody in his office told me where I could get a good typist cheap, and that typist was Anne.

I remember asking, "If she's good, why is she cheap?" and Miss Munson – or Miss Baker, whichever it was, I can't remember – looking a little queer.

"Well, I don't know exactly. She's had some kind of trouble – illness in the family, I think, something quite tragic, though it's hard to find out much about her – she's a nice, normal-looking kid, but she keeps herself to herself as if she had the plague. Her people live way down south – a father and stepmother; and I suppose she has to send money home. Anyway, she's anxious for all the work she can get. And her work is good, Frank; I've seen it."

Frank is my name; Frank Carter.

"She won't come to your rooms though," the woman added. "That's a thing she's always very particular about – so particular it's funny. She won't work except in her own apartment."

Anne had a shabby little place off 42nd St. She'd had it for years, I learned later, although she was still a young girl – very young to have been living alone so long.

At least I thought she was living alone. There was no name but hers listed at that apartment number according to the little directory by the front door. And when I walked into the sitting-room that was the only real room she had (the bed was an in-a-door affair), the door into the tiny kitchenette was open. And I saw no one in there.

Not that I was looking for anybody else. Or would have been after I saw Anne.

She wasn't a regulation pin-up girl. She was too quiet for that. Her prettiness was so quiet that you didn't realise, until you'd looked at her awhile, that it was perfect to the point of beauty. The first thing you noticed about her was that she looked clean and trim and dainty. And I'll still swear that she was clean, inside and out – I'll swear that to the end and beyond.

I offered her the standard rates, and asked if I could stay and dictate to her that afternoon, or if I'd better come back in the morning. But she said, "Stay. I've got some other work to do, but I can do it tonight."

I noticed, as she said it, that she glanced uneasily toward the other side of the room. As if there might be somebody there, somebody she'd rather not have there. That was what first made me glance toward the kitchenette. But it was so small that I'd have sworn nobody could have been in there. Not unless it was an almost paper-thin person hiding between the refrigerator and the open door.

Anne said again, with a relieved note in her voice, "This is a good time for you to stay." And I stayed.

For three hours we worked steadily. I dictated, and she wrote, never even looking up from her typewriter. And then all of a sudden her fingers began to move more slowly on the keys; not really slowly, but without their original crisp speed.

I had been walking up and down the room – I don't find it easy to dictate sitting – and suddenly I stopped. Stopped walking and stopped talking. Beside a chair that had been empty when I came in, and wasn't empty now.

Anne was sitting in it too, working, her fingers moving busily over the keys of a typewriter that wasn't there.

I took one startled glance across the room, saw that she was still in her old place at the typewriter table. Another showed me that there wasn't any mirror on the wall, though a mirror would have reflected the typewriter as well as the girl.

Then I took a jump backward – a pretty fast jump – away from that chair, and looked again.

She was still there, the second Anne. The same hair and face, the same figure and dress, the same busily moving fingers. I even saw, looking down, that the strings of her left shoe were coming untied, and I looked across the room and saw that the original Anne's left shoe was coming untied in just the same way, and just the same place.

Then she looked up and saw me, and the thing that I was staring at. The thing that shouldn't have been there. And for a second her face crumpled up like that of a child about to cry.

Then she said steadily, though with pain in her voice, "Do not mind her, Mr Carter. It is my sister Mary – my twin sister. She will not speak to you, nor pay any attention to what you say. She lives in a world of her own. She always has – ever since my mother was killed in an automobile accident when we were little."

So that was it, I thought. The illness in her family wasn't down south, it was up here, with her. And she had trouble getting work because of the crazy sister. Couldn't go out to an office, of course – couldn't leave her alone. And people who came in were startled, as I had been.

I stammered, "I see. I'm sorry," and went on dictating. But I found it hard to concentrate on my story again; unpleasant, somehow, to think of how quietly Mary must have stood there, those three hours, pressed into that narrow space between the kitchenette door and the refrigerator; into those few inches that I hadn't thought would hold any human being.

She'd watched us from there, her sister and me. Watched us, and then crept in at last so softly that I hadn't heard her. So softly that the door hadn't even creaked as she swung it outward to release herself from behind it.

It should have creaked. It must be a very good door.

We worked another half-hour; and all that time Mary's fingers moved just as Anne's moved, only with no keyboard beneath them. Typing on air. Imitating her sister was the one thing she had brains enough to do, I supposed. Probably she'd even noticed that Anne's shoestrings were coming undone, and had untied her own to match. It wouldn't be pleasant to be watched like that, always, every minute of every waking hour.

I gave up, after that half-hour. I told Anne, "I'm tired, and you must be. Suppose we go out to dinner?"

I felt sorry for the kid. I wanted to show her that her sister hadn't scared me off, and besides, I liked her. Even then I knew that I liked her a lot.

She looked scared. She said, "No. Thank you very much, Mr Carter, but I can't. I can't leave my sister."

"Bring her along," I said. "And stop calling me Mr Carter. My name's Frank."

She hesitated a moment. She said then, "You would be embarrassed, Mr Carter. Mary would not eat anything – she never eats before strangers – but she would pretend she was. She always imitates every move I make."

That was what I'd guessed; I suppose I felt proud of being right, and I still wanted to be kind. I said heartily, "Well, let her. It's nobody's business but ours. Come along."

And she gave in. She let me take her. Dinner dates didn't often come her way, poor kid; not with a sister like hers.

The hour was early for dinner, and we found a little table in a corner of a quiet restaurant. Nobody seemed to notice Mary, although she kept just lifting her spoon up and down, up and down from the bowl of soup I had brought to her; I told the waiter the second lady had no appetite. After the meat was brought and Anne began to eat it Mary used her spoon like a fork. But presently I forgot her; Anne and I were busy talking, and Anne was enjoying everything like a child. Her eyes were big and shining, as if she'd never been in a restaurant at night before.

We were beginning dessert when I looked around and noticed that Mary wasn't there. She'd gone as suddenly and silently as, earlier, there in the apartment, she had come.

I expected Anne to be disturbed, wildly upset even, but she wasn't. She only said, quietly, "She must have gone home."

"You can trust her to get there all right?" I asked.

"Yes. She will be back sooner or later." For a moment the gayety went out of her face. "You can always trust Mary to come back."

It was her look-out, not mine; I said nothing more. I took her to the theatre, and she enjoyed that as she had enjoyed the restaurant. Like a little girl, having a great treat. She seemed to have forgotten all about the work she was supposed to do that night. Her eyes sparkled like diamonds, and when I took her home I kissed her at the door, and her mouth was fresh and sweet. So sweet that I forgot to wonder if Mary was waiting for her, behind the door; the wonder that, as we walked down the hall, had been crawling up and down my back like a cold worm.

During the next few days I kept telling myself that it was silly, superstitious, to have that cold, creepy feeling about

Mary. To be afraid of an idiot girl. Except for bad luck – that accident that had made both girls motherless and knocked her silly – she'd have been as warm and sweet and exciting as Anne was. But the way she moved – you never saw her coming or going, you only knew suddenly that she was in a room or that she wasn't – got on my nerves. I couldn't help it. I couldn't help that any more than I could keep away from Anne. I finished my story, and dictated another and another. And always Mary was in and out, like Anne's reflection got loose from a mirror; and whenever she came some of the life seemed to go out of Anne – most of the energy and sparkle. I kept noticing that; I didn't like it.

Then one day I asked Anne to marry me. I remember how quietly she sat there, with her hands folded on her knees and the tears dropping down on them, brightly, soundlessly, her big eyes wide and wistful like the eyes of a child staring into a candy store, and knowing that it can never have any.

"I am sorry, Frank. I would like very much to marry you. But I can't; I can't leave Mary. And you could never stand it – having her there always, year after year. Everywhere. For there would never be any place, Frank, where I was, where she would not come. She could not be kept out."

And then I saw Mary, sitting across the room. She hadn't been in the apartment when I came (I was sure of that, I had learned to look behind doors), but she was there now. And for once she wasn't imitating Anne. No tears were falling from her eyes; they were watching us, but watching me more than Anne, and there was an intent look in them; an eager, avid look. Like a hungry cat's.

I saw her reflection in the mirror above Anne's little mantel. It came to me, with a start, that it was the first time I had noticed that.

I said roughly, "You've got your own life to live. Why don't you send Mary away – to some good place where they'd look after her better, probably, than you can? I can afford it. She'd soon forget you."

"No – no! I can't!" Anne cried out as if in pain. Or terror. "It's impossible, Frank! You don't know what you're asking."

"I do know," I said stubbornly. "Sometimes you've got to be a little hard on one person, honey, to be kind to more than one. We've got our rights too, you and I."

She laughed then, a queer little laugh. She said, "I have no rights, Frank. I am not – like other people. I oughtn't ever to have gone out with you. I didn't want to hurt you; I was just hungry; hungry to – to be like other girls. To live. Sometimes I get so hungry that I understand how Mary herself must feel. Outside – farther outside even than I am."

"What do you mean?" I had a queer sense of something alien, cold. Of inexplicable, black cold.

She said, "It doesn't matter. Please go now, Frank. For good."

I didn't; I argued. But she would only say over and over, "Please go now, Frank – it's no use. Please go." We both lost control of ourselves; I shouted and she cried. And all the time that still figure in the chair across the room just sat there, quietly watching us. She didn't look stupid or scared or sympathetic; she looked strong and sinister; sure of herself. Almost amused.

Once I saw Anne dart a glance at her; a strange, sidewise glance, and then – I *knew!*

It wasn't love or pity that bound Anne to Mary. There was fear in Anne's eyes – stark fear.

I caught my girl in my arms; I tried to pull her to the door. I said, "Come outside with me, honey. Somewhere where we can talk alone." I meant to send doctors back to take Mary – trained men who could handle her if she got violent. I suppose I thought she might; I don't really know what I thought.

But Anne pulled away from me. She was suddenly calm. "It's not so simple as that, Frank. Places don't matter. No walls, no locks, no distances, could ever keep Mary away from me. She *is* me."

I said hotly, "That's crazy!" But again I felt that queer inner chill.

She smiled and shook her head. "If you won't believe me go to Charleston and ask my father. He'll explain; I can't. If I even tried to I'd sound as mad as you think Mary is."

And in the end I went to Charleston. Went telling myself that Anne was hysterical and that it was no wonder, after years of life with a lunatic, quite possibly a dangerous lunatic. Went knowing that I was, somehow, unreasonably afraid.

I didn't expect to like Anne's father. I had no use for a man who'd so shirk his own responsibilities, shift all the burden to his daughter. Mary might have given her stepmother the creeps, been unbearable around the house – I could understand that; but he should have put her away years ago. Never have let her fasten herself around Anne's neck.

But I found him a gentle, ineffectual-seeming little man with a soft voice and a sensitive face. When I walked into the sleepy-looking little stationery store he ran, he greeted me with a smile that was very like Anne's.

I said, "May I have a talk with you, Mr MacNair? I've just come from New York. I met your daughters there – Anne and her twin sister."

His face turned white at that. The smile went away. He said, after a minute, "Yes, of course, Mr – Mr – I didn't catch the name. How is Anne? How are – they?"

I had lunch with him. I told him everything – how I wanted Anne, why she wouldn't marry me.

"It's not right, Mr MacNair," I ended. "Anne has a right to her own life – to a chance to get something out of it, poor kid. You must be Mary's legal guardian; you ought to be able to do something about it."

He looked miserable. He said unhappily, "My boy, for fourteen years – ever since Anne was eight – I have been wanting to do something about it. I have tried – for many years I tried. But nobody on earth has any control over Mary. You see – Anne is my only daughter."

I stared. I didn't say anything. For a minute I wondered if the whole MacNair family was mad. Or if I was.

He went on, "It began when Anne was eight years old, you see. When her mother was killed. She and the child were in the car together, on a country road, when it crashed. People came in time to pull the little girl out, but my wife was – burned. Anne must have heard her screaming. And for hours afterward she kept crying, 'I tried to pull her out, Daddy – I tried, but I couldn't! I couldn't!'

"I didn't take any notice of that, then; I set it down to shock. Anne wasn't much hurt, but she was cruelly shaken – beside herself. And she couldn't really have tried to help her mother; she'd been found pinned beneath the wreckage, helpless to move. Later, much later, I talked with one of the men who'd been first on the scene, and he said that he'd been surprised when they found my little girl where she was, pinned – he'd thought, as he first came up, that he saw a child silhouetted against the flames. Been badly scared, he said, for fear she'd be burned before he could reach her. He had thought she was – trying to pull at something."

He paused a moment, his mouth tightening.

"I don't like to think of that, sir," – with a pitiful kind of dignity – "of my wife. Afterwards, for a long time, Anne wasn't well. She was nervous and cried easily, and the housekeeper I engaged didn't get along with her. She said the child disobeyed her and played in the yard when she was supposed to be in the house – things like that. Anne always denied it; whenever there was any mischief done she'd say, 'It was Mary.' I thought Mary was one of those imaginary playmates children make up. Then one day we found Anne safely inside the house when the housekeeper had sworn she was out of it and there'd been no chance for her to slip back in; I concluded the woman was being completely unreasonable – picking on the child. That was why I married Charlotte Trumbull sooner than I would have otherwise; I thought Anne needed a mother – more intelligent care. But Charlotte didn't get along with Anne either. She maintained that the child wouldn't stay in her bed at night – kept creeping around the house like a little ghost.

"One night I saw her myself, after midnight, on the stairs. I called to her and she didn't answer. I followed her and took her by the shoulder – and it was like catching hold of a piece of muslin. My fingers went through the whole shoulder as if it were a nightgown – closed on each other. Through something that was too thin, too – *wet* – for flesh. It was like thrusting your hand, wrist-deep, into a cloud.

"And then I heard a voice from the top of the stairs – Anne's voice: 'Did you call me, Daddy?' She'd come out of her room and was standing there, wide-eyed and puzzled, fresh from sleep – and I looked down again at the thing I had under my hand. It was still there – Anne's face, Anne's curls, Anne's night-things, perfect as a reflection in a mirror – and then it quivered, as your reflection in a pool quivers when you disturb the water, and was gone.

"But Anne had seen. She smiled. She actually beamed. She said, 'You've found Mary, Daddy. You see now – Mary's real; I don't tell stories.' And I ran back up the stairs and grabbed her and carried her back into her room as if all the devils out of Hell were after us. I locked the door and knew, even as I locked it, that no lock could keep that – *thing* out; that uncanny fleshless thing that was my daughter's twin."

He stopped and mopped his brow. "That was the beginning. Charlotte wouldn't believe it at first, but presently she had to; we saw the two of them together – often. The situation grew worse as Anne grew older; we couldn't send her to school or camp, of course; there was – too much confusion. She had to give up all young friends of her own age. We tried doctors; the thing seemed to come oftener if Anne were ill or tired, but tonics, exercise, all such things, failed. Sometimes the shape would stay away for days, weeks even, but always it came back. As a rule it did nothing in particular, only wandered about aimlessly or imitated Anne's motions, but it was – unnerving. And there were a few times—" He stopped again, then said slowly, reluctantly, as if the words were being forced out of him:

"There is no malice in my daughter, Mr Carter, but it is only fair to tell you that there is, sometimes, in that spectre. One night when Anne was eighteen, Charlotte, my wife, fell downstairs. She is permanently crippled – lame. And she has always sworn that Mary pushed her. Her fear of them – of even Anne – made all our lives intolerable after that. So when my daughter wanted to go to New York I did not oppose her so much as I should have liked to – the family doctor said, too, that she might be stronger, happier, in new surroundings; that the thing might not come back there. For he *knows*, Carter – after all these years he too knows. If you do not believe me, ask him."

I did believe him. I even felt sorry for him. It would have taken a stronger man than he to save Anne – I wasn't so sure, any longer, that I could do it myself.

He asked me a few questions. How Anne was – how strong she seemed – and, in a way, how Mary was. Had I ever touched her? Ever seen her reflection in a mirror?

He seemed depressed when I had seen her reflection.

"That is a bad sign; a very bad sign. When Anne was ten or twelve you could not see Mary's reflection in a mirror. But as time passed she seemed to grow stronger – more substantial. It was not until the day before Charlotte's accident on the stairs that we ever saw her reflection in a mirror. But of course that accident may really have been one – Charlotte may simply have slipped; for years she had been very nervous."

He didn't believe that, I knew. He believed that his daughter was possessed of – or haunted by – a devil in her own likeness. But I did not. All the way back to New York, on the swift plane that carried me away from the sleepy old Southern city, I tried to figure out exactly what I did believe.

The ancient Egyptians believed in what they called the *ka*, a "Double", a body within a body; they mummified their dead and built elaborate tombs, believing that the *ka* might come and go like a live man from that house of death.

They thought that sometimes it might leave the body of a living man and make journeys that he could not. Modern occultists meant much the same thing, apparently, when they talked of astral bodies. Well, suppose that that long-ago night when she heard her burning mother's cries, Anne's Double had come loose from her physical body? Had tried to help but failed, because it lacked strength, solidity? And had never rightly been able to get back inside again – to make safe anchor within her? A lot of what we had all felt about the creepiness of "Mary" could be set down to imagination, superstition – she was only a kind of floating doll after all, without real consciousness of her own.

Even if she had tried, a time or two, to do harm, what of it? We all have evil impulses, desires we never acknowledge to our normal, waking consciousness. Sex does play a part between parents and children; little girls are often jealous of their fathers' attention to even their own mothers. Anne might subconsciously have wished her stepmother dead; Mary might have tried to do something about it, there on the stairs. But she hadn't actually killed the woman. And Anne could never have been very happy since her mother's death; if she were well and happy her whole being might integrate, coalesce, again; Mary might vanish.

Anyhow, I loved her. I couldn't leave her; leave her alone, shut up for life with that weird, more than half-bodiless thing. Any more than I could have deserted a child, or a comrade in battle.

I went straight from the airport to her apartment. I found the door half-open, and Anne in the midst of packing, standing in the middle of a confusion of clothes and suitcases. Alone; blessedly alone.

She burst into tears at sight of me. "Oh, Frank, Frank, I should have left sooner! But I never really thought you'd come back; how could I? How—"

And I swept her into my arms. I knew, then, that she hadn't the strength to fight me any longer.

I won't try to tell about the weeks that followed. You can't describe love. We were happy; completely happy; and

Mary never came at all. We almost forgot her; it seemed silly to go on with the plans I'd made; to buy a ranch in the West where we could be alone together and there'd seldom be anyone to notice Mary if she did appear.

But the ranch would be a good place for me to write. I thought, too, that there might be less chance of Anne's getting nervous there. Brooding over the idea of Mary's coming back, and so perhaps, by sheer force of fear, invoking her.

In the fall of '49 we found exactly what we wanted: an old adobe ranch house in the mountains of southern Arizona. Its deep recessed porch looked out over the most marvellous view that I've ever seen; a wilderness of jagged peaks and steep, massive slopes, their golden-brownness dotted with green saguaros. Slopes that curved for a little way and then dropped, sheer, into a valley that looked like a knife-cut slashed in the bowels of the earth.

Anne was all right until after Christmas. It was on New Year's Eve that she caught the cold.

She was feverish for a day or two. I slept on the living-room couch so as not to disturb her. Something was wrong with our telephone – it went bad very suddenly, with that contrariness that inanimate objects sometimes seem to have – but old Mr Barker, from the nearest ranch, offered to go for a doctor. He'd been a good neighbour; glad, I think, being old and alone, of somebody to talk to, and of a chance to eat Anne's cooking. I thought his offer a godsend, but it made Anne positively hysterical. She did not want a doctor.

She kept saying over and over, "He'd see her! The doctor would see her! She's standing over there in the corner, Frank. Smiling. She's planning something. Oh, don't let her come any nearer – don't, Frank, don't!"

Neither old Barker nor I saw anything. But I didn't let him go for the doctor; perhaps I should have.

Toward evening of the second day Anne had a more lucid interval. She said: "Frank, do you remember? Was my apartment door open that day you came back from

Charleston?" And when I said yes, she drew in her breath sharply: "I was afraid of that. It shouldn't have been open – I always kept it shut and it had a spring lock."

I said comfortably, "You just forgot it that day, honey. You were upset – trying to run away from me when you didn't want to get away."

She said, "You never would have found me if that door had been shut. I wouldn't have opened if you'd only rung the bell." Her flushed face was drawn and her mouth set.

Then, in a moment, she was delirious again. She cried out in terror: "She's bending over me! . . . bending . . . I can't breathe. Oh, stop her, Frank – stop her!"

For a few minutes I was terrified too; afraid that the cold had turned into pneumonia. For it seemed as if she would choke to death. But the spasm subsided as suddenly as it had come.

On the third day she slept peacefully. Deeply, tranquilly, with a faint smile on her lips, as a child sleeps.

Once or twice I thought I didn't quite like that smile; there was a faint shade of mockery in it; something not like her. As if her face were a mirror, reflecting another, unseen face. But I told myself that was nerves; I tiptoed round the house, to keep from waking her.

Toward evening she did wake, long enough to eat, and she was entirely like herself; sweet and frank and friendly. But she soon slept again. I did too, on my couch by the fire.

About midnight I woke up. And saw her kneeling before the embers, the faint light shining in her hair. It must have been moonlight really, coming in through the Venetian blinds, that were open, though I'd thought I'd closed them. It couldn't have come, as it seemed to come, from her.

Nor could it have been – as it seemed to be – red . . .

But before I had time to wonder about it she turned and looked at me. Smiled at me, and there was such witchery in her eyes and in her mouth as I had never seen in any woman's face.

"I'm all well now, Frank." She held out her arms. No man could have resisted.

In the early morning I got up. She was still lying there, wide-eyed, flushed and rosy, in the dawn. It was I who felt feverish, shaky; somehow drained. I wanted, queerly, to get away. I went into the bedroom, for a clean shirt, for the morning; no fear, now, of disturbing Anne.

But Anne was still lying there in bed, fast asleep.

I staggered back into the living-room. Fast, hoping to prove that I'd been dreaming. But she was still lying there, that thing on the couch, smiling up at me.

She said softly, "I'm a better lover than Anne. You know that now."

I stood there, gaping. And her smile widened.

"After tonight we'll let her sleep soundly always, won't we? Every night, so that I can come to you? I've been wanting to come to you for a long time; I've been wanting a body for a long time. But I couldn't get one – not until her love for her father and her jealousy of her stepmother made a way for me to get in."

I said stupidly, "It was you, then, who lamed Mrs MacNair?"

She laughed. "Not for that old fool's sake – I never cared for old men. I couldn't even have the fun of killing the poor dowdy old frump; Anne's wish wasn't strong enough, and I wasn't far enough in yet. It's taken me time. But I knew Anne would bring me better game in the end; she's young and pretty – pretty enough to catch most men. But neither she nor any other woman of earth can give a man what I can give . . . Come!"

And she held out her arms again. And I came.

I didn't love her; I never loved her. I still loved Anne. But I couldn't withstand the other one. It was true that she could give a man what no woman on earth could – what no other lover outside hell could. Night after night she gave it to me.

And Anne slept more and more, by day as well as by night. Sometimes she'd look at me in a puzzled way and say, "I'm sorry, Frank. I don't know why I can't seem to get stronger. It is hard on you." And I would grin and shrug and soothe her; and the day would seem like a dream, an unreal, half-alive time of waiting for the darkness to fall. For Mary's arms.

Night after night we'd lie on that couch before the fire, and love and whisper. I've said that she talked now; but I'm not sure that I ever really heard a voice. That part may have been all inside my head, her thoughts coming to meet my thoughts. She did think; she was terribly real, whatever she was. About that I have no idea. She may have been some passionate, wicked woman who had died and wanted to get back to earth, or she may have been some evil spirit who had never worn flesh. I know one thing – that she was utterly, altogether evil.

It scared me sometimes, by flashes – brief flashes of my normal consciousness, like waking up for a minute, out of a dream – to realise that Anne was constantly getting weaker. That this creature was draining out her life in the effort to get vitality, substance enough out of her body to maintain her own dreadful, half-embodied earthly existence.

Old Barker noticed it on his visits. He said once, "Hadn't you better let me get a doctor for Miz Carter yet? She seems mighty poorly – mighty slow about pulling around." But I shook my head: "No, Barker. It's good of you, but she's prejudiced against doctors." I don't know what made me say that.

He said, a worried look in his eyes, "You look as if you could use one, too."

That was true. I knew that I too was getting weaker. I couldn't write any more. I couldn't think much. All the vitality was being drawn out of me in those flaming hours with that creature whom I had once thought creepy, cold.

One night I tried remonstrating with her. "Mary, Anne can't stand much more of this. Neither can I. You'd better slow up a bit – you don't want to kill the geese that lay the golden eggs."

She laughed; that soft shrill laugh of hers that may never have made any sound at all.

"You mean you are not man enough for me, my Frank? Do not let that humiliate you. No man could be – for long.

But tonight you are. Come here." And again she pressed her mouth to mine.

I forgot everything for a while. Everything but the hellish delight of her. But presently I did manage to remonstrate again.

"Mary, whatever you do with me you can't afford to get rid of Anne. You can't replace her as easily as you can me. You've said yourself that it took you a long time to get in – to be able to make yourself a body out of hers."

She made a little face. "What use is a body if you do not enjoy it while you have it? Kiss me again, my Frank."

To her we were only instruments that served her pleasure. When we were useless – that is, dead – she would regret nothing but the loss of that pleasure. And begin looking about for new instruments.

I had moments of despair; of fear and horror. But I don't suppose I ever would have done anything about them if Anne hadn't found out.

I woke late one morning – it must have been almost noon – from a deep sleep. A heavy, stupor-like sleep. And it was Anne who stood there looking down at me. Not the other.

Her eyes were wide and frightened. She said, "You look ill, Frank. You look white – almost as if you were dead. Nursing me never got you down like this." Then she put her hand on my shoulder; her voice was quick and rough. "Is it – Mary?"

I couldn't answer. I felt the red burning up under my skin until my face, however white it had been, must have looked brick-coloured. I felt as if my whole body was. I turned away my head.

She gave a short, strangled cry. As hurt a cry as if I'd stuck a knife into her. Then she sank into a chair and began to weep.

I lay there; too miserable, too ashamed, to try to do anything. After a while she said: "It's all my fault. I never should have married you. I never should have let you come to see me. I knew that something awful might happen if I did. But I – I wanted so much to be like other girls – to live.

I wanted you. And so did she. I might have known that she'd never have kept away so long – been so quiet – if she hadn't wanted me to marry you. To get you where she could get at you!"

I got up then. I went to her and put my arms around her. I said, "I love you, Anne."

But she pulled away from me. "What difference does that make? She's stronger than you – stronger than I. Stronger than anyone who has a body! But she can't do without a body. Well, she can't have mine any more!"

And she turned and ran out of the house. Straight for the place where the cliffs fell sheer.

I caught her at the edge of the mountainside. At the very place where the slopes turned to cliffs. She fought me, but I dragged her back; carried her back to the house. I seemed to have all my strength back then.

She lay quietly when I put her down on the couch. She said as quietly, "You shouldn't have done that, Frank. Because, you see, I must die – that's the only way out."

I said, "You shan't."

But she shook her head. Wearily, like a tired child. "It's the only way to save you, Frank. To save myself. I should have known that she was back. I did know it, there when I was ill. But I didn't want to know – I didn't want to remember. She's taken my life, but she shan't have yours. I'll die today or tomorrow, or the day after – you can't stop me, Frank. There's no other way. Even if I left you, would she?"

She began to cry, softly and drearily, like a child who has cried so long that it no longer has the strength to cry aloud. She cried herself to sleep.

I sat there by her, all afternoon. I saw the shadows lengthen, the sun sink toward the jagged western peaks. The golden-brown glare that burned the land begin to dim a little.

In an hour it would be twilight. The delicate Western twilight. In another hour it would be dark, and the materialised Mary would come. And I would forget all about Anne.

And then all of a sudden Mary was there. Standing beside us, looking down at Anne with an angry, scornful face.

"It would have been better for the poor fool if she had stayed stupid. Now she will have to be bedridden, without strength to walk. Perhaps without strength to think, if she should be stubborn and try to refuse food. I must take enough more of her life to see to that."

She bent over, swiftly. Her whole body dropped down, like a cat's, upon Anne's. She pressed her lips to the sleeping girl's lips. It looked as if she were sucking up her breath.

I rose. I went to the bedroom. There was a gun in one of the drawers there – a gun that I had bought as a curiosity, because one of the famous old Western marshals was supposed to have carried it. I loaded it; I came back into the living-room with it in my hand.

Mary was still very busy. I came quite close to them without her seeing me. I took deliberate aim. I knew that there was no use in firing on the one I wanted to fire on – on that thing out of Hell! But there were some things, at least, from which I could save Anne. I shot her through the head.

I woke up, days later, in a Tucson hospital. I have been very ill; they think that I breathed in smoke while trying to rescue my wife from our burning home. Old Barker found our bodies together just outside the door; Anne's badly charred. An adobe house with cement floors cannot burn easily, but the interior of ours was gutted. I remember setting fire to the curtains; I remember pouring kerosene over the couch where Anne lay, and firing that; while all the time fists that had no force beat me, and cries of fear and satanic rage rang in my ears. But I did not drag Anne's body out; I know that. I was faint – with smoke and horror – when I staggered out myself.

They have asked me, very gently, if Anne, my wife, had been discouraged, unbalanced, because of her long illness. They might not have been so gentle if a woman's fingerprints had not overlaid mine on the gun they picked up from the cement floor; the corpse's fingerprints, they think. That puzzled me at first; I couldn't think why or when Mary had touched the gun.

But last night I found out. Yesterday I went from the hospital to a hotel. In the afternoon I had scattered the ashes that used to be Anne from a mountain peak – so that they will drift through that valley into which we used to look down when we were happy. The ride back took me until after dark. And when I turned on the light in my hotel room – the room that had been so clean and pleasant and empty that afternoon when I had left it – I saw her sitting there. A charred figure, on the bed.

But she still smiled – smiled with teeth that showed unpleasantly through the blackened places where her lips had been.

"I'm not as pretty as I was before you tried to burn her, am I? But I'm here. I'll always be here – or wherever you are – whenever it gets dark."

I said, "But you can't be. Anne was burned – I scattered her ashes this afternoon."

She laughed; her old laugh. "Not in time. If you'd been able to burn her the day she died I wouldn't have been able to come back. But I've had time now – time to learn how to use your body a little. Your *ka* wasn't so well anchored when you were sick, there in the hospital. I'll always be with you now, Frank. You'll never be able to get rid of me."

And she began singing softly and combing her hair – hair that fell away in ashes while she combed it.

All night long I walked. I walked the quiet downtown streets where Eastern-looking stores mingle with Indian trading-posts; I walked the lovely still streets of the residential area where Spanish-style houses loomed up like thicker masses of night shadows behind avenues of palm and orange trees. And all the time I heard soft footsteps behind me – knew what I should see if I looked over my shoulder. For two nights I have walked so.

Tomorrow afternoon – no, it is this afternoon now – the Sheriff's office will give me back my gun. And I shall use it again. Then perhaps I shall find Anne in some place where Mary cannot follow. And Mary will be powerless for awhile – until she finds some other instrument she can use.

JOEL LANE

Slow Burn

JOEL LANE lives in Birmingham, England. His publications in the weird fiction genre include four short story collections: *The Earth Wire*, *The Lost District*, *The Terrible Changes* and *Where Furnaces Burn* – the latter a book of supernatural crime stories set in the West Midlands – as well as a novella, *The Witnesses Are Gone*.

His short stories have appeared in various magazines and anthologies including *Black Static, Weird Tales, Cemetery Dance, Gutshot, The End of the Line, Evermore, The Museum of Horror*, *Gathering the Bones*, *Shadows Edge* and two *Mammoth* series: *Best New Horror* and *Best British Crime*. A booklet of his short crime stories, *Do Not Pass Go*, was published in 2011, and his articles on classic weird fiction writers have appeared in *Wormwood*, *Foundation*, *Supernatural Tales* and other periodicals.

"'Slow Burn' was one of several weird crime stories that appeared for the first time in *Where Furnaces Burn*," reveals Lane. "Unlike most of that cycle of stories, it's not set in an urban underworld, but rather in one of the Black Country's most strange and compelling areas of natural beauty – the Wren's Nest nature reserve, an ash forest growing on limestone rocks.

"The book as a whole was equally influenced by the occult detective and *noir* fiction sub-genres, and some of the stories – including this one – tried to create fragments of a regional mythology."

EVERYONE KNEW THE fires at the Wren's Nest were the work of untraceable kids with spray cans and lighters. But we had to investigate, if only to make some of them less confident about doing it again. The tracksuited youths huddled on the bare streets of the estate around the nature reserve told us as much by their turned backs as we could have learned from interrogating them. The charred debris of fire-starting equipment among the burned trees and shrubs told its own story. *Why* wasn't a question for the police, though I wondered at the time whether adolescent rage was enough of an explanation.

When Elaine and I had been courting, we'd come here a few times in the spring of 1980. In those days, the paths were less clearly marked and it was easy to get lost. The limestone cliffs, after millions of years on dry land, still had their own secret geography. The layered ash woods filtered the daylight, made you feel sheltered by some kind of ancient building. Elaine and I walked for hours, holding hands, sometimes pausing to kiss. We searched the exposed rock faces for tiny fossil shells, and chased each other through labyrinths of creepers and ash-fronds. But we never tried to make love there, for a reason we agreed some time afterwards: we both felt watched.

Coming back in the autumn, twenty years later, felt strange. The place no longer seemed peaceful. Black cinders were scattered through the undergrowth, and scorched trees had fallen into the deep gullies. It was hard to see where the effects of fire ended and those of seasonal decay began: dead leaves and black fungus covered everything. Ash trees are called that because of how they look in autumn. The years of police work meant that wherever I looked, I saw places to hide bodies. The sunlight flared randomly off branches as if they were on fire.

Near one of the signposts that guided visitors through the nature reserve, we passed a large wooden effigy of a trilobite fossil. Its ridged surface was charred and split open. The real "Dudley Bug", which had given the town its municipal symbol, had been found here. The Wren's Nest was high above the surrounding area, though it didn't feel like it. Further on, the footpath led us around the edge of a pool long since rendered inert by blue-green algae. Beer cans and condoms floated on the dark surface. The limestone rim was yellowed and crumbly like old cheese.

I wondered why Elaine and I had stopped coming here. The place had a way of confronting you with sudden views – sheer hillsides, layered depths – that made you feel on the edge of the unknown. Maybe it was just vertigo. Maybe it had to do with the way our relationship had become focused on the home, on maintaining our own peace and security, not taking chances. If we came here again, it would feel like the end of something.

Most of the fires had started near the edge of the reserve, where the warden's office had been destroyed for the second time in five years. It was a blackened hulk, marked off by scene of crime tape. An earlier police team had already gone through the wreckage, though the fire had started some distance away. The wind blew flakes of ash into our faces. We circled the high metal fence around the disused mines, looking for any discarded items that might hold fingerprints. It was colder out here than among the trees. The bloodshot sun was setting behind the estate.

The old limestone mines had been shut down for decades, due to the effects of subsidence. I'd heard something about a fire in one of the mines, around the time I joined the force. The area was sealed off to stop kids trying to get into them. Looking through the steel chain-link fence, I began to wonder if the fires might have some kind of symbolic meaning. The dark, shapeless buildings inside made me think of ancient burial vaults. Once again, I had the sense of being watched.

This time there was a specific reason. The man standing a little way to my left, who in the fading light I'd taken for a colleague, was looking at me in a rather defensive way. He was aged seventy or so, with a ragged beard and shabby clothes, and his hands were trembling – which could have been due to drink or illness. I nodded to him and said: "Cold day to be out here."

"It is. You won't find anything."

His comment surprised me. "Why's that?"

He smiled, glanced at the fence, then looked back at me. "You don't remember me, do you?" I shook my head. "Morton. You'd recently joined the Birmingham force when I retired. Bad health. I had an accident." He raised his gloved right hand: the fingers were bent in like the legs of a dead crab.

"Good to see you." I vaguely remembered his name, but not his face. "What brings you here?"

"That's a good question." He cradled his right hand in his left without looking at it. "I suppose there's not much else to do."

"Why won't we find anything?"

Morton shrugged; his inert hand made the gesture oddly puppet-like. "Because you can't see it. There's a lot I could tell you, but I don't think you'd understand. The others didn't."

He was mad, I realised. But my unanswered questions about the Wren's Nest made me say: "Do you want to talk? I finish at six, we could have a chat then if you like." Morton suggested the pub at the north end of the nature reserve. I watched him walk away slowly, bent over, his arms folded against his chest. Maybe he spent all his time here.

Our search team walked down to the Wren's Nest housing estate that bordered the nature reserve. It was a different world. Whole streets of pale terraces were marked for demolition, their windows covered by wire grids. The barking of dogs echoed from concrete walls. Groups of thin youths on street corners eyed us suspiciously as we approached, then turned away. I could see why the local police had needed some external support. Had the arsonists been driven by a hatred of the past, I wondered, or by an obscure need to connect with it?

* * *

The Crow's Wing pub had originally been an office building of some kind, maybe the local job centre when there were still jobs. It had been refitted with dark red carpeting, the kind whose pattern is more easily felt than seen, and coal-effect gas fires. Morton was sitting at a small table in the corner, next to the silent jukebox. He was smoking a thin roll-up. An empty pint glass was by his living hand. "Like another?" I asked.

"Cheers. Pint of Banks'."

There were a few other people in the pub: a man studying the racing page of a newspaper, a young couple talking with hushed voices, a white-haired drunk lost in his own world. I got Morton's pint and a half for myself from the tired-looking barman and returned to his table.

Morton took a deep swallow of beer and shuddered. "Did you tell your colleagues you were going to talk to me?" I said no. "They'd have told you not to bother. For once, it's not a conspiracy. They think I'm a lunatic." His accent was a blend of Scottish and Black Country.

"You might be," I said. "Doesn't mean you've got nothing to say worth hearing."

"I can see a brilliant future awaits you." He looked at me steadily, then rested his cigarette between the fingers of his dead hand. "Mad or not," he said, "I'm going to tell you why they shut down the mines. People kept going down there and not coming out. They found a few of them in the tunnels, curled up tight, stiff like fossils. Then a tunnel collapsed, killed a whole shift of mine workers. The company said there'd been a fire. That was the only way to explain the state of the bodies."

Morton closed his eyes, reached across with his right hand to pick up the cigarette. His fingers trembled, and I noticed they were scarred with many small burns. The roll-up glowed white in his mouth, then dull red. He coughed and drained his pint. "Another?" I asked.

"Cheers." A few more drinkers, all ageing men, were at the bar. When I returned with Morton's drink, he was looking at a copy of the *Express & Star* he'd picked up from the next table. He pointed to a headline: THEY DON'T BELONG HERE. "What belongs here doesn't belong in the world," he said. "Know what I mean?"

"Not really, no."

He rolled another cigarette, slowly. The air in the pub was becoming grainy with smoke. "In 1980, a teenage boy went missing from the estate. His friends said he spent a lot of time out here. We searched the whole area with dogs. On the second day, one of the team noticed that a sealed mine entrance had been damaged by subsidence. There was a narrow gap a boy could have squeezed through.

"It was a long shot, but we had to try. Three of us managed to force the opening a little wider and went down there with torches. It was cold down there, cold and damp – but somehow I felt a heat on my skin, like a fire was close by.

"We found him in one of the side tunnels. Lying on his side, curled up, with his hands over his face. His wrists and ankles were tied up. Some other kids must have left him there. We couldn't be sure it was the missing boy, because the face was terribly burnt. His clothes weren't even scorched, but his head was charcoal."

Morton paused. His eyes were staring inward; I glimpsed confusion and fear in them. "What happened then, I'm still not sure. Two of us picked up the body. As we started back towards the mine entrance, the walls around us began to shake." His hand mimicked the tremor, perhaps intentionally. "And then part of the tunnel roof collapsed behind us.

"The shock, in a nearly enclosed space, was enough to make me and Finch drop the body. Some debris bouncing off the tunnel wall knocked the torch out of Sumner's hand. He couldn't see to pick it up. We were groping around in the dark when something came out of the tunnel. I thought it was a loose rock, glowing with some kind of luminous mould, but then I realised it was crawling over the rubble to get to us. Shimmering like a cold flame. Wasn't human, but it had hands – and a kind of melting white face. It reached out to take the dead boy. I tried to pull him back. Felt something grab hold of my arm. A deep, terrible chill – it made me feel numb all over. I must have blacked out. A few minutes later, Finch was shining the torch in my face. The body had disappeared. There was no feeling in my left hand.

"We didn't know what to report. In the end Sumner told them there was some kind of toxic waste down there; it was too dangerous to explore further. I was in hospital by then. My left hand and forearm slowly changed, over two or three days." Morton gulped his pint. He was looking pale. "The flesh turned dark like a bruise, then darker. It started to flake away. By the time they cut it off, it was more like charcoal.

"The official report said I'd been affected by some toxic material that had leaked into the mine from the surrounding rock bed. They built higher fences round the derelict mines to keep people out. Later I tried to tell my superintendent what had happened. He said the poison had obviously affected my mind. I was invalided out of the force. Done fuck all since except come here and wait."

Morton started rolling another match-thin cigarette. I didn't know what to say. His scarred fingers trembled as they placed the roll-up in his mouth. He thumbed the lighter twice. It didn't catch. Silently, he passed it to me and I lit his cigarette. He closed his eyes and drew a breath, wincing with pain.

"Don't know why I keep coming back," he said. "The local boys don't know why they keep starting fires. It's a ritual they don't understand. But I'll tell you one thing. Whatever we saw down there had no intention of getting out into the world. It was a misfit, an exile. It had come out of the fire."

When we left the pub, I offered Morton a lift. He shook his head, pointing to the footpath that led back into the nature reserve. There was a moon, so I expected he could see where he was going. Though perhaps he could find his way in the dark. I walked down into the estate, where my car was parked. The smell of smoke remained with me as I drove back to Birmingham.

* * *

A week later, I heard that Morton had been found dead in the Wren's Nest. A heart attack, apparently, with the cold finishing him off as he lay among the rusting ash trees. I went to his funeral, along with some of my older colleagues. He had little by way of family and friends left. A sense of chill made me leave as soon as the service was over.

A few nights after that, I went back to the Wren's Nest. I had some irrational notion of finding what he'd been looking for, or paying tribute to his search, or giving his spirit the chance to talk to me. People I know dying always knocks me off balance. You don't get used to that.

It was a bitterly cold night. Rain in the daytime had left the ground muddy, and stars of frost were glittering in the beam of my torch. I walked carefully up the wooded hillside to the limestone cliffs, and on past the blue-green water. The gullies on my right were featureless pits; they could have led to the depths of the earth. The chill soaked through my overcoat and gloves, made my skeleton want to curl up like a foetus.

At last I reached the open area where the blackened warden's office stood near the steel fence that enclosed the mines. People were scattered around the fence, alone or in groups. More were coming from the woods all around. The moon was glowing through a hazy scar tissue of cloud. I could hear voices, but not words.

There were white-haired men with bottles, teenage boys and girls, and some rough-looking people in between – travellers maybe, or just off the estate. Some of them had built a mound of fuel: charcoal bricks, newspaper, rubbish soaked with lighter fluid. The crowd began to gather round it, and one of the old men lit a match. It flared up, died back down, then burned steadily. The crowd pressed in around it, warming their outstretched hands. I felt it was Morton's funeral pyre. Maybe the others did too. Despite the heat, my hands were numb.

The fumes were getting to me, or some of the youngsters were smoking weed. I could feel myself becoming detached from everything except the fire. My mind was floating like a curled-up flake of ash. The more I gazed into the red and gold heart of the flames, the more I could see. The faces of people I'd lost. A map of the place where I'd grown up, only ten miles from here. Letters and runes. Other people were pressing behind me, their breath stale with alcohol and decay, eager to be shown what to do. And then I saw it.

Held in the flames like a reflection in water, a pale shape was forming. It had a thin, spineless body, but its hands were wide and reaching towards us with bloodless fingers. Its face was a swirl, a thumbprint, without eyes or mouth. I could hear its voice in my head like the roaring of a great fire. *Wait. Do nothing. The land will burn. The time will come.* And as we all stood watching, it showed us what would happen. Then, one by one, we turned away and walked back into the night.

STEPHEN VOLK

Celebrity Frankenstein

STEPHEN VOLK is best known as the creator of the multi-award-winning drama series *Afterlife* and the notorious 1992 TV "Hallowe'en hoax" *Ghostwatch* which jammed the switchboards at the BBC, terrified the nation, and even caused questions to be raised in Parliament.

He co-wrote the recent feature film *The Awakening* starring Rebecca Hall and Dominic West, and his other screenplay credits include Ken Russell's *Gothic* starring Gabriel Byrne and Natasha Richardson, and *The Guardian*, directed by William Friedkin. He also scripted one of Channel Four's *Shockers* and won a British Film Academy Award for his short film *The Deadness of Dad* starring Rhys Ifans.

A collection of his stories, *Dark Corners*, appeared in 2006, and his short fiction has previously been selected for *Year's Best Fantasy and Horror*, *Best New Horror* and *Best British Mysteries*. He has been a finalist for the Bram Stoker Award, British Fantasy Award and Shirley Jackson Award, and is the author of the stand-alone novellas *Vardøger* and *Whitstable*, the latter published in May 2013 to coincide with the Peter Cushing Centenary. The author also writes a regular comment piece for *Black Static* magazine about the craft and business of making horror.

As Volk explains: "Often I've heard the observation that pop stars these days are mere commodities, manufactured to the specifications of an industry hungry to create something or someone, thrust them in the limelight, then drop them just as quickly. People talk of 'Svengalis' and 'puppet-masters', but I thought of Dr Frankenstein's rejection of his creature and the parallels struck me as delicious fun to play with. Even if the fun ends in tragedy.

"The title was a given. Almost every TV show, here in Britain anyway, has *Celebrity* in the title (*Celebrity Bitchslap News* possibly taking the prize for the most inane and depressing of the bunch).

"Unnecessary to point out, probably, is that my inspiration here came from Elvis, Britney, Michael Jackson's antics, *The X-Factor*, *American Idol*, and Tom Cruise on the sofa, as well as Mary Shelley – who certainly knew a thing or two about fame in her lifetime, but to my knowledge never had her own chat show."

IN MY MIND the gap was non-existent between falling asleep and waking up, but of course weeks had gone by. Obviously. There were many procedures to be done and one had to be recovered from, and stabilised, groggily, still under, before the next began. I had no idea of the doctors taking over in shifts, or working in tandem, to achieve the programme-makers' aims. I was out of it. Meanwhile the video footage of the surgery circled the world. Screen grabs jumping from cell to cell. I learned later that at the moment the titles began running on the final segment of the Results show, we'd already had the highest ratings the network had ever had. *Any* network ever had. This was history, if I but knew it. If I was awake. Then I *was* awake . . .

Salvator's eyes took a while to focus. Some filmy bits floated in the general opaqueness like rats' tails, which troubled me for a few seconds. That and a certain lack of pain which came from being pumped with 100%-proof Christ-knows-what anaesthetic and various other chemicals swashed together in a cocktail to keep me stable. The *new* me, that is. If you could call it "me" at all.

I raised a hand to examine it front and back. It was Murphy's hand, unmistakably. I'd know that blunt-ended thumb and slightly twisted pinkie anywhere. The tan ended at the stitches where it was attached to Vince Pybus's tattooed arm. I revolved it slightly, feeling the pull in my forearm muscles – not that they were mine at all. Except they were. There was the tremendous urge to yell something obscene, but I remembered being counselled not to do that on live TV for legal and other reasons, not least being the show might get instantly pulled. But the word "Fuck" seemed appropriate, given a new entity had been given life, of a sort, with no actual "fucking" involved. As befits suitable family entertainment. Primetime.

Anticipating my thoughts, some guardian angel out of my field of vision put an oxygen mask over my mouth – whose mouth? I felt a coldness not on my lips but on Finbar's, wider and more feminine than mine, a Jim Morrison pout – and I drank the air greedily: it stopped the feeling of nausea that was rising up from my guts. Or somebody's, anyway.

I raised my other hand and it was trembling. It also happened to be African-American, muscled and smooth. My man Anthony's. I flattened its palm and ran it over my chest, hairless, Hispanic, down to the hard, defined muscles of Rico's stomach. Maybe alarmingly, I didn't have to stifle a scream but a laugh. And almost as if it wanted to drown me out in case I did, up came the Toccata and Fugue, blasting loud enough to make the walls of Jericho crumble, and my hospital table tilted up, thirty, forty-five degrees, and shielding my eyes with Anthony's hand from the army of studio lights, I blinked, trying to make out the sea of the audience beyond.

"Are you ready for the mirror?" said a voice.

It was Doctor Bob and I saw him now, brown eyes twinkling above the paper mask, curly hair neatly tucked under the lime green medical cap. I nodded. As I had to. It was in my contract, after all.

I looked at Moritz's face as the reflection looked back. Long, lean, pale – not un-handsome, but not Moritz either.

Finbar's lips, fat and engorged, maybe enhanced a little cosmetically while we were all under, gave him a sensuality the real Moritz lacked. Moritz, who lay somewhere backstage with his face removed, waiting for a donor. Next to armless Vince and armless Anthony, a fond tear in their eyes no doubt to see a part of them taken away and made famous. I saw, below a brow irrigated with a railway-track of stitches where the skull had been lifted off like a lid and my brain had been put in, Salvator's darkly Spanish eyes gazing back at me like no eyes in any mirror in Oblong, Illinois. Blind Salvator, now, who was sitting backstage, whose grandfather had been blind also, but had only eked a rotten existence as a beggar on the streets of Valladolid. Yet here was Salvator, his eyeless grandson, rich and American, and about be richer still from the story he now had to tell, and sell. Salvator could see nothing now – true, but he had seen a future, at least.

"Wow," I said.

Doctor Bob and the other Judges were standing and applauding in front of me now, wearing their surgical scrubs and rubber gloves. Doctor Jude's cut by some fashion house in Rodeo Drive, her hair stacked high and shining. The gloves made a shrill, popping sound. Doctor Bob's facemask hung half off from one ear. I was still in a haze but I think they each said their bit praising us.

"I always believed in you guys."

"You're the real deal. That was fantastic."

"You know what's great about you? You never complained and you never moaned in this whole process."

It was the Host speaking next. Hand on my shoulder. Sharp charcoal suit, sharp white grin: "Great comments from the Doctors. What do you think of that? Say something to the audience."

With Alfry Linquist's voice, I said: "Awesome."

Soon the clip was on YouTube. Highest number of hits ever.

I got out of the hospital bed and they handed me a microphone. I sang the single that was released that Christmas and went straight to number one: "Idolised". One of the biggest downloads ever. Global.

As soon as I could record it, my first album came out. Producer worked with Frank Zappa (not that I was real sure who Frank Zappa was). *Born Winner*, it was called. The Doctors decided that. Guess they decided way before I recorded it. Like they decided everything, Doctor Bob and his team, the Judges. Went triple platinum. Grammys. Mercury. You name it. *Rolling Stone* interview. Jets to London. Private jets courtesy of Doctor Bob. Tokyo. Sydney. Wherever. Madness. But good madness.

(The other madness, that came later.)

I wish I could've been me out there watching me become famous. Because from where I sat there wasn't time to see it at all. Grab a burger and Pepsi, then on to the next gig. I was loving it. So people told me. So I believed.

Big appearance was I guested on the next Emmy awards, telecast across the nation, giving out a Best Actress (Comedy or Musical) to Natalie Portman, my Justin Bieber fringe covering my scars. The dancers gyrated round me, Voodoo-like. I spoke and the tuxedos listened. I sung alongside Miley Cyrus and got a standing ovation of the most sparkling people in entertainment. Face jobs and chin tucks and jewellery that could pay off the debt of a small African country.

It was weird to have a voice. Somebody else's voice, literally that voice box in your throat not being the one you were born with. Strange to have a talent, a gift, a kind of wish come true that you carry round in your body and it's your fortune now. Alfry was my voice but I guess I carried him. Without my brain and my thoughts he couldn't have gotten to the top. Without Anthony and Vince's big old arms and Allan Jake Wells's legs and Rico's perfect abs, without any one of those things neither one of us could've made it. But, this way, we all did.

The Judges gave us a name and it was complete and to say we were happy was an understatement. I just knew Anthony wanted to get those biceps pumped right up fit to explode and I could feel Rico's insides just churning with a mixture of nerves and excitement, and I said, *Okay buddies, this is here, this is now, this is us and this is me. No going back*. And I could feel every cell of them saying it with me.

And every night after performing I counted the scars on my wrists and shoulders and round my thighs and ankles and neck and said, "Doctor Bob, thank you so much for this opportunity. I won't let you down."

But all dreams got to end, right?

Bigtime.

I appeared on talk shows. Pretty soon got a talk show myself. Letterman eat your heart out. Guests like Lady Gaga. George Michael. (Outrageous.) Robert Downey, Jr. (Phenomenal. Wore a zipper on his head to get a laugh. Gripped my hand like a kindred spirit.) Title sequence, black hand, white hand, fingers adjusting the tie, cheesy grin on Finbar's Jagger lips. Salvator's eyes swing to camera. The cowboy-gun finger going bang.

All this while Doctor Bob and his people looked after me, told me what to sign, what to do, where to show up, which camera to smile at, which covers to appear on, which stories to take to court. Which journalists to spill my heart to. Rico's heart. And I did. I did what I was told. Doctor Bob was like a father to me. No question. He created me. How could I say no?

There were girlfriends. Sure there were girlfriends. How could there not be? I was unique. Everybody wanted to meet me, see me, touch me, and some wanted more of me. Sometimes I'd oblige. Sometimes obliging wasn't enough.

That money-grabbing crackpot named Justine, housemaid in some Best Western I'd never stayed at, hit me with a rape allegation, but truth is I never remembered ever meeting her. It was pretty clear she was a fantasist. We buried her.

Like I say there was a downside, but a hell of an upside. Most times I thought it was the best thing I ever did, kissing my old body goodbye. Didn't even shed a tear when the rest of me in that coffin went into the incinerator, empty in the head. Just felt Doctor Bob's hand squeezing Vince Pybus's shoulder and thought about the camera hovering in my face and the dailies next morning.

But the peasants were always chasing me. The peanut-heads. The flash of their Nikons like flaming torches they held aloft, blinding me, big time. I had nowhere to hide and sometimes I felt chained to my office up on the 99th Floor on the Avenue of the Stars. Felt like a $1,000-a-night-dungeon in a castle, the plasma screen my window to the outside world. Doctors checking me, adjusting my medication so that I could go out on the new circuit of night clubs, appear on the new primetime primary-coloured couch answering the same boring questions I'd answered a hundred thousand times before.

Sometimes I growled. Sometimes I grunted. Sometimes I plucked a sliver of flesh from my knee and said, "I'll deal with you later." And the audience howled like I was Leno, but they didn't know how bad the pain was in my skull. It was hot under the lights and sometimes it felt like it was baking me.

"We can fix that," the Doctors said, Doctor Jude with her legs and Doctor Bob with his nut-brown eyes. And they did that. They kept fixing it. They kept fixing me, right through my second album and third, right through to the *Best of* and double-download Christmas duets.

The problem was rejection. Balancing the drug cocktail – a whole Santa Claus list of them – so that my constituent body parts didn't rebel against each other. That was the problem. The new pharmaceuticals did it, thanks to up-to-the-minute research, thanks to a scientific breakthrough. All sorts of medical miracles were now possible. The show couldn't have gotten the green light without them. As Doctor Bob said, "It was all about taking rejection. All about coming back fighting."

I told my story in a book. Ghostwriter did a good job. I liked it when I read it. (The part I read, anyway.) Especially the part about Mom. Though Dad wasn't that happy. Tried to stop publication, till the check changed his mind. I did say some parts weren't true, but Doctor Bob said it didn't matter as long as it sold, and it did sell, by the millions. My face grinned out from every bookstore in the country. Scars almost healed on my forehead. Just a line like I wore a hat and the rim cut in, with little pin-pricks each side. Signing with Murphy's hand till my fingers went numb. Offering the veins of my arm for Doctor Jude to shoot me up, keep me going, stop me falling apart. I wondered if anybody had told her she was beautiful, and I guess they had. "You nailed it. You've got your mojo back. I'm so proud of you – not just as a performer but as an human being," she said as she took out the syringe.

On to the next job. Getting emails from loons saying it was all against nature and my soul was doomed to Hell. Well, doomed to Hell felt pretty damn good back then, all in all. Except for the headaches.

But pretty soon it wasn't just the headaches I had to worry about.

One day they held a meeting at Doctor Bob's offices and told me that, "in spite of the medical advancements", the new penis hadn't taken. *Necrosis* was the word they used. Bad match. I asked them if they were sure it wasn't because of over-use. They said no, this was a biomedical matter. "We have to cut Mick Donner off, replace him with someone new." So I had to go under again and this time had a johnson from a guy in psychiatric care named Cody Bertwhistle. Denver guy, and a fan. Wrote me a letter. Longhand. Told me it was an honour.

I don't know why, and there's no direct correlation, but from the time Mike Donner's got replaced by Cosmic Cody's, things went on the slide.

Maybe it was chemicals. Maybe the chemicals were different. They say we're nothing but robots made up of chemicals, we human beings, don't they? Well if a tiny tweak here or a tad there can send us crawlin'-the-wall crazy, what does it mean if you get several gallons of the stuff pumped into you? Where are you then?

These thoughts, I'll be honest, they just preyed on me. Ate me up, more and more. Maybe that's the cause of what happened later. Maybe I'm just looking for something to blame. I don't know. Probably I am.

Maybe Doctor Bob knows. Doctor Bob knows everything.

After all, before me made us, he made himself. Out of nothing, into the most powerful man in television. A god who stepped down from Mount Olympus after the opening credits with the light show behind him like *Close Encounters* on acid.

I remember standing under the beating sun with four other guys next to a sparkling swimming pool lined with palm trees outside this huge mansion in Malibu. Servants, girls, models, gave us giant fruit drinks with straws and thin Egyptian-looking dogs ran around the lawns biting at the water jerking from the sprinklers. And Kenny started clapping before I'd seen Doctor Bob in his open-neck Hawaiian shirt walking across the grass towards us, then we all clapped and whooped like a bunch of apes. Poor Devon hyperventilated and had to be given oxygen. I'd felt strangely calm. The whole thing was strangely unreal, like it wasn't really happening, or it was happening to somebody other than me. I couldn't believe that person who was on TV, on that small monitor I was looking at as it replayed, *was* me. Maybe I was already becoming somebody else, even then. We toasted with champagne and he wished us all luck, and I don't know if it was the champagne or the warmth of the Los Angeles evening, or the smell of gasoline and wealth and the sound of insects and police sirens in the air, but I felt excitement and happiness more than I ever had in my life before, and I didn't want it to end.

We were buddies, that was a fact. Through the entire competition he was less of a mentor, more of a friend, Doctor Bob. Then, once I'd won, well, our friendship went stratospheric. And I was grateful for it. Then.

We played golf together. He paid for me to train for my pilot's licence. Took me up into the clouds. Every week we had lunch at The Ivy. Hello Troy. Hello Alex. Hello Sting. Hello Elton. Hello Harrison. Hello Amy. Still at Sony? He wanted me on display. I was his shop window. I knew that. Sure I knew that. But I always thought he was watching me. If I took too long to chew my food. If I scratched the side of my neck. It started to bug me. If I squinted across the room, or stammered over my words I felt he was mentally ringing it up. Cutting his chicken breast like a surgeon, he'd say, "You are okay?" I'd say, "Of course I'm okay. I'm great. I'm perfect." And he'd stare at me really hard, saying, "I know you're perfect, but are you okay?" One day I said, "You know what? Fuck your Chardonnay."

That was the day I took that fateful walk in the Griffith Park, up by the observatory. Just wanted to be on my own – not that I could be on my own any more, there being at least half-a-dozen of us in this body, now, that I knew of. Didn't want to even *contemplate* if they'd stuck in a few more organs I didn't know about. The semi-healed scars itched under my Rolex so I took it off and dropped it in a garbage can beside the path. Walked on, hands deep in the pants pockets of my Armani suit.

You know what I'm gonna tell you, but I swear to God I didn't do anything wrong. I wouldn't do that to my mom, I just wouldn't. She raised me with certain values and I still got those values. Other people can believe what they want to believe.

She was making daisy chains.

This little bit of a thing, I'm talking about. Three, maybe four. Just sitting there beside the lake. I watched her plucking them from the grass and casting them into the water, just getting so much enjoyment from the simple joy of it, so I knelt down with her and did it too. Just wanting a tiny bit of that joy she had. And we spoke a little bit. She was nice. She said she wanted to put her toes in the water but she was afraid because her mom said not to go near the water, she might drown. I said, "You won't drown. I'll look after you." She said, "Will you?" I said, "Sure." So that's how come there's this photograph of me lifting her over the rail. I was dangling her down so she could dip her feet in the water, that's all. They made it look crazy, like I was *hurling* her, but I wasn't. The front pages all screamed – *People, Us, National Enquirer* – he's gone too far, he's out of control, he's lost it. Wacko. I hadn't lost it. She wasn't in *danger*. We were just goofing around. And who took the shot anyway? Her mom? Her dad? What kind of *abuse* is that, anyway?

Parents! Jesus! After a fast buck, plastering their kid all over the tabloids? They're the freaks, not me. And that poor girl. That's what made her start crying. Her mom and dad, shouting and calling her away from me. "Honey! Honey! Get away from the man! Honey!" And I'm like . . .

Doctor Bob went ballistic. Brought me in to the Inner Sanctum, Beverly Hills, and ripped me a new one. (Which he could have done literally, given his medical expertise.) I just growled. I snarled. He looked frightened. I said, "See those chains over there?" pointing to his wall of platinum discs, "I'm not in your chains anymore." He shouted as I left, "You're nothing without me!" I turned to him and said, "You know what? I'm everything. You're the one who's nothing. Because if you aren't, why do you need me?" As the elevator doors closed I heard him say, "Fucking genius. Fucking moron."

I could do it without him. I knew I could.

But after Griffith Park, it wasn't easy to get representation. I still got by. Put my name to a series of novels. Thrillers. Sorta semi-sci-fi, I believe. Not read them. Celebrity endorsements. Sports and nutritional products. Failing brands. Except I was a failing brand too, they soon realised.

Then this lowlife cable network pitched me a reality series, à la *The Osbournes*, where a camera crew follow me around day in, day out. Twenty-four seven. Pitched up in my Mulholland Drive home for three months. But the paycheck was good. Number one, I still needed my medication which was legal but expensive, and two, I reckoned I could re-launch of my music career off the back of the publicity. So it was a done deal. Found a lawyer on Melrose that James Franco used. The producers sat on my couch fidgeting like junkies, these cheese straws in shades, saying they wanted to call it *American Monster*. I was like,

"Whatever." The lights in my own home were too bright for me now, and I had to wear shades too. I'd have these ideas on a weekly basis, like my eyes were out of balance and I'd think a top-up from a hypo would get me back on the highway. It did. Periodically.

More and more I needed those boosts from the needle to keep me level, or make me think I was keeping level. Meanwhile the ideas wouldn't go away. I didn't know if the bright lights were inside or outside my skull. The bright lights are what everybody aspires to, right? The bright lights of Hollywood or Broadway, but when you can't get them out of your head even when you're sleeping they're a nightmare. And rats go crazy, don't they, if you deprive them of sleep? Except the drugs made you feel you didn't need sleep.

One of these ideas was there were germs around me and the germs I might catch would affect my immune system and inhibit the anti-rejection drugs. I was really convinced of this. I took to wearing a paper mask, just like the one Doctor Bob wore when he took my brain out and put it in another person's skull. Wore it to the mall. To the supermarket. To the ball game.

Then I guess I reached a real low patch. The reality show crashed and my new management bailed. Guess it wasn't the cash cow they were expecting. Clerval always was a ruthless scumbag, even as agents go, feet on his desk, giving a masturbatory mime as he schmoozes his other client on the phone, dining out on his asshole stories of Jodie and Mel.

Some reason I also got the idea that germs resided in my hair, and I shaved that off to the scalp. Felt safer that way. Safer with my paper mask and bald head, and the briefcase full of phials and pills, added to now with some that were off-prescription. Marvellous what you can find on the Internet, hey?

Didn't much notice the cameras anymore, trailing me to the parking lot or to the gym, jumping out from bushes, walking backwards in front of me down the sidewalk or pressed to the driver's window of my Hummer. Didn't care.

I guess somewhere deep down I thought the photographs and photographers meant somebody wanted to see me. Someone wanted me to exist, so it was worth existing, for them. How wrong can you be?

It felt like it was all over. It felt like I was alone.

Then one day I got a call from Doctor Bob. No secretary. No gatekeeper. Just him. He said, "Listen, don't hang up on me. You know I'm good for you, you know we made it together and if I made some mistakes, I'm sorry. Let's move on." I reckoned it took a lot for him to pick up the phone, so the least I could do was listen. "I'm going in to the network to pitch a follow-up series. And if they don't clap till their hands bleed I'll eat this telephone. It's the same but different: what every network wants to hear. Hot females in front of the camera this time, and you know what, I'm not going to even *attempt* to sell it to them. The pitch is going to be just one word. We're going to walk in and sit down, and we're going to say: *Bride*.

I said: "We?"

He said, "I want you in on this. You're on the judges' panel."

And that's what happened. Contract signed, everything. It was my baby. My comeback. It meant everything to me. I went back to the fold. Doctor Jude kissed my cheek. I *did* have my juju. I *had* nailed it. I *was* fantastic, as a performer and as a human being . . .

Overnight, I was booked on *The Tonight Show*. I was back up there. I was going on to announce *Bride*. They wanted Doctor Bob to sit beside me on the couch but he said, "No, son. You do it. You'll be fine." And I was fine. I thought I was fine. But when the applause hit me and the lights hit me too I got a little high. I was back on the mountain-top. I wanted to sing – not sing, run, run a million miles. And I loved Doctor Bob so much, I said it. I wasn't ashamed of it. I said it again. I shouted it. I jumped up and down on the couch saying, "I'm in love! I'm in love!" because that's what it felt like, all over again.

And, though it hit the headlines, I thought, what's the big deal? And, when my security pass didn't work at the rehearsal studio, I thought, what the hell? But when Doctor Bob didn't return my calls, then I knew something was turning to shit. Then I got a text from the producer saying my services were no longer required: there was a cancellation clause and they were invoking it. I was out.

I thought: Screw Doctor Bob.

Screw *Bride*.

I did commercials, appearances, while the series ran and the ratings climbed. If the first series knocked it out of the park, series two sent it stratospheric. I tried not to watch it but it was everywhere like a virus, magazine covers, newspapers. I kept to myself. I sunk low. I shaved my head again. I wore my mask. I took my meds.

Sleepless, I wandered Hollywood Boulevard amongst the hookers of both sexes. They looked in better shape than I did. Scored near Grauman's Chinese. Did hopscotch on the handprints in the cement. Watched the stretches sail by to fame and fortune. Watched pimps at their toil. Sometimes someone wanted to shake my black hand, other times wanted to shake my white.

In McDonald's I picked up a discarded *Enquirer* and saw what I didn't want to see: photographs of Doctor Bob leaving The Ivy with the winner of *Bride* on his arm. Lissom. Tanned. Augmented. A conglomerate of cheerleader from Wichita, swimmer from Oregon and pole-dancer from Yale. There she was, grinning for the cameras with her California dentition, just like I used to do.

Yes, I sent him texts. The texts that they showed in court: I admit that. Yes, I said I was going to destroy him. Yes, I said I was more powerful than him now and he knew it. In many ways I wanted him to suffer. I hated him, pure and simple.

But I didn't kill her. I swear on my mother's life.

Yes, she came to my house. Obviously, because that's where they found the body. But she came there, drunk and high, saying she wanted to reason with me and persuade me to mend broken bridges with Doctor Bob. When the prosecution claimed I abducted her, that I drugged her, that was all made up. She came to me doped up and in no fit state to drive home. I told her to use the bedroom, drive home with a clear head in the morning. It was raining, too, and I wasn't sure this girl – any of her – would know where to find the switch for the windshield wipers. Her pole-dancer arms were flailing all flaky and I saw the scars on her wrists and on the taut, fat-free swimmer muscles of her shoulders.

I put two calls in to Doctor Bob but they went to "message" so I hung up. She had two blocked numbers on her phone and my guess is she called someone to come pick her up while I was out.

I had an appointment with a supplier because my anti-rejection drugs were low. Maybe I shouldn't have left her but I did. Fact is, when the police found my fingerprints all over the carving knife – of course they did, it was in my house. From my kitchen. Anyway, *their* fingerprints were all over the damn thing too.

I didn't break the law. Not even in that slow-mo car chase along the interstate where I kept under the speed limit and so did they.

I know I was found not guilty, but a good portion of the American people still believed I killed her. Thirty-two wounds in her body. Had to be some kind of . . . not human being. And I am. I know I am.

But the public didn't like it that way. They blamed American justice. Blamed money. Yes, I came out free, but was I free? Really free? No way. I was acquitted, but everyone watching the whole thing on TV thought it was justice bought by expensive lawyers and I was guilty as sin. They near as hell wanted to strap me to the chair right there and then, but there wasn't a damn thing they could do about it.

God bless America.

I had to sell my place on Mulholland Drive. Live out of hotel rooms. Pretty soon I was a cartoon on *South Park*. A cheap joke on Jon Stewart. Couldn't get into The Ivy any more. Looked in at Doctor Bob, eating alone.

Now, where am I?

Plenty of new pitches to sell. Trouble is, I can't even get

in the room. Maybe it's true that the saddest thing in Hollywood is not knowing your time is over.

Now the personal appearances are in bars and strip joints smelling of semen and liquor. Not too unlike the anaesthetic, back in the day. I ask in Alfry's voice if this signed photo, book, album is for them. They say, no, it's for their mother. And that's the killer. Nobody wants to say the autograph of the person who used to be something is for them.

Night, I flip channels endlessly on the TV set in some motel, the cocktail in my veins making me heavy-lidded but nothing less than alert. If I see a clip of me I write it in my notebook. Radio stations, the same. Any of my songs, I chase them for royalties. I'm human. Everybody wants a piece of me, but I'm not giving myself away any more. Not for free, anyway.

I look in the bathroom mirror and I see flab. Scrawn. Bone. Disease. Wrinkles. Puckers. Flaps. I'm wasting away. I'm a grey blob. What they didn't say when they build you is that you die like everybody else. Only quicker. Six times quicker. The techniques weren't registered and peer-reviewed, turns out. Nobody looked into the long-term effects of the anti-rejection regime. That's why I've been eating like a horse and my body keeps nothing in but the toxins. When I was passing through Mississippi and collapsed at the wheel, the intern at the hospital said the protein was killing me, the fat, cholesterol, all of it. My body was like a chemical plant making poison. I said, "What? Cut the munchies?" He said, "No more munchies. No more midnight snacks. One more hamburger will kill you."

I'm a nineteen-year-old concoction, hurting like hell. Each part of me wants the other part of it back. It's not a spiritual or mental longing, it's a physical longing and it's pain and it's with me every sleepless second of the goddamned day.

My only crime was, I wanted to be somebody.

Trouble is, I was six people.

At least six, in fact.

To be honest, I lost count after the second penis.

Maybe you can hear the music in the background, in the next room. They're playing "Teenage Lobotomy" by the Ramones on the tinny radio beside my king-size bed.

While I'm here, sitting on toilet pan, coughing up blood.

Truthful? I'd be writing this the old-fashioned way, paper and pen, except Murph's fingers are feeling like sausages and I'm getting those flashes again in the corner of Salvator's left eye right now. They're like fireworks. Hell, they're like the fourth of July. That's why I'm talking into this recorder. The one Doctor Bob gave me, way back. The one I needed for interviews, he explained. "They record you, but you record them. You have a record of what you say. They get it wrong, sue their ass." Doctor Bob was full of good advice, till it all went wrong, which is why I guess I'm sitting here, wanting to set it all down, from the beginning. Like it was. Not like folks say it was. Not like the lies they're saying about me out there.

Half-an-hour ago I rang for a take-out and a mixed-race kid in a hoodie rang the doorbell, gave me a box with a triple bacon cheeseburger and large fries in it. Gave him a fifty. Figured, what the heck?

I've got it in my hand now, the hamburger, Anthony's fingers and Vince's fingers sinking into the bun, the grease dripping onto the bathroom floor between my feet, feet I don't recognise and never did. The smell of the processed cheese and beef thick and stagnant and lovely in its appalling richness – a big fat murderer. The intern was right. One more bite *will* kill me. I know it. The drugs were too much. The side-effects, I mean. Like steroids shrink your manhood, this shrinks me. The dairy, the fat. And nobody gave me a twelve-step. Nobody took me in.

I texted Doctor Bob just before I started talking into this thing. He'll be the first to know. He'll come here and he'll find me. Which is how it should be. There's a completeness to that I think he'll understand. For all that came between us, and boy, a lot did, I think we understood each other, deep down.

That's why I know, absolutely, this is what I have to do.

Whether he listens to this story – whether anybody presses "Play" and listens, is up to them. Whether they care. Whether anybody cares, any more.

All I know is, I'm taking a big mouthful. God, that tastes good . . . A great big mouthful, and I taste that meaty flavour on my tongue, and that juice sliding down my throat . . . And the crunch of the iceberg lettuce and the tang of the pickle and the sweetness of the tomato . . . God, oh God . . . And, you know what?

I'm loving it.

ROBERT SHEARMAN

Blue Crayon, Yellow Crayon

ROBERT SHEARMAN is an award-winning writer for stage, television and radio. He was resident playwright at the Northcott Theatre in Exeter, and regular writer for Alan Ayckbourn at the Stephen Joseph Theatre in Scarborough.

For BBC Radio he is a recurrent contributor to the afternoon play slot, but he is probably best known for his work on TV's *Doctor Who*, bringing the Daleks back to the screen in the BAFTA-winning first series of the revival in an episode nominated for a Hugo Award.

His first collection of short stories, *Tiny Deaths*, was published by Comma Press in 2007. It won the World Fantasy Award for Best Collection. His second collection, *Love Songs for the Shy and Cynical*, published by Big Finish Productions, won the British Fantasy Award and the Edge Hill Readers Prize, and was joint winner of the Shirley Jackson Award. A third collection, *Everyone's Just So So Special*, won the British Fantasy Award. In 2012, the best of his horror fiction – half taken from these previous collections and half new work – was published by ChiZine as *Remember Why You Fear Me.*

"I wrote this story whilst I was serving a year's term as resident writer at Edinburgh Napier University," recalls Shearman. "It was a heady time. Space in which to work! An office with my name on the door! A stream of students who would ask me for writing advice – and, no doubt, be scuppered by my vaguely unhelpful replies. I was in ego-boost heaven.

"The only downside was the five-hour commute to the office. I live in London – that name on the door that made me feel so smug was a very long way from home. Every Wednesday morning I'd take the train up to Scotland, and every Friday evening I'd take the train back home again. I assumed that over time I'd get used to the journey. It was not to be.

"It never seemed to matter which carriage I sat in – sooner or later, there would be a noisy child sitting close to me. The sort of child who wanted to fill each and every painstaking hard-fought-for mile with screaming and shouting. I have nothing against children at all. I dimly remember being one myself. But I have a theory that children mutate into something alien when put in a metal box and flung about at high speeds.

"The following story is based upon a real event where a child was acting up most aggressively across the aisle from me. I glared at his parents in that ineffectual way we British do when we want to make a complaint without actually daring to say anything; true to form, the parents ignored me.

"I closed my eyes tight and pretended that through sheer will alone I could sleep, and I honestly prayed that the child would disappear. When I next dared to open my eyes, some minutes later, the child was gone. The parents sat in their seats, talking quietly, perfectly happily. I assumed the child was in the lavatory, and I dreaded his inevitable return. I determined to enjoy the peace for as long as I could. I dozed a bit.

"Whenever I thought to open my eyes to check, the child still hadn't returned. And he never did. We arrived in Edinburgh some hours later; we all got off the train; the parents got off too, and never seemed to remember they had had a child in the first place.

"I went straight to my office, and started to write."

Andrew Kaplan was coming home, at last, and it'd be for a *real* holiday, not like that time last August when the company called him back to work after only four days' leave, they'd guaranteed he wouldn't be needed in until January 5th, that would very nearly give him two weeks. "Great," his wife had said, when he'd phoned her and told her the good news, and Andrew asked whether his daughter would be excited too, and his wife assured him that she would be. The flight from Boston was packed with British people who'd be getting to see their families, and there was a revelry in the air, nothing too outspoken, nothing drunken or boisterous, they were respectable denizens of middle management – but there were polite smiles everywhere, everyone seemed to be sporting a smile, and the stewardesses were wearing tinsel on their name badges, it all seemed very festive.

The aeroplane took off half an hour late, but Andrew wasn't too worried, he knew that nine times out of ten any delay is made good in transit. But when the pilot came over the intercom and apologised once again that they were going to have to circle Heathrow for the fourth time – "The runways are all full, everyone wants to get back for Christmas!" – Andrew began to worry about his connecting flight from London to Edinburgh. By the time that all the passengers had filed off the plane and made their way to baggage claim no one was smiling any more. Andrew was almost resigned to the idea that he'd missed the connection, but then he dazedly realised that his suitcase was the first on to the conveyor belt – and that never happened! – and if he *ran* he might just make it to the check-in desk on time; and so that's what he did, he *ran*, and his case was heavy, laden down with so many special presents for his family, but he didn't let that stop him – he raced down the travelator from terminal three to terminal two, apologising as he pushed other passengers to one side – and it was going to be okay, if he kept up this pace he was going to make it with *minutes* to spare, and he burst into the departures hall and looked up at the monitors for his flight details – and there they were, it hadn't taken off yet! – and there was a word in red right beside it, and the word was CANCELLED.

And for a moment he felt quite relieved, because it meant he had no reason to run any more, and he'd done his best, hadn't he? And for another moment he was quite angry. And then he just didn't feel anything very much, he was just so tired.

No more flights to Scotland tonight. Sorry. Yes, the inconvenience is highly regrettable. There will, of course, be compensation, and somewhere for Mr Kaplan to rest until service resumed in the morning. But Andrew didn't want an airport hotel, or, God knows, did they just mean some sort of darkened lounge he could sit in? – it's all he had thought about on the flight over, that after three months away he was going *home*. He remembered what his wife had said, one of those last times he'd managed to get through to her on the phone – "We've never been apart so long before." He'd asked her whether his daughter was looking forward to Christmas, and his wife had said, "Of course she is, she's five years old, Christmas is all she thinks about!" And she'd explained that they had already decorated the tree together, and sent out the cards, and been carol singing – all the things they'd always done as a family, and this time he'd been away for them, and she didn't press that point, she didn't try to make him feel guilty – but then, she didn't need to. And Andrew stood in the airport terminal and fumed; by rights he should be flying home right now, by rights he should be somewhere in the air over Birmingham. "I need to get back," he said to the woman behind the counter, "I need to get back tonight, whatever it takes." It was Christmas Eve tomorrow, he needed to know that when his daughter woke up on Christmas Eve her father would be there ready for her.

He was told there was a last train to Edinburgh, leaving from Kings Cross station within the hour. He joined the queue for a taxi, then pleaded with the people in front to let him go first, then paid them all ten pounds each. The taxi fare cost him fifty quid, but by this stage of the proceedings

Andrew didn't care about money any more – on the radio there was playing a non-stop medley of Christmas hits, and Andrew wasn't in the mood for them, and the driver seemed quite put out when Andrew told him to turn them off. Andrew apologised with a healthy tip that used up all his spare cash. Andrew tried to call his wife to tell her he'd be late home, but his mobile phone was confused, it was still hunting for a signal from an American network provider. He asked the taxi driver whether he could use his phone. The taxi driver refused.

He bought a ticket with his credit card. The train was already filling up. He dragged his suitcase down the platform, and carriage after carriage he couldn't spot an empty seat. He was starting to despair – and there, at the very last compartment, there were seats galore, the train was almost deserted. He couldn't see why, he looked for a sign that said it was a different class, or required special reservation, but no, nothing. He climbed aboard, heaved his case into the empty luggage rack, plopped himself down wearily into a seat. He had a whole table to himself. He smiled at the people around him – "Pretty lucky!" he said, but they didn't reply. There were a couple of businessmen sitting together, a young mother with a girl, an elderly mother reading a magazine, a middle-aged man who was asleep. Andrew decided to take his cue from this last passenger; he closed his eyes, and by the time the train pulled out of the station Andrew was snoring gently.

"Bang!"

And Andrew was awake, and there was the little girl, and she was leaning over his table as if she owned it, and she was pointing a gun at him, except it wasn't a gun, it was two fingers, with a third wiggling underneath as a trigger. "Bang! Bang! Bang!"

Andrew wasn't sure whether to respond or not. With his own daughter he tried to play along as much as possible, no matter what strange pretending game she flung at him, that was what a daddy was supposed to do. But this wasn't his daughter, and he didn't know whether he should encourage her, frankly he didn't know whether he should be talking to her at all. So he sort of half went for it; he clutched at his chest, he said, "Ugh!" quietly, as if he'd been shot, as if he were dying, but it was all a bit pathetic, and even as he did it, Andrew could feel himself blushing red with embarrassment.

The little girl didn't seem to mind. She looked delighted by this unexpected piece of playacting. "Bang! Bang!" she went, she shot him twice more for good measure, and Andrew didn't know what he was supposed to do this time, he was already dead, wasn't he? And she laughed out loud, and then, with a scream, turned and ran down the aisle to the other end of the carriage. She didn't shoot at any of the other passengers, and Andrew didn't know how he felt about that, whether he was annoyed or just a little bit proud.

He looked towards the girl's mother, but she didn't appear even to have noticed, she was staring dully out of the window. He looked around the rest of the carriage, with a rueful smile – kids! – but no one caught his eye. The old woman was still reading her magazine; the businessmen had run out of things to say, and were looking away from each other; the middle-aged man was still asleep.

Andrew rather envied him, because here came the girl again, running back down the aisle, whooping. Andrew wondered how anyone could sleep through a racket like that.

His head felt muzzy, he knew he was teetering upon the edge of sleep, and if only he could fall in the right direction he'd be dozing soundly all the way home. Why wouldn't the girl shut up, why wouldn't she just sit down and shut up – he'd never let *his* daughter run riot on a train, especially not when it was late at night, especially not when there was a passenger onboard who was clearly fighting jet-lag – and he felt a resentment for the mother who was *still* not doing a thing to help, *still* just looking out of the bloody window, really! – and he tried to force the resentment down, because he knew if he let it the resentment would keep him awake, it'd growl away at his innards, he'd be unable to relax. And here came the girl again—

"Ssh!" he said, and glared at her, and put his finger to his lips. And she stopped dead, and looked surprised, and a little hurt maybe that her one playfellow, the one person who had given her a damn, had turned against her. Her bottom lip trembled. She began to cry.

"No, no," said Andrew, "ssh!" And he put his finger to his lips again, but this time with a smiley face, see, all smiles, he wasn't cross with her, not really. But it was no good. The tears were in full flow now, the girl let out a misery that was profound and was sincere, and was very very loud, she began to scream the place down. He hadn't realised you could scream tears out like that.

Andrew panicked a bit, looked quickly at the other passengers. But no one seemed to mind. The woman didn't raise her eyes from her magazine. The businessmen turned their heads in the child's direction, but with supreme indifference – and then quickly turned away again, as if annoyed that the pair of them had been caught looking at the exact same thing.

And the mother said, very softly, but stern, "Come and sit down." And for a moment Andrew stupidly thought she might mean him. But the girl sulkily turned, and went back to her seat. "Get out your colouring book. Play with your crayons." The little girl was still crying, angry little sobs, but she did what she was told. And all the while the mother didn't so much as glance at her, her attention still upon the window and whatever she could make out from the darkness.

The little girl took out her crayons. She looked down at her colouring book. Grim, not a hint of a smile. The crying had almost dribbled to a halt, there was just the odd little moan punctuated with sudden sniffs. Andrew watched her, carefully; the little girl didn't seem to notice he was spying on her, but then, then, in one instant she turned her head towards Andrew, right at him – and what was that in her smile? Rage? Triumph? Something adult anyway, something almost sneering, and it made Andrew feel small and ashamed.

And then she was at work with her crayons. She wasn't colouring anything in, she was *attacking* the book, stabbing down hard with the bright blue stick, slashing at the page. And now, in her left hand, she produced a yellow crayon, and she was stabbing down with that too, she was showing no mercy, the crying had stopped, she was instead giving grunts of effort as she stabbed as hard as she could. And Andrew realised only he could see this, the mother took no interest whatsoever, and Andrew thought he should alert her, because this was wrong, something was terribly wrong – and as the child spattered blue and yellow cuts deep into the paper she looked at him again and he could see there was spit bubbling out of her mouth, was it even foam? And Andrew opened his mouth to say something, he didn't know what, but before he got the chance—

The woman had turned from the window. She didn't look angry, or annoyed, or frustrated – that was the oddness of it – her face looked perfectly composed and neutral. "Enough," she said, calmly, and stood up, and she was pulling the little girl up too, by the shoulders, and up into her arms. And the little girl began to scream again, and this time it was a scream of fear, she knew she was in trouble now – and the mother didn't care, she was into the aisle, and carrying the girl up to the other end of the carriage, the girl struggling and kicking and lashing out, and yet for all that still holding on tight to her crayons and her colouring book. And the mother and child were gone.

The sudden silence was a shock. Andrew closed his eyes right away, to see if he could find that drowsiness again, but the silence rang right round his head.

He looked out of the window. It was black out there, just black. He couldn't see a thing, not a single house, or a tree; it was as if someone had painted over the windows, and there was a glossy shine to the black that began to give Andrew a headache.

Presently the woman came back, and sat down in her seat. Andrew was pleased to see the noisy little girl wasn't with her.

He closed his eyes again. A couple of minutes later, when he opened them, he saw that one of the businessmen had fallen asleep. He closed his eyes once more; when he opened them, a few minutes after, he saw that the second businessman had succumbed too, and his head was lolling against his partner's, and they seemed huddled together for warmth and protection. It almost made Andrew laugh out loud – and he decided that he'd like to take a picture of them with his phone, and send it to his wife. She would find it funny, and she could show it to their daughter too! He took out the phone, but it still hadn't found a signal.

Next time he closed his eyes he wanted to see whether he could make the old woman fall asleep too. But she didn't, she remained forever glued so sourly to her magazine. Never mind.

The mother was staring out at the blackness of the night.

He wondered where the little girl had got to.

The mother then took a thermos flask out of her bag, and poured herself a cup of tea. She sipped at it, turned back to the window.

Andrew closed his eyes one last time, tried to fall asleep. The train rocked from side to side as it sped down the tracks, it made him feel like a baby, it made him feel drowsy. But all the while he listened out for the return of the little girl, he knew the little girl would be back soon, must be, he was tense with anticipation of the noise she would make.

He refused to open his eyes for a good ten minutes. He kept himself busy by reciting, silently, and in strict chronological order, the captains of the English cricket team since Len Hutton. When he reached the present day, he opened up – and looked – and the girl *still* hadn't returned. The mother had put away her tea now, the old woman was still reading, the businessmen and the middle-aged man all still asleep.

Where was she?

He got to his feet. No one looked up. He walked down the aisle to the end of the compartment. The electronic door trundled open for him with a hiss.

The girl wasn't to be seen. He tried the far door, but it was locked, this was the end of the train. A sign said the toilet was vacant, and Andrew knew that little girls aren't always very scrupulous about locks. He hesitated, then knocked gently upon the door. "Are you all right?" he called.

There was no answer, and that annoyed him, she must have been in there for twenty minutes now, twenty at the very least, time for him to recite the English cricket team and back again! And he realised he needed the toilet anyway, he hadn't been since halfway over the Atlantic Ocean, and so when he knocked again it wasn't just as an interfering busybody, but as a man who had waited long and patiently for the lavatory and was now claiming his due right to pee.

He pushed upon the door, very tentatively, and it swung open, and he peeked his head around the door, fully prepared to make protestations of surprise when he saw the little girl inside – but there was no one there – and he supposed that was a good thing, he hadn't really wanted the embarrassment of a girl with her undies round her ankles – but where was she then? Where had she got to? And the answer crept over him, and any urine that had been nestling in his bowels froze to ice and was never going to come out now, not ever.

The mother had thrown her overboard. She must have thrown her overboard. She had had enough of her tantrums, and had picked her up, and marched her down the aisle, and to the window, and chucked her out. And he could imagine the little girl's screams being cut off as she was sucked into the night, and how her body would have fallen down the side of the speeding train, as if she were flying, as if she were a witch, a little witch who'd lost her broomstick, falling until her head smashed against the track.

And then the mother had calmly returned to her seat. And all the while since had been staring out into the blackness. The blackness into which she had tossed her child.

No.

That couldn't be it.

Think.

He had had his eyes closed. And what had happened, surely – yes – was that the girl had walked past him to the *other* end of the compartment – tiptoed past, probably, unusually quietly, but girls were peculiar things, weren't they, maybe she was playing some sort of game? – she was now no doubt terrorising another compartment altogether. And the mother? The mother who had just sat in her seat the whole time (half-an-hour more like, really) whilst her daughter ran amok somewhere without supervision? That made her a bad parent, perhaps, but he could live with that, he wasn't the best parent in the world either, was he, was he? She could be a bad parent, that still made more sense than that she was a murderer.

He sighed with relief, and only then realised he'd been holding his breath, that he'd been scared. And he actually went to the toilet; he couldn't do anything especially useful in there, but he splashed some lukewarm water on to his face, he wiped it off with a paper towel. It was better than nothing, better that than he'd had a wasted journey.

And with full confidence he walked back down the aisle to his seat at the other end of the compartment. And he was going to sit down, he really was, and that would have been the end of the matter – but there was just a moment's hesitation, the need to satisfy some stupid lingering doubt – or maybe it was something to do with velocity, he was already on a trajectory to the next compartment, why stop short, why not walk straight on and look?

The electronic door wouldn't open for him. He tugged at it. It wouldn't budge.

It wasn't *locked*, nothing like that, what would be the point? But it was jammed, very definitely jammed, and there was probably nothing suspicious in that, no cause for alarm, it wasn't as if his compartment had been deliberately segregated from the rest of the train (why on earth did that pop into his head?). But he pulled at the door with all his might, he grunted with the effort. Until he became convinced that all the passengers behind him were watching, and laughing. And then he stopped, and he turned about, and of course no one was watching, no one even cared.

He stood there, bit his lip. Tried to work out what to do.

The girl was small, maybe she was hiding somewhere in the carriage? (Silently, for over half-an-hour?) He walked down the aisle again, and he looked this way and that, he looked underneath the tables and upon all the rows of seats. And he thought, has she got off? Could she simply have got off? The train hadn't stopped at any stations yet, it was two hours' journey until York – but maybe they had *reached* York; he hadn't thought he'd fallen asleep when he'd closed his eyes before, but maybe he had without realising it, he was jet-lagged to tiny bits, maybe they'd passed a *dozen* stations and he hadn't even noticed, maybe the train had stopped and the little girl had got off – late at night – on her own – and her mother had stayed onboard and waved her goodbye – for some reason – and—

"Excuse me," he said softly to the old woman with the magazine, "has the train stopped anywhere yet?"

The old woman looked up, at last, and stared at him, and she didn't reply – and it didn't seem to Andrew that she was being rude, there was utter blankness in that expression, maybe she didn't understand English? (Although the magazine was in English, wasn't it?) She continued to stare, she wouldn't look away.

And he said, "What happened to the little girl?" And at that her mouth began to open, very slowly, it was almost as if he could hear the creak of those old lips parting, and muscles that had lain dormant for so long began to grind as they were forced into action – and suddenly Andrew didn't want to see what would happen next – he didn't want to see that mouth open – he didn't want to see what might be inside – and he whipped his head away from her, he backed off, he fought down a sudden swell of panic and breathed and breathed again and felt his heart steady. He looked back at the old woman, he forced himself to, and she was once more staring intently at her magazine, it was as if he'd never approached her in the first place.

He saw that her eyes weren't moving, she wasn't *reading* anything, it was all staring, just stares. He walked past her and turned around to look at the pages, and saw that across the centrefold was a picture of a young woman, a model, prettier than the old woman could ever have been. He wondered if she'd been gazing upon this one picture for the entire journey. He wondered why.

He went back to the end of the carriage. He pulled down the window, and took a deep breath of fresh air, and felt better.

And he could see that it was possible, look. See how the window opened nice and wide? A little girl could squeeze through there, no problem. He himself could squeeze through, probably, if he hunched his shoulders a bit. That was all it would take, and then he'd be with the girl, they'd both be off this train and the wretched journey would be over. And the blackness was *perfect*, he could see the beauty of it now, this close up, his face so close it was *grazing* it. So shiny, new even – and the little girl hadn't suffered, he could see that now, she had just flown away into the dark and would never have hit the ground, the wind so fast and carrying her off safely. And he knew then that he would do it too. He would do it. He would do it. He would step out into the blackness. He would do it. He would never see his wife or daughter again, but then, was he ever going to have seen them anyway, what, really? Because he couldn't believe that, he couldn't picture that, the three of them together, around a Christmas tree, laughing, hugging, it was beyond imagining, it seemed so fake – and there was nothing fake about the blackness, that was the only truth, why not accept it? He would do it. And the wife and daughter might be sad, for a bit, he wondered if they would. But they'd never find his body, it'd be lost within the black. – And he wondered whether his luggage at least would make it home, he had Christmas presents for his family, he'd like them to have something nice to open on the big day.

He stepped forward. He felt something hard under his foot. He toyed with it for a moment, rolled it under his sole, then frowned, wondering what it was. He lifted the foot to see.

There were two crayons. One blue, one yellow.

He picked them up. He looked at them for a while.

When he walked back into the compartment the lights seemed dimmer somehow. As if the darkness had seeped in from somewhere, or was it just because he was tired? Because he was so tired. And the old woman was asleep now, her head slumped awkwardly, uncomfortably, and she'd dropped her magazine on the floor – and Andrew thought he should pick it up for her, but he never wanted to go near her again, and as he passed her down the aisle he pressed his body hard against the opposite row of seats.

Everyone was asleep. Except the mother, who was no longer looking out of the window, she was looking at *him*. And smiling.

"Ssh," she said, and she put her finger to her lips. "Let's not wake them."

"No," said Andrew.

She tapped at the seat next to her. "Come and sit down," she said. And Andrew did.

The woman took out her flask and poured herself a tea. She asked whether Andrew would like one. He thanked her, said no. And she nodded at that, as if that was what she'd been expecting, and smiled, and sipped at her tea, and looked back out of the window again, as if her audience with Andrew was at an end.

Andrew felt he should leave her, get up, return to his own seat. But he felt so heavy.

He was still holding the crayons, bunched together tight in his fist.

"Excuse me," he said, and the woman looked at him. "Excuse me," he said again, and held the crayons out to her.

He wondered what she'd do. Whether the woman would look shocked. Or remorseful. Whether she'd get violent, or cry, or confess. But her face didn't change at all, it was most disappointing.

"Is that some sort of Christmas present for me?" she said.

"Yes," said Andrew. "No. I mean. For your daughter."

"Do you have a daughter?"

"Yes."

"Then why don't you give your presents to her?" And her eyes twinkled, because she was teasing him – was she teasing him?

"No," he said. "I mean. You don't, I. I thought. I think your daughter may have dropped them."

She took them from him then, looked at them hard, studied them even. "I don't think these can be my daughter's," she concluded finally, and handed them back.

"Why not?"

"Because I don't have a daughter."

Any more, thought Andrew – he dared her to say it, *any more*. "Oh," he said.

The woman smiled. And went back to the window.

"No," said Andrew. "I mean. Hey."

She looked back.

"You don't have . . . ?" – and he so much wanted to ask directly, he'd seen her with her, hadn't he, the whole carriage had – although he knew that if he woke them up they would all deny it, he knew that with sudden cold certainty, if they even talked to him, if they even acknowledged him at all. He wanted to say, but I saw you with the girl, the girl you got rid of, what did you do to her? And instead he said, "You don't have a daughter? Well, have, have you ever wanted one?"

The woman raised her eyebrows at that, amused, and Andrew blushed.

"I don't have anyone," she said. And she held his gaze this time, daring him to contradict her – but, no, it wasn't that, she wasn't daring him at all, she spoke with the confidence of utter truth, she knew he wouldn't contradict her, why would he try?

"I'm sorry," said Andrew. "So, you've no one to spend Christmas with?"

"No."

"I'm sorry." And he felt an urge to invite her home, she could stay with his family, she could be his family, he felt it rise up inside him, if he had been breathing more freely then it might even have popped out.

She stared out at the night. He stared at it too. And it seemed to him they were hurtling through a void, they were nowhere at all, nowhere, that the tracks would end and the train would fall into the void deeper and deeper and they would be lost, it seemed to him this may have already happened.

"Are you seeing your family for Christmas?" she asked.

And he told her.

He told her of the presents he had for them in his suitcase. For his daughter he had some dolls bought specially in Boston, all of them famous figures from the American Revolution, she wouldn't find them anywhere else! And for his wife he'd picked up some perfume at Duty Free. But now these gifts felt a bit paltry. What would his daughter want with a figurine of Paul Revere? But little girls were so good at playing games, weren't they, he had seen her have hours of fun with a cardboard box, she had pretended it was a car, and a dinosaur, and a spaceship, and she'd said to Andrew, play with me, *pretend* with me – but Andrew wasn't very good at pretending, when his daughter shot him with her fingers and Andrew fell over he always tried a bit too hard and he was sure she was embarrassed by his efforts; she had taken that cardboard box, pretended it was a time machine, and a zoo, and a *father*, he'd come home once and she'd got a box and was pretending it was *him*. He didn't know what to do with his own daughter, and each time she'd grown, and aged, and changed. And what would his wife want with perfume? But he had a better present for them, something he couldn't wrap, should he tell? He'd be coming home for good. For good. No, not this time, but soon, very soon. Because for the last year and a half he'd been doing these trips to the States, and his wife had said to him, you're missing out on your daughter's childhood! and he had said, but it's my *job*, I have to go where they tell me, do you think I have any choice? But now he was coming home for good, by April he'd be back in Britain, they said some time in the spring, it'd be May at the latest. He'd be home, and his wife had said, you're not only running out on her childhood, you're running out on *me* – and she wouldn't be able to say that any more. She wouldn't be able to complain about a bloody thing. And when he told them both, and he'd tell them on Christmas morning, he'd keep it as a proper present, how happy they would be! Because his wife was wrong, he wasn't trying to avoid her, that was ridiculous, he loved her, he was pretty sure he loved her, being at home with her again would take some adjustment but it would be worth it. He was scared. Of course he was scared. He couldn't remember his wife's name. How odd. The jet-lag. His own wife's name, and he was fairly certain she'd had one. He couldn't remember his daughter's name. He wondered whether he might have written them down somewhere, maybe they were on his mobile phone, along with the names of his bosses and his secretarial staff and all his clients, but no – no – he'd call them now, he'd ask – but there was still no signal, the phone said it couldn't find a network provider. And he was scared, because he knew when he got home there would be *that* conversation, because *that* conversation always happened when he got back, sooner or later. And when he'd tried calling his wife recently she'd been so curt with him, she sounded so very far away – and when he told her he'd be home for Christmas for a whole two weeks she sounded almost sarcastic – "Great," she'd said – that was all – "Great." And she never let his daughter come to the phone any more, she was too busy being asleep in bed or playing with cardboard boxes or being dead. And he knew then. Oh God, he knew then. His wife didn't love him. Not any more. She had once. Not any more. And his daughter. His daughter, his daughter was dead. She was dead. And his wife hadn't even told him! She hadn't told him, because he was in Boston, what good would it do? She hadn't told him because she was angry with him, she'd had a daughter, and she'd slipped through his fingers, she'd got lost in the blackness of the night. Though, to be fair, maybe she had told him, didn't he remember that time – wasn't there a phone call – wasn't there a conversation, and a lot of tears, and he'd had to go to a meeting, they were waiting for him, he wasn't going to listen to this shit, "Bastard!" she'd said, she'd screamed her tears out, he hadn't realised you could *scream* tears out like that, "now, now," he'd said, "I'll be home for Christmas, we can talk about it properly then." "Great," she'd said. Oh God. Oh God. He'd had a daughter, and she was lost, and he was lost too.

The woman who had never been a mother and had never had a daughter took his hand. She smiled. She asked if he would like that cup of tea now. He said yes.

"Wipe away your tears," she said.

"Yes."

She poured him a cup. It was steaming hot. It tasted bitter.

"You get some sleep," she said. "Don't you worry. I'll wake you when you get home."

"Yes. Thank you. Yes."

He settled back in his seat. It felt so soft suddenly, and it was peaceful, there wasn't a sound. And the train rocked from side to side as it sped down the void, it made him feel like a baby, it made him feel drowsy.

"Can I keep the presents?" she asked. He didn't know what she meant for a moment. "The crayons?" He gave them to her. She put them in her pocket. She smiled again, took his hand again, squeezed it. She let him sleep.

It wasn't the woman who woke him up. It was a station guard, shaking his shoulder gently. "Come on, mate, end of the line," he said. There was no one else in the compartment, and the lights were on full. "Come on, some of us have Christmas to get home to!"

Andrew fetched his luggage from the rack. It felt lighter than he remembered. He stepped out on to the platform.

Edinburgh was icy, and wet, and right, and home, and he breathed the air in, and felt awake.

He caught a taxi. The taxi driver was playing a medley of Christmas songs. Andrew didn't mind.

He couldn't find his keys. He hammered at the front door. "Let me in!" he cried. And then, to take the desperation out of his voice, "Let me in, it's Santa Claus!"

And his wife opened up. There she was. Oh, there she was.

"Do you love me?" he said, and he could see that she did, her eyes shone with it, he hadn't realised how very obvious love could look. "I love you," he told her, "I love you," and decided not to add that he couldn't remember her name.

"Where is our daughter?" he said. "Is she all right? Is she alive?"

He didn't wait for an answer, he ran up the stairs, ran to the bedroom. His daughter was in bed, and stirred at his noise. "Daddy?" she said. She rubbed at her eyes. "Daddy? Is it really you?"

"Yes," he said, "yes, darling, I'm home, I'm home, and I'm never leaving again!" He wouldn't leave, sod the job, sod Boston, he'd found something he thought had been lost, he wouldn't let go. And she was better than he remembered, she'd reached the age at last where he would never feel uncomfortable with her, or anxious, she was perfect, she was *shiny*, what luck.

He pulled her out of bed, right by the shoulders, held her, hugged her, and he kissed her head and he kissed her hair. And he knew her name, it was all right. She smelled to him of earth, and mud, and dead leaves, but it was all right. He rocked her in his arms. And after a while he stopped, but the rocking just kept on going, and he didn't know what it was.

MICHAEL KELLY

October Dreams

MICHAEL KELLY is a Canadian author, editor, and publisher. Two of his short stories were reprinted in *The Mammoth Book of Best New Horror Volume 21*. His fiction has also appeared in a number of other publications, including *All Hallows*, *Black Static*, *Dark Horizons*, *PostScripts*, *Shadows Edge* and *Supernatural Tales*, and is collected in *Scratching the Surface* and *Undertow and Other Laments*.

More recent fiction appears in *Imaginarium 2013: The Best Canadian Speculative Fiction*, *The Grimscribe's Puppets* and *The Weird Fiction Review*. Kelly is a Shirley Jackson Award and British Fantasy Award finalist, and he edits and publishes *Shadows & Tall Trees*.

His latest book is *Chilling Tales: In Words, Alas, Drown I*, while the sixth volume of *Shadows & Tall Trees*, due in 2014, sees the periodical change to an annual anthology.

"Perhaps unsurprisingly, 'October Dreams' was written in October," reveals the author, "shortly after I'd re-read Ray Bradbury's *The October Country*, a book I revisit every autumn. The story was written in a relatively short amount of time – less than half an hour, if I recall – and was my attempt at a simple, short Hallowe'en shiver."

HER DREAMS WERE October dreams.

The girl was at that strange, carefree, happy age of dreaming and longing where one doesn't realise that they are unlikely to ever be that happy again. She dreamed of damp earth, crackling leaves, and wood smoke; warm spiced cider and cool winds; candied apples, and capering ghosts; grinning pumpkins and the boundless night.

The girl dreamed orange and black.

Then the girl grew older. She excelled in high school. And her dreams changed. They were filled with boyish grins, twining limbs, and soft smiles. She went to University. She found a job.

The world grew serious.

And still she dreamed, but she dreamed less, because now she wasn't a girl, but a woman, all grown up. And grown-ups, she knew, rarely dreamt. Grown-ups weren't expected to dream.

She fell in love and got married. And he wasn't the man of her dreams – who could be? – but he was good and kind and loved her. What dreams she still had she put on hold, and had a child, a girl, beautiful beyond words. She named her Autumn. And the woman who was once a girl was happy, yes, but it was a different happy. It wasn't the wild exuberance of infinite possibilities. It wasn't orange and black. It was contentment. And she was content to be content.

And life, as it does, passed.

The woman who was once a girl grew old. Her daughter Autumn dreamed too, but they were different dreams. Autumn found a good job, got married, moved away, and had children of her own. The woman's husband, who never knew of her dreams, grew infirm and passed away.

The woman who was once a girl wept quietly.

She grew older. She grew lonely.

She dreamed, again, of leering jack-o'-lanterns, burning leaves, fresh-baked harvest pies, wet sidewalks, and pumpkin-scented winds. She dreamed of witches, demons, ghouls and zombies.

She dreamed of darkest night.

She dreamed of the dead.

Time passed. The world quietened. The woman quietened. She waited . . . waited, and dreamed her October dreams. She could smell the season, the slow rot. Still she waited. And finally there came a knock on the door, and she could hear them outside, chuckling, shuffling, rustling like orange leaves in a damp wind, tiny feet stomping, nervous and excited chatter.

The old woman who was once a young girl with dreams smiled, eased herself painfully from her chair, and moved to the door. She pulled some candy from a bowl, opened the door, wishing – *hoping* – for a trick, a child-like prank. She stood there, grinning. And all the children turned, scampered and skittered away, shrieking, as if they'd seen a ghost.

Or something worse.

ALISON LITTLEWOOD

The Eyes of Water

ALISON LITTLEWOOD lives near Wakefield, West Yorkshire, with her partner Fergus. As well as appearing in *The Mammoth Book of Best New Horror*, her short stories have been selected for *The Best Horror of the Year*, *The Year's Best Dark Fantasy & Horror*, *The Best British Fantasy 2013* and *The Mammoth Book of Best British Crime 10*. Other credits include the anthologies *Terror Tales of the Cotswolds*, *Resurrection Engines*, *A Carnivàle of Horror*, *Magic*, *Where Are We Going?* and the charity anthology *Never Again*.

About her second exotic story in this volume, she explains: "I'm often inspired to put pen to paper after visiting places that are particularly atmospheric, or simply different from those I'm used to. There's something about being somewhere new that makes you alert to the things that make a place unique.

"The most intriguing places I visited in Mexico were the *cenotés* – half-immersed caves dotted around the Yucatan Peninsula. Some were quite bare, while others were lined with tree roots and others lit up like some magical grotto. What was just as fascinating, though, was their history. The Yucatan is a dry place, and the *cenotés* were a source, not just of mystery, but of life. That is reflected in their significance in the beliefs and religious practices of the area.

It was impossible not to write about a place with such a rich heritage.

"I've heard theories saying that caves in fiction represent our unconscious minds, or the mysterious part of ourselves we cannot understand. I wouldn't be surprised, as I seem to have a natural fascination with them – my story in last year's *Best New Horror* was also set in a cave.

"When this story was originally published as a Spectral Press chapbook, I envisaged Alex as male. It was the editor of this volume who suggested changing her to female, and I'm really happy with how it turned out!"

THE WORLD ABOVE and the world below were divided by a few feet of earth, but out here, it seemed impossible the other could exist. Above, market stalls; brilliant sunshine; a car park surfaced in dust; an ever-present circle of Mexican girls, no more than five or six years old, holding out handfuls of embroidered handkerchiefs. No one wanted handkerchiefs, but they bought them anyway at the sight of the downturned mouths that said, "I'll cry if you don't."

I passed stalls selling lace and dresses, brilliantly coloured pottery and carvings. When I didn't stop the women pointed the way to the cave, being helpful. They called out, "Maybe later." I knew this was so they could catch me on the way back, claiming a prior arrangement, but I nodded anyway. It was my first trip to a *cenoté* – one of the many flooded caverns that fractured the Yucatan Peninsula – and I was already half-immersed.

The narrow path led away from the stalls and towards a dark hole in the ground. As I approached I saw that steps had been cut into the stone; the steeper sections were bridged with wooden treads. There was a rope in place of a handrail and a sign bearing the caution, WET STONE ARE SLEPERING. I wondered if Rick had noticed it. He'd be down there already – I'd seen his battered pick-up in the car park – a sign that he belonged, if only in part, while I was merely a tourist.

The sign was right, it was slippery, and I clutched at the rope. I couldn't see anything for a few steps, then caught a glimpse of the palest blue below; I went on, careful where I placed my feet, until I reached the bottom. I looked up and saw the cave. The water was spot-lit, creating a turquoise glow that darkened to indigo at the edges. Stalactites hung everywhere, save for a brilliant white spot where light speared through a hole in the ceiling. There were vines too, slender and dark, threading down to touch the water; then I realised they were the roots of trees growing above, outside in some other world.

The *cenoté* was beautiful. It was also empty: no Rick, no tourists. I wondered what it would be like to be here alone in the dark, and shuddered.

A splashing sound: there was someone down here after all. A shape spun out of the brilliant white place where the beam of sunlight hit the water. The shape turned into arms, elbows, a head. It shook itself and the spray sent shock-waves across the water.

"Get in here, Alex," Rick called out. "It's sweet. Wash the sweat off."

I was wearing a swimsuit under my shirt, so I slipped it off as I headed for the pool. The water was clear, and small black fish were swimming in it. I wanted to dip my head into the cold, to dive down and see what lay beneath. I wanted to swim into the circle of light and see what happened.

Rick laughed, his voice echoing. It was too loud, too brash – too male perhaps, or just too foreign. I didn't like it, and for a split-second, I wished him gone; then saw his grin and found myself grinning back. We swam. He told me about his projects, what it was like to really explore, to dive the *cenotés*, passing from one cave into another. How they had discovered a whole new system. It was infectious, his enthusiasm, always had been. I envied him. His smile was the same as ever: clean, white, broad. His skin was smooth then, and his body was whole.

* * *

My mobile rang as I dropped off the dive tanks, and I dug for it in my rucksack. I had been out with a group off Cozumel Island. I hadn't seen much apart from the underwater sculpture just offshore, Christ with his head thrown back towards the light, feet anchored to the seabed. Apparently it was lucky to touch the figure; I wasn't a churchgoer but did it anyway, knowing it was pointless. I could breathe all the time, while the free-divers around me struggled to attain sufficient depth. At least their moment of contact had cost them something.

I found my mobile. I didn't recognise the number and I didn't recognise the voice, bubbly and distorted, as though coming up from the deep.

"It's Kath," she said, and I frowned; I didn't know anyone called Kath, but couldn't say so because she was crying and I couldn't stop her long enough to speak.

Then I caught the word "sister", and my stomach lurched because I did know who it was, after all. I remembered a broad, stocky girl of twelve or thirteen, her hair tied back in plaits that Rick liked to tug when his mother wasn't looking. We had been friends back then, though I had always preferred to run with the boys.

Kath must be in her twenties now, a couple of years younger than Rick. I swallowed and stared out across the beach, the waves whipped into white-tops by the steady breeze, and I wondered when I had managed to swallow sand.

"Are you there?" she asked, and "Are you hearing me?" and she sounded so desperate I wanted to shout down the phone that no, she wasn't alone, I was there. Instead I just croaked, "Yes?"

"They say they found a body. They say it's Rick. But I don't—"

The crackling was broken only by the waves and the boats and the sounds of voices shouting on the wind.

"It can't be him," she said. "I'm flying out, but I can't get there yet. Please, Alex, can you help? We have to know it isn't him."

I found myself nodding, my throat closing up. I *knew*. My eyes teared even while I told myself that it wasn't true, couldn't be true. *Twenty-three*, I thought. It stuck in my head while I tried to think of words to say: *twenty-three*. It was so fucking wrong, and I looked straight into the sun, feeling the sting of salt spray in my eyes, blinded for a moment. I remembered a shape thrashing in a brilliant point of light, the head and arms and legs emerging, twenty-three years old and already marked by some fate he couldn't see.

I never doubted my capability to identify Rick until I was standing in front of the body. I had planned to give one simple nod, then do whatever I could to make sure his sister didn't have to see him this way. The room was filled with the sound of fridges barely ticking over. The smell was at once sweet and unbearable; it couldn't be compared to anything else.

Rick didn't have a face. My mind hadn't got around that yet; the words *twenty-three* were still there, circling like buzzards, and now there was this new thought. My lips pressed together, keeping everything down and in, but inside my head was screaming: *He hasn't got a face*.

The hair was there, at least in part. Towards his forehead – where his forehead should have been – there were only tufts. The skin had been torn away. His eyes were still there but the lids had gone and I couldn't look at them. His nose was a small, soft mound. I found myself staring at it and my stomach contracted. Thank God nothing came up; if it had I would have vomited over the corpse.

I turned away from it and felt a hand on my shoulder. "Take your time," the attendant said in strongly accented English, and I almost laughed. Time wasn't going to help. The man without a face could have been Rick, could have been anybody. I wondered whether that would comfort his sister.

I turned back, taking in the shreds of muscle still clinging to his skull, the places where bone shone through. I forced myself to try and make out what shape the face would have been.

"Are there any other signs?" the attendant said, and I blinked.

"What?"

"Signs that you would know. There are no tattoos, but – a scar, maybe. An old scar."

I shook my head. Rick led a charmed life: *had* led a charmed life. As long as I'd known him he'd been into sky diving, zip-wires, rock climbing, anything that gave him a buzz. He'd never broken a bone, never had an injury I knew of. And then I had that image again: a girl with frizzy hair running after us while we rode our bikes, at least until the day she'd grown sick of being left behind and shoved a stick between the spokes of his wheels.

I heard her crying in my mind. "I never knew," she'd said. "I just thought it'd slow him down."

Rick had teased Kath about that scar on his knee for years.

I turned back to the body and pulled aside the sheet. One knee was smooth, but the other had a white ridge underlining the patella. The left – had it been the left? I couldn't remember.

"Miss?"

I closed my eyes, opened them again. "It's him," I said.

"You're sure?"

"I'm sure."

He nodded, looked happy, then overwrote the expression with sympathy. I didn't care. Kath wouldn't have to see this now. I thought of her horrified expression, back when she'd pulled that stunt with the bike; I wondered if it would have made her feel better to know that she had marked him then, claiming him as her own in readiness for a day like this.

"He was found by a surfer," the mortuary attendant explained, "in the *ojos de agua.*"

I frowned. My Spanish wasn't great, but I knew of a *cenoté* called *Dos Ojos* – two eyes. And *agua* – something I asked for every day.

The attendant sighed. He sat back, putting his hands behind his head. "Your friend was diving in a *cenoté*. It was not on the tourist routes, no? Not safe. This *cenoté* had many systems. Many caves. Eventually, the caves come out in the sea. The sweet water – fresh water – it comes through the cave and goes into the sea. At high tide, it is like – how you say – a bathtub. You try swimming in a bathtub when the plug is pulled?"

I frowned.

"I have felt it myself, in a *cenoté* near my village. I had to get to the steps and keep hold." He demonstrated, clenched his fists. "So I didn't get pulled down. Your friend, he get pulled down."

"And the eyes?"

"*Sí.* The sweet water, it bubbles up through the sea, like the water boils in that place. It is the *ojos*. The eyes of water."

"But Rick was a good diver. He wouldn't have gone in alone." I only said this because I didn't want to ask about what was really in my mind: Rick's face.

"It happens." He dismissed my friend with a wave of his hand.

And so I had to ask: "How did his face get like that?"

"He was beaten," the man said. "Sucked down. Dragged against the rocks, all through the tunnels." He sat forward, scraping his chair against the tiles. "I am sorry."

I wiped my damp palms on my shorts, shook hands and left. It wasn't until I stood outside, the sun like hot metal on my head, that I thought about his words: *dragged against the rocks*. And yet – Rick's face was entirely gone; but the rest of his body had hardly been bruised at all.

Kath's flight was due in at 5:00 p.m., but I'd forgotten how long it took to get through customs at Cancun, to have the necessary papers checked and stamped. When she finally appeared it was disorienting to find I recognised her at once. It was the same Kath, the same stocky build, the same hair already frizzing in the heat. She didn't speak to me, just dropped her bags and put her arms around my neck.

I hugged her back. Her skin was cool but heat radiated from her anyway, like a child in a fever.

I tried to explain what had happened while I drove away from the airport. I thought she'd want to sign the papers, get the body home as quickly as she could; and I'd go back to my tour, start trying to forget. So her words took me by surprise.

"When are we heading out?" she asked.

"Out?"

"I want to see where it happened." Her voice was small but impossible to counter. "I want to see where my brother died."

My mind was blank.

"I'm coming with you," she said, as if that was the only thing to be decided.

The village was a small cluster of buildings, some painted pink or blue, but most left dust-coloured. "Down there," I said. One of Rick's colleagues, an American, had shouted directions down a crackly phone. I turned onto a side street, heading past a small white church. There was a group of men outside it, pulling a crucifix into position, hauling on ropes and steadying the base, no doubt preparing for Easter. They stopped working as we passed, shuffling back, staring. One old man grinned, his face a sudden mass of wrinkles, his eyes impossibly blue. *Eyes of water*, I thought, and grimaced.

Beyond the village we took a narrow track and headed straight into the thorny scrub forest. The Mexican jungle wasn't how I'd imagined. The trees were interspersed with agave and palms, the spaces between filled with thorns and spines, everything parched and brittle.

After a while we saw a *palapas*, an open-sided hut thatched with palm fronds. When we rounded it we found a clearing full of tents, generators, pick-ups, cars. There were stacked crates, bottles of water, barbecue equipment, diving kit, plastic tubs containing what looked like firewood. Two men leaned over a trestle table with paperwork spread upon it. One of them, a slender Mexican, approached, holding out his hand to shake before we'd even stepped out of the car.

"So sorry, *Señorita*," he said, and Kath closed her lips tight.

"I am Arturo. You will stay with us tonight. Tomorrow, we show you everything." He waved at the sky; it was already greying, though the humidity and heat remained. "Eat with us." He gestured. People were emerging from a path that led into the jungle, talking and laughing. Some of them carried more of those plastic tubs. I turned to see Kath dragging her bag from the back seat; heard whistling from the *palapas*. A man with a wetsuit stripped to his waist was stringing extra hammocks beneath it. I nodded, thinking how much Rick would have loved this.

Arturo bent over the plastic tubs, his eyes wide. The tubs didn't contain firewood. They contained bones, tagged and labelled, darkened to the colour of mahogany. "We didn't expect so many," he said. "The Maya used this place. *Cenotés* were sacred places, then. Not just for swimming." His eyes met mine. "They were gateways to the Underworld. Places to offer sacrifice." He waved a hand over the tubs, indicating a femur, a skull. "Many sacrifices."

I took a sip of mescal, vicious in its raw bite. Kath bent low over the bones, peering in.

"Is this what Rick was doing?" I asked. "Finding bones?"

Arturo nodded. "The Maya had no water, apart from the *cenotés*. The god of rain – Chaac – he gave this water. So they give him these *señores y señoritas*."

"Did you know Rick well?"

"In the rich places, Chichen Itza, Dzibilchaltun, they give gold, jade, as well as persons. It was an honour to be given to the gods. It was said that a sacrifice – they would not die." Arturo chuckled. "They did not die, but they did not come back, no?"

"And Rick?" My voice rose. "Did you notice he'd gone? Did you look for him?"

Arturo met my gaze. "Of course," he said. "He was one of us. A good diver. What happened, it was a – freak accident, no? We never had – tides like that before. This is a safe expedition. Organised."

I felt Kath's hand on my arm. "Go on," she said to Arturo. "I want to know everything."

I stared at her as Arturo started up again about sacrifices, the way sometimes their beating hearts were torn from their bodies; about how some were simply thrown into the *cenotés*, *cenotés* with no stair and no ladder. He opened one of the tubs, took something out. "Another kind of sacrifice," he said. "This one is defleshing. They cut the skull – here, here – and peel the muscle down the face."

I stared at it. The skull was misshapen, the forehead steeply sloping and tall, alien-looking. I remembered reading something about how boards were clamped to Mayan babies' heads, elongating them to show their status. I looked closer. There were cuts across the bone, showing where the muscle had been stripped. I remembered raw flesh tagged with flakes of skin, pale bone shining through from beneath, the soft mound of a nose. Pale eyes washed almost transparent, impossible to read their expression.

"Sacrifice," I said later, as Kath and I settled into our hammocks, pulling mosquito nets over the top. "Strange, isn't it, that they threw bodies into the *cenoté*. Do you think they knew they were poisoning their drinking water?"

She didn't answer.

"How they demanded blood," I said, "it's hard to understand. A good thing no one does that now."

"Don't they?" she said, quietly. "Remember the village."

I cast my mind back, trying to work out what she meant, and thought of the men gathered around the crucifix. I remembered the waters off Cozumel, free-divers plunging down to touch the submerged Christ. Rick, being pulled down into blackness.

"Do you remember that day with the bikes?" I asked, suddenly. "When Rick hurt his knee?"

It took her a while to answer. “I lied,” she said. “I knew what would happen. It was the price I wanted him to pay, for always chasing off, leaving me alone.”

She fell silent for so long I thought she was asleep. I listened to the snores coming from neighbouring hammocks, to insects singing in the night. And her voice came again, so low and broken I almost didn’t hear it.

“I hated him then,” she said. “I was his sister and I hated him. I wanted to see him bleed.”

I woke in the night. I wasn’t sure what had awakened me; I opened my eyes and saw heavy shapes suspended from the ceiling, people in their hammocks swathed like pupae. I half-sat, brushing netting from my face, and saw someone standing just outside the *palapas*. It was Rick. I could see it in the tousled hair, the way he stood, the white arc of his teeth. The moon cast a dark shadow at his feet.

I swung myself out of the hammock and looked up once more, knowing he would be gone, but he was not. He raised a hand and waved.

The scar on his knee – had it been the left, or the right? It must have been someone else laid there on the slab. Everything could be well again, made new. I realised I should be calling out to him, but he turned away and walked into the dark.

“Wait,” I hissed, and headed after him. Now I couldn’t see him any more. There were only the tents huddled in the clearing, the dark mass of trees. I realised I was standing by the path that led into the jungle and I started down it, pushing past dry, clawing spines.

“Rick,” I called. Only the air came back, pressing in close and warm. I went on, emerging into a small clearing. Rick was there, standing at the opposite side, smiling.

“Rick, where the hell have you been?”

He tilted his head, beckoning me on. I started towards him, looked down, and realised what I was about to do. I stopped so suddenly I slid, pin-wheeling my arms for balance. There was a hole in the ground. It was a metre across and almost perfectly circular, and when I looked into it, the blackness was so complete it appeared solid.

I looked up, searching the shadows for Rick. The clearing was empty. When I looked back down the path, I saw only my own footprints written in the dust.

My head ached. Last night no longer seemed real. We stood in the clearing, the sun blazing, looking into the hole. Arturo knelt down next to it. "It looks like a well," he said. "It's only when you lower yourself inside you discover it's a cave. From there a passage leads to another, and another, all the way to the sea."

I peered down but still couldn't see anything, only darkness. Someone brought a spotlight and when Arturo switched it on a little more rock wall was revealed, but nothing more. I imagined being lowered into that hole, thrown down it maybe, and swallowed.

Arturo looked at me. "You can't go in," he said, and my stomach contracted. Then he added: "You can swim on the surface only."

I looked up at Kath and found she was looking at me too. I couldn't breathe. *Of course.*

They dragged a metal structure over the hole. It was connected to a winch and a metal chair hung from it. I kicked off my shoes and Arturo helped me into the chair, then raised his eyebrows. When I nodded he fixed a rope across my lap and put a flashlight into my hands before stepping back. They had already started the winch.

I saw the earth floor of the jungle, then there was only rock. The chair bumped against it and I closed my eyes. When I opened them I saw only the dark. I reached out and found nothing there. I could faintly see my own arm but there was nothing else, nothing I could touch. My heart thudded with the creaking of the winch so that the two things seemed connected.

"You're nearly there." The voice was distorted. "You will want the light, *Señorita.*"

The light: of course. I fumbled, switched it on. A bright beam struck out and I saw black webbing wrapped all around me; the roots of plants, clinging to the cave wall. I reminded myself that it was only a *cenoté*, like the one I'd visited with Rick. His face rose before me, pulped and misshapen; I blinked and it was gone.

"Are you all right, *Señorita*?"

I began to shout "Yeah, fi—," and caught my breath as my feet struck cold water.

"Miss Alex?"

"Fine. I'm there." I had a sudden image of the chair continuing to sink and fumbled to release the rope that bound me to it. The water was up to my knees, then my thighs. How deep was it? How far to the opening that had dragged Rick under and through? With a grunt I slid from the chair and water took me, splashing my face. I couldn't touch the bottom. They could have warned me, I thought; no one had even asked if I could swim. Resentment rose as I tilted my head, looking back towards the light. It was a long way away.

For a moment I thought of sacrifices thrown into the cave, the way they must have watched that same circle of light until they could no longer tread water and sank into the dark. This time, when I caught my breath, it came with a gasp. *No*. Soon I could swim back to the chair and they would lift me out. I would feel the sun on my face.

I took deep breaths and shone the light around the cave. I wondered if there were fish – blind, white, maybe – and pulled my legs up close. I let the ripples grow silent.

The Maya used this place. Cenotés *were sacred places, then.*

Arturo's words whispered around the walls.

They were gateways to the Underworld . . . The god of rain – Chaac – he gave this water.

I thought of some presence somewhere beneath me, undefined and huge and with eyes that saw everything, regardless of the dark or the distance. I caught my breath; I knew I should leave, now, before panic set in. I swam back to the chair and dragged myself onto it. "Pull me up!" I shouted.

Nothing happened. The chair didn't move. Then I heard a low sound, but not the winch; it deepened, growing hoarse, reverberating around the cave before tailing away. Then came the rumble of a distant motor. The other sound had gone. I tried to remember what it had been like and thought of slender animals with amber eyes that did not blink.

The chair began to swing. I held tight to the sides, letting it take me upwards and out, back towards the light.

"It is unnerving, no?" Arturo leaned over me, releasing the rope. "Especially with only one light. Usually we have a group. Three lights each. But this, I felt you should see."

I stared at him. Kath was watching me, her expression anxious. I nodded, letting her know I was fine. I didn't feel fine. My knees shook as I stepped away from the hole. I wanted to sit on the ground, taste the dust on my tongue.

"It is a wondrous place, no? Your friend – he love this place. He wanted to see it alone. We say he should not do this, but he did it anyway. He was like that." Arturo turned to Kath, nodding at her. "We thought he had gone away for a while. I am sorry. Sorry." He couldn't stop nodding. "But cave exploration, it is dangerous. We go together, *sí*? Not alone. Much of the caves – it is very deep. No one has been through them all." He paused. "If it is any comfort – your brother, he wish to see everything. And perhaps he did. Perhaps he saw things we will never see."

We ate *fajitas* and refried beans as the light faded, sitting in our hammocks. We had already packed our bags. First thing tomorrow we would be on our way, back to officialdom and bureaucracy, the task of getting the body home. I could no longer imagine returning to my tour after that, couldn't visualise it any more.

Kath chewed steadily, staring into space.

The thing that had happened to Rick – I couldn't find a way of looking at it. When I tried, all I saw was that black, empty space; putting out my hand to touch the wall and finding nothing there.

His face had been stripped. The muscles peeled away.

"You heading out?" The voice was loud, chirpy, and I turned. It was the American, the one who'd given us directions to the camp. He came over, waving his hand.

"In the morning," I said. "Early." Kath didn't say anything.

"He was a brave guy, your friend."

"You knew him?"

"We all did."

"You all liked him?"

"Sure." He looked at me.

"He had a wild streak," I said. "Arturo said Rick went off alone, into the *cenoté*. He said he loved the place."

"Wouldn't surprise me. He always liked to push it." He shrugged. "Not sure whether 'loved' is the right word, though."

"Why's that?"

"He was fascinated by it, sure. He was always talking about what was down there. But he said to me once – Rob, he said to me, there's something wrong with this place."

"Wrong?" Kath spoke at last. "What do you mean? He knew there was something dangerous?"

"Not dangerous, no. He thought he'd seen something down there once. It freaked him out. There's a place where you go down through the halocline, then through a squeeze, then upward again. He said he saw something in the place you come up through the halocline again."

The halocline. I had heard of that: a place where lighter fresh water meets the heavier salt water beneath. I'd seen pictures of it, a place that blurred and swirled, where light was distorted. In some of the pictures you would swear that the fresh water was actually air; you'd soon find out it wasn't, if you took off your mask. As illusions went, the halocline could be deadly.

"What did he think he saw?"

"Wouldn't say." Rob shrugged. "Probably nothing. Your mind plays tricks on you down there, you know? Look, I'm sorry about what happened, okay? I just wanted to say that, before you go."

I could only nod as he walked away and Kath went back to staring into space.

I didn't sleep, not at first. I stared up at the rough ceiling of the *palapas*, watching the shadows deepen. And yet I knew when Rick was there.

I sat up and saw his pale skin shining in the moonlight. I couldn't see his face but his chest was whole, and that made it worse somehow; the shadow that lay above. He didn't beckon or say anything, just led the way as he had before, and I followed.

I couldn't hear his footsteps; couldn't hear my own. Even the insects were silent as I went down the path. I didn't need to keep Rick in sight to know where he was going.

At first, when I reached the clearing, I couldn't see him; then I did. He stood off to the side, next to some piles of equipment. When I edged around the *cenoté*, he was gone; there were diving tanks on the ground where he had been. I didn't want to think about what he was telling me. I couldn't do it; but I knew I couldn't go back either. I had to face this, to see whatever it was he wanted me to see.

I gathered the tanks and one of the lights. There was a pile of wetsuits; I found one my size and pulled it on. Then I stared at the winch. It was a problem, and yet I could see the solution straight away, as if I'd planned this. I'd winch the equipment down to the water then climb down the cable. When it was done, I'd just have to hope I could climb back up; either that, or hold on until someone came. In the wetsuit I should be all right until morning, providing nothing happened down there.

I tried not to think about Rick's face as I started up the winch. The motor was loud but I ran it until I thought I heard a distant splash. The equipment was down: it was time.

The hole was a narrow well leading to blackness. I leaned out and took hold of the cable, wrapped my legs around it and started to slide.

This time I had switched on the spotlight before lowering it and the surface of the water shone blackly beneath me. The cable hissed under my hands and I tried to grip tighter, to slow my descent. *The cable are slepering*, I thought, and grimaced. It wasn't funny; it was also too late. I already knew I would never be able to climb out. Then I heard a sound, the same cry I had heard before; something like a jaguar, but impossibly close, and in the next moment I was falling.

I hit the surface hard, came up thrashing through water that was dead cold. I couldn't get my breath, just kept gasping at the shock of it. I was trapped. I was drowning. I thought of sacrifices, how long they might have lasted. I forced myself to take steady breaths, reminded myself that I wasn't hurt, that I could float. The wetsuit was doing its job, warming me. Tomorrow, help would come. Now . . . now I could follow my friend. I focused on that, on Rick's grin, the way he would have laughed at my fear.

When I'd retrieved the equipment I shone the lamp downwards into the water and I dived. It took a while to find the bottom; the cave went deep. I stretched out a hand and found answering fingers of stone reaching upward, their surface almost as dark as everything else. Then something moved. It was a dream of movement, maybe nothing at all, but I headed towards it. The water ahead swirled as if disturbed by a diver's flippers; then it settled and I saw a rope marking the route into the caves. I shone the light along it. There. Something else, swimming ahead of me: Rick.

I followed, ducking through a gap and into a new space. I had no idea how big it was, but it felt endless. I was dwarfed, despite the fact that my world had contracted to only this: the sound of my breathing; the dark; a thin, pale rope.

I kept going for what seemed a long time. I started to wonder if the remaining air would last long enough for this journey and back again; pushed the thought away.

Alex.

I stopped.

Alex.

It was sensory deprivation, that was all. I already knew how sound could seem distorted down here, how the dark could make the mind play tricks. I remembered that noise I'd heard, the cry of a jaguar; closed my eyes. When I opened them Rick was there, his face whole this time, pushed up close to mine. His eyes were wide open. I started, blinked, and then there was nothing but the halocline blurring and shifting, the flashlight sparking blues and greens from its heart. It was the place the American had spoken about.

I went down through the blurring water, saw where the tunnel narrowed and balked. *There's a place where you go down through the halocline*, he had said. *Then through a squeeze.*

I wasn't a great diver: I knew this. I wasn't like Rick, who would do anything, go anywhere. The squeeze was a dark hole that didn't get any better when I shone the light into it. It was full of particles that danced and swam and confused everything. It was too narrow for my tanks. I'd have to take them off and push them in front of me, a manoeuvre I'd heard about but never tried. It was no good. I'd have to go back, wait in the pool until help arrived. I'd have to confess I'd wanted to see the place where Rick had died but that I got scared; that I didn't have my friend's courage.

I took off the tanks. Without allowing myself to pause, I entered the tunnel.

The tanks were unwieldy, too buoyant, catching on the roof. My breathing quickened; I couldn't seem to slow it down. I knew if they got stuck I'd be trapped down here, tethered to them until the air ran out. The walls touched me, welcoming. Closing in. I was in a tomb, a narrow, dark tomb, and I couldn't breathe.

Then the tanks moved and I lunged forwards, felt them pull away from me at the other end. I was through. I saw the halocline at once. It was just like before except brighter, as if there was some source of illumination within it; it was turquoise and cerulean and sapphire, all the colours of the Caribbean, the shades moving and passing into each other like veils. Then I saw what was on the other side.

A woman was waiting there. She stood clear of the water on a stone platform that jutted from the cave wall. I craned my neck to look at her. She wore a simple tunic, black stones about her neck and feathers in her hair. Her fierce eyes were turned on me.

I was caught on some surge of water, had to look away. When I looked back I expected her to be gone, but instead I saw someone standing next to her. It was Rick.

I swam towards them, still pushing the tanks. I looked up again into clear air. Their clothes didn't cling; the feathers stuck out from the woman's hair. They were dry. And yet . . . that was what the halocline did, wasn't it? Caused illusions. And Rick, after all, was dead, lying on a slab in some overheated mortuary.

My dive tanks bumped against the platform edge. They were bobbing on the surface; no more water.

I climbed out, knowing that it was all wrong, that there shouldn't be any air down here. And yet when Rick smiled, gesturing towards my mouthpiece, I took it off and pulled in an experimental breath.

I turned to Rick, but it was the woman who spoke.

"You travelled through the body of the life-giver," she said. "What gift do you bring?" Her voice was quiet but resonated like the cry of the jaguar. She was dangerous, this woman. I could sense it, see it in her eyes. They were dark and yet liquid: *eyes of water*, I thought.

"The waters are restless. They will have sacrifice. What do you bring, traveller?"

I shook my head.

She made a low growling in her throat. Her eyes shone. "My god is a jealous god," she said. "It is the giving time."

My throat felt clogged, as if I wasn't breathing at all. I looked at Rick. It *was* him I'd seen on the slab, I knew that now.

She threw back her head and laughed. "We are the servants of Chaac. Be sure that your gift is enough, or Chaac will take what he needs. The things he desires."

I thought of Rick's face, the remnants of skin, the soft mound of a nose. Defleshed. What had he offered, to have failed so badly? When I looked at him he didn't say a word.

"What does Chaac require?" I asked.

She smiled. It was a casual smile, but it made me want to tear the eyes from my head. She had small, white, pointed teeth. She went to Rick, trailed her fingers across his chest. "Blood," she said.

I looked at my old friend, searching for some trace of the boy I had known. "Rick, help me."

Her laughter rang out, mocking. It echoed around the cave, deepening until my chest ached.

"Ask him," she said. "Ask him what he gave. Ask him if it was good enough." Her voice was harsh, peremptory, and my mouth opened of its own accord.

"Rick?"

His head jerked as if he had just woken. He glanced at me, looked away. And I knew, then, even before he mouthed the word: "You."

"Rick?"

He wouldn't look at me.

The woman waved a hand. "Choose," she said. "What will *you* give?"

I thought, wildly. I had nothing. Some money, back home; I could borrow more, use it to purchase – what had Arturo spoken of? Gold. Jade. But when I looked into this woman's eyes, I knew it would never be enough.

Then I thought of Kath, on the outside, not so far away. Sleeping in a hammock in the warm, close night. I could come back here, bring her with me. Rick's offering hadn't been enough, but perhaps she would be. It was all I could think of. I looked at Rick. He was staring down at the floor, his eyes half-closed. It would be a fine revenge, to bring her here: his sister. Still I couldn't bring myself to say the words.

"Speak," she said.

I shook my head and her eyes snapped to mine. And I decided.

"I have nothing to give," I said. "I have nothing. I can't make – I can't give you a sacrifice." I wanted to continue, to say something about how that didn't happen, it wasn't done any more, and forced myself to shut my mouth. She would flay the flesh from my bones. Rip the face from my body.

Something in her look told me I had to continue.

"There's only me." My throat constricted around the words. "It's all I have. I can't bring anything else. I can't offer anyone else." I looked at Rick and saw that other version of him: the faceless one. She would give me to Chaac, to the water, and it would take me down. Flense my body. Eat me and spit out the bones.

"Do it now," I said, and let my head fall. I closed my eyes. "Quickly. Please." I didn't open them again. I didn't have to as the thunder of water filled my ears.

There was cold all around. Other than that I couldn't feel anything: my body was numb, my hands, my face; especially that. I reached up and touched my skin. It felt smooth, but maybe it did, afterwards. I opened my eyes and found I was blind. Then everything started to come back, the light, the air, and I started to shake. My face, though, was warming; I felt the sun on it, the blessed brightness. I was in the water, but something about it was wrong. It roiled and surged like something restless.

When I looked around I could see the coast. In the distance were boats, people swimming. Further inland was the edge of the jungle; it must be a long way to the camp where Kath would be waiting. I had no idea how to get back there, or how I would explain. No doubt they'd say I'd pulled some prank, or that I'd delved too far; that I had merely been lucky to survive my fool's dive.

They'd say the changes in pressure had got to me. Made me hallucinate.

I allowed myself to move with the water. Whatever they said, however it happened, I was here, in the eyes, the *ojos de agua*. Somewhere far below, water gushed from a cave mouth that led out of the earth. The dark was waiting there, something that didn't sleep and didn't die.

And I had pledged myself to it.

When I closed my eyes, I saw my friend's face. His whole, complete face. I remembered what he'd done: *You*, he'd said. When I remembered the woman, I couldn't quite bring myself to hate him for it.

Rick had always been the one to go farther, to see things no one else had seen, the one who laughed at what made others fear. But I hadn't betrayed him. I'd been to the place he wanted me to go, seen the things he wanted me to see; but I hadn't given any life but my own.

I wondered when the creature of the *cenoté* would claim it from me.

I started to strike out for the shore, thinking of the free-divers plunging down towards their crucified god. I thought about how we offered ourselves, wondered if, after all, it was some need we had, to throw ourselves before some idea or thing. Maybe, sooner or later, all of us had something or someone waiting to collect. If so, maybe it wasn't so bad; better than being trapped in the endless dark, unable to go forward, unable to go back. Whatever I had given, for now, it was enough. And the thing in the cave – it was the life-giver, too.

The breeze was picking up and I swam harder. It became easier as the feeling flooded back into my limbs. It felt as if my body were re-forming itself, my arms and legs becoming solid, capable, more real; defined by their motion as I swam out of the bright place where the sun struck the water.

STEPHEN JONES & KIM NEWMAN

Necrology: 2012

ONCE AGAIN, WE mark the passing of many notable writers, artists, performers and technicians who, during their lifetimes, made significant contributions to the horror, science fiction and fantasy genres (or left their mark on popular culture in other, often fascinating, ways) . . .

AUTHORS/ARTISTS/COMPOSERS

Richard Alf, chairman and co-founder of the San Diego Comic-Con, died of pancreatic cancer on January 4, aged 59.

American comic strip artist **John Celardo** died on January 6, aged 93. In the early 1950s he succeeded Bob Lubbers as the illustrator of the syndicated daily and Sunday *Tarzan* newspaper strips, which he continued until 1968. Celardo also worked for various comic book titles, including *Jungle Comics*, and he illustrated a *Land of the Giants* strip on packages of the Topps Chewing Gum trading cards.

Author **Phyllis MacLennan** died on January 8, aged 91. After working in Military Intelligence during World War II, she made her SF debut in *Fantastic* in 1963. MacLennan published six more stories, some of which appeared in various anthologies, and her only SF novel was *Turned Loose on Irdra* (1970).

UK film composer **David Whitaker** died on January 11, aged 81. He composed the scores for *Scream and Scream Again*, Hammer's *Dr. Jekyll and Sister Hyde* and *Vampire Circus*, *Vampira* (aka *Old Dracula*), *Dominique* (aka *Dominique is Dead*) and *The Sword and the Sorcerer*.

American horror writer **Howard** [Lance] **Hopkins** died of a heart attack while walking home in the snow on January 12. He was 50. An editor and writer for Moonstone Books, Hopkins's short stories appeared in a number of small press publications during the 1980s and 1990s, and he self-published many horror novels through his Golden Peril Press. These included *Grimm* and spin-off series *The Chloe Files*, *Night Demons*, *The Dark Riders* and *The Nightmare Club* series for children. Under the pseudonym Lance Howard he also published more than thirty Western novels.

Italian SF author **Carlo Fruttero** who, with regular collaborator Franco Lucentini, edited the SF magazine *Urania* (1964–85), died on January 15, aged 86.

British photographer and author Sir **Simon** [Neville Llewelyn] **Marsden**, 4th Baronet, died on January 22, aged 63. His atmospheric black and white photographs of old ruins, graveyards and reputedly haunted houses appeared on numerous book covers and record albums, and collections of his own work include *The Haunted Realm*, *Visions of Poe*, *Phantoms of the Isles*, *This Spectred Isle: A Journey Through Haunted England* and *Vampires: The Twilight World*.

British composer **Ted Dicks** (Edward Dicks), who wrote the music for such 1960s hits as "Right, Said Fred", "Hole in the Ground" and "A Windmill in Old Amsterdam", died on January 27, aged 83. Dicks also composed the theme song for *Carry on Screaming!* and wrote the scores for *Virgin Witch* and the 1970 TV series *Catweazle*.

British comic strip artist **Mike White** died over the weekend of January 28–29 after a long illness. Best known for his work on the "Roy of the Rovers" football strip for six years, his first strip appeared in *Valiant* in 1965. He went on to work on Jack Adrian's violent and controversial "Kids Rule – OK" in *Action* and for *2000AD* he collaborated with writer Alan Moore on various strips, including "Abelard Snazz", "Future Shocks" and "Time Twisters" (the memorable "The Reversible Man" story).

Gretta M. Anderson (Gretta McCoombs), who edited and published the American horror, fantasy and SF periodical *2AM Magazine* (1985–95), died of a heart attack on January 29, aged 55.

American bookseller and SF and fantasy writer **Ardath Mayhar** (Ardath Frances Hurst) died on February 1, aged 81. After writing some poetry and pseudonymous Westerns, she made her genre debut in 1973 and became a full-time author in 1982, publishing more than sixty novels, including *How the Gods Wove in Kyrannon*, *Soul-Singer of Tyrnos*, *Warlock's Gift*, *The Black Tower* and *Shock Treatment*. Mayhar's short fiction was collected in, amongst other titles, *Slewfoot Sally and the Flying Mule and Other Tales from Cotton Country*, *The Crystal Skull*, *The Twilight Dancer and Other Tales of Magic, Fantasy and the Supernatural*, *Strange Doin's in the Pine Hills* and *A World of Weirdities*. She received the SFWA Author Emeritus Award in 2008.

British SF and fantasy writer **John Christopher** (Christopher Samuel Youd) died on February 3, aged 89. He made his genre debut with a poem in a 1949 issue of *Weird Tales*, and published his first novel, *The Winter Swan*, that same year. Best known for his YA "Tripods" trilogy (1967–68, adapted for a BBC-TV series in the mid-1980s), his other novels include *The Death of Grass* (aka *No Blade of Grass*, filmed in 1970), *The Year of the Comet* (aka *Planet of Peril*), *A Wrinkle in the Skin* (aka *The Ragged Edge*), *The Little People*, *Pendulum* and *Bad Dream*. The author's many books for children include the "The Prince in Waiting" and "Fireball" trilogies, along with *The Lotus Caves*, *The Guardians*, *Empty World* and *A Dusk of Demons*. *The Twenty-Second Century* collected some of his SF work under the "John Christopher" by-line, and his many other pseudonyms included Christopher Youd, Hilary Ford, William Godfrey, Peter Graaf, Peter Nichols, Anthony Rye, Stanley Winchester and Samuel Youd.

Eighty-seven-year-old **John Turner Sargent, Sr,** who was CEO of publishing imprint Doubleday & Co from 1963–78, died of a stroke on February 4, following a long illness. Among the authors he worked with were Stephen King and Peter Benchley, and Sargent was rumoured to have been the Doubleday executive who ordered the US edition of J. G. Ballard's *The Atrocity Exhibition* pulped in 1970 because it included a story about his close friend, Jacqueline Kennedy.

American comic book artist **John** [Powers] **Severin** died on February 12, aged 90. He was best known for his work on EC's *Two-Fisted Tales* and *Frontline Combat*, and Marvel's *Sgt. Fury and His Howling Commandos*, *The Incredible Hulk*, *Conan the Barbarian* and *King Kull*. In the 1970s he contributed to Warren Publishing's *Blazing Combat* and *Creepy*. Severin was one of the founding artists on *Mad*, and he worked for 45 years on the humour magazine *Cracked*.

American author and stage director **Mark Bourne** died of a heart attack on February 25, aged 50. He worked with Ray Bradbury to adapt the latter's stories for the theatre and planetarium performances, and his fiction appeared in *The Magazine of Fantasy & Science Fiction*, *Realms of Fantasy* and *Asimov's*. Bourne is credited with first using the word "morph" in an SF story in 1993.

British actor (*The Terrornauts*, *Out of the Unknown* etc.) turned TV scriptwriter **Richard** [Michael] **Carpenter** died of a blood clot on February 26, aged 82. He scripted the series *Catweazle* (1970–71), *The Boy from Space* (1971), *The Ghosts of Motley Hall* (1976–78), *The Baker Street Boys* (1983), *Robin of Sherwood* (1984–86), *The Borrowers* (1992) and *The Return of the Borrowers* (1993), along with the film *Stanley's Dragon* and *I Was a Rat* (based on the Philip Pullman novel). Carpenter also wrote a number of novelisations of his work.

American comic book artist **Sheldon Moldoff** died on February 29, aged 91. His work appeared in *Action Comics* #1 (which introduced Superman), and he also worked on the Golden Age versions of Hawkman and Hawkgirl. After drawing *Moon Girl* for EC, in the late 1940s he packaged the horror comics *This Magazine is Haunted*, *Worlds of Fear* and *Strange Suspense Stories* for Fawcett Comics. From 1953–67 Moldoff was one on Bob Kane's primary "ghost artists" on *Batman*, and he is credited as co-creating the characters Bat-Girl, Batwoman and Ace the Bat Hound, along with supervillains Mr Freeze, Poison Ivy, Clayface and Bat-Mite.

Canadian-born technical artist **Bruce Cornwell**, who worked on Frank Hampson's "Dan Dare, Pilot of the Future" comic strip in the *Eagle*, died on March 2. He also had work in *The Dalek Book* and *The Dalek World* in the mid-1960s.

Conceptual movie artist **Ralph** [Angus] **McQuarrie**, who created the iconic designs for such characters as Darth Vader, R2-D2, C-3PO and Chewbacca in *Star Wars*, died on March 3, aged 82. He had been suffering from Parkinson's disease. A technical illustrator for Boeing before he started designing movie posters, he later contributed concept art to *The Empire Strikes Back*, *Return of the Jedi*, *Close Encounters of the Third Kind*, the original *Battlestar Galactica* TV series, *Raiders of the Lost Ark*, *E.T. The Extra-Terrestrial*, *Cocoon* (which won him an Oscar for Best Visual Effects in 1986), *Star Trek IV: The Voyage Home*, **batteries not included* and Clive Barker's *Nightbreed*. McQuarrie was also the conceptual artist for the *Back to the Future* ride at Universal Studios.

British film archivist and journalist **Philip Jenkinson**, who presented the BBC-TV shows *Late Night Line-Up* and *Film Night* in the late 1960s and early 1970s, died on March 4. He was 76. Amongst the many celebrities he interviewed were John Ford, Ramon Novarro, Gloria Swanson and Boris Karloff. He also wrote a regular column about films for the *Radio Times* and appeared in the 1977 Christmas special of *The Morecambe & Wise Show*.

Academy Award-winning American songwriter and screenwriter **Robert B.** (Bernard) **Sherman** died in London on March 5, aged 86. In collaboration with his younger brother, Richard M. Sherman, he contributed songs to such movies as *The Absent-Minded Professor*, *Moon Pilot*, *In Search of the Castaways*, *The Sword in the Stone*, *Mary Poppins*, *Winnie the Pooh and the Honey Tree*, *The Gnome-Mobile*, *The Jungle Book* (1967), *Chitty Chitty Bang Bang*, *Winnie the Pooh and the Blustery Day*, *The AristoCats*, *Bedknobs and Broomsticks*, *Snoopy Come Home*, *Charlotte's Web* (1973), *Winnie the Pooh and Tigger Too*, *The Slipper and the Rose: The Story of Cinderella*, *Little Nemo: Adventures in Slumberland*, *The Tigger Movie* and many other titles. The Sherman brothers wrote the song "It's a Small World (After All)" for an installation at the 1964 New York World's Fair, since when it has reportedly become the most translated and performed song ever.

Forty-one-year-old New Zealand-born SF and horror writer **Paul Haines** died of cancer in Australia the same day. A winner of the Ditmar and Aurealis awards, his stories were collected in *Doorways for the Dispossessed*, *Slice of Life* and *The Last Days of Kali Yuga*.

German SF author **Hans Kneifel**, who wrote more than eighty *Perry Rhodan* novels, along with many other shared-world and stand-alone books, died om March 7, aged 75.

Influential French illustrator **Jean** [Henri Gaston] **Giraud** (aka "Moëbius"), who co-founded the magazine *Metal Hurlant* in 1975, died in Paris after a long battle with cancer on March 10. He was 73. Best known for his comics work around the world, he also created concept and storyboard art for such films as *Alien*, *Time Masters*, *Tron*, *Masters of the Universe*, *Willow*, *Little Nemo: Adventures in Slumberland*, *The Abyss*, *Space Jam* and *The Fifth Element*. He was the Artist Guest of Honour at the 2007 World Fantasy Convention, and was inducted into the SF Hall of Fame in 2011.

M. A. R. Barker (Professor Muhammad Abd-al-Rahman Barker), who created the world of "Tekumel" as a setting for the role-playing game *Empire of the Petal Throne* (1975), died on March 16, aged 83. He also wrote five novels with the same setting, beginning with *The Man of Gold* in 1984.

American SF fan turned author **Gene DeWeese** (Thomas Eugene DeWeese) died on March 19, aged 78. He had been suffering from Lewy body dementia. Best known for his tie-ins to *Star Trek*, *Lost in Space*, *Amazing Stories*, "Ravenloft", "Dinotopia" and *The Man from U.N.C.L.E.* (with Robert "Buck" Coulson, under the pseudonym Thomas Stratton), DeWeese's more than 40 books also include *The Blackhoe Gothic*, *Nightmares from Space*, *Whatever Became of Aunt Margaret?* and *The Adventures of a Two-Minute Werewolf* (which was made into a TV movie in 1985). Some of his short fiction was collected in *The Wanting Factor* and, under the pen-name Jean DeWeese he published nine Gothic novels, including *The Reimann Curse*, *The Moonstone Spirit* and *Nightmare in Pewter*.

Italian poet, novelist and screenwriter **Tonio** (Antonio) **Guerra**, best known for his work with director Michaelangelo Antonioni and other leading Italian directors, died on March 21, aged 92. His many films include *Perseus Against the Monsters* (Spanish version, uncredited), *The Tenth Victim*, *Blow-Up*, *Cinderella – Italian Style*, *Ghosts – Italian Style*, *Zabriskie Point* and *Flesh for Frankenstein* (uncredited).

Swiss-born British academic and novelist **Christine Brooke-Rose** died the same day in France, aged 89. Known for her experimental novels, starting with *Out* in 1964, she also wrote the 1981 non-fiction volume *A Rhetoric of the Unreal: Studies in Narrative and Structure, Especially of the Fantastic*.

British author and journalist **Peter Phillips** died on March 28, aged 92. During the 1940s and 50s he wrote around twenty of SF stories, including "Dreams Are Sacred" (*Astounding*, 1948), which was adapted as "Get off My Cloud" in 1969 for the BBC TV series *Out of the Unknown*.

British editor and publisher **Nick Webb** died on April 10, aged 62. He began his career at Penguin before moving on to Granada and Arrow. He was managing editor a Sphere and also worked at Duckworth and Simon & Schuster UK. While senior fiction editor at Pan Books in the late 1970s he commissioned Douglas Adams to novelise his radio series *The Hitchhiker's Guide to the Galaxy*, and Webb also wrote Adams's official biography, *Wish You Were Here* (2003), following the author's premature death.

American SF author and editor **K.** (Kathy) **D.** (Diane) **Wentworth** died of pneumonia caused by complications from cervical cancer on April 18. She was 61. Her novels include *The Imperium Game*, *Moonspeaker* and *House of Moons*, along with two collaborations with Eric Flint, *The Course of Empire* and *The Crucible of Empire*. As co-ordinating judge for the L. Ron Hubbard Writers of the Future Contest she edited the annual *Writers of the Future* anthologies from 2009 until her death.

American film composer **Joel Goldsmith**, the eldest son of composer Jerry Goldsmith, died of cancer on April 29, aged 54. Best known for his music for the *Stargate SG-1*, *Stargate: Atlantis* and *SGU: Stargate Universe* TV series and spin-off movies, his other credits include *Laserblast* (with Richard Band), *The Day Time Ended*, *Dr. Heckyl and Mr. Hype*, *Island of Blood*, *Double Jeopardy*, *The Man with Two Brains*, *Watchers*, *Moon 44*, *The Rift*, *Maniac Cop 3: Badge of Silence*, *Man's Best Friend*, *Rattled*, *Vampirella*, *Kull the Conqueror*, *Monster!* (1999), *Chameleon 3: Dark Angel*, *Haunting Sarah* and *War of the Dead*, along with episodes of the 1990s *Outer Limits*, *Witchblade* and *Sanctuary* TV series. Goldsmith also composed around 20 minutes of additional music for his father's score for *Star Trek: First Contact*.

American small press horror writer **Michael Louis Calvillo** died after a long battle against cancer on April 30, aged 37. His novels include the Bram Stoker Award-nominated *I Will Rise*, *As Fate Would Have It*, *Lambs* and *Death and Desire in the Age of Women*. He also published the novellas *Bleed for You* and *7 Brains*, and some of his short fiction is collected in *Blood & Gristle*.

Best-selling American children's book writer and illustrator **Maurice** [Bernard] **Sendak**, best known for his Caldecott Medal-winning *Where the Wild Things Are* (1963, filmed in 2009), died of complications from a recent stroke on May 8, aged 83. His more than 80 other books include *In the Night Kitchen* (1970), *Outside Over There* (1981) and *Bumble-Ardy* (2011). Sendak also received the US Congress National Medal of Arts, the Hans Christian Anderson Award, a National Book Award and the Astrid Lindgren Memorial Award.

Philippines-born comic book artist and letterer **Tony DeZuniga** died of complications from a stroke on May 11, aged 71. One of the first Filipino artists to have his work accepted by American publishers in the late 1960s, he co-created such characters as Jonah Hex and Black Orchid for DC Comics. Amongst many other titles, DeZungia worked on *Conan the Barbarian*, *Conan the King*, *Doc Savage*, *Dracula Lives*, *Ghosts*, *House of Mystery*, *House of Secrets*, *Man-Thing*, *Monsters Unleashed*, *Phantom Stranger*, *Red Sonja*, *Savage Sword of Conan*, *Swamp Thing*, *Vampire Tales*, *Weird Mystery Tales*, *Weird War Tales*, *Weird Western Tales* and *The Witching Hour*.

American SF fan and photographer **Jay Kay Klien** died of oesophageal cancer on May 13, aged 80. He published a small number of short stories, his photographs of conventions appeared in numerous magazines, including *Locus*, and he was Fan Guest of Honor at the 1974 World Science Fiction Convention. Klein was inducted into the First Fandom Hall of Fame in 2011.

Film scholar and critic **Paul Willeman** died the same day, aged 77. Among the books he contributed to were *Roger Corman: The Millenic Vision* and the original edition of the *Aurum Film Encyclopedia: Horror*. Willeman wrote the bulk of "continental" film entries for the latter, highlighting the careers of people such as Jesus Franco and Paul Naschy.

Mexican author **Carlos** [Manuel] **Fuentes** [Marcías] died on May 15, aged 83. Best known for his magical realist works, he also strayed into genre fiction with *Aura*, *La* *cabeza de la hidra*, *Terra Nostra*, *Inez* and *La Silla del Aguila*. From 1959–73 he was married to actress Rita Macedo and received a state funeral in Mexico City.

Filipino comic book artist **Ernie** (Ernesto) **Chan** (aka Ernie Chua) died of cancer on May 16, aged 71. The many titles he contributed to include *Chamber of Chills*, *Claw the Unconquered*, *Conan the Barbarian*, *Dark Mansion of Forbidden Love*, *Doc Savage*, *Ghosts*, *Haunt of Horror*, *House of Mystery*, *House of Secrets*, *Jonah Hex*, *King Conan*, *Kull the Conqueror*/*Kull the Destroyer*, *Savage Sword of Conan*, *Secrets of Haunted House*, *Secrets of Sinister House*, *Swamp Thing*, *Tales of Ghost Castle*, *Tales of the Zombie*, *Weird Mystery Tales*, *Weird War Tales* and *The Witching Hour*.

British literary agent and editor **Hilary** [Harold] **Rubinstein** died on May 22, aged 86. The nephew of Victor Gollancz, he entered publishing in 1950 and founded the Gollancz SF line, bringing his friend Kingsley Amis to the list. In the mid-1960s he became an agent at A.P. Watt, where he represented the estates of H.G. Wells, Rudyard Kipling and G.K. Chesterton. Rubinstein retired from the firm in 1992.

Hugo Award and Caldecott Medal-winning American artist **Leo Dillon**, best known for his artistic collaborations with his wife Diane, died of lung cancer on May 26, aged 79. Together they created numerous print and album covers, posters, greeting cards and more than 40 children's books. Among the authors whose works they illustrated are Harlan Ellison, Ray Bradbury, Ursula K. LeGuin, Michael Moorcock and R. A. Lafferty. Some of their work was collected in *The Art of Leo and Diane Dillon* (1981), and they jointly received the World Fantasy Award for Lifetime Achievement in 2008.

Ray [Douglas] **Bradbury**, arguably the greatest and most influential writer in our genre(s), died on June 5, aged 91. After moving with his family to Los Angeles in 1934, he joined the Los Angeles Science Fantasy Society where he met Forrest J Ackerman, Hannes Bok, Edmond Hamilton, Ray

Harryhausen, Robert A. Heinlein and Henry Kuttner, amongst others. He contributed to various fanzines in the late 1930s, before he broke into the pulp magazines in 1941, contributing short stories to *Weird Tales*, *Super Science Fiction* and numerous other titles. In 1947 some of his best fiction was collected in *Dark Carnival* by Arkham House. In the decades that followed, Bradbury published numerous novels and collections, including such classics as *The Martian Chronicles*, *The Illustrated Man*, *Fahrenheit 451*, *The Golden Apples of the Sun*, *The October Country*, *Dandelion Wine*, *The Day It Rained Forever*, *Something Wicked This Way Comes*, *The Halloween Tree*, *From the Dust Returned* and many other titles. He scripted John Huston's 1956 movie of *Moby Dick*, *It Came from Outer Space* and other projects, and his own work has been widely adapted for film, TV and theatre, notably for his own television series, *The Ray Bradbury Theater* (1985–86). His many awards include the World Fantasy Award for Life Achievement, SFWA Grand Master, Bram Stoker Life Achievement Award, World Horror Grandmaster and a National Medal of the Arts. On what would have been his 92nd birthday – August 22, 2012 – NASA announced that it was naming the landing site of the Mars Curiosity rover "The Bradbury Landing" in honour of the late author.

American SF writer **Jim Young** (James Maxwell Young) died of complications from glioblastoma (a malignant brain tumour only diagnosed several days earlier) on June 12, aged 61. A former US diplomat, he wrote two novels (*The Face of the Deep* and *Armed Memory*) and his short fiction appeared in *The Magazine of Fantasy & Science Fiction* and elsewhere. Following his early retirement, he worked as an actor, appearing in a number of short films and as Adolf Hitler in *Nazis at the Centre of the Earth* (2012). Young married and then divorced editor Kathryn Cramer in 1989.

Influential American film critic and champion of the *auteur* theory, **Andrew Sarris**, died of complications from a stomach infection on June 20, aged 83. From the 1960s onwards, his reviews appeared in *The Village Voice* (in which he famously championed Hitchcock's *Psycho*) and the *New York Observer*. Sarris also edited an English-language edition of the French magazine *Cahiers du Cinéma*, and he wrote the acclaimed reference work *The American Cinema: Directors and Directions 1929–1968*.

Tony Award-winning American composer and lyricist **Richard Adler**, who co-wrote (with Jerry Ross) the 1955 Broadway hit *Damn Yankees!*, died on June 21, aged 90. It was filmed in 1958 with Ray Walston as the Devil. He was married to actress Sally Annn Howes from 1958–66.

Seventy-one-year-old writer, director and producer **Norah Ephron** died in New York of leukaemia on June 26. Among her less successful credits are the John Travolta angel movie *Michael* and the 2005 remake of *Bewitched*.

Former *Saturday Night Live* writer and producer **Tom Davis** (Thomas James Davis), who also scripted the 1993 movie *Coneheads*, died of head and neck cancer on July 19, aged 59. He had a small role in that film, and also appeared in *Blues Brothers 2000* and *Evolution*.

New Zealand children's author and former librarian **Margaret Mahy** died after a brief illness on July 23, aged 76. The author of around 40 novels, 20 collections of stories and 100 picture books, some of her best-known titles are *The Tricksters*, *Aliens in the Family*, *The Haunting*, *The Changeover: A Supernatural Romance*, *Memory*, *A Horribly Haunted School*, *Alchemy* and *Portable Ghosts*. She was the first writer out side the UK to win the Carnegie Medal.

British film critic and writer **James** [Patrick Blackden] **Marriott** died in a drowning accident on July 28, aged 39. A Senior Library Assistant at the University of Bristol, he edited *Horror: The Complete Guide to the Cinema of Fear* (aka *Horror! 333 Films to Scare You to Death*, co-credited to Kim Newman), and his other books include the reference volumes *Horror Films* (under the pseudonym "Patrick Blackden") and *The Descent*. Mariott also contributed pieces to *21st Century Gothic*, *The Exorcist: Studies in the Horror Film* and *SFX* magazine.

Incisive and acerbic American author, playwright and screenwriter [Eugene Luther] **Gore Vidal** (aka Edgar Box/Katherine Everad/Cameron Kay), died of complications from pneumonia on July 31, aged 86. Along with a number of critical essays, he wrote such genre-related novels as *Messiah*, *Kalki*, *Duluth*, *Live from Golgotha* and *The Smithsonian Institution*, plus the 1957 play *Visit to a Small Planet*. Vidal's screenplays includes *Suddenly Last Summer*, *Visit to a Small Planet*, *Myra Breckinridge* and *Caligula*, along with episodes of TV's *Omnibus* ("The Turn of the Screw", 1954) and *Climax!* ("Dr. Jekyll and Mr. Hyde", 1955). As an actor, he was in *Suddenly Last Summer* (uncredited) and *Gattaca*, and appeared as himself in episodes of *Rowan & Martin's Laugh-In*, *Family Guy* and *The Simpsons*.

Stalwart British illustrator **Alan** [Joseph] **Hunter** died on August 1 following a long illness. He was 89. Influenced by the work of Virgil Finlay, he became a commercial artist and draughtsman, and his SF art career began in the early 1950s illustrating for such magazines as *New Worlds*, *Science-Fantasy* and *Nebula Science Fiction*. He then went on to publish his often complex line illustrations in numerous semi-prozines and fanzines on both sides of the Atlantic, including *Fantasy Tales*, *Whispers*, *Dark Horizons*, *Ghosts and Scholars*, *Science Fiction Chronicle*, *Algol/Starship*, *Vector*, *White Dwarf* and many others. In 1981, Hunter was Special Artist Guest at Fantasycon VII.

Fifty-one-year-old French SF writer, critic and musician **Roland C.** (Charles) **Wagner** was killed in a car crash near Bordeaux on August 5. His partner and daughter who were in the same car only suffered minor injuries. His first novel, *Le Serpent d'angoisse*, appeared in 1987, and he went on to publish around fifty more (many under the pseudonym Richard Wolfram), including *HPL (1890–1991)*, an alternate history biography of H. P. Lovecraft.

Tony, Emmy and Oscar-winning American composer and songwriter **Marvin** [Frederick] **Hamlisch** died after a short illness on August 6, aged 68. His movie soundtracks include *The World's Greatest Athelete*, *The Spy Who Loved Me*, *D.A.R.Y.L.* and *The Return of the Six Million Dollar Man and the Bionic Woman*, while his songs have been used in *Ski Party*, *The Devil and Max Devlin*, *The Fan*, *Big*, *Shrek the Third*, *Land of the Lost* and episodes of TV's *Batman* (1967), *The Tick* and *Fringe*.

Legendary American comic book artist **Joe Kubert** died of multiple myeloma on August 12, aged 85. Born in Poland, he travelled to America with his parents as an infant. He began is comics career in 1942 and went on to work with most of the major publishers on such titles as *All-Star Comics*, *Tor*, EC's *Two-Fisted Tales*, *The Brave and the Bold*, *Our Army at War* ("Sgt. Rock"), *Hawkman* (who he had also illustrated back in the 1940s) and DC's *Tarzan*, amongst many other titles. In 1976 he founded The Kubert School to train future comic artists, including his sons Adam and Andy.

Sixty-six-year-old American author **Adam Niswander** died of respiratory failure the same day, having spent several months in the hospice of a VA hospital in Arizona. Best known for his Shaman Cycle of novels, *The Charm*, *The Serpent Slayers*, *The Hound Hunters*, *The War of the Whisperers* and *The Nemesis of Night*, along with the stand-alone *The Sand Dwellers* and *The Repository*, his short fiction was collected in *Blurring the Edges of Dream*. Niswander also founded the Lovecraft convention MythosCon.

American-born Irish SF writer **Harry Harrison** (Henry Maxwell Dempsey), best known for his Stainless Steel Rat SF crime series, the Deathworld series and the 1966 novel *Make Room! Make Room!* (filmed as *Solent Green* in 1973), died in England on August 15, aged 87. Harrison began his career as an artist for such EC comics as *Weird Fantasy* and *Weird Science*, often collaborating with Wally Wood, and he was the principal writer on the *Flash Gordon* newspaper strip during the 1950s and 1960s. Harrison sold his first story in 1951 to *Worlds Beyond*, and he went on to become a prolific contributor to the SF magazines (under his own name and such pseudonyms as Felix Boyd and Hank

Dempsey), most notably to John W. Campbell's *Astounding/Analog*. His other novels include *Planet of the Damned*, *Bill the Galactic Hero*, *A Transatlantic Tunnel Hurrah!*, *Star Smashers of the Galaxy Rangers*, *Skyfall*, *West of Eden* and *The Hammer and the Cross* (written with Tom Shippey). As an editor, Harrison not only had short stints at *Rocket Stories* (as Wade Kaempfert), *Amazing Stories*, *Fantastic* and *Impulse*, but also compiled numerous anthologies, including the annual *Best SF* series (1968–75) with his friend Brian Aldiss, with whom he jointly founded the critical journal *SF Horizons* and the World SF organisation. As Leslie Charteris he wrote the 1964 novel *Vendetta for the Saint*, and he collaborated with artist Jim Burns on the 1979 graphic novel *Planet Story*. Amongst other awards, Harrison was named a SFWA Grand Master in 2009.

Fifty-six-year-old Chicago fan and convention organiser **Ken Hunt**, who was head of logistics for Chicon 7, the 70th World Science Fiction Convention held over August 30–September 4, 2012, died on August 20 of complications following a cascading cardiac event and emergency surgery.

British landscape painter **Michael** [Harvey] **Embden** died of cancer on August 21, aged 63. During the 1970s and 1980s he also produced more than 100, mostly SF, cover paintings for books by Roger Zelazny, Poul Anderson, Gordon R. Dickson, Tad Williams, C. J. Cherryh and Patricia Kenneally, along with an illustrated edition of H. Rider Haggard's *She* (with Tim Gill) for Dragon's Dream in 1981.

American SF and fantasy author **Josepha Sherman** died of early-onset Alzheimer's disease on August 23, aged 65. She began publishing in 1986, and her novels include the Compton Crook Award-winning *The Shining Falcon*, *The Horse of Flame*, *Child of Faerie Child of Earth*, *A Strange and Ancient Name*, *Windleaf*, *Gleaming Bright*, *King's Son Magic's Son* and *Son of Darkness*. She edited a number of anthologies, including *Lammas Night*, *Trickster Tales* and *Urban Nightmares* (with Keith R. A. DeCandido), and compiled the 2008 study *Storytelling: An Encyclopedia of Mythology and Folklore*. Sherman also wrote tie-in books for *Star Trek*, *Xena Warrior Princess*, *Buffy the Vampire Slayer*, *Highlander* and *Andromeda*, often in collaboration with other authors.

Eighty-three-year-old American folklorist **Shirley Climo,** who authored 24 books of retold fairy tales and fables from around the world, died the same day.

Italian film poster artist **Arnaldo Putzu** died on September 1, aged 85. He had been suffering from Alzheimer's disease. Best known for his iconic posters for the *Carry On* series, during the 1960s and 1970s his work in Britain included Hammer's *Creatures the World Forgot*, *Frankenstein Must Be Destroyed*, *Countess Dracula* and *Legend of the 7 Golden Vampires*, along with UK posters for *From Russia with Love*, *Dorian Gray*, *Voices*, *Blood on Satan's Claw*, *Flesh for Frankenstein*, *The Island at the Top of the World*, *Westworld*, *The Golden Voyage of Sinbad* and many others. Putzu also painted most of the covers for the children's magazine *Look-In*, from 1973 until 1981.

Oscar-winning lyricist **Hal David** (Harold Lane David), best known for his numerous hit collaborations with Burt Bacharach (including "The Look of Love"), died of complications from a stroke the same day. He was 91. Among the many movies to feature his work are *Casino Royale*, *On Her Majesty's Secret Service*, *Lost Horizon* (1973) and *Moonraker*.

American literary agent **Wendy Weil** died on September 22, aged 72. The genre authors she represented included Karen Joy Fowler, Carol Emshwiller and James Morrow.

English teacher turned video games pioneer **Mike Singleton** died of cancer in Switzerland on October 10, aged 61. Among the influential games he created were *The Lords of Midnight*, *Doomdark's Revenge*, *Midwinter*, *Midwinter II: Flames of Freedom*, *Star Trek: The Rebel Universe* and *Lord of the Rings: War in Middle-Earth*. He also worked with LucasArts developing the games *Indiana Jones and The Emperor's Tomb* and *Wrath Unleashed*.

American writer and editor **Charles E.** (Edward) **Fritch** (aka Eric Thomas and Christopher Sly), whose story "The

Misfortune Cookie" was adapted for a 1986 episode of TV's *The Twilight Zone*, died on October 11, aged 85. A member of the "The Group" – along with Richard Matheson, William F. Nolan, Charles Beaumont, George Clayton Johnson, John Tomerlin, Chad Oliver and others – he edited the SF magazine *Gamma* (1963–65 with Nolan) and was the last editor of *Mike Shayne Magazine* (1979–85). Some of his short fiction is collected in *Crazy Mixed-Up Planet* and *Horses' Asteroid*, both published by Powell.

Patrick O'Connor, a former editor at US imprints Pinnacle and Popular Library, died on October 13, aged 87.

American comic book artist **Marc Swayze** (Marcus Desha Swayze) died on October 14, aged 99. During the Golden Age he worked on the adventures of Captain Marvel and the Marvel Family for Fawcett's *Whiz Comics*, co-creating Mary Marvel with Otto Binder.

Paul Kurtz, founder of Prometheus Books in 1969, died on October 20, aged 86. In 2005 Prometheus launched the SF/fantasy imprint Pyr.

South African-born American author **Janet Berliner** (aka Janet Gluckman) died in Las Vegas of complications from an auto-immune disorder on October 24, aged 73. Her novels include The Madagascar Manifesto series (with George Guthridge), *Execution Exchange* (with Woody Greer), *Rite of the Dragon* and *Artifact* (with Kevin J. Anderson, F. Paul Wilson and Matthew J. Costello), while her short fiction appeared in *Shayol*, *The Magazine of Fantasy & Science Fiction* and various anthologies. As an anthologist, she edited *Peter S. Beagle's Immortal Unicorn*, *David Copperfield's Tales of the Impossible* and *David Copperfield's Beyond Imagination*. Berliner won a Bram Stoker Award in 1997 (with Guthridge) for the story "Children of the Dusk".

American artist **David Grove**, who painted the movie poster for Disney's *Something Wicked This Way Comes* (1983), died of emphysema on October 25, aged 72. During his career, Grove produced numerous book covers and film posters, and some of his work was collected in the 2011 volume *David Grove: An Illustrated Life*.

French critic and editor **Jacques Goimard** died of Parkinson's disease the same day, aged 78. While an editor at Pocket Press, his *Le Livre d'or de la science-fiction* series published nearly 50 volumes from 1978–87. He also co-edited a number of SF and fantasy anthologies, including a "Year's Best" from 1978–82.

American book dealer **John D. Squires**, a world authority of the life and works of M. P. Shiel, died after a long illness on November 2, aged 64. Squires also contributed to *The New York Review of SF*.

American SF author **Kevin O'Donnell, Jr**, best known for his four-volume Journeys of McGill Feigham series, died of complications from cancer on November 7, aged 61. He sold his first story to *Analog* in 1973, and his other books include *Bander Snatch*, *Mayflies*, *War of Omission*, *ORA:CLE*, *Fire on the Border*, and the horror novel *The Shelter* (with Mary Kittredge).

Russian SF writer **Boris Strugatsky** (aka S. Vititsky), the younger brother of frequent collaborator Arkady, died of complications from leukaemia on November 19, aged 79. Their acclaimed novel *Roadside Picnic* was filmed by Andrei Tarkovsky in 1979 as *Stalker*. Both brothers were Guests of Honour at the 1987 World Science Fiction Convention in Brighton, England.

Disney development and design artist **Mel Shaw** (Melvin Schwartzman) died of congestive heart failure on November 22, aged 97. He began his career in animation in 1933, and went on to work in various capacities on *Bambi*, *Fantasia*, *The Rescuers*, *The Fox and the Hound*, *The Black Cauldron*, *The Great Mouse Detective*, *Beauty and the Beast* (1991) and *The Lion King*. In the late 1940s, Shaw and his business partner Bob Allen redesigned "Howdy Doody", the marionette featured in the 1950s NBC-TV show of the same name.

American underground cartoonist **Spain Rodriguez** (Manuel Rodriguez), the creator of the post-holocaust hero Trashman, died of cancer on November 28, aged 72. A former biker gang member, during the late 1960s he published his own comics magazine, *Zodiac Mindwarp*.

Rodriguez's other titles include *Sherlock Holmes' Strangest Cases*, *Alien Apocalypse* and *Nightmare Alley*.

American cartoonist and film critic **Jeff Millar** (Jeffrey Lynn Millar) died of bile duct cancer on November 30, aged 70. With illustrator Bill Hinds he created the syndicated *Tank McNamara* comic strip, and his zombie story "Dead and Buried" (with Alex Stern) was the basis for the 1981 movie of the same name and the novelisation by Chelsea Quinn Yarbro. Millar's other stories appeared in *Orbit Science Fiction* and Damon Knight's *Orbit 17*.

Julie Ann Jardine who, with her then-husband Jack Owen Jardine, wrote *The Swords of Lankor* and *The Mind Monsters* (both 1966) under the pseudonym Howard L. Cory, died in November, aged 86.

Christopher [John Dusser] **Davies**, one of the three founders of UK publishing imprint Dorling Kindersley (DK), died on December 2 after a lengthy illness. He was 71. Davies was with the company, best known for its illustrated books (including the infamous *Star Wars* debacle – four million copies sold but seventeen million printed!), from 1974 until his retirement in 2005.

American writer **Michael Alexander** died of cancer on December 4, aged 62. He published his first story in *The Magazine of Fantasy & Science Fiction* in 2010, and he also contributed to *Analog*.

Croatian fan, translator and convention organiser **Krsto A.** (Anton) **Mazuranić** died on December 21, aged 70. He was the editor-in-chief of *Future* magazine (1993–97) and is credited for bringing SF to Croatia and the rest of the former Yugoslavia.

Eclectic British composer Sir **Richard Rodney Bennett** died in New York City on December 24, aged 76. His many credits include Hammer's *The Man Who Could Cheat Death*, *The Nanny* and *The Witches*, along with *Billion Dollar Brain*, *Voices*, *Sherlock Holmes in New York*, *The Tale of Sweeny Todd* and the 2000 TV mini-series of *Ghormenghast*. In 1964, Bennett also contributed incidental music to the BBC's *Doctor Who*.

Archie [Edmiston] **Roy**, Professor Emeritus of Astronomy at the University of Glasgow, died on December 27, aged 88. A Founding President of The Scottish Society for Psychical Research, between 1968 and 1978 he published six SF and horror novels: *Deadlight*, *All Evil Shed Away*, *The Curtained Sleep*, *Sable Night*, *The Dark Host* and *Devil in the Darkness*.

Controversial American convention promoter and publisher **Rick Olney** (Richard L. Olney) died on December 28, aged 58. He was often accused of abruptly cancelling events and not paying his artists.

PERFORMERS/PERSONALITIES

British stuntman and fencing master **Bob Anderson** (Robert James Gilbert Anderson), who doubled for David Prowse's Darth Vader during the light-sabre duels in *The Empire Strikes Back* and *Return of the Jedi*, died on January 1, aged 89. A former Olympic fencer, Anderson also worked on *From Russia with Love*, *Casino Royale*, *One of Our Dinosaurs is Missing*, *Star Wars*, *Superman II*, *Highlander*, *The Princess Bride*, *The Lord of the Rings* trilogy and *The Hobbit: An Unexpected Journey*, along with the TV series *Highlander* and an episode of *Doctor Who*.

Cockney character actor **Harry Fowler** MBE (Henry James Fowler) died on January 4, aged 85. A stalwart of British cinema from the 1940s through to the 1980s, his credits include *Went the Day Well?*, *Mister Drake's Duck*, *Fire Maidens of Outer Space* and Hammer's *The Nanny*. He was also a regular on the short-lived 1982 TV series *Dead Ernest*, and appeared in an episode of *The Young Indiana Jones Chronicles* and the *Doctor Who* serial "Remembrance of the Daleks".

South African-born **Bob Holness** (Robert Wentworth John Holness) died in England on January 6, aged 83. Best known as a TV quiz-master on such shows as *Blockbusters* and *Call My Bluff*, Holness was the second actor to portray James Bond when he voiced the character in a 1957 South

African radio dramatisation of *Moonraker*. He later turned up as an announcer in an episode of the 1970s TV series *Thriller*.

1940s Hollywood actress **Natalie Draper**, the niece of Marion Davies, died on January 13, aged 92. She appeared in small roles in a number of films, including the 1945 version of *The Picture of Dorian Gray*.

British character actress **Marion Mathie** died on January 20, aged 80. She appeared in Hammer's *Dracula Has Risen from the Grave*, along with episodes of TV's *Adam Adamant Lives!* and *Department S*. She reportedly left an estate worth £1 million in her will.

American announcer and voice actor **Dick Tufeld** (Richard Norton Tufeld) died of congestive heart failure on January 22, aged 85. Best known as the voice of The Robot on TV's *Lost in Space* (1965–68), he was also worked on such other Irwin Allen shows as *Voyage to the Bottom of the Sea* and *The Time Tunnel*. Tufeld's other voice credits include various animated TV series, an episode of *Space Patrol* and as the Rambler-Crane Series Robot in the 1998 movie version of *Lost in Space*.

Dependable Hollywood leading man **James Farentino** (James Ferrantio), who starred in the 1994 TV series *Blue Thunder*, died of heart failure following complications from a broken hip on January 24, aged 73. His credits include *The War Lord*, *The Possessed* (1977), *The Final Countdown*, *Dead and Buried* and *The Cradle Will Fall*, along with episodes of *The Alfred Hitchcock Hour* and *Night Gallery* (Fritz Leiber's "The Girl with the Hungry Eyes"). He was married four times, to actresses Elizabeth Ashley, Michele Lee, Debrah Farentino and Stella Farentino.

British-born character actor **Ian Abercrombie** died in Hollywood on January 26, aged 77. He began his film and TV career in the mid-1960s, and appeared in *Sole Survivor* (1970), *The Hound of the Baskerviless* (1972, starring Stewart Granger as Sherlock Holmes), *Wicked Wicked*, *The Questor Tapes*, *Young Frankenstein*, *The Island at the Top of the World*, *Blood Beach*, *The Ice Pirates*, *Catacombs*,

Warlock, *Repossessed*, *Puppet Master III: Toulon's Revenge*, *Army of Darkness*, *Addams Family Values*, *Test Tube Teens from the Year 2000*, *Rattled*, *The Lost World: Jurassic Park*, *Mousehunt*, *Johnny Mysto: Boy Wizard*, *Wild Wild West*, *Jack Frost 2: Revenge of the Mutant Killer Snowman* and *Garfield 2*. He was also in episodes of *Get Smart*, *Search Control*, *The Six Million Dollar Man*, *Battlestar Galactica*, *Voyagers!*, *Tucker's Witch*, *Fantasy Island* (as Inspector Lestrade), *Otherworld*, *Alfred Hitchcock Presents* (1986), *Faerie Tale Theatre*, *Tales from the Crypt*, *Twin Peaks*, *The Flash*, *Babylon 5*, *Touched by an Angel*, *Beyond Belief: Fact or Fiction*, *Buffy the Vampire Slayer*, *G vs E*, *Star Trek: Voyager*, *Birds of Prey* (as Alfred Pennyworth), *Charmed* and *Moonlight*, and he was a regular on the Disney Channel's *Wizards of Waverly Place*. Abercrombie also contributed voice work to numerous video games and cartoon shows, including playing both Darth Sidious and Chancellor Palpatine in *Star Wars: The Clone Wars*.

British stage, screen and radio actor **Frederick** [William] **Treves** died on January 30, aged 86. He appeared on TV, often as authority figures, in *A for Andromeda* and *The Andromeda Breakthrough*, *The Avengers*, *Randall and Hopkirk (Deceased)*, *Doomwatch*, *Doctor Who*, *The Invisible Man* (1984) and *The Young Indiana Jones Chronicles*. Among his small number of film credits are *The Elephant Man* (based on his great-uncle's famous medical case) and *Afraid of the Dark*.

Actor and stage magician **Tony Giorgio** (Joseph Anthony Giorgio), who (under the name Lu Sifer) appeared as Satan in *Night Train to Terror* (1985), died of cardiopulmonary failure on February 1, aged 88. He also had small roles in *The Wrecking Crew* and Disney's *Escape to Witch Mountain*, along with episodes of *I Dream of Jeannie*, *The Six Million Dollar Man*, *The Bionic Woman* and *Fantasy Island*.

Respected American actor and director **Ben Gazzara** (Biagio Anthony Gazzara) died of pancreatic cancer on February 3, aged 81. Best remembered for his three movie collaborations with director John Cassavetes in the 1970s,

Gazzara also appeared in *When Michael Calls* (based on the novel by John Farris), *The Neptune Factor*, *Maneater*, *Control* and *Summer of Sam*.

The same day saw the death by cancer of another American actor/director, **Zalman King** (Zalman King Lefkovitz), at the age of 69. Best known for his erotic movies such as *Two Moon Junction*, *Wild Orchid* and *Red Shoes Diaries*, King also appeared in *Some Call It Loving*, *Blue Sunshine*, *Galaxy of Terror*, *Endangered Species* (which he also executive produced) and episodes of *The Alfred Hitchcock Hour*, *The Munsters*, *The Man from U.N.C.L.E.* and *Land of the Giants*.

Seventy-five-year-old **Bill Hinzman** (Samuel William Hinzman), who portrayed the graveyard zombie in the opening scenes of George Romero's seminal *Night of the Living Dead* (1968), died of cancer on February 5. After working with Romero again on *Jack's Wife* and *The Crazies*, Hinzman traded on his *NOLD* reputation, often playing other walking dead roles in such films as *The Majorettes* and *FleshEater* (aka *Zombie Nosh*), both of which he also directed, along with *Legion of the Night*, *Santa Claws*, *Evil Ambitions*, *The Drunken Dead Guy*, *Shadow: Dead Riot*, *The Spook Show*, *It Came from Trafalgar*, *Underground Entertainment: The Movie* and *River of Darkness*. As a cinematographer, Hinzman worked on *The Crazies*, *Captured Alive*, *Santas Claws*, *Scream Queens' Naked Christmas*, *The Dead Walk: Remaking a Classic* and *Children of the Living Dead*.

Josephine Streiner, who also played a zombie in *Night of the Living Dead*, died the same day, aged 93. She appeared in the documentaries *One for the Fire: The Legacy of "Night of the Living Dead"* and *Zombies: A Living History*.

Eighty-two-year-old American leading man [Joseph] **Peter Breck**, who starred as the middle son of Barbara Stanwyck's character in the 1960s TV series *The Big Valley*, died in Canada of complications from advanced dementia on February 6. Discovered by Robert Mitchum and best known for his roles in numerous TV Westerns, he also appeared in *The Crawling Hand*, *Shock Corridor*, *The Sword and the*

Sorcerer, *I Still Dream of Jeannie* and *The Unnamable II: The Statement of Randolph Carter*, along with episodes of *The Outer Limits* (1960s and 1990s), *The Six Million Dollar Man*, *The Incredible Hulk* and *Fantasy Island*.

French actress and novelist **Franca Maï** (Françoise Baud) died of cancer on February 8, aged 52. She starred in Jean Rollin's erotic vampire movie *Fascination* (1979).

Whitney [Elizabeth] **Houston**, Patrick Bateman's favourite singer in the novel *American Psycho*, was found dead in the bathtub at her room at the Beverly Hilton Hotel on February 11, aged 48. The official cause of death was given as "accidental drowning combined with effects of atherosclerotic heart disease and cocaine use". The singer and actress had been battling drug addiction for many years, and although traces of marijuana, the anti-anxiety drug Xanax, the muscle-relaxer Flexeril and the antihistamine Benadryl were also found in her system, they were ruled as not having contributed to her death. Houston appeared in *The Preacher's Wife* and the 1997 TV movie *Cinderella*, which she also executive produced.

Irish character actor **David** [Blake] **Kelly**, who played Grandpa Joe in Tim Burton's version of *Charlie and the Chocolate Factory* (2005), died of pneumonia on February 12, aged 82. His other credits include *The Hunchback of Notre Dame* (1982), *Merlin of the Crystal Cave* (based on the novel by Mary Stewart), *Agent Cody Banks 2: Destination London* and *Stardust* (based on the book by Neil Gaiman), along with episodes of TV's *Adam Adamant Lives!* and *Whoops Apocalypse*.

Lina Romay (Rosa María Almirall Martínez, aka Candy Coster/Lulu Laverne), Spanish actress, director (mostly porno) wife and muse of director Jess Franco, died of cancer on February 15, aged 57. Among her many film credits, including more than 100 for the prolific Franco, are *La maldició de Frankenstein* (1972), *La fille de Dracula*, *The Sinister Eyes of Dr. Orloff*, *El misterio del castillo rojo*, *Les avaleuses*, *The Perverse Countess*, *Les possédées du diable*, *Die Marquise von Sade*, *Caged Women*, *Jack the Ripper* (1976), *Justine de*

Sade, *Revenge in the House of Usher*, *La tumba de los muertos vivientes*, *Faceless*, *Tender Flesh*, *Lust for Frankenstein*, *Vampire Blues*, *Vampire Junction*, *Incubus*, *Killer Barbys vs. Dracula*, *Snakewoman* and numerous porno titles.

The last known leading lady of the silent film era, Romanian-born **Pola Illéry** (Paula Iliescu), died in Scranton, Pennsylvania, the same day, aged 103. Her final screen appearance was in the 1938 French film, *Le tombeau hindou* (aka *Le tigre du Bengale*), based on the novel by Thea von Harbou. She fled to the United States at the outbreak of World War II and became an American citizen in 1946.

1940s Hollywood actress and former fashion model **Elyse Knox** (Elyse Lillian Konbrath), who starred opposite Lon Chaney, Jr in Universal's *The Mummy's Tomb* (1942), also died on February 15, aged 94. In her 12-year career she also appeared in *Arabian Nights* (uncredited) and the serial *Don Winslow of the Coast Guard*. She was the mother of actor Mark Harmon.

British character actor **Peter Halliday** died on February 18, aged 87. His credits include *The Anatomist*, Hammer's *Captain Clegg* (aka *Night Creatures*, with Peter Cushing), *Virgin Witch* and *Madhouse* (with Vincent Price). On TV he starred as John Fleming in *A for Andromeda* and *The Andromeda Breakthough*, and appeared in episodes of *The Avengers*, *Out of the Unknown*, *UFO*, *Doomwatch*, *Beasts*, *The Tripods* and several series of *Doctor Who*.

Swedish actor, director and author **Erland Josephson**, best known for his roles in Ingmar Bergman's films and TV productions, died of complications from Parkinson's disease on February 25, aged 88. His many credits include *The Magician* (aka *The Face*), *Hour of the Wolf*, *The Magic Flute*, *The House of the Yellow Carpet*, *The Sacrifice*, *Control* and *Prospero's Books*.

British-born **Davy Jones** (David Thomas Jones), lead singer with the 1960s pop group The Monkees, died following a heart attack in Florida on February 29, aged 66. The Monkees had their own TV show on NBC from 1966–68 and created their own spin-off movie, *Head* (1968).

Character actor and playwright **Hal Borske** (aka Haal Borske) died of complications from a stroke in February. He was frequently a member of Andy Milligan's repertory company in such films as *The Naked Witch* (1967), *The Ghastly Ones*, *Torture Dungeon* and *Monstrosity* (as Frankie the golem). He also made an uncredited appearance in the gay comedy *Dragula* (1973).

Welsh-born British character actor **Philip Madoc** (Phillip Jones) died of cancer on March 5, aged 77. Usually cast as villains, he appeared in *Daleks' Invasion Earth: 2150AD* (with Peter Cushing), Berserk (with Michael Gough), *Doppelgänger* (aka *Journey to the Far Side of the Sun*) and Hammer's *Dr Jekyll and Sister Hyde*, along with episodes of *Out of This World* (hosted by Boris Karloff), *The Monsters* (1962), *The Avengers*, *The Champions*, *Randall and Hopkirk (Deceased)*, *UFO*, *The Rivals of Sherlock Holmes*, *Space: 1999*, *Survivors* (1976), *Doctor Who*, *A Very British Coup* and *Spine Chillers*.

Rudy Ricci (Rudolph J. Ricci), a friend of George R. Romero who helped create *Night of the Living Dead* (1968), died of complications from a fall on March 8. He was 72. Ricci also turned up as a zombie in that film and as a motorcycle raider in the sequel, *Dawn of the Dead* (1978). He is also credited with the story for *The Return of the Living Dead* (1985).

British actress **Faith Brook,** the daughter of veteran actor Clive Brook, died on March 11, aged 90. Her credits include *Jungle Book* (1942), *The Curse of King Tut's Tomb*, and episodes of TV's *Invisible Man* (1959), *One Step Beyond*, *The Adventures of Don Quick*, *Thriller* (1974) and *Spooky*.

French actor **Michel** [René Jacques] **Duchaussoy,** who appeared in *Man with the Transplanted Brain* (1971), based on the novel by Alain Franck and Victor Vicas, died of a heart attack on March 13, aged 73. Duchaussoy also appeared in the 2006 comedy *Poltergay* and an episode of *The Young Indiana Jones Chronicles*, and he was the voice of Archibald in the *Arthur* animated movies. He was awarded the Légion d'Honneur in 2011.

French actress, film editor, scriptwriter and script supervisor **Natalie Perrey** died in Paris on March 25, aged 83. Best known for her collaborations with director Jean Rollin, her credits with him include *La vampire nue*, *Le frisson des vampires*, *Suce moi vampire*, *Vierges et vampires*, *La rose de fer*, *Lèvres de sang*, *Les deux orphelines vampires*, *La finacée de Dracula* and *La nuit des horloges*.

American leading man **Warren** [Albert] **Stevens** died of chronic lung disease on March 27, aged 92. Best remembered for his role as the ill-fated doctor in *Forbidden Planet* (1956), he was also in *Gorilla at Large*, *Cyborg 2087* (aka *Man from Tomorrow*) and *The Return of Captain Nemo*, along with episodes of TV's *Inner Sanctum*, *Science Fiction Theatre*, *Alfred Hitchcock Presents*, *One Step Beyond*, *Men Into Space*, *The Twilight Zone* (1962 and 1986), *The Outer Limits*, *The Man from U.N.C.L.E.*, *Voyage to the Bottom of the Sea*, *The Time Tunnel*, *Tarzan*, *Star Trek*, *Land of the Giants* and *Wonder Woman*.

American character actor [Francis] **Luke Askew**, best known for his supporting roles in *Cool Hand Luke* and *Easy Rider*, died following a long illness on March 29, aged 80. He also appeared in the movies *The Beast Within*, *The Warrior and the Sorceress* and *Dune Warriors*. Askew's TV credits include episodes of *The Six Million Dollar Man*, *Fantasy Island*, *The Greatest American Hero*, *The Powers of Matthew Star*, *Knight Rider*, *Automan* and *The 4400*.

Prolific Japanese voice actor **Takeshi Aono** died on April 9, aged 75. His numerous *anime* credits include the *Space Crusier Yamato*, *Fist of the North Star* and *Dragon Ball Z* series.

Canadian-born actor and playwright **Ronan O'Casey** died in Los Angeles on April 12, aged 89. In England from the late 1940s until the early 1980s, he appeared in the 1956 version of *1984* (as Rutherford), *Satellite in the Sky* and the BBC TV series *The Trollenberg Terror* (1956–57). As a literary executive at Commonwealth United, he also associate-produced *The Magic Christian* (1969).

Canadian actor **Jonathan Frid** (John Herbert Frid), who portrayed vampire Barnabas Collins in nearly 600 episodes on the daytime soap opera *Dark Shadows* (1967–71), along with the spin-off movie *House of Dark Shadows* (1970), died on April 13, aged 87. He also appeared in *The Devil's Daughter* and *Seizure*, and had a blink-and-you'd-miss-him cameo in Tim Burton's 2012 remake of *Dark Shadows*. Frid later starred in a 1980s Broadway revival and national tour of *Arsenic and Old Lace*, and he was featured in the 2010 *Dark Shadows* audio drama, *The Night Whispers*.

The same day saw the death of 81-year-old singer, songwriter and actress **Marilynn** (Marilyn) **Lovell** after a long battle with multiple sclerosis. Although she appeared in episodes of TV's *The Munsters* and *Captain Nice*, she is best remembered for writing and performing songs in the early 1970s horror films *The Return of Count Yorga*, *Deathmaster*, *Terror House* and *Scream Blacula Scream*.

Quirky American character actor **William Finley** (William Franklin Finley III), who starred as doomed songwriter Winslow Leach in Brian De Palma's horror rock opera *Phantom of the Paradise* (1974), died of complications following surgery on April 14, aged 71. He also appeared in De Palma's *Sisters* (aka *Blood Sisters*), *The Fury* and *The Black Dahlia*, Tobe Hooper's *Eaten Alive* (aka *Death Trap*), *The Funhouse* and *Night Terrors*, along with *Silent Rage*. On TV he appeared in episodes of *Tales from the Crypt*, *Sabrina the Teenage Witch* (as an apparently uncredited werewolf) and *Masters of Horror*.

American character actor **Ron Palillo** (Ronald Gabriel Paolillo), who played Arnold Horshak on the 1970s sitcom *Welcome Back Kotter*, died of a heart attack the same day, aged 63. He appeared in the movies *The Invisible Woman* (1983), *Jason Lives: Friday the 13th Part VI*, *Hellgate* and *Trees 2: The Root of All Evil*.

Twenty-six-year-old Bollywood actress **Meenakshi Thapar**, who made her debut in the 2011 Indian horror film *404*, died on April 19 when she was allegedly kidnapped and later strangled and decapitated by two aspiring actors attempting to extort a 1,500,000-rupee ransom from her family.

British-born Hollywood actress **Patricia** [Paz Maria] **Medina** died on April 28 in Los Angeles, aged 92. She appeared in *Don't Take it to Heart*, *Moss Rose* (with Vincent Price and George Zucco), *Francis*, *The Magic Carpet*, *Aladdin and His Lamp*, *Siren of Bagdad*, *Phantom of the Rue Morgue*, *Mr. Arkadin* (aka *Confidential Report*), *The Beast of Hollow Mountain*, *Snow White and the Three Stooges* and *Latitude Zero*. Medina also appeared on TV in a couple of episodes of *Thriller* (hosted by Boris Karloff), *The Alfred Hitchcock Hour* and *The Man from U.N.C.L.E.* (with Price again), before she retired from acting in 1978. She was married to actors Richard Greene and Joseph Cotton.

Busy American character actor **George Murdock** (George R. Sawaya, Jr), who was often cast as authority figures in movies and on TV, died of cancer on April 30, aged 81. A semi-regular on the original *Battlestar Galactica* series (1978–79) as Dr Salik, he appeared in Disney's *Blackbeard's Ghost*, the *Night Gallery* pilot, *A Howling in the Woods*, *Earthquake*, *The Sword and the Sorcerer*, *Star Trek V: The Final Frontier* (as God), *Timescape*, *The X Files* and *Looney Tunes: Back in Action*, along with episodes of such TV shows as *The Twilight Zone*, *The Wild Wild West*, *Tarzan* (1966–67), *Cimarron Strip* (Harlan Ellison's "Knife in the Darkness"), *The Sixth Sense*, *Search Control*, *The Six Million Dollar Man*, *The Invisible Man* (1975), *The Hardy Boys/Nancy Drew Mysteries* ("The Mystery of the Haunted House"), *Struck by Lightning*, *Knight Rider* (1983–84), *Nightmare Classics* ("The Strange Case of Dr. Jekyll and Mr. Hyde"), *Star Trek: The Next Generation*, *What a Dummy*, *The New Adventures of Superman*, *Team Knight Rider*, *Early Edition*, *The X Files*, *Smallville*, *Eli Stone* and *Torchwood: Miracle Day*.

American-born British actor and stage magician **John Forrest** (John Forsht, aka John Klox) died in France in April, aged 80. As a child actor, he appeared in the 1946 *Great*

Expectations (and later the 1967 TV series) and the body-swap comedy *Vice Versa* (1948).

British actress **Tracy Reed** (Claire Tracy Compton Pelissier) died of liver cancer in West Cork, Ireland, on May 2, aged 69. The step-daughter of director Sir Carol Reed and cousin of actor Oliver Reed, she appeared in *Dr. Strangelove or: How I Learned to Stop Worrying and Love the Bomb*, *Devils of Darkness* and *Casino Royale* (1967), as well as episodes of Hammer's *Journey to the Unknown* (Robert Bloch's "The Indian Spirit Guide"), *The Avengers*, *Out of the Unknown* (John Wyndham's "Random Quest") and *U.F.O.*, before retiring from the screen in 1975. Reed was considered as a replacement for Diana Rigg in *The Avengers*, before Linda Thorson got the role, and her first husband was actor Edward Fox.

British character actress, scriptwriter and poet **Charlotte Mitchell** (Edna Winifred Mitchell) died of pneumonia the same day, aged 85. She had been suffering from breast cancer and myeloma. Mitchell appeared in the movies *The Man in the White Suit*, *Village of the Damned* (1960), *Blood on Satan's Claw* and *Out of the Darkness* (1985), and was also in an episode of TV's *Shades of Darkness*.

American character actor **George Lindsey**, who portrayed Gomer Pyle on the CBS sitcom *The Andy Griffith Show* (1964–68) and various spin-offs, died after a lengthy illness on May 6, aged 83. His other credits include episodes of *The Twilight Zone*, *The Alfred Hitchcock Hour* (including Ray Bradbury's "The Jar"), *Voyage to the Bottom of the Sea* and *Fantasy Island*. For Disney he appeared in *Charley and the Angel*, *Treasure of Matecumbe* and an episode of TV's *Herbie the Love Bug*, and he voiced animated characters in *The AristoCats*, *Robin Hood* and *The Rescuers*. According to actor Leonard Nimoy, Lindsey was Gene Roddenberry's first choice to play Mr Spock on *Star Trek*.

Bee Gees singer and songwriter **Robin** [Hugh] **Gibb** died of cancer in London on May 20, aged 62. With his siblings he appeared in the misconceived movie *Sgt. Pepper's Lonely Hearts Club Band* (1978).

Emmy Award-winning American character actress **Kathryn Joosten**, a regular on *Desperate Housewives* and *The West Wing*, died of lung cancer on June 2, aged 72. Her other numerous TV credits include episodes of *3rd Rock from the Sun*, *Prey*, *Buffy the Vampire Slayer*, *The X Files*, *Charmed* and *Joan of Arcadia*. She was also in *Hellraiser: Inferno*, *Bedtime Stories* and *Mega Python vs. Gatoroid*.

British-born actor turned game-show host **Richard Dawson** (Colin Lionel Emm) died of complications from oesophageal cancer the same day, aged 79. Best known for his recurring role in *Hogan's Heroes* (1965–71) and as the host of *Family Feud* from 1976–85, he also appeared in *Munster Go Home!* and *The Running Man*, along with episodes of *The Outer Limits*, *The Alfred Hitchcock Hour*, *Mr. Terrific* and *Fantasy Island*. Dawson's first wife was actress Diana Dors.

British actress **Caroline** [Frances] **John**, who played Doctor Who's companion Dr Elizabeth Shaw opposite Jon Pertwee's Time Lord in 1970, died of cancer on June 5, aged 71. She recreated the role of Liz Shaw in *The Five Doctors* (1983) and a number of spin-off video and audio productions. John also appeared in the 1982 TV version of *The Hound of the Baskervilles* (starring Tom Baker as Holmes), *The Woman in Black* (1989), and episodes of *The Rivals of Sherlock Holmes*, *The Memoirs of Sherlock Holmes* and the mini-series *A Very British Coup*.

Veteran American character actor **Frank Cady** died on June 8, aged 96. A regular on the 1960s TV sitcoms *Green Acres*, *Petticoat Junction* and *The Beverly Hillbillies* as general-store owner Sam Drucker, he appeared in the movies *The Sky Dragon*, *The Great Rupert*, *The Next Voice You Hear . . .*, *When Worlds Collide*, *The Atomic City*, Alfred Hitchcock's *Rear Window*, *The Bad Seed* (1956), *7 Faces of Dr. Lao* and Disney's *The Gnome-Mobile* and *The Million Dollar Duck*, along with an episode of TV's *The Monster Squad*.

Canadian-born Hollywood leading lady [Therese] **Ann Rutherford** died of heart failure on June 11, aged 94. Best known for her role as Scarlett O'Hara's younger sister in *Gone with the Wind* and her recurring role as Mickey Rooney's girlfriend in the popular *Andy Hardy* movies, she also appeared in *A Christmas Carol* (1938, as the Ghost of Christmas Past), *The Ghost Comes Home*, *Whistling in the Dark*, *Whistling in Dixie*, *Whistling in Brooklyn* and *The Secret Life of Walter Mitty* (with Boris Karloff). Rutherford was married to *Batman* TV producer William Dozier and retired from acting in 1976.

Japanese singer **Emi Itô** (Hideyo Itô) who, with her twin sister Yumi, performed as part of the music duo The Peanuts, died on June 15, aged 71. The sisters appeared as the tiny Shobijin Fairies in Toho's *Mothra*, *Godzilla vs. the Thing* and *Ghidorah the Three-Headed Monster*.

Iconoclastic American actress and artist **Susan Tyrrell** (Susan Jillian Creamer, aka SuSu) died on June 16, aged 67. In April 2000 the Oscar-nominated actress lost both legs as the result of a rare blood disease. Her films include *Wizards* (1977), *Midnight Lace* (1981), *Night Warning*, *Forbidden Zone*, *What's Up Hideous Sun Demon*, *Fire and Ice*, *Angel* and *Avenging Angel*, *Flesh + Blood*, *The Offspring*, *Big Top Pee-Wee*, *Rockula*, *Digital Man*, *Powder* and the video compilation *The Boneyard Collection*. She also appeared in episodes of TV's *The Hitchhiker*, *Shades of LA* and *Tales from the Crypt*.

Veteran British stuntman **George Leech**, who worked on eleven James Bond films from *Dr. No* (1962) to *A View to a Kill* (1985), died on June 17, aged 90. His other credits include *Chitty Chitty Bang Bang*, *Superman* (1978) and *The Masks of Death* (starring Peter Cushing as Sherlock Holmes).

Welsh-born British comedy actor **Victor Spinetti** died of cancer on June 18, aged 82. Best remembered for appearing with The Beatles in *A Hard Day's Night*, *Help!* and *Magical Mystery Tour*, the Tony Award-winning actor's other screen credits include *Digby the Biggest Dog in the World*, *The Little Prince*, *The Lion, the Witch and the Wardrobe* (1979), *The Princess and the Goblin*, *The Adventures of Indiana Jones: Attack of the Hawkmen*, *The Adventures of Indiana*

Jones: Adventures in the Secret Service and *Wednesday*, a horror short written and produced by David McGillivray.

Former professional model and pin-up girl **Kay Christopher** died of complications from diabetes the same day, aged 86. After signing a contract with RKO Radio Pictures, she appeared as Tess Trueheart in *Dick Tracy's Dilemma* (1947) and made an uncredited appearance as a nurse in *Mighty Joe Young* (1949) before leaving the industry in 1954.

Memorable American character actor **Richard** [Hugh] **Lynch**, best known for his villainous portrayals, was found dead at his home on June 19, aged 72 or 76 (reports varied). Instantly recognisable from his blond hair and scarred features (he accidentally set himself on fire in 1967 after taking LSD), his numerous movie credits include *God Told Me To* (aka *Demon*), *Good Against Evil*, *Deathsport*, *Vampire*, *The Ninth Configuration*, *The Sword and the Sorcerer*, *Cut and Run*, *Invasion USA*, *The Barbarians* (aka *The Barbarian Brothers*), *Bad Dreams*, *Aftershock*, *Alligator II: The Mutation*, *Trancers II*, *Puppet Master III: Toulon's Revenge*, *Merlin* (1993), *Necronomicon*, *Scanner Cop*, *Cyborg 3: The Creation*, *Terminal Virus*, *Werewolf* (1996), *Curse of the Forty-Niner*, *Ancient Warriors*, *Corpses Are Forever*, *The Mummy's Kiss*, *Wedding Slashers*, *Mil Mascaras vs. The Aztec Mummy*, *Halloween* (2007), *Laid to Rest*, *Dark Fields* (aka *The Rain*), *Resurrection*, *Gun of the Black Sun* and *The Lords of Salem*. A regular on the short-lived TV series *The Phoenix* (1981-82), Lynch also appeared in episodes of *The Bionic Woman*, *Battlestar Galactica* (1978), *Buck Rogers in the 25th Century*, *Galactica 1980*, *Manimal*, *Blue Thunder*, *Automan*, *The Last Precinct* ("Never Cross a Vampire"), *Werewolf*, *Super Force*, *Star Trek: The Next Generation*, *Highlander* and *Charmed*.

Dependable British actor **Anthony Bate** died the same day, aged 84. He appeared in episodes of TV's *Out of This World*, *The Avengers*, *The Saint* ("The House on Dragon's Rock"), *The Champions*, *Shadows of Fear*, *Out of the Unknown*, *The Guardians* and Nigel Kneale's *Beasts*, along with the 1974 films *Ghost Story*.

British character actor **James** [David] **Grout**, often typecast as policemen and best known for his recurring role as Chief Superintendent Strange in TV's *Inspector Morse* (1987–2000), died on June 24, aged 84. He also appeared in *The Abominable Dr. Phibes* (with Vincent Price), *The Ruling Class*, and episodes of *The Guardians*, *Thriller* (1973), *Orson Welles' Great Mysteries*, *BBC2 Play of the Week* ("Fairies", as Sir Arthur Conan Doyle) and *The Box of Delights*.

Former professional American football player **Ben Davidson** (Benjamin Earl Davidson), who played Rexor in *Conan the Barbarian* (1982), died on July 2, aged 72. He was also in the pilot for *Lucan* and an episode of *Fantasy Island*.

Beloved American actor **Andy** [Samuel] **Griffith**, who starred in the TV series *The Andy Griffith Show* (1960–68) and its various spin-offs, *Matlock* (1991–95) and *Salvage 1* (1979), died of a heart attack on July 3, aged 86. He also appeared in such movies as *Angel in My Pocket*, *The Demon Murder Case* and *Spy Hard*, along with episodes of *The Bionic Woman* and *Fantasy Island*.

Much-loved British comedy actor, director and scriptwriter **Eric Sykes** CBE died after a short illness on July 4, aged 89. He starred in his own eponymous TV series from 1960–65 and 1972–79, and his other credits include *Theatre of Blood* (with Vincent Price), *The Others* and *Harry Potter and the Goblet of Fire*, along with episodes of *The Return of Sherlock Holmes* ("The Six Napoleons") and *Gormenghast* (as Mollocks).

Academy Award-winning actor **Ernest Borgnine** (Ermes Effron Borgnine) died of renal failure on July 8, aged 95. The burly star's movie credits include *The Vikings*, *Willard* (1971), *The Poseidon Adventure* (1972), *The Neptune Factor*, *The Devil's Rain*, *The Ghost of Flight 401*, Disney's *The Black Hole*, *Escape from New York*, *Deadly Blessing*, *Alice in Wonderland* (1985), *L'isola del tesoro*, *Merlin's Shop of Mystical Wonders*, *Gattaca* and *Small Soldiers*. He was also a regular on the short-lived TV series *Future Cop*

(1976–77), voiced Mermaidman in *SpongeBob SquarePants* (1999–2011), and appeared in episodes of *Captain Video and His Video Rangers*, *Highway to Heaven*, *Early Edition* and *Touched by an Angel*. Married five times, Borgnine's wives included actresses Katy Jurado and, very briefly (32 days), Ethel Merman.

American stuntman and stunt co-ordinator **Conrade Gamble II** died on July 12, aged 45. The Gulf War veteran was a stunt double for actor Ving Rhames and he worked on *Spider-Man 2*, *The Skeleton Key*, *Evan Almighty*, *G.I. Joe The Rise of Cobra*, *The Green Hornet* and episodes of the TV series *Alias*.

American voice actress **Ginny Tyler** (Merrie Virginia Erlandson) died on July 13, aged 86. Her credits include Disney's *Son of Flubber*, *The Sword in the Stone*, *Mary Poppins* and *Winnie the Pooh and the Honey Tree*, along with *Doctor Dolittle* and episodes of TV's *The New Casper Cartoon Show* (as the voice of Casper the ghost), *Mister Ed*, *Space Ghost*, *The Adventures of Gulliver* and *The Fantastic Four* (as Sue Richards/Invisible Girl). Tyler also narrated a number of Disney record albums, including *Bambi* and *Babes in Toyland*.

The body of **Sage** [Moonblood] **Stallone**, the son of actor Sylvester Stallone, was found in his Hollywood Hills home the same day. He was aged 36 and died of heart disease. Sage Stallone was the co-founder/president of Grindhouse Releasing, dedicated to restoring obscure exploitation films, and he appeared in the movies *The Evil Inside Me*, *Reflections of Evil*, *Chaos* and *Moscow Zero*.

Oscar-winning Hollywood and Broadway actress **Celeste Holm** died on July 15, aged 95. She had been hospitalised with dehydration following a fire in Robert De Niro's apartment in the same Manhattan building, but had requested to be allowed home two days before her death. Although best known for such movies as *The Snake Pit*, *All About Eve* and *High Society*, she also appeared in *Jack and the Beanstalk* (1956), *Cinderella* (1965), *Death Cruise*, *Midnight Lace* (1981) and *Murder by the Book*, along with episodes of

TV's *Wonder Woman*, *Lucan*, *Fantasy Island*, *Matt Houston* and *Touched by an Angel*. In her later years a bitter feud with her two sons wiped out Holm's $2 million fortune and left her dependent on social security.

Welsh-born actress **Angharad** [Mary] **Rees** CBE, who played Jack the Ripper's murderous daughter in Hammer's *Hands of the Ripper* (1971), died after a long battle with pancreatic cancer on July 21, aged 63. Her other film credits include *Jane Eyre* (1970), *Baffled!*, *The Curse of King Tut's Tomb* and *The Wolves of Kromer*, and she appeared in episodes of TV's *The Avengers*, *Thriller* (1974), *Bedtime Stories* and *Robin of Sherwood*. After she retired from acting, she designed jewellery for a shop she owned in London. From 1973–94 Rees was married to actor Christopher Cazenove.

British actor **Simon Ward**, the father of actress Sophie Ward, died after a long illness on July 23, aged 70. He played (uncredited) one of the schoolboy's in Lindsay Anderson's *If . . .* (1968) before going on to appear in Hammer's *Frankenstein Must Be Destroyed* (with Peter Cushing), *Quest for Love* (based on a story by John Wyndham), *Dracula* (1974, as Arthur), *Holocaust 2000*, *Dominique* (aka *Dominique is Dead*, based on a *Weird Tales* story by Harold Lawlor), *The Monster Club* (based on the book by R. Chetwynd-Hayes), *Supergirl* (as Zor-El) and *Wuthering Heights* (1992). Ward also appeared in an episode of TV's *Orson Welles' Great Mysteries* (Arthur Conan Doyle's "The Leather Funnel" with Christopher Lee) and the 1989 mini-series *Around the World in 80 Days*.

American comedy actor and singer **Sherman** [Alexander] **Hemsley**, who starred in TV's *All in the Family* spin-off *The Jeffersons* (1975–85), died of complications from lung cancer on July 24, aged 74. He appeared in the movies *Love at First Bite*, *Alice in Wonderland* (1985), *Ghost Fever* and *Casper: A Spirited Beginning*, along with episodes of *The Incredible Hulk*, *Fantasy Island*, *The Twilight Zone* (1985), *What a Dummy*, *The New Adventures of Superman* (as The Toyman), *The Secret World of Alex Mack* and the 2004 pilot of *Mr. Ed* (as the voice of the titular talking horse). Hemsley was also the voice of B. P. Richfield on *Dinosuars* (1991–94).

American actor **Chad Everett** (Raymon Lee Cramton) died the same day of lung cancer, aged 76. His many TV credits include episodes of *The Man from U.N.C.L.E.*, Hammer's *Journey to the Unknown*, *The Highwayman*, *Shades of LA*, *Touched by an Angel* and *Supernatural*. He also appeared in the movies *The Intruder Within*, *Star Command*, *When Time Expires*, *Psycho* (1998) and *Mulholland Dr*.

British actress **Mary Tamm**, who portrayed the first incarnation of Tom Baker's companion Romana (1978–79) on BBC TV's *Doctor Who*, died after a long battle with cancer on July 26. She was 62. Tamm was also in the film *Tales That Witness Madness* and episodes of *Jane Eyre* (1983), *Doghouse, Worlds Beyond*, *The New Adventures of Robin Hood* ("Witches of the Abbey"), *Crime Traveller*, *Jonathan Creek* ("Satan's Chimney") and *Twisted Tales*. The actress's husband, Marcus Ringrose, died of a suspected heart attack hours after giving a eulogy at her funeral on August 7.

American character actress **Lupe Ontiveros** (Guadalupe Moreno) died the same day of liver cancer, aged 69. Often cast as Latino housekeepers or maids, she appeared in the movies *The Goonies*, *Dolly Dearest*, *Universal Soldier*, *Candyman: Day of the Dead*, *Mr. St. Nick* and *Dark Mirror*, along with episodes of TV's *Tales from the Crypt* and *Reaper*.

Gruff American character actor **R.** (Robert) **G.** (Golden) **Armstrong** [Jr.] died on July 27, aged 95. Often portraying sheriffs and generals, his numerous movies include *The Legend of Hillbilly John* (based on the stories of Manly Wade Wellman), *Race with the Devil*, *The Car*, *The Pack*, *Heaven Can Wait* (1978), *Devil Dog: Hound of Hell*, *The Time Machine* (1978), *The Legend of the Golden Gun*, *Evilspeak*, *The Beast Within*, *Children of the Corn* (1984), *Predator*, *Dick Tracy* (as Pruneface), *Warlock: The Armageddon*, *Purgatory* and *Keeper of Souls* (aka *The Waking*).

On TV Armstrong appeared in the recurring roles of the ghostly Lewis Vendredi on *Friday the 13th: The Series* (1987–89) and The Old Man on *Millennium* (1997–98), along with episodes of *Alfred Hitchcock Presents*, *Great Ghost Tales* ("The Monkey's Paw"), *The Twilight Zone*, *The Alfred Hitchcock Hour*, *The Time Tunnel*, *The Invaders*, *The Sixth Sense*, *Tales of the Unexpected* (aka *A Twist in the Tale*), *Salvage 1*, *Fantasy Island*, *Darkroom*, *Beauty and the Beast*, *Silk Stalkings* and *Quantum Leap*.

Hollywood actor and singer **Tony Martin** (Alvin Morris), who co-starred in *Ali Baba Goes to Town* and the Bob Hope Jack the Ripper comedy *Here Come the Girls* (1953), died the same day, aged 98. His biggest hit was in 1950 with "There's No Tomorrow", later adapted for Elvis Presley as "It's Now or Never". After divorcing actress Alice Faye in 1941, Martin was married to Cyd Charisse for 60 years until her death in 2008.

British comedy actor **Geoffrey Hughes**, who was the voice of Paul in *Yellow Submarine* (1968), died of prostate cancer on July 27, aged 68. He also appeared in episodes of *Randall and Hopkirk (Deceased)*, *Shadows of Fear*, *Doctor Who* ("The Trial of a Time Lord") and *Polterguests*, along with small roles in the films *Blood of Satan's Claw* and *Revenge* (aka *Terror from Under the House*).

American character actor **Norman Alden** (Norman Adelberg) also died on July 27, aged 87. Best known as Lou the café owner in *Back to the Future* and Bill the colour-blind cameraman in *Ed Wood*, he also appeared in *The Nutty Professor*, *Ben*, *Everything You Wanted to Know About Sex* *But Were Afraid to Ask* and *They Live*, along with episodes of TV's *My Favorite Martian*, *Batman*, *Planet of the Apes*, *Electra Woman and Dyna Girl* and *Fantasy Island*. Alden contributed voice work to Disney's *The Sword in the Stone*, *Transformers: The Movie* and the *Super Friends* series (as Aquaman).

American character actor **John Finnegan** (aka J. P. Finnegan), who was a semi-regular on the TV series *Columbo*, died of pneumonia on July 29, aged 85. His movies include *The Natural*, *School Spirit*, *Spellbinder*, *The Hunchback Hairball of L.A.*, *Last Action Hero* and *Mars Attacks!*, along with episodes of *McCloud* ("McCloud Meets Dracula"), *Lucan*, *The Amazing Spider-Man*, *Galactica 1980* and *Highway to Heaven*. Finnegan also voiced the villainous Warren T. Rat in the animated *An American Tail*.

New Zealand-born actor and Oscar-nominated screenwriter **Jonathan Hardy** (aka Jonathon Hardy), who was the voice of galactic ruler Dominar Rygel XVI in TV's *Farscape* (1999–2004), died in Australia the same day. He was 71. The bushy-browed actor also appeared in *Mad Max*, *The Scarecrow* (with John Carradine), *Death Warmed Up* and *Bloodmoon*, along with an episode of *Twisted Tales* (aka *Twisted*).

Roy Steffens (Roy Steffensen), who scripted and starred in the live 1955–56 TV show *Captain Z-Ro*, died on August 2, aged 98. He later became a TV art director on such shows as *The Bionic Woman* and *The Hardy Boys/Nancy Drew Mysteries*.

American actor and drama teacher **Al**(bert) [Cornelius] **Freeman, Jr.** died on August 9, aged 78. He appeared in the movies *Finian's Rainbow* and *Castle Keep*.

American actress **Phyllis** [Schuyler] **Thaxter** (Phyllis St. Felix Thaxter), who portrayed Ma Kent in *Superman* (1978), died of complications from Alzheimer's disease on August 14, aged 90. Her other credits include Arch Oboler's *Bewitched* (1945) and episodes of TV's *Suspicion*, *Alfred Hitchcock Presents*, *Thriller* ("The Last of the Sommervilles"), *The Twilight Zone*, *The Alfred Hitchcock Hour* and *The Invaders*.

American character actor **Biff Elliot** (Leon Shalek), the first person to portray PI Mike Hammer on screen, died on August 15, aged 89. He appeared in such movies as *Brainstorm*, *Blood Bath* (aka *Track of the Vampire*), *The Navy vs. the Night Monsters*, *Destination Inner Space* and *The Dark*, along with episodes of TV's *Lights Out*, *Science Fiction Theatre*, *Alfred Hitchcock Presents*, *Voyage to the*

Bottom of the Sea, *Star Trek*, *Planet of the Apes* and *The Next Step Beyond*.

Dependable American actor **William Windom** died of congestive heart failure on August 16, aged 88. Best known for playing Dr Seth Hazlitt on CBS-TV's *Murder She Wrote* (1985–96), the actor won an Emmy in 1970 for his performance in the series *My World and Welcome to It*, based on James Thurber's essays and cartoons. He also appeared in the movies *Brewster McCloud*, *Escape*, *The Mephisto Waltz*, *Escape from the Planet of the Apes* (as The President), *Taste of Evil*, Disney's *Now You See Him Now You Don't*, *The Man*, *Space Rage*, *Attack of the 50 Ft. Woman* (1993), *Miracle on 34th Street* (1994), *Children of the Corn: The Gathering*, *Raising Dead* and *Dismembered*. Windom was also a prolific guest star on TV shows, appearing in episodes of *Lights Out*, *The Twilight Zone*, *Thriller* (1962), *The Wild Wild West*, *Star Trek* ("The Doomsday Machine"), *The Invaders*, *Rod Serling's Night Gallery* ("They're Tearing Down Tim Riley's Bar"), *Ghost Story*, *Love American Style* ("Love and the Ghost"), *The Bionic Woman* ("Black Magic", with Vincent Price), *The Incredible Hulk*, *Fantasy Island*, *The Greatest American Hero*, *Automan*, *Highway to Heaven* and *Knight Rider*.

Ninety-five-year-old American comedienne **Phyllis Diller** (Phyllis Ada Driver), known for her outrageous appearance and distinctive laugh, died on August 20. Often credited as the first stand-up female comedian, she appeared in *Doctor Hackenstein*, *The Boneyard* and episodes of TV's *Get Smart*, *Night Gallery* ("Pamela's Voice") and *Tales from the Darkside*, as well as making a cameo appearance in the 1960s *Batman* series. Diller also contributed voice work to *Mad Monster Party?* (starring Boris Karloff), *Alice Through the Looking Glass* (1987), *The Nutcracker Prince*, *A Bug's Life*, *The Nuttiest Nutcracker* and *Casper's Scare School*.

American actor **Jeffrey Stone** (John Forrest Fontaine) died in Malaysia on August 22, aged 85. After being the model for Prince Charming in Walt Disney's *Cinderella* (1950), his credits include *The Thing That Couldn't Die* and an episode of TV's *The Outer Limits*. He is also credited with coming up with the original idea for the 1964 movie *Unearthly Stranger*, and in 1966 he wrote and directed *Strange Portrait* starring Jeffrey Hunter. His second wife was actress Corinne Calvert.

Dependable American character actor **Steve Franken** (Stephen Robert Franken) died of cancer on August 23, aged 80. His numerous screen credits include *The Time Travelers* (1964), *Westworld*, *The Reincarnation of Peter Proud*, *It Happened at Lakewood Manor* (aka *Ants*), *Terror Out of the Sky*, *The Fiendish Plot of Dr. Fu Manchu*, *The Ghosts of Buxley Hall*, *Transylvania Twist*, *Breakfast of Aliens*, *Munchie Strikes Back* and *The Omega Code*, along with episodes of *One Step Beyond*, *My Favorite Martian*, *Bewitched*, *The Wild Wild West*, *Batman*, *Night Gallery*, *Kolchak: The Night Stalker*, *Man from Atlantis*, *Supertrain*, *Fantasy Island*, *Freddy's Nightmares*, *Harry and the Hendersons* and *Threshold*.

His number was finally up: American puppeteer, actor and voice artist **Jerry Nelson**, who played the instructional Count von Count in TV's *Sesame Street*, died the same day. He was 78. Nelson also portrayed such characters as Floyd Pepper, Robin the Frog, Crazy Harry, Dr Julius Strangepork and Marjorie the Trash Heap in such other Jim Henson shows as *The Muppet Show* and *Fraggle Rock*, and his movie credits include *The Dark Crystal*, *RoboCop 2* and *Muppets from Space*.

The first man to set foot on the Moon (July 20, 1969), **Neil** [Alden] **Armstrong**, who uttered the immortal phrase "That's one small step for man, one giant leap for mankind", died on August 25, aged 82. The former US astronaut underwent heart-bypass surgery earlier in the month to relieve blocked coronary arteries.

Busy American actor **Michael Clarke Duncan** died on September 3 of complications from a heart attack he suffered in July. He was 54. Best known for his roles in such movies as *Armageddon*, *The Green Mile*, *Cats & Dogs*, *Planet of the Apes* (2001), *The Scorpion King*, *Daredevil*, *George and* *the Dragon*, *Sin City*, *The Island*, *The Last Mimzy*, *Slipstream* (2007), *Cats & Dogs: The Revenge of Kitty Galore*, *The Sibling* and *Green Lantern*, he also appeared in episodes of TV's *Weird Science* and *Chuck*, and voiced numerous animated cartoons and games.

Dependable American actor and nightclub singer **Lance LeGault** (William Lance Legault), who portrayed Alamo Joe Rogan on the 1987–88 series *Werewolf*, died of heart failure on September 10, aged 77. He began his acting career as a stunt double for Elvis Presley in four films in the early 1960s, and his other credits include *Coma* (1978), *Captain America* (1979), *Nightmare Beach*, *The Silencers* (1996), *Dark Breed*, *Mortal Kombat: Annihilation* and *Scorpio One*, along with episodes of such TV shows as *Land of the Giants*, *Logan's Run*, *Wonder Woman*, *The Incredible Hulk*, *Battlestar Galactica* (1978–79), *Buck Rogers in the 25th Century*, *Voyagers!*, *Knight Rider*, *Automan*, *Quantum Leap* and *Star Trek: The Next Generation*.

Although best known for playing Agatha Christie's Hercule Poirot on BBC radio, 89-year-old British actor [Albert] **John Moffatt**, who died the same day, appeared in episodes of TV's *The Indian Tales of Rudyard Kipling* and *Mystery and Imagination*, along with the 1982 film *Britannia Hospital*.

American actor and stuntman **Stephen Dunham** [Bowers] died on September 14, his 48th birthday, after suffering a heart attack several days earlier. He appeared in *The Mummy* (1999), *Get Smart* (2008) and *Paranormal Activity 4* (with his wife Alexondra Lee), along with two episodes of the TV series *The Chronicle*.

American character actor **John Ingle**, best known for his recurring role as Edward Quartermaine in the soap opera *General Hospital* for almost two decades, died on September 16, aged 84. He also appeared in *Amazon Women on the Moon*, *Heathers*, *RoboCop 2*, *Repossessed*, *Stepfather III*, *Death Becomes Her* and *Skeeter*, along with episodes of TV's *Highway to Heaven* and *ALF*. Ingle also narrated and voiced "Cera's Father" in *The Land Before Time* animated movies.

Twenty-eight-year-old American actor **Johnny** [Kendrick] **Lewis** died on September 26 after falling from the roof of a Los Feliz building where he had been renting a room. He was suspected of killing his 81-year-old landlady and her cat before accidentally plunging to his death as he attempted to flee the scene. The troubled actor, who used to date singer Katy Perry, was later cremated and buried at sea. Best known for a recurring role in TV's *Sons of Anarchy*, he also appeared in *AVPR: Aliens vs Predator: Requiem* and a 2005 episode of *Smallville*.

Austrian-Hungarian born character actor **Herbert Lom** (Herbert Charles Angelo Kuchacevich ze Schluderpacheru) died in his sleep in London on September 27, aged 95. Usually cast as a villain, but best remembered for his role as the increasingly insane Chief Inspector Charles Dreyfus in the series of *Pink Panther* comedy films, he also appeared in *The Ladykillers* (1955), *Mysterious Island* (1961, as Captain Nemo), Hammer's *The Phantom of the Opera* (in the title role), *Doppelgänger* (aka *Journey to the Far Side of the Sun*), *Mark of the Devil*, *Count Dracula* (1970, as Prof. Van Helsing opposite Christopher Lee's vampire), *Dorian Gray* (1970), *Murders in the Rue Morgue* (1971), Amicus' *Asylum* and *—And Now the Screaming Starts!*, *Dark Places*, *And Then There Were None* (1974), *The Dead Zone*, *King Solomon's Mines* (1985), *Whoops Apocalypse*, *Ten Little Indians* (1989), *Masque of the Red Death* (1989) and *The Devil's Daughter*. On TV, Lom appeared in a two-part episode of *The Man from U.N.C.L.E.* that was re-edited into the 1967 feature film *The Karate Killers*.

American actor [Robert] **Michael O'Hare**, best known for playing Cmdr Jeffrey Sinclair in TV's *Babylon 5* (1994–96) and the spin-off movie *Babylon 5: The Gathering*, died on September 28, aged 60. He had suffered a heart attack three days earlier that had put him into a coma. O'Hare also appeared in *C.H.U.D.*, *The Trial of the Incredible Hulk*, *The Ambulance* and an episode of *Tales from the Darkside*.

Busy British-born Canadian character actor **Bernard** "Bunny" **Behrens** died the same day, aged 85. His film credits include *The Changeling*, *Resurrection*, *Galaxy of Terror*, *Firefox*, *What's Up Hideous Sun Demon*, *The Man with Two Brains*, *Haunted by Her Past*, *Ghost Mum* and *The Possession of Michael D.* (aka *Legacy of Evil*). On TV Behrens played regular Gustav Helsing in the 1990–91 show *Dracula: The Series*, and he also appeared in episodes of *The Bionic Woman*, *The Greatest American Hero*, *Highway to Heaven*, *The Twilight Zone* (1985), *Friday the 13th: The Series* (aka *Friday's Curse*), the 1980s revival of *Alfred Hitchcock Presents*, *War of the Worlds*, *Forever Knight* and *Kung Fu: The Legend Continues*. He was also the voice of Obi-Wan Kenobi in the National Public Radio dramatisations of *Star Wars* (1981), *The Empire Strikes Back* (1983) and *Return of the Jedi* (1996).

Austrian-born Hollywood actor and fashion photographer **Turhan Bey** (Turhan Gilbert Selahattin Sahultavy) died of Parkinson's disease in Vienna on September 30, aged 90. During the 1940s – with many of the studios' American stars off fighting in World War II – he became an exotic leading man for Universal in such serials and films as *Junior G-Men of the Air*, *Drums of the Congo*, *The Mummy's Tomb*, *Arabian Nights*, *Crazy House*, *The Mad Ghoul*, *Ali Baba and the Forty Thieves*, *The Climax* and *Night in Paradise*. Bey's other films include *Shadows on the Stairs*, *Footsteps in the Dark*, *The Gay Falcon*, *The Falcon Takes Over* and *The Amazing Mr. X* (aka *The Spiritualist*). After retiring from the screen in 1953, he returned 40 years later to appear in *Possessed by the Night*, *The Skateboard Kid II* and *Virtual Combat* (aka *Grid Runners*), along with episodes of TV's *SeaQuest DSV*, *VR.5*, *The Visitor* and *Babylon 5* (for which he received an Emmy nomination).

Classical British actress **Daphne** [Helen] **Slater** died in Switzerland on October 4, aged 84. On TV she appeared in a now apparently lost 1959 BBC adaptation of John L. Balderston's time-travel play *Berkley Square*, along with episodes of *Out of the Unknown* and *Shadows*. Slater also starred opposite Peter Cushing in the first BBC version of

Pride and Prejudice in 1952, and with Stanley Baker in a 1956 version of *Jane Eyre*.

Former NFL football player and pro wrestler turned actor **Alex** [George] **Karras** died of kidney failure and complications from dementia caused by repeated head injuries on October 10. He was 77. Karras played "The Hooded Fang" in the 1978 children's film *Jacob Two-Two Meets the Hooded Fang*, and he was also in *Blazing Saddles* (as Mongo), *When Time Ran Out* and an episode of *Faerie Tale Theatre* ("Goldilocks and the Three Bears"). He was married to Canadian actress Susan Clark.

Dependable American leading man **Gary** [Ennis] **Collins** died on October 13, aged 74. Following a small, uncredited role in *King Kong vs. Godzilla* (1962), he appeared in the movies *Killer Fish*, *Hangar 18* and *Watchers Reborn*. On TV he starred as Dr Michael Rhodes on the short-lived series *The Sixth Sense* (1972), and guest-starred in episodes of *The Six Million Dollar Man*, *The Bionic Woman*, the 1970s *Thriller*, *The Fantastic Journey*, *A Twist in the Tale*, *The Love Boat* ("Ship of Ghouls" with Vincent Price) and *Fantasy Island*. Collins was separated from his second wife, former Miss America Mary Ann Mobley.

British comedy actor and author **John Clive** (Clive John Frederick Hambley), who was the voice of John in *Yellow Submarine*, died on October 14, aged 79. His credits include *A Clockwork Orange*, *Straight on Till Morning*, *Go For a Take*, *Queen Kong*, *The Pink Panther Strikes Again*, *A Dream of Alice* and a number of *Carry On* and softcore sex films. He appeared in episodes of *The Gnomes of Dulwich*, *Roberts Robots* and *The Young Indiana Jones Chronicles*, and in 1989 he directed a TV version of Charlotte Perkins Gilman's *The Yellow Wallpaper*.

Dutch actress **Sylvia** [Maria] **Kristel**, who starred in the original *Emmanuelle* (1974) and a number of softcore sex sequels and spin-offs, died of cancer of the liver on October 18, aged 60. Her other movie credits include *The Nude Bomb* and *Dracula's Widow*, but drugs and alcoholism eventually blighted her career. Kristel reportedly had affairs with, amongst others, Ian McShane, Warren Beatty, Gérard Depardieu and Roger Vadim.

British character actor **Joe Melia** (Giovanni Philip William Melia) died on October 20, aged 77. He appeared in supporting roles in the films *Modesty Blaise* (1966), *Peter Pan* (1976) and *The Sign of Four* (1983), while his TV credits include episodes of *Sherlock Holmes* ("A Study in Scarlet" with Peter Cushing as Holmes), *The Hitch Hiker's Guide to the Galaxy* and *Ghostbusters of East Finchley*.

Swedish actress **Anita** [Barbro Kristina] **Björk**, once described as the "new Garbo", died on October 24, aged 89. She appeared in *Die Hexe*, *Hamlet* (as "Ofelia", 1955), *Phantom Carriage* (1958) and *Lady in White* (1962). Following the suicide of her first husband in 1954, Björk had a lengthy affair with Graham Greene after the writer became infatuated with her.

Perennial grandad **Clive** [Robert Benjamin] **Dunn** OBE died on November 6 in Portugal from complications following an operation earlier in the week. He was 92. Best known for his role as Corporal Jones in the BBC sitcom *Dad's Army* (1968–77), Dunn also appeared in small roles in the films *What a Whopper*, *The Mouse on the Moon*, *The Magic Christian* and *The Fiendish Plot of Dr. Fu Manchu*, along with episodes of TV's *Five Children and It* (1951), *The Avengers* ("Something Nasty in the Nursery") and *Metal Mickey*. In the early 1970s he had an annoying #1 hit with the song "Grandad", which remained in the British charts for 28 weeks.

American voice actress **Lucille Bliss**, best known for playing Smurfette in the Hanna-Barbera *Smurfs* cartoons, died on November 8, aged 96. She began her career as an uncredited voice in Disney's *Cinderella* (1950) and went on to contribute work to such movies and TV series as *101 Dalmatians* (1961), *The Secret of NIMH*, *Robots*, *The Flintstones*, *Duck Dodgers*, *Avatar: The Last Airbender* and *Invader ZIM*.

British character actor [John] **Roger Hammond** died of cancer the same day, aged 76. His many credits include *The*

Pied Piper (1972), *Queen Kong*, *The Hunchback of Notre Dame* (1976), *Morons from Outer Space*, *A Christmas Carol* (1999), *Arabian Nights* (2000), *Bedazzled* (2000), *Around the World in 80 Days* (2004) and episodes of TV's *Doctor Who*, *The Avengers* ("Return of the Cybernauts"), *Catweazle*, *The Tripods*, *The Adventures of Sherlock Holmes* and *Ghost Busters of East Finchley*.

American actress **Deborah** [Iona] **Raffin**, who starred in *The Sentinel* (1977), died of leukaemia on November 21, aged 59. Her other movies include *Gold Told Me To* (aka *Demon*), *Grizzly II: The Concert* and *Scanners II: The New Order*, along with episodes of *Hammer House of Mystery and Suspense* ("Last Video and Testament") and the 1980s *Twilight Zone* TV series. With her music producer husband Michael Viner, she founded the successful audio book business Dove Books-on-Tape in 1985. They sold the company in 1997.

American leading man **Larry** [Martin] **Hagman**, who starred as astronaut Major Anthony Nelson in the 1965–70 NBC-TV sitcom *I Dream of Jeannie*, died from complications of throat cancer on November 23, aged 81. The son of legendary Broadway actress/singer Mary Martin, he also appeared in the movies *Fail-Safe*, *A Howling in the Woods*, *Son of Blob* (which he also directed), *The Return of the World's Greatest Detective* (as "Sherman Holmes") and *Superman* (1978), along with an episode of *Rod Serling's Night Gallery* and pretty much every other US TV series of the 1970s and 1980s. From 1978 onwards he portrayed J. R. Ewing in *Dallas* and its various spin-offs and continuations.

Quintessential British leading lady **Dinah Sheridan** (Dinah Nadyejda Mec) died on November 25, aged 92. Her first role, at the age of 12, was in a stage tour of *Peter Pan* starring Charles Laughton as Captain Hook and his wife Elsa Lanchester as the titular character. A film star during the 1940s and 1950s, later in her career Sheridan appeared in episodes of TV's *Zodiac*, *Hammer House of Horror* ("The Thirteenth Reunion") and *Doctor Who*. Her first husband was actor Jimmy Hanley, and one of their three children is Hammer heroine Jenny Hanley.

British actress **Dolores Mantez** died on November 30, aged 73. She played series regular Lt Nina Barry on Gerry Anderson's *U.F.O.* (1970–73), and her other credits include episodes of *The Avengers* and *Randall and Hopkirk (Deceased)*.

Veteran American character actor **Harry Carey, Jr** (Henry G. Carey), the son of character actor Harry Carey and a member of the "John Ford stock company", died on December 9, aged 91. He appeared in numerous Westerns (often alongside John Wayne), plus *Monkey Business* (uncredited), *Billy the Kid vs. Dracula* (with John Carradine), *Cyborg 2087*, *Gremlins*, *UFOria*, *Cherry 2000*, *The Exorcist III* and *Back to the Future III*. On TV his credits include episodes of *Men Into Space* and *Knight Rider*.

Eccentric British astronomer and broadcaster Sir **Patrick Moore** (Patrick Alfred Caldwell-Moore) died the same day, aged 89. Besides inspiring generations of children to keep watching the skies through his BBC-TV series *The Sky at Night*, which he presented for more than 700 record-breaking episodes, he also wrote more than 20 SF novels for younger readers. His non-fiction books include *Science and Fiction* (1957), and he also turned up playing himself in the 1966 short film *The Master*, *Red Dawrf A-Z*, *Doctor Who* ("The Eleventh Hour") and various episodes of *The Goodies*.

India-born **Kenneth Kendall**, who became the first person on British television to read the news in 1955, died on December 14 following a stroke. He was 88. Kendall appeared (invariably as a newsreader/interviewer) in *The Brain* (aka *Vengeance*), *They Came from Beyond Space*, *2001: A Space Odyssey* and episodes of *A for Andromeda*, *Suspense* ("Virus X"), *Doctor Who*, *Adam Adamant Lives!*, *Dead of Night* and *The Dark Side of the Sun*.

British character actress **Daphne** [Margaret du Grivel] **Oxenford**, the voice of the BBC children's radio programme *Listen with Mother* (1950–71), died on December 21, aged

93. She appeared in Hammer's *Frankenstein Must Be Destroyed* (uncredited) and episodes of *Shadows of Fear*, *Doctor Who* (1987) and *Murder Rooms: The Dark Beginnings of Sherlock Holmes* (Stephen Gallagher's "The Kingdom of Bones"). Her scenes as an elderly Dame Agatha Christie were deleted from the 2008 *Doctor Who* episode "The Unicorn and the Wasp", but were restored in the DVD version.

Emmy-winning American actor **Jack Klugman** (Jacob Joachim Klugman), who starred in such TV series as *The Odd Couple* and *Quincy M.E.*, died of prostate cancer on Christmas Eve, aged 90. His other credits include *Poor Devil* (with Christopher Lee), *Camera Obscura* (2010), and episodes of TV's *Inner Sanctum*, *Alfred Hitchcock Presents*, *The Twilight Zone*, *Around the World in 80 Days* (1989) and *The Outer Limits* (2000).

American character actor **Charles Durning** died the same day, aged 89. A former professional boxer, he appeared in the movies *Sisters* (aka *Blood Sisters*), *Twilight's Last Gleaming*, *The Fury*, *The Muppet Movie*, *When a Stranger Calls* (1979), *The Final Countdown*, *Dark Night of the Scarecrow*, *Solarbabies*, *Project: Alien* (aka *Fatal Sky*), *Dick Tracy* (1990) and *When a Stranger Calls Back*, along with episodes of *Tall Tales* ("The Legend of Sleepy Hollow", 1985), *Amazing Stories*, *Early Edition* and *Touched by an Angel*. Durning played Santa Claus in *It Nearly Wasn't Christmas*, *Elmo Saves Christmas*, *Mrs Santa Claus*, *Mr St. Nick*, *A Boyfriend for Christmas* and *Captured Hearts*.

British leading man **Jon Finch** was found dead in his flat on December 28. He was 70 and had suffered from diabetes for many years. Although he began his career on TV in the 1960s (including the short-lived BBC SF series *Counterstrike*), it was his appearances in Hammer's *The Vampire Lovers* and *The Horror of Frankenstein* that led to him starring in Roman Polanski's *Macbeth*, Alfred Hitchcock's *Frenzy* and *The Final Programme* (aka *The Last Days of Man on Earth*, based on the novel by Michael Moorcock). However, after reportedly turning down a number of key roles, including that of James Bond in *Live and Let Die*, and being forced by illness to pull out of *Alien* after just one day's filming, his career floundered somewhat. Later credits include *Doktor Faustus* (1982), *Merlin of the Crystal Cave*, H. P. Lovecraft's *Lurking Fear*, *Darklands*, and episodes of TV's *The New Avengers*, *The Martian Chronicles* mini-series, *Hammer House of Horror* ("Witching Time") and *The Memoirs of Sherlock Holmes*. In the 1980s he was married to actress Catriona MacColl.

Former beauty contest winner and model **Gloria Pall** (Gloria Palitz, aka Voluptua) died of heart failure on December 30, aged 85. Because of her striking figure, she had small parts (often uncredited) in *Abbott and Costello Go to Mars*, Disney's *20000 Leagues Under the Sea*, *The Night of the Hunter*, *Jailhouse Rock* and episodes of TV's *Space Patrol*, *Commando Cody: Sky Marshall of the Universe* and *The Twilight Zone*. Pall wrote 13 books about the movie industry, including her memoirs.

FILM & TV TECHNICIANS/PRODUCERS

Acclaimed Japanese designer **Eiko Ishioka** died of pancreatic cancer on January 21, aged 73. Best known for her outlandish Oscar-winning costumes for *Bram Stoker's Dracula* (1992), she also worked on *The Cell*, *The Fall*, *Immortals* and *Mirror Mirror*, and designed the costumes for the stage musical *Spider-Man: Turn Off the Dark*.

Prolific Emmy Award-winning American TV director and producer **John Rich** died on January 29, aged 86. Although best known for directing comedy, his credits include two episodes of the original *The Twilight Zone* series.

American cinematographer **Ric** (Richard) **Waite** died of a heart attack on February 18, aged 78. His credits include *Dead of Night* (1977), *Revenge of the Stepford Wives*, *Red Dawn*, *The Triangle* and episodes of TV's *Wonder Woman* and *Nowhere Man*.

Japanese visual effects art director **Yasuyuki Inoue** died of heart failure on February 19, aged 90. His numerous credits for Toho Studios include *The War of the Gargantuas*, *King Kong Escapes*, *Destroy All Monsters!*, *Yog – Monster from Space*, *Godzilla on Monster Island* (aka *War of the Monsters*), *Godzilla vs. the Smog Monster*, *Catastrophe 1999: The Prophecies of Nostradamus*, *Terror of Mechagodzilla*, *Battle in Outer Space 2*, *Deathquake*, *Godzilla 1985* and *Princess from the Moon*.

Oscar-nominated cinematographer **Bruce** [Mohr Powell] **Surtees** died on February 23, aged 74. Best known for his work with Don Siegel and Clint Eastwood, amongst the movies he shot are *The Beguiled*, *Play Misty for Me*, *Conquest of the Planet of the Apes*, *High Plains Drifter*, *Firefox*, *Tightrope*, *Pale Rider*, *Psycho III*, *Ratboy*, *Back to the Beach* and *The Birds II: Land's End*.

Production illustrator **Robert Temple Ayres** died of heart failure on February 25, aged 98. His most famous work was the map used in the opening titles of TV's *Bonanza*, and he also worked on Disney's *The Black Hole*.

Former Hollywood juvenile actor turned producer and TV director **Jerome Courtland** (Courtland Jourolman, Jr) died on March 1, aged 85. His directing credits include episodes of *The Flying Nun* and *Fantasy Island*, while for Disney he produced *Escape to Witch Mountain* (1975), *Pete's Dragon*, *Return from Witch Mountain*, *The Ghosts of Buxley Hall* and *The Devil and Max Devlin*.

Japanese director **Nobru Ishiguro**, best known for the popular anime film and TV series *Space Cruiser Yamato*, died on March 20, aged 73. His other credits include *Megazone 23*, *Robotech: The Movie* and episodes of *Astroboy* and *Legend of the Galactic Heroes*. Ishiguro was also the co-author of a 1980 history of Japanese animation.

Stylish British production designer turned film director and scriptwriter **Robert** [Bernard] **Fuest**, best remembered for the macabre comedies *The Abominable Dr. Phibes* and *Dr. Phibes Rises Again* (both starring Vincent Price), died on March 21, aged 84. Following his work as a designer on *Out of This World* and *The Avengers*, Fuest's other directing credits include *Wuthering Heights* (1970), *And Soon the*

Darkness, *The Final Programme* (based on the novel by Michael Moorcock), *The Devil's Rain*, *The Gold Bug* (1980, based on the story by Edgar Allan Poe), *Revenge of the Stepford Wives* and *Mystery at Fire Island*, along with episodes of TV's *The Avengers*, *The New Avengers* and *Worlds Beyond*.

American-born film producer **Hal E. Chester** (Harold Ribotsky, aka "Hally Chester") died in London, England, on March 25, aged 91. He began his career as a child actor in 1938 (as one of Monogram's "East Side Kids" and Universal's "Junior G-Man"), before becoming a producer with such films as *The Beast from 20,000 Fathoms* and *Night of the Demon* (aka *Curse of the Demon*).

British cinematographer **Brian Morgan** died on April 6, aged 69. His credits include the TV series *Children of the Stones* and *Robin of Sherwood*, and an episode of *She-Wolf of London*.

Charles McNabb, who was part of Ricou Browning's underwater support team on *Creature from the Black Lagoon*, *Revenge of the Creature* and *The Creature Walks Among Us*, died the same day, aged 84.

American film producer **Martin Poll** died of pneumonia and kidney failure on April 14, aged 89. He began his career by producing a number of films in Germany and France for international release, along with 31 half-hour episodes of the 1954–55 *Flash Gordon* TV series. His later credits include *The Possession of Joel Delaney*, *Night Watch*, *Arthur the King*, *Haunted Summer* (with Alice Krige as Mary Shelley) and the TV mini-series *The Dain Curse*. In 1956 he opened the Gold Medal Studios in New York and three years later was sworn in as the Commissioner of Motion Picture Arts for that same city – the only individual to ever hold that title.

Emmy Award-winning American TV director **Paul Bogart** (Paul Bogoff) died on April 15, aged 92. His credits include *Shirley Temple's Storybook* ("The Legend of Sleepy Hollow", 1958), *Hansel and Gretel* (1958), *Ten Little Indians* (1959), *Golden Showcase* ("The Picture of Dorian

Gray", 1961), Carousel (1967), *The Canterville Ghost* (1986, starring John Gielgud), and episodes of *'Way Out* (hosted by Roald Dahl), *The Nurses* ("Night of the Witch") and *Get Smart*. Bogart also directed the 1984 comedy sequel *Oh, God! You Devil*.

British visual effects designer **Peter Wragg**, who created the spaceship and other props for BBC-TV's *Red Dwarf*, died on April 15, aged 65. He also worked on *Thunderbirds Are GO*, *Threads*, *The Moonstone* (1997), and episodes of *Captain Scarlet and the Mysterons*, *The Flipside of Dominick Hide*, *Another Flip for Dominick*, *Doctor Who*, *The Hound of the Baskervilles* (1982) and *Ghostbusters of East Finchley*.

Emmy-winning musical variety and game show producer and host **Dick Clark** (Richard Wagstaff Clark), chairman and CEO of Dick Clark Productions, died from a massive heart attack following a hospital procedure on April 18. He was 82. Although best known for such TV shows as *American Bandstand*, he also produced or executive produced the movies *Psych-Out*, *The Werewolf of Woodstock*, *The Dark* (1979), *The Man in the Santa Claus Suit*, *The Demon Murder Case*, *The Power* (1984), *Night Shadows* (aka *Mutant*), *Remo Williams: The Adventure Begins* (aka *Remo: Unarmed and Dangerous*), *Remo Williams* (1988) and *Death Dreams*. Clark also appeared in *Wild in the Streets*, *The Phynx*, *Spy Kids*, and episodes of *Batman*, *Sabrina the Teenage Witch* and *The X Files*.

Jim (James) **Isaac**, who co-produced and directed the superior sequel *Jason X* (2001), died of cancer on May 6, aged 51. He began his career in special effects, and worked on such movies as *Gremlins*, *Enemy Mine*, *House II: The Second Story*, *Virtuosity* and *eXistenZ*. Isaac's directing credits include *The Horror Show* (1989), *Skinwalkers* and *Pig Hunt*, and he also worked in various capacities on *Return of the Jedi*, *The Fly* (1986), *DeepStar Six*, *Naked Lunch* and *Children of the Corn V: Fields of Terror*.

Pioneering British-born hair stylist **Vidal Sassoon** CBE died of complications from leukaemia in Los Angeles on

May 9. He was 84. Sassoon was famous for creating Mia Farrow's distinctive and much-copied hairstyle in Roman Polanski's *Rosemary's Baby* (1968). Sassoon met the second of his four wives, Canadian-born actress Beverly Adams, while styling her hair on the Amicus film *Torture Garden* (1967). They were married for almost 14 years, until their divorce in 1981.

American sound effects editor **Jerry Christian**, who worked on Alfred Hitchcock's *Psycho* and *The Birds*, died on May 26, aged 86. He eventually became head of Universal's sound effects department, and won an Emmy Award for his work on Steven Spielberg's *Duel*. His other credits include *Jaws*, *The Six Million Dollar Man* and *Knight Rider*.

American visual effects designer **Matt** (Matthew) **Yuricich**, who won a Special Achievement Oscar for his work on *Logan's Run* (1976), died on May 28, aged 89. A talented matte artist, he also worked (often uncredited) on *Prince Valiant* (1954), *Forbidden Planet*, *The World the Flesh and the Devil*, *Tarzan the Ape Man* (1959), *Atlantis the Lost Continent*, *Lost Horizon* (1973), *Soylent Green*, *Westworld*, *Young Frankenstein*, *Doc Savage: The Man of Bronze*, *Futureworld*, *Damnation Alley*, *Close Encounters of the Third Kind*, *Star Trek: The Motion Picture*, *The Last Chase*, *Blade Runner*, *V*, *Brainstorm*, *Ghostbusters*, *2010*, *Fright Night* (1985), *Poltergeist II: The Other Side*, *Solarbabies*, *Masters of the Universe*, *The Monster Squad*, *Field of Dreams* and *Bill & Ted's Bogus Journey*.

Japanese director and screenwriter **Kaneto Shindô** died on May 29, aged 100. He was the oldest film-maker in Japan. As a writer, his credits include *Onibaba*, *Kuroneko* (which he also directed) and *Jishin rettô* (aka *Deathquake*).

British cinematographer **Christopher** [George Joseph] **Challis** died on May 31, aged 93. He began his film career in the late 1930s and was a second unit cameraman on *The Thief of Bagdad*. Challis went on to work as a lighting camerman/camera operator on such Powell-Pressburger productions as *A Matter of Life and Death* (aka *Stairway to Heaven*), *Black Narcissus* and *The Red Shoes*, before becoming director of photography on *The Tales of Hoffman*, *Footsteps in the Fog*, *Chitty Chitty Bang Bang*, *The Private Life of Sherlock Holmes* and *The Little Prince*.

Hollywood art director and production designer **Stan Jolley**, the son of veteran character actor I. Stanford Jolley, died of gastric cancer on June 4, aged 86. Best known for his work with producer Irwin Allen on *Voyage to the Bottom of the Sea*, *Land of the Giants*, *City Beneath the Sea* and *The Swarm*, his many other credits include *The Phynx*, *Night of the Lepus*, *Terror in the Wax Museum* and *Knife for the Ladies*, along with episodes of TV's *Mister Ed* and *Get Smart*. Jolley was also responsible for designing such Disneyland attractions as the Golden Horseshoe Saloon, the Storybook Land Canal Boats and the interior of Sleeping Beauty's Castle.

Sixty-three-year-old American production designer **J.** (John) **Michael Riva**, the grandson of actress Marlene Dietrich, died after suffering a stroke on June 7. His many credits include *Ilsa Harem Keeper of the Oil Sheiks*, *The Hand*, *Halloween II* (1981), *The Adventures of Buckaroo Banzai Across the 8th Dimension*, *The Goonies*, *The Golden Child*, *Scrooged*, *Congo*, *Evolution*, *Stealth*, *Zathura*, *Spider-Man 3*, *Iron Man*, *Iron Man 2* and *The Amazing Spider-Man*. Riva also directed an episode apiece of TV's *Amazing Stories* and *Tales from the Crypt*, and he was a visual consultant on the 1999 remake of *House on Haunted Hill*.

British-born TV producer and director **Norman** [Frances] **Felton**, best-known for co-creating the 1960s series *The Man from U.N.C.L.E.* and *The Girl from U.N.C.L.E.*, died in California on June 25, aged 99. He also produced the TV pilots *Ghostbreakers* (1967) and *Baffled!* (1973), along with the series *Strange Report* (1969–70).

Hollywood film producer **Richard D.** (Darryl) **Zanuck**, the son of legendary 20th Century Fox executive Darryl F. Zanuck, died of a heart attack on July 13, aged 77. He was involved in such films as *Sssssss* (aka *Ssssnake*), *Jaws*, *Jaws 2*, *The Island*, *Cocoon*, *Cocoon: The Return*, *Deep Impact*, *Planet of the Apes* (2001), *Reign of Fire*, *Big Fish*, *Charlie* *and the Chocolate Factory* (2005), *Sweeney Todd: The Demon Barber of Fleet Street* (2007), *Alice in Wonderland* (2010) and *Dark Shadows*.

American producer and director **William** [Milton] **Asher**, the son of veteran Universal horror producer Ephraim M. Asher, died of complications from Alzheimer's disease on July 16. He was 90. Best known as the producer/director of TV's *Bewitched* (1967–72), Asher also directed 100 episodes of *I Love Lucy*. His other credits include episodes of *The Twilight Zone* and the *Bewitched* spin-off *Tabitha*, and the films *The 27th Day*, *Night Warning* (aka *The Evil Protégé*) and *I Dream of Jeannie . . . Fifteen Years Later*. For AIP, Asher created the popular "Beach Party" musical movie series and directed *Beach Party*, *Muscle Beach Party*, *Bikini Beach*, *Beach Blanket Bingo* and *How to Stuff a Wild Bikini*. He was married to *Bewitched* star Elizabeth Montgomery from 1963-74.

Experimental French film-maker **Chris Marker** (Christian François Bouche-Villeneuve) died on his 91st birthday on July 29. His credits include the 1962 experimental SF short *La Jetée*, which was remade as Terry Gilliam's *Twelve Monkeys* (1995). Marker (who took his pseudonym from the Magic Marker pen) reportedly studied philosophy with Jean-Paul Sartre in the 1930s and never granted an interview.

British camera operator **John Harris** died in July, aged 87. He began his career as a clapper-loader and focus-puller for Gainsborough Pictures in the early 1940s, and the many films he worked on include *The Collector*, *Chitty Chitty Bang Bang*, *Tales from the Crypt* (1972), *The Creeping Flesh*, *Vault of Horror*, *—And Now the Screaming Starts!*, *Live and Let Die*, *The Man with the Golden Gun*, *Lisztomania*, *The People That Time Forgot*, *Orca*, *Superman* (1978), *Superman II*, *Millennium* (1989), *Popcorn* and the TV movie *I Still Dream of Jeannie*.

Documentary film-maker **Mel Stuart** (Stewart Solomon), who directed *Willy Wonka & the Chocolate Factory* (1971), died of cancer on August 9, aged 83. He was a first cousin of Stan Lee.

Oscar-winning Italian special effects artist **Carlo Rambaldi** died after a long illness on August 10, aged 86. Best known for creating the title character in Steven Spielberg's *E.T. The Extra-Terrestrial*, Rambaldi's credits include *La vendetta di Ercole*, *Perseus Against the Monsters*, Mario Bava's *Planet of the Vampires* and *A Bay of Blood*, *La notte dei diavoli*, *Frankenstein '80*, *Flesh for Frankenstein*, *Blood for Dracula*, *Deep Red*, the controversial 1976 remake of *King Kong*, *Close Encounters of the Third Kind*, *Alien*, *Nightwing*, *The Hand*, *Possession*, *Conan the Destroyer*, *Dune*, *Cat's Eye*, *Silver Bullet*, *King Kong Lives* and *Cameron's Closet*.

American film editor **George A. Bowers** died of complications from heart surgery on August 18, aged 68. His many credits include *The Pom Pom Girls*, *Galaxina*, *The Adventures of Buckaroo Banzai Across the 8th Dimension*, *The Stepfather* (1987), *The Preacher's Wife* and *From Hell*. Bowers also directed the creepy 1980 horror film *The Hearse* starring Joseph Cotton.

British-born Hollywood producer and director **Tony Scott** (Anthony D. L. Scott), the younger brother of Ridley Scott, committed suicide on August 19 by jumping to his death from the Vincent Thomas Bridge in Los Angeles. He was aged 68. As a director, his films include *The Hunger* (based on the novel by Whitley Strieber), *Crimson Tide*, *The Fan* and *Deja Vu*. Through the brothers' Scott Free Productions, he was involved with such projects as *The Hunger* TV series, *The Andromeda Strain* (2008) and *Coma* (2012) mini-series, and the movies *Tell-Tale*, *Prometheus* and *Stoker*.

Canadian producer **Jake Eberts** (John David Eberts), who founded Goldcrest Films in the 1970s, died of uveal melanoma on September 6, aged 71. His credits include *The Name of the Rose*, *The Adventures of Baron Munchausen* (1988), *The Princess and the Cobbler*, *Super Mario Bros*, *James and the Giant Peach*, *The Wind in the Willows* (1996), *Chicken Run* and *The Illusionist*.

British exploitation producer and director **Stanley A.** (Alfred) **Long** died on September 10, aged 78. Although best known for a string of sexy softcore movies in the 1960s and 1970s, he began his career as an uncredited camera operator of Roman Polanski's *Repulsion* before going on to photograph such films as *The Sorcerers* (starring Boris Karloff) and *The Blood Beast Terror* (starring Peter Cushing). As Al Beresford, he and Michael Armstrong co-directed the 1986 fix-up horror movie *Screamtime*, while his distribution company Alpha Films released such titles as *Night of the Living Dead*, *Dawn of the Dead*, *Shivers*, *Rabid*, *The Brood* and *Maniac* in the UK. His autobiography, *X-Rated: Adventures of an Exploitation Filmmaker*, was published in 2008.

British film and TV animation producer **John Coates** died of cancer on September 16, aged 84. He worked as a production supervisor on *Yellow Submarine* and the 1979 version of *The Lion, the Witch & the Wardrobe* before going on to produce the "Soft Landing" sequence in *Heavy Metal*, *The Snowman*, *When the Wind Blows*, *Father Christmas*, *The Wind in the Willows* (1995) and *The Snowman and the Snowdog*.

American cinematographer **Harris Savides** died of brain cancer on October 9, aged 55. His credits include *Se7en* (additional photography), *The Game* and *Zodiac* (2007).

American TV producer **Henry Colman** died on November 7, aged 89. Best known for such popular series as *The Love Boat* and *Hotel*, he also produced the 1975 TV movie *The Dead Don't Die*, written by Robert Bloch, and Colman himself scripted an episode of the superhero series *Isis*.

British director, producer and sceenwriter **Bob** (Robert) **Kellett** died on November 27, aged 84. Best known for such bawdy film comedies as *Up Pompeii* and *Are You Being Served?* (both based on popular television series), he also directed three episodes of the 1970s TV series *Space: 1999* and was second unit director on *Haunted* (1995), based on the novel by James Herbert.

American-born visual effects producer **Eileen** [Mary] **Moran** died in New Zealand on December 3, aged 60. She began her career at Digital Domain, working on such movies as *Lake Placid* and *Frequency*, before moving to Weta

Digital in 2001, where she supervised the effects on Peter Jackson's *King Kong* (which she co-produced), the *Lord of the Rings* trilogy, *The Lovely Bones* and *The Hobbit: An Unexpected Journey* (also as co-producer), along with *I Robot*, *X-Men: The Last Stand*, *Eragon*, *The Bridge to Terabithia*, *4: Rise of the Silver Surfer*, *30 Days of Night*, *The Water Horse*, *Jumper*, *The Chronicles of Narnia: Prince Caspian*, *The Day the Earth Stood Still*, *District 9*, *Avatar*, *Rise of the Planet of the Apes*, *The Adventures of Tintin: The Secret of the Unicorn* and *Prometheus*.

American animation director, producer and storyboard artist **Rusty Mills** died of colon cancer on December 7, aged 49. His credits include episodes of *Animaniacs* and *Pinky and the Brain*, along with the 1995 special *Tiny Toons' Night Ghoulery*.

British special effects cameraman **Harry Oakes** died on December 11, aged 91. He began his career in the late 1940s as a clapper-loader and then focus-puller for Hammer Films, working on such titles as *Man in Black*, *The Quatermass Experiment*, *X the Unknown*, *The Curse of Frankenstein*, *Quatermass 2*, *Dracula*, *The Revenge of Frankenstein*, *The Hound of the Baskervilles*, *The Mummy*, *The Terror of the Tongs*, *Taste of Fear* and *The Damned*. He then worked with Gerry Anderson on the TV series *Captain Scarlet and the Mysterons*, *U.F.O.*, *Space: 1999*, *Terrahawks* and *Space Precinct*, along with the films *Thunderbirds Are GO*, *Thunderbird 6* and *Doppelgänger* (aka *Journey to the Far Side of the Sun*). Oakes's other credits include *Superman* (1978), *Dracula* (1979), *Flash Gordon* (1980), *Superman III*, *Legend* and *Aliens*.

Veteran American TV director **Don Medford** (Donald Muller) died on December 12, aged 95. The prolific Medford helmed episodes of *Tales of Tomorrow* (35!), *Alfred Hitchcock Presents* (both 1960s and 1980s series), *The Twilight Zone*, the pilot for *The Man from U.N.C.L.E.* (released theatrically as *To Trap a Spy*), the pilot for *Ghostbreakers* (1967), *The Invaders* and *Something is Out There*, along with the 1978 TV movie *The Clone Master*.

British puppeteer **Violet Phelan Philpott** (Violet Yeomans) died on December 14, aged 90. In the early 1960s she created the puppets for TV's *The Telegoons*, based on the popular BBC Radio series *The Goon Show*, and in 1972 she created Zippy for the popular ITV children's series *Rainbow*.

American screenwriter and director **Danny Steinmann** (aka Danny Stone/Peter Foleg), died on December 18, aged 70. Best known for *Friday the 13th: A New Beginning*, he was an associate producer on the Gene Roddenberry pilot *Spectre*, and he co-wrote and directed *The Unseen* under the Foleg alias.

British producer and writer **Gerry Anderson** MBE (Gerald Alexander Anderson) died of complications from Alzheimer's disease on December 26, aged 83. Often in collaboration with his former wife Sylvia Anderson, he co-produced the puppet (Supermarionation) and live-action TV series *The Adventures of Twizzle*, *Torchy the Battery Boy*, *Four Feather Falls*, *Supercar*, *Fireball XL5*, *Stingray*, *Thunderbirds*, *Captain Scarlet and the Mysterons*, *U.F.O.*, *Space: 1999*, *Terrahawks* and *Space Precinct*. His other credits include the films *Thunderbirds Are GO*, *Thunderbird 6* and *Doppelgänger* (aka *Journey to the Far Side of the Sun*).

Oscar-winning New Zealand sound editor **Mike Hopkins** (Michael Alexander Hopkins) drowned in a rafting accident on December 30. He was 53. Hopkins's credits include *Death Warmed Up*, *Mr Wrong*, *Braindead*, *The Frighteners*, *Aberration*, *The Lord of the Rings* trilogy, *The Ring 2*, *King Kong* (2005), *Transformers* and *Fresh Meat*.

USEFUL ADDRESSES

THE FOLLOWING LISTING of organisations, publications, dealers and individuals is designed to present readers and authors with further avenues to explore. Although I can personally recommend many of those listed on the following pages, neither the publisher nor myself can take any responsibility for the services they offer. Please also note that the information below is only a guide and is subject to change without notice.

– The Editor

ORGANISATIONS

The Australian Horror Writers Association (*www.australianhorror.com*) is a non-profit organisation that was formed in 2005 as a way of providing a unified voice and a sense of community for Australian (and New Zealand) writers of horror/dark fiction. AHWA aims to become the first point of reference for writers and fans of the dark side of literature in Australia, to spread the acceptance and improve the understanding of what horror is in literature to a wider audience, and in doing so gain a greater readership for established and new writers alike. Email: *ahwa@australianhorror.com*

The British Fantasy Society (*www.britishfantasysociety.org*) was founded in 1971 and publishes the newsletter

Prism and the magazines *Dark Horizons* and *New Horizons*, featuring articles, interviews and fiction, along with occasional special booklets. The BFS also enjoys a lively online community – there is an email news-feed, a discussion board with numerous links, and a Cyberstore selling various publications. FantasyCon is one of the UK's friendliest conventions and there are social gatherings and meet-the-author events organised around Britain. For yearly membership details, email: *secretary@britishfantasysociety.org* You can also join online through the Cyberstore.

The Friends of Arthur Machen (*www.arthurmachen.org.uk*) is a literary society whose objectives include encouraging a wider recognition of Machen's work and providing a focus for critical debate. Members get a hardcover journal, *Faunus*, twice a year, and also the informative newsletter *Machenalia*. For membership details, contact Treasurer Jon Preece: *machenfoam@yahoo.co.uk*

The Friends of the Merril Collection (*www.friendsofmerril.org/*) is a volunteer organisation that provides support and assistance to the largest public collection of science fiction, fantasy and horror books in North America. Details about annual membership and donations are available from the website or by contacting The Friends of the Merril Collection, c/o Lillian H. Smith Branch, Toronto Public Library, 239 College Street, 3rd Floor, Toronto, Ontario M5T 1R5, Canada. Email: *ltoolis@tpl.toronto.on.ca*

The Horror Writers Association (*www.horror.org*) is a world-wide organisation of writers and publishing professionals dedicated to promoting the interests of writers of Horror and Dark Fantasy. It was formed in the early 1980s. Interested individuals may apply for Active, Affiliate or Associate membership. Active membership is limited to professional writers. HWA publishes a monthly online *Newsletter*, and sponsors the annual Bram Stoker Awards.

World Fantasy Convention (*www.worldfantasy.org*) is an annual convention held in a different (usually American) city each year, oriented particularly towards serious readers and genre professionals.

World Horror Convention (*www.worldhorrorsociety.org*) is a smaller, more relaxed, event. It is aimed specifically at horror fans and professionals, and held in a different city (usually American) each year.

SELECTED SMALL PRESS PUBLISHERS

The Alchemy Press (*www.alchemypress.wordpress.com*), Cheadle, Staffordshire ST10 1PF, UK.

Alliteration Ink (*alliterationink.com*), PO Box 20598, Dayton, OH 45420, USA.

Bad Moon Books/Eclipse (*www.badmoonbooks.com*), 1854 W. Chateau Avenue, Anaheim, CA 92804-4527, USA.

Bards and Sages Publishing (*www.bardsandsages.com*), 201 Leed Avenue, Bellmawr, NJ 08031, USA.

Bibliofear, 13 Macclesfield Road, London SE25 4RY, UK.

Big Time Books (*www.bigtimebooks.com*).

Blood Bound Books (*www.bloodboundbooks.net*). Email: *editor@bloodboundbooks.net*

Bold Strokes Books, Inc. (*www.boldstrokesbooks.com*), PO Box 249, Valley Falls, NY 12185, USA. Email: *publisher@boldstrokesbooks.com*

Books of the Dead Press (*www.booksofthedead.com*). Email: *besthorror@gmail.com*

Cemetery Dance Publications (*www.cemeterydance.com*), 132-B Industry Lane, Unit #7, Forest Hill, MD 21050, USA. Email: *info@cemeterydance.com*

ChiZine Publications (*www.chizinepub.com*). Email: *info@chizinepub.com*

Chômu Press (*info@chomupress.com*), 70 Hill Street, Richmond, Surrey TW9 1TW, UK. Email: *info@chomupress.com*

Curiosity Quills Press (*curiosityquills.com*) PO Box 2540, Dulles, VA 20101, USA. Email: *info@curiosityquills.com.*

Damnation Books LLC (*www.damnationbooks.com*), PO Box 3931, Santa Rosa, CA 95402-9998, USA. Email: *admin@damnationbooks.com*

Dark Minds Press (*www.darkmindspress.com*), 31

Gristmill Close, Cheltenham GL51 0PZ, UK. Email: *mail@darkmindspress.com*

Dark Regions Press/Black Labyrinth (*www.darkregions.com*), 300 E. Hersey Street STE 10A, Ashland, OR 97520, USA. Email: *cmorey@darkregions.com*

Donald M. Grant, Publisher, Inc. (*www.grantbooks.com*), 19 Surrey Lane, PO Box 187, Hampton Falls, NH 03844, USA.

DreamHaven Books (*www.dreamhavenbooks.com*), 2301 East 38th Street, Minneapolis, MN 55406, USA.

Earthling Publications (*www.earthlingpub.com*), PO Box 413, Northborough, MA 01532, USA. Email: *earthlingpub@yahoo.com*

Edge Science Fiction and Fantasy Publishing/Hades Publications, Inc. (*www.hadespublications.com*), PO Box 1714, Calgary, Alberta T2P 2L7, Canada. Email: *publisher@hadespublications.com*

Enigmatic Press (*www.maynard-sims.com*), 3 Cutlers Close, Bishops Stortford, Herts CM23 4FW, UK.

Eternal Press (*www.eternalpress.biz*), PO Box 3931, Santa Rosa, CA 95402-9998, USA.

Ex Hubris Imprints (*www.pstdarkness.wordpress.com*). Email: *postscripts2darkness@gmail.com*

FableCroft (*fablecroft.com.au*).

Fedogan & Bremer Publishing (*fedoganandbremer.com*), 3918 Chicago Street, Nampa, Idaho 83686, USA.

Guntlet Publications (*www.gauntletpress.com*), 5307 Arroyo Street, Colorado Springs, CO 80922, USA. Email: *info@gauntletpress.com*

Gray Friar Press (*www.grayfriarpress.com*), 9 Abbey Terrace, Whitby, North Yorkshire Y021 3HQ, UK. Email: *gary.fry@virgin.net*

Hieroglyphic Press, 25 Chanctonbury Road, Burgess Hill, West Sussex RH15 9EX, UK. Email: *evans_lichamleas@yahoo.com*

Hippocampus Press (*www.hippocampuspress.com*), PO Box 641, New York, NY 10156, USA. Email: *info@hippocampuspress.com*

The House of Murky Depths (*www.murkydepths.com*).

IDW Publishing (*www.idwpublishing.com*), 5080 Santa Fe Street, San Diego, CA 92109, USA.

Jurassic London (*www.pandemonium-fiction.com*), 153 South Lambeth Road, London SW8 1XN, UK. Email: *jared@jurassic-london.com*

Megazanthus Press (*www.nemonymous.com*).

McFarland & Company, Inc., Publishers (*www.mcfarlandpub.com*), Box 611, Jefferson, NC 28640, USA.

Miskatonic River Press (*www.miskatonicriverpress.com*), 944 Reynolds Road, Suite 188, Lakeland, Florida 33801, USA. Email: *keeper@miskatonicriverpress.com*

Mortbury Press (*mortburypress.webs.com/*), Shiloh, Nantglas, Llandrindod Wells, Powys LD1 6PD, UK. Email: *mortburypress@yahoo.com*

Mythos Books, LLC (*www.mythosbooks.com*), 351 Lake Ridge Road, Poplar Buff, MO 63901, USA.

NewCon Press (*www.newconpress.co.uk*).

Noose and Gibbet Publishing/Karōshi Books (*www.nooseandgibbetpublishing.com*). Email: *info@nooseandgibbetpublishing.com*

Nightjar Press (*nightjarpress.wordpress.com*), 38 Belfield Road, Manchester M20 6BH, UK.

Night Shade Books (*www.nightshadebooks.com*), 1661 Tennessee Street, #3H, San Francisco, CA 94107, USA. Email: *night@nightshadebooks.com*

Nodens Books (*www.nodensbooks.com*), PO Box 493, Marcellus, MI 49067, USA.

Omnium Gatherum (*omniumgatherumedia.com*).

Prime Books (*www.prime-books.com*), PO Box 83464, Gaithersburg, MD 20883, USA. Email: *prime@primebooks.com*

PS Publishing Ltd/PS Artbooks Ltd (*www.pspublishing.co.uk*), Grosvenor House, 1 New Road, Hornsea HU18 1PG, UK. Email: *editor@pspublishing.co.uk*

The RAS Press, 1745 W. Kenneth Road, Glendale, CA 91201, USA.

The Red Penny Papers (*redpennypapers.com*).

Salt Publishing (*www.saltpublishing.com*), 12 Norwich Road, Cromer, Norfolk NR27 0AX, UK.

Sarob Press (*sarobpress.blogspot.com*), La Blinière, 53250, Neuilly-le-Vendin, France.

Savoy (*www.savoy.abel.co.uk*), 446 Wilmslow Road, Withington, Manchester M20 3BW, UK. Email: *office@savoy.abel.co.uk*

Science Fiction Trails, PO Box 3000 PMB 132, Edwards, CO 81632, USA.

Screaming Dreams Publishing (*www.screamingdreams.com*), 113–116 Bute Street, Cardiff Bay, Cardiff CF10 5EQ, UK. Email: *steve@screamingdreams.com*

Shadowfall Publications (*www.shadowfall publications.com*).

Shadow Publishing (*www.shadowpublishing.webeasysite.co.uk/*), 194 Station Road, Kings Heath, Birmingham B14 7TE, UK. Email: *david.sutton986@btinternet.com*

Spectral Press (*spectralpress.wordpress.com*), 5 Serjeants Green, Neath Hill, Milton Keynes, Buckinghamshire MK14 6HA, UK. Email: *spectralpress@gmail.com*

Spectre Press, 56 Mickle Hill, Sandhurst, Berkshire GU47 8QU, UK. Email: *jon.harvey@talktalk.net*

Spinetinglers Publishing (*www.richardmoule.wordpress.com*), 22 Vestry Road, Co. Down, BT23 6HJ, UK.

Stony Meadow Publishing/Dark Moon Books (*wwwstonymeadowpublishing.com/www.darkmoonbooks.com*), 13039 Glen Ct., Chino Hills, CA 91709-1135, USA.

Subterranean Press (*www.subterraneanpress.com*), PO Box 190106, Burton, MI 48519, USA. Email: *subpress@gmail.com*

Tartarus Press (*tartaruspress.com*), Coverley House, Carlton-in-Coverdale, Leyburn, North Yorkshire DL8 4AY, UK. Email: *tartarus@pavilion.co.uk*

Ticonderoga Publications (*www.ticonderogapublications.com*), PO Box 29, Greenwood, WA 6924, Australia.

Written Backwards (*www.nettirw.com*). Email: *written@nettirw.com*

SELECTED MAGAZINES

Albedo One (*www.albedo1.com*) is Ireland's magazine of science fiction, fantasy and horror. The editorial address is Albedo One, 2 Post Road, Lusk, Co. Dublin, Ireland. Email: *bobn@yellowbrickroad.ie*

Ansible is a highly entertaining monthly SF and fantasy newsletter/gossip column edited by David Langford. It is available free electronically by sending an email to: *ansible-request@dcs.gla.ac.uk* with a subject line reading "subscribe", or you can receive the print version by sending a stamped and addressed envelope to Ansible, 94 London Road, Reading, Berks RG1 5AU, UK. Back issues, links and book lists are also available online.

Black Static (*www.ttapress.com*) is the UK's premier horror fiction magazine, produced bi-monthly by the publishers of *Interzone*. Six- and twelve-issue subscriptions are available, along with a new lifetime subscription, from TTA Press, 5 Martins Lane, Witcham, Ely, Cambs CB6 2LB, UK, or from the secure TTA website. Email: *blackstatic@ttapress.com*

Cemetery Dance Magazine (*www.cemeterydance.com*) is edited by Richard Chizmar and includes fiction up to 5,000 words, interviews, articles and columns by many of the biggest names in horror. For subscription information contact: Cemetery Dance Publications, PO Box 623, Forest Hill, MD 21050, USA. Email: *info@cemeterydance.com*

Dark Discoveries (*www.darkdiscoveries.com*) sets out to unsettle, edify and involve with fiction, interviews and non-fiction and is published irregularly. JournalStone Publications, 199 State Street, San Mateo, CA 94401, USA. Email: *info@darkdiscoveries.com*

The Ghosts & Scholars M. R. James Newsletter (*www.pardoes.info/roanddarroll/GS.html*) is a scholarly journal published roughly twice a year. It is dedicated to the classic ghost story and, as the title implies, to M. R. James in particular. Two-issue subscriptions are available from Haunted Library Publications, c/o Flat One, 36 Hamilton

Street, Hoole, Chester CH2 3JQ, UK. Email: *pardos@globalnet.co.uk*

The Horror Zine (*www.thehorrorzine.com*) is a monthly online magazine edited by Jeani Rector that features fiction, poetry, interviews and reviews.

Locus (*www.locusmag.com*) is the monthly newspaper of the SF/fantasy/horror field. Contact: Locus Publications, PO Box 13305, Oakland, CA 94661, USA. Subscription information with other rates and order forms are also available on the website. Email: *locus@locusmag.com*. You can also now subscribe to a digital edition at: *weightlessbooks.com/genre/nonfiction/locus-12-month-subscription*

Locus Online (*www.locusmag.com/news*) is an excellent online source for the latest news and reviews.

The Magazine of Fantasy & Science Fiction (*www.fandsf.com*) has been publishing some of the best imaginative fiction for more than sixty years. Edited by Gordon Van Gelder, and now published bi-monthly, single copies or an annual subscription are available by US cheques or credit card from: Fantasy & Science Fiction, PO Box 3447, Hoboken, NJ 07030, USA, or you can subscribe via the website.

Morpheus Tales (*www.morpheustales.com*) is billed as "the UK's darkest and most controversial fiction magazine" with quarterly print issues and reviews appearing on the website and myspace versions (*www.myspace.com/morpheustales*).

[Nameless]: A Biannual Journal of the Macabre, Esoteric and Intellectual . . . (*www.namelessmag.com*) features fiction, articles and reviews in an on-demand paperback format. Cycatrix Press, 16420 SE McGillivary Blvd., Ste. 103-1010, Vancouver, WA 98683, USA. Email: *info@namelessmag.com*

The Paperback Fanatic (*www.thepaperbackfanatic.com*) is an attractive full colour magazine devoted to sleaze and exploitation authors, artists and publishers. It is available by subscription only. Email: *thepaperbackfanatic@sky.com*

Rabbit Hole is a semi-regular newsletter about Harlan Ellison® that also offers exclusive signed books by the author. A subscription is available from The Harlan Ellison® Recording Collection, PO Box 55548, Sherman Oaks, CA 91413-0548, USA.

Rue Morgue (*www.rue-morgue.com*), is a glossy monthly magazine edited by Dave Alexander and subtitled "Horror in Culture & Entertainment". Each issue is packed with full colour features and reviews of new films, books, comics, music and game releases. Subscriptions are available from: Marrs Media Inc., 2926 Dundas Street West, Toronto, ON M6P 1Y8, Canada, or by credit card on the website. Email: *info@rue-morgue.com. Rue Morgue* also runs the Festival of Fear: Canadian National Horror Expo in Toronto. Every Friday you can log on to a new show at Rue Morgue Radio at *www.ruemorgueradio.com* and your horror shopping online source, The Rue Morgue Marketplace, is at *www.ruemorguemarketplace.com*

Shadows & Tall Trees (*www.undertowbooks.com*) is published occasionally. Editor Michael Kelly's trade paperback magazine is open to previously unpublished submissions of quiet, literary horror fiction. Email: *undertowbooks@gmail.com*

Space and Time: The Magazine of Fantasy, Horror, and Science Fiction (*www.spaceandtimemagazine.com*) is published quarterly. Single issues and subscriptions are available from the website or from the new address: Space and Time Magazine, 458 Elizabeth Avenue #5348, Somerset, NJ 08873, USA. In the UK and Europe, copies can be ordered from BBR Distributing, PO Box 625, Sheffield S1 3GY, UK.

Subterranean Press Magazine (*www.supterraneanpress.com/magazine*).

Supernatural Tales (*suptales.blogspot.com*) is a twice-yearly fiction magazine edited by David Longhorn, which is moving to PoD format. Supernatural Tales, 291 Eastbourne Avenue, Gateshead NE8 4NN, UK. Email: *davidlonghorn@hotmail.com*

Video WatcHDog (*www.videowatchdog.com*) describes itself as "The Perfectionist's Guide to Fantastic Video" and is published bi-monthly from PO Box 5283, Cincinnati, OH

45205-0283, USA. One-year (six issues) subscriptions are available from: *orders@videowatchdog.com*

Weird Tales (*www.weirdtalesmagazine.com*) Nth Dimension Media Inc., 105 West 86th Street, Ste 307, New York, NY 10024-3412, USA.

DEALERS

Bookfellows/Mystery and Imagination Books (*www.mysteryandimagination.com*) is owned and operated by Malcolm and Christine Bell, who have been selling fine and rare books since 1975. This clean and neatly organised store includes SF/fantasy/horror/mystery, along with all other areas of popular literature. Many editions are signed, and catalogues are issued regularly. Credit cards accepted. Open seven days a week at 238 N. Brand Blvd., Glendale, California 91203, USA. Tel: (818) 545-0206. Fax: (818) 545-0094. Email: *bookfellows@gowebway.com*

Borderlands Books (*www.borderlands-books.com*) is a nicely designed store with friendly staff and an impressive stock of new and used books from both sides of the Atlantic. 866 Valencia Street (at 19th), San Francisco, CA 94110, USA. Tel: (415) 824-8203 or (888) 893-4008 (toll free in the US). Credit cards accepted. World-wide shipping. Email: *office@borderlands-books.com*

Cold Tonnage Books (*www.coldtonnage.com*) offers excellent mail order new and used SF/fantasy/horror, art, reference, limited editions etc. Write to: Andy & Angela Richards, Cold Tonnage Books, 22 Kings Lane, Windlesham, Surrey GU20 6JQ, UK. Credit cards accepted. Tel: +44 (0)1276-475388. Email: *andy@coldtonnage.com*

Richard Dalby issues an annual Christmas catalogue of used Ghost Stories and other supernatural volumes at very reasonable prices. Write to: Richard Dalby, 4 Westbourne Park, Scarborough, North Yorkshire Y012 4AT. Tel: +44 (0)1723 377049.

Dark Delicacies (*www.darkdel.com*) is a Burbank, California, store specialising in horror books, toys, vampire merchandise and signings. They also do mail order and run money-saving book club and membership discount deals. 3512 W. Magnolia Blvd, Burbank, CA 91505, USA. Tel: (818) 556-6660. Credit cards accepted. Email: *darkdel@darkdel.com*

DreamHaven Books & Comics (*www.dreamhavenbooks.com*) became an online and mail-order outlet only in early 2012, offering new and used SF/fantasy/horror/art and illustrated etc. with regular catalogues (both print and email). Credit cards accepted. Tel: (612) 823-6070. Email: *dream@dreamhavenbooks.com*

Fantastic Literature (*www.fantasticliterature.com*) mail order offers the UK's biggest online out-of-print SF/fantasy/horror genre bookshop. Fanzines, pulps and vintage paperbacks as well. Write to: Simon and Laraine Gosden, Fantastic Literature, 35 The Ramparts, Rayleigh, Essex SS6 8PY, UK. Credit cards and PayPal accepted. Tel/Fax: +44 (0)1268-747564. Email: *simon@fantasticliterature.com*

Horrorbles (*www.horribles.com*), 6731 West Roosevelt Road, Berwyn, IL 60402, USA. Small, friendly Chicago store selling horror and sci-fi toys, memorabilia and magazines that has monthly specials and in-store signings. Specialises in exclusive "Basil Gogos" and "Svengoolie" items. Tel: (708) 484-7370. Email: *store@horrorbles.com*

Kayo Books (*www.kayobooks.com*) is a bright, clean treasure-trove of used SF/fantasy/horror/mystery/pulps spread over two floors. Titles are stacked alphabetically by subject, and there are many bargains to be had. Credit cards accepted. Visit the store (Wednesday–Saturday, 11:00 a.m. to 6:00 p.m.) at 814 Post Street, San Francisco, CA 94109, USA or order off their website. Tel: (415) 749 0554. Email: *kayo@kayobooks.com*

Iliad Bookshop (*www.iliadbooks.com*), 5400 Cahuenga Blvd., North Hollywood, CA 91601, USA. General used bookstore that has a very impressive genre section, reasonable prices and knowledgeable staff. They have recently expanded their fiction section into an adjacent building. Tel: (818) 509-2665.

Porcupine Books offers regular catalogues and extensive mail order lists of used fantasy/horror/SF titles via email *brian@porcupine.demon.co.uk* or write to: 37 Coventry Road, Ilford, Essex IG1 4QR, UK. Tel: +44 (0)20 8554-3799.

Reel Art Collectibles (*www.reelart.biz*), 6727 W. Stanley, Berwyn, Illinois 60402, USA. Nicely designed Chicago store selling movie material, classic comics, vintage toys and rare books. They also host celebrity signings and have regular warehouse sales. Tel: 1-708-288-7378. Facebook: *Reel Art, Inc.*

Kirk Ruebotham (*www.biblio.com/bookstore/kirk-ruebotham-bookseller-runcorn-cheshire*) is a mail-order only dealer who specialises in mainly out-of-print and second-hand horror/SF/fantasy/crime fiction and related non-fiction at very good prices, with regular catalogues. Write to: 16 Beaconsfield Road, Runcorn, Cheshire WA7 4BX, UK. Tel: +44 (0)1928-560540. Email: *kirk.ruebotham@ntlworld.com*

The Talking Dead is run by Bob and Julie Wardzinski and offers reasonably priced paperbacks, rare pulps and hardcovers, with catalogues issued *very* occasionally. They accept wants lists and are also the exclusive supplier of back issues of *Interzone*. Credit cards accepted. Contact them at: 12 Rosamund Avenue, Merley, Wimborne, Dorset BH21 1TE, UK. Tel: +44 (0)1202-849212 (9:00 a.m.–9:00 p.m.). Email: *books@thetalkingdead.fsnet.co.uk*

Ygor's Books specialises in out of print science fiction, fantasy and horror titles, including British, signed, speciality press and limited editions. They also buy books, letters and original art in these fields. Email: *ygorsbooks@gmail.com*

ONLINE

All Things Horror (*www.allthingshorror.co.uk*) is a genre interview site run by Johnny Mains that mainly focuses on authors, editors, artists and movie stars of the 1960s, 1970s and 1980s. It also caters to reviews of both films and books, and features a short fiction section that is open to submissions.

Cast Macabre (*www.castmacabre.org*) is the premium horror fiction podcast that is "bringing Fear to your ears", offering a free horror short story every week.

Fantastic Fiction (*www.fantasticfiction.co.uk*) features more than 2,000 best-selling author biographies with all their latest books, covers and descriptions.

FEARnet (*www.fearnet.com*) is a digital cable channel dedicated to all things horror, including news, free movie downloads (sadly not available to those outside North America) and Mick Garris's online talk show *Post Mortem*.

Hellnotes (*www.hellnotes.com*) offers news and reviews of novels, collections, magazines, anthologies, non-fiction works, and chapbooks. Materials for review should be sent to editor and publisher David B. Silva, Hellnotes, 5135 Chapel View Court, North Las Vegas, NV 89031, USA. Email: *news@hellnotes.com* or *dbsilva13@gmail.com*

The Irish Journal of Gothic and Horror Studies (*irishgothichorrorjournal.homestead.com*) features a diverse range of articles and reviews, along with a regular "Lost Souls" feature focusing on overlooked individuals in the genre.

The Monster Channel (*www.monsterchannel.tv*) bills itself as "the first and only independent interactive horror channel!" The 24/7 streaming channel includes first run indie horror movies, retro VHS gore and hosts horror classics.

Pseudopod (*www.pseudopod.org*), the premiere horror fiction podcast, continued to offer a free-to-download, weekly reading of a new or classic horror fiction by a variety of voices. The site remains dedicated to paying their authors while providing readings for free and offering the widest variety of audio horror fiction currently available on the net.

SF Site (*www.sfsite.com*) has been posted twice each month since 1997. Presently, it publishes around thirty to fifty reviews of SF, fantasy and horror from mass-market publishers and some small press. They also maintain link pages for Author and Fan Tribute Sites and other facets including pages for Interviews, Fiction, Science Fact, Bookstores, Small Press, Publishers, E-zines and Magazines,

Artists, Audio, Art Galleries, Newsgroups and Writers' Resources. Periodically, they add features such as author and publisher reading lists.

Vault of Evil (*www.vaultofevil.wordpress.com*) is a site dedicated to celebrating the best in British horror with special emphasis on UK anthologies (they seem to like this series a bit better now). There is also a lively forum devoted to many different themes at *www.vaultofevil.proboards.com*